A Celebration of Storytelling

Editing by GD Deckard

From

Dark Owl Publishing, LLC

Arizona

Also from
Dark Owl Publishing

Anthologies

Something Wicked This Way Rides
Where genre fiction meets the Wild West.
(coming October 1, 2021)

Collections
The Dark Walk Forward
A harrowing collection of frightful stories from John S. McFarland.

The Last Star Warden:
Tales of Adventure and Mystery from Frontier Space, Volume I
Sci-fi pulp fiction at its finest by Jason J. McCuiston.
(coming March 1, 2021)

Bottled Spirits & Other Dark Tales
A collection of strange fiction from the twisted vision of Adrian Ludens.
(coming May 1, 2021)

No Lesser Angels, No Greater Devils
Beautiful and haunting stories collected from Laura J. Campbell.
(coming May 1, 2021)

Novels
The Keeper of Tales
An epic fantasy adventure by Jonathon Mast.
(coming March 1, 2021)

Buy the books for Kindle and in paperback
www.darkowlpublishing/the-bookstore

Table of Contents

Table of Contents

Forward

First, we want to thank you as readers for your interest in Dark Owl Publishing. This is our first anthology, and we believe that the tome you hold in your hands is a shining example of what we will be producing from now on.

A Celebration of Storytelling honors and showcases the art of writing in the main four genres of fiction: fantasy, thriller and horror, mystery and crime, and science fiction. Each tale contains a festival, fair, carnival, or celebratory event to honor the antiquity and the importance of writing and scripture: to record history or to alter it, to entertain all types of populations, and to explore and explain the world around us.

This anthology stems from a previous publisher who had to close their business. Dark Owl Publishing picked up the four separate anthologies and decided to keep the same spirit of the works to give the authors the publication of their stories that they so greatly deserved.

We are honored to have fifty-eight stories from thirty-nine authors. Their talents have embodied the mission of this anthology. From all walks of life, they have unique abilities to excite and inform, to render realism and alter imagination, to amaze, delight, terrify, and fascinate us as readers. Their work is more than worthy of this, a celebration of storytelling.

We do want to send out some very important thank yous. First, to Christine Morgan, who has a story in this anthology titled "By Bread Alone". Christine did the first round of copy editing for the anthologies while they were still under the old publisher. Her work was extremely important, for, as a good copy editor should, she found those mistakes we seem to miss when we initially read through stories. As the previous publisher said, and we agree, our "gratitude for her support with this project, both as an author and an editor, is never-ending."

Second, we also want to thank GD Deckard for being the final Lead Editor of this anthology. With his experience, we needed him to help with the final details, such as making sure the stories flow well and checking for any more mistakes that publishers certainly can miss. GD's kindness and willingness to help a fledgling publisher truly tells us we are making the right decisions and that we will be able to produce more high-quality content with confidence and strength.

And last but certainly not least, we want to say thank you to the truly incredible authors who wanted to keep their stories in this anthology. We cannot say how much it means to us for them to trust our vision and our goals as we move forward in our endeavors. They deserve more than just their stories in this publication; we hope you will follow them via their links in the About the Authors section and purchase more of their work. In addition, you as readers will be lucky enough to see more work by them as Dark Owl grows!

In all, Dark Owl Publishing is a woman-owned business dedicated to taking care of our authors and getting their work out to the public in ways they might otherwise not be noticed.

Our goal is to never cater to one group of people over another. We want to give all authors a chance, no matter what their life situations are. We want to find all kinds of authors in the writing community to get their quality work out to readers who might otherwise miss them. Open submissions and diversity anthologies will help with that mission.

We want readers to be happy, which means making authors happy, too. We believe this anthology is the first of many works to come that succeed in that mission.

In addition, if you are interested in becoming part of the Dark Owl staff, please visit our website to learn more about opportunities available to you as an author or other member of our continually growing company.

Thank you for your support as we progress and produce more quality content for you!

Andrea Thomas and Staff
Dark Owl Publishing
July 2020

PART ONE:

A PAGEANT OF FANTASY

STORIES DANCE

JONATHON MAST

Ever dance with a story?

Oh, she was beautiful. We swayed together as the band played bad country music badly. Incandescent bulbs had been strung over the stretch of asphalt that served as the dance floor. Above that a great dark sky smiled at us. Couples danced together, staring into each other's eyes. Around us people snacked on freshly made funnel cake at picnic tables. Just beyond was the midway, full of garish games and "thrilling" rides. The sound of a carousel jangled just over the sound of the crowds. Beyond that a parking lot filled with Fords and Chevys and a lot of dust.

But here in my arms, I held a story made flesh.

She looked up at me. She was the one I'd been looking for for so long. I'm not one to fall in love quickly, but I think I knew her well already. There was no woman like her.

Her eyes were—

Well, her hair was—

No. I can't tell you what she looked like. And does it really matter? What did matter was that she was in my arms. She wore a faded blue dress, but despite her very plain clothing, she felt regal. Something about the way she held herself, like she knew she was royalty, even if she didn't look it.

She smiled at me. "I'm so glad I met you tonight." It's what you're supposed to say in an evening like this.

"I'm glad I met you," I answered, because that's how you're supposed to answer.

She looked distant then. "You should probably go soon. I don't want to die."

I raised an eyebrow at her.

"I told you I was a story."

"Yeah?" I cocked my head.

"I'm not a happy story. I'm not a romantic comedy or anything like that. I'm old. So old." She stepped away and hugged herself. She shivered. "Old stories never have happy endings."

"Well. Maybe you and I can write a new ending." I gave her a mischievous smile.

She looked away and shook her head. "When you're a story, you have to just... live yourself out. Over and over again. You can escape your pages for a night or two, wiggle your way out of the prison of ink and paper, but you can't escape who you are." She sighed. "But that's what I am. If we stay together, if I'm happy with you, I'll die again, until the next carnival, the next festival, the next county fair. Because that's what happens."

"I won't let you die." I wrapped my arms around her. She fit there.

She sighed. "Here's what's going to happen: My father will show up and scream something about how I'm too good for you, or you're not good enough for his little girl. You'll get angry and stand up to him. And then he'll take out a gun or something, and he'll try to get at you. I'll get in the way. I'll die. It's just that simple."

"I don't think you know me well enough if you think I'd stand up to a guy with a weapon." I winked at her.

"The problem is stories are... contagious. You'll get caught up in it. You'll stand up to him."

"You're really weird."

"Oh?"

"It's what I like about you," I whispered in her ear. Then I kissed the tip of her nose.

And she put her hand up against my face. It was... it was so intimate, how she did it. Like we were the only two on the dance floor. Like there wasn't bad country plunking out of horrendously tuned guitars thirty feet that way.

And she closed her eyes.

I took her hand off my face and kissed it, real gentlemanly-like. "We could go see the parson right now. I think I saw him eatin' corn over yonder."

Anna blushed. "Duke, you know I can't marry you." I loved it when she blushed. The color of her cheeks was so pretty against the faded blue dresses she always wore.

Around us, people danced in time to the guitar and violin players. Sunset painted the sky like nothing I'd ever seen before, it was so gorgeous. It was a prime night for marrying, and that's for sure. I'd bet the parson was going to get a lot of business tonight from all the sweethearts. It wasn't every day all the boys came home from a cattle drive together.

And here in my arms was my Anna, the girl who'd waited for me. "You're my girl. Course you can marry me!"

"But my father!"

I just grinned at her. "Let the old coot come. It's the county fair. He can't do nothing here!" I let loose a great whoop.

And just like that, the boys were right there. "What's up, Duke?" Travis asked.

"Anna's scared her pa is gonna get in the way of our love."

Travis whooped. The other boys joined in the war cry.

I nodded toward them. "Think they can protect us, honey?"

She stomped a foot and crossed her arms. "You don't know my pa. He's got a thing for horses. Only the best. And he'll come right in on a whirlwind and take me away from you, and you'll never see me again."

"I'd like to see him try."

Now, see, that's the stupidest thing a guy can say in a situation like that. Let me give you a little bit of friendly advice: Never say something like that. Because whoever you're talking about is going to show up and try it, and you're going to look like a fool. And me, sure, I'm used to looking like a fool, but I still don't like it, especially in front of my girl.

"Duke Nelson!" The gruff voice thundered over the fair, calling my name. And there he was, the big man himself. Drooping mustache. Huge hat. And he rode a horse that had been groomed so well he fairly shone. The man didn't care he was riding right onto the dance floor, he just clip-clopped right up to us. A stylized sun was stitched onto his saddle.

The boys, my loyal friends, skedaddled. Thanks, boys.

"Mister Fairborn." I nodded as if it weren't nothing special.

"Get away from my daughter." He pulled out his pistol and casually waved it my way.

The crowd gasped and moved away. The sheriff stepped close, but her pa raised an eyebrow at him. He backed off. Being a cattle baron meant you could get away with this kind of stuff, I guess.

"We're gonna get married, old man," I said.

"My daughter ain't marrying the likes of you," he sneered at me like I was a lame colt.

I bunched up my fists, getting ready for a fight.

But Anna stepped between us. "Pa, let's go back home."

"Look. Someone with sense around here," he said.

"Like hell!" And with that I seized Anna's hand and pulled her back to me. I grinned at the shocked expression on her face. Why wouldn't I grin at that beautiful face?

But her father raised the pistol, right at my chest, and it thundered louder than any storm I'd lived through on the plains.

But Anna was faster. She stepped between us.

And her blue dress wasn't so blue anymore. A red stain spread on it.

She fell over. I grabbed at her.

My Anna took her last breath in my arms.

I stumbled as the woman pulled her hand away from my face. The bad country was still going. The incandescent bulbs buzzed overhead. The night chill started to creep into my skin. Once more I smelled the funnel cakes.

She offered a sad smile at me.

"What was that?" I asked.

"Me."

"I was someone else."

"You entered into my story," she answered. "Into me. You were part of me." She stepped closer and put her head against my chest. "Just dance with me a little longer, before I send you away. Before my father comes."

"Am I really here?"

"Well, you're a part of my story for the moment. Hopefully not for long. I really don't want to die again tonight."

"Maybe you're part of my story tonight," I whispered into her hair. "Right here. Right now." We swayed together a little, but a thought dug into the back of my brain. "How do I know right now isn't part of your story? Something from the past?"

"You're here. Not in an imagined Old West."

"Imagined?"

"Stories don't always take place in history."

I breathed in. "I was confident there. Thought I could take him on, one-on-one."

"It's part of the story. The man is overconfident. Thinks he can take my father down. And every time he's wrong." She shook her head. "Every time."

"How many times?" I asked.

She put her hand against my face again.

I took her hand and put it in mine. "Meredith," I breathed.

And she smiled. Her entire face lit up. Even through the majestic peacock feathers of her masquerade mask, her hazel eyes blazed. I'd never seen anyone quite like her. Every other woman at the ball must be jealous of her. Every man must be jealous of me. They must be wondering who I was, dressed as a masked stable boy.

They would never guess I really was a stable boy.

"You can't touch me like that," I whispered. "Not here. Not where others can see."

"Damn them," she answered with a giggle. "I am tired of hiding our love." She spun around me as the orchestra began another waltz, majestic and alien to anything I had danced to before. She finished her spin and smiled at me again. "The only one we need to fear is my father. Watch for him; he wears a mask made of mirror. He's always had a thing for mirrors."

And around us on the dance floor, people whispered as they danced. The men stared down their noses. The women raised their eyebrows higher and higher.

And my Meredith. Oh, my Meredith.

It was a royal masquerade for the queen, but Meredith was the star here. None could shine brighter than her. And here she was.

Mine. I had eyes only for her.

"Cedric!"

The harsh, harsh voice cut through the music. The orchestra stuttered to a stop. I'd forgotten to watch for him, lost in Meredith's beauty.

I turned to see a man in a bright green suit and a mask made of mirror. It had a strange pattern etched in the mirror—like a circle with rays coming from it. He stepped forward and yanked my mask away from my face.

"It is you," he growled.

"It is," I answered.

"Step away from my daughter."

I looked at her and then at her father. "No. I don't think I shall."

He reached to draw his foil. Around us, people gasped. The master of the masquerade strode forward, his heels clicking on the marble floor. "See here, Lawrence, you can't do this! Not here!"

"I'll pay to have your floor cleaned of the blood," Meredith's father spat.

"If you intend to duel me, you'll need to provide me a weapon," I said, crossing my arms. I was accustomed to shoveling horse shit in my daily tasks; I had learned to do it verbally as well. I made sure to keep my terror out of my voice.

"I won't duel you, boy. I'll simply kill you where you stand for sullying my daughter, for stepping above your place!" He lunged, his foil gleaming in the light of hundreds of candelabra, slicing through the air faster than any of my horses could run.

Meredith was faster.

She stood between us. And then she screamed between us. She fell.

Her father and I reached her in the same breath.

Her last breath.

And again my feet were on asphalt. Again the bulbs overhead. Again the funnel cakes.

"I am a very old story," she said as she removed her hand from my cheek.

I looked around. We were in no grand ballroom celebrating a masquerade. No, just the county fair. Just people from the surrounding towns brought together with the promise of rides, games, and greasy food.

No one carried swords. There were plenty of county sheriffs around if anyone tried causing trouble. One walked by, the radio on his shoulder staticking.

"How long do we have?" I asked.

She shrugged as we continued swaying.

This song had gone on a long, long time. No one seemed to mind, though. All the couples stayed on the dance floor.

"There's too much security here. It's not like back then. The sheriffs would stop it before there was that kind of violence, wouldn't they?"

"Well," she answered, "I'm sure a father could have a pocketknife. Or conceal and carry. It is a thing, you know."

"Who is your real father?"

"Who told me first?" She shrugged again, raising her hand to my cheek.

And then we laughed. Everyone laughed. It's what you did when Titania made a joke. All the fae joined together and twittered and guffawed and sniggered.

The queen raised her hands. "Let the Festival of Tales begin!"

Around us, brownies and pixies and goblins and gnomes and creatures of every color and smell joined in the celebration. The games began by the border with the woods. The dance began in the meadow. And of course, the stories began on the stage.

Zazzabell winked. She whispered, "Come with me."

I grabbed her hand. "We can't leave."

"Oh, I don't want to leave! I just want to put a glamour on you."

We ducked behind one of the massive tree roots that bordered the meadow. Fireflies danced in the moonlight everywhere, but they never tattled. Not on the fae.

Zazz grabbed my hand and kissed the inside of my wrist. I felt the muscles in my arm reweave themselves over my bones. My ribs expanded. My neck thickened.

"Which glamour is this?"

"Oh, you look like Grignor."

"Your intended?"

"No one would yell at me for being with him. Not even my father. And now you are him." She kissed me.

Oh, how she kissed me.

And we flew back to the festival meadow, our wings glimmering in the reflected light of the fireflies.

"And what shall we do?" I asked her.

"Oh, the games!" she laughed.

So we flew down to another border of the meadow and dared to play man-chess and flitter-flam. I let her win every time. We laughed so hard.

The little sprite that ran the flitter-flam game groveled as she handed back the balls so we could pitch them for the next round. "I am pleased to see you in such fine spirits, Grignor."

"I must be in fine spirits when playing with my intended!" I answered.

"Certainly, my lord," the sprite answered.

I wish I'd noticed. But that sprite, she chittered to an ant who scuttled to a spider who whispered to a dragonfly that zipped to the royal pavilion. She'd noticed that Grignor was never so merry.

And all at once the games fell silent as a fae bearing the seal of the king, the golden sun, strode the alleyway. "Ah! Flitter-flam! A favorite game of mine!" And with that Oberon the king was beside me. "Ah! Grignor! I see you play. Would you care to make a wager?"

"Of course, my lord," I answered, bowing.

Zazz shrunk from my side, trembling.

Oberon grinned. "If I should win, you will lose every glamour and everyone will see you for the pustulent thing you are. And you will be cursed to relive this night forever, the story told until the end of time at every festival held under the stars. It will be written and kept bound."

Zazz gave a sour face. "Father, why must you include the cycles? You always love the cycles!"

The king continued as if he hadn't heard. Perhaps he hadn't. "But should you win, I shall give you your heart's desire. Whatever you wish, I shall make it so. The moon? It will be yours. The sun? It will shine only for you. A woman's love? None will stand in your way." He paused. "Do we have a deal?"

The humans say to never strike a deal with the fae. But the fae, we know a harder truth: Never make a deal with royalty. But when else could I ever receive a chance like this? I knew how to play flitter-flam like none other. And if I won, he was oathbound to allow Zazz and I to wed.

"My lord, nothing more would please me."

And so we played. As the lower caste, I pitched first. Oberon watched, one eyebrow raised. Zazz watched through her fingers. Oberon's guards watched, nudging each other.

The other games stopped running. People began crowding close as Oberon took his first pitch.

"Flam!" shouted the crowd.

My heart fell.

I took my second pitch. The musicians at the dance stopped playing. Why bother playing when there were no dancers? They had all stopped to watch.

Oberon took his second pitch.

"Flam!" the fae shouted and giggled.

I took my final pitch.

The storyteller at the stage sat down and wept. No one was interested in his saga. They had all come to watch.

Oberon smiled at me. "Ah, Grignor, I suppose if you're this bad at this game, I should cancel your nuptials. After all, if you can't handle this kind of pitch, how can I entrust you to give me strong grandchildren?" And he winked. "But I suppose once your glamours are gone, you'll just wither up and blow away anyway, won't you? And do it again and again and again."

He turned his back to the playing field and pitched the ball without even looking.

"Flitter-flam!" the crowd cried.

Zazz's face. I have never seen defeat like that. I have never witnessed someone lose all hope in just so few minutes.

I had never lost so much so quickly.

Oberon turned to me. "So. Now I take your glamour from you." And he waved a hand.

But Zazz stepped between us. "Father, no!" she pleaded.

But the spell was complete. It rang through the air. And Zazz rang.

Her wings drooped, withered, fell off her. Her dress turned to dust. Her face wrinkled. And then her fingers. And then her knees.

And then like a dandelion she rotted away.

Oberon and I stared at his daughter, the delightful rose withered and dried up.

And her hand was on my cheek again as we swayed on the dance floor in the Midwest August heat.

I looked around me. None had left the dance since I'd started swaying with the story made flesh. "What's going on with everyone else?"

"They're sinking into my telling, too. They'll stay here now until my father arrives."

"And what happens if he doesn't come?"

"He'll come. He always does."

And that's when he arrived. A man with a long-sleeved button-up shirt and jeans. His silver hair was mostly hidden by a baseball cap bearing the logo of a team I didn't recognize. No, it did look familiar.

It looked like a sun.

"Git away from my daughter!" he thundered.

And so I stepped away. "All right." I smiled. "I didn't realize she was taken. Here. She's all yours." I turned and walked away.

The old man sputtered. "Wait!"

"Oh?" I turned to face him again.

"You're not, that is, you're not going to, aren't you going to say she and you belong together?"

"Nah. Not if it means her dying. I figure she probably deserves better than me anyway." I winked. "I'm also not fond of getting into family squabbles. I've got enough of my own, after all."

More sputtering.

And I walked away. Just like that.

And my story lived. The story I had loved every time it had been told since she first stepped between me and the fae king. She didn't die this time.

Here's the problem with stories: If you don't tell them to the end, they don't know what to do. They just sort of... stop.

So my story and her father just stood on the dance floor, sputtering. They couldn't move on without someone to turn the page, and I wasn't going to do it for them. Not if it meant her dying.

That's where I come in. You see, you might say this wasn't her story at all. It was mine.

The county fair was pretty big, all things considered. I prowled from the dance floor where I'd met her and down to the midway. Colored lights flashed. Teens reigned the midway this time of night, trying to impress each other and maybe sneak a kiss or maybe something more.

My story, as she showed me her retellings, had given me all I needed. Her father was a fan of horses. A fan of mirrors hiding things. And a fan of cycles.

I looked around. She was imprisoned somewhere with horses, mirrors, and cycles. What might that be? A hall of mirrors? One of the rides that spun at ridiculous speeds?

And then I found it: The carousel.

By this time of day, it was abandoned. No little kids begging to ride. And most dates had forgotten how nice it was to simply sit and spin on a horse. And the center of the carousel held mirrors. All around the border, the tent-like top bore stylized suns.

I smiled at the wooden horses. These majestic animals hid a secret, and I was glad to find it.

You see, stories live in all sorts of ways. Through spoken words. Through television. But my story, my beloved from of old, had told me exactly where she was: In a book. Pages and ink. And now that her story had paused, now that I had refused to play along, she was caught.

But not just her. Her father, too.

I approached the center of the carousel and gazed at my reflection. Hateful things, mirrors. They only show what's true, and who wants to see that?

Ah, but stories! Stories are so much cleverer than reality, aren't they? After all, if they weren't, you wouldn't be reading this story now, would you? No, you know the truth, good reader, don't you?

I took the mirror off its panel to uncover the inner mechanisms of the carousel: Books.

Volumes and volumes of books.

What should I do now, gentle reader? Should I release them all? Should I let them flit around the world to their hearts' content? Should I burn the pages and free them in a very different way? Or should I make myself the master of the fair and play stories with the humans that come to visit us here?

I did not know.

Oh, that's not true. Of course I knew what I intended. But if I told you how it ended, where would be the fun in that?

WHAT THE WIND WHISPERS TO THOSE WHO LISTEN

KELLY KURTZHALS GEIGER

He was born onto the soil, as all her children had been, and as all farmers were. The soil full of minerals and magic needed a fair trade of offerings. The baby squalled his first breath and she noticed how different he was.

He had bright orange hair, hair that was licked by flames and kissed by demons. The mountain demons controlled the weather and all the farmers' blessings and curses, and they had wicked senses of humor when it came to babies. The brazen dual sunshines strode through the barn's one carved window, casting a warm halo on the boy's downy red head. But his hands, oh his horrible hands. His smooth golden hands, soft and delicate, did not look like a farmer's hands at all. The flower-petal fingers uncoiled to the air and sent a wave of sick dread across his mother's chest.

"Mathilda!" The attending midwife gasped when she gathered the newborn from the ground and into his traditional swaddle made of fresh thrush. "He's..."

"He's not right," Mathilda finished her sister Irmah's sentence.

Irmah pursed her lips and brought the boy to the cauldron to bathe. Mathilda rested her back against the smoothed wall. Irma dunked him once, twice, then a third time, as was customary for newborn farmers: once for the demons, twice for the Tyrans, and a third for the soil.

By the second immersion he no longer squalled. His face shone clear in the gathering glitterlight and he peered about his surroundings with an unusual curiosity that frightened Irmah. Her weathered brown hands shook as she smoothed back the orange strands covering his dented head. The sod barn smelled of sweltering blood.

"What are you going to do?" Irmah asked.

Mathilda's heart churned. "Give him to me," she said. She took the child to her breast, latching him onto her, giving herself to him despite a tightening in her lungs that told her to resist and wondering what she had done to deserve such a betrayal. It wasn't anything she could remember. Mathilda worked hard, with piety and fastidiousness. "Light seven candles at the shrine for the Tyrans," she instructed her sister. "And one for the demons."

The Tyrans, their city overlords, would take kindly to the news of another newborn male farmer. They didn't need to know about his hands. The demons, she was certain, already knew.

When Irmah closed the shabby wooden barn door behind her pale grey tired face to go light the offerings, Mathilda leaned the child down onto the dirt and rubbed his soft golden hands with stones and loose soil. She would come to do this every morning for seven crossings of the moons with her baby son in the daybreak of the rising suns, and he would oblige her patiently, though his hands would never take on the rough rancor of a farmer.

Mathilda's husband beat her as soon as she recovered enough from the childbirth. The beatings he would come to do repeatedly, most often in the cool dusk of the setting moons when his eyes grew hard and his breath teemed of alcohol. After a while, he forgot the original cause of his anger.

Mathilda never forgot.

They named the boy Ervyn after his greatest-great-grandfather, although he did not deserve such a name, but because he was the seventh son of a seventh son. And once the sheen of his birth was off him, they set him to work in the fields alongside his brothers and sisters who were wary of such a strange new child, at first. Their plain tan faces stole glances at his shining clear white one, his red hair rising like burning embers from beneath groping green squash vines. He smiled when he caught his siblings staring, and it soon became impossible to resist the charm of his tinkling bellchime baby laugh.

When the Tyrans came for their crops during the darkest red of the fall harvest suns in preparation for their Great Feastival, Mathilda presented Ervyn to them, as was customary. She had covered the boy's delicate silken hands with a pair of dingy canvas work gloves, hoping the Tyrans would not ask to see his hands.

"Why are the child's hands thus clothed?" The elder Tyran asked first thing, tottering on his cloven hooves and reaching with talon clawed hands. The elder frowned at the boy Mathilda kept tight in her arms. His horns glinted through the dark red light of the fall season suns.

Mathilda trembled. Tyrans took children born with lesser deformities than Ervyn's away from their homes in the farming village of Moerow and brought them to the capital city of Kywerth. What became of them, no one really knew. But most believed the final outcome lay atop a Tyran's dinner table.

"'Tis but a blight on his hands, contagious poison that must run its course through his body to cure itself," Mathilda replied with a voice that broke more than she'd hoped.

One of the officers stepped forward to investigate and Mathilda slunk backward one small step in her best black cloth shoes. "I must warn you, my Lord, 'tis a very contagious blight. Farmers all acquire it at some point in our lives, so we are immune, but I fear such a blight has not reached the city of Kywerth."

The officer paused, uncertain, and Mathilda held her breath. "Why have I not heard of such a blight?"

Mathilda looked behind her at the row of farmers beside her come to present their new summer children. They did not begrudge her lie told and stood stoic and unmoving, as they often told lies to the Tyrans themselves when necessity arose.

"We don't wish to trouble your lordships with troubles belonging only to poor farmers," Mathilda replied.

"Well, I must see these hands for myself to determine the worth of the child to the farmers," the officer said, and Mathilda's heart clung to her throat.

The boy squirmed in her arms and reached one of his gloved hands out toward the officer as if he understood and wanted his petal-fingers to be freed and seen. The officer moved to remove the glove.

"Stop," the elder Tyran commanded. "If it is a blight unkind to the people of

Kywerth, I will not have you expose us to it."

Mathilda bowed and ducked backward out of the line as the next farmer moved forward to present her new child. Mathilda turned her face to conceal her joy. Deformed as the boy was, seven crossings of the moons had passed since she'd birthed him, and she had reluctantly formed an attachment.

* * *

Ervyn grew amid bursting beanstalks that coiled their vines toward each other and cornstalks that stretched their silks toward the sky, hoping to touch it. He played in the long roaming fields but could not be forced to work, nor would he take to it naturally. His nearest sister in age, Reuthie, had been given her row to hoe when she turned two, only two full harvest seasons prior, and had known instinctively what to do with it as had all her siblings before her. But Ervyn didn't take his hoe to the ground to coax persistent weeds away from their hosts. Instead, he straddled the long rod like an imaginary horse, striding down lanes of surprised tomatoes and flustered beets. The vegetables, much like the humans, didn't know what to make of this foreigner dancing among them with unfamiliar fingers. The vegetables cowered and dreaded being trounced upon, much less plucked by such a child once they became ripe.

Mathilda scolded him and set him back to his row once, twice, and then gave up a third time. He took the reprimands with the wisdom of one who understands somehow they don't need to follow instructions. The time of the harvest was approaching again, when the Tyrans would come demand their crops for the Feastival, and by the time three full harvest seasons passed Ervin could sense before she could that Mathilda did not possess enough time to pause from her work to punish him. So he continued his mischief untethered by guilt.

* * *

One day, under the sweltering heat of the dual green summer suns, as Mathilda and her family pulled string beans from their vines and loaded them into small bushels which they could carry on wagons for washing and sorting, Reuthie paused from her picking and drew one velvety bean leaf to her mouth. She stretched the edges taut and pursed her lips and blew a single note into the air, high and clear.

"Reuthie!" Mathilda snapped. "Idle hands are a demon's fortune."

Reuthie stifled a giggle and made one more noise with the leaf, because of how much fascination it was giving little Ervyn, who was not so little anymore but a big boy of five full seasons. Having grown bored by the lack of results his antics caused, he had resigned himself to tending his place in the fields until he could devise himself another distraction. His presence among his brothers and sisters felt significant, as if a Tyran lord himself had deigned to stoop his back to kneel in the soil with them. Reuthie in particular, being the closest in age, felt the most determined to please her odd brother.

Ervyn's eyes followed her every movement, and when she produced the sound from the leaf, his eyes grew wide with amazement and delight. He set aside his half-filled bean bushel and chose a leaf of his own after several moments of careful consideration. He pulled the leaf into his soft hands which were smudged only slightly from the soil but otherwise as delicate and silky smooth as ever. He wrapped his golden petal fingers around the leaf as if they made parts of a whole, and then he stretched the leaf taut to his lips as he'd seen his sister do. And when he blew into it, every single person in the bean field stopped to unfurl their backs and turn their heads at the sound he made—high and clear. But Ervyn blew not just one note, as Reuthie had done. He manipulated the leaf with his fingers and adjusted his air flow until he devised a tune so soft and lilting even Mathilda forgot to scold him, all from only a plain leaf that rivaled any tune made on a proper instrument.

And thus it was that Ervyn discovered music.

First, he chose a hollow reed from the best among the plants that grew in the ditch between cattails and muck. He dried the reed and poked strategic holes in it along one side from a place of knowledge he neither knew nor understood. He played melodies on his reed instrument that he invented, sweet rhapsodies and sacred hymns which calmed the farmers and made them nostalgic for emotions they'd never felt and things they couldn't explain.

The reed instrument changed Ervyn. He no longer desired to hunt for mischief. He became a responsible worker in the fields, turning over the raw dirt with his hoe to force its magic, and coaxing seedlings to bear fruits. The fruits also delighted in the boy's sweet berceuses and delicious adagios, and grew fuller and heartier as a result.

Mathilda humored him this reed instrument, since she saw no harm that it had given the boy such a sense of peace. She watched his delicate fingers trip over the little holes he carved and wondered at the creation of it all, including how she had created such a creature with only her simple womb. And she felt justified in her choice to save him from an unknown fate with the Tyrans when he settled and took his rightful place beside the family in the clodded rows of ground. All their lives depended on the magic wrought forth from the soil. If the lands were not tended properly, the fruits they birthed would refuse to come forth. Tyrans punished farmers whose crops did not yield. Fervent whispers on late evenings before cracking firelight belied tales about Tyrans who ate flesh as easily as crops.

Ervyn's fingers grew longer and impatient with the reed instrument after he had mastered it. He mused privately on it for a while, and from no example he'd ever seen before, he fashioned a string instrument by combining a rusty old tire hubcap, a narrow flat wooden stick, a scrap of canvas pulled tight, and five strings of foxwire. He spent long hours honing and tuning his new stringed instrument in the cold blue winter evenings after the fields were turned and turned again to prepare for spring planting and his large family gathered in dim candlelight that cast shadows across the carved sod walls. Before the smaller pale moon turned crescent and the larger moon had begun to poke its head along the ridge of mountains where demons dwelled, Ervyn found the patterns on the strings he needed, and he played.

Inside the sod domicile, everyone went still. Ervyn sat alone beneath the glint of stars and the surprised winter moons, and he strummed an opus so layered and complex the stars themselves blinked in harmony. The swarm of rising and falling notes were strummed in a variety of styles: stroking and picking, although Ervyn did not know or invent names for the techniques he used. He wrapped the fingers of his right hand along the instrument's neck and fingered the strings in intricate patterns he intuited as the fingers on his left hand drew forth vibrating pitches, creating themes that wound between longing and hope.

Farmers in nearby homes drew near to listen and marvel, carrying candles which licked playful patterns beneath their appreciative faces. Irmah stole a glance at Mathilda, who stood bewitched by Ervyn's music. Mathilda's face turned dour when she recognized the same look her sister had given her when the child was born: fear and dread.

Mathilda's husband stumbled outside past where Ervyn played on the small stone landing and he blustered through the farmers down the weed-choked path toward their community square of Moerow. Ervyn paused his tune only slightly at the disturbance and then forgot even himself to his music.

Ervyn remembered his father only again when startled awake in the wee hours of pre-dawn by the sounds of flesh being struck and his mother's stifled cries. He looked at Reuthie who lay at the far edge of the girls' bed directly to his right. She stared wide awake at the low thatched roof above her head and met Ervyn's stare only briefly before she turned her back to him.

When the dual suns rose with the blue morning winter light, the family tended quietly to the morning chores and a simple breakfast of fried tomatoes over skillet potatoes supped from wooden bowls. They ignored the bruises that bloomed red and purple on Mathilda's face and arms. Ervyn followed his family toward the fields to begin the day's task of sowing and churning long rows of soil by hand for them to stir forth magic enough to welcome new spring seedlings.

When he reached the stone door stoop, he found his new string instrument and his old hollowed reed both lying crushed and mangled against the sod wall where he had sat and played.

His brothers and sisters watched as he went first to his string instrument whose neck was broken and strings were torn loose and wild. Then he took up his old reed that had been snapped in half and trounced upon until flat.

His brothers and sisters watched Ervyn draw the instruments into his arms and march them solemnly to the trash heap. He deposited them and then turned back without a word.

* * *

The following spring a drought struck the farmers with a fierce vengeance, the strength of which none of them had seen in their lifetimes, but only heard about in their fireside tales. The soil cracked and cried out in pain. The sky showed no mercy, burning its wretched dual unrelenting suns. The clouds portended no rain, and the farmers cursed the demons of the mountains for this punishment they didn't understand. Seeds wrought from the babies of the fruits of the previous summer's harvest were eaten instead of planted, for the ones that went into the soil dried to dust and then vanished forever, useless and wasted. The farmers grew thin and suspicious of each other with bellies hollow and full only of bitter blame.

When spring dragged into summer and no harvest yielded to pledge to the Tyrans, families fought, delaying the inevitable sacrifice.

Then, in the dusty gloaming of the orange summer sunrises, two full suns before the Feastival when Tyrans were to come collect, Mathilda stared across her mud dwelling at the sad starved faces of her eleven children—seven boys and four girls. The children refused to meet her gaze, because they knew a decision was being made. Which of them would she give in the place of the empty harvest?

"Ervyn," she said, her voice choked with thirst and shame, "take Reuthie to the city. Give her and yourself to the Tyrans, but don't tell them yet there is no harvest. That way, we might be spared some of their cruelty and more loss to our own, finding it out sooner instead of when they would."

She said the thing she needed to say and then she moved to the cast iron stove because she couldn't face them any longer. And though it made sense to give her youngest to the Tyrans, especially poor Ervyn who would have been taken to Kywerth anyway upon discovery of his physical distortion, it seemed to Mathilda that her heart would split inside her chest and gouge her with its shards.

Ervyn and Reuthie took no possessions. Ervyn's most beloved things had been destroyed and not replicated, and Reuthie owned only a scrap of wire tied with twine which she used as a doll. She didn't believe it worth carrying. They passed the Moerow community square where little trading posts sat empty and farmers wilted on sad stoops, praying forgiveness from the mountain demons for whatever crimes they didn't know they'd committed, besides cursing them for their cruelty.

The children walked with reluctant elongated shadows across the landscape as unending as time, past the yard of bones where their ancestors were kept naked for burning beneath the suns, and onward. They didn't speak because their words were caught behind their tongues, wedged by knots of disbelief.

When the dusty path meandered past lonesome tumbleweeds and rounded the bend of the bare mountain causeway that sheltered their view of the Tyran's city, Reuthie gasped. Farmers never ventured this far beyond the mountains where the demons resided and so they'd never seen the city of Kywerth before. Huge white columns buttressed up against smooth white walls and sprouted to high domed towers like giant mushrooms. The spiral tips on each dome touched the smaller sun as if they were holding it aloft in the sky.

"Let's hide," Reuthie said, grasping Ervyn's arm, her eyes wide as moons. "Let's run away and hide!"

"To where?" Ervyn countered. The ruthless mountain demons would certainly not feed or shelter them, and they couldn't go home.

Reuthie began to cry weak tears. "Please."

Ervyn looked at his older sister and he held out his hand, palm up, his flower-petal fingers reaching for hers. She snuffled and wiped her eyes and put her small brown hand in his weird wild golden one. She'd never touched his hands before, and she was surprised at the softness of the fingers that comforted her all at once like a warm hug.

"I'll protect you," Ervyn said.

"How? When we're going there so they can kill us and eat us?" More tears she didn't have to waste streamed down her dirty disheveled face.

"Maybe they won't," Ervyn said. "Maybe it's just a myth."

Reuthie frowned at his sudden assuredness and calm. "What do you mean, a myth?"

"A story the farmers tell when children go away. So they don't have to feel bad about sending them because they no longer can afford to keep them." Reuthie still looked skeptical, so he asked, "Have you ever seen a Tyran eat a human?"

She took a deep shaky breath. "I've seen them take them," she said. "And I've seen people never come back."

"Take them, yes, but eat them?"

Reuthie had to admit she hadn't. She shook her head.

"Well, I don't believe it," Ervyn said. "They eat vegetables, like we do. I think it's a myth the Tyrans made up in the first place so we're afraid of them. So we keep growing their vegetables for them for a Feastival no farmer has ever seen, because they're too lazy to do it for themselves."

He spoke such a profound amount of words and ideas for a boy of only six full seasons, so many more words than Ervyn had ever strung together all at once in his short life. These two facts combined made Reuthie nearly inclined to believe him. She glanced at the imposing mushroom-shaped towers once more. "Well, in any case," she finally admitted, "I'm sure they've already seen us standing here like fools. It's too late to turn back now."

She took the first step forward and Ervyn followed, still holding his sister's hand in his and casting a wan smile at her. She didn't turn her head. "Ervyn, how come you're so smart?"

"I don't know," he said, his faded cloth moccasin boots crunching in the loose sand-colored gravel. "I think the wind just whispers notes to me and I can hear them because I listen."

Reuthie decided then that he was right. She was starving, they both were, but she fed off his confidence which was as inexplicable and magical as the weather. She grasped his soft fingers once more and moved forward toward the gleaming white city.

* * *

No sentry waited at the white wrought iron gates at the end of the path, since nobody expected two farmer children to arrive unannounced, and there were no enemies save the mountain demons to guard the city against. A drought meant the demons overslept the winter, drunk on laziness and power.

Ervyn and Reuthie paused in the eerie silence. Ervyn held tightly to Reuthie's hand on his left, and he put his petaled fingers of his right hand up to the gate and pushed. It opened with a sigh and a soft metallic creak. The gate door, just like the cloth curtains that divided the rooms in their four-roomed sod domicile, seemed to exist only for division's sake.

The sand-colored gravel beneath their feet gave way to smooth caramel-colored cobblestones. Around them rose great white structures with delicate carvings etched along all sides with elaborate details: a winged beast here, an angelic figure there. So much beauty to drink, Ervyn's fingers itched with an unbridled ferocity for the first time since his instruments had been broken.

Then, they heard a sound they couldn't understand but which seemed familiar all at once, like the cries of a triumphant bird. Ervyn moved toward the sound but Reuthie held him back. Ervyn squirmed out of her grasp, compelled toward the labyrinth.

The children wove through the twisted shaded cool paths between towering structures until they came to a round clearing amid the buildings. They stopped short. Thousands of Tyrans seated on stools facing a raised dais turned their horned heads at the intrusion of the two young farmers. The sound stopped, and only then did Ervyn and Reuthie realize its origin when the creature standing straight upon the dais dropped its curved brass instrument from its mouth. The creature was a human boy, only with bloated cheeks and full lips like a bullfrog.

Four Tyrans leapt from their stools to seize the children.

Then they noticed Ervyn's hands.

Gasps and mumbles reverberated through the crowd. Reuthie and Ervyn's legs petrified. The crowd parted for the elder Tyran who came forward on cloven hooves.

"What are you doing here?" The elder asked.

"There is no harvest offering this season," Reuthie spoke when Ervyn could not, telling the truth against her mother's instructions.

The elder flicked his furry grey eyes at Reuthie's explanation. Then he reached out one taloned claw toward the boy and Ervyn obliged, offering one of his golden petaled palms into the elder's grasp. The elder perused the long delicate fingers without a word and the entire colony waited with craned necks and stifled breaths.

The elder's black lips curled upward and parted to bear elongated teeth. A smile.

He ushered Ervyn to the dais in a flurry of beating hooves and murmurs. The bullfrog-boy gaped and then stepped aside to make room for Ervyn amid the commotion. Reuthie was pushed backward by the crowd of Tyrans.

When the sea of bodies ebbed, Ervyn was left standing alone on the center of the dais. Into his hands the elder Tyran placed a stringed instrument, not completely unlike the rough one the boy had fashioned himself from odd bits and pieces, but a much more beautiful thing, as graceful as a swan. Its body was pure white and its strings and head were glimmering gold.

The elder Tyran retook his stool in the row nearest the edge of the dais and motioned for Ervyn to begin. Ervyn searched the crowd for Reuthie's small brown head. Once he ascertained she was unharmed at the border of the round stone clearing, he bent his head to his beautiful white swan, and he strummed.

He stroked the swan softly, at first, as if to wake her from her long slumber. She rose and stretched and came to life beneath his fingers. Together Ervyn and the swan began a tale of loss and longing so serene the clouds and the suns were still. The bullfrog-boy watched Ervyn's fingers, rapt in the spell. Then he brought his brass instrument to his pursed lips and took up the melody at the bridge, adding depth and layers to the tale. Tyrans wiped burgeoning tears from their furred faces. Then, when the last strain of the music swelled to the coda and faded to a trickling diminuendo, the crowd paused in reverence for only a moment to sup the last lingering aftertaste of sound before exploding into a cacophony of beating talons and stomping hooves.

And thus, Ervyn's first concert was a success.

* * *

The Great Feastival followed. Ervyn and the bullfrog-boy, whose name the children learned was Stethen, the sixth son of a sixth son, were guests of honor. Stethen explained he had been taken by Tyrans during the harvest presentation three seasons prior, and so they were comforted that no harm would come to them. They did not know that while they devoured savory stewed tomatoes and deep-fried squash atop tenderly salted barley porridge, the Tyran council convened at a nearby table to decide upon the fate of Reuthie, a wholly ordinary farmer whose lack of talents they had passed over seasons before. Killing her crossed their minds, to keep safe their secrets and true desires from the farmers. Eating her was also not entirely out of the equation, for Tyrans did eat humans after all, when necessity arose.

Ervyn watched them, listening without hearing. He turned to his sister. "Can you cook like this?"

She paused from shoveling her food to consider the question and its underlying meaning. She chewed and swallowed and dropped her pewter fork to the side of her white ceramic gold-leafed plate. "No," she said.

Ervyn glanced again at the Tyran council, who took no notice of the children while busy contemplating their predicament. Reuthie knew then. "I know only how to farm. And how to make a sound from a leaf, or a doll from wire and twine," she added. A farmer girl of only eight seasons in age hadn't use for skills other than that.

"Then one of those will have to do," Ervyn concluded.

Reuthie nodded, tears welling in her eyes. "I'll think of something," she said.

* * *

That night, the children climbed a rickety wooden staircase stained with whitewash. From the windows at each landing they could see now that between white marble towers with their ornate carvings stood regular wooden structures made from white pine with roofs of crisscrossed holly branches. They were given a soft cotton-stuffed bed to share in a room inside the top of the tower with a window overlooking the city. The stars seemed closer up this high, the moons almost reachable.

"Humans built this place," Ervyn told Reuthie when their escorts had gone. "The Tyrans could never do this all themselves, with claws for hands and hooves for feet."

Ervyn climbed into the bed, softer and lusher than any he'd ever known, but Reuthie remained at the window. She stared out into the sprawling white city and plotted how she could also come to be invited to stay.

When the Tyrans came to steal her from the darkness, as they had decided in order to avoid disturbing their new musical protégé, Reuthie surprised them by sitting awake and cross-legged in the center of the room. Ervyn stirred only slightly when the Tyrans tiptoeing unsuccessfully on cloven hooves into the chamber stopped short to see what she had done.

Reuthie bowed her head and held something out for them in supplication. The officer in charge came forward, the same Tyran who had once almost originally discovered Ervyn's hands and he was tricked by Mathilda.

He took the doll Reuthie had fashioned. It was an ugly crude rag doll, made from strips of fabric she'd torn from the pillowcase she'd been given to sleep upon. The blue-patterned cloth had been manipulated into a dress, the body plump with stuffing and tied at the waist with a bit of blue napkin fitted carefully to a bow. Two buttons stood in for eyes pulled from Reuthie's own farmer overalls and a mouth painted in a bright red smile from remnants of the stewed tomato dinner. In lieu of hair, the doll had been given a bonnet to match her dress.

"I can do better," she said. Ervyn stirred now from his slumber and startled at the crowd of Tyrans invading the bedchamber.

The Tyran handed Reuthie back her doll.

"Please!" She cried. "I'll do anything to stay."

The officer had no pity for the forlorn girl. "We've been ordered to dispatch of you, for the secrets of Kywerth must never be revealed."

"There must be a way," Ervyn interjected. "Have you not human slaves?"

"We do..." the officer began.

"Then give her a position," Ervyn snapped, "or I will not play your instruments."

To prove his point, Ervyn took the petal-like fingers of one hand to bend back the fingers of the other and stretched them near to breaking. When one of his fingers cracked with a hollow and dull sound, the officers caved.

Ervyn and Reuthie were led to the elder Tyran in the pitch dark of night through winding corridors and bizarre chambers filled with mystical objects that drew their attention and craned their necks. Still, they were forced onward.

The elder wore a robe and sat on a chaise astride his canopied bed. The other Tyrans bowed their heads in the presence of such an intimate setting. Ervyn and Reuthie did the same.

Ervyn began to plead for his sister when the elder, who had been briefed, chose to circumvent the need for more elaborate proceedings and dispatch with formalities.

"I understand the girl child wants to be invited into the city of Kywerth to become a slave," the elder said, before directing his attention wholly to Reuthie. "Only by promising to never return to your home, never once, could you be allowed to remain, no matter what you see or are asked to do here."

"I promise," she said without a moment of hesitation. "I promise," she repeated solemnly.

And thus Reuthie swore a promise which she would not keep.

* * *

Reuthie became a kitchen slave where she was taught the elaborate cooking of secret dishes the Tyrans had invented. Two crossings of suns later, after the elder Tyran and his officers set out to collect the non-existent harvest from the farmers of the drought, mysterious meat arrived into the kitchens and Reuthie knew then the fate she had only narrowly avoided.

She and Ervyn avoided eating the meat.

* * *

As time crawled forward, the children began to forget their former lives as farmers. Once Ervyn's snapped finger completely healed, he could play every instrument the Tyrans invented for him: horns, flutes, strings with bows, and a large wooden box made of ivory keys. Each of them he mastered with proficiency as easily as if he had fathered the instruments himself. His fingers bloomed and each night slaves were sent to his private room in the tower to caress and stroke his fingers, preserving them as finely as pure gold and polishing them to shining.

Neither Ervyn nor the slaves spoke about the farms from where they came, and so the memories drifted into the distance like vague dreams lost upon awakening.

The Tyrans delighted in such lives made of music and gaiety and rich food and drink and excess. As seasons passed and fine vegetables filled the kitchens and their plates, Ervyn and Reuthie eventually also forgot about the mysterious meat. Not because they really forgot. Instead they willingly chose to not remember the meat, and thereby disturb the rich comfortable lives they had stumbled upon by fate and luck.

The meat, though. The meat always loomed, a threat tugging dark dangling threads at their consciences.

* * *

When seven summer seasons passed and Ervyn became a near-man of twelve and Reuthie a young woman of thirteen, the air crackled dry and dust ground the air like sandpaper on a breath. The red harvest suns crossed in dueling blazes of fiery hot judgment, and so Ervyn and Reuthie felt the drought hugging the city like death's dry kiss. The same drought which had brought about their unexpected circumstances, and they remembered.

Reuthie begged her brother to leave then, to go and warn the farmers of their imposing doom and rescue them from the Tyran's dinner tables. But Ervyn refused. The farmers had sent them here, he reminded her, to be eaten in their stead.

So Reuthie went alone. The gates, she learned, were locked after all but only from the inside, to keep secrets safe and tucked away within the white walls. She'd never even attempted to leave the city before, having kept her promise all these seasons.

She snuck out through an opening in the kitchen behind the iron cauldron and through the ashes.

And she ran, past the mountain demons and down the trail and out of sight.

* * *

Ervyn smelled the fire before he saw it.

He paused from his practice on a new golden horn with a curved tail and pearl-covered finger holes to rush to the window of his tall white tower. The city was ablaze in a fiery ecstasy. Flames danced and grew powerful, devouring white rooftops like demons descended from their mountaintops to wreak havoc and oblivion.

Farmers burst through the gates and trampled through the streets with torches and Tyrans took hoof from their homes, screeching and howling, leaving behind their broken and driven through the opened gates toward the mountains.

Ervyn scrambled down his tower and pushed his way through the terrified Tyrans toward the round clearing and the dais.

His mother didn't recognize him at first, so grown and changed had he become. No longer a boy with deformed fingers, but a young man with arrogance and pride of his talent.

Mathilda stared out from the center of the dais at this unknown son. Her hair blew wild and ragged as the light from the torch she held waved hungry sparks and coughed dark smoke. Ervyn curled his long golden fingers into fists.

"Mother, no!" He cried, but his words only fed her burning resolve. With a demonic smile of yellowed teeth and ash-streaked crevices in her wrinkled face, Mathilda touched the flames to the wooden box with the ivory keys. The flames tasted the elegant carvings and were pleased, rising in triumphant satisfaction.

Ervyn couldn't move.

The instrument blossomed fire for its one last performance, a crumbled discord of strings collapsing on each other in defeat.

He didn't feel his mother grab him by the arm and pull him away.

* * *

The Tyrans retreated to a land somewhere beyond the mountains. If they eventually came to build cities of their own there, the farmers couldn't discern and didn't care because they were freed.

With only the unseen mountain demons left to appease, the work of a farmer evolved. Droughts and floods were countered and fought with careful preparation. Craftsmen, former Tyran slaves, devised storage and more elegant housing structures based on what they'd learned in their years in Kywerth.

But when hunters devised weapons and meat began to appear upon plates in these new comfortable wooden homes alongside vegetables fresh or canned, the origin of the meat was not questioned. Reuthie became especially essential to the grooming of chefs and the growth of the food industry, and she handled both meat and vegetable with deft cunning.

Only Ervyn could not bring himself to music again, his will broken beyond repair like his former instruments.

He farmed. Though if he hated being thrust back into the fields, no one could discern because he never said. He also never said whether the strained sounds of Stethen's bullfrog horn calling folks to arise and work gave him a vague sense of melancholia.

His fingers grew dark and tattered and weary. The more he farmed, the less his fingers appeared different than those of other farmers, save for a slightly longer length and an occasional odd gesture. An echo from his past. Mathilda noticed these gestures, though she did not remark upon them.

As seasons passed Ervyn found alcohol poured into his hardened shell soothed the emptiness, as his father had found before him. And as his father had done, he curled his fingers to strike when blind fury overtook him, and he didn't remember how or why it began that way.

When his seventh son was born with soft tendril fingers Ervyn said nothing. He let the boy alone, only occasionally to whistle a sad tune through a bean leaf to make the child smile.

The seventh son of a seventh son grew determined to avoid such a downtrodden state as his father, being particularly averse to the fits of fury which seemingly came from nowhere to a child who did not understand. So when the seventh son accidentally discovered his own talent for a game using a stick and a ball, he shoved those talents aside and he farmed with fervor. He found a kind of peace in farming which his father never had, though farming never gave him the kind of joy his game of stick and ball had done, nor the kind his father had felt when he first played his white swan instrument. Those shadow memories faded into a hollow silence that resonated at the bottom of a bottle and the sly creaking of a rocking chair on a porch overlooking the fields.

When the seventh son welcomed his seventh child, a daughter, he named her Ervyna because by the time the second smaller moon had drifted away to forge its own path in the cosmos and the second sun had all but burned out, farmers no longer discounted females. The need for farmers had also been diminished by the larger more powerful sun, dwindled with the stakes of competition and automation. So the female child named Ervyna used her soft yearning fingers to write elaborate words scratched on scraps of paper wherever she could find them, encouraged by her grandfather and his tunes whistled through a bean leaf.

And thus it was his story is told.

JUST LIKE 1815

ANDREW McCORMICK

"The Governor-General's conference is over. He will see you now."

The two diplomats from the Union of States rose from their seats. They had been seated in the New Orleans Government House's stuffy reception area for well over twenty-five minutes. The whole time, the raucous ear-splitting noise originating from outside the compound, due to impromptu festivities celebrating yesterday's World Series victory, had been distracting. Despite voicing their concerns, the male receptionist had politely declined to close the portico doors, citing a problem with the air conditioning.

"They only want to rub their damn victory in our faces," the younger diplomat groused. The older diplomat said nothing.

The receptionist stood shakily. "If you gentlemen would care to follow me?" He indicated they should go down a hallway. He rubbed his reddened eyes discreetly and tried unsuccessfully to suppress a toothy grin. When they reached His Lordship's private office, the receptionist knocked twice, then threw open the thick oaken doors.

The Governor-General sat at his desk, his high-backed chair turned away from them. He appeared to be listening to the triumphant roars emanated from Pakenham Park on the other side of Government House. The tele-box was on, which the Governor-General could watch out of the corner of his eye, replaying the Seventh Game of the 1962 World Series.

The receptionist coughed slightly. Lord Bernard Law Montgomery, His Majesty's Governor-General of the New Orleans Crown Colony, swirled his chair to face the diplomats. Grunting, he waved the pair to chairs, being careful not to spill wine from his goblet. Judging from the bottle's label, the claret originated from an award-winning British Columbian winery outside Portland. The bottle's half-filled contents indicated His Lordship must have been "in conference" with John Barleycorn for some time.

"Your Lordship. Union of States Minister-Without-Portfolio, Richard Nixon. And Union Consul to the New Orleans Crown Colony, John Kennedy." Bowing slightly, almost falling over with the effort, the receptionist left.

Reluctantly, the tele-box was turned off. "I would imagine you would rather not watch Willie Mays slide past Johnny Roseboro again, eh, what?"

Montgomery chuckled to himself as he laid the remote down on his large, ornately carved mahogany desk. "Minister Nixon. Consul Kennedy. How kind of you to visit at this early hour to offer your congratulations." He suppressed a burp. "I assume that was your purpose. Damn decent of you, I must say."

"Thank you for receiving us," Nixon said simply.

"Quite remarkable, this base-ball game of yours. Faster than cricket, I grant you, but not nearly as exciting. Though that last game was quite thrilling. Run scoring in the bottom of Inning Nine. Last minute victory and all that. Our New Orleans

Redcoats defeating the New York Yankees." He paused, musing. "The Redcoats beating the Yankees. Just like the Battle of New Orleans. Just like 1815, eh, what?" He smiled, and then guffawed like a donkey, as if just now realizing the angle the sport pages had been trumpeting for days.

"Yes," Nixon said. "An exciting World Series. For New Orleans."

"Thank you," Montgomery noticed his goblet was not full. He picked up the claret bottle. After pouring, he asked if they would care for some. They declined.

"Well, then. If I may ask, what might be the reason for this unexpected call? I must confess I was surprised to hear you were here with no scheduled appointment. Did my best to clear up my desk to receive you." He took another sip. "Good God, I hope it isn't yet another complaint about blocked trade on the Mississippi." Montgomery sighed, and then went on, as if lecturing again at the War College.

"We have been quite specific as to the amount of river tonnage we will receive coming down the Mississippi River. Any further arguments on raising the quota, I regret, would only waste your time and mine. Your Midwest grain shipments will just have to find another outlet." He took another swallow, and then smiled at the diplomats. He seemed to be enjoying himself.

"Now, if you'll excuse me, I must prepare for the festivities this afternoon. No rest for the weary, you know. I do hope you two will attend the Redcoat victory parade in a few hours, eh, what? As my guests?" Montgomery guffawed most unpleasantly.

"We understand your time is valuable," Kennedy said. He looked over at Nixon, who nodded solemnly. Kennedy lowered his voice significantly.

"Actually, Lord Montgomery, we have been looking for an opportunity to confer privately with you for the past twenty-four hours. The, ah, Redcoats beating the Yankees provided some unexpected cover for the much more pertinent business we need to discuss without further delay."

"Eh?"

"Minister?" Kennedy said to Nixon.

Nixon rose and produced several papers from within his ermine robe.

"Yes, Lord Montgomery, something urgent has come up which may require your personal touch." He spread the papers on the desk. They appeared to be photographs.

"My personal touch, you say?" They could see he was flattered. He leaned further forward. Pinned ostentatiously to his chest was his Victoria Cross, awarded by King George IX for Montgomery's victory at El Alamein over General de Gaulle.

"Yes," Kennedy said. "We are hoping you will be able to alert His Majesty's government to a potentially grave situation. It concerns Cuba."

"Cuba? Which one? East Cuba or West Cuba?"

"Primarily East Cuba. The British Mandate. Although it also concerns the Confederacy's West Cuba Mandate."

"I see," although Montgomery clearly did not. Outside, a loud off-key rendition of "God Save The King" came from the direction of the Park.

"With your permission?" Nixon said. Montgomery didn't look up as the Union diplomat closed the balcony doors.

As he stood beside Montgomery, Nixon leaned down and circled a few areas in one of the photographs with his fountain pen.

"These images, taken from our satellites, reveal that the British Empire is currently establishing a missile base outside the city of San Cristobel. We have further confirmed the missiles will be capable of carrying atomic weapons, which is a clear violation of the 1954 League of Nations Non-Proliferation Atomic Compact."

Montgomery grumbled as he put on gold-rimmed spectacles and looked closer.

"These photographs should have been given to the League at once," Kennedy said. "But President Stevenson fears that if the Confederacy is alerted to a British threat, it would aid President Wallace's reelection. As we both know, President Wallace is hardly a dove when it comes to East Cuba."

Confused, Montgomery put his goblet down and took out a pack of Savannahs.

"Cigarette?" Neither diplomat accepted. Montgomery lit his cigarette and puffed vigorously. White trails of smoke clouded his seventy-five-year-old features.

"Assuming all this to be true," he said, after exhaling. "And I'm not saying they are. Why show these to me?"

"Our government has little influence with either London or Charleston."

"Your own damn fault, backing Egypt during that Suez thing."

"It is hoped," Nixon went on. "That you might persuade Whitehall to dismantle those missiles."

Montgomery laughed. "Now, why should I tell Harold McMillian to do that?"

"You do have some influence, we would imagine, with your distinguished war record. And you do have credibility when it comes to anti-atomic sentiment. After all, you *did* council Whitehall against using the Bomb on Paris."

"Even if your efforts were unsuccessful," Kennedy said.

"True, true, all too true," Montgomery absently fingered his Victoria Cross medal.

"But why are you so bloody concerned about our *alleged* missiles in Cuba? I would think you would welcome them. They'd put some restraint on Wallace's saber rattling."

Nixon handed over a second set of photographs.

"*These* photos show that the Confederates have begun their *own* atomic base. Right outside Cienfuegos, near a place called *Bahia de Cochinos*."

"Translates to '*Bay of Pigs*,'" Kennedy added. "If I correctly recall my prep school Spanish."

"The Confeds have *atomic* weapons?" Montgomery looked thunderstruck.

"We detected atomic tests in Carlsbad Caverns over nine months ago."

"Good God."

"We have strong reason to believe the Confeds are not aware of your missile base," Nixon said." We cannot approach McMillian ourselves, being diplomatically isolated. We hope that you, as a former war hero, can act as an intermediary."

Nixon returned to his chair. As he sat down, he gently stroked its armrests. "Time is essential. Once Wallace learns of your British base, as he will, he would launch his missiles without a second thought, given his animosity toward England. A preemptive attack on East Cuba, not to mention a probable strike against New

Orleans, will insure his reelection. As for us, given his aggressive immigration and expansion policies, six more years of President Wallace is not an option."

Montgomery frowned. "Nor us. We favor an independent Mexico as you do."

Nixon leaned forward from his chair and rested his hands on Montgomery's desk. The Governor-General regarded the Union Minister with concerned eyes.

"Let us put our cards on the table," Nixon said. "Our proposal is this. Alert McMillian of the existence of the Confederate base. Let him be aware you received the information from us. Use these photographs, which, most assuredly, can be verified from your own satellites, as well as from any neutral country's surveillance, such as Cathay, Brazil or Prussia. If Wilson denounces them strongly at the league, combined with the element of surprise, it will put the Confederacy in a most awkward and embarrassing position, to say the least."

Nixon paused. "Go on, then," Montgomery said. Nixon went on.

"Given the universal tension at present, with the world seemingly poised to begin World War Four, only with this one *beginning* with atomic weapons, the Confederacy will have no choice but to be forced to back down. It will deflate Wallace's support and greatly improve the chances for Senator Lyndon Johnson to be elected. In return, we ask that England quietly dismantles their base, once the crisis is over. After all, we realize those English missiles could just as easily hit Washington City as they could Charleston."

Montgomery was silent for over a minute. This was an awful lot of sudden information for the old warrior to process, Kennedy mused.

Montgomery took a slow sip of claret. Wiping his chin, he said, slowly, "I understand the urgency. This must be revealed before their election, which is only weeks away. But, pray, have you considered the consequences? I mean, what if Wallace decides to launch his missiles, *anyway?* My God, he could, loose cannon as he is."

"A risk we must take," Nixon said. "Hopefully, the horrors of Hiroshima, Paris, and Montevideo are as upsetting to the citizens of the Confederacy as they are to the rest of the civilized world."

"Hopefully." Montgomery pushed with his arms to stand up from his chair. "Very well. I suppose I must do what I can." Unconsciously, he licked his lips.

"How soon can you contact London?"

"Within the hour. Even on Sunday, there must be *someone* on duty in the Foreign Ministry." He chuckled. "I sincerely hope McMillian will be able to gather a quorum of ministers for an immediate cabinet session. They all do so love to keep their weekend whereabouts hidden, eh, what?"

Kennedy and Nixon chuckled perfunctorily back at him. British minster love-nests were currently the major topic in all the British tabloids.

"Contact Consul Kennedy directly at the Union Consulate," Nixon said. "We must insist on an answer in less than twenty-four hours. Otherwise, we will be forced to reveal both the British and Confederate bases at the League ourselves."

"Good, good," Montgomery said. "A little tight deadline never hurt anyone. Especially when we're dealing with the lustful passions of Members of Parliament."

His Lordship escorted the pair of diplomats to the lobby. At the door, they shook hands and exchanged vague farewells. As they were about to leave, Nixon turned and said loudly so the receptionist could hear. "I still think Roseboro tagged

Mays out on that steal of home, but there's no help for that. You can expect delivery of our World Series wager of six cases of Ohio Bourbon within the week."

Caught off-guard, Montgomery spluttered, "Thank, thank you."

"It is the least we can do."

The Union diplomats left Government House and got in their horse-drawn carriage at the columned entrance for their return to the Union Embassy. They had opted for not driving the Embassy's hybrid limousine, correctly anticipating the swelling throngs of New Orleans celebrants jamming the narrow streets.

Joyous celebrators flowed into every street they passed; many held bottles of Bayou Beer in their hands. Obviously, the Sunday Blue Laws were not being enforced.

As they rode in silence, Kennedy gazed out the tinted window and saw numerous signs along their way, hand-made as well as shop-printed. All had the same message.

"Just like 1815," he read aloud.

"Just like 1815." Nixon repeated.

"Because of one copperhead snake bite."

"What? Oh, yes, how the American general died, of course." Nixon chuckled. "Back when there was only *one* America. General Johnson, Jackson, something like that. Riding in the wrong swamp at the wrong time. Leaderless, the Union army was routed." He laughed. "True, the English *should* have withdrawn and left New Orleans, since the War of 1812 had been over for weeks, but they didn't. With us later losing the War of 1818, New Orleans stayed British. As a result, the Mississippi River was closed to us as an avenue for commerce, the Southern States grew restless, they seceded, and the rest, as they say, is history."

"If only we had won," Kennedy mused. "How different things would have been."

"Oh," Nixon said as he closed his eyes to rest. "I imagine things would have been pretty much the same."

The carriage slowly clip-clopped its way down the cobblestone streets.

CHACONNE

BRUCE MEYER

We met when we were pan-handling the same corner, and rather than tell me to get lost or me tell him to fuck off he told me his story. "Why was he working the cows for change?"

He replied he was just trying to get some change so he could buy a cup of coffee and a subway token so he could jump in front of a train.

"But why not stick around to tell someone your story? I got ears. You gotta have some story."

That made him listen, and the more he listened, the more he told me. He was not the sort of man to hide behind the masks everyone wears. He knew what the masks meant and how to wear them and he'd tell you what they meant. James Bennett was a natural-born teacher and he taught me how to survive the end of the world.

He'd been a scholar of Italian Renaissance literature at the university and had risen to the top of his profession, establishing himself as an authority in the field of *commedia dell'arte*. He was admired by his students as a *bon vivant* whose bawdy sense of humour was attributed to the *Arlequino* he had absorbed by osmosis from his research.

Several strokes were against him from the start. He was a non-Italian teaching in an Italian department, and his passions led him to believe he could conduct his life as if he were a Tuscan *cavalieri*. He told me he'd made a clown of himself. I knew what he was talking about. "We're all clowns," but I added, "we have to listen to our own beat even if it is not the one the world wants to hear."

The passion that did him in was a graduate student who bore a striking resemblance to the Mona Lisa, though her eyes were not as soft and gentle as La Giaconda's nor did her dark hair fall with the grace and beauty that enticed thieves and emperors to risk everything for her. When I passed Ms. Giaconda on the sidewalk, she looked right through me. She was Italian by birth, sophisticated, and beautiful in a sculpted way. Something about her beauty, her white marble complexion, spoke of coldness, with an element of the reptilic about her. I find that a turn-off. One look at her and I could have told him she was dangerous. Bennett was certain he was in love with her and she was in love with him. But in reality—and there is always a *but* behind every reality—nothing was farther from the truth.

And though Lizina Albero had become the centre of his world, an offering of forbidden fruit in the academic garden, he saw the house of cards he had built collapse. It was grand theatre, a scenario worthy of a frame but not a painter. What had it all been for? Lizina was just another student with a pleasant smile when she needed to smile and shrewdness when she needed to serve her own ends.

In April of 2012, Lizina brought the matter of her affair with James Bennett to the attention of the university's Sexual Harassment Officer. By autumn of 2012,

Jim had lost his sense of humour. He also lost his wife, his job, his home, and most of his mind. Take away a man's world, leave him with only his naked silences, and he will fill the void with babble and the trash of false dreams.

In short order, he was brought before a tribunal of his peers and dismissed from the university. His lawyer, an old school friend, did not even show up to defend him. When Bennett went home, Lizina had already spoken to his wife and the locks on the front door had been changed. On the night of his defeat, the 20th of October, Bennett tried to check in to a downtown hotel only to be told that his credit cards had been cancelled and he had nowhere to go. He wandered the streets all night and at dawn sat down on a bench at Bloor and Spadina, loosened his black and white tie with clown faces that someone had given him years before as a joke, and wept beside the tumbled oversized black marble dominos stacked at the corner.

He should have seen it coming. He knew the jealousies of his department. His so-called friend and colleague, Gabriel Sole, had long wanted to eclipse him, while giving him the friendly sort of advice one gets from a bartender or a priest in the intimacy of confession while both dish out stuff to roll the head. Bennett came to realize that Sole was his Iago. Sole coveted Bennett's research on *commedia* and clowns. Dashing and dark, Sole was *Scaramouche*, the fiery lover, the dark presence who in faculty meetings knew how to humiliate Bennett subtly and reduce the stupid Anglo to a simpering *Arlequino*.

When Bennett walked along Bloor Street towards Bathurst early on the drizzly morning of October 21, he saw Lizina and Gabriel, arm in arm, kissing outside of a coffee shop, sharing an aubade of lovers parting at dawn, a veritable Romeo and Juliet who might as well have been debating ornithology in their birthday suits as standing there balancing lattes and briefcases with their free hands. Jim knew his betrayal had been a farce from beginning to end. Good luck to Gabe, Jim told himself. Life is a comedy where everyone is a clown. Each man in his time plays many parts until the party is over and with the judgment knell of midnight the truth is unmasked. But in that moment of absolute humiliation, he no longer felt as if he was *Arlequino*, but the dupe of the drama, *Il Dottore*, the impotent professor, or worse, a hobbling *Pantalone* who would never recover the vigor that had once driven him in his hubris. That was the beginning of the bad part for Jim.

After one night in the Fred Victor Mission when someone stole his Paul Smith socks, he decided he would use his negotiable skills and get a job, a fresh start. But as the days of November wore on the problem of "no-fixed-address" became an impediment. The morning we met, he'd asked me as we stood huddled with some other guys outside a coffee and doughnuts place on Bloor Street what other accommodations might be available. He'd had a terrible night among the coughing, agitated bodies spread on cots. Wasn't there somewhere else to go?

"Seaton House. It is the filing cabinet for the unwanted men of Toronto. It is dangerous. Someone will steal your shoes. That is a level of unkindness one step beyond stealing your socks. And winter is coming on. If you thought the Freddy Vic smelled, wait 'til you get a whiff down there in the S.O.B."

He didn't get my drift.

"S.O.B.," I explained to him, "was the name for the area around Seaton House, an abbreviation used by taxi drivers for Seaton, Ontario, and Berkeley Streets. It is an acronym for a place you don't want to go. There's a room upstairs, monitored day and night, where the methadone addicts—the guys coming off heroin who are touch and go—lie under white sheets like snowdrifts who have melted into themselves. I once looked in through the window of that darkened room. The dude at the window, the watcher, told me to come and have a look. The bodies were arranged in tidy rows in the dim light. One or two of the sleepers had their knees crooked, but the rest were just these shapes who were adrift in their own perished dreams, each his own personal Franklin Expedition. And from a distance as I looked in, the room was an arctic landscape of men suffering from their own desires.

"You don't want to go there," I told him. "You don't want to go there."

Jim can be a resourceful guy, so, he found us a basement room in Kensington Market, an "apartment" below a butcher's shop that smelled of a gas leak and damp rot, with two cots, a hot plate, and a chair we could take turns sitting in. We dubbed it Plato's Cave. He'd run into an old gym buddy of his who loaned him a couple of hundred bucks. I thought it was heaven after the street. Jim thought it was hell, but I said, "hey, you must have a pretty good grasp of Dante, right? So, what's your problem?"

"Hell is a narrative, a place where people are trapped in their own stories, and I am living in it now," he said. "I am living my story and it won't end."

"*But,*" I responded, "there was a way out and up, right?"

Jim finally asked me how I knew so much about Dante. I think he was being sarcastic. I told him even a PhD candidate in Math with an Engineering degree had read his Dante and Tasso, too, and that shut him up. *Jerusalem Delivered.* Could be. Had been. Dante got out alive. Tweegie and Bennett delivered.

Our first night in the cave, he asked me about my last name which I hadn't told him and I said, "yeah, Mike Tweegie, and don't say anything about me seeing a puddy-tat."

"Great, he said, here I am living in hell with a caged mathematician who has a fear of cats, and nothing adds up."

But I assured him that it did. Even when the numbers sailed away from me on the horizon of my mind's eye and the alphabet of equations began to resemble hydro lines, I knew it would lead somewhere. I'd been bad once. I'd written all over the wall of the York Club, so much so, they had to send in masons to turn each brick around. Now I'd met him.

That first night, I heard him weeping in his cot, so I climbed in with him and we just held each other. It was good to hold another human being again. I tried comfort him. "Hey, I said, we should put a sign on the door, a nice professional-looking brass plate. *Bennett and Tweegie, Spelunkers and Mountaineers.* I'm your Virgil," I told him.

He began to talk more and more now—constantly, in fact—about the world ending, that everything in his life was a sign of the life's demise and that the Mayans were right. It was all going to disappear in a puff of smoke or the thud of a dark invisible comet just as the sun was coming up on Friday, December 21, the solstice of 21/12/12, and that if there was something he could do to stop it, something that would make his miserable life worthwhile, something he could die believing in, he would seize it and make the world his own again. Damn, he wanted to save the world. I liked that. He especially went on with his date rant after we'd pass a former graduate student on the street during our evening wanderings.

Wanderings aren't a bad thing to pass the time. Vagabonds, the original clowns, did this as both a hobby and living. Remember Hamlet's players and their king? The nineteenth century poets, Bliss Carman and Richard Hovey, made pointless walking into a popular poetic theme, a motif that was taken up by W.H. Davies and even Samuel Beckett. I'm sounding like a literary critic, eh? Jim and I were ambulatory Vladimirs and Estragons, waiting for something to happen, and wandering broke the monotony of the wait. I once wandered non-stop for three weeks, just up and down the Bayview Extension, through the labyrinths of Rosedale and the rat's maze of Cabbagetown and into those great little places to hide where the other street people seldom hang. Now, I had a companion to wander with. Every now and then Jim would say something slightly upsetting, and I'd think of Rumi in his cave and how he murdered his only friend in the world, but I didn't figure Jim for being homicidal. I mean, a man who grieves the loss of Paul Smith socks isn't exactly homicidal in my books.

During one of our November evening wanderings along Yorkville, Jim ducked into a classical music store. He knew the owner and the shop had been one of his favorite haunts. He said he'd dropped a lot of money there and they'd let him browse so we'd be warm for a few hours. There was music playing. Something early Baroque.

As we stood in the CD store, I was suddenly struck with a horrific pain at the centre of my soul. It began with the low bass notes in the opening bars repeating and repeating on the store's stereo. I thought a monster was coming to eat me. The low moaning notes were overlaid with the weeping of a violin, a voice struggling to make sense of a great tragedy, a heart consoled with trivial explanations and afterthoughts that somehow didn't matter in the great scheme of things.

"This music mads me!" I screamed and put my hands over my ears.

Jim looked startled and embarrassed as I writhed on the floor. The sad, tragic violin notes were like a knife slicing through everything that had been my life. I wept. The clerks came running and gathered around. One asked if she should call an ambulance. Another wondered if I was epileptic. Jim told them all to stand back and give me air.

He knelt and whispered in my ear. "That is Vitali. It is his 'Chaconne pour Violon,'" he said in a gentle voice. "Would you like me to ask them to turn it off?" he asked softly, but when I pulled my hands from my ears, I suddenly felt a clarity that I hadn't known in years, a sense that the world I had given up for dead around me was alive and brilliant and as ordered as a Fibonacci sequence, its miracles blossoming in my blood. I remembered reading what Toni Morrison had once said about a young woman named Marie Cardenal and how she had been changed by hearing a Louis Armstrong trumpet solo. I was now part of that experience of transformation. The gathering helped me up from the floor.

"What is a chaconne?" I asked. "I need more. I need more."

Jim begged the indulgence of the store owner. She brewed a pot of coffee and the three of us spent the evening listening to chaconnes and ciacconna, passacaglia, and grounds. Bach, Bertali, Busconi, Pachelbel's "F Minor Chaconne for Organ"—one of the most beautiful pieces of music I have ever heard—all passed through the night and into my heart.

Numbers and equations started coming back to me with a tremendous alacrity. I suddenly felt as if my life and its disorganization was not a cess pit of madness or a disorder but simply a song, a melody, a very limited human expression in its brevity where a voice in the music longs for a lost or inaccessible order. I had once thought that mathematics could do that for me, but in the infinite universe of numbers and possible questions and probable and palatable solutions, I heard the voice inside me dwindle and grow silent as if it could say nothing more. Now, I felt I could speak again, effortlessly, limitlessly because to say something, anything, is to add a few grace notes to the beautiful cacophony that is the human experience.

Jim was quiet, withdrawn, and pensive. He sat there with his chin on his fist and his elbow propped on his knee like Rodin's Thinker. We started talking about the chaconne as a lost form of music that was constantly struggling to be reborn in every age. The chaconne had been the music one dared not play in the seventeenth century, yet it was the music everyone wanted to hear, and was to its own era what the blues has been to ours. As a dance, it was popular into the eighteenth century. That's when Vitali's sad violin lament was written. He transformed the chaconne in all its blues brilliance into the soulful *crie de coeur* that Vitali—a name that echoes the word for life—harnessed in his "Chaconne pour Violon." That is what had driven me to the floor. The chaconne was forgotten through the nineteenth century until in the early twentieth Busoni reinvented Bach's horny-rhythmed little dance as a piano masterpiece. Heck, now that I think of it, I realize that Bruno Mars's "The Way You Are" is a chaconne. The tune overlays a repetitive bass line. Bob Dylan, Johnny Cash—they are the *chaconnieri* of the world we know and take for granted.

Jim had been thumbing through a music reference book that the clerks kept behind the cash register of the CD store so they could appear knowledgeable if anyone sprang a pop quiz on them.

"Here it is," he said, holding up the book. "The chaconne was Mayan in its origins and had come to the Old World via the survivors of Cortez's expedition who destroyed Aztec civilization and converted Mexico to the sexless ways of Christianity."

I pictured Bernal Diaz and a group of Aztec captives in a small coastal *bodega* on his return to Spain. The Aztecs huddled in a corner like guys from the street. They played their beloved music for the last time before being seized by the Inquisition and having it tortured out of their bodies. They knew the world would end four times and begin again, each time destroyed by one of the elements, the last of the destructions by fire. They were the survivors of the fiery death of Tenochtitlan and lived to sing the requiem of all they lost. The chaconne spread through the streets of Europe where the musicians of the *commedia* took it up as their banner of bawd. Masked, the players thrust out their loins to both men and women alike, inspiring the comedies of Shakespeare and the etchings of the French master Jacques Callot. It was a music that matched the lives, passions, and professions of outcasts and street walkers—the *pasar calle* whose rhythmic struts became the signature of the *passacaglia*. And even as those Aztec *chaconnieri* burned at the stake for refusing to abandon their rhythm, they shouted their hymn to life. The last sound from their lips was the song of a phoenix rising from the ashes.

A group of Italian travelers heard a chaconne in the smelly, smoky confines of a vagabond *taverna*–the kind of inn Cervantes knew and captured in *Don Quixote*–and they could not get the music's lustiness out of their heads. They hummed it to the point of madness, a vitality that spoke of real life rather than heavenly reward. They carried it home with them to the scandalous courts of Italy and Naples and the world of Caravaggio and The Seven Mercies. A linguist later told me that the *chaconne* and its Italian derivation *ciacconna* may have come from a Mayan word for a medicinal plant known as the *cinchona*, an evergreen that in the dead of December blossoms in Central and South America at the solstice like the Glastonbury Thorn. The flowers of the *cinchona* contained large doses of quinine to cure a dying child or an enfeebled old man from the scourging sleep of malaria. The chaconne was the music of life in the midst of death.

Just after midnight Jim stood up and went to the window. "I know now what it is we must do to save the world," he said. "We must make an offering of synchronicity to the sky." Jim turned from the window. "We must make the world dance."

I had been cured by a chaconne. I was ready to begin again. Jim saw the cure in a different way. The world needed to begin again and in a new way. As we walked back to our stinking cave, and cars disappeared one by one from the traffic of the foggy night on Bloor Street, Jim told me his plan.

He knew street musicians who busked near Yonge and Bloor. One guy, an almost blind beggar who sold pencils and whose body was twisted from birth, played an empty white shortening bucket he had salvaged from a garbage pile in the heart of Chinatown. He would provide the beat, a pulse that could speak precisely through the indifference of a street corner and reach directly into the nervous system of a passerby. Another was an elderly drifter from Louisiana who had long ago given up his dream of jamming in a jazz band. He would carry the core bass melody, that repetition of four notes in the "ground" or bass line. Jim and I would build our own instruments out of whatever we could find—he told me he had played the cello before his demise and that if he could find the wood and wire he would construct his own version of a *viola da gamba*.

I was told to duct tape together as many narrow-necked bottles as I could, containers of different shapes that would serve as a chamber organ, the instrument of choice for chaconne composers such as Schmelzer and Biber whose music brought the *ciacconna* to its apotheosis during the 1640s in the lascivious courts of the Vatican cardinals. I found what I needed in the back of an LCBO. Having crafted our instruments, we would gather on the sixth hour of the twenty-first day of the year and play the world back into existence with a song to worship the rising sun, return of light to the world. The bass line would be the steady pulse of the turning planet. The beat would be the presence of time. And our variations on the narrowly defined theme of three or four notes would be the voice of humanity crying with a synchronicity and vitality needed to restart time from its dead, singular, zero point.

Hollywood, the pint-sized percussionist, Zeke the axe, me as Pipes on the "organ," and Jim on his viola da gamblin' as Zeke called it because that's all you have left after you've played your last hand, gathered on the corner of Bloor and

Avenue Road as the dawn was breaking on the morning of the twenty-first, the day rising of the winter solstice when the world would shed its darkness and its history. And if the planet survived past the sixth hour or the twelfth day of the twelfth month of the twelfth year—the spirit of harmony in all things—would be everlasting, reaffirmed and renewed in a world without end.

Jim had convinced them of his plan, though he had not told them of its complete details. The two new guys wanted to know where they were going to play. Jim had spent the last of his money on the gig. He pointed upwards to the top of the Park Hyatt.

"The music," he said, "will carry over the sleeping university from the rooftop terrace of the bar and wake the world either to its fate or its salvation."

He had chosen as the signature piece for the eternal moment Bertali's "Ciacconna." Zeke wasn't sure it made much sense or music, for that matter, though he said he was still drunk and didn't know what he was doing and didn't really give a damn as long as he could play.

Hollywood said he was game because this was his moment to shine, and though Zeke was still the worse of it he went along with the gamble. "I guess it's warmer in jail than out here and I ain't one to stand out in the cold if my friends are going inside." And so, he came in with us. We were a quartet.

We marched unnoticed through the lobby of the hotel and took the elevator to the Rooftop Lounge.

"Just like Carnegie Hall," exclaimed Hollywood as the elevator climbed. "Next stop Hollywood!"

Security never stirred. I looked at Jim in the mirrored and polished brass box. His face was glowing. With one tremendous shove, Jim burst open the portal to the lounge and then flung wide the French doors to the parapet terrace. Zeke stopped at the bar and slipped a bottle of Jack Daniels into his pocket.

We began to play at approximately 6:03. Sunrise.

We weren't that bad considering we had only practiced for an hour or so the day before.

We opened with a very moving version of Pachelbel's "F Minor Chaconne," or what sounded as if it could be that piece. The music wafted over the intersection, over the top of the museum and its giant, obtrusive crystal addition, and across the sleeping campus where not a student was stirring.

By the time that piece was over I knew the odds were against us. The light was rising along Bloor and over the top of the condo behind the Church of the Redeemer and soon it would break through the portal of the bell arch on that church and the intersection below would light up with the rest of the city, a golden glow shining brighter than an ancient idol on the empty streets with no one there to worship it.

And just as we were about to break into the Bertali, Jim leapt up on a tabletop beside the balustrade, stripped off his clothes, and shouted to the dawn to proclaim his belief to the sleeping city.

"Let there be synchronicity!" he shouted. "And if the world is not to end this day, let us all be reborn as new brothers and sisters in the human comedy! Let us play the world back to life and bring heaven and earth together once again for the everlasting joy of humanity!"

"Here! Here!" shouted Zeke. And we began to play.

Hollywood's beat thumped like the works of a clock, and Zeke's four notes repeated over and over in a steady defiance to time and change with an irresistible constancy to which he hollered, "Hallelujah!"

Jim put his make-shift *viola da gamba* under his arm and pressing it against his naked breast stroked the music from it as if it was his lover. And I blew on those bottles, my neck turning this way and that to capture the beat and the majesty of the melody. And by God we were magnificent.

The sun broke through the arch of the bell tower of the Church of the Redeemer, and I heard the shadow of its summons echo through the streets and off the glass walls that were lit with the golden light of a new dawn as if it was chiming the hour of redemption. And as we laid down our variations on the theme over top those four simple notes, the music drifting sure as a damp morning breeze toward the lake and the infinite heavens above as the security men arrived to wrestle our instruments from us. Yet, in the mayhem of that final struggle, 6:12 a.m. on December 21, 2012 passed, and the world was reborn, everlasting, with all the love and suffering it had always known.

As the police loaded us into the squad cars, I looked over at Jim and he was beaming.

"I am a new man today," he said. "Thank you, Tweegie, for your love and devotion."

"What will you do with your new life?" I asked him. I had an inkling of what I would do with mine once we did our time for break and enter.

"I have taken a new name," he said. "I am Giaccomo Bennetti. I am master of the *commedia dell'arte*, and I shall carry the message of the human comedy into the streets of this city, where the rebirth we have witnessed here today will live among the people forever."

And when I saw him again, four years later as the blossoms broke like laughter on the slant bank of old Taddle Creek outside Hart House, he was wearing a mask from the *commedia*, the face of *Il Dottore*, the experienced man whose knowledge has gone amiss. He was tacking up a poster advertising for players who wanted to take the people's art and voice into the busy streets and crowded downtown avenues of Toronto to delight those who hunger to know what lies behind all the masked faces they pass without a second thought, and to teach what it is to love the world as one would a wild and hopeless dream.

THE BLACK MASQUERADE

TIM JEFFREYS

The festival of The Black Masquerade took place every year, on the day of the spring solstice. The people of Kieldaig would dress up in grotesque masks and costumes of their own devising. Then, starting at dawn and continuing on until long after sundown, they would dance through the streets following a haphazard band of musicians. There were tuba players and bagpipers, flutists, and children with tin drums strung around their necks. All of those too would be wearing masks.

Once, it was believed that spirits inhabiting the highlands surrounding the village came down from the woods and peaks for a day to dance with the villagers. The spirits loved to dance and show off, it was said, but they kept to the highlands because they understood that their appearance horrified the living. The villagers wore their grotesque masks and costumes so that the spirits could move amongst them undetected. In this way the villagers honoured the highland spirits, and the spirits—sated and satisfied at being given a chance to spend a day dancing amongst the villagers—would send down enough rain from the slopes to keep the villagers' crops alive through the rest of the year.

By the time Niall Lockhart was born, the people of the village, barring a few of the most elderly residents, no longer believed in mountain spirits. But the tradition of The Black Masquerade went on. It was an excuse to dress up, and get drunk, and dance in the street, and as can be imagined, nobody wanted to give that up. And it was the one day of the year Niall Lockhart looked forward to the most.

* * *

The year he turned eighteen, Niall saw a beautiful young woman dancing amongst the crowds during The Black Masquerade. Her face was bare, and instead of a costume she wore a long loose white cotton dress through which the sunlight at times penetrated and revealed the outline of her body. Falling still as dancers continued to jostle around him, Niall pushed back the mask he wore in order to look at the woman unhindered. Radiant in the spring sunshine, her fair hair like a halo of gold, her soft eyes full of joy, her mouth open in laughter, she twirled and threw up her arms and kicked her feet with the rest. Briefly, Niall caught the woman's eye and she too paused in her dance to smile at him before the crowd closed in and swallowed her up. Niall even called out *No* and reached out a hand as the dancers enveloped him too, but it was no use, and by the time he was able to push his way through the throng to where he thought the woman had been standing, she had been swept away and was nowhere to be seen.

He couldn't get the woman's face out of his mind. When he lay in bed the memory of how she'd smiled at him, so warmly, so invitingly, kept him awake into the early hours. For a week he walked the village asking about her, describing her to everyone he met, but nobody remembered seeing her and no one knew who she was.

"You should never remove your mask during the dance," his grandmother scolded him. "That's when they see you. That's when you're vulnerable."

Having searched in vain for the woman every day since the festival, Niall's head hung in despair. He'd hardly touched the meal the old woman had prepared for him. "What are you talking about?"

"She was one of the spirits. Don't you see? Every year they take someone—or try to! Remember your Uncle Vincente? They took him one year."

Niall scoffed laughter. "Uncle Vincente went to Germany to find work. Anyway, she wasn't even wearing a mask."

With some effort, his grandmother sat forward in her chair and leaned towards him across the dining table. She took hold of his wrist. Her old hands were surprisingly strong. "How do you know that what you saw wasn't a mask? Can't the spirits wear masks too? All she would've had to do was take you by the arm—like this! Like I'm doing now!" Her fingers tightened on his wrist. "And lead you off into those mountains. And you like a love-struck fool following her wherever she goes. And then when you get up there, into those high places, the mask comes off and you'll find yourself alone with something you weren't expecting. Nothing in life is ever what you think it is, especially the most enticing things. There's always a catch. Remember that."

But Niall still tossed and turned at night, and sat with glazed eyes during the day, remembering the woman's smile, and how the sunlight had penetrated her dress to show the outline of her lithe young body. Was it possible she was one of the highland spirits, as his old grannie claimed? "Pah!" he said to himself. "Ridiculous!" But he resolved to find out. So, one bright sunshiny day he set off on a hike into the hills beyond the village with his sleeping bag and a bedroll on his back and a rucksack stuffed with bread, cheese, oatcakes, and some strips of herring stolen from the pantry. He was content to be alone on those slopes, following the footpaths through landscapes green and brown, with that vast ever-charging sky above him, perching on gnarly outcrops to eat, and crossing over the little wooden bridges spanning the steely fast-flowing streams. The surroundings so beguiled him that he almost forgot why he was there.

* * *

It was on his second day of wandering that he came across a peculiar sight. On a flat plain overgrown with matgrass, near to a small shallow lake, there stood a desk. And sitting at the desk was a square-jawed man. The man's hair was white at the temples and he wore a pin-striped suit. He appeared oblivious to the chill of the low wind. On the desktop in front of him sat some kind of counting machine, of the kind Niall had seen used in the bank in Invergorden. But instead of money, the man appeared to be counting pebbles.

On first seeing the man, Niall had glanced all around, looking for a building or a crowd of people, perhaps a film crew, as he was sure the man and his desk had to be connected to *something*. There couldn't just be a desk and a man in a suit there alone amidst all that matgrass. He watched dumbfounded as the man got up and hurried down to the edge of the water, leaned over and scooped up two handfuls of pebbles from the lakebed, ran back to his desk, and began busily counting them off on his machine. After a moment, as if sensing Niall's presence, the man halted his counting and glanced up.

"Hello," he said, smiling.

"Hel-hello," Niall said. "I thought I'd imagined you. What... what're you doing?"

"Just working," the man said. "So much work to do." He stood from his chair. "Hey, perhaps you'd like to come and work for me."

"Um, no thank you," Niall said. "I came here to find someone."

"Really? Who's that?"

Niall squinted at the man. Then, feeling foolish, he described the woman he'd seen only briefly on the day of the Black Masquerade, the woman whose features were nevertheless etched on his memory.

"I don't even know her name," he concluded.

"You sound like someone in love," the man said.

"Do you know her?" Niall asked.

"Perhaps I do," said the man, smiling again. "But if you want my help, you're going to have to earn it. Come and work for me."

Niall took a few steps closer to the desk. "What are you doing?"

"Counting the pebbles from the bottom of the lake."

Niall glanced down at the lake, then back at the man. "What for?"

"Oh, it's very rewarding work," the man said. "A very sought-after position. Here's an idea. You fetch the pebbles, and I'll count them up. Then when you get tired, I'll fetch the pebbles and you can count them up. That way we'll be done in no time. And as a reward, I'll tell you where to find this young woman you're looking for."

"Oh okay," Niall said. Though dubious, he let the pack fall from his back. He thought perhaps the man was mad. He'd have to be, out here in the middle of nowhere, counting pebbles from the bottom of a lake; but if there was a chance he knew where the woman Niall was looking for lived, Niall thought it might be good to humour him for a while. So he spent some time running back and forth to the lake, scooping up handfuls of pebbles from the icy water, which the man would drop through his counting machine and toss into a bucket which was hidden under the desk. He ran the pebbles through the machine quicker than Niall could collect them, and Niall soon tired.

"I really don't see the point of this," Niall said, when he stopped to catch his breath. "Who cares how many pebbles are at the bottom of that lake?"

"Someone does," the man said. "And it's important we count them."

Niall shook his head. His hands had become achy and red from the repeated dips in the lakewater. He tucked them into his armpits to warm them.

"It really does seem pointless."

The man shook his head. "No, no. It's very important, I assure you."

"And what about my reward? You said you'd tell me where the woman lived."

The man sat back in his chair. "Well, I can tell you that she lives in a little dry stone cottage."

"And?"

"A dry stone cottage beside a wide shallow stream. Over that way I think." The man pointed towards a high hill.

"How far?" Niall said. "How long will it take me to get there?"

The man stood. "It's your turn to do the counting. Sit down here at the machine, and I'll bring you pebbles to count."

"I honestly don't see the point of it."

"Is this your first job, young man?" the man said. "You'll need to work hard if you want to make an impression."

"But this isn't a job, it's just a pointless made-up task."

The man laughed at this, his head falling back. Then the humour left his face. He glanced up at the sky. "We need to put in a few more hours of it yet." Then before Niall could say anything more, he turned and strolled down to the lake.

Niall sat down at the desk. His fingers still ached. His stomach rumbled too. "A very sought-after position," he said to himself. "Ha!"

The man returned with pebbles cupped in his hands and dumped them down on the desk. Then before Niall could begin feeding them into the machine, he was off again to the lake for more.

"Wait," Niall said. "Just a minute. I need to..."

"Quick," said the man, returning a second time. "We've a lot to get through today."

The pebbles began to pile up on the desk faster than Niall could count them. Niall put them through the machine as fast as he could, but they began to scatter and fall to the ground. Every time the man returned from the lake, Niall nodded and smiled at him, hoping to assure him that everything was under control. But it soon became apparent that he couldn't keep up. He wanted to jump up and shout out about how ridiculous what they were doing was, how he hadn't signed up for this, all he'd wanted was a bit of information. But he kept putting the pebbles into the machine. And he kept nodding and smiling at the man every time he returned with more pebbles, afraid that if he didn't the man wouldn't tell him what he wanted to know. Finally the man stood over him, shaking his head.

"You need to improve your productivity, young man."

"*What?*" Niall said, releasing all the pent-up frustration. "I'm working as fast as I can, can't you see that? But you're going too fast. It's too much. I'm getting cold. My hands are numb already. And my feet. And the whole thing is just..."

"What?" said the man, cocking one eyebrow. "What is it?"

"Stupid," Niall said.

The man sighed. "You're not showing the required commitment. I'm afraid I'm going to have to let you go."

"*Commitment?*" Niall barked laughter. "To counting the pebbles from a lake? That's... That's... that's the stupidest thing I ever heard!"

"Perhaps it's not the right role for you. You haven't met your targets, I'm afraid. You haven't achieved your agreed targets."

"Targets?" Niall was speechless for a moment. Then he stood. "Fine. Just tell me exactly where to find the woman I told you about and I'll be on my way."

"I can't do that," the man said, his eyes now fixed on a grey spearhead of rock in the distance. "You didn't work hard enough to get paid."

"*Paid?* What do you mean, paid? I only wanted..." Jerking to his feet, Niall stamped over to where his pack and bedroll laid in the matgrass and snatched them up. After he slung his pack onto his back, and turned to address the man one last time, he saw that the desk and chair and the counting machine were gone. Vanished. The man too was gone. Hearing laughter and shrieks of glee, he glanced towards a dome of rock on his right in time to see a small, hunched, bat-eared figure disappearing over the crest of it.

"What the hell?"

Enraged to think that he'd been tricked, he started to follow the figure, but then he stopped. He thought of his grandmother saying, *Can't the spirits wear masks too?*

Shaking his head, he started walking again, looking out all the while for a dry stone wall cottage. He could only hope that the man, or whoever or whatever it was he'd just encountered, had at least been telling the truth about that.

* * *

That afternoon, Niall found himself walking along the edge of a shallow stream. After stopping for a hasty lunch, he had spied some kind of house or cottage far away in the valley ahead and seen also that the stream would lead him straight to it. He was still fuming about the time he'd wasted earlier in the day. That was the most infuriating thing, not that he'd been tricked, but that he'd wasted so much time on such a senseless task. Counting pebbles from the bottom of a lake indeed!

Orange light was already blazing up the sky between the two distant peaks, and the house or whatever it was he'd seen was still some miles away. Night fell swift here in the highlands, and soon he would be bedding down. How long could he stay out here before his food supplies ran out or the weather turned? A day or two more? Grimacing, he turned his head and spat, thinking again of the wasted hours.

Somewhere in the midst of all this irritation and anguish, he happened to look down and saw that there was a banknote stuck to his right leg. It was a fifty-pound note, in fact. The wind blew it flat against his thigh just above the knee. He managed to grab the note before it was whipped away by the wind. He held it up in front of his face and stared at it.

Impossible!

He caught sight of something in his peripheral vision, and turning his head, he saw more banknotes blowing by. At once he began to snatch at them and chase after them as they tumbled along on the wind. He was laughing. Soon he had a thick wad of notes in his hand, and the wind carried still more. Some caught in the grass and were immediately snatched up by Niall. Others floated on the surface of the stream like lily pads. He grabbed at a couple of these too, but they disintegrated in his hands. Pausing to stuff a bundle of notes into his backpack, he immediately began collecting more.

He was half aware that he had strayed off course, but he thought, *To hell with it!* He'd be going back to Kieldaig a rich man! People would've laughed at him if they'd seen him setting out. They were probably laughing now. But they wouldn't be laughing when he returned loaded down with cash! His mind tripped over itself thinking of all the things he could buy. A house! A car! Some nice clothes! He'd be the best dressed man in Kieldaig! And then what? Then what would he do with all his money? Suddenly picturing himself sitting alone in a room in a mansion house, he stopped and let the money in his hands flutter away on the wind. What would be the use of all that money if he didn't find *her*—the woman who had smiled at him on the day of the Black Masquerade? What was the use of money if there was nothing to spend it on? No one to share it with?

On the crest of a hill he saw a figure then, a tall figure silhouetted against the sky. It was from the direction of this figure that the banknotes had been blowing. As he watched he saw this figure reach down, pick a bundle of something from the ground and release it onto the wind. As first as they fluttered they had looked like banknotes, tens and twenties and fifties just like the ones Niall had filled his rucksack with, but by the time they reached Niall they were no longer banknotes, they were leaves. Dead leaves fallen from the trees.

Fooled again!

With an outraged cry, Niall slung the pack from his back and opened it up. Full, it was, of rotting leaves just like the ones fluttering around him now, fluttering around him as if to taunt him. Yelling again, he began to dig the leaves out of his pack with one hand. Then he turned to the figure on the crest of the hill and shouted the worst insults he could think of and danced around in anger and shook his fists. He thought he heard laughter returning. Then the figure turned away, giving an indication of a grotesque and elongated profile, before disappearing down the far slope of the hill. It was some minutes before Niall ceased his cursing and angry gesticulating. When he at last looked for the stream he'd been following before he began chasing money all across the strath, he was dismayed to realise night was beginning to fall, and he gave one final thwarted bellow.

Laying out his bedroll, he cursed the mountain spirits and their tricks. They didn't want him to reach the house where the beautiful woman lived, it seemed. But he would. He would. Ha! Just see! He would get there tomorrow.

* * *

The next day, as Niall breakfasted on the last of the oatcakes, thin spindrifts of snow began to fall.

Just a flurry, he thought. *It's common enough here in the highlands.*

He waited for the snowfall to stop, but instead it fell heavier, sticking to the ground. In no time it had obliterated the path he'd planned to take that day. The path to the cottage where, he'd hoped, the beautiful woman lived. And with his food almost gone, he knew there was nothing for it but turn himself around and head for home. He didn't want a walking party finding his frozen body huddled behind some rock in spring. He didn't want to be remembered as a young fool who'd gone off alone into the highlands and died of exposure, all because a woman had smiled at him during the festival of the Black Masquerade.

When he arrived back in the village, a group of children stopped their games to follow him and jeer.

"Did you find her?" they asked, hiding sniggers behind their hands. "Did you kiss her?"

"Piss off home," he told them, throwing wild kicks their way, making them scatter.

He knew that would not be the last of it.

In a village like Kieldaig nothing was ever forgotten.

He heard windows being thrown open as he made his way along the village streets. People he passed stopped to stare. He did his best to ignore the voices that called out to him.

Piss off, he thought. *Piss off, the lot of you.*

Rather than the fool who'd gone on a mad quest and frozen to death up in the highlands, he realised now that he was forever doomed to be the idiot who'd wandered into those high places looking for love and returned empty handed. People would be talking about it for years, the same way they still griped about how old Logan Harris had only won the pony show thirty years ago because behind his wife's back he'd been sleeping with Maggie Stewart. Maggie, that year, had been the pony show judge.

Maybe, Niall thought bitterly, *freezing to death would have been better.*

The village streets seemed suddenly small, like a trap drawing him inwards, and he realised he'd have to leave.

At least his old gran was pleased to see him back.

"Don't get used to me," he told her as he entered through the front door. "I'm away to Invergorden."

"What?" she said. "When?"

"Soon."

* * *

Sometime after Niall left Kieldaig, the tradition of the Black Masquerade died out. In Invergorden, he found a job as a sales rep for a pharmaceutical company, and—being a hardworking and personable sort—he gradually worked his way up the company hierarchy. The money was good, but the hours were long, and he soon began to resent his position. He would daydream about other things he could be doing with his life if he wasn't travelling from city to city with his suitcase full of pillboxes and sampler bottles. He went on smiling at the customers though, wearing his smile like a mask, a mask he eventually failed to recognise as such. For a time he enjoyed spending the money he earned, but eventually he grew bored and restless and left the money to accumulate in his bank account.

Then one day, in a crowded hotel bar, a woman smiled at him. Her smile reminded me of the smile of that beautiful woman he'd seen dancing amongst the crowds at the Black Masquerade when he was eighteen, so full or warmth and invitation. Her name was Ailsa. He fell in love right there, and later married her. They had a few happy years together, but in time Niall discovered Ailsa was not the woman he thought she was. Behind his back, she'd had many affairs, and his marriage was a sham. He was distraught on discovering this. There was no option for the two of them except to divorce.

Following the separation, Niall quit his job, gave up his share of the house he'd bought with Ailsa, sold his car and the rest of his belongings, and bought a caravan, which he parked by the edge of a loch. From that day on, he spent his days painting watercolours and making little clay models which he sold to tourists. He woke at dawn to see mist rising off the water and enjoyed a silence so profound it was as if someone had stopped time. Then at dusk he watched the sun set. He looked at the stars in the night sky and went to bed happy, quietly awed by the splendour and the beauty and magnitude of things. And by how unknowable it all was. Now when he smiled it was genuine, joyful, not a mask he wore to impress others.

Lying there in bed Niall sometimes thought about the time he'd trekked in the highlands above Kieldaig, and the spirits he'd encountered there. And when he did, he thought of this time fondly. It had been a lesson; he saw that now. And at last he realised what the spirits had been trying to teach him.

It was this: that life, *real life*, was the true masquerade.

REGATTA RONNIE

DWAIN CAMPBELL

Bang! The shotgun blast, muffled by concrete walls, is barely heard in the shabby, sweat-tainted confines of Her Majesty's Penitentiary's gym. Yet, Regatta Ronnie catches the start and commences rowing like the madmen he is.

"Complete fruitcake?" I ask Mike Rowsell, the other guard on station.

"Nuttier than an almond grove, Murph."

"Then why isn't he in Arkham Asylum, getting treatment and Thorazine in his orange juice?"

Mike purses lips, thinking that one over. I notice an offending gravy splotch on his slate gray uniform shirt. Obviously he's already raided a food stall outside the walls. "No malice in Ronnie Slaney, Bayman extraordinaire. Not a violent offender, and he's sane as a parson before a psychiatrist. If we let him row with the races on the lake, he'll cause no trouble." Left unsaid, bar him in his cell, forbid his lunatic obsession, and four of us will have to sit on him in the Special Handling Unit. Not cool, with us shorthanded on a holiday.

Newfoundland's Royal St. John's Regatta on Quidi Vidi Lake is the oldest sporting event in North America. But more so, it is fair day, and by noon, on a rare glorious morning like this when the sun is splitting the rocks, there will be 30,000 merry makers on the lakeshore just outside our walls. Not so merry in here, because the prisoners get understandably sullen at missing out on the good times. To top it off, no grounds privileges, on account of the yard gates being wide open to accommodate our union's fundraising booth. That increases the Surly Index immeasurably.

Soon, and dimly, for they are in the gazebo across Quidi Vidi, the Church Lad's Brigade Band cranks out "Up the Pond", anthem of the Regatta and signal that the teams are on the return leg and going for the finish line. Sure enough, Regatta Ronnie redoubles his efforts. Man, he's ripped up top like Captain America. I'm some glad he's docile.

Mike follows my gaze. "He's an inshore fisherman of the Old Breed. Doesn't even own an outboard motor. Rows his skiff out to his cod traps, when he's not buttonholed in here."

"Regular customer? Collects Air Miles courtesy of the Crown?"

Mike guffaws. "When he gets caught. Ronnie can see the French islands of St. Pierre and Miquelon from his fishing stage. Smuggling brandy and wine into Canada is his birthright, or so he thinks. The Mounties figure different, and two months ago they caught him and his wife red-handed, not a quarter mile from home." Mike pauses, a sad cast to his eyes. "That last caper went south, catastrophically, and..." *Bang,* the winner of the race crosses the finish line. With that, Ronnie springs off the rowing machine and does a victory lap around the dilapidated equipment, beating his chest like King Kong.

He's an odd stick, no mistake. With a severe crew cut and sleet worn, leathery face, he is a classic Marlboro Man. Eyes are a fierce blue, ears jumbo large, and hands, scarred from a lifetime of hauling lobster traps and fish nets, have the span of a catcher's mitt. No tattoos; that sets him apart from our garden variety punks doing piddly two-years-less-a-day sentences. As said, from the waist up he's trim, Mixed Martial Arts grade, but his legs are spindly in contrast. Makes sense; Newfoundlanders rarely walk the length of themselves, and the old gams never get a workout. As a result, his body is all askew, ill-proportioned.

Regatta Ron draws near to grab a Gatorade. I think to make conversation. "Mr. Slaney, catch your wind, sir." He's fifty-five; it doesn't hurt to be polite to an older inmate. "Twenty minutes easy until the next race."

He stiffens, blue eyes sparking dangerously. He squares onto me, and it's all I can do not to step back. "That's the Domino's Pizza Juvenile Female race. You thinks I take on little namby-pamby skirts, b'ye? You thinks I is a goddamned pervert?" He's in my face, and I recollect the alarm button is by the far door.

"Whoa, Mr. Slaney. No harm meant. My friend is new guy on the block, just learning the ropes. New guy, new wife, new baby, all newy." Mike is so darned smooth in deescalating confrontations. He's got the golden touch with dynamic security, which in the trade means you have a personal relationship with the inmates and work that to advantage.

Sure enough, Ronnie simmers down. "Wife, eh? I got a wife, loves her dearly, so I do." For some reason, that puts Mike on his toes, tense at the ready, though our man is edging away. "Finest wife in Placentia Bay."

Mike leans in, sotto voice, "He only rows the men's races. And about that wife..." At that instant our dour Lieutenant goosesteps into the gym, all business.

"Rowsell, I need you in Visitation. Every bloody family from the Bay is in town, and half them are popping in to see our darling guests." The Lieutenant aggressively jerks his thumb and Mike makes tracks like Speedy Gonzales. "Murphy, I got an easy job for you, but it's important. Cover lunch break on the tower over the north wall. We got half a dozen joes on the booth, so don't get keyed up about the open entrance. You watch out for bags tossed over the wall and into the yard. Crumpled chip bags and the like which might contain Oxys, benzos, Happy Pills, crap like that. When spelled, get back up here lickety-split to spring me, for I'll be babysitting Slaney." If Regatta Ronnie heard "baby-sitting", he didn't let on. Thank God. The boss settles down to schedules and time sheets, not even looking at Ronnie.

Glad to be away from Ronnie's hyper-charged energy field, I beat it with alacrity. You are surprised a Corrections Officer can sling fancy words like "alacrity"? Let's just say a B.A. in English is not a hot-foot credential into the World of Work, and with a baby on the way I had to get employment *tout suite*. Hence, this Corrections uniform.

The stairs down to the exercise yard are grimy, outright dingy. The prison is ancient, sections of it dating back to 1859. Yeah, we're talking Dickens era awful. I exit into blessed fresh air, grateful for not encountering a rat, and I don't mean a Mafiosi snitch.

Man oh man, what a grand day for the Regatta. Sunny but not overly hot, and with scarce a breeze to ripple the lake. Instantly, I hear the staccato rat-tat-tat of our Crown and Anchor wheel in full spin. Somebody put their back into it, for the wheel is just tatting to a stop as I approach. Three diamonds prompt the usual theatrical groans as Jenny Peyton from Admin scoops in quarters. One strawberry-haired kid is squealing though, for he plopped fifty cents on diamond and he's collecting big time. No fool, he then beelines for a concession stand that sells too greasy, too expensive burgers. That mite will have a well-earned bellyache before long.

"Raking it in, Jen?" She processed my Human Resources forms, and I know her for a good sort.

"A mint, Murph. Weather like this, we'll deposit a ton of coin." Deposit most of it. Scuttlebutt suggests dollars will be skimmed for a few bottles of Christmas Party Lamb's Amber Rum.

Pleasantries done, I walk thirty paces west and ascend to the glassed-in cupola set upon the wall overlooking the lake. From this lofty perch I take in the Regatta in all its glory.

On the first Wednesday in August, for a couple of centuries now, workaday St. John's puts down tools, ropes and quills and goes into festive mode. The rowing races, serious-minded athletes plying oars in sleek shells, are but an excuse for a gigantic garden party. The top of the lake is beaded by a hundred colourful food stands, and folks are face and eyes into fries swimming in gravy, hot dogs in soggy buns, and excruciatingly sweet candy apples. There are as many games of chance run by Lion's Club and Knights of Columbus barkers, obviously successful since many a person has a kitschy, cheap-o prize tucked under one arm. Across Quidi Vidi Lake, there is a small village of bouncy castles, pony rides, and dinky little merry-go-rounds, all proceeding to a beer tent the size of Buckingham Palace. Even this early I can see professional booze hounds lined up for the ID check and tickets. Two years ago, I would have been in the queue, a carefree gent with no worry greater than a frightful student loan and the last vestiges of acne.

Now that young man is in line-ups to buy Pampers and Johnson's Baby Shampoo.

Here, in my glass tower, I listen to the babble of a thousand joyous conversations. "Is that you Jack? What are you at, old man?" Or, "Tammy girl, where you been to these three years past? You're so slim you can hide behind a snake—Weight Watchers?" Or, "Ninety-one, and I got another Regatta under my belt. God won't take me, sure." As I watch, two massive Royal Newfoundland Constabulary horses, ridden by natty coppers, sidle through the throng to delighted *ohs* and *ahs*. Law abiding citizens, enjoying summer to the hilt, that's the Regatta.

What a contrast to the incarcerated within these walls. Drug dealers, burglars, car thieves, domestic hellraisers, the dregs and flotsam of society. At least they are small time. The real bad actors await trial and then passage to Dorchester Penitentiary on the mainland. Those guys are hard on the nerves, and I am lucky there are only a couple on my usual cell block.

Crews are leaving the boathouse quay to assemble at the start line. This is the ExxonMobil Male General Workers race, so Regatta Ronnie will be settling himself on the rowing bench. He must have a sixth sense, to know what is happening out here on the pond. There's a story to him; Mike was broadcasting heebie-jeebie vibes to that effect. I'm curious, but savvy enough to know curiosity kills cats.

I wrench away from preoccupations and the Regatta doings. I'm supposed to be watching the inside of the walls to catch disguised packets of drugs tossed over the walls for inmates to find tomorrow. I can't afford to screw up and have my Nazis-Lite Lieutenant put a reprimand in my probationary file. Once a fella signs a mortgage, he is slave to the Man. Perhaps we are all prisoners of a kind.

Yet, the Regatta tableau is irresistible, if not mesmerizing. The men's teams are now lined up, each shell held in position by the cox. The crowd's attention shifts momentarily as an older gentleman in a natty tweed suit steps into view brandishing a shotgun. Curtly, a megaphone voice asks, "Ready, number one?" The cox in the first shell raises his hand. "Ready number two?" And so it goes, for each eager crew that has trained for months for this exact moment. Then, after a suspenseful pause, *bang,* they are off in a froth of oars. There is a swell of cheering from the crowd as the shells arrow for the far end of the lake, where they will come about and return for the finish. I'm guessing it's a two, maybe three, kilometer course.

Regatta Ronnie will not cover a centimeter, but that won't stop him from rowing his heart out. Funny what happens, when sanity careens sideways and flips over the guard rail.

I'm relieved by another probationary guard. There is just time to nip out the gate for a bite before liberating the Lieutenant from his babysitting gig. I descend to the gate and nod to three colleagues on peacock display in formal dress uniforms which otherwise only get worn in the Remembrance Day parade. I'm tempted to get Indian food, but the line-up is too long. A hot dog cart is free, and in ordering I decide to experiment with dynamic security.

Thus, on returning to the gym, I present Ronnie with two hot dogs. "Thought you might need to carb up, Mr. Slaney. You're firing on all cylinders, burning high octane gas."

Ronnie eyes the dogs hungrily, but warily. "Mustard, ketchup and relish?"

"Took a chance on all three."

He relaxes, marginally. "Best kind, Newy." Then, to my amazement, he gulls the dogs in four Godzilla chomps. He inhaled them, by God.

A trollish burp, and then, "Lord thunderin', that hit the spot. My missus Sally makes hot dogs on Saturday nights." Invoking the Missus prompts a thought. "Look kid, you getting off at 8:00?"

"Nope," I answer glumly. "Agreed to overtime." Remember those Pampers? They're expensive.

"Well... hurrumph... make sure you're scarce for that last men's race. That'll be just as the sun goes down, getting' gloomy around 9:00. By scarce, I mean gone from this dump of a gym."

My gut thunks. "Am I getting Escape from Alcatraz drama from you, Mr. Slaney?"

His piercing eyes glaze for a microsecond, and I kick myself for using pop culture references. Regatta Ronnie is from another universe, out in the disconnected sticks.

"Just sayin' that Officer Newy, if he wants his nose clean, will be cleaning toilets at the other end of this Lakeside Hotel during the last men's race." With that, he abruptly jogs to an exercise bar bolted into paint flecked walls and does stretches.

Damn, I need write this up, notify the Lieutenant. But I'm reluctant, because it sounds like the maybe escape plan is for the end of the day, and I don't want to wrestle Ronnie downstairs if they decide to lock him up. Besides, this may be a fleeting psychotic delusion that he'll forget in five minutes' time. Consequently, I dither. It is the easiest thing to do. Cowardly rookie, that's me.

We are quite forgotten, Ronnie and I. All afternoon he does his thing, racing up Schizophrenia Lake then back down again. He is inexhaustible, powered by warp nacelles. Energy hums off him like the angry whine of electricity in high tension transmission wires. Rather than seeming drained after a race, he's amped up to the nth degree. While he goes bananas on the rowing machine, I sit bored on a gouged vinyl bench and pretend to look vigilant. Between races, Ronnie asks, "You still here?", then shakes his head like I'm the biggest idiot in God's Creation. He may be right. After an eternity and a half, the Lieutenant remembers I get a supper hour, and the same bucko who relieved me in the tower arrives to supervise the Regatta Ronnie Show.

"Anything I need to know?" he nervously asks on the transition. Nervous, because he knows Ronnie is a complete wild card. Ronnie doesn't help by breaking out in cackling song.

Ronnie row the boat ashore, hallelujah
Ronnie row the boat ashore, hallelujah
Sally help to trim the sails, hallelujah
Sally help to trim the sails, hallelujah

"God almighty," breaths the relief, looking green about the gills. "Does he bite?"

"Just watch him like a hawk," I warn, and scram with unseemly haste toward the staff area. We are hours shy of the last race, so bucko will be fine.

Then the dreaded All Call. Disturbance in Visitation. I am on the Response Team, so with stomach rumbling I rush to the area where prisoners get to chat with relatives. Wasted adrenalin, because Mike Rowsell is on point and he's doing his patented Stay Calm Carry On spiel with a guy who just got a Dear John good-bye from his girlfriend, in person. Understandably, he's bouncing off the cinder block walls. I linger in the corridor with a few other responders, just in case it gets physical.

"Regatta Ronnie winning all his races?" an older balding guard asks with a smirk. He's nursing a Styrofoam cup of coffee that I suspect is deadlier than hemlock. Prison coffee constitutes cruel and unusual punishment.

"Setting records, every contest." Might as well ask. "Ronnie ever try a prison break, or anything outlandish?"

"Nah, Captain Ahab don't cause much trouble if he gets catered to. Even the prisoners got that figured out. He's all talk and no action."

That settles it. I'm not going to write up Ronnie's warning. All talk, like buddy says. I'm off the hook, conscience.

Eventually, Mike and his charge emerge. All well on the Western Front. The other Corrections Officers escort the spurned lover to his cell, not unkindly. Mike and I are left, and we gab.

"Ronnie keeps the peace, I gather."

"Yeah, and between races he rambles nonstop about his wife, and Mike, he was talking about..."

"The wife," Mike cut in. "She was more off the rails than Ronnie. I remember when that wonky old she-bear used to visit. Crazy as a loon on meth, and that's being charitable."

Wait. "Was?"

"That last smuggling run was a tragic screw-up. Ronnie tossed the booze over the side as the Mounties closed in. Sally went bonkers, howled like a banshee, and jumped overboard after the contraband. Ronnie dived to rescue her. The cops tried to save both, but only managed to fish out Ronnie. Sally Slaney, lost at sea."

"She's dead?" Hackles on the nape of my neck.

"Playing Patty Cake with the octopuses," Mike confirms, shaking his head at the weirdness of it all. "Only, Ronnie doesn't buy it. He thinks she's home baking molasses bread and knitting socks. We don't argue, because it gives him a reason to get out on good behavior."

"God Almighty," I breathe.

We saunter to the lunch room. Supper for me is supposed to be microwaved mac 'n cheese; comfort food ordinarily, but my wife mixes in onion and I loathe onion. I am wrinkling my nose at the Tupperware container when Jen and pals roll in, balancing trays of mooseburgers. "Lookie, lookie, people. Donation from a food truck that pulled out early on account of the fog." Saved from my wife's concoction, by God. But hey, fog? The sun was on high beam just a while ago.

Jen reports. "There is a bank of fog offshore as solid as the Great Wall of China. It's starting to snake through the sea cliffs and onto the lake. They've moved the Men's Championship Race up by half an hour. Should get going any minute now." I glance at the lunch room TV screen that displays local coverage of the Regatta. A camera pans to the far end of the lake where roiling fog has nearly reached the turnabout buoys. I don't know if I've ever seen a sea fog churn like that, sort of like a cyclonic cloud. Reminds me of that Stephen King story "The Mist," and believe me, I don't need to go there today.

I stand mesmerized, mooseburger forgotten in my hand. No way this Fortean fog is related to Regatta Ronnie and his crazed warning to vacate the gym during the last race. Pure coincidence, right?

"Crowds are thinning," Mike comments between appreciative chews of his burger. "Just diehard racing fans and the beer tent mob out there now." He watches the screen as the championship race crews assume starting position.

"Mike," I blurt. "Let's grab a few burgers and head to the gym. See Ronnie row the last race."

Mike shrugs assent. Good for a lark, as far as he's concerned. As for me, I think his calming superpowers might be needed if Regatta Ronnie goes completely strange-o. And with Ronnie, that's saying a lot.

We clearly hear the starting shotgun on TV. I practically jog through the narrow corridors, which has Mike looking askance. I bloody well should confess about Ronnie's warning, and how I should have recorded it and alerted the higher ups. However, that takes more character than I can muster.

We stumble into the gym, winded. I am surprised to see the Lieutenant himself and two of his cronies watching Ronnie row like Hercules. Okay, this is good, for whatever happens, there are five on deck and the senior man on hand. A Special Forces helicopter could land on the roof to snatch him away, and we'd handle it.

Regatta Ronnie is a spectacle. He's pulling so hard the machine is practically jumping an inch off the floor on each stroke. I swear, the bolts violently jangle like a rain of shrapnel on a tin roof. My eyes catch Ronnie's, and there is not a hint of sanity in them. He offers a feral, manic grin, one flecked with mad-dog spittle. It is then I notice.

All day, every race, the rowing machine has pointed toward the finish line. Like one would, that makes sense even to lunatic. But this race, Ronnie has reversed the machine and is rowing straight at the faraway turnabout line, where the preternatural fog is swirling like a mini Hurricane Katrina.

"Ouch." That from Mike, who had reached down to pull up socks and got sapped by a wicked arc of static electricity. He takes his uniform cap off, and I literally see hairs start to rise from his scalp.

What the blazes?

Ronnie emits three whooshing grunts, like a whale gushing spray, signal of a supreme effort, then...

...the far wall explodes.

The lot of us are hurled into the corridor like five pins hit by a Howitzer shell. A deadly spray of metal and masonry chips the wall above us. Brick dust billows from the gym, even as a small tsunami of chilling water spills out to lap around our splayed limbs. Bruised and battered, I disentangle from Mike and stagger into the gym.

Weight benches, treadmills, bikes, all are overturned. I slosh threw the watery mess, sick at the thought of finding Ronnie's mangled body encased in warped metal. But he's not there, and neither is the rowing machine. A gaping eight-by-eight-foot hole in the wall is there however, right in front of where Regatta Ronnie did his disappearing act. I look out to see a dozen alarmed people in the yard below. Chunks of brick and mortar litter the grass.

"Ronnie Slaney is at large," I shout down. Instantly, several gawkers peel away to search the yard and patrol the wall perimeter. I see loungers at the gate have sprung to action and the big doors are swinging shut. Time is critical, for a maelstrom of agitated, smoke-gray fog is surging over the walls. If Ronnie gets out, he will be hell to find.

The Lieutenant, bleeding from several nicks and abrasions, appear beside me, fit to be tied. "Slaney must have planted a bomb on your watch, Murphy," he hisses venomously. My heart sinks a mile. I'm toast.

"Or my watch, or yours, sir," Mike remarks evenly. "The gym video will tell the tale." Mike's forehead will require stitches and a concussion check from the penitentiary doc.

Reminded of the video, the boss grits teeth in impotent rage. He is likely recollecting he did paperwork when he "babysat" Ronnie, an interval in which, quite unnoticed, Ronnie could have planted a Hiroshima bomb against the wall. "Get a plumber," he shouts, and splashes off in a fury.

A plumber? To do what? There are no broken water pipes in this exterior wall. Where is this water coming from?

I bend down to wet my fingers, and raise them to lips.

Salt water. Oh my. Oh my... God.

I wonder what Sally is cooking for supper tonight.

FINDERS KEEPERS

DANIELLE DAVIS

I remember it clearly because I was dating Todd then. To celebrate our two-month anniversary, he wanted to take me to the movies. There was a new Terminator movie out, and he was fair to bursting to see it.

"We'll go on opening night. That's always the best showing," he confided with the air of one who knows. He always seemed to know the best way to do everything. "Even if we have to stand in line for a couple of hours, it'll be worth it. Because that's how much you mean to me." Then he chucked me under the chin with his bent forefinger the way his dad always did with his mom. I always asked him not to do it. Same story with the way he'd always say, "Have a little faith, Faith," and then laugh like it was the first time he'd ever said it.

Not that it mattered.

Though standing in line for two hours sounded thrilling, I had been more interested in going to the *Festum Extraordinarium,* or the Circus of the Extraordinary, that was coming to the FedEx Forum that weekend. Nobody really knew how to explain the *Festums Extraordinarium* then. They'd only just begun cropping up thanks to the new discoveries in Scotland, the Canary Islands, and in Antarctica, where someone figured out how to cross into the fey realm and return back. With proof.

But back then the whole idea was still new. And one was coming to Memphis for the first time.

Part acrobatic circus, part carnival of wonders, the *Festum Extraordinarium* was different for every city. It depended on what creatures and acts the owners had acquired along the way. Sometimes different *festums* would trade certain acts, if the creatures were, well.... *extra* extraordinary, but folks could usually count on each *festum* being different than the last.

They were such strange attractions that they became their own *thing*–even though it became common knowledge that "festum" meant "circus" in Latin, people never called them circuses. No. They were always *festums.*

Anyway, Todd had zero interest in them because they didn't feature famous people or explosions and because the kind of people from school that would recognize him at a movie theater didn't usually attend them. He liked to be recognized, Todd. It validated certain things for him that he never articulated, but that I later came to understand anyway.

Funny the things you see later, after the filter's worn away.

I'd talked him into getting tickets, even though he was still quite vocal about his dislike for it. "Fairytales? Mythological creatures?" he scoffed. "Watch, this is all going to turn out to be one big hoax, like global warming. It's so quixotic, I'm surprised you're even interested in this sort of thing." Which was Todd-speak that indicated he thought *me* immature and naïve for my curiosity.

And at that point in my life, I worried he was right. Todd had a masterful way of misdirecting, of being able to share his opinion on a thing without actually mentioning it. His superhero power was that of being oblique. I admired it so much. It always seemed to involve some delicate turning of a phrase or careful nuance of body language as he said it.

In return, I became as finely calibrated as a tuning fork to the way he said things. With a casual phrase, he could have me anxiously trying to remember what I said that wasn't to his liking. One glance could make me feel like a goddess, or rethink my entire outfit choice for the night. I was so interested in this guy, the handsome guitar player who hit on me when he came through my checkout line at the grocery store, that I wanted to get it right. All of it. Around him, I felt a sort of frantic electricity as I strove to behave as expected with the least amount of correction from him.

So for me to insist anyway was a big deal. It was an even bigger deal that he listened.

* * *

You know how the FedEx Forum is more like a huge covered arena? Despite Todd's disdainfully hovering eyebrow or his slight commentary on the people that shuffled through the entrance with us, I was excited. I expected the arena in the middle to be decked out like a traditional circus, with small bumpers designating different performance sections and the bleachers rising all around the whole area like a mountain range of squeaky, foldable seats.

Instead of walking through the doors to the sight of a filling amphitheater, we saw a tent planted in the middle. It looked like an old circus tent, except the topmost supports were asymmetrical, giving the whole tent a slanting, crooked appearance. The tent material was thick enough that it was impossible to see any light filtering through, and it was patterned in an unsettling combination of thick black and purple stripes.

"They can't even get the tent set up properly!" Todd snickered as he placed a hand possessively over my shoulders as we looked for our seats. It was an awkward embrace for a thin aisle, so I had to contort sideways and crab-step down the stairs to avoid the oncoming traffic of people going up.

We had to ask an usher where to find our seats, since none were printed on the tickets. He informed us there were no assigned seats, and that we were to enter the *festum* tent when we were ready. I noticed a curious half-smile on his face as he said it—and that wasn't all I noticed—but Todd didn't. The moment he heard we didn't have seats, he began craning his neck around to see if anyone else was seated. Perhaps getting special treatment he should ask about.

"Did you see that?" I hissed in his ear as we walked away from the usher. Todd steered me toward the entrance to the *festum*.

"Do you mean the don't-give-a-damn-about-my-job attitude or the mildew smell of his uniform?" Todd didn't look at me as he spoke. He was too busy scanning the crowd for faces he knew.

"No, the weird way his hair was around his usher's cap. It kinda looked like he had..." *Horns* is what I'd been about to say. But my internal tuning fork for Todd's mood began to vibrate in a way that made me pause. I didn't want him to think I was naïve. I also didn't want to see the amused condescension on his face as he informed me about the special effects the guy probably used to heighten the mood of the place. Just a gimmick. A hoax. Like everything else we were about to see tonight. This would be said in the tone of someone who knows about such things.

"...dandruff," I finished lamely, hating myself a little. But it produced a positive effect.

Todd smiled down on me, the smile he used when he was proud I was on his arm. "Eww. Someone should have told him." In a tone that implied he would have liked to.

I glanced over my shoulder at that, just a little peek, and found the usher staring at me with that strange half-smile. Like he knew what I had almost said. And he knew why I hadn't said it.

Of all the things I saw that night, he was the most normal.

* * *

I'm not going to try to explain everything that went on under the canvas ceiling of the *Festum Extraordinarium* that night. It was both incredible and otherworldly.

There were smells I couldn't identify but that made my body flush with terror, shooting adrenaline speeding through my body. Then the scent would change, and I'd feel a tingling wetness in my lower belly and thighs and hear my own breathing panting quickly through my lips. When I glanced at Todd beside me, though, his face would show some other emotion, like triumph or confusion, so I knew that whatever we were smelling, it acted in different ways for different people.

I saw, or thought I saw, a woman transform into something with a serpent's body and waving green tendrils for hair. Then, when I'd blink, she'd be a performer in a brightly colored leotard, waving a hula hoop once more.

Certain areas of the rooms we were shepherded through—all by ushers who looked identical to the usher that told us about the seats outside the tent, as if there were multiple copies of him stationed throughout the *festum*—would shimmer like a 3-D image. Tilting my head one way made the room look like a fully furnished Victorian sitting room. Tilting it another made the room look like a dungeon, where a body hanging from one corner leered at me and winked.

Even now, my memories of that night play tricks on me. Some of the things I remember have reappeared in my dreams, while others seem to happen in varying orders of events. Sometimes the fairy room appears at the end of the tour, and at other times it's somewhere in the middle.

But it's the room I remember most vividly. Partly because of what was in it. But partly because of the woman standing outside of it.

Goldie Torres. That was how she introduced herself. A plain, unassuming black woman with hundreds of long, perfect braids of hair that fell to her hips like a beaded curtain. I remember she was in a navy polo shirt and plain khaki skirt, like she was a tour guide at the zoo or something. Only her shirt bulged in places that it shouldn't have, and sometimes the bulges moved as if fat snakes were writhing underneath.

Somehow—and I don't remember how—we'd lost the crowd we'd walked in with. That's one of the other things about my memory: I remember vividly some rooms where we're surrounded by people, even up to the room before the fairy one, but I don't remember at what point we lost them. However it happened, we ended up alone.

Goldie had something about her that I liked immediately. It could have been the soft, intelligent way she spoke. Or the way she never seemed to make unnecessary movements, and when she did move, it was with a fluid grace that made her appear confidently relaxed. It was very soothing overall.

And in her presence, Todd finally shut up.

He'd been commenting almost nonstop in my ear since we walked in, though the things he commented on were mundane, like the scent of a room or the temperature in the tent or the way one of his shoes was rubbing a blister on his right foot. He didn't make a single comment about any of the oddities I saw. It was as if he couldn't see them. Wait, no... he'd have commented on an empty tent. But whatever it was he saw didn't seem to be the same thing that I did.

But around Goldie, I didn't hear one offhanded comment about anything. So it was in complete silence that we entered the fairy room.

The room was small—maybe ten by twelve at the most. Black curtains acted as walls that sealed us off from the rest of the world once the curtain door was drawn shut. Two-tier shelves lined the room and made a three-sided box, from where we stood at the entrance around a support pole in the center. Small tea lights hung like the gaps in a chain-link fence all around the curtains. Still, though there had to be two hundred of them, it was still too dark to see how they were attached to the fabric.

On the shelves were jars. And in them were fairies. At least two dozen of them, each within their own oversized Mason jar covered by a thin mesh duct taped over the opening.

Goldie acted as the tour guide. She moved as fast or as slow as we did around the room and told us about each fairy we bent to examine.

In one jar, a small naked figure stood staring defiantly up at us with eyes made of ice chips. "An ice fairy," Goldie said in a soft voice. The figure was about as tall as my hand if I measured from wrist to the tip of my middle finger and looked to be male, though his genital area was smoothly rounded like a child's doll. His skin glittered all over with a fine dusting of hoarfrost. On his head were small, frosted icicles of hair that stood up like a hedgehog's quills. His hard wings, attached to his back near his shoulder blades, formed sharp geometric triangles of ice fractals. They fanned the air in spurts like a butterfly.

In another, a spider fairy. As tall as the first, this one appeared to be female, but with the same rounded genitals and small, pert breasts that had no nipples or areolas. Her wings, though, consisted of firm black spines that flexed and unfolded as a spider's legs might. The sections in between consisted of thin cobweb strands that fluttered gently when the fairy moved its wings. Goldie told us these fairies were born flightless, with only the spider leg spines in place. The fairy had to collect actual spider thread and weave its own wings before it could fly. Like the spider, the fairy caught small insects in its wings for food. But when I leaned forward, squinting, I asked about the large hairy tusks that curved out of her mouth and covered the bottom half of her face. Goldie informed me those were the fairy's mandibles and pointed out the sharp black barbs at the end. "That's what the females use to inject the poison into their mates after intercourse." I stared into the fairy's eyes, the two large black orbs on top and the smaller four in a row below them, and I wondered what she was thinking.

Another jar on the opposite side of the room contained nothing but a darkness that even the candles behind it couldn't seem to penetrate.

"What's that one?"

"A starry night."

"Why's it named that?" But when I moved closer, I noticed the two small pinpricks of white light that came into view.

"Those are what it uses to attract prey. Much like the..." Goldie frowned at the ceiling, searching for the word. "You know, the fish with the light on its head...?"

"Anglerfish?" I supplied, and Goldie snapped her fingers as she grinned at me. "Yes! That's it."

I gave Todd a sideways glance, surprised he didn't comment on my useless knowledge of deep sea creatures. It was the sort of thing he would have done earlier in the night. I was starting to enjoy the fact that in here, within the *festum*, I seemed protected from it. The thought made me smile.

Goldie knew them all. She offered small bits of information at just the right times. This one only fed on the morning dew it collected from holywoods, a rare species of flower found mostly in the Caribbean. That one defended itself by shooting poisonous darts as fine as slivers from the dark spots on its back. The one with the metal shavings in the bottom was an alchemical fairy that made intricate geometric sculptures from them when it got bored.

All had stories. And all were just as fantastic as the next.

Finally, at the end of the tour, Goldie stood before us near the door with an expectant smile on her face. She was looking at me. Todd, oddly enough, just stared at one of the lights on the curtains with a small frown on his face as if he was trying to remember something elusive.

"Now," Goldie grinned, "we have a moment to ourselves. You have an interesting name, Faith. It has great significance to some of our kind."

"Our kind?" I repeated. But Goldie didn't answer. Instead she just smiled at me in a way that suggested I already knew the answer.

"I've seen a lot of people come through today. But only a few who were worth actually seeing." She brought her face close to mine. "*You* are worth seeing." Her breath smelled like honeysuckle. In my peripheral vision, I saw movement from something under her shirt and heard a sound like many voices whispering. *Wait, wait,* they called.

She walked behind me and strode over to a fairy jar resting on the upper tier of the opposite corner shelf. When she returned, she held out the jar, cradled carefully in her long-fingered hands, and gestured for me to take it.

Inside was a small fairy sitting on the clear glass bottom with her arms loosely circling her knees. A burgundy cascade of hair covered her naked figure. She was grinning at me. When I brought the jar up to eye level, she lifted one hand to wiggle her fingers at me in a mischievous wave.

"What in God's name am I supposed to do with a fairy?"

"You like her?" Goldie asked. "You may take her. She will bring you luck."

I cast a wary eye at the fairy, who gave an enthusiastic nod as if to lend support to Goldie's words. When she grinned, I saw her teeth were sharp needles.

"What kind of fairy is she?" My voice sounded cautious, but in truth, I was already planning how I was going to keep her in my room without my parents finding out. How to keep her hidden at school—maybe in my locker...?—and if she'd help me pass my Calculus midterm next week.

The fairy chastised me with a theatrical frown, as if to say *for shame*, and shook her head.

"Her power is unique. Her kind is called a finder fairy, though the name is a bit deceptive. She doesn't so much find things that are lost, like your car keys, so much as she reveals things that were once hidden."

"And what sort of thing do I need found?"

Goldie's eyes filled with a sense of knowing. I had no doubt, then, that she knew what was on my soul and had compassion for what she saw there.

"Where are her wings?" I asked in surprise, for I just noticed she didn't have any.

"They are there. But she doesn't want you to see them yet. Don't worry, that will change once she trusts you."

The whole situation was surreal and yet my intuition told me this was going to happen.

"I can't accept this."

"Then borrow her for a while. Come visit me again the next time we're in town, and bring her back with you."

That, I found, I could accept.

Todd, meanwhile, still stood in the same stance I'd left him in. When I put my arm through his, he jumped, startled, and asked in a distracted voice if I was ready to go. I glanced back at Goldie, who nodded, and then told him yes.

I slipped the fairy jar in my purse, careful not to jostle her, and left.

On the ride home in my Prius, Todd broke up with me. It wasn't me, he said, it was him. He couldn't handle a girl who could change her own tires and who laughed loudly in crowded places like nobody else was around and who danced in the rain without caring if other people saw her do it. In general, he concluded, one who didn't act like she didn't need a damn hero to rescue her.

"And I need to be the white knight," he pleaded. "I need someone who lets me do the heavy lifting once in a while. I'm afraid we're just not compatible."

He was right about that part, but wrong about the rest. I had no idea where his rambled list had come from, since I didn't know how to do any of those things. But my intuition told me this was necessary. So, however little I understood it, I let Todd Basker break up with me on our two-month anniversary.

And that was just the first step.

* * *

Years later, I tried to give the fairy back. She brought me all manner of luck, but she required a lot of attention. By that time, scientists had been able to identify almost two hundred species of what they called *fey fauna*, and the subject was already being taught in school Biology classes.

But I never saw anything called a "finder fairy" ever appear in the lists. And trust me, I looked.

As a last resort, I called the manager of the FedEx Forum and asked for the contact number of the last *Festum Extraordinarium* that rolled through there. He said no such one ever had. When I faxed him the ticket stub I'd saved from that magical night, he laughed, congratulated me on a well-executed prank, and hung up.

Since then, I've gone to several *festums*, but few of them have fairy rooms, and of the ones that do, none of them are guided by a strange, black woman named Goldie Torres. And none of them have heard of a finder fairy.

She sits on my desk now, in my dorm room at Rhodes University. Though she sits in plain sight now, my roommate hasn't once commented on it. It's as if Mary can't even see her.

So I'll tell you this: if you ever have a chance to capture or acquire a finder fairy, *do it.* Pay any amount, go to any length. Because even though I was willing to give mine back, it's not like they're not worth the effort. And honestly? After a while you get used to the work.

And another thing. If you ever attend a *Festum Extraordinarium* and make it, strangely alone, to a fairy room run by a woman named Goldie Torres? Tell her thanks for me. I think she'll remember my name.

DANCER

Bradley H. Sinor

I walked into the Red Lion. I'd been there before, when it was a classier place, but this time all I wanted was a drink, and I didn't care where the drink came from.

The only table I could see was close to the stage where the dancers entertained the scum that frequented the place. I'm sure it was available because it was under a bright light. Said scum wouldn't want a spotlight shining on what they were probably doing.

The crowd was boisterous, which was different from the last time I was there. The few people that were there preferred to be alone and silent while they watched the girls taking their clothes off.

The song ended and the brunette gathered her discarded clothing and headed for the dressing room.

A hand-lettered sign hung on the door.

KEEP HANDS OFF THE DANCERS!

Dancing red and green lights played over the translucent stage floor in time to a semi-country song.

The next dancer emerged.

She wore a long dress of sea-green that terminated just above bare feet. Honey yellow hair touched her hips, shaking in a match with her movements. She turned and turned again swiftly, a strobe light framed her movements of frozen seconds.

There were four dancers in all, counting the blonde. One was still behind the stage and the other two were spread around talking to patrons and cadging drinks from them while trying to keep what clothing they wore on. This dancer was the prettiest; the others were fair. But there was something about her that struck a familiar chord. The house lights rose while the music changed.

Megan.

Memories were born.

A summer dawned, words that were meant to last forever, and sudden tearing as we walked away from each other.

Megan loosened the thin strings that ran from the top of her low plunging dress over her shoulders. Her dress slid down, revealing twin pear shaped breasts. A small globe dipped out of the ceiling, lights streaming from it, first over Megan's bare skin, then out over the audience.

She played to the men who sat around the edge of the stage and to those, to her, dark forms beyond it. Blue light ran in streams from her hands out into the shadows.

The composure that had held her apart melted away. Megan was a good performer. She caught the beat and went on. No one noticed her slip. The last song of the set was a gloom-haunted tune full of low piano notes and a muted drum solo. Not once during her dance or while she gathered her dress up from the floor did her eyes come anywhere near me.

There was a slight delay in the next dancer starting. A scarecrow-thin soldier had dropped money into the jukebox in defiance of the custom that allowed the dancers to pick their own music. As the girl finally emerged, she discovered that the song she had wanted was not playing.

A voice was clear, cutting through the din quite sharply, and so very familiar.

"Will you buy me a drink?" Megan said from just behind me.

* * *

We sat at a small table away from the spotlight, in the shadows. I indicated the crowd and she shrugged, saying only "bachelor party."

"What should either of us say now?" she said after a very long, loud silence.

I sipped on the beginning of my second drink, a beer like the first. I prefer them over harder drinks. A greenish bottle of what looked like malt liquor sat in front of Megan. If I knew places like the Red Lion, it was probably as alcoholic as Kool-Aid.

"I really don't know," I said. "You know, it may sound trite, but you haven't changed at all, Megan."

"Thank you. But I know when you're lying. My mirror doesn't do anything to hide the truth."

There were changes in her. Not many, but they were there, masked in the dim light. Perhaps in other places I could see them. But for now, it could have been a long gone yesterday that I was looking at across the table.

"You've changed, though, Barnabas. Physically and otherwise. There are harder lines and scars that the beard doesn't completely cover," she said.

The music had finally begun again. The dancer was a small girl with stringy red hair and a green flower tattooed on her left shoulder. Her movements, like the others, were rough and ill-timed.

"Why?" I gestured around us at the bar.

She gave a sad shrug. Once she had been a math major with dreams of teaching, perhaps in a small college somewhere.

"The money, I guess. It pays four hundred a week, plus any tips I earn. When Wayne left me, I had to do something to pay my own way."

"He left you?"

"Yes, a divorce two years ago," she half-chuckled. "It wasn't working out between us because I had met John. It was good for a while, but he made me think that I wasn't good enough for him. I didn't want another divorce then; I still don't. Gods, it hurt when he said he wanted out. Yet, there was nothing that I could do to stop him."

"But why this?"

"I finally found something that I was good at and could get paid doing it. Until something else comes along."

I tried to find some word. Something that might comfort her from the memories. But for once in the long life I was totally speechless. I took one of her hands and give it a gentle squeeze.

"Maybe we would have lasted," she said. "So, tell me, what has come for you? Did you ever start selling your artwork?"

"A few pieces here and there. Other things have distracted me for a time. They were strong influences."

"Did you ever find someone for yourself? A woman who could love you just for you?"

I had. I found her and then lost her. Just as Megan had been taken from me. Only it was with the finality of death.

The arches are a strange construction that bend time and space and probability. No one I knew of had ever encountered or understood them and even fewer knew of their existence. It had been through one of the arch doorways that I had found and then lost the green-eyed woman called Sumara.

"I wonder now if you are even of this world anymore," Megan said.

I could not answer her.

* * *

The girl with the tattooed arm began the final dance of her set. She wore only a kerchief around her waist and a necklace that hung between tiny breasts. The small piece of cloth was so the police could not arrest them for performing nude in public. Megan said that they all had to meet that requirement.

She spoke to me, but her words were lost in the flair of music and conversation from all sides. I was ignoring everything except the necklace that the dancer with stringy red hair wore. It was a notched metal triangle hanging from a rough gold-like chain.

It was a Karadi. A key to the use of the arches.

"Where did she get that?" I demanded of Megan.

She was puzzled, not really understanding what I was talking about at first. I pointed to the dancer.

"It isn't hers; I know that for sure," she said, squinting at the bright light that illuminated the stage. "I think it's from the junk box."

"What's that?"

"An old trunk full of a bunch of stuff that we use in the acts. Nothing special or valuable. If it was, it would have been gone a long time ago. Nobody really owns it. I've used that necklace myself a couple of times. I like it a little. Once I had to take it and clout a drunk between the eyes with it."

"Didn't like what you were doing?"

"He liked my dance. The problem was he wanted to grab a quick feel. And that is not allowed."

The music droned on, barely audible from the laughing and shouting of the patrons.

"Where did this stuff come from?"

"The girl who got me the job and showed me the ropes pretty much said it's been here as long as the Red Lion. I think a lot of it was left over from the old pub that used to be on this site. That place partially burned about twenty years or so ago. At least that's what Sheba told me," Megan said.

I had a feeling I knew the answer before I asked the next question.

"What was the name of this burned pub?"

"I think it was called the Inn of the Crossed Scabbards or something like that."

She did not have to say any more. I had known an inn called by that name in that other world I had reached through the arch. There had been strange tales about the place. If it could exist here and there, there might a way to use the arch.

"I've got to get that necklace."

"Is it that important?" she asked.

I nodded. The Karadi could manipulate an arch to the whim of the user. I could step though to any place, any time or any when.

"Will you help me?"

"Y... yes. The dancer's name is Misty. She'll be getting off for the evening in just a few minutes. I heard her say something about meeting someone at the airport or somewhere. So she's probably gone downstairs to change," Megan said.

* * *

She led me down a short hallway past walls with graffiti six feet high and the tattered remnants of beer posters. Behind a stack of empty beer bottle cases we found a pitted staircase that led into inky blackness. Megan flipped a small switch and a line of flickering neon came to life.

"The dressing room is down here. If she's not there, Misty should be getting there any time now," Megan said.

I followed her down the stairs.

"Misty? Is that her name?"

"No, it isn't. The owners have a rule that we aren't supposed to tell anyone our real names. We all have to use other ones. That way if some dangerous creep takes a liking to one of us, he can't track us down to our houses," she said.

That was a wise precaution.

"What is Misty's real name? I don't think that I would qualify as dangerous creep."

"Dangerous maybe. Creep, no way. Her real name is Elaine Yarbroo. There are not too many of them around, so it would be easy to find her."

"What about you? What name do you use?"

She was quiet for a moment. "Sheba."

I looked askance at her.

She explained. "I took that name when Sheba quit. I took her place."

"The stage name protects you from customers you don't like; that's good. At least you give your real name to men that you want to have it."

She answered me with a stare that cut me to the soul. For that moment I hurt as badly as the day I had taken the dagger in my shoulder at the Battle of Four Sabers.

"Your shill name and what you do with it is your business. I'm sorry." That was the best I gave her; it was all I had.

* * *

A sudden sound of footsteps brought a small shape around the corner and out of the shadows to stop at the foot of the stairway. It was Misty. She was clad now in a University of Oklahoma sweatshirt and jeans. She smiled when she saw Megan and gave me an odd look.

"'Lo Meg. Who's that?" she asked. "He your new guy?"

I had the feeling that she wasn't used to seeing Megan with anyone else, at least not at work.

"Someone very special to me a long time ago. You might call him a shadow out of my very sordid past."

She cocked an eyebrow first at Megan, then at me. "Well, well. You and I will have to have a long talk about her sometime. But right now, I have got out to the bus station. Mike's coming in on the 10:25."

"Before you go," I started.

Megan shook her head.

"Go on, Elaine, I do need to talk to you later about something that's important," Megan said.

"Okay, but make it very late tomorrow. I haven't seen Mike in a long time," she said, smiling.

"Yeah, so you can get some sleep."

"That too." She made it up the creaky stairs and out of sight almost before the sound of her voice had faded away.

"She always travel that fast?" I asked Megan.

"Most of the time. I think that's why they call her Misty. All anyone sees of her when she doesn't want them to is just a bit of drifting mist," she said.

I could see what she was talking about. The girl seemed to exist in a different timeframe from everyone else.

"Why did you stop me from asking her?" I demanded. "She might have had the Karadi with her."

Megan shook her head.

"I don't think so. Everybody has their own special odd little quirks. One of Elaine's is that she cannot stand to wear any kind of jewelry."

This did not fit.

"Then why was she so prominently using it when she danced?" I said.

The idea that this all might be a carefully laid trap suddenly did not seem so absurd. I wondered what I really knew about Megan, beyond an eight-year dead memory.

"You are going to have to start learning to trust other people. As for Misty, she uses the necklace as something to get the shill's attention. Besides, I told you that things like that can help in a tough situation," she said.

I relaxed, but just a bit. There was no way to explain to Megan that for most of the last few years, I had stayed alive by not trusting more people than I had to.

* * *

The dressing area was a room in the midst of another room. The walls were actually the backs of a number of huge crates piled one on top of the other. Light came from four large pole lamps. Several lockers, a makeup table and a full-length mirror had been arranged in the area.

"So where is this junk box?"

"Right here," Megan answered. She pointed to an ancient army footlocker. It was the kind you can pick up in a surplus store for a ridiculous price. A small padlock held it closed.

Megan knelt beside it and began to work the numbers. I glanced around, peering at the room nervously. There was something familiar about the place. It was mostly a feeling that I could not pin down.

I had dined several times at the Inn of the Crossed Scabbards, as well as gone there to drink and watch the dancing girls. So it seemed far too close to be pure coincidences.

Megan had begun to search through the locker. She was careful, laying each thing separately on the floor for my observation. There were negligees and other bits of clothing, some quite exotic looking, jewelry and even what turned out to be a collapsed hula hoop.

"You use this?" I said, a little disbelieving.

"Tu-Tu uses it. That's her specialty when she dances. I always thought it was kind of stupid looking, myself."

As the moments passed, she began to toss thing after thing out and onto the floor. I could see the frustration growing on her face. It was mirrored, I suspected, on my own.

"It's not here," she said. She dropped to the floor in surrender.

"Are you sure that Mist... Elaine couldn't have taken it with her?" I stared, helplessly at the clothing on the floor and the empty footlocker.

"I'm certain. As I said, she can't stand to wear any kind of jewelry. That's what frustrates her boyfriend so much. She can't wear his ring."

"Then it must be here." It was all I could think of to say. I've been described as a man with a lot of resources. Right than I wished I knew how to draw on them.

Megan tossed her head back and stared at the ceiling. Her hair fell clear of her ears for the first time. Hanging from her lobes were earrings in the form of tiny silver serpents, crouched to strike.

"You still have them?" I said. I had made them for her as a gift just after she had been in a car accident. "I would have thought that what's-his-name would have made you get rid of them. If he ever knew who they were from."

Megan's ex-husband and I had not gotten along. Not surprising, considering matters. I had tried to beat his brains out one afternoon in the middle of a chapel on the army base where he was stationed.

"He never asked, so I never said anything." She chuckled. For the first time since I had seen her on that stage, Megan smiled like the lady I had once loved. "What is so important about that necklace? You make it sound like a life-and-death matter. I mean, it certainly wouldn't look any good on you, I must say."

"I agree. You always had good taste in clothing. But as for that little knick-knack, it is many things that you could not even conceive of."

* * *

Megan rested her head on my shoulder. I had not really said very much more about the Karadi, the arches or the world that I found there. I did not know if we could ever regain what we had had, or if we should even try. But for that moment, it was a very nice feeling that filled the both of us.

She cried. The tears were few but quite real. After a time, I felt her hand touch my chin, gently turning my face toward her. I did not know what I felt as we looked at each other. She kissed me then.

"Such a touching scene!"

The beefy-faced bartender stood on the stairway, his huge frame almost blocking it from view. Farrah Fawcett's smiling form on his t-shirt was in stark contrast to the air of pure malevolence about him.

Megan's hand tightened on mine. I made ready to push her aside and leap to my feet, if necessary. The thong holding the dagger at my wrist seemed to loosen by itself.

"What do you want?" I demanded. It occurred to me I sounded like Humphrey Bogart just then.

"That's not the question," he said. "It should be more what do *you* want."

"Do you know this guy?" I asked Megan.

"He's only been working here a week or two. I've barely even spoken to him," she said.

"This isn't what you think." I hoped he just thought that one of the girls had decided to turn a trick on the premises. There was a gnawing feeling in the pit of my stomach that he knew better.

"I know what it is, Mr. Tobin. Besides, Sheba isn't that type."

That tore it. If he knew me, he probably was looking for the same thing that I was. The Karadi. I had several questions, like why he had not just taken it before. But they could wait until I controlled things.

The bartender took a few steps closer. He was not armed, or did not appear to be, so I knew what had to be done. I threw myself at him, headlong, in a bull rush. Had Megan not clung to me, the blow that sent me into darkness would probably never have engulfed me.

* * *

The ropes around my wrist were tight. The bartender knew his job well. I had to keep flexing my hands in order to stave off numbness.

I had awakened to find both Megan and myself trussed up like deer for the slaughter. I had the distinct feeling that it was exactly what this fellow had in mind.

We were in a different part of the basement. Dust lay over everything and looked as if it had been there a very long time. Ancient packing cases and broken furniture confirmed my guess.

I had to twist to find our "host". And when I did, I knew I was at last in the right place. I only hoped that this could become the right time. The bartender stood, his back to us, in front of an arch.

It extended a full foot out from the rest of the brick wall. All the edges were engraved with glyph symbols. Whether the big man was truly a human who accidentally discovered the arch, or one of the quasi-living guardians I had heard about, mattered little. Storm clouds of grey and black, crisscrossed by sudden bursts of lighting, danced in the confinement of the arch.

"Barnabas, what is that?" said Megan.

"It's what I would have gone looking for after I held the Karadi. It's a transport arch. One of my scientist friends called it a matter disintegrator reiterator that can reach to other worlds in the universe. On the other hand, some of the sorcerers I knew said it was a bending of the Power to create, or find as you will, worlds of demons and other spirits."

Memories come at odd times. During my youth I was much in awe of the work of a writer named Arthur C. Clarke. As I lay bound only a dozen feet from the arch, I remembered him saying *Any sufficiently advanced technology is indistinguishable from magic.* I did not know if the arch was the work of magic or science. I just knew it would work.

"Barnabas, I'm scared."

"So am I, honey. So am I."

* * *

"If only I had the Karadi, I'm certain I could get rid of this fellow. But if he has it, then what's the use. He can call on the power of the arch. Providing he knows how," I said.

"I've got it," Megan said. Her face ran to red with the revelation.

"Why didn't you give it to me?" I demanded.

"I wanted to keep you with me or make you take me with you away from here. I just want to be left alone," Megan said.

That was all I needed. Big, fat, and ugly still had his back to me. I think he was trying to set the controls of the arch. That is a very difficult thing to without the Karadi. Why he had not bound our feet I can't even guess.

His hearing was sharp. I had covered barely half the distance, some dozen feet, when he whirled around facing me, a German Mauser held in his massive hand.

He fired twice and missed me. I managed to strike him almost dead center in the middle of his huge chest. We both tottered together. He fell backwards, while I stayed on my feet. The force of my blow sent the bartender falling into the midst of the arch.

There was an explosion. His fat form shimmered and then disappeared. The storm in the arch waned for a moment, reborn in a breath stronger than ever. The explosions continued and the room shook.

In some manner, the sudden insertion of the bartender's body had short-circuited the arch. The enormous power within it was building up to a forced explosion.

"Megan, we've got to get out of here." Not even the Karadi would be able to stop what was about to happen.

Megan's head was slumped to her chest. A red stain grew on her blouse. I cut my ropes on a rough piece of metal binding, slashing my flesh to ribbons in the process.

One of the bartender's bullets had struck her square in the heart. I ripped her blouse away, hoping I might do something to save her. The blood stained her bare skin like the stage light had only an hour before.

She was dead.

Even though it was not by my hand, I knew I had killed her. The bullet had also shattered the Karadi; its broken pieces lay afloat in her blood.

No! I had lost her once. And then lost Sumara to death. I would not let it go on. For a mad moment, I thought to plunge myself headlong into the arch. The chaotic forces alone would probably kill me.

The explosions continued. The basement shook uncontrolled. The musty air was full of plaster and the distant smell of fire.

The arch!

There might be a way. The Karadi had shattered into five major pieces. Several slivers remained, but I discounted them. I laid one on Megan's forehead, one between her breasts, one on her stomach and squeezed one each into her palms. Theoretically, they could still act as a shield against the chaotic forces in the arch.

The mind of the user determines where the arch sends one. I hoped that with no direction it would simply drift into chaos, until a time when I could find another Karadi and use it to revive her.

I kissed her still-warm lips. A tear rolled from my cheek to hers. Then as carefully as I would carry a newborn child, I lifted Megan into the arch. Her body shimmered and seemed to drift away.

I only hoped that I had acted fast enough.

Smoke filled the basement, so I think that I recall clawing my way up the stairs.

* * *

The fireman said they found me on the floor outside of one of the restrooms. I was trying to crawl to safety, they said. I had to take their word for the whole matter. My first memory was of a paramedic sticking an oxygen mask on my face.

There were only two casualties of the boiler explosion, which is what they called it, that destroyed the Red Lion; Megan Cameron, topless dancer, and Melvin Williams, bartender.

I did not even tell my name. I just walked into the fog until the red glow of the fire was a distant thing, and then cried.

TWO FIRES

HANSEN ADCOCK

Bronn's deadline for reaching the caldera of Old Wizard fell upon the Night of Demons. The man knew people would say he was mad and a fool for trying, but it had become his main goal, even an obsession. He wanted to prove himself, and this time he also wanted to sample Old Wizard's charge.

Hollow rapping sounded on the plank door of his hut. The distant stench of burning scored his nostrils. He limped down the steps adjoining the bedroom and kitchen to answer the summons.

"What do you want?"

"Wood for the banefire, sir?" Four boys younger than ten years apiece loitered on his doorstep with a wheelbarrow full of fallen tree branches, mangled, unwanted, carpentered furniture, and spare kindling from the neighbouring huts. None of them were recognisable behind the guising masks obfuscating their features—carved and hand-painted facsimiles of forest animals, in this case a rabbit or a hare, a wild boar, a bear, and an elk in honour of the Horned Lord, the forest god Glanegians believed ruled over all of nature.

Muttering, Bronn limped deep into his hut and found a lump of tree-stump he had been planning to whittle into something decorative and set it atop the heap of fuel offerings.

"Thank ye, sir," elk-face said. "Going to be a big 'un tonight."

"Is it? My understanding was that there were two banefires at this time of year, in Glanige?"

"We're in charge of one this year, and some other boys fr'm south of the river are doing the other. Will ye be joining us this time, sir?"

"Parading up and down with all of my belongings between two infernos? I don't think so. We'll see."

Rabbit-head and boar-face nudged each other and giggled.

"Ask."

"No, *you* ask him."

The boy with an elk-mask sighed. "Mr. Bronn, we wanted to know something. Are ye a Murridan?"

"One of the Little Folk? Do I look as if I surfaced from a burial mound to you?"

"No... but they can guise as human people, and ye have funny skin, and ye study magic..."

"Get along with you," Bronn said with an exaggerated glower. "I never did hear such ridiculous nonsense."

The boys pushed their cart down the dirt lane, laughing. Bronn dallied until they moved out of sight, slammed the door, and hobbled back to his sleeping-quarters, tossing himself onto the second-hand four-poster, and let his crutch topple onto the rush matting.

Every year, their questions and comments burned him more than any fire could.

On the last Night of Demons, the village schoolboys had enquired as to whether he was one of the Harridan—although those witches were always women—and all because he wanted to learn about the Arcane Lore (superstition, demons, stories about the Murridan and the Harridan, and so forth, in order to disprove it empirically), took an interest in natural philosophy, did not participate in common superstitions, and possessed one leg shorter than the other. Not to mention the fact that his skin was a different colour to that of the locals: a dark indigo in contrast to their pale, freckled flesh.

His eyes wandered to the mason-jar of formaldehyde on the bedside cabinet. Inside it, a wizened, curled thing floated, its separate vertebrae and insectoid, faceted eye-orbs clearly visible. It stared back at him, unmoving, unseeing.

"Soon," he told it, though he was unsure whether it could hear. "First, a few necessary preparations. Then we leave, Mythadonna."

His satchel gaped next to him on the bed, half-packed. He placed a camping stove and a flask inside it, trying to create space, musing on how he would squeeze the jar into the bag. Perhaps he could carry the flask, although if he did so the citizens of Glanige would assume he was on his way to the public-house for the annual fireside tale-telling and drinking shut-in and invite themselves along. That was the only problem with Glanegians. They were so amiable they were almost rude.

Mythadonna, according to his working hypothesis, was a faerie corpse. He found the creature during the first night of summer, inside one of the dozen Neolithic burial mounds which surrounded the village's outskirts and provided, in the minds of its inhabitants, a sacred ring of protection from ill luck or supernatural evils.

Disturbing those barrows in any way would earn someone days of castigation and a week in the stocks having decaying fruit, vegetables, and mouldering meat thrown at them. Therefore, Bronn had visited the hollow hills in the third stretch of the morning, when the other Glanegians were abed. He had been interested in the larger mound on the village's western side, near the beach, which possessed an opening that lined up with the exact point on the horizon where the sun would rise at the end of the Night of Demons. This alignment was common legendary knowledge, but he measured the line between the tomb's entrance and the constellations with a sextant and found that the rumour was true. With his shovel and bag of tools he had entered the mound and discovered that the opening extended as a stone shaft, stabbing right through the hill, lined with shelves of bone-filled coffins and ancient weapons—spearheads, mainly—along with pewter jewellery, chalices and plates curlicued and engraved with serpentine patterns and creatures of warped design. The skeletons in the coffins grew shorter and more fine-boned the further into the barrow he crept.

A tiny, ornate chest had waited at the shaft's end, unlocked. Inside that lay the inert form of Mythadonna, no more than the length of his ring finger, curled on her side, naked, her skin blackened and stretched taut over her skeleton by some unknown mummification process, mouth agape. Despite him wearing gloves and taking the utmost care, her wings crumbled away from her spine when he lifted her—if they *were* wings, they resembled desiccated leaves more than anything else—and he put her in his coat pocket without understanding exactly why he had done so. He supposed he wanted to feel closer to the bizarre and inexplicable, in order to make sense of it.

Of course, he kept the specimen hidden from inquisitive eyes, never permitting visitors into his home, and subjected her—or it—to months of study. Mythadonna's home had been the jar of preserving fluid since that night. Over time, the moniker Mythadonna seemed to suit her—the name of the midnight flowers on top of the cliffs which one of the Harridan was said to have planted before the burial mounds even existed.

Bronn always maintained that he would return the specimen to its original resting-place, but now his annual attempt to climb Old Wizard had come around again, and the seed of a wild plan took root in his head. He would take Mythadonna with him. This time, she might provide him with the luck he needed to make it to the summit. The volcano often had streaks of lightning shooting into and out of its caldera into the ominous clouds above it, and he knew, from his natural philosophy studies, that lightning was natural energy, the animating force. If he were to somehow obtain some of that energy... Mythadonna might live, either proving or disproving his hypothesis.

The jar stowed in his bag at last, Bronn picked up his crutch, shucked the bag onto his shoulders, bit his lip, and heaved himself onto his good leg. He thought about leaving a fire burning in his hearth while he was out, to "ward off" evil spirits and the Little Folk, but decided against it this year. Waste of fuel. Ghosts did not exist. The only supposed Murridan for leagues around was the dead one he had trapped in a container for months, and nothing had occurred as a consequence to his ancient grave robbery.

In the fields, the ritual had already begun. Paces-high stacks of unwanted wood and kindling donated by the Glanegians now roared and danced with towering banefires, one at each end of the field opposite his hut, which had been used to grow turnips and wurzels. The entire village, a sprawling mob, along with their confused herds of cattle, pets, and other items they wished to protect from evil, gathered at the field's edge, spilling into the lane. As Bronn left his hut, the first few villagers were guiding their livestock in between the two banefires, although the animals did not appear to think highly of the event.

"Bronn!" voices called. "How do! Come and join in, man!"

He looked over the sea of fire-lit, carven, painted faces in the darkness, and the bobbing lights that people had fashioned by setting melted candles into hollowed-out turnips, and shook his head.

"It's bad luck if ye don't walk betwixt 'em!"

"Don't say we didn't forewarn ye!"

Bronn glanced at the heap of pre-slaughtered cows, pigs, and sheep next to the first banefire, ready for the winter sacrifices to the Horned Lord. He shook his head again before moving away.

Such a waste of life and wood.

The solemn music of Glanige's three churches tolling their bells swelled the air, along with the smoke, and Bronn began to leave the village. He knew that smoke was meant to be protection against the more malign spirits of the dead and the Murridan, but that still did not mean he wanted to hang around, breathing it in.

A blue-black crow soared overhead for much of his journey, chacking as he hobbled past the last few mud-and-straw huts, past the estuary, and crunched his way along the line of Broken Beach, the sea-polished glasses and shells sparkling underfoot in a myriad of different shades of grey, which would look beautiful in daylight. Old Wizard lurked a couple of stretches away, grim and hulking in the darkness.

The first time Bronn tried to trek up Old Wizard, he was a boy of fifteen, and his parents had still been living in Glanige. Pol and Glinda Dwarrows possessed the same deep indigo skin as their son, having emigrated ten years before from far Dal-Rhiatah in the extreme north-west of the globe, fleeing from slavery, and the war that occurred at that time to abolish it in their country. They had tried to deter him from making the climb, worrying about the congenital defect in his leg, but that only made him more obstreperous—he was sick and tired of his leg controlling what he could and could not do, the questions and teasing he endured in school, the humiliation of not being allowed to play sports or roam anywhere far from home unescorted because of it. Old Wizard became a challenge, a *rite of passage*, something he could surmount alone to prove to himself, and everyone else, that he was stronger and more capable than they gave him credit for. It also provided a sense of adventure, a special aim to work towards. In the year before his first attempt he trained hard in privacy, lifting weights, learning all he could about mountain climbing and knots from library books, and obtained several lengths of rope from the chandler on the lane next to his, along with knives, chisels, and other tools he would use to gain purchase on the rock.

Two days before his fifteenth birthday, he revealed his plan to his parents and asked them to tell no one else, in case he failed. They were not pleased, but consented to the idea provided that if he was not back in four to five stretches, they could send help after him.

On that first climb he reached the halfway point, paused to eat his rations, and realised he did not yet have the stamina or strength to continue and still be able to make the descent afterwards. Every year since then he had tried and failed to gain the highest point and gaze into the volcano. He was now twenty-three, with good strength in his arms, upper body, and functioning leg. Perhaps now, he would achieve his dream.

As he drew closer to Old Wizard's root, the crow flew into the moon and on to somewhere he couldn't see, croaking. The ascent began at a gentle gradient, easy enough to walk, but he did not rush, because soon he knew he would have to crawl.

As he walked, leaning on his crutch, his mind travelled backwards to Glanige and its inhabitants. The Night of Demons marked the end of the old year and the beginning of the new, when the spatio-temporal dimensions of the World Tree lay close enough to touch, even overlap, and things that would not ordinarily be able to contact human beings were said to make the effort to do so at this turning-point. The churches continued to peal their bells in a superstitious ritual to comfort the Dead, providing a surreal backdrop to Bronn's laboured breaths and grunts when the climb became steeper and steeper.

Once the slope towered too high to crawl up, he rested, squatting on his haunches, and drank soup from his flask to drive out some of the cold. He bound a thick blade to the underside of each of his boots, and started the difficult part of the ascent, grasping for handholds, hoisting himself up, or chipping at the rockface with a chisel to create handholds when he found none. Sweat pooled on his back under his gansey, and his breath rasped in the back of his throat.

The bells sounded ever more distant, the air taking on a thin, silvered quality which he often associated with the aftermath of a heavy snowfall, and by the middle of the night he had passed the halfway point, or so he guessed. The village lights appeared smaller and further away than he could ever remember. Fuzzy-minded, he rested on a narrow shelf of igneous rock and gnawed his way through a packet of jerky and drank the remainder of the soup.

Something darted at his head, beating his scalp, snatching the piece of dried meat from his hand, and he swayed, cursing, fearing the possible fall—

"Apologies," a voice spoke right beside him. "Long flights always make me hungry."

Slowly, Bronn turned his head.

Perched on the shelf next to him was a figure swathed in a cloak fashioned out of many different birds' feathers, with a long, pale face which ended in a strange twisting and pinching of the nose, and the mouth underneath it looked almost invisible... as if the person had a flesh-covered beak. And the eyes...

He stared as the bird-man swallowed the pilfered food and licked his white, arachnid fingers.

"What... what are you? How did you get up here?"

The man—if he was male, he looked androgynous—regarded Bronn with huge, slanted, obsidian eyes, the pupils ringed with a thin band of tawny gold.

"I am a guide," he said at last. "I flew here."

"You flew?" *The air must be giving me hallucinations*, Bronn thought. *But can hallucinations converse with the people having them?*

"Yes. I was the crow. It's my other aspect."

Puzzle pieces fell into place.

"The Glanegians worship animal gods," Bronn said. "One of them is said to be a centuries-old mage who was incarcerated in the body of a crow for two hundred years. Is that...?"

"I am Corvus the First, the Crow King, yes. I would not call myself a god, though the worship does me no harm."

Bronn averted his face, stuffing the flask back into his satchel, checking Mythadonna's jar was still safe. "I'm dreaming. When I look up, you will be gone."

"Look, then."

He looked. The Crow King was still incredibly there, warm and alive and wild. His black hair stuck in different directions, littered with twigs, leaves, burrs, and tiny feathers. His breath stank like something ancient and sweet.

"Fascinating," Bronn murmured. "But how can this be real? The gods are stories. Psychological constructs using archetypes from the Collective Unconscious. I never knew hallucinations were so vivid."

The Crow King cocked his head. "I made myself visible to you on this night, outside the magical seal around yonder human village, to warn you of the creature you carry. In its dormant state, it is harmless, but should you succeed in bringing it to life, you will come down from this volcano a changed man, if you come down at all, and it will change your village, and then perhaps the world. Those changes may not be to your liking, Bronn Dwarrows. Those beings wreak havoc and pestilence."

Bronn refused to ask him how he knew his name and ulterior motive. "The creature—you mean the specimen from the burial mound?"

"The exact same. I would ask you to hand it over to me, so that I can dispose of it safely."

"I spent a lot of time trying to ascertain what Mythadonna is. If I can prove she is a genuine Murridan, I will be the first natural philosopher to prove the existence of that race. I'm afraid I'm not parting with her. Not yet."

"That was a command, not a question."

Bronn dug his knife out of his pocket and brandished it at the apparition.

"If you try to rob me up here, you will regret it, sir."

The Crow King cocked his head in the other direction. "A little blade won't be enough to stop me, if I decide to wrest the fae girl from you. Your courage is amusing."

"But how would you carry her away, in bird shape, without damaging her?" Bronn asked, thinking he was being clever.

"My intent is to destroy the creature in all thoroughness. Such a species should not be allowed to exist in this world."

"There are more of them?"

"Were. Many hundreds of years ago. I was one of the mage-kings who worked to extinguish them. They were dangerous in large hives, and extreme pests as individuals. Every year's end and every summer's beginning, they would open the hills and lure human folk underground, or fly into the world and sour food, wither crops, drive people insane, and kidnap children to breed with in captivity once they matured. There was no surcease to the trouble they caused. Women were often taken to deliver their young as midwives, then returned to this world with their memories muddied and blurred, if they ever returned at all."

Bronn shook his head, put his knife away, and tried to resume his climb.

The Crow King raised a fine eyebrow. "You are ignoring me?"

"Yes. I would stay to make a further... study of you, to make sure you're not... a hallucination... take photographs..." Bronn panted, "but I have this task to do first. I need... to make the top by dawn... want to see the storms."

No response came. When he glanced down, the rock ledge lay empty, and a single, black feather spiralled past his face on its earthward journey.

Low, menacing grumbles travelled to his ears from above, and the sky flashed cobalt blue and white.

Almost there. Almost...

His fingers scrabbled upwards, found empty air, then curled over a stone lip—

A bristling cloud of blurred grey, black and white descended upon his head and upper body, scratching, stabbing, tearing, shrieking. A mob of birds, from nowhere.

Screaming, he let go of the rockface with one hand to flail at his attackers, then to protect his eyes. The onslaught lasted for what felt like aeons, until at last the birds tired and withdrew. He dangled there, heaving, panting, bleeding from multiple lacerations, shaking too much to trust himself to move.

He glanced down. The cloud of birds was drifting down and coalescing back into the shape of the Crow King, who glared back at him.

"I do not wish to kill you," the Crow King said, "but seeing as the laws of my kind forbid us to take without consent, I have to find a way to force you to give the creature to me. Hand it over."

"If you don't want to harm me, then you have no power over my decisions," Bronn snarled. "You can have her *after* I'm finished with her."

He heaved himself up and over the stone lip, his boots landing on blackened, hardened crust engraved with hairline cracks. Further ahead, a break in the volcanic rock issued steam and glowed scarlet, and many leagues beyond that, another stone lip rose like a tiny mountain range, extending its way around most of the crater.

He had made it. This was Old Wizard's caldera. Bronn wanted to dance and jump around for joy, but eased himself into a crouch and stretched his aching, lame leg out in front of him. He fumbled his satchel open and withdrew Mythadonna's jar, setting it on the ground next to him. The sky loured and boiled overhead, groaning like a massive tree being felled, and every hair on his body crept and stiffened, his scalp tingling.

Be quick.

Bronn unscrewed the jar, tipped the fluid out in his haste, and laid the tiny body upon the cracked rock, afraid of breaking it. He took magnets and wire out of his satchel and arranged them around Mythadonna in a configuration which he theorised would be enough to draw down the lightning, checking all around him for the presence of the Crow King, then descended part of the way down the volcano's side to wait.

The night cracked. Everything bleached white.

Pulse pounding in every limb, Bronn blinked and blinked until he could see again. He still clung to the rock, unharmed. Branches of lightning played between the top of Old Wizard and the storm clouds above in a never-ending display of jagged electrical trees, dissipating and reforming. The resulting boom was enough to cause tinnitus, and he appreciated why the people of Glanige called the volcano by its nickname. It was cantankerous and frightening, it possessed too much power, and seemed to take delight in throwing it around.

He squinted into the sky and gawked. The clouds had amassed into the rough outline and features of the Horned Lord—two cavernous eye sockets, and two never-ending antlers with row upon row of eye-boggling tines—but as he watched, the illusion began to dissolve.

That's silly. Volcanoes have no intelligence. Clouds have no mind. Concentrate.

He scrambled up and peeked into the crater.

Mythadonna was gone. No sign of the body anywhere, or any evidence of it having been burned. Had Corvus the Crow King taken it? He guessed not. The lightning would have fried him alive if he tried to steal her.

What a disappointment. Still, he could return to the village confident in the knowledge that he had succeeded in a task no one else thought he could do, or that anyone else had ever dared to try. At last, instead of feeling like a mere boy, he felt like a man.

Bronn clambered down Old Wizard, containing his excitement. He would now be able to tell anyone that cared to ask about his adventure, instead of being called mad for trying. He could pen a letter to his mother and father, who moved to a rest home further inland when he entered his twenties, and tell them the good news. He wondered what time of night it was. The bells had ceased ringing, and the air felt colder.

They'll have taken the last burning brands from the banefires to relight their hearths at home. It's dark now, so it must be almost dawn. The first day of the new year.

The Crow King did not appear in his human aspect during Bronn's return to Glanige, but a crow followed him overhead, complaining in a raucous voice.

On his weary limp down Broken Beach, something pulled his hair, *hard*, and slapped him around the side of his face.

He whirled around. Nothing there.

Something bit his earlobe with needle-pointed little teeth. He shrieked and swatted at the thing, and it fell onto the sea-glasses with an aggravated hiss.

He stared.

Mythadonna glared up at him, wingless, defenceless, and hideously angry. She must have crawled onto his coat and let him carry her down the volcano unawares. Now she wanted his attention, *and she was alive.*

"Can you speak?" He did not dare to raise his voice above a whisper, and knelt down with difficulty, fatigue chewing his bones.

Mythadonna's twisted, ugly little face grinned at him.

"What have you done with my wings, boy?"

"Me? Nothing. I found you in a—"

"Oh, I knows where you finds me. It was in a place you had no right to be in, meddler. You took what isn't yours to have."

He watched her shivering there, covering her modesty with both arms, and experienced a stab of remorse.

"I'm sorry, I... curiosity, I suppose... let me help you up—"

"No," she spat. "Where be the others?"

"Others?"

"My people. Where be my family, my hive? The *Murridanagh*?"

Bronn recalled what the Crow King had said on the volcano.

"I'm afraid they don't exist anymore."

Mythadonna screeched like a glass violin until blood dripped from the end of his nose.

"You will pay for what you has done," she seethed. "Every sunrise on the first day of the year, light floods my tomb and wakes the spells graven on my casket, replenishing my wings ready for when a new era of the *Murridanagh* begins. This year I is not there, thanks to you, and now my wings be gone! And you has woken me before the time when I should be waking!"

"I... well, I can take you back there now—"

"Too late!" She gestured to the east, where the sun warmed the horizon. "It seems we is lumbered with one another..."

Before he could protest, she swarmed up his leg and clawed up his coat until she sat atop his left shoulder, chuckling in a way that replaced his pity with something like fear.

"...For I sees that, like me, you have a physical wrongness. If you wants, I could even up your body by destroying the longer leg. I be flying no longer, but still I has so much magic, itching to gets out..."

"No!" he gabbled. "Not that! Couldn't you make the lame leg strong and functional instead?"

"My power knows not how to repair, only breaks, disorders, and disarrays. Tell me, how many mortals be living in Glanige now? A hundred? Two hundred? Whom shall I sends into madness? Any cattle I can strikes with sickness and ride to death all through the night? And babies... oh, I loves babies. At this turn of the year the mortal folk used to introduce their newborns to the community. Do they still be doing that?"

"Yes," Bronn said, his heart sinking below his ribcage.

"*Good.* I shall likes it here after all. I'm a newborn to everyone here. Why don't you takes me into the village and be introducing me?"

Oh, gods. What Hell have I brought to my people?

Near the first of the barrows, Bronn noticed a dark figure. The Crow King was waiting for him. He limped faster, hope lighting a little banefire in his innards.

"Congratulations," the Crow King commented with heavy sarcasm. "You did not listen to me, and now you are paying the price."

"I consent!" Bronn panted. "You can take her off me. I'm done with her now. My hypothesis is proven."

The Crow King shook his head. "Now that she lives, she belongs to herself and herself only, not you. You no longer have the right to give her to me, or anyone else. I cannot help you."

"There must be something you can do! Wait—"

The Crow King gave him a mocking bow and melted upwards, until only a large crow flapped into the air. The crow slipped into the sunrise without another sound.

Bronn trudged into the morning-lit village with weary bones and a heavy soul, a tiny demon on his shoulder, and knew that quite soon he would no longer be welcome in Glanige, perhaps anywhere else, ever again.

NEED TO KNOW

KB NELSON

"So, I won't get old, I might never die—that's what you're offering me, right? Gimme a minute, Nasia, I'm feeling kinda blindsided here." Jessica unwound her lanky form and fetched the bottle of Chardonnay from her mom's fridge. "Shall I top off your wine too? I think it's going to be a long night."

She was fresh from battle with Friday after-work traffic, having driven directly from her office in Seattle to her mother's apartment in Ferndale. As soon as she was in the door and had kicked off her shoes to curl up on the couch, her mom had pressed a tumbler of white wine into her hand.

"Really, Nasia, you still don't own even one wine glass? For guests?"

"Ha! You should know better than that!"

Nasia had always embraced a migratory lifestyle; every so often she would discard all her possessions, move, and restock from a new second-hand store. Along with acquiring a new, second-hand name. But she had enjoyed watching Jessica develop a taste for the finer things in life after she left home.

The plan had been for one of their periodic girls' weekends: hit the Scotch bar, maybe rent a kayak, probably compare latest TV or food obsessions while Nasia probed for information about Jessica's personal life. But after a brief review of their latest favorite novels, Nasia steered the discussion to more sober matters. Like whether or not death was optional.

"You know, Naz, I would've bet you couldn't shock me anymore. And lost."

Nasia hadn't heard Jess call her "Mom" since her daughter was in her teens. Other than the occasional slip into old habits.

At the time Nasia had sported the name Mary and appeared to be only about ten years older than her daughter. Now she looked like Jessica's younger sister, and as time continued to pass and she didn't age, Nasia knew she would eventually appear to be Jessica's daughter. But based on previous experience, she knew that the original parent-child dynamic would never change.

Jess continued, "Anyway, I thought the thing was, well... This was it. Your body wouldn't ever age, couldn't ever die."

"Well, that is almost true. I have always known my capacity to regenerate does have limits. But to my surprise, its ability to stop ageing apparently does as well. I have noticed little signs like morning creakiness in my joints. It is like nothing I have ever experienced before, and I cannot say I like it very much. No grey yet, though; thank goodness for small blessings!"

"Yeah, you, queen of the seasonal hair color," Jess quipped. "What a hardship if you should actually have to cover some grey. I can't remember the last time I saw your natural brunette anyways."

Nasia followed her daughter's deflection into a more comfortable topic. "I see you put in some highlights. I like! It looks as blond as when you were little." She affected a coy look. "Would you believe I've actually started paying attention to ads for age-defying moisturizers?"

Eyebrows raised. "Holy smokes, for real?" Jess paused. Nasia allowed silence to build until Jess continued. "So, you know, we've never really talked about... like, how did you choose this body when you, uh..."

"Okay. So, when I chose this host body, I needed someone who was socially invisible as well as available without delay. Choosing a healthy, wellborn host was out of the question. See, my host body at the time had been damaged beyond what I could repair. When I found Atalia—that was her name, if you recall. Anyway, I knew that she had had a miserable life; hardship was typical for common people. I could easily heal her injuries, but between malnutrition and general poor health they would have been fatal to her without my help. It was simply a case of right place, right time."

Jess eyed her mother's short sturdy form and said, "So you started out as a half-starved peasant." She brought up her phone. "Life is good. Let's order pizza."

* * *

The Nasia that Jess was visiting in Ferndale was a persona created at the end of Jessica's high school years. Graduation was the type of watershed event Nasia relied on to change her identity. When Jess moved to attend university, she helped her set up a little suite and visited frequently. School chums came to know Nasia as their friend's flamboyant, protective, older sister. Daring cosmetics and centuries of acting practice ensured she appeared to be quite unlike Mary, Jessica's demure mother. Nasia was always aware of the chance she might bump into one of the few of Jessica's high school friends who were also on campus. Although dodging them was always simplest.

Nasia's solo lifestyle combined with a rather infertile body had led to few pregnancies and births over her long life. She had, however, witnessed more unwanted pregnancies, botched abortions, still-births and maternal deaths than she cared to remember. She'd shared only a small sample of the stories with Jess. Most women she and her daughter knew took present-day reproductive technology for granted. Nasia had made sure Jess appreciated modern birth control and understood that for the first time in Nasia's long life, motherhood was her choice, not happenstance.

Explaining her true nature to her own child was therefore something Nasia had needed to do infrequently throughout her life. She had no tried and true path to follow. In any case, what worked a few centuries previously would be all but useless, the frames of reference being so dissimilar. She decided to reveal the truth when Jess was riding the bumps of her early teens, what with everything else already in flux. In retrospect, probably not the best choice.

Jessica's reaction started with the expected puzzlement and disbelief, but swiftly flamed into adolescent fury. "So, you've been keeping a humongous secret all this time? And you always tell me that I'm supposed to be open and honest with you! Now I'm supposed to lie to my friends the same way you've been lying to me? What a fucking hypocrite!" Jess's straight-armed, fist-clenched pose had been cute when she was a toddler. Now, barely thirteen but taller than her mother, glowering down at her with incandescent anger, she was anything but cute.

"What even *are* you?" With a tearful, "I hate you!" she ran out of the kitchen into her bedroom and slammed the door.

As with all the other dramatic incidents which had been exploding once every couple of weeks, she reappeared after a few hours, when supper was on the table. *Adolescent appetites, keeping families together since forever,* Nasia thought.

It had taken several weeks for Jess to come to grips with the idea. As she worked through it, she would toss out an occasional question or two. They tended to be of a practical nature. And of course, from a teen, self-centered.

While drying the dishes one night she said, "So, you decided to have a kid. What, you just hung around the bus station and looked for some guy to be my dad? Did you even consider who *I* would turn out to be? You didn't even think of that, did you?"

Nasia took a slow breath. "That's not entirely accurate, there are better places to look for a, uh, brief relationship, than a bus station." She ignored Jessica's look of astonishment and continued. "You realize I had to research to ensure that I wasn't planning to procreate with one of my own great-great grandsons. Had to move around. And one of the reasons I never considered using an anonymous sperm bank. Genetic testing wasn't really an option back then."

"Oh my God, you're not joking, are you? Okay, stop talking, this is insane!"

Jess had first noticed that most of her friends had fathers, even if they didn't live in the same home, around the time she started kindergarten. Nasia had responded to her questions about her father with some variation of, "I don't know who or where he is," followed by a distraction or change of subject. As Jess got older and more persistent, Nasia became deaf to any inquiry.

But that hadn't stopped Jessica's curiosity; if anything, it stoked it. Out of the blue one day she announced, "I know I'm part Dutch." She'd come to that conclusion because she was tall and fair like the De Vries kids down the block.

To which Nasia replied, "If you like."

"Humph! You are so *frustrating!*"

Now that Jess understood her mom's bizarre truth, it was obvious why she wouldn't want a relationship her own child's father. Or anyone, for that matter. Why she never had close friendships or volunteered at the school.

History class that year was doing a unit on the French Revolution. One afternoon as they were driving to the mall Jess asked if she had actually watched the beheadings.

"It sounds so gross and disgusting. Were people more bloodthirsty then?"

"Well, first of all, no, I did not see it, I was not even in Paris at the time. I think I was in Athens around then. I was pretty good at sniffing out social upheaval and staying away. Keeping a low profile, you know."

"So, what was Athens like?"

"That's the other thing. I really have no memories of that time. Don't roll your eyes at me, young lady! I am not trying to evade. Think about this. Do you remember the shoes you wore when you were five? Or even your birthday party? That was only eight years ago."

"So, it's all just a blur? Or, uh, is it more, like, your memory banks get full and you have to dump stuff? Then it's just not there at all?"

"Well, it is more like snapshots. Here, this might explain it. You know how you remember yappy Luna from next door? She was always such a cheerful dog. She loved it when you rubbed her tummy. You were so sad and angry when we moved away, you said you would miss her more than your friends."

"Totally! I still think about her whenever I see a Corgi. What's your point?"

"Do you remember the names of the people who lived there? What car they had? The color of their house?" They turned into the mall parking lot as Jess considered the question.

"Uhh, Mr. and Mrs... Harrison? Okay, I see what you mean, I have a snapshot of Luna but not of the rest of the place. Because I cared about the dog."

"Exactly. For me, my snapshots sometimes get all jumbled up, get lost and found again, sometimes one shows up unexpectedly. But there are some, like when I joined with Atalia, that are always clear. Always there." Nasia steered into an open spot, turned off the car and continued.

"Things with strong emotions tied to them—they make the strongest, most lasting memories. Like the day you were born and I first held you." She reached in her purse for a tissue.

"Oh jeez, Mom, are you crying? You think you'd be toughened up by now. I think you're getting weepier; you're going to be bawling as we pass the Hallmark store pretty soon."

"Oh shut up, smart aleck." She mussed Jessica's hair and then reached in for a hug.

A few days later Jess had trotted out a new inquiry. "So, like, who exactly are you? Is this Atalia person still in there? What was she before this, uh, 'hosting' thing happened?" Jess had grudgingly accepted her mother's insistence that she really didn't know what her origins were. Trying to find those memories was like looking into a black void.

"When Atalia and I joined, I healed her and rejuvenated her as I had promised. She and I had some issues, like any new roommates who had just met. But unlike roommates, we could not just agree to disagree on things, move on and forget about it. For example, her ambition to marry, that was a tough one. Or even taste in men. She really did like the bad boys, which is how she wound up injured in the first place."

Jess was confused. "She liked someone who would hurt her? That's just stupid."

"Oh honey, love is stupid. But that's a discussion for another day.

"Anyways, after forty or fifty years there were very few differences of opinion; you really could say we were one personality. After a couple of centuries, pretty well all traces of her had faded away."

Now, two decades after this conversation started, Nasia had offered Jess first dibs on becoming her new host. It wouldn't be Jess herself who would be virtually immortal. But close enough to it.

* * *

Nasia waited until she heard Jess stirring before she fired up the coffee grinder. She knew her daughter would appreciate the luxury of having someone else make the coffee while she lazed in bed, or pull-out couch as it happened to be. After a few minutes the coffee maker alerted them with its "ready" beep.

"I really should look into getting one of those machines with a timer and automatic grinder," Jess said as she got up, raising her voice to reach around the corner. She pulled her housecoat out of her overnight bag. "Maybe in the future we'll all have coffee robots." She recalled the previous evening's conversation as she halted mid-sleeve and said, "Oh. Right."

"Good morning, sunshine!" rang out from around the corner. Delicious aromas drew Jessica into the kitchen where her mother mixed pancake batter while bacon started to sizzle.

Nasia had always been a morning person. Since she only needed about four hours of sleep to wake refreshed and energized, she was also an evening person. Jess hugged her mom good morning and murmured, "Mmm, coffee. I'll think about breakfast in a minute."

"Look at the beautiful day. When was the last time you went to a good old-fashioned country fair? The Lynden Fair is on this weekend. I went last year, and it is everything a country fair should be. Chickens and quilts and the whole nine yards. I would bet you can even tolerate a ride on the Ferris wheel. Now that you are all grown up."

Jess silently stared over the rim of her coffee cup.

Nasia laughed, "Okay, okay, you wake up first."

A shower, a leisurely breakfast and few hours later they were on the road. Jess fiddled with the radio while Nasia drove. Unable to find a program which satisfied her, she continued to scan stations until her mother said, "You know, we could just talk. Last night was about my stuff, what's new with you?"

"Right, your 'stuff.' Anyways. Well, I've started seeing someone. Actually, I was going to tell you last night, before we got sidetracked."

"Oh-ho! Who is it, where did you meet him, dish, dish!" chirped Nasia, all the while thinking, *Oh please let this one not be a dud.* She had spent centuries confirming that it's better to be happy and single than in a bad relationship. As well, she'd learned that everyone has to figure it out for themselves.

"You're going to laugh. I tried online dating and damn if it didn't work! He's a tax attorney—yeah, I said you'd laugh! He's actually an interesting guy; we had a couple of dinner dates then went hiking once. He's divorced but no kids. Skis at Snoqualmie."

"So far so good. Do I get to meet him? No pressure, just a simple hello with your sister; it's not like he's meeting your mother." Nasia glanced to the side and winked.

"You planning on coming to Seattle anytime soon? We're going to see Cirque du Soleil. It's coming through next month; you could join us."

"Planning dates a month in advance. Sounds like you are really moving along with this guy. Does he have a name?"

"Marty, his name is Marty. And before you ask, yes, he's taller than me. Like, well over six feet." She absently repeated, "Marty," and Nasia studied the little smile which creased the corners of her mouth. Nice.

The fair was easy enough to find. Before they were even off the highway, signs directing them to Free Downtown Parking! started to appear. With a Free Shuttle to the Fair!

"Gotta love small towns," said Jess.

Once on the fairgrounds they started to meander along the midway. They walked in comfortable silence as they watched the riders' expressions of delight or terror zip by. The pervasive fragrance of straw became overtaken by the sweetness of fried dough as they made their way towards the kiosks.

"Oh God, funnel cakes, how disgusting." Nasia laughed. "No line-up yet. Should we get two or just split one?"

"Yeah, just one, my metabolism isn't quite what it used to be," Jess said, looking annoyed that everything she said or thought about today reminded herself of her mortality. "I'll get it, you grab us a place to sit."

Nasia wandered past the petting zoo, watching the usual assortment of timid and brave children. And timid and brave parents. She found a vacant picnic table in a sunny spot. An elderly man seated at the table next to it greeted her.

"Lovely day, huh? Not so hot, like last week." He nodded at Jess as she arrived and set down a paper carton of fried dough and sugar, and two sodas. "You ladies just here for the fine food or you gonna get your innards jiggled too? Me, I'm just watching the entertainment. I'm up from Bellingham with my favourite little gal, she's on that crazy Octopus ride, just finishing now. Loves the darned thing; wants to go every year."

Nasia saw a bouncy ponytailed girl exiting the ride and waving in their direction. "Your granddaughter?"

Jess added, "She's lovely. You must be very proud."

"My granddaughter? What, is Hailey up here, where?" He turned and checked out a noisy gaggle of pre-teens, then turned back. "Oh, here's my little gal now." He called to a short, dowager-humped woman who strolled up as the young girl trotted past them to meet her friends. "Hey, Nancy, did you see Hailey up here?"

"Oh don't be foolish George, you know they've gone to Whidbey..."

He broke in, "...for the rest of August, yes of course. Now that I think of it, weren't they going to..."

She completed his sentence, "...Skype just after lunchtime? Yes, I was just coming to say that we'd better be getting home." She greeted Nasia and Jess. "Hello girls! What a gorgeous day!" Her laugh lines deepened as she squinted into the sun and flashed a broad smile. "Did you go on the rides before eating your funnel cake? Speaking from experience, that's the best order to do it in. Of course, you could just sit here like..."

"...like the smart one of this couple and take a pass on both, like me. And you know Gina would be sitting right here with me." George turned to address the two women. "That's our daughter, beautiful like her mom but sensible like her dad."

"Oh fiddlesticks, at least I have a soulmate in Hailey. My sense of adventure just skipped a generation."

Jess jumped into the conversation. "I'm just up for the weekend. We used to catch a fair almost every year before I moved to Seattle. I'm happy to enjoy some second-hand adrenaline and catch some sun, but I expect my sister here with the 'sense of adventure,' as you say, will want to torture herself with a few rides before the end of the day."

"Well you girls enjoy the rest of your afternoon. We're done here. Come along old man, let's get a move on."

As the couple walked and talked Jess was fascinated by their dovetailed exchange. "Should we have that leftover roast beef for supper? I could warm it up..."

"...in the gravy, sure that sounds good, maybe on some of that sourdough bread." Their conversation traded back and forth as they walked into the parking lot.

Jess gazed after George and Nancy and murmured, "Wow, they've probably been married twice as many years as they were single."

* * *

Later that evening both women were pecking away on their electronics. Nasia sat at the kitchen table with her laptop and Jess was cross-legged on the couch with her tablet. Without looking away from the monitor, Nasia said, "Even if you do not know it yet, I can tell that hosting is not for you."

"What?"

"My mother's intuition has kicked in. You think you need more time to consider it, but I know you will come to the same conclusion. Immortality is not for you."

Jess looked up from her tablet. "It's an amazing opportunity. But you're wrong, I don't need more time and that's because it's not a new idea to me. I've thought about it before, lots of times, what would it be like to be you. To see the things you've seen, to learn and to do. To read science fiction and know that you'll be able to look back on it like we look at Jules Verne's books now."

"Absolutely!" Nasia jumped up from her chair. "What is the most fun is that things happen no one could foresee. In the fifties everyone was looking forward to flying cars, but it is the internet that has totally changed the way we live. Maybe some think tanks were discussing it, but as far as I'm concerned, nobody saw it coming. Right now, I am impatient for virtual computers, no more lugging around a device. But I also know that I have no idea what will have the biggest effect on my life in five or six decades."

"But..." Jess set aside her tablet and sighed. "To love, and to lose everyone you love."

"You are right. The loss... You would think I would have learned to avoid attachments in my life but hearts—even immortal ones—do not work that way." Nasia settled back into her chair. "You know, my wish to have a child was not something I took lightly. I told you years ago that you were my first planned pregnancy. But we never really talked about how crazy it was for me to make that decision. Having a child in my life always made it much more complicated and created some of my most painful memories. But my most precious ones too."

"So you get it! This primal urge, how I want to have kids whether it makes sense or not. And I've always wanted to grow old watching them grow up. And, yeah, to be an old grey-haired granny." Jess unconsciously ran her fingers through her bangs and continued.

"But this, what you're offering me, it's not just my decision. This concerns you as much as me, right? Or maybe even more so. That's what I've been thinking about all day."

"Oh honey, I am not in any rush. You are not my only option, just my first choice. Well, my easiest choice. Roommates, remember?" Nasia thought of times past when she would gladly have offered her gift to one of her children, but circumstances made it impossible. An ancient memory drifted up: her newborn grandson squalling as her daughter convulsed and died. No need to share that disturbing image.

"I am sure I have decades to go before my aging will become obvious." She turned her kitchen chair back to the table. "How would you feel about having a little sister?" She ignored Jessica's gape and pointed at her laptop. "Come take a look at this."

"I'm just emailing Marty; one second," Jess said as she hit Send. She got up, looked over Nasia's shoulder and read:

HOW STRONGLY DO YOU AGREE OR DISAGREE WITH THE FOLLOWING: I AM LOOKING FOR A LONG-TERM RELATIONSHIP THAT WILL ULTIMATELY LEAD TO MARRIAGE.

Nasia clicked on the Absolutely Disagree button.

"Mom, seriously, eHarmony?"

"Why not? It seems to have worked for you, and it says here that there is someone for everyone. No one will ever say I am not willing to learn things from my kid! Here we are, I am just about finished registering—oh look, it says I am awesome. This website *is* a good judge of personality."

Jess grinned and shook her head as the last few questions flashed by. She turned to go back to her tablet and heard, "So we should go clubbing tonight; you will be my wingman. Last time I was looking for someone to date, smartphones did not even exist. Hell, the internet did not exist! Okay, how does this Tinder thing work?"

* * *

Five weeks later Nasia, Jess and Marty were standing in the rain waiting to pass through Cirque du Soleil's security/purse check. The line-up was just long enough to allow for conversation. Jess and Marty chatted quietly as they huddled under his umbrella. Nasia declined the offer to join them, standing aside to let the rain run from her hood onto her face and drip off her nose.

Marty raised his voice to include her. "Your sister was right, Nasia, you're amazing, just a ball of energy! I haven't seen you sit still yet. You must've been right ready to crash when I phoned Jess last night. Seriously, she told me you got to her place in Sea-Tac at six a.m. so you could avoid the traffic through Seattle. You must have left Ferndale at, what, three thirty?"

"Hey, less traffic equals greater serenity."

He checked the tickets and addressed Jess. "You're *sure* Nasia doesn't mind sitting by herself?"

"Trust me, she's not one for just being polite."

"She is right, Marty, trust her! Really, getting a ticket at all on such short notice was more than I could hope for. This will be fun!"

"And anyways, no she didn't crash, she sat up surfing on her computer for a while after I went to bed. That's not unusual; she's never needed a lot of sleep." Jess gave Nasia's hood an affectionate tug, releasing another rivulet of rainwater. "At least she respects my quiet hours."

Marty shook his head and said, "Must have been absolutely brutal for your mom when you guys were little, being a single parent of two with one kid who doesn't sleep much." From previous conversations with Jess, Nasia knew about her common ground with Marty, that they both had absent fathers.

"Uh, yeah, I guess so, I never really thought about it from her point of view." Jess changed the subject, as she usually did when someone started talking about her mother. "Do you think they're going to confiscate my bottle of water? Is this like airport security? Can you see what they're doing up there?"

Marty didn't need to stretch to see over the crowd. "I think you'll be okay. You can always empty it on the ground if they don't want you bringing outside liquids in. Nobody's going to notice another puddle."

* * *

Security had been uneventful, as expected. The show was spectacular, also as expected. Breathtaking and beautiful. After the show Nasia waited for Jess by the popcorn station. They took one last turn around the merchandise floor while Marty fetched the car. Nasia slid the umbrella from under Jessica's arm as they exited the show tent. She raised it and grabbed the opportunity for a private chat while they walked arm in arm.

"That's quite the nice fella you have there. Marty. Sounds like a country singer, but but Mr. Tall, Dark and Handsome has more of a Mick Jaggar vibe if you ask me. Short for Martin I assume?"

"Actually his name is Maret. He's from Indonesia, born in Jakarta. He's named for his birth month, March. Apparently that's a thing there. I'm actually only a couple of months older than he is. He told me his mom moved here with him when he was about three, so he doesn't have an accent, although if you pay attention the odd word comes out with a bit of a sexy foreign lilt!"

Nasia stumbled, steadied herself on Jessica's arm and blurted, "I'm okay!"

With a tiny catch in her voice she continued, "Yeah, I picked up on a bit on an accent, thought he was maybe Dutch or German, with a last name of Hengfeld."

"Actually it's Hengfelt, with a T. He told me it's quite an uncommon way to spell it. Can't imagine going through middle school with name like Heng*felt*, though, can you? I'll have to ask him about it sometime. Look, here he comes now."

Marty jingled his car keys as he walked toward them. Jess moved from under her mother's umbrella to take his arm with easy affection. He looked up into the Scotch mist and said, "It's not really raining anymore. You can probably put that down."

Jess looked at her mother. "Nasia, you okay? You look like you saw a ghost."

"What? Oh, sorry, just wool-gathering here. I, uh, I had a mental image of that Cirque performer who died last year. Can you imagine what it must have been like to be in the audience?" She smiled at the two and rubbed her chin. "Glad I didn't think about it until now. If it had been on my mind while the show was going on,

I think that might have been too much suspense!"

She furled the umbrella and pirouetted, face towards the sky. Kicking up splashes, she hurried toward the car waiting for them in the no parking zone at the curb. "Anyways, you are right, the rain has stopped. We better get going before the parking patrol sees us."

"All right, all right, wait up!"

Later, back at the apartment the two women sat with cups of chamomile tea, snuggled on the couch in their pajamas. Nasia had allowed Marty to maintain the fiction that he didn't usually stay over after a date. Though his sentiment was strangely outdated, she was happy to have the evening alone with Jess.

"So that was kind of adorable. Does he really think that I would disapprove of my sister having a man stay over? Like, whose toothbrush and razor does he think I noticed in the bathroom?"

"Oh, he asked me to hide those away. You're right, in a way he's so strait-laced it's almost cute. Yeah, yeah, I know, tax attorney, almost an accountant." She took a sip of tea. "I think his mom was really conservative or something. Makes him think that everyone's judging him."

"Does she still live in the States or did she eventually move back?"

"Neither, she passed away, quite a few years ago, I think. Sounds like she was quite the strong, practical woman. He said she put the fear of God into him when he was a teenager with regard to not getting a girl pregnant. She had an unwanted pregnancy so made damned sure he'd never be the cause of one. He says he knew more about birth control at the age of fourteen than half of his friends do now."

"Well, it worked out that he never had kids. Makes dating a divorced guy a lot easier." Nasia focused on steadying her voice as she inspected a fingernail. "Do you know if he even wants to be a father? Or have you actually discussed anything that, uh, substantial?"

"Yes. Yes we have." Jess sighed and set her cup aside. "Mom, I really like him. I'm falling in love. But, well, you know how I feel about wanting to start a family. I want to get pregnant and have my own child." She laid her head in Nasia's lap.

Stroking Jessica's hair, Nasia was glad that her smile was hidden. "So, it sounds like there is a problem in that department? Dealbreaker, even?"

"Not exactly. Apparently Marty's bitch of an ex was so determined to not have kids that she made him have a vasectomy to prove that he loved her. So I know, even if we wanted to become pregnant, if we got that far, it wouldn't be his biological child."

Nasia stifled a shout of *Yes!* and instead made an observation. "Well, you have said that you were going to have a baby by age thirty-five, whether or not you are in a relationship. So, this does not actually change the, uh, the logistics of becoming pregnant. You just need to decide if you are going to do this on your own or with Marty. Assuming he is even on board."

"When we talked about that whole thing with his ex, he seemed to genuinely regret that he no longer had the option to be a daddy. I pointed out that although both he and I had biological fathers, neither of us had daddies. So it works both ways: he could become a daddy even if he wasn't a biological father. Though I'm pretty sure he thought I was talking theoretically.

"He certainly carries some anger about how his ex literally managed to leave permanent scars."

Jess sat up and yawned. "I've got to get to bed before I fall asleep right here. I'll see you in the morning. Good night. I'd say don't stay up too late, but I know better."

Nasia watched her head into the bathroom and close the door. She leapt to her feet and did a silent little happy dance as she dabbed away a few tears.

Hengfelt. Over three decades ago, a drop in her bucket of time. She could still recall every detail of the tall gorgeous man she met in Jakarta. The delirious few months they spent together. How she decided to conceive his child and then vanished from his life as soon as she succeeded. Had he had any male relatives there? A brother perhaps? She had no idea.

But with no potential for genetic problems if they were to have children, there was no need for either Jessica or Maret to learn they were at best, first cousins, if not half-siblings.

"Hey, Jess," she called through the bathroom door. "We can check out the sperm banks tomorrow. Maybe we can get a deal. Buy one get one at fifty percent off?"

"Good Lord, Naz. Good night."

CONVERGENCE

Nickolas Urpi

I

Papa had left again, as soon as he had returned.

They had laughed, danced, embraced, and flooded each other with kisses. He teased her, shaking a mooncuttle he had just caught in her face. Its long, dead tentacles flapped about her cheeks and she cried, while laughing. Her father removed it and put it back in the sack with the others, all the blackish-beige cephalopods that glimmered in the dark waters beneath the caverns outside of Tarante, feeding on moonlight.

When they had finished laughing, and he washed the inky mess from her face (making sure to pinch her nose as he did so), he walked to the window to look out over the city. When he saw the purple ribbon of light streaking across the sky, his face darkened, and his lips tightened. Ladja knew when she saw him that the good times had come to an end and that he would leave again, despite having come home with a full load of the elusive mooncuttles. The Convergence was coming, and Papa always left when the Convergence came.

In a flash, Ladja was left alone, with the bowl of whitish hair cupping her head and a net full of mooncuttles in the smoking cupboard above the hearth, which had gone cold. She wouldn't need it with the Convergence coming. Mrs. Pirio would be by the following day with baked breads for her, so she wouldn't be in want of food for another three days. Papa would pay her upon his return. In the meantime, Ladja was to wait, not going out, not drifting from the house. She would sharpen his arrowheads, which were all already sharpened, and dust the house, which was already dusted.

She climbed out the roof-window of their apartment and sat on the red tiles with her arms wrapped around her knees, watching the Convergence take shape. Each player was getting into position, the moons rising up, closer than she had ever seen them before. She felt as though she could see every rivet, every canyon, every blemish that summed up the spherical glowing orbs, already orange from the coming spectacle.

By the next morning, they would converge and there would be no morning, no noon, no night, only ever-present in-between. She thought back of the days when she would be dressed up in her magical horse outfit, holding hands with her mother, and watching the sparkles from her sparkler dance in front of her eyes. She could not remember her mother's face, only the softness of her voice and the squeezing touch of her hand, wrapped around her own.

She listened back with her memory to her mother describing the Convergence and the festival that took place for the duration: *"Every year, Phyrcia and Gailon, the two moons that surround our planet, suddenly change course, without rhyme or reason, by the will of the heavens or the will of the sun, and they come together with the sun to create one big star. One big orange star with purple ribbons streaming out of it, wavering like thunder. And for three days, this bright star, with the small white twinkling stars in the sky falling around it like a crown, warms the earth. For three days it isn't cold. It isn't hot. It's just warm, and beautiful. The sky is orange and purple. But you know all that, you've seen it."*

Ladja nodded. "The festival."

"Hush!" Mama laughed. "I'm getting there. In Byrlio, we have a festival, a great carnival to celebrate the convergence: to celebrate the miracle. They don't know what the miracle is for, or what it promised; there are so many stories. But they light fireworks that burn the sky, they set off firecrackers and fry dough with honey, they sprinkle meat with spices and dress up dogs like fairies and sprites and let them dance around, they release balloons to honor the dead, hold public dances where couples and children come together and spin until their feet hurt and their calves are too stiff to stand, they have games of races and javelin throws and sack races, they have giant spinning machines that lift you into the air and twirl you around, they put you in carts and take you around the city. People dress up like deities, old kings and queens, paint themselves like Thrakians, and wear extra hooves like centaurs; people breathe fire like horses, and drink wine that is hot and sweet, they shave ice off giant blocks and drizzle them with the juice of fruits and nuts..."

Ladja fell asleep before her memory could play out, just as everything took its place.

When she awoke, the Convergence was fully blooming, all the stars weaving their crown around the trifecta of celestial bodies. At long last, Ladja determined that she was tired of listening to the distant hum of the festival, wondering what it was like to be amongst the lively and the vivacious. She resolved to find her mother, who was lost during the Convergence, they say, to the Labyrinth. They never said where the Labyrinth leads, only that it appears, by magic, during the Convergence, and that it can be followed to the Temple of the Night.

Ladja was hesitant to open the door, remembering the words of her father and how her mother had disappeared, but the sound of laughter and singing pulled her out of her fear and she stepped into the outside world, forged anew in sight by the Convergence.

II

"There you are," Mama said, laughing as she opened the cupboard.

Ladja was hiding amongst the tablecloths, wearing one of them as though it were clothing.

"You found me!" Ladja laughed, as Mama pulled her out and embraced her.

"I'll always find you," Mama said. "It was a good disguise; you can't ever hide yourself from love, Ladja, don't you know that?"

Ladja had lost the doorway as soon as she stepped out into the fresh, warm air of the Convergence. Everything was beautiful. People were dancing down the street, their faces covered in masks and their bodies cloaked in capes. The capes and masks were a traditional dress of the Convergence, except for those who played the parts in the theaters and the parades.

Ladja quickly immersed herself in the jovial atmosphere, horses prancing through the streets while their admirers sang songs of their speed and noble ancestry. She passed by the booths where custard-stuffed breads were sold at a penny a piece, where fieldnuts were roasted and crushed with sugar into a paste, where hams and wild boars were roasted on a rotating spit, and fruit juices were poured over ice, shaved off of monolithic blocks that couldn't melt during the Convergence.

She purchased the gracefruit juice with a penny she had found fallen from someone's pocket. She walked around, smiling as she drank and licked the sticky, cold ice. Everything seemed to be awash with pleasure. The soldiers of the town stripped naked, save for their helmets and shields, and with wooden spears, with leather wrapped around the ends, reenacted battles lost to memory. She watched the dragon parade, the horse parade, the Thylacine parade, and laughed at the comics who danced through the streets, slapping each other in a game of endless tag. She only stopped to weep when she saw mothers and daughters, linked hand in hand. She wondered why her father had to hate the Convergence festival; she missed him too. It was as though a thin pane of glass always separated them. They could see each other clearly enough, but not touch fully—completely.

When she awoke from her reveries, she found herself down an unfamiliar street, with a parade approaching that she also did not recognize. They started surrounding her.

They were more than surrounding her, they were marching around her in a circle, their brightly painted masks shining like the copper sun in the sky the other three-hundred and sixty-two days of the year. They swirled around her in concentric patterns that had no balance. They reached out their hands to her, poking her with their fingers and grabbing her by the shoulder.

Ladja screamed and tried to push through them, but their ranks would not break. They pulled at her, herding her up the street while chanting her name.

She bit the hand of one of them and pushed through them. He gave way, falling against the wall while she slipped out of their grasp.

"Ladja! Ladja!" they all called, pursuing her through the streets. She ran through the laughing crowd, who stepped back, believing the pursuit to be a parade chase. They laughed and laughed while she ran and ran, the whole group of Daylights pursuing her, shattering their ranks like glass and dispersing into the crowd.

Ladja ducked and turned, a Daylight waiting for her at every corner. She dodged a hand, only to find that her shirt was latched onto by the fingers of one of their priestesses. The priestess' clutch dug further and further into her, and on her shoulder where she struggled to bite it. She saw the other Daylights converging on her positions.

Sweat stung her eye and she was afraid the Daylights would drag her away to their temple. A sweet-floral scent filled her nostrils, piercing the pain of her present anguish and waking her to an idea. She grabbed the ice fork lying on the granita-server's table and plunged it into the priestess' hand.

The priestess' shrieking shocked the crowd, and when they all turned to look, Ladja had vanished. The Daylights scattered yet again, bouncing off every wall in the hopes of catching a glimpse of the girl.

Ladja was hiding under a pile of carpets for sale in the seamstress' booth, flattening herself completely so that the natural lumps of the carpet would hide her from the sight of the Daylights.

Without the passage of the sun, it was impossible to know how long she was there under the carpets. It felt as though she had been there hours, but she knew it could not have been that long as most of the people whom she could see through the carpet fold were still there. She waited for turnover, at least two more rounds of spectators and customers flowing through the festival until she would emerge from her hiding place. Once in a while, she saw a Daylight, but usually they were heading, in a hurry, towards the temple.

A mask fell in front of her from an anonymous source of whom she only saw the dark cloak pass. It was the mask of a raven, complete with shimmering purple feather plumes and a hard beak carved from wood. Ladja reached forward and snatched the mask. She put it on as she slipped out of the carpets. The wooden beak was pulling the mask from her face as she walked, so she found a corner to disappear into and ripped the beak off the mask. Luckily the beak was hollow and only barely sealed onto the mask, which had a complete nose, and she threw the beak aside and wore the mask as it was. She still needed a cape, however, to escape suspecting glares from the Daylights.

After some rummaging about, Ladja discovered two things: one, that the festival does not sleep, people are awake at all hours and never seem to tire, the whole duration of three imperceptible days; and two, that the actors and actresses that performed the tragedies and comedies oftentimes threw away capes they had just used, as they became marred at the edges from dragging across the stage.

Ladja snuck behind one of the performances and pulled a dark navy coat from the discarded pile. This she double wrapped around herself to make it fit her petite size. The obscurity of the combination of mask and cloak instilled her with a newfound confidence to tackle the mystery of the Labyrinth.

III

"Ladja!" Father laughed.

"What?" Ladja yelled, her face burning with anger.

"You know what," Father replied, picking her up and putting a cloth over her wound.

"I'm done with this," Ladja replied. "I'm done with this!"

She threw down the whittling knife and turned away from him.

"Fine, give up," Father said, taking the knife from her. "Give up on this and anything that seems too hard."

Ladja made no reply, but her fingers softened from their tight grip of her knees.

"Give up and see where that gets you," Father said. Then he leaned down to her: "You never give up if you want something, Ladja, never."

Ladja did not realize how difficult the Labyrinth would be to find. To begin with, the Labyrinth was an ancient concept, and she reasoned, therefore, that the newer parts of the city would be unlikely to contain its entrance. Most of the ancient part of the city, however, had already been built over many times and was now hardly old at all, save for some walls and rocks that held no clue whatsoever. She grazed her hand over the bricks, holes from eons of rain puncturing them. She let her fingers slip from the wall and turned to resume her journey when she saw a Daylight staring at her, dumbstruck.

She turned to run and slipped on a step. She collapsed into the brick, her mask slipping from her face and tumbling onto the floor, revealing her face.

"Ladja!" Daylight exclaimed. "Come with me!" He reached for her.

Ladja screamed and kicked at his hand. He pulled at her, dragging her away. She kicked at him and lunged for the mask. He shouted and jumped for her.

She whirled around, the mask securely latched onto her face.

The Daylight collapsed onto the floor, weak as though struck with a knife and holding his trembling hand out—pleading for mercy. All she could see through his mask were his eyes, wide and glimmering with fear. Ladja, herself frightened of the Daylight, stood up.

They both quaked with terror.

At last, the Daylight arose and receded away into the end of the street, until he disappeared entirely into the crowd.

Ladja scampered away, retreating into a jeweler's shop, where she hid behind any adult she could find. It was full today with men and women purchasing gifts for lovers, gifts which they had saved up all year to purchase. The glass beads and rings abounded, and gems of all shapes and colors flashed in Ladja's eyes. She waited until her breath calmed down and then decided to begin again.

Ladja scoured the streets for clues, noting down patterns on used papyri that had been sacks for sausages. She wrote the words she thought might be important. Soon enough, her papyrus was covered in "clues," none of which apparently lead in any direction or brought her any closer to her destination.

She noticed, though, as the crowds filtered towards a play in the back of the ancient quarter, a cat siting by the edge of the clocktower. The clocktower rose above the town and looked down at every quarter, from the ancient to the new, the rich to the poor, the priests to the laymen, the farmers to the builders. It had been reconstructed countless times over the years such that, as there was no written record of it, there was no way to know when it was built. It was timeless.

"In there?" Ladja asked, pointing to the tower. "Is that where the Labyrinth is? In there?"

The cat snuck through the crack in the door, which was supposed to be closed but rarely was. The clockkeeper was unreliable and oftentimes left it ajar, which was enough for smaller mammals to sneak through.

Ladja pursued the cat, a white-spotted orange creature, without rhyme or reason to its decisions. The young girl entered the clocktower and felt her nose itch as it was struck with that damp musty smell. It was only subdued by the Convergence's warmth and easy air. It was as if there were the effect of a breeze without the movement of one. Everything was a hushed stillness in the tower. The laughter from the festival echoed off the cold, wet stones and seemed diminished, as though the tower were a place apart from where she was: a place where the festival was just a memory still resounding.

"This must be it," Ladja conjectured. "This is the origin of the Labyrinth, the key."

A meow rumbled like a roar down the winding stone steps towards Ladja. She looked up to see the cat staring back at her from the top of the winding staircase.

Ladja pursued it, careful not to slip on the wet stones that tightly choked the empty cylindrical center.

She let her feet carry her as she flew up the steps, dangerously flirting with slipping on the condensation that formed just above each step. The cat's calls came progressively closer to her ears and soon enough, she found herself at the top of the tower, overlooking a vast space called a city, enclosed by a layer of hills obscured by the purple haze of distance. Above her she could see the Convergence, still radiant in its streaming and vibrant.

The cat stood in the corner, leaning over a gargoyle, frozen in its stone prison, and looked at Ladja, its tail keeping time with the clock that ticked above them. Ladja looked out over the city, noting the crowds and vendors still at work. The traffic of their feet obscured the ground from view, eliminating the possibility of finding a secret pattern in the cobblestones that lined the square. Ladja walked around the edges of the bell tower, the cat watching her make her rounds, trailing her hand along the edges of the wall while she peered over at the celebration.

"Is it this way?" Ladja asked the cat, pointing over the walls towards the hill.

The cat made no response.

She inquired again when she had gone a little further. She even thought to look up at the clocktower itself and the walls, and the floor of the patio, wondering and questioning if there were a secret riddle in the legend of the Labyrinth.

But she found nothing.

There was no wind, and the clocktower made no sound. Time itself seemed to stand still, as without the sun it was impossible to determine at what point of the Convergence they were in.

"It's hopeless! Hopeless! And it's all your fault!" Ladja screamed at the cat, who only hissed its reply, before turning around and disappearing into the tower.

She heard its paws tap their way down the stairs.

At some point she began to cry, and at another she stopped. She heard the faint murmur of people, broken up by laughter and the vivacious popping of firecrackers in the center of the festival, now so far removed from her. She whispered to herself indecipherable words and then pretended to sleep. The light was too bright, however, for rest, and she sunk into melancholy.

IV

Ladja leaned over the edge of the clocked tower, her night mask dangling from her fingers as she looked out into the crowd. Her failure in uncovering the Labyrinth's mystery was still very much a presence in her mind, and as a result she felt too lethargic to make the climb down to the bottom of the tower. Instead, she decided to let her mind wander into the clouds, and let the rhythm of the festival's beating heart play into her ear.

To amuse herself, she began to draw with her finger in the air.

Then she drew along the heads of the characters she saw below, even the Daylights that rummaged about, searching for her amongst the crevices. They couldn't scare her any longer. They, and the festival, were too far away.

The lines she drew formed images, but they moved too often, as the children ran and the adults shifted, chasing them. Some of them remained still and waved to her. They formed one large colorful mass, like God's palette had fallen from the sky, splashing into a rainfall of paint.

She drew again, with her finger, making circles and circles and circles and circles...

Ladja froze.

Her circles never completed themselves. They couldn't. The people were moving, individual drops in a pond. They had no center.

"The festival is the Labyrinth," Ladja whispered to herself, speaking an ancient incantation. "The people, the Celebration, the Convergence, the Labyrinth... everything."

"Ladja! Ladja!" a fearful voice called out from the depths of the clocktower.

"Papa!" Ladja called down. "I'm up here."

Papa emerged from the stairwell and fell to his knees, his arms outstretched in a sweaty mess as his little girl fell into them.

"Papa! I thought you don't come to the festival?"

"Mrs. Pirio came into the woods looking for me when she found you missing! Are you all right?"

"Yes, I'm fine," Ladja said, putting her hands on either side of her father's cheeks and stretching out her fingers. "You're very silly, Papa."

Papa laughed, a tear mingling on his cheek with his sweat. "Don't ever do that again—not ever."

A thunderous boom cracked from above, drawing all eyes to the sky, now split into two as the Convergence split open. At first, none could see what had emerged, as the sun's light was still too strong to look up into the sky for details. All they could determine was that something was blocking the light, and whatever it was, was approaching.

Ladja slipped from her father's arms and bolted down the stairs.

"Ladja!" he called after her, chasing her down the stairs. She paused only to look out the small windows of the clocktower at the figure still descending from the sky with its arms outstretched in either direction.

The ribbons of purple shot down and wrapped around the figure, clothing and wrapping her, pulling down from the heavens like an infinite series of fabric. The moons slowly fell to the side of the sun, beaming with their bright, white light as the sun collapsed below the horizon's ridge.

Ladja emerged from the bottom of the tower, running towards the figure, which had created a natural space in the crowd as they all gaped at the mysterious thing that had fallen from the Convergence. The young girl embraced the figure, dressed as night and still radiant from the white moonlight.

"Mama," Ladja said, burying her head in her mother's arms. Her mother leaned down and embraced her, letting Ladja's tears soak into her purple robes. "I missed you."

"I missed you too, Ladja," Mama replied, stroking her hair. "My smart little girl. Thank you for finding me."

"I didn't give up," Ladja whispered. "Never."

"I know."

They both turned to look at Papa. He stood at the edge of the crowd, with a trembling lip and still eyes, paralyzed with emotion and disbelief.

"Lenore," he sighed. Ladja pulled them together and the crowd erupted into a loud cheer, drowning out the years of sorrow and loss Papa had poured into his tears. They remained buried head in hair and head in chest until they no longer had the strength to hold themselves up.

The crowd faded away, laughing still as the last embers of the festival of the Convergence burned away into a chilling breeze from the north. The autumn air shook at the trees and painted them gold for the next day's first light.

They had much to discuss, and walked around in the dual moonlight, telling their tales and experiences amongst the fallen masks and firecracker dust.

And when they fell asleep in their beds, the sun had just begun to sing yellow light gently over the city, the roosters trumpeting its arrival.

And time began anew.

PLAYS LIKE THE GREATS

STEVE GLADWIN

Hawk Webster—that was the guy. Although I guess he might as well have been Lester Hawkins or Coleman Young. Or even Cole Webster. Yes, you know that one kinda sits right.

Hey, don't get too close! They say I've got pretty much all the diseases you've heard of, and even some stuff ain't been invented yet. Just stick a chair way over there now. 'Sides, this stuff ain't infectious. I mean you can't catch cancer or emphysema or meningitis. They could stick me in the Guinness Book of Records. Course, I can still see the funny side. Helps. But that don't take away the fact I ain't got much time left.

It's jazz—as it's turned out—that's killed me. I've always loved jazz, loved it since I can remember, even before I could play it, and that didn't turn out to be as long as I'd have liked. Loved all of it—the smoky clubs, the quiet feeling, the hush until the band takes up the tune and the roar when they do. Best of all would be being up there on the stage, with the chanteuse polishing her tonsils from one end to the other, or the drummer kicking it off and never letting up.

For me, king of them all, better than the walking bass and the high hat, even a trumpeter like Clifford or Miles, or fine sliders like Jack T and Vic D, that's got to be the sax man, the one up there blazing a trail of golden notes all the way to heaven. You like that one? Golden trail to heaven. Ain't no doubt about it.

My pop bought some jazz CDs at one of them car-boots. Nothing much worth having, but some no-taste sad sap was dumping them for peanuts. I mean, stuff like Monk with Coltrane or Sonny, some Sonny with Miles, Clifford and Max, Hawk and Pres playing the old Kansas City rematch, and best of all a gennelman called Mr. Ben Webster.

I never heard Ben play, but my I wish I'd had the chance. Big huge contradiction of a man. He could be up there blowing up a storm on the fast, energetic stuff, but just as easy he could dip right down and sing across the ballads like a violin player's bow, leaving the sweetest trail little more than a thread. Ain't ever been no-one like Ben, not even Lester, for although the Pres could get that fragile, broken, hardly blowing sound, no-one could blow on a thread like Ben. If I'd only settled for that, maybe you and I would be having a different conversation, buddy.

But yeh, where was I? All them drugs are fit to start me rambling. A mighty contradiction was Benny. All that talent and beauty and care, when he almost seemed to be making love to his horn. But not twenty minutes ago he'd have turned up late with blood on his cuffs on account of the poor sap he'd given a beating to for whatever on earth reason he conjured up. See, for all that golden tone, they still called him the Beast, and there were plenty of times that rep was well deserved.

He didn't even have his own place, you know. Lived with his sweet old mamma who'd always had god big and wanted her Ben to play his sweet horn for Jesus. So, I guess it was all peck on the cheek and, "you take care now, Mom." Once he shrugged that off, the preppy smile was gone and out came the Beast. They said he once had three fights before he even reached the club.

But none of us are perfect, and I certainly ain't, as my current predicament shows you. Time to go back to where it started. Back to four years ago, when I first met Hawk Webster.

* * *

When you're as big a jazz fan as I am, you'll go a long way to find some being played live. Not that here in Wales it was ever good for much, apart from trips to Brecon for the festival. There was some good stuff on, mind, but both times I got as far, the wind was so bad blowing off the beacons you could hardly hear some of the outdoor acts.

But this time it was just some field in the middle of nowhere. The countryside was all green and rolling, going all manner of colours evenings, when it was kissed by some of the best sunsets.

That was how I found the *Leap Year Jazz Fair.*

It wasn't just the name that was weird, let alone it being mainly freezing and the end of February! There were plenty of other ways this turned out to be one weird festival. Nothing to look at, as you might think, just a collection of dirty looking yurts and benders in the middle of a field, hippy dreads and the whole pseudo pagan look like druids, and the rest. Dreads and coloured boots, foul smelling roll-ups and dogs on strings. Even the toilets were just pits dug in the ground, and a long drop to take a shit in. People queuing and flaunting their bog roll like it was the most natural thing in the world.

If the music hadn't made the grade, I wouldn't even have stayed the night. As it was, I wasn't quite brave enough to risk the long drop in the dark. There was a nice pub just up the road where a couple of the late-night gigs were being held. Nothing beats that feeling of being able to sit there in your slippers and take it all in, like this whole place is your home. Even better, all the stoned, smelly hippies and weirdoes had to take off and try not to fall over their tents in the pitch-black, while I was snug and warm in a retro four-poster bed. The room even had a fire—with real, actual logs!

Saturday afternoon was when they held the memorabilia auction in the second biggest of the benders; all kind of people bringing in this instrument and this sheaf of music like they were on *Antiques Roadshow*, while lots of other stuff—none of it cheap—was cluttering up the tables.

But it was the old battered sax case on the floor I was interested in. I couldn't see what it was doing where it was, so I supposed it mustn't be part of the rest of it.

Couldn't resist a peep, course not. Dust all over it enough to set me coughing as I tackled the rusty old clasp. I raised up the lid and—there he was.

I hadn't seen him come over, and he certainly hadn't been part of the actual auction; I had the oddest feeling he must just have come with the sax. Turns out I was right. Huge, black guy, smiling there in his porkpie hat, sort of a shambling, genial bear with a suit two sizes too big. Needless to say, he towered over me. The bear gave me a grin, but I didn't feel like I was prey.

"This yours?" I wasn't quite sure what reaction I'd get.

"Seems to be. Or," he added, picking at the corner of his mouth with a toothpick. "Maybe it's just waiting on whoever's got the lips."

His voice was also bear deep. I felt daft and not just cos his six-foot-something was like a giant to my scarcely much over five-and-a-half. I'd tried to play a mate's sax in the past, but got a sound like a wounded dog in a tunnel. Further experiments had only ended up making the menagerie wider and his neighbours even less tolerant. Still, I gave it a go for a couple of weeks, until dog finally gave way to bellowing seal and it was my neighbours banging on the ceiling.

I shook my head. "I can't play. I tried it."

"You ain't tried this one."

"If it's yours, I wouldn't want to ruin your memory of it."

The guy wasn't the sort to take a "no," and I didn't feel much like getting on his bad side. Besides, he already had the tenor out of the case and was slinging it round my neck, showing me how to attach the lanyard.

You'd think that all the other people buzzing round the jazz honey pot might have shown some interest, but they had their own bargains to negotiate, collections to add to, and there was always the beer tent. No ice-creams in February, but plenty of chocolate and cakes.

They hardly seemed to register my first scratchings and yodellings, even when it came out like a cow being waterboarded. And all the time the giant in the porkpie hat stood there, like I was his finest pupil.

By this time, my face was a beetroot, my hair wet and flopping, even in February. He gave me a look, like he was thinking hard.

"What people always do, see, is *try* to play. Ends up taking all of their blow and gives nothing in return."

I nodded, still needing to get my breath back.

"What you need instead is to feel. Feel right down inside to the heart of the horn."

Just one more time, then. I took a few breaths and then, instead of trying to end up with cheeks like Miles Davis, I did what the man said and reached *in*. I played out on a thread of sound like my hero. I blew into the horn like there was hardly any need for blowing. I blew like a Ben Webster.

Then there were all this whooping and clapping and the giant in the pork pie hat was giving it like the best of them. I guess he must have modelled himself on either Webster or Hawkins, because he stood there like a just as solid version of them both.

I just stood there gobsmacked. "I can't play like that," I burbled. "How?" But the truth was I had, for instead of the latest in the tortured animal parade, I had wound out my golden thread and spun it in the air, until, for a few more seconds, I was playing one of the great standards, although I wasn't quite sure which one!

That was it, then, my few minutes of jazz glory. I couldn't see anyone in the tent I knew, but had already bumped into a few faces that weekend, including an old mate who was also staying at the same pub, whom I'd talked jazz to until long past midnight. So, this was nothing I was going to dine out on. It would be with *me* for a long time yet, mind.

I frowned. I unhooked the lanyard and handed the sax back over but my new pal, this big smile on his face was handing it back. "It's yours," he grinned. "Take it away with you. Play it like that, and it will serve you well."

"I can't," I protested, hardly able to believe this turn of events. "It must be worth a fortune."

"Sound is, maybe. Ain't nothing special about the horn."

Of course, I took it. It was what I'd always wanted, even if I'd only just realised it. And the growing crowd were giving it some, as if the main act was standing right there in front of them, instead of warming up in the big tent next door.

A weird thing happened, then. It was as if everything around me just faded, so it was just me and him and the golden horn, still in the air between one pair of hands and the other.

"*Treat it right,*" as his voice also faded. "*It will treat you fine.*"

Something else then, which I couldn't quite believe. "*I come as part of the deal. One day only.*"

I don't remember staying for the remainder of the acts. I must have gone back to the pub.

* * *

What do you need to create some jazz? Take a walking bass rhythm with the sound of the sticks beneath it. Add the floating jaunty sound of a Ben, or the full rounded blare of the Hawk, before you know it, Hank or Oscar's tinkling piano slides in, and then the fun really starts.

On Ben's version of "Bye Bye Blackbird," the tune doesn't so much get played so you can recognise the standard when it comes back in at the end, but sort of squeezes itself in one instrument at a time, so that—if you like—the jam's there from the start. The party has already started and you'd better get up to speed.

I live in a little valley in Mid Wales and it was to there I returned with my battered sax case and its contents. I'd had a couple of pints of the local real ale at that weird little festival, and lunch time drinking's never suited me. It was already eight by the time I'd negotiated the inevitable trail back between Llandrindod Wells and Newtown—a real farmer's road, if ever there was. Home well by nine and nothing much in the house. It would have been easier to grab a bag of crisps and a liquid supper at the local, but I was in a hurry to find out what the sax guy meant.

Charley, my girlfriend, was working that night—she's a staff nurse in A and E—which might be a good job if things were about to get weird. She doesn't really get my love of jazz either—more of a Manic Street Preachers or Catatonia girl, but she'll try to listen and puts up with it all right—not that she's much choice, poor cow. She starts off liking the tune, but then afterward she says it just becomes so much background, blah, blah.

It seemed weird trying it in our bedroom. Well, mine, but she shared it most nights she was on the right shift. But then it was mine first, and that's why the walls were full of moody black and white jazz: Monk in his fedora filtering his genius on the keys through a swirl of smoke from the chewed cigar in his mouth, Miles, blowing up a storm over the chest of drawers, where even behind those cool shades you could still catch the *Don't fuck with me* look. Sonny all grizzled grey beard, like an elongated extension of his sax. Then there was Ben himself, straight off the cover of *Days of Wine and Roses*. Grey suited and benevolent with all that frustrated held-back muscly anger.

I wasn't sure what I expected, but not what happened next. I laid the bashed up old case on the bed, still not believing something like this could be mine without even a deposit. Again, I struggled to open the rusty clasps. No sooner had the lid opened, than a dark figure seemed to unfold itself from the case and I all but pissed my pants. *Well*, I thought, once I'd recovered. *He did say he was part of the deal.*

"I didn't," I struggled to say, "think you meant it quite so literally."

The jazz man tipped his hat at me. "A one day only deal. Not quite once in a lifetime, but close enough."

The details about how we'd met were already becoming fuzzy like last night's dream with blurred edges. I suddenly had a great thirst on me and I'd have liked nothing better than to go and drink with the rest of them up the road. I never thought he'd meant it, but then the sax was the sax and no deal without him.

"Genie out of a bottle," I said, trying to make light of it all. "Jazz man from a sax case."

"You got the wishes thing right. And the name's Cole Webster. Two for the price of one. So, what will it be for the first one—if I can grant it, that is?"

There was something in that grin I didn't quite care for, but hey, what can I say. I didn't have the common sense gene on alert. So, of course I blundered in with that first wish, like I'd imagine most folks do.

I gave it a few seconds, but my mind was set. "I want to be able to play the sax properly." The sax made a hollow ringing sound as I tapped it.

His grin grew wider and a bit less shit-eating. "Well, you've sure made a good start," he said. "You know that old joke about how do I to get to Carnegie Hall?"

"Man, you just gotta practice?" And man, everyone knew that joke.

Then he was gone, back to wherever he came from. I examined the empty case to try and work out the trick how he'd folded himself out of it, but it looked just ordinary. I was thinking about the pub because I fancied forgetting the lot of it for a few hours, but then I looked up at the poster on the wall—no Charley tonight, deaf neighbour one side and no-one for half a mile the other. Why not.

For this I needed a record player—the only way to not just capture the jazz, but the time and place, sweat, smoke, and cheap booze it was recorded in. Just some cheap compilation I'd had for years. Half the tracks Ben was playing with Hank Jones and the rest with the one and only Oscar Peterson. I used to see Oscar years ago on *Parkinson* and *The Two Ronnies* when I was a kid, ripple of chord upon chord and ski-slope glissandos. Low level grunting but not quite as bad as Glenn Gould for getting in the way of the business in hand. Then he just seemed like some fat, cheerful black man, rings on his hand and the kinda grin that said he could do anything. And boy, could he.

Later I would see Oscar for what he truly was—a man with a true gift for the ivories—and never better than when he was with Hawk or Ben. And the stuff he did with both them—man.

Hey, but I'm getting to be a jazz bore. Back to *The Frog*, which was the name of the cheap CD. I was all for listening with itchy fingers like I usually do. A bit of air sax would usually creep in, but hey, didn't I have the real thing. A few bars of Ray Brown's walking bass and old Ed Thigpen quietly there rattling the sticks, and then—even before my man Oscar comes tinkling in—Ben slides up like he always does, but this time he's got company, maybe even a rival.

To start with I play with him, just in the background at first, but as my confidence grows and we're note for note, almost like one fat sound. Here's Oscar, no accompanying grunts for once, but who cares because the ivories aren't my tinkle. I'm a horn man, an unholy alliance because—and this is where the impossible happens—now I'm so confident I'm riffing round the Big Man, going up and over his fluting swoop, his breathy sound as unique as it ever is, but now here's me with something new that ain't his. Brasher like Sonny, with a bit of Coltrane soul.

I'm still there at the end, and why stop there, when there's "The Wee Small Hours of the Morning" to follow, and "How Deep is the Ocean." And it's almost like I'm not here in my room, but somewhere in the smoke-filled past with the gods up there on stage, and me with them playing this same golden horn, and surely man, this has to be a dream.

In the end I went down the pub as normal. But if the usual crowd were expecting me to be full of life and bounce, they were going to be disappointed, I could hardly keep my mind off the sax and on the pint in hand.

At one point, seeing that I'd hardly touched the first, Trev put his hand on my forehead to check my temperature. It's true that I could usually sink them like the best of them, but that was all pre-three wishes. A whole lot of that was.

So, the buzz of inconsequential detail, and forced laughter continued to buzz around me, but my heart was in a smoky jazz club, my mouth on a damp reed and fingers playing over a whole host of keys. As for my soul—well that was with Big Ben, as I daresay Hawk Webster would have expected. And always at the back of my mind that awful fear that next time my clumsy fingers would just clatter over the keys, my mouth rasp against the reed, and normal squeaking atonal service would be resumed, as the familiar phalanx of cats resumed their nightly yowl off. But, for that brief, forty minutes, it had all combined and whatever happened, I would never forget it.

You want to know if I could still play like that the next day? You just bet I could.

* * *

The best of Role Models for the new Young Turk of Jazz.
Jazz Roots in Town - Summer Extra - Chris Driffield

I profess to have been round the block a few times, when it comes to *This year's new discovery,* or *the new sound that's set to set the world alight.* Many a "new discovery" has ended up over-promoted before they could achieve a consistent level, or fractured beyond immediate repair in the hectic rush of their first few years. Others have blazed briefly, only to blow it all out in a rush of drink and dope. For Ellis Watkins however, at thirty-one, mature for a jazz player, that age and maturity, and an open and honest approach has really given his growing number of fans hope that he may live up to the name he has—possibly unwisely—

chosen for himself. I spoke to him before the second of two late-night guest spots at Ronnie Scott's, and it was this impossible legacy that we discussed first.

Well, Ellis, you can't say that this isn't a bit of a hard one to live up to.

Sure, well, you know, you can only try.

So, you admit that you chose the name yourself?

Yes, Chris, I wandered into that particular bear pit and offered myself to the baying crowd.

What's the story behind it; *Plays Like the Greats*. Were there any particular greats you had in mind?

Initially there were only two, I suppose. I knew I could never play with the sheer force of Sonny Rollins, or with the spirituality of Coltrane. And Lester's unique fractured sound, well you may as well ask me to sing like Billie Holliday while I'm at it. So, they were the main two really—Ben and Hawk.

Hawk and Ben. The Beast and the Bean. Is there a leaning towards either one in particular?

I can't really separate then. You'll think this is daft, mind, but I often imagine them as sort of composite character. With Hawk's huge sound and—

Ben's fighting skills.

(laughs)

Something like that. I call him Hawk Webster and I suppose that's who I am when I'm playing. Means I can switch from one to the other.

So, Ellis, you played the sax at school as a teenager and promptly gave it up.

Yeh, he said my mouth wasn't the right shape.

But it clearly is, some twenty-odd years later. Did you have some radical dentistry between times?

Nothing so exciting. I suppose it must have been my laying off and coming to it fresh again. And finding the right sax of course.

Indeed. A year to the day, almost, since you lost it after a gig in Berlin and offered a reward of twenty thousand pounds.

And I'd have found it, if some kind German jazz fan hadn't gone and looked for it specially. That guy wouldn't take anything, you know. What a prince.

If you don't mind me saying this, Ellis, your voice clearly started off in the valleys of Mid Wales and now it's gone a bit more transatlantic.

Oh, fair play to you, I can still "boyo" with the best of them. But this next tour of the U.S. will be my third in three years. Some of that has to rub off.

People have also noticed that you've bulked up a bit; must have been all those American portions.

And I wear the same kind of porkpie hat. But I'm not black yet, last time I looked.

And you're *not* strictly limited yourself to Hawk Webster now? Bit of Sonny creeping in—sometimes Coltrane soulful. Especially with all those experimental runs.

I've been trying to work in a bit of Gerry Mulligan as well, only the baritone is tougher than it looks. And I'll leave the soprano to Coltrane and Barbara Thompson. Art Pepper—he's high on my list.

Watch out for his lifestyle, though. I shouldn't think a spell in St. Quentin is high on that list?

No way. (laughs)
Well, I'd better let you get back. Maybe we could pick this up again after the tour?
Sure. My pleasure, man!

* * *

My second wish then, in case you haven't guessed yet, was to play like the greats. *That's* where the name came from, my man.

* * *

It started off well enough. If you work in a music shop like Ellis did, then you're going to spend a fair bit of time picking up the instruments and having a jam; talking jazz and blues, reading jazz, rock and blues—hey, even breathing it. Rock he was cool with and blues was even a bit more *it* than jazz, the times he felt that way. Women he went for, especially the "jazz chantoosies," as he called them—saying it like he was born in Brooklyn. Ella, Sarah, Billie, and Dinah, two legends who died young, and two who lived and sang on.

When it started, I was on permanent nights and we just weren't seeing each other, just an occasional screw, followed by an exhausted sleep, and an occasional breakfast thrown in, if you were lucky. Ellis was no mean cook and he liked to treat his women well. Listen to me, I'm making him sound like he had a whole history when he met me. All that only came later.

Fair play to him, Ellis was a bit of a looker, but when I met him, he just seemed to have found this way of burrowing under his personal stone, so no-one could prise him out unless he wanted them too. He was still there, active in the world, but somehow, he didn't engage with it in any of the ways that matter. I had to kick at that old stone a bit to dislodge it, but you should have seen me kick.

If you're going to play with the sound he had and the boyish charisma that came along, then you're going to pick up a fair bit of female attention. There are the ones that wind their curls with a *Gee, shucks* expression of wonder on their faces, or those that pretty much slap their rack in your face like it's a challenge, wear too much or the wrong sort of perfume, skirts up past the crotch, flaunt their lipstick-bright, cock-sucking lips and I'll show you all the tricks. But none of it bothered me—because it was Ellis, right. Why would I bother about Ellis?

And when it all started up, this sudden expected talent! When my man began to play the magic like he'd been blowing it all his life—well that was fine too, because he'd taught me to like Ben and Hawk and Coltrane and Sonny and Dexter and all the rest. Even though if there was anything after rock, I preferred piano. But Igor Levitt and Monk are both geniuses, right?

Hey, I'm sorry, but one of the things he taught me, Ellis, was that jazz men sometimes talk the talk so much, that it becomes a kind of code. The rest need not apply, left cold outside wondering how to chip in with the one *I am not worthy* comment.

So, then he could play just fine, sure, but something about it wasn't just play. If anyone had said to me then that my normal home-loving Ellis had had a spell cast on him, then you know—maybe! He was him, but not him. He was Ellis transported with this dull glaze in his eyes when he played, which I first took for dope or worse—having seen so much of its victims being brought in night after night.

Luckily, he was transported in bed—by which I don't mean he brought the sax into the sex—that would have been one kink too far. No, what he brought was the swoop and the dive and above all the sweet, sweet timing when he practiced his flutter tonguing. Who was this girl to complain?

And man, could he hold it all back, like some jazzy Moses with the whole of the Red Sea at his back. And holding me inside, until—Jesus, when we both came together it felt like the end of the world and the garden of Eden at the same time. So, of course we made the jokes; if that's what jazz does for you lover, you just practice for as long as you want. And me going into work all baggy eyed from the lack of sleep, which was being well compensated for elsewhere. All the looks and jokes in the changing room—if you can't handle it, maybe you'll introduce me, et cetera.

So, then I had this idea. Take his talent out into the world and see where it goes. None of this I'm past twenty-five and no-one's going to be interested shit! The right contacts just fell into place at the right time and well, it just took off. A year in and I'm there setting up a European tour for him, hospital and bedpans behind me and promising career down the pan. My mum went ballistic!

But I was someone now. I was the full-time manager-cum-secretary to *Ellis Watkins*, who styled himself *Plays like the Greats*, and what's more on those increasingly rare occasions when we weren't too knackered, my body was the instrument this particular great would tune, my reed he would kiss and tongue, my keys which he would cover with caresses from feather light to pounding brass. And always at the heart of it the rhythmic bass and pulse of the drum. Ellis wasn't just sax now, he was pure loving jazz, and I was the standard he loved playing the most.

Everything stops. All good things must, et cetera. It started with the girls. For what I'd been stupidly oblivious to with the Brit girls, soon became so obvious with mademoiselles and frauleins, and senoritas and the rest, that I realised how daft and naïve I'd been. But at first, so what. We were too busy to care and the jazz and the love—when we could snatch it, was so special, and then there was the money and the jazz again and man, always the jazz. When I got Ellis to myself, jazz soon became sex and sex, jazz and that was like a jam that lasted forever.

Then one drunken hazy night, I caught him doing one of those gushy acting all-innocent, please Mr. Ellis Nordic types by the side of the tour bus, and I knew then with that dull achy, you silly bitch feeling that never goes away, that he must have been grabbing any opportunity for years. I laughed when he wilted so quickly and then I pulled hard on her pigtails as she tried to get past me and made her squeal. Even then I managed to fetch her arse a good one as she scrambled into her knickers. But although there were plenty of other accidents I could have acted on, by that time, it was all I could do to stop him getting hold of the drugs.

* * *

Wish Three then. Have you been paying attention, or what? I wanted to play the sax like a dream, then play it like the greats. There was only one wish left then and I had to do something so darned foolish. If Hawk had really been Hawk and Ben, Ben, instead of some lousy genie looking for the next prime fuck-up, I might just have retired with the whole lot of it! Wished for a garden shed, or lots of customers, even though this particular cee-lebrity didn't work the counters anymore. Or maybe a really cool wedding for Charley and me—like I've been promising for years—extended honeymoon in the Seychelles or some such tropical paradise.

But instead I had to say the damndest fucked-up thing.

There's Hawk Webster in front of me, all made up and sleek, but still with his buttons straightening over his belly, and wasn't that a stain on his porkpie? Still he towers over me and I'm thinking you know what, all in all I could dig it if this were it. Like maybe I could put the third wish on hold, or else give it to some old wish selling charity or some such. And I swear I was about to do it. Only instead, a truck of shit flew into my mouth and dumped a load in my brain while it was at it. My head became full of the wrong sort of thoughts about later-than-late nights and other female company, the rustle of nylon and the shedding of underwear and new lips coming down, down, a brand-new set of pink keys to play on.

With the girls, there was the company and the laughter and the needing new ways to relax when the bourbon was running dry or weren't enough anymore.

I want to live like the greats, is what this dumb sonofabitch wished.

You'll have to 'scuse me cos I have to use the pan; I'm squirting from both ends on these new drugs. But they say the more squirts I put up with, the more weeks I'm likely to have left. But I know how long I ain't got, even if they want to pretend otherwise. Now, you just go and have yourself a smoke while I deal with this. There are better places to be around.

* * *

I'm nearly past done now. And sides, I'm bone tired and fucked up ten ways before sundown.

Shall I tell you about the fair. The one where it all started with the sax case. Well, soon as I knew I was pretty done for, soon as I worked out the bits from my wish that I didn't want, that I'd gotten stuck with anyway. Soon as it wasn't all just tits and ass and blow and enough white lines to make a motorway—I decided to consult my friendly neighbourhood jazz genie on the matter of a possible get out. And that was when the smug fuck presented me with my own personal ticking time bomb.

I don't know why I didn't think of it before, but you know the answer to that better'n I do. So, here goes.

"I want to take that last wish back," I said to his porkpieness. "And if you say I can't, then tell me if there might be another get-out. Like, can I just take the sax back to the fair. Let someone else with the talent give it a whirl. It's been a good gig, but the encore's long gone done and dusted."

His answer surprised me. "Sure, can," he replied. "Easiest thing in the world. There's always a get-out. Well (shit eating grin in place), 'specially at the *Leap Year Jazz Fair*. Those kinda things only come around every four. And therein lies your answer."

Sounds easy enough, right, you've just have to wait until the fair comes around again. Turns out there's been just over three and a half years gone by since. All *I* have to do is wait another six months and I suppose if I can't make it under my own steam, there's such things as ambulances—and even satnavs that cover places not on the map. I can wait it out six months, right?

Except that my dumb ass final wish asked for me to live like the greats. And that was fine through all the girls and the partying and the playing and drinking and doping. All cool, right?

I just wish I didn't also have Dexter's throat cancer and Big Ben's brain tumour, let alone Bird's drug habit and Lester's bust liver. Because everyone knows how many jazz-folk died young, right. And if you ain't got that straight in your head, then don't you be letting your fingers loose on my old saxophone.

A Tale of Bears and Honey

Christopher Wheatley

The thief Crazy Cavan found himself poised, one leg half out of a second-story window, in the private quarters of the Western Palace of His Majesty Hyronomous Tubak the Magnificent (Howling Mad Hyronomous as he was un-fondly referred to by his subjects, those that weren't languishing in the dungeons, hanging from poles outside the city gates or force-marching themselves endlessly in pursuit of the Glorious Battle for Supremacy over the Ubuloos[1]).

No-one said anything about bears, was the first thing that went through Cavan's mind when the moment was over, closely followed by the dumb realisation that his leg was still sticking out the window, dangling absurdly over the balcony, along which was lumbering quite quickly a small, mean-looking and certainly vicious bear, which no doubt regarded the proffered limb as something of a treat, all wrapped up and ready for eating.

Cavan hastily retracted the leg, slammed shut the window and threw down the bolt just as the furry menace flung itself bodily against the frame. It left a trail of slobber as its gnashing maw slipped out of sight, only to reappear again in a succession of eager jumpings and pawings which left the would-be-thief but little secure in his comfort.

Cavan drew the curtains and spent some moments cursing every god, goddess and deity he knew (all except for Thamber, God of the Bears, who for obvious reasons Cavan thought best not to anger).

The rattling resumed at the heavy wooden door behind him, along with muffled voices calling for keys. The actual key, which the thief hoped was the *only* one, was right now stuck in the lock, where Cavan had left it after turning the latch in an effort to discourage sudden intrusions of the sort which would probably lead to such embarrassing questions as: "Who are you?", "What are you doing in the King's Chambers?" and "What's that in your pockets?"

Swiftly he put his ear to the door, just in time to discern the words: "Intruder", "get the axe", and "smash it down!".

Looking wildly about, Cavan's eyes lit upon an unfinished plate of food which lay on the ornate dressing-table. Quickly, he scooped up the platter, replete with half-eaten steak (medium-rare) and ran to the window at the far end of the long wall, the end *sans bear*. Without delay, he thrust up the shutter and stuck his head out into the sunshine.

The bear, not insensible to the noise, whirled round, spraying froth from its mouth, and began lumbering in the direction of the thief, fast building up a goodly amount of momentum. Cavan dropped the meat onto the balcony–*plop*–and

---

[1] A small flightless bird which inhabits the rocky coastal regions of several continents. It may be inferred from this that the King was (and is) several planks short of a staircase.

slammed down the window. Moving to one side, so as not to distract the beast, he waited long enough to observe with relief that steak, to a bear, is a treat not to be taken lightly, and then he sprinted with pumping legs back to the initial window.

Just as he was about to exit this, and just as there came an almighty crash at the door, which bulged alarmingly but did not break, Cavan remembered the Object, which was still sitting on the divan as he had left it, wrapped in sackcloth and tied up with string. The thief rushed back to gather it up (it was cylindrical, about two and half feet long by a foot and a half across)—to leave without it would make a bad day even worse—for it was this particular item that was the cause of his visit.

Securing the bundle under one arm, Cavan hot-footed it back to the window. As calmly as possible (given the calamity at the door, which even now shook under another thundering impact), he inched up the frame, allowed himself a quick peek to ensure that the beast was still occupied at the far end of the balcony, and slipped silently out, pulling the window down again behind him.

The thief now stood on the narrow veranda, in the noon-day sun of high summer, about two stories up from the royal gardens, which appeared at this moment to be hosting a party of some persuasion, for a veritable host of high-born ladies and gentlemen, together with their high-born offspring and high-born pedigree dogs, fashionably dressed in seasonal attire (even the dogs), strolled, frolicked or stood chatting amiably among the manicured lawns, immaculate hedges and colourful flower-beds. Somewhere out of view, a band played jaunty tunes and the sound of laughter rose through the air. *Fewmits*, thought the thief and, taking one quick look down below, slid across the railing and dropped gracefully to the ground, just as the sound of splintering wood reached his ears.

Cavan landed, rolled and came to his feet to be met with the startled gazes of an aged Baroness, two ladies-in-waiting, one terrible-eyed lapdog and a Duke of the Royal Navy[2]. Cavan bowed deeply, winked broadly and disappeared at pace into the nearest hedge. As he had hoped, it was some seconds before the astonished onlookers recovered their wits enough to sound the alarm.

Bursting through the hedge and into the middle of a picnic, the thief wasted no time but accelerated away, upturning cups, saucers, baskets and at least one duchess as he dashed across the grass, practically throwing himself between a gap in the hedge wall and skidding to a halt at a crossroads formed by two gravel paths flanked by rosebushes. Quick glances showed peril in both directions. Shouts from behind spurred him to choose one at random and he pounded fast as he could down a wide, pretty avenue.

Up ahead, a white-bearded old captain, evidently ahead of the game, squared his face and shoulders, crouched down with arms outstretched and a determined look in his one remaining eye. Cavan did not slow; if anything he sped up, and left the ground at a point some feet ahead of the old man, somersaulting clear the captain's head over and regaining the path on the far side with barely a check in his stride.

Flying out of the avenue, Cavan swerved away from another lawn and dashed thankfully into a copse of trees which stood to one side. Once into the shade he

---

[2] Freshly returned from the Second Great Ubuloo Crusade, where he had distinguished himself magnificently.

did not stop but, panting hard, spared a glance behind, which showed that as suspected he had not entirely shaken pursuit. At least four guardsmen, resplendent in red and definitely unhappy at being made to run in half-plate armour in the heat, barrelled after, their wicked-looking pikes gleaming in the sun.

Cavan dodged and ducked, seeking to put as much greenery as possible between the two parties, cutting a right angle and veering off again. He rushed up a little rise, down the other side and without warning left the trees, crashing through a large bush in a shower of leaves. He had time to gather a brief impression of a narrow open space boxed in by hedges before falling headlong into a pond.

Even as he gasped to the surface the thief knew something was wrong. The water felt super sticky and... well, not like water at all. Struggling upright, he became aware of voices as he desperately rubbed the syrupy liquid from his eyes. As he did so, Cavan beheld a number of young ladies dressed as faeries surrounding the pond and staring at him open-mouthed.

One, a dark-haired beauty with stick-on shimmery wings, turned on the unfortunate thief a severe and imperious gaze. "Who are you?" she said with regal authority, "and what do you mean by throwing yourself into our honey-pool?"

"*Honey?*" spluttered Cavan. He looked down and his hands and clothing. Indeed it was, and he was covered with it. He looked about and noticed a number of servants stood to either side, each dressed in strange transparent black veils and carrying long black wooden devices with tubes and funnels on the ends. It occurred to the thief that he had seen their like before. "*Bee-keepers?*" he said aloud in wonder.

"Bee-*catchers*, actually," determined a haughty, pouty, blonde lady, with a withering look.

"You're all mad," said Cavan in disbelief, then was spurred into action by the sounds of nearing pursuit.

Rummaging under the thick surface, he quickly retrieved the precious parcel and struggled free, aided by the force of several folded parasols, wielded by said ladies, which struck him mercilessly about his arms and his back.

Once more into his stride, Cavan ran on, spraying drops of honey all about, disappearing into a thick flower bed and glooping free on the other side into a rough-grassed area obscured from the main lawns by a row of high trees. Cries from behind warned that the search was still in full swing. Cavan, who was justifiably feeling things could have gone better thus far, staggered through another line of bushes and came up against a wall.

His first thought was that it was not high enough to be the outer wall that he sought. His second thought was to nevertheless go over. Swiftly he removed his belt, threaded it through the string around his bundle and secured the whole over one shoulder. With firm but sticky hands, he hoisted himself upward. It was an old wall, and not difficult to climb, encumbered and exhausted though he was.

As Cavan attained the summit, and was just casting about to get his bearings, the bricks upon which he was sitting slid out from under, sending himself and the entire top row of blocks and mortar crashing to the ground. As the dust settled, he laid for some moments, looking up at the sun and ruefully reflecting on his life so far. But, being a professional, and also quite aware what capture would lead to, it was not long before he painfully pulled himself upright, glad, at least, to discover no blood or broken bones.

The enclosure was walled on all sides, with a small door to the right, doubtless leading to yet another garden. Cavan regarded the debris, which had crashed down upon a number of large wooden boxes. White wooden boxes, curiously designed and now split asunder. A buzzing sound penetrated his bruised consciousness and then it came to him—hives.

Hives.

Bees.

Honey.

The briefest of split-seconds passed before, eyes wide and mouth screaming, Cavan plunged through the door, breaking it clean off its rusty hinges and followed very, very closely by a considerably-sized swarm of hornets.

Princess Valespia, daughter of His Highness Hyronomous Tubak, at this time was sat upon her white canopied platform, just to one side of the band, watching the dancers before her sway and frolic to a popular tune. Under the great white parasol it was cool and shady, yet nevertheless the princess felt irritated. She turned to Lady Usula, who was fanning herself with a construction of bird-feathers. "The dancing is particularly poor this year, don't you think?" said the princess.

"Oh, yes," sighed Lady Usula, who knew better than to ever disagree with royalty, "one is so hard pressed to discern any originality, any *flair* at all..."

"Quite so," chimed in Lady Betsda, next to her, "it really is *such* a bore."

"Well bless my soul," exclaimed Duchess Ralia, from Princess Valespia's right, "who on earth is that contestant right at the back—his style is *most* extraordinary!"

Valespia squinted and raised the field-glasses to her eyes. The man in question indeed made for a peculiar sight, dressed in bright gay colours which seemed to catch the sun and sparkle whenever he turned, which was constantly. A small thrill ran through the princess—never had she witnessed such invention! The man capered and leapt and slapped first his head, then his thighs, then each leg in turn, twisting and turning like a fish on a riverbank. How high he jumped! How energetically he rolled upon the grass, only to spring back to his feet and begin slapping himself all over again.

At last, evidently exhausted by his efforts, the incredible man leapt whole-bodied into a nearby barrel of rainwater, disappeared for full thirty seconds before springing back into view, landing soundly on two feet and looking around as if rendered senseless by the genius of his own display.

"Bring that man here at once!" Velaspia commanded.

Two burly men-at-arms, who up till now had been busy passing a fag back and forth and swapping notes on who was favourite to win this years' Most Comely Maiden Award, jumped swiftly into action, adopted the universal expression of bouncers the world over[3], each grabbed one of Crazy Cavan's arms and half-carried him to the Princess.

The thief submitted without resistance, kneeling before the platform with head hung low.

For a moment there was silence.

"Good man," began the Princess, "I believe I can speak for the whole party in

---

[3] Somewhere between supreme disinterest and righteous judgement.

saying that never before have we witnessed such an incredible spectacle..."

"Your highness," pleaded the man, without looking up, "I most humbly beg for your mercy, not for myself, you understand, but for my five poor motherless children..."

"Pardon me?" interrupted her highness, "what the devil is this man talking about? Look here, do you not understand? Lord Albit, pass him this ribbon. Sir, I now pronounce you winner, first class, of the annual Princess's Contemporary Dance Tournament. Here are your five gold pieces, and here is your royal certificate."

Cavan looked up suspiciously, as if at any moment the cruel jest would be over and the guards would haul him off to the torture cells. He accepted the awards dumbly, realisation slowly growing that this was not, in fact, a joke. He closed his eyes and allowed a small smile to spread across his face.

"You are required," commanded the Princess, "to return here five days from now for a private showing at the palace when your trophy shall be awarded you. Thereafter you understand that I may require your services as dance tutor and choreographer to the royal ballet. Now, is there anything else we may do for you?"

"Thank you, your majesty," said Cavan humbly and, metaphorically crossing all of his fingers and toes, added, "if your guards could just escort me to the gates. I fear I have somewhat lost my bearings..."

And that is how Crazy Cavan came into possession of a rare treasure, the which he was to deliver to a mysterious stranger that very night, in return for the princely sum of one thousand golden coins. And as he sat some time before then, and some hours after his ordeal at the palace, quietly sipping his third restorative ale of the night at the Lucky Duck Tavern, curiosity got the better of the thief and, secure in a private booth, he part-unwrapped the package, to examine more closely the object within.

It was a large golden chalice, quite beautifully wrought, engraved with all manner of birds, beasts and human figures in varied poses, encrusted around the rim and base with diamonds, emeralds and rubies.

Carved upon one side, in elegant, flowing script, were the fateful words: Gratefully Awarded to the Winner of Her Majesty Princess Valespia's Contemporary Dance Tournament.

Crazy Cavan stared as his own distorted reflection in the gleaming surface of the cup. For rather too long he stared at it. It was some moments before he realised that the weird, high-pitched and dangerously unhinged laughter in his ears came from his own mouth.

The Gods, he decided, as he carefully re-wrapped the trophy, could kiss his hornet-stung bottom.

RUDRAYANI VISITS OUIDAH

GUSTAVO BONDONI

The dust and the humidity hung together in the air. Impossibly so. Harriet thought that, at any moment, they would combine to form mud and fall in dense drops.

But it didn't happen, and she sweated and coughed as the dilapidated Toyota 4-Runner traversed the eight miles that separated Cotonou airport from the town of Ouidah. It had no air conditioning, so the driver had ordered all the passengers to keep their windows open.

Luckily for Harriet, only five others shared her trip. She'd watched in horror as pickups piled dangerously with people left the airport under the watchful, smiling gaze of green-uniformed policemen. No one seemed to care.

The scenery was a disappointment. She'd known intellectually that Ouidah was on the coast, but it hadn't registered on an emotional level. In her heart, any drive through Africa this close to the Equator should have involved impenetrable tropical jungles, not dusty tarmac roads, even if said roads did wind through lush, low greenery. The road even had white intermittent lines recently painted down the middle. Certainly not Conrad's Africa, then.

At least the Voodoo festival was going to meet every expectation because... well, because it was the world's biggest Voodoo festival.

Ouidah was a town of orange-colored dirt and low buildings. A thin black woman in her mid-thirties with short hair stood where the SUV stopped holding a sign that said "Harriet" in black marker on cardboard. Harriet smiled at her and held out a hand. "Dr. Maga?"

"Yes. I'm glad you could make it. Welcome to Benin." Angelique Maga spoke in Oxford-perfect English with only the faintest trace of some Romance language in the mix—Portuguese, most likely, or maybe French.

"Thank you."

"Is that all your luggage?"

"Yeah. A wise person once told me there were two kinds of luggage: carry on and lost."

"He must have gone through Heathrow a lot."

They laughed and walked along the dirt alley that served as a causeway between the national road and the town proper. A group of small children eyed her as they passed, but even golden hair and the possibility of foreign candy wasn't enough to drag them away from their game of soccer.

Ouidah, or at least this part of it, was set on a grid pattern, with pale dirt roads— a different kind of dirt from the orange stuff, clearly—dividing the town into perfectly ordinary city blocks, albeit very sparsely settled ones. As they walked her host pointed out the sights, promising to take her to the Modern African Art Museum once she got some rest. They reached a pale-yellow house with wooden shutters and Angelique turned onto the path.

"Welcome to my home," she said.

It was a house. It wasn't a hut or a Bedouin tent. A perfectly normal house with a couple of bedrooms, a kitchen, a living room and tiled floors. A huge weight she'd been carrying suddenly lifted from Harriet's shoulders.

Angelique must have noticed. "You were expecting something else?"

"I... I didn't know what to expect, and I was afraid to ask." She felt her cheeks burning. "I'm sorry."

"Oh, that's all right," Angelique replied. "You weren't totally off base. Most of the houses around here wouldn't meet Western standards, but we do get a lot of tourists at the beach hotels, so the construction industry can build high-quality stuff if you pester them about it. Contractors around here call me the 'Crazy Book Lady', but they never turn me down when I call. British pounds go a long way."

"So, when does the party start?"

Angelique turned serious. "It's not a party," she said. "It's the biggest congregation of Voodoo magicians in the world, and people take it very seriously. This is a religious festival, and we need to treat it that way." Then she relaxed. "After everyone drinks enough rotgut, that's when it becomes a party. But be careful before. If you offend people, they might stick pins in you."

"Of course. I'm sorry," Harriet replied, wondering if Dr. Maga was serious, but too frightened to ask.

"Don't worry about it. Now tell me. How does a sociologist from Illinois end up in Ouidah for her dissertation?"

"I'm researching the contrast between the ceremonies of the major monotheisms and traditional non-European faiths, and I stumbled on the information about this celebration. Unfortunately, most of what's out there was written by travel writers. They're a weird breed, travel writers. They'll spend pages talking about the booze and very little about the actual religious underpinnings of the stuff they're watching."

"You don't get web traffic with religious underpinnings."

"Well, that's why I had to come over here. This festival needs a scholarly observer."

"And I don't count?" This was delivered with a raised eyebrow and a slight smile. Combined with the British accent, it was devastating.

"I never meant to imply that," Harriet said quickly. "I didn't think it was your area of interest."

"Oh, I'm definitely interested. But we can discuss that later. Here comes my husband."

* * *

Midafternoon showed her a side to the town she hadn't imagined. "Is it always this crowded?" Harriet said.

"No," Philippe replied. Angelique's husband was not at all what Harriet had expected. He was a white man from France, with several scars and a limp, about fifteen years her senior. He'd mentioned being a scientist at a cutting-edge facility in Paris in his younger days. Despite that, he seemed more at home in the tropics, and in Ouidah specifically, than Angelique did. "These people are all here for the festival." He pointed to a man in yellow pantaloons. "Does that look like a man from Benin to you?"

"No. He looks Indian," Harriet replied.

Angelique, who'd been following a few steps behind, interjected: "He's probably Nepalese," she said. "I've heard that hundreds of people from a town just outside Kathmandu arrived last night. The festival is getting bigger every year."

"But... why would anyone from Nepal come here? Voodoo has nothing to do with the Hindu faith."

"That's where you're wrong," Angelique said. "Voodoo takes from every faith. Its original followers were taken from all over Africa, and they borrowed from everyone they encountered. I wouldn't be surprised if we found a connection to India we've missed so far. Heck, the two religions are so similar, I'd be surprised if there wasn't a link."

"Similar?" Philippe said. "In what way?"

Harriet never got a chance to answer. The crowd around the art museum suddenly shouted in dismay and parted ahead of them to reveal a pickup truck piled with people surrounded by a bunch of angry men. They were shaking the truck and shaking their fists at the driver.

One man opened the door and pulled the unresisting driver out onto the street. Much shouting ensued, but it didn't escalate beyond that. Most of the gesticulation seemed to be concentrated around the pickup truck's left front tire. Some animal, apparently, had been hit. A white leg stuck out under the wheel.

Philippe and Angelique strode quickly through the onlookers and Harriet tagged along. The men made way for them respectfully, although they were still shouting in agitation amongst themselves.

"What's happening?" Harriet asked

"The driver ran over a goat. This isn't a good day to lose your goat," Angelique explained.

"Why?"

"The ceremonies are tomorrow."

"Ah." Harriet remembered that goats were sacrificed at the ceremony. She'd thought it was only one goat that was used, but now, looking around the crowd, she saw goats everywhere, tethered to fences, held protectively in arms and led on leashes. Apparently, this was a really bad time to be a goat.

Philippe spoke and the shouting died away. Eventually, the man in the pickup—alone, now; his passengers had melted into the crowd—was allowed to drive on. As they turned to leave, something made Harriet look back.

A Nepalese man wearing yellow pants, muscular bare chest glistening in the heat and humidity, stared at them. She turned to show him to Philippe, but when she pointed, the fellow was gone.

She spent the rest of the afternoon thinking about him. Why had he been so interested? There were plenty of other white tourists among the throng, most of them the kind of folk you might expect to encounter at Burning Man—people completely alienated by mainstream life hoping that they could find something deeper somewhere—and Harriet and Philippe certainly weren't anything special. But the look the man had given her in that instant their gazes had met was unsettling. It was, somehow, a knowing look.

She hoped there hadn't been anything important at the Ouidah Modern Art Museum... because if there was, she had missed it completely in her preoccupied state.

Before she knew it, it was time to go to bed. The festival was tomorrow.

Her window, open to the cool night air, buzzed with more insects and birds than she'd ever imagined existed.

Harriet took a long time to fall asleep.

* * *

"I'd seen videos of the rituals, but I never imagined there would be this many people."

"The videos online are a few years old," Angelique replied. "The festival has just exploded over the last two events. At any moment, the government is going to send police down to keep us all safe, and that's when it will end."

Harriet mopped the sweat from her brow. "And I couldn't really believe that they'd hold a Voodoo ritual in the middle of the day. It doesn't seem like something that should be done in plain sunlight."

"Why not? Voodoo is the most natural of religions. Think about it: a group of freed slaves, thousands of miles from their homes, in a foreign place where people speak a strange language... they won't look into some deep philosophy for their worshipping; they'll take inspiration from the world around them. It's a religion that belongs in the sun." She paused and winked. "Although, I'll admit that a lot of the better stuff happens at night."

"Oh. I didn't see any videos of that."

"By the time night comes around, everyone is pretty drunk... and the kind of people who upload videos to YouTube aren't around with their cell phones... not if they want to keep them at least. But if we're careful, we might be able to see a couple of the rites."

The crowds ebbed and flowed, and there seemed to be a couple of focal points. One was a small courtyard between two houses in an otherwise unremarkable residential neighborhood, while the other, much more public, was in a plaza across from the basilica.

Despite the crowds, their little group had no trouble getting through the narrow lanes. At first, Harriet thought it was because there were two obvious foreigners in the group, but she soon realized that wasn't the case. The other foreigners in the crowd were being blocked and jostled just like everyone else.

But not Angelique. The crowd ahead of her parted like the Red Sea. A soft word here, a raised eyebrow there, and the people around her nodded and moved aside.

"How come the festival is held here? Is this a Voodoo capital or something?"

Philippe smiled. "You mean like New Orleans or Port Au Prince? Not remotely. It's the center of the Voodoo universe once a year, and that's it. Ouidah doesn't even have its own Voodoo church, and the population isn't really part of any of the popular Voodoo movements you see on the net. In fact, they ascribe to West African Vodunism more than anything else."

Harriet had read that in the source material, but long experience had taught her that books never quite got the situation exactly right, and that numbers often felt different on the ground. Apparently, this time was an exception. She wrote that down on the tiny notepad she'd brought for the purpose.

It felt strange to be taking notes by hand, but Angelique had warned her against bringing her cell phone along. The festival had been perfectly peaceful over the years, but why tempt a drunken hand with a modern trinket? Petty theft was one thing the authorities had never been able to control.

"What about rape?" she asked. It was what everyone she'd spoken with stateside had told her to be careful of.

"The wizards don't allow that," Angelique replied with finality. "This is a festival for all."

The way she said it made Harriet feel that the subject was not even worth revisiting. If someone had told her she'd feel perfectly safe in the middle of a massive Voodoo festival in Benin, she probably would have laughed at them. But she did.

Even the edict about cellphones seemed completely unnecessary: every other person in the crowd appeared to be filming the events around them with perfectly modern-looking devices.

They stopped at a light blue door at one end of the courtyard, and a man emerged. He was tall and overweight and wore a bright, brand-new white tunic embroidered with elephants, dazzling in the midday sun. He nodded towards Angelique and walked down an alley.

He was followed by two more men, equally brilliantly attired, and two matronly women. Philippe filed in behind them, sweeping Angelique and Harriet along. Behind them came everyone else. The procession carried drums, bells and rattles. Someone had borrowed an ambulance, and the siren pierced the humid air.

They walked along the dusty road for some blocks, and Harriet found herself moving rhythmically as she progressed. It amazed her that a crowd of several hundred people, armed with several different ways of creating rhythm, could keep time so beautifully. There was nothing discordant about anything.

A man slotted in beside her, and a flash of yellow made her turn her head. It was a member of the Nepalese contingent, but whether it might be the same man or another was beyond her. He nodded a greeting.

"Hello," she said. Despite the sacred nature of the procession, there was no taboo about talking, laughing or shouting. Everyone she saw seemed to be both happy and loud.

"Ah. You speak English?" Again, she was surprised at a very crisp bit of pronunciation. Not quite Angelique-Oxford-perfect, but good enough for a procession in Benin.

"Yes. I'm from America."

He bowed slightly. "Ah. I am from Khokana. It is in Nepal."

"Pleased to meet you. I didn't know Voodoo was big in Nepal."

"It is complicated... much of what you see here is... related to what you would see at my temple."

He said it carefully, a man picking his words to avoid confusion. Or was it to avoid clarity? She didn't know, and wasn't about to insult him by asking. "I hear a lot of you came for this ceremony."

"Enough of us," he replied.

That was all they could discuss before the eddies of the crowd pushed him away into another group.

The procession entered a large space enclosed by whitewashed brick walls. It might have been a soccer stadium, as the dusty remains of a grass field with painted lines on it could barely be made out beneath their feet.

The white-tunicked leaders of the procession advanced onto a stage in the center of the pitch, and again Harriet experienced a moment of culture shock. The platform was one of those modern pieces made of black material and shiny metal strips—the kind you saw at major rock concerts. It made her think about how she saw the ceremony versus how the locals and the other Vodunists saw it. For her it was an anachronism, a throwback to a different time. For them... it represented their daily faith, as modern as the iPhones they were filming the proceedings with. There was no need to construct a rickety wooden platform in the name of tradition. They were creating tradition.

They sat on a bleacher, under an awning, essentially the VIP section of the soccer field. Everyone else sat on the dirt in the sun, and no one complained. Quite the contrary, everyone she saw was smiling and chanting along when appropriate or simply watching and filming the rest of the time. She estimated a couple of thousand people in the crowd.

"Is everyone here?"

"No. There are about twenty ceremonies happening in different parts of town, and one on the beach a couple of miles out." Philippe looked around. "But this is the ceremony that matters. The men and women up there are the wizards that shout loudest. Loud enough to be heard over the rest. Mawu can hear them. Legba can hear them. The Queen Mother—" he pointed to a woman in white— "is the strongest of all the ones holding court this year, although not the strongest ever. There are more Queen Mothers on Earth than this."

Then came the first goat.

A man carried it reverently to the stage and gave it to one of the men in white. A sacrificial knife was raised, but Harriet missed the blow. She didn't turn away because of any squeamishness but because, out of the corner of her eye, she saw a commotion among the yellow-pantaloon crowd.

One Nepali youth, on seeing the goat, tried to run towards the stage. He would have made it, too, if a couple of his elder companions hadn't tackled him and dragged him back to the isolated patch of dirt they'd claimed for their own.

She gave it little thought. Several members of the crowd had already achieved ecstatic trances. Why not one of the Nepalese?

As afternoon dwindled to evening, she noticed that many of the attendees trickled away. "What's happening? Is it finishing already?" She was disappointed. While the ceremony had been a wonderful, animalistic series of rites and bloody animal sacrifices, it seemed to be missing something. Maybe it was because she'd been sitting in the shade under the awning instead of out in the sun where the crowd was denser. Also, she noticed that drink was circulating freely among the people in the crowd in bottles and large white jugs. She doubted they were serving virgin cocktails.

"Not quite. People are going off to get an hour's rest before sundown. That's when the good stuff starts," Philippe said. He grinned at her. "Have you ever seen an old James Bond movie called *Live and Let Die*?"

"Not that I remember. I might have watched it with my dad when I was a kid. It was more his speed than mine."

"That's refreshing. You'd be surprised by how many people formed their entire image of Voodoo from that single movie. I was going to point out how different it was from what you saw today. In that one, the rituals were dark and depraved, with undertones of tropical lust. You could tell that wasn't the case today. You could call this a family affair."

He was right; there were dozens of kids scattered through the crowds. "Except for the drinking."

Philippe shrugged. "Only Americans have those hang-ups about alcohol. I remember going to debutante balls when I was fifteen, and we all drank wine. This was in France in the eighties, so we're not talking about the middle ages or anywhere uncivilized after all." He said it with the conviction of one who knows that his country of origin represents the epitome of human culture.

"All right. Yes, it's a family thing. So now it goes on at night?"

"No. Now we send the kids to sleep and only a select few of the people here go on at night. Those who know where everything is."

"And what's that like?"

He smiled. "Well, it's a pity you don't remember the film. It would save a lot of explanation..."

* * *

Angelique ordered a drink, essentially fruit and rum and ice and sugar tossed in a blender. It looked refreshing, so Harriet ordered her own and was stunned to realize the mix was mostly rum. Angelique had been downing it like water with little effect.

"Excuse me," Philippe said. "I'm off to get more drinks."

"And I'm off to get some of the drinks out of my system," Angelique said, and headed for the ladies' room.

The bar was Ouidah's best nightspot, with modern everything and international prices. But the best part was a balcony looking out onto the street where they could watch the festival go by. The crowd was much more animated now, with more bare torsos in evidence—although the women maintained their decorum—and much more dancing. Still no one seemed out of synch, and Harriet envied the grace of their movements. Nightfall was still an hour away.

Suddenly, unexpectedly, her view was blocked by a young man who sat in front of her.

"You're the scholar," he said, "aren't you?"

"The scholar? I didn't know I was famous."

"Everyone is famous in such a small place. Especially foreigners."

"There are quite a few of those."

"But only one here to study this perversion."

She peered at him. "Didn't you try to run onto the stage this afternoon?"

He shook his head. "I wouldn't dirty my feet with that stage. I was trying to save the goat."

This made no sense. What did goats have to do with anything... and if he thought the ritual was somehow unclean, why had he flown all the way down from Nepal to see it? "Are you part of an animal rights group?"

He laughed. "Of course not. They're our enemies, too."

She was getting more and more confused. "What, exactly, is it you're a part of?"

"We worship Rudrayani."

Harriet took a second to remember what she knew about that particular goddess. Unless she was mistaken, Rudrayani was a manifestation of the Hindu goddess Durga with a major following in Nepal. That had to be it. "The warrior goddess," she said.

He nodded. "Among other things. You must help us to defend her flock."

An image came to her of a ritual in a pool in Nepal. Goats that had been worshipped until the day before were thrown into a pool and viciously slaughtered by the worshippers using only their hands and teeth. The man who killed the goat would lead the sacred procession. "The... the goats?"

"Yes. They are sacred, and this wholesale massacre is simply unacceptable to Rudrayani. Where is the respect? Where is the reverence? Nowhere."

It still made no sense. "But with that criteria, you should be burning down half the slaughterhouses in Eastern Europe."

He shrugged. "Those are just ignorant businessmen. This is different. This quasi-religious usage echoes across the firmament and disturbs Rudrayani. She hears the magicians."

Harriet nearly laughed at that. Millions of supposedly sacred animals slaughtered for food every year, ignored. But the few dozen that were used in Voodoo rites over a weekend in Africa were an issue? It was the kind of religious thinking she'd encountered extremely often over the course of her studies, but it never ceased to amaze her.

The man spoke into her silence. "Will you help us?"

"I'll report what I see, and I'll definitely note the concerns of the temple of Rudrayani."

He peered at her shrewdly. "You won't denounce them?"

"I'm a neutral observer. I need to be objective."

Anger colored the man's features, but Philippe chose that moment to return from the crowded bar. "Am I interrupting something?"

"No," Harriet replied. "Please sit down."

"Excuse me," the young man said with a sour look at the Frenchman. "I need to go."

"Trouble?" Philippe asked once he was gone.

"No... just weirdness."

"Oh. Then you're just getting warmed up for tonight."

* * *

An enormous bonfire illuminated the beach outside the town. They'd hitched a ride on a pickup truck which was full to overflowing when they hailed it. As soon as the passengers saw Angelique, however, several of them decided to get out and walk so they group could take their place.

At night, the dancing was more frenzied, much less innocent than what had happened during the day. It didn't take a lot of imagination to imagine the dancers pairing off and disappearing into the inky night after the dance was done... but there was no indication that the dance would ever be finished.

It went on and on and on, driven by a drumbeat much more urgent, much more organized, than what had played during the day. Harriet felt the tug of the beat. She'd always loved to dance, but this was irresistible; she felt it in her bones, in some primal part of her that had inherited the love for drumbeats from the first humans to discover percussion.

Then she was dancing. She'd lost her shoes somewhere, and a large man dressed as Baron Samedi gyrated in front of her, perfectly complementing her own motion. A tiny corner of her mind protested that Baron Samedi wasn't a figure in West African Vodunism.

Shut up and let me dance, she told the voice.

Harriet took a long pull from a jug someone handed her. The spirits burned her throat on the way down—this definitely wasn't the top-shelf rum they'd served at the bar. It was exactly what she wanted. She drank every time it was offered, and she could have sworn she felt the alcohol leaving her body through her sweat glands.

How long she danced, she couldn't say. She was perfectly aware of her surroundings, maybe a bit buzzed but certainly not drunk, but she couldn't find the desire to stop dancing. Exhaustion grew, but she still moved. She'd never felt that good in her life.

She stumbled.

That killed the trance. But it wasn't her body that had failed her; she hadn't lost the rhythm due to tiredness or clumsiness. Inconceivably, the music itself had broken. Discordant strains had crept in.

Harriet listened. Something that sounded like a cross between a bagpipe and a flute was sending its music across the beach. Cymbals, moving at their own rhythm, clashed with the drums.

It sounded anything but African, anything but Voodoo.

The dancers around her seemed unaware that anything was amiss. They continued to gyrate, lost in the world of endless percussion, incapable of perceiving the jarring tones.

But for Harriet, the magic was gone. She followed the sound of the whining music until, behind a small dune, she found the Nepalese contingent playing an assortment of unfamiliar instruments.

They chanted, too, but so quietly that it seemed each verse was meant to be heard only by the person reciting it.

Harriet felt the hairs of her arm stand on end. There was electricity in the air, power coming together around her. She stepped back.

Clouds, illuminated from within by their own lightning, rolled into the clear sky, blocking the cold pinprick of the stars, and took station above her. A couple of drops fell.

Something huge stepped out of the cloud and onto the sand.

It was a luminous woman, twenty feet high with six... no, eight arms. Each hand held a sword or shield. A couple of the arms worked together to aim a bow and arrow. Harriet gaped as the monstrosity lowered itself to the ground on an invisible rope.

Paralysis lasted only a moment. She threw herself to the ground as a curved blade hissed over her head, followed by a dry chuckle. Whatever this was, it hadn't meant to kill her, only to scare her. The knowledge lodged fully formed in her head along with the certainty that if the figure had meant to hit her, there would be pieces of Harriet lying on the ground in several places.

She recognized the figure: it was Durga, the Hindu goddess. And she was in her full warrior manifestation.

No, she realized, it wasn't Durga. It was Rudrayani. She was here about the goats.

It was ridiculous.

Harriet ran through the sand. "Dr Maga! Philippe!" she cried.

The dark swallowed up her voice, so she headed toward the bonfire.

Unfortunately, she realized, Rudrayani was headed in the same direction. The sword sang over her head and Harriet heard more laughter as she picked herself off the sand.

Despite the deity, she ran towards the light. Her mind, that rational part of her that was still trying to make sense of things was asking questions: was she seriously considering it a deity? Why not a hallucination? It was a more likely explanation, after all that firewater.

Something tripped her. It was a hand, connected to an arm. To her immense relief, the arm was connected to Philippe.

"Sorry," he said. "I couldn't think of any other way to stop your running without getting up. That thing has made it very clear that she doesn't want me on my feet." He touched a bald spot on the top of his head.

"What the hell is going on?"

"Trouble among the pantheons. It happens sometimes." He looked up at the towering, multi-armed goddess. "Never on this scale, though."

"You mean the gods are real?"

Philippe sighed. "Of course they're real. Why do you think so many people worship? Why do you think they come down here in droves?" He paused. "I know the answer. Just like every other scholar, you think people are stupid. Well..."

Whatever he was going to say next was lost in a gasp.

Harriet turned her gaze back to the monster approaching the bonfire. She'd brought her bow into play and was scything down the dancers. She watched in horror as the guy dressed as Baron Samedi—a beautiful, well-muscled young man—went down with a shaft protruding from his neck.

And yet the dancers didn't stop. They seemed unable to break out of the rhythmic movement even as they were felled by the warrior goddess. Each time one died, it seemed that two more appeared to take his place.

"No," Philippe whispered, and his hand tightened its grip around her ankle.

A figure strode through the sand towards the conflict. At first, Harriet didn't recognize her... and then she saw: Angelique. She moved confidently, seeming to grow with each step.

No. Not seeming to grow. She was growing. By the time she entered the ring around the fire, she stood as tall as the Hindu monstrosity.

Calmly, Angelique faced her rival. The dancers rallied around her, swaying about her feet.

Rudrayani's followers gathered around her as well, no longer playing their instruments.

The two goddesses—she assumed her friend was actually a Queen Mother, the strongest of all, channeling Mawu herself—faced each other. The problem, in Harriet's eyes, was that one was armed to the teeth, and the other... the other was just a mortal woman temporarily gifted powers beyond anything she should suffer.

The instant lasted forever. It seemed to Harriet that even the fire stopped flickering as time stood still.

Then Rudrayani swung her sword. It hummed straight and true towards Angelique's neck.

And stopped, as if held by an invisible hand.

The feeling of electricity in her hairs started again. Harriet felt the tension rising, and rising even more. The air hummed.

She jumped to her feet, ignoring Philippe's questions and ran into the circle. She shook one man until he responded and ran away in terror. Slapped a dancing woman and sent her on her way. She went around the circle until there were no more innocents waiting to die.

Then she looked out at the Nepalese. They were at risk, too.

But she shook her head. Let them take care of their own. She didn't have much time; Angelique couldn't hold much longer. The amount of electricity around her seemed too much for the world to bear.

Harriet ran.

As she dove for cover behind a dune, the universe exploded around her. She was tossed through the air like a rag doll and saw the dark sand coming up to meet her.

Then blackness.

* * *

Harriet woke in a house. Not Angelique's house. Not a Western house. There were no tiled floors in this place, and no electric lights. A pungent candle burned beside her bed and an old man looked down on her.

He smiled an ancient, toothless grin.

"My son danced with you last night," the man said.

She wanted to protest that he was too old to have such a young, virile son, but then she heard the truth in the old man's soft words.

"He died."

"He has died before, and will die again. It is in his nature."

"Angelique..."

The man looked down. "She is truly dead. I'm sorry. But she will be remembered."

With that, she slept again.

* * *

When she woke, she was in the clinic, and a tall doctor with skin so dark it was almost black had replaced the old man.

"How are you feeling?" he asked her in English. "You took a nasty bump to the head."

"I'm all right. I think."

"I'm glad to hear it. It was a rough night. Do you remember anything about the accident?"

How to explain to this urbane professional? She shook her head.

"We think it was a still—where they brew the alcohol for the festival—but we're not sure."

"I don't know," she mumbled.

He shone a light into her eyes, checked her reflexes and said, "I see no reason to keep you here unless you have a bad headache or anything else to report. Other than the bump to the head, all you've got is some bruising and scrapes."

"No, I'm fine." It was true. Whatever was in that candle had been pretty potent.

Someone had brought her possessions to the hospital. She didn't bother to go find Philippe. She knew he would be gone, so instead, she hiked towards the bus stop.

On the way, a packed pickup stopped beside her and every single passenger descended to make room. She accepted the ride gratefully.

At the bus stop, a small stand sold Voodoo fetishes. Desiccated bats, carved faces and... and a perfect, beautiful likeness of Angelique. The woman who ran the table refused her payment for one. "You saved my brother," was all she said, apparently all the English she knew.

Harriet remembered the old man's promise. Again, the truth rang through his words. Angelique would be remembered. At first through fetishes, then, soon perhaps, there would be another deity in the tradition, one named after her friend.

She smiled at the thought. A woman named after an angel, part of the Vodun pantheon.

It made sense. This was a religion making its own traditions.

THE HUMAN CONDITION

HANSEN ABCOCK

Monday, February 29th. New Moon. First Day of Welcome.
21.00

Stephen is a newcomer but does not realise it. He has lived in this town all his adult life, with nobody but himself, the landlord, an older woman named Jill who resides in the room opposite him, and his cat, Greytooth.

Stephen looks out of the window of his room in the boarding-house and sees the Festival being set up in the town centre. The travelling show comes once every year, and each year Stephen hates it.

He sits down at his laptop and writes another letter of complaint to the Council, one to the *Daily Express* and one to the *Times*. Every year, this is common practice for him. Everyone else ignores his complaints.

23.00

The noises are loud and wild to Stephen, even with the window closed. He gave up trying to work hours ago but does not dare to go to bed. He is afraid of the dreams. He is afraid of walking in his sleep.

* * *

Tuesday, February 30th. New Moon. Second Day of Welcome.
00.00

"DO YOU KNOW WHAT A GHOUL IS?"

Stephen walks up and down the same length of street next to a dead man—who is not dead. The living are always on the right-hand side of the street. He can't see what is on the left.

He treads on something that cries out in awful pain and looks down to meet the hostile gaze of a mutilated man, who somehow seems less real than the ghost beside him.

03.00

Stephen emerges from the clammy confines of the night terror, his gasps returning to normal breaths. His heart speeds and slows down.

This happens only once a year, he reminds himself. *Only for a week, once a year.* By next Monday the nightmares and the sleepwalking should dissipate. The waiting will be long and hard, but he is a patient man.

05.30

He swings his legs out of bed to inspect his feet. The soles are covered with black grime. It must have rained in the night. The now almost customary footprints lead unerringly from the door to his bedside.

He does not see any point in returning to sleep.

The revels abate at first light, but some of the travellers will still be awake, manning stalls, selling oddities (such as frogs' dreams in jars), or telling the fortunes of passers-by.

Stephen makes a point of never going to the travellers' market or their shows. He went only once, many years ago, to please an old girlfriend. In his opinion, they tricked her out of her money and treated her with disrespect.

In actuality, the atmosphere that the travellers brought with them made his skin crawl and his courage shrivel.

08.00

The landlord looks up as Stephen enters the kitchen of the boarding-house.

"Bacon and eggs? Porridge? Toast?" he asks. It's not every day that your landlord asks to make you breakfast.

"Just a black coffee, please," Stephen says. His head feels like the fiery pits of Hell, but he manages to force the drink down and get his system into something resembling wakefulness.

"You got in rather late last night," Jill from the room opposite does not hesitate to tell him. "Three in the morning! Clattering and banging around, cursing, whimpering... What was going on? It was enough to wake the dead!"

Stephen gives her a look and says nothing. It's going to be a long, difficult week.

23.30

Stephen's eyes close as soon as he hits the pillow. As soon as they shut, he starts to dream.

He gets out of bed and looks in the mirror in the bathroom across the hall. He is sweating blood, and calmly washes his face. Black sludge comes out of the tap marked "life" and dark blue ink out of the one marked "essence." Both burn his skin.

Flesh-eating horses stare at him from grass verges as he walks, the pet rabbit he had when he was nine cradled in his arms. He cries and laughs in equal measure.

* * *

Wednesday, February 31ˢᵗ. Waxing Crescent. Third Day of Welcome.
03.00

Stephen wakes up half-hanging out of the bed. His skin feels sticky and there is a musty, musky smell in the room. He is so exhausted, he falls back to sleep.

08.40

"You're up late," his landlord remarks.

Stephen downs two cups of coffee and rests his head on the table for a few minutes.

Jill comes in and demands to know who left the sink taps on in the bathroom all night.

Stephen wearily lifts his head, and Jill begins to ask what he thinks he was doing last night, getting in at such a late hour again, waking her up with loud noises? She has half a mind to lodge a formal complaint with the landlord, who looks none too thrilled at the prospect.

Stephen goes outside, in silence, to smoke a cigarette. He has given up smoking, but in the last week of February he takes it up again to cope.

There is a dead cat on the doorstep, but it is not Greytooth. Greytooth stays far away from him at this time of year.

* * *

Thursday, February 32ᵈ. First Quarter. Fourth Day of Welcome.
00.00

Stephen resolves not to go to bed. He sits at his writing desk and contemplates leaving, going on to another town for a few days...

His mouth opens and a frog spews out in a wet, slimy ball. It wriggles feebly and expires on the desktop. He watches it with detached interest.

Forked lightning pierces his eye through the windowpane, but he does not jump. Something invisible seizes him from behind, a comforting terror, and whispers in his ear, telling him what he should do next.

He is lonely. He should find company. Seek human life. There is a girl locked in sleep whom he should kiss...

03.35

Stephen is woken by a spluttering, screeching noise, to find himself standing in Jill's room, next to her bed. He does not remember falling asleep, though he must have done so.

Jill glares up at him, and savagely wipes her arm across her mouth. She spits in his face, leaps out of bed, and wallops him over the head and shoulders with her pillow, shouting at him to "clear off."

But when he goes to the door, he can't clear off. It's locked. He has no idea how he managed to get in.

Jill, at last, calms down enough to stop hitting Stephen and unfastens the door for him. She gives him a long, strange look, and he goes back to his room with glowing cheeks.

He does not sleep anymore that night.

08.00

Over breakfast, which for Stephen consists of two cups of black coffee followed by a measure of whiskey, Jill marvels at how he managed to sleepwalk through a locked door last night, the key of which was fastened securely around her neck. She wonders aloud if he ever used to work as an escapologist, then tells him that of course he can't have, he's far too young and innocent-looking.

Stephen doesn't feel like talking. He gives her a wan smile and wishes Greytooth was here.

Then Jill starts to lecture him about young men secretly harboring an unconscious desire for older women, and assures him that he needn't feel ashamed. She knows he was asleep.

He mutters his thanks and goes for a walk. On the way to the top of the road, he passes a man who stops, frowns at him, and asks if he is all right.

"I'm fine. Just tired," Stephen says.

"I'm sorry about your cat," the man tells him.

"Cat?"

"You know. The one who passed away."

"My cat's not dead."

"It looked to be that way, when you were carrying it the other night."

Stephen suddenly remembers his dream about the rabbit, and the dead cat on the doorstep of the house he rooms in, and feels rather sick.

23.59

It snows fast and hard, in large white dollops. The heating is not effective, so Stephen curls up in bed to keep warm. He wonders, albeit vaguely, where he sleepwalks to whenever he leaves the building. Before he can come to any conclusion, he falls asleep.

Faceless people emerge from the mist, laugh and say hello, before passing and fading out of sight again. The fog is so thick and cold, he can't feel his own body. Stephen cannot even tell if he is standing the right way up.

The fog takes on a pinkish tinge. People bump up against him, until he realises they aren't looking for a fight. They must be dancing. Or are they standing still and is he the one dancing? But Stephen can't dance, and he knows it.

The laughter continues, and although it's not directed at him, he can't be sure if it is mocking or friendly.

* * *

Friday, February 33ᵈ. First Half. Fifth Day of Welcome.
09.00

Stephen staggers downstairs with a thumping ache behind his eyes. He's not been one for partying hard, but this is how he would imagine a hangover to feel.

When he enters the kitchen, the landlord turns around and gawps at him. His mouth works up and down as if he is having problems swallowing something.

"What's wrong?" Stephen asks and winces. One side of his face is incredibly sore. He touches it and it flares up again, so he lets his hand drop. "What's happened?"

He goes back upstairs and looks in the mirror. Quite a sizable tattoo of some intricate knot work has been done on his cheek, starting next to his eye and curving inwards, down to his jaw line and overlapping it, onto his neck.

"I didn't know you were the type!" the landlord says when Stephen comes back into the kitchen. "Were you at the revels last night, then?"

"No." Stephen grimaces.

"Was about to say. Would be a bit funny if you did, 'cause you're that bloke who's written so many negative letters about it to the papers, aren't you?"

Stephen nods emphatically, but inside he starts to wonder.

23.30

Stephen decides this has gone far enough.

No more snow has fallen, and the day remains cold. He plans to follow his somnambulist footprints from the night before. He waits until everyone else has turned in for the evening.

The house is quiet. He treads softly downstairs and out of the door.

The torch Stephen thought to bring is not needed. The moon lights his path. He is a shadow, one with the shadows. He almost feels like someone else, and for a moment imagines himself to be Greytooth, prowling, stalking... what? Himself? Impossible.

He is nearing the showground. Houses give way to snow-covered bushes and undergrowth, followed by a clearing. Greytooth waits at its edge.

Greytooth's cheekbones lift in a feline smile, and he fixes Stephen with a long, unusual stare. It is unusual because Greytooth normally meows and winds himself about Stephen's ankles in a figure of eight upon meeting him, but he does not do so this time. The cat is still.

"Hello," Stephen murmurs, and squats down to pet his long-absent friend.

Greytooth stands up on all fours, and inches ever so slightly away from his outstretched fingers.

Greytooth eyeballs him.

Greytooth opens his mouth and says, "So, you've decided to come awake at last."

Stephen is unable to move for a moment.

The cat leads him further in, amongst crowds of people. Some are in their pajamas, slack-faced, addle-eyed, walking at a slow, unchanging pace, disregarding the others, who are awake. The awake revellers are tolerant and kind enough to give the sleepwalkers some space. One or two somnambulists have their arms held, and are led, all unwitting, by conscious guides. A few are led by pets, mostly guide-dogs.

Remaining stallholders are still shutting up shop, clearing the items for sale into crates and drawing curtains, draping tarpaulin. They smile and wave as Stephen goes past; he does not recognise them. A woman wearing a bandanna and a shawl eyes him up and down, smiles suggestively. A young man winks at him.

There is something about these people which still unnerves him, though Stephen does his best to be polite, smiling, nodding, waving back. Who are these people, in actuality? Where do they come from? Do they ever need to sleep?

Greytooth does not give him long enough to dawdle, and they arrive at the end of his footprint trail. All around them, the people like him, both awake and asleep, drunk or sober, drugged or dreaming, come to a halt and cluster into a large audience facing a wide stage.

The stage is empty, but impressive. It is open to the air on all sides but one. Floodlights throbbing blue, green, lilac, then yellow punch fingers into the night sky and sweep over enchanted faces. It is warmer here.

Stephen senses the anticipation, the friendly expectation of everyone in the crowd, colouring his own feelings. This is the first time, in a long while, that he has felt connected to something bigger than he is.

* * *

Saturday, February 34th. Waxing Gibbous. Sixth Day of Welcome.
00.00

The show starts.

This isn't a dream, Stephen thinks. *This is better than a dream.*

Greytooth watches with him, curled up against the side of his ankle. It is impossible to guess what he is thinking, which is normal for a cat.

"Have I stood here every night, in my sleep?"

Greytooth nods. Then, mysteriously, he says, "Every human being has two sides."

"What?"

"Just be quiet. Watch the show."

"What do you—"

"I said, watch. It will become clear later."

"Do you think my daughter saw this?"

"It would be excellent for her if she had. I don't know. I'm trying to concentrate."

Up on stage, a woman dances with a dragon. Real flames shoot out of its nostrils, but she is unhurt. She leaps and ducks away, or through them, making it part of the dance. A man walks on, smiles, and disappears.

"You'd almost think it was real," Stephen whispers to himself.

Greytooth mews in amusement. "What makes you think it isn't?"

A woman comes through the crowd towards Stephen, carrying a tray of drinks and odd things to eat. Behind her, on stage, a wizened little man sprouts fur and horns, then eats himself whole, tail-end first. Inside him is nothing, and now the nothing is all on the outside. Then the empty space skews back into the man again. The audience screams, gasps, claps with delight.

"It's always different every night," the vendor says. "They go wild for it."

Her teeth gleam white, unnaturally sharp in the moonlight. She has a grin like a predator, but Stephen is not threatened, and accepts a plastic cup of something alcoholic which nearly lifts the top of his head off.

He looks at the woman, nerves and arteries singing in his body, and dares to ask: "Do you know me?"

"Stephen," she says, and holds out a long, manicured hand. "I've known you for a long time. We all have. You stand in this exact spot every night we come here in the year. I've never seen you awake, though."

She offers him something to eat, but he declines. The drink is more than enough and some of the nibbles are slowly moving by themselves.

"Suit yourself," the vendor shrugs before moving away. "I'm Melanie."

"I've never, um....?" Stephen asks his cat.

"Kissed her? Heavens, no. Friends only." Greytooth bares his teeth. "A creature of her kind normally eats a man who makes the first move. Best to wait."

"Um, and if she does make a move on me?"

"Accept it. It'd only last a month, anyway. They're fickle."

Onstage, four people in cowls conjure Death, then bleach his skeleton, before reducing him to ash. They snort the ash, sprout wings, and fly over the heads of the audience, narrowly missing a few. The spectators crane their necks. Some laugh. Others cover their faces. A few swear, and a young child cries.

A be-cowled angel picks Stephen up and bears him aloft.

"Greytooth...!" he yelps in surprise.

"You'll be fine." The cat, shrinking below him, looks him in the eyes with his own, two shrinking burning headlights in the crowd. "Good luck."

01.00

Stephen's feet come to rest on the planks of the stage.

The winged, hooded person—he can't tell whether male or female—releases the hold on his back, and flaps off somewhere unseen.

Millions of eyes rest on the stage. Rest on him.

His knees go weak. He grins in complete embarrassment, bordering on fear.

A tall imposing man with a long white beard, wearing a black cape, enters stage left, and bows to Stephen.

He is unsure how to react to this, but inclines his head to the stranger, whose mouth twitches in amusement.

"Welcome!" the man addresses the audience. "For our next act, we have a volunteer from the audience! Stephen! Nice of you to be awake this time."

A smattering of titters.

"I," the stranger announces, "am going to cut this man in half, without killing him, and put him back together!"

"What?" Stephen is hoarse.

"Don't worry—we've done this before with you once, and it worked perfectly." The magician winks at him. "I haven't killed a volunteer so far. Have I, ladles and jelly-spoons?"

They cheer. Greytooth shouts, "Knock 'em dead, Stevie-boy!"

The magician instructs Stephen to lie comfortably on the floor.

He doesn't know what else to do. He does as he is told.

The magician stands facing the crowd, on the other side of him. "Do you believe in magic, sir?"

"I never have—well I thought I don't. Didn't. But then I'll have to, er, I mean... I don't know."

"We shall see!"

The magician closes his eyes, and holds his arms out above Stephen, palms facing downward. An expression of peace and serenity crosses the old man's face, and Stephen feels himself slowly lifting...

He is now levitating five feet off the stage floor, perfectly relaxed in his disbelief.

Some laughter. The audience claps.

01.30

The magician makes a violent gesture with one hand at the sky. A bolt of electricity forks down from the clouds, into Stephen's middle.

For Stephen, everything goes white for a couple of seconds. Then he feels his top and bottom halves separating, floating apart. It does not hurt. It seems natural, like continental drift.

Once his sight returns, he strains his neck upwards, to peer along at himself. His legs are far away. It is like looking at the coastline of another country. He tries to waggle his foot. He can't.

After a couple of minutes, his foot twitches spasmodically, as if it can't decide what to do with itself.

The audience holds its breath, like crickets chirping, but without a sound.

The magician smiles benignly down at him. "How are you feeling, Stephen?"

"Bit drafty."

Everyone roars with laughter, and so does Stephen, but underneath his laughter there is a current of fear: what if they decide, as a cruel joke, to walk away and leave him there? He'd never be whole again.

The magician brings his hands together with a soft clap, and the two halves of Stephen's body thunk into each other, like a train joining onto a carriage, and he feels his skin, bones, nerves, innards, all knitting together, like a thousand tiny ants crawling.

He is reunited with his legs.

The magician lets him down gently. He stands, using knees shakier than ever, and the audience screams and jumps up and down in wild abandon. The magician takes hold of Stephen's hand and they both bow together, Stephen rather dazedly.

They exit stage right, the cheers echoing in Stephen's head.

The magician takes him backstage and sits with him while he vomits into a bucket, patting him on the back, and tells him the first time you're awake is always the hardest, and that he'll get over the shock.

Stephen rests there. He doesn't watch the remainder of the show. Being part of it made it lose its appeal.

03.30

It's the after-show party.

The magician, who introduces himself as Kip, invites Stephen along, "for being such a courageous human volunteer," and leads him out of the stage arena.

The punters are dispersing and going back home. Some will remember the journey, and others won't. Some will recall dark dreams when there were none.

Kip leads Stephen across the dirt plaza, into a voluminous black tent. If the magician had not lifted the flap, he wouldn't have guessed there was a tent there—it matches the dead of night exactly.

The interior of the tent, warm with bustle, is a flood of light, noise and colour. Strange people and humanoid beings, in even odder clothes, stand around in groups talking, raising their voices and laughing. Others circulate. The smaller, more hyperactive ones run or fly or pirouette around the circumference. People are showing one another unearthly tricks for fun, or at least, they seem unearthly to Stephen.

In one corner, sitting on mats and cushions, a group of half-transparent musicians with gills play a quiet, yet persistent melody that winds through the air and around the happy people unseen, insinuating itself between the words of conversations.

There is a buffet. Kip leads Stephen to it and leaves him to mingle. He has "things to do."

Stephen inspects the food. He is hungry, having been up all night. What he thinks is lobster turns out to be scorpion. What looks like salad suddenly writhes and flails a tentacle or two. There is bread, although mouldy. He sticks to that.

He has just pulled the blue crust off and is about to put the middle of the bread into his mouth, when Greytooth winds into view, very much at home.

"You're overwhelmed," the cat says with sympathy. "You obviously don't realise you're at the troll-and-hag side of the table. You don't need to eat that. You don't know where it's been. Here, let me show you where the good stuff is... don't worry, it's not raw fish..."

Greytooth leads him further along.

There are apples that taste like honey. Wine that looks like water. Bread and milk. Grass (bizarrely). Pebbles that taste a bit like dew and a bit like mist which dissolve on your tongue. Many different types of fruit, some spiky, others leathery and shrivelled, some strange colours that Stephen cannot name. Some more of that fiery drink Melanie gave him earlier, the sort that nearly popped the top of his head off.

Greytooth is distracted. "Look, I would watch you scoff all night. Believe me. But I have things to do... so... if you need me, I'll be over there."

Stephen looks. "Next to that blue Persian? She's pretty."

Greytooth walks away stiffly, tail in the air. "He's a *he*."

Stephen hides a smile. Already he's downed two measures of the knock-your-head-off drink. Things swim pleasingly in and out of focus. He begins to let go.

A couple of people dance with him. One has hooves. The other has a tiger's face.

Unfortunately, alcohol does not make the strangeness of these people less real, so he decides to throw himself into it, half-convinced he'll wake up in his own bed soon. Unless *this* is reality, and the rest is a dream?

As the night segues into the darkest hour before dawn, things get more raucous. Willowy dryads do impossible contortions and challenge their friends to better them. The band in the corner get louder, faster, and shoutier—sometimes racier—with an odd tempo that slows down and speeds up faster each time. People dance and skid around on sweat until they collapse. A half-man, half-monkey crashes onto the table and spins around on his head. Someone else takes his head off and loses it, because a bunch of satyrs are using it to play volleyball. Somebody sets light to the tent and tames the flames into golden lizards, which she then eats.

Stephen, drunk and only a little worried, stands in a darkened corner, sipping and watching people get themselves into trouble, laugh, enjoy it, then move on, leaving the trouble where it lay, and the cycle repeats itself. The music is so loud he can hardly think. It vibrates through his feet, right through his ribcage and his head. He might as well be a piece of music.

05.00

Stephen is just entertaining this thought, when a woman who is half-hag on one side and toffee-haired teenage girl on the other sidles up to him and tries to get him to come with her somewhere private.

It is then that Melanie comes to his rescue. The hag-girl looks at Melanie, shrugs, and walks away.

"You're 'er," Stephen slurs in surprise.

"Sorry?" she shouts.

"You're here!" he shouts back.

"Where else would I be?" She nips him playfully on the end of his nose.

Was that a first move? he wonders.

Before he can think about how to react, a young girl with wide bat-ears turns around and nudges him, then points to the other side of the tent, where Kip is walking up to a podium, looking serious.

Once behind the podium, Kip claps his hands for silence. The sound is magically amplified, and bounces around the tent like a thunderbolt. The band stop playing with something close to relief, sweaty and bedraggled. People stop dancing and shouting. Everyone turns to look at Kip. After the commotion, the absolute peace is eerie.

"This is the penultimate night—or should I say, morning—we will be staying here," Kip begins, and delivers a long and heartfelt speech. People applaud and chuckle occasionally, but Stephen isn't listening. He's drunk, he's tired, he's watching Melanie's face and trying to guess what she's thinking.

She looks back and widens her eyes at him meaningfully.

"S-sorry," he stammers. "I was just—"

She gives him a short push. "Go on! Don't embarrass him!"

He looks around, sees every single face in the tent eyeballing him, and realises Melanie is not trying to wind him up. Kip wants him up on the platform.

Flattered but bewildered, Stephen begins to regret telling most of the people here—he lost count of how many—the details of his disturbing dreams with a lack of inhibition; none of them showed much surprise, though a few laughed. Now, he feels they know too much about him. There is a knowing look in their faces as he makes his way through them.

Every individual stares him in the eye, unblinking, and they part like the Red Sea, allowing a narrow corridor of space through which he can walk.

Is it just him, or are those warm, friendly smiles slightly fixed? Are the stares a little cold? Are the hands at his back, propelling him along, rather firm? Or are they simply touching him for good luck, what with him being the only human person there?

Kip reaches an arm down and helps Stephen up next to him.

"A round of applause, please, for our latest addition to the family!" Kip shouts.

There is whistling, cheering, the waving of hands in the air. A couple of elephant-folk stamp their feet, and the tent shakes up and down.

Stephen is not sure he heard correctly. What new addition? There are no babies here. Then he feels Kip's hand clamp down on his shoulder, and realises with a sick feeling that Kip means him.

05.30

The noise dies. Stephen says, "I'm sorry?"

"We've been waiting with bated breath for this happy day, Stephen."

"Pardon?"

"The day when you finally come to join us. It's how we take on new staff."

"But I don't want to work in a... in a circus!"

"We're not a circus. We're your brethren. You're one of us."

"But—"

"Friends!" Kip addresses the sea of upturned faces. "Here we have a classic example of one of our own kind, sorely affected by the Human Condition. He is half and half, never whole. One side of him is dormant whilst the other is awake. Two unbalanced polarities. I am going to wake this man up. I am going to do it *properly.*"

Kip stretches his arms out, placing one hand palm-downwards in the air above Stephen's head, the other palm facing Stephen's left ear.

"I didn't agree to this!" Stephen hisses. "Whatever it is you think you're doing—"

"I am going to connect your polarities. Hold still."

"I didn't... you can't force me to work with this bunch. I can't do magic. I'm normal. And I haven't signed any contract."

"Ah. Stephen. You've eaten our food and drunk our spirits. According to our laws, that binds you to us."

Stephen ducks out from underneath the old man's hands, saying he's going now. He jumps from the platform, runs to the side of the tent with his arms wrapped around his head. Nobody attempts to give chase, but they are slow to move out of the way. They all stare.

He lifts the tent fabric and rolls under it, back into the cold steel light of dawn.

06.00

Trudging. Melted snow. Churned-up mud. Hangover.

His head reels. He trips. Throws up. Wipes his mouth with a handful of snow. Wants to die. Keeps walking.

On the way to his living quarters, Stephen is caught in a thunderstorm filled with swirling snow. Lightning tickles him twice but he pays it no attention. Goose-pimples erupt along his arms, face, neck and back. His blood simmers.

The door handle explodes into a million tiny pieces when he touches it.

He walks in and wipes his feet, creating miniature whirlwinds which die after thirty seconds. He tells the landlord the doorknob is broken, then goes to bed.

12.00

Sunlight strikes him in the face, and he has to get up. He forgot to close the curtains before retiring.

Greytooth is on the window-ledge, wanting to be let in.

Stephen does so.

"If you're going to speak, don't. I feel absolutely foul. I'm never drinking again."

"Meow."

He goes down, into the kitchen, and fixes himself a sandwich. The bread looks grey and unappetising, and whatever he's put in it—already he has forgotten, everything in the fridge seems the same—doesn't look like much.

The first bite is difficult to swallow. He chews it over and over for ten minutes before forcing it down. It tastes like cardboard, cotton wool, foil, thorns, bleach—everything a human is definitely not meant to eat. He gags, spits it into the bin, and throws the rest after it.

At first he thinks it is still a hangover. But as the afternoon wears on, and he cannot even drink tap water, he begins to suspect that something is wrong.

23.00

He dreams a dreamless sleep. Or perhaps he sleeps a dreamless dream?

* * *

Sunday, March 1ˢᵗ. Full Moon. Seventh Day of Welcome (Overdue).

He is plagued by strange faces, half-remembered déjà vu, and odd irritations.

The first face of the day hangs above the bed on waking, then slowly fades away. From then on, they seem to be in every reflective surface: hovering in the mirror behind him as he brushes his teeth, staring out at him from blank TV screens, watching or walking with him when he strolls past shop windows. He ignores them.

He carries on, with a calm demeanour, when little details he forgot he had dreamed the night before come to fruition, seemingly by chance. It puzzles him and makes him feel disorganised and disorientated.

When he stops to watch a display of television sets in one shop window, they all change channel after he sneezes.

The roadside weeds his feet touch bloom into exotic specimens, then wither and die in a moment, leaving piles of dead leaves. He feels like autumn, and he doesn't like it.

Objects which should—by rights, in his opinion—be inanimate, grow mouths and attempt conversation. After hissing at a post-box to "shut up," and receiving odd looks from passers-by, he learns that the voices can only be heard or understood by him. What language do they speak? Can a tree talk English, even if it originates from a different part of the world, or are his ears hearing one thing while his brain tricks him into thinking it's another?

"What's happening to me?" he asks aloud.

"Well, you're awake," a nearby rock humphs.

"I wasn't talking to you!"

"Excuse *me* for *breathing.*"

He runs back to his room on tiptoe, trying not to create holes in the tarmac, which is an odd sight for those watching. He aims to lock himself in when he gets there, pinch himself all over, splash his face with water, whatever he can think of—

"I'd like a word," his landlord says in the doorway. "Come through."

He goes through. They sit down.

"I won't beat around the bush, mate," the landlord says. "I've been having a fair few complaints about your behaviour... strange noises... things broken...you know."

"You're throwing me out, aren't you?" His hands curl into fists.

"I'll give you a month to get yourself sorted, but after that you'll have to go."

"I've got nowhere else to go!"

He has. He just doesn't want to go back.

"Contact the Housing Association."

He coughs and finds himself upstairs in the bathroom. He opens the door and walks back down to the kitchen, where the landlord gapes at the vacant seat with a frozen expression.

"How did you do that? What... happened?"

He loses his temper. "I don't know! I'm a freak! All right?"

The glass in the window behind the landlord cracks, bows outwards and shatters. The lights flicker in a staccato signal. Cupboard doors and drawers bang open and closed, cutlery and saucers ratting against each other, a noise like demented castanets.

The psychic storm abates, and the lost, now homeless young man says, "Don't bother. I know what you're going to tell me. I'll leave now. Just let me get my stuff."

His stuff consists of a battered briefcase containing a moth-eaten old suit, reams of notes and rough drafts, and his laptop. He leaves the laptop behind. He has a feeling that he won't need it where he's going.

Greytooth has gone again.

The man walks out of his old lodgings and into a half-familiar street. None of it is real to him anymore. He has forgotten who he is. The name is slippery, and trying to recall it is like holding onto a bar of soap—if he clings too tightly to who he is, it's no longer on the tip of his tongue, where he manages to make it stay.

He walks past a poster taped to a bench: TRAVELLING REUNION SHOW: ALL WEEK. He knows he's going the right way, and that's enough. He hopes they are still there.

Though he knows they will be. Greytooth will be there.

Then he will leave with his new brothers and sisters, and Stephen will be reunited with himself. Cured of humanity.

THE TRAVELING ZOO OF THE MYSTERIOUS AND EXTINCT

GREGORY L. NORRIS

Every few days, they performed the ritual of ashes. Oberth's mother gathered up the darkest cinders from the remains of the night's fire, ground them, and mixed them into water. Then, with painstaking attention to detail, she re-dyed the boy's hair and eyebrows. Whatever remained of the potion was massaged into his face and throat, as though his skin, already darkened permanently by the constant sun, was not to be trusted.

"For protection," she said whenever he asked why she was so determined to disguise him.

"From whom? No one cares," he argued, which gained him that look from her dark eyes.

"God cares," she said.

Oberth shrank from his mother's gaze and suffered the ritual. As she finished, his mother rattled off the day's list of expectations.

"Attend to the herd, draw extra water from the well, and we'll need wood for the fire."

Of course, he thought but kept the words to himself. He imagined them in his throat, levitating on tiny clouds, until he swallowed them down and they joined all the others he'd eaten rather than speak them and incur her anger. He assumed his mother loved him—as much as she was able to. But Oberth also understood that her love was fragmented, and beside it were jagged instances of intense hatred for the father he'd never met and never would.

"Now go, and be careful," she said.

He bounded away, disliking the unnatural, glazed sensation of his cinder-dyed curls and the smell of fires past on his cheeks. Within minutes of performing the first of his chores, sweat would make the ashes run, shattering his disguise. Not that anyone but the few women left would see his unmasking, and most of them still wore outfits of mourning black and walked around Vezucadia with heavy eyes that never looked directly at you.

* * *

Oberth's hair felt damp and itchy. He'd finished with their small herd of goats and was at the community well when a great spectacle drew his focus from the task to the cleft in the time-eroded rocks that surrounded the oasis on three sides. The boy's heart raced at the image of the procession, presently too far away to identify beyond the plumes of dust they kicked into the gray morning sky.

"Visitors," he gasped.

No one came to Vezucadia, not since the Time of Sorrow. These visitors were dressed in colorful garb and carried banners. Fresh fear slithered over Oberth's flesh at the possibility that the soldiers responsible for Vezucadia's sorrow had returned. If so, running would do him little good. He waited, watched. The procession drew closer, enough to see the men riding on horseback or seated atop wagons weren't armed. Their horses pulled carts. Other, more fantastic animals Oberth didn't recognize walked among the procession, many of them also drawing wagons. Several had long necks, funny faces, and blunt horns. Four of the giants lumbered like cattle, only they were many times larger and were gray-skinned and leathery-looking, with tusks, massive ears, and elongated trunks for noses.

The procession moved with an orderliness he didn't think possible from one so grand. Oberth tended the small herd of goats with less precision. He counted twelve wagons, twice that number of horses, and more people clad in bright plumage than the few living in Vezucadia. Their scarves and headdresses rode the wind around them like tongues of flame connected to shoulders. It was a glorious sight, the kind glimpsed once in a lifetime. But it also terrified him, for they were marching nearer and headed to the very place he occupied: the Well of Tears, as the women in town sometimes called it when they thought he wasn't within earshot while drawing water.

Oberth thawed. He took two hasty steps away from the well and toward the crumbling stone hut he and his mother knew of as home, and they were the most arduous movements of his young life. Eyes still trained on the spectacle traveling into Vezucadia's center, he panicked. His feet tangled. Oberth tripped. For a terrible moment, he imagined the giant animals trampling over him, stomping him into the aggregate and dust. Their footfalls rumbled across the ground, making his heart race even faster. Somehow, he got his legs under control and scampered away, a scream lodged in his throat.

It was the end of the world, he was sure.

"*Mama*," he attempted, but Oberth's voice wasn't there.

Several long seconds later, he found it and shrieked for her at the limit of his lungs.

* * *

They waited behind the door, which didn't keep out the sand when the wind demanded entrance and wouldn't do much better if giant animals charged at the timeworn wood.

"Soldiers," his mother said in barely more than a whisper.

"They don't look like soldiers," Oberth said.

His mother whirled from the door to face him. "And how would you know what soldiers look like?"

Her tone was poisonous, her eyes wide, damp, crazed.

"They look like colorful birds," Oberth said, unable this time to trap the words. "Like flowers in bloom."

She exhaled loudly through her nostrils, the sound reminding him of other times when she cried alone, thinking him asleep. His heart continued its mad pulse in his chest, impersonating an animal in a cage. His mother moved away from the door and to the hearth, where she poked at the embers beneath the pot containing their untouched supper. The air in the room pressed down, thick and heavy. The knock that hammered the outside of the door struck Oberth's ear like a thunderclap.

His mother gasped, froze. The knock sounded again, this time far less deafening in intensity.

"Don't answer it," she hissed, all color gone from her face, all emotion, too, save her horror.

She maneuvered over to him and clutched Oberth in a tightness that verged on strangulating. They waited, neither speaking, the air almost too dense to breathe. Eventually, their uninvited visitor left. Long minutes later, music drifted into the hut from the direction of the well.

* * *

His mother slept. In the fire's ember-light, Oberth watched her, wondering of the pain and terror that plagued her days and haunted her nights.

Colorful visitors had arrived in Vezucadia, where only a handful of childless women and one boy adorned in ashes lived. Oberth's curiosity smothered his fear. Sleep would prove impossible on this night. The music—mysterious, beautiful—haunted his memory.

Oberth crept to the door and opened it. The warm night breeze swept in, breaking apart the stagnancy. He slipped outside into a darkness broken up by a sliver of moon overhead and, nearer to the house, the fires of the new encampment. Upon the breeze was the pungent smell of animal scat and urine. Tents as colorful as the people who'd raised them glowed in the moonlight against the otherwise gray landscape.

Oberth sneaked through the distance, past the low stone wall that marked the hut's front boundary, onto the road pounded into the earth over the years, and away from the shuttered homes where Vezucadia's few souls endured the night, doubtless shaking with the same fear as his mother. Spare sounds came from the direction of the town's center, which was lit brighter than on any other night the boy recalled. Lanterns glowed inside tents, and among the illumination he made out figures moving back and forth like spirits, things only half there.

Oberth reached the well. The giant animals rested beyond the line of tents. Oberth desperately wished to see the wonders again, even if only by moonlight. Walking with his head aimed low, he skirted the well, approached the first of the tents, and froze. A figure stepped out of the darkness and loomed before him.

Oberth spun back in the direction of the Well of Tears and, beyond it, home. Another tall shadow blocked his escape.

* * *

The two colorful figures dressed in clothes so bright they nearly hurt Oberth's eyes marched him into the tent and before a figure resting in a funeral pose on a bed of equally ostentatious pillows. At first, Oberth wondered if the person was dead—he believed the body to be that of a man, given he general shape beneath its clothes, but he couldn't be sure until the corpse unsteepled his fingers, stood, and spoke.

"Finally, someone brave enough to respond to our invitation," his captor greeted in a deep voice.

"Invitation?" asked Oberth.

"We knocked on every door, humbly to offer what we bring here in exchange for a meal or even a kind word. But, finding none, we waited for you to seek out us. You are the first, Mister—"

"Oberth," he said.

The man, tall and festooned in elegant finery that partially hid his face, bowed. "A pleasure to greet you, Oberth. I am Master Tulle, at your service."

An exotic mélange of desert and spices filled Oberth's next shallow sip of air. "Master Tulle," he addressed. "You cannot keep me here."

"Keep you?" Tulle laughed as he straightened. "You're the one who's interrupted my nap. Stay, go—the choice is yours."

The guard dressed in vibrant plumage stepped aside and lifted the tent flap. Escape back into a night dappled in moonlight awaited. Oberth's relief was short-lived, because he understood that to leave would also result in disappointment.

"This is a zoo?" Oberth asked.

"Eh? More curiosity on the young mister's part, I see," Tulle said. He waved Oberth over to a table upon which grails carved from wood sat beside a bucket filled with well water. "Will you join me for a drink?"

Oberth hesitated.

"Suit yourself. What is this place called?"

"Vezucadia," Oberth said.

Master Tulle sipped before responding. "A grand name for such a small, unfriendly place. Why have we seen no other men? Apart from you, of course, Mister Oberth."

Oberth wandered over to the table. Master Tulle towered over him, but Oberth sensed no danger. In fact, the very opposite from the man in the vibrant costume. "They were all slain before my birth."

"By whom?"

"Warriors from a distant land. Holy men, they claimed, en route to liberate another place they claimed was even holier."

Though partially hidden by his garb, Oberth gleaned the look that washed over Tulle's face. "I see."

"You do?"

"Crusaders and their crusades," Tulle said, not bothering to hide his disgust. "When did this slaughter take place?"

Oberth shrugged.

"And how old are you, young mister?"

"Six. Almost seven."

Master Tulle finished his drink, set the grail down, and then reached into the tangle of curls atop Oberth's head. Oberth recoiled. Tulle rubbed his fingers together, clearly aware of the residue left behind, but he said nothing on the matter.

"Our fates are similar, each affected by the madness of religious zealots who have granted themselves the divine power to determine who is worthy of life on this world and who isn't," Tulle said. With flourish, he waved the same hand, and his plumage snapped in response, like a bird's feathers. "We have fled Assyria and the conflict that grows between two such religions. You asked about this zoo. I operate and protect a traveling collection of the mysterious and extinct."

Tulle's words captivated Oberth. "Extinct?"

"Relics from lost times—creatures that once were but are no more anywhere else in the world. Some that are the last of their kind and must be protected before they are killed off, hence the reason we travel."

"Where do you go?"

"To Africa, where some of my animals originated. In Africa's deep jungle, we will hide and live far from the coming bloodshed—bloodshed made on the ridiculous argument over the names of gods."

Oberth's eyes narrowed. "That isn't a ridiculous thing!"

Tulle laughed, though the response lacked all humor. "Isn't it? Which god deemed it necessary to dye your hair in ashes so none would know your true father's heritage?"

"What do you mean?" Oberth pressed. "The ritual is so no harm comes to me."

"What harm do you mean? Harm from the other widows of Vezucadia, and to disguise pale hair and paler skin, like those of the crusaders that laid waste here before you were born?"

Oberth heard the words and tensed. Tulle returned to the table and drank.

"I'm sorry—you are correct, of course, young mister," Tulle said. "I am tired and thirsty from our long travel, and it is late. Perhaps tomorrow you will return and we will show you wonders few eyes in this modern world would be blessed to see. Good night."

Tulle turned away, showing Oberth his back. As he did, Oberth noticed something about the man's shape, an incongruity that didn't appear correct.

Oberth approached the tent flap again, held open for him to exit through. He walked out, confused in equal doses by the ill fit of Master Tulle's plumage and the meaning behind his words.

The ashes. The soldiers who'd killed all of Vezucadia's men and boys, before he was born. *Born.* His hair was that of a crusader—she'd told him the soldiers had murdered his father. On the walk back to the hut, Oberth knew that was a lie. So was the reason behind the ritual of ashes.

He approached the door, entered quietly through it, and fell into her clutches. She tore Oberth's grip from the handle and held him by the shoulders.

"*Why?*" she demanded.

"I wanted to see—"

She struck his face. The pain was minor, the unexpected humiliation the real wound. "I try to protect you, and you walk toward danger without seeing!"

His mother raised her hand for a second blow. This time, he winced in anticipation, and she caught herself before the punishment was delivered. Oberth shook free.

"It's a zoo, with animals," he said through sobs.

"I don't care what it is."

"They only wanted water and for us to share food while here. They've traveled far—"

"We have no food to share."

"They're going to Africa. Said they'll show me the wonders they brought with them from Assyria."

"The sooner they leave—"

"*Mama*," Oberth cried and rubbed his cheek.

Her expression turned from one of flames beneath the skin to ice. "You are not to go near them again, Oberth. Not ever!"

* * *

He huddled on his blanket, his tears drying up but not his hurt. He hated the hut, hated all of Vezucadia and his life there. Mostly, he hated her. If Master Tulle was correct—and Oberth knew he was because he sensed the traveling zoo's leader was a man of truth—she had lied about his father, about *him*. A crusader? One of the men responsible for so many tears, so much sorrow.

He thought of the cliffs in the distance, one in particular. The one she would never look at save a time in the season before when, during an unexpected spell of rain, she grew distant, even frightening, and would stare past the open door in its direction.

"The Mother's Rock," she said, "where so many went when they learned they were with child. They climbed to the top and hurled themselves down to their deaths and those of their unborn babies."

The revelation had haunted Oberth since, leaving visions in his imagination of the canyon floor littered with bones—the larger of the mothers along with tiny, perfect skeletons in the hollows of their bellies.

And he remembered something more, what she'd let slip as the rain pounded down like tears from the clouds.

"I almost joined them."

Oberth rolled over. The room's darkness engulfed him and, long minutes later, so did sleep.

* * *

He went about the chores of the day, tending to the animals and wondering of Master Tulle and the curiosities in his traveling zoo. At the well, he drew water and carried it back to the hut, from the cut of his eye studying the colorful tents and mysterious creatures that would soon depart for Africa.

In the dusty prison of their home, he found her asleep in a curl, her black cloak like a stain of cinders in his thoughts. Oberth sulked to his room. There, the terrible knowledge he'd glimpsed tormented him. Released into his understanding, it likely always would. So would not seeing the mysterious and extinct housed within Master Tulle's traveling zoo. Though not old, Oberth was old enough to realize that once the zoo vanished from Vezucadia, the loss of such a thing would haunt him forever.

She was asleep.

Oberth returned to the gray landscape outside and didn't stop until he was once more surrounded by the vibrant color of the traveling zoo.

* * *

"Young Mister Oberth," Master Tulle greeted. "Welcome back."

Tulle extended his hand. The boy walked past the two guards keeping watch and into the protection of Tulle's arm.

Oberth offered up the meager gifts in his satchel—fruit, olives, and unleavened bread. "It isn't much, sir."

"Enough, my friend—and we thank you."

Master Tulle led Oberth out of the tent and through to the wagons. The air there was rich from the smell of the animals.

"Have you opened your mind to the possibilities of a world much vaster than the one you know?"

Oberth nodded, aware that the smile had returned to his face, the lingering sting of his mother's slap gone.

Tulle showed him the giants corralled and feeding on the sparse vegetation around the town's center. The ones with long necks grazed on the tallest of branches. The gray behemoths pulled up grass with their nose-trunks.

"Elephants and giraffes," Tulle said.

"They're incredible," Oberth sighed.

"There are many such animals where we're going, in Africa. Now, I will show you creatures few have seen—and fewer will see tomorrow."

A shiver teased the hairs at the nape of Oberth's neck. He fought it, failed. The chill tumbled.

"Follow me, Mister Oberth."

Master Tulle led him among the wagons, most of which contained animals caged behind metal bars. One held a pair of creatures that looked like cats, only these were much larger. The big cats paced. One threw itself at the bars where Tulle and Oberth stood at a safe distance.

"Tigers, ones with sabers for fangs," Tulle said.

In another caged wagon were three smaller creatures with fur-covered bodies but heads like birds. Adding to this confusion were the animals' wings.

"Gryphons, the last in Assyria," Master Tulle said.

Farther along, Tulle showed him a wagon with a closed chamber. Opening the doors revealed a nest made of tree roots. The nest contained two large eggs of a pale blue color flecked in gold. The nest was suspended over several flat rocks that radiated heat.

"What are they?" Oberth asked.

"Mysteries."

"You don't know?"

Master Tulle's mouth, only partially visible through his vibrant headdress, curled into a wide smile. "Just think of the wonder revealed to us should they hatch!"

There were other curiosities, other mysteries, but none so cryptic as what Tulle showed him in the last of the wagons. It contained an oblong, carved stone box with the head of a creature that looked like a man, though not exactly.

"What is it?" Oberth asked.

"A sarcophagus. It contains the bones of our ancestors, removed from Assyria and the centuries of looming conflict that will destroy it."

"Bones," Oberth sighed.

Again, his imagination wandered to the Mother's Rock and thoughts of his own origins while studying the sarcophagus that contained Master Tulle's and his people's.

"And now, you have seen everything."

Oberth blinked and returned to the moment. "No, there must be more, some mystery that I've missed."

"I'm afraid not, young mister," Tulle said. He extended his arm and the length of colorful fabric drifted wing-like behind him. "You've witnessed all of our mysteries. And it was my pleasure to share them with you, for neither you nor many others will ever glimpse these strange sights again."

Tulle walked Oberth to the well.

"Thank you, Master Tulle," the boy said. "I'm grateful. I'll remember you and your zoo always."

Tulle fixed him with a look through slitted eyes. "What I've shown you might chase you in dreams as well as daylight. When you're older, less willing to believe in the fantastic—beyond religious dogma, that is—you could find yourself questioning if I and this zoo were even really here."

They shook hands, and again Oberth thought, *His fingers...something is different, not quite right about them.*

"We leave soon, young mister," Tulle said. "It was good to have met you on our long and dangerous journey to Africa."

"You as well, Master Tulle."

Oberth turned, a heaviness in his chest, and walked from a world of color and mysteries back to the gray reality of his life with its cinders and secrets.

* * *

She wouldn't speak to him in words, but the language of her body came clearly to Oberth as she slammed down his plate, spooned stew onto it, and thrust the meager meal under his face.

"Mama?" he asked, which was the wrong decision.

"You went there, despite my telling you not to," she snapped, her anger so sharp that Oberth nearly dropped his spoon. "Why?"

The words were past his lips before he could trap them. "To see wonders of this world and creatures that are almost extinct before they're gone forever."

"Foolish boy," she admonished. "A waste of time when there is always so much work to be done here!"

Rage filled Oberth. He slammed his plate down on the table, mimicking her outburst, and stood from his chair. "Why do you hate me so, Mama?"

"Don't speak like that to me!"

"It's because of him—the one who is really my father. The one who came to Vezucadia with the other soldiers. The one whose hair you disguise with ashes so the women will never know your son was his. You hate me because of what he did."

"Oberth—"

His legs were moving quickly toward the door before he could order them to stop or she could get there first. "I love you, Mama. And so I give you this gift—to never again be forced to look upon me and see my true *Baba*."

He opened the door. The afternoon had mostly surrendered to shadows, but enough light remained for Oberth to see the zoo of the mysterious and extinct had resumed its travels. A bright patch of color was visible at the cleft in the rocks leading out of Vezucadia.

"Oberth!" she cried.

"Goodbye, Mama," he said.

Oberth ran.

And ran.

The crumbling relic of Vezucadia fell behind him. Oberth passed the Well of Tears and the open area where the zoo and its wonders had made camp, the space once more empty and left unmarked save for the tracks of numerous wagons and the footprints of giants.

Faster, he raced along the road, conscious that dusk was falling, the shadows stretching out like reaching hands seeking to corral him within the confines of the desolate town.

Sweating, he put on a burst of speed. Long seconds later, Oberth passed the Mother's Rock. He cast a look in its direction and, to his horror, a scream clawed at his ear. But he soon realized it was only the wind and raced on, following that waning burst of color until he thought he would drop from exhaustion.

"Master Tulle," he called. Summoning the last of his energy, Oberth repeated the words, shrieking them.

One of the guards at the rear of the procession turned around and spotted him.

"Hold up," the guard called.

* * *

They led him to the wagon containing the bones of their ancestors. Master Tulle stepped down from the reins.

"Mister Oberth, what are you doing here?"

Catching his breath in great, deep swoops, Oberth said, "The other night, when we first met. You said it was my choice to stay or go. I choose to stay with you."

Tulle eyed him in the dying daylight.

"And you were wrong. I did not see all of your wonders, Master Tulle. The most mysterious of all," Oberth said. "You and your people."

Master Tulle laughed. "You are an intelligent young man, Mister Oberth."

Tulle removed the headdress that covered most of his face. His forehead was taller, shaped differently, his eyes, nose, and mouth closer together than on any of the people Oberth had ever met.

"Who are you?" Oberth asked.

"Cousins of men. Men of a different offshoot than you and yours. And just as extinct as the tigers with sabers for teeth, the gryphons, and all the other wonders that reside in this zoo, for we are the last of our kind."

"I want to go with you and the animals to Africa," Oberth said.

"You?"

"I'm a hard worker—and the last of my kind, in danger of becoming extinct. *Please*," Oberth begged.

Master Tulle didn't answer straight away, and the next few seconds tolled with the weight of minutes, hours. But then Tulle smiled, and hope filled Oberth's heaving chest.

"Come aboard. You can ride with me," Tulle said.

Oberth hopped onto the wagon. The procession resumed its slow, steady march forward beneath the light of the rising moon and headed toward a distant land.

THE WRATH OF NABU

Nickolas Urpi

i

"Come, children! Hurry!" Nalabakh yelled, his clawed hand outstretched to gather the children into his arms.

The sparks in the distance brightly sparkled in their eyes. They were tepid to trust him, but knew they had no choice. The four of them scrambled into his arms, the two oldest pushing the younger ones ahead to protect them.

His clawed wings then surrounded them, and his ram's head glowed a luminescent blue as he hardened into stone. The children were so pressed together, even in his large body, they could hardly breathe. Only a space here and there about Nalabakh's neck allowed some air to circulate, but the spaces were tight for a reason.

In another moment the slaves of Nabu were upon Nalabakh's hardened stone body and with their teeth and claws scraped and bit at him, savagely reaching for the children inside.

The slaves of Nabu were long, lizard-like creatures with heads that resembled leopards. Their claws were long sharp hooks, and their tongues forked. Their bodies were scaled, and they stood like sapiens. The children cried from inside Nalabakh's stone sanctuary, as the rank breath of the slaves seeped into their nostrils like a poisonous fume.

One of the slaves managed to insert a treacherous claw through the space in Nalabakh's neck and reach down to the children. The children pressed against each other to avoid it, and yet it came closer and closer as the slave reached further into the space.

The slave suddenly emitted a terrifying screech, his claw pulled out of the hole as he was wrenched from the body of Nalabakh. Another screech followed a horrifying slashing sound, and the slave was dead.

Two figures had burst forth from the village that had surrounded the burning city and began to slaughter the slaves, biting and clawing at them and tearing them in two. The children could see through the small openings, in the light of the white moon and orange fire, the figure of two gargoyles, the kin of Nalabakh, whom they had seen watching them from atop the temples while they played in the streets in what seemed a lifetime ago. The gargoyles were killing the slaves and driving them back to the burning City of Nor, where the children had once lived and thrived but two days hence.

In the Great Fire of Nabu, many were killed, but the four children, steadfast friends, were playing outside the city gates when the slaves of Nabu descended from the sky and wrought death on the city. Many of the sacred guardians of the city rushed to its defense, but they were powerless against the great number of slaves and the power of Nabu, who was strong in the city that once worshipped him.

The four children had run into the forests and hidden for the duration of the day, when the slaves were blind and weak. At nightfall, the slaves were awake again with sight and began to pursue the children. They were, in turn, pursued by the gargoyles, the last remaining of the guardians who scoured the countryside looking for survivors, the city in the meantime burning continuously, as though the fire fed on its memory of the screams.

When the last of the slaves could be heard howling through the plains and decrepit to the city, one of the other gargoyles grabbed Nalabakh's head and breathed a white fire into his eyes. A white-blue glow spread over his whole body until his features were lost in the illumination. The other gargoyles peeled a full, thick layer of stone skin from him and his body relaxed into flesh. The children scrambled out from his arms and he heaved his breaths as though he had never breathed before.

There were four children, two boys and two girls, their heads covered in curly red and brown hair, their eyes a soft violet color, and their white and gold tunics stained with blood and dirt.

They were frightened and huddled together as they gazed at the three gargoyles standing before them, hideous and terrifyingly huge: Nalabakh with his ram's head, the second a griffon, named Yarabakha, and the last with the head of snake, named Ilubakh. Their bodies all resembled mammals with human-like arms, and each had a pair of bat's wings on their back with claws. Nalabakh was the only one with a long trail of spikes down his back to the end of his long serpentine tail.

"Jelu is hurt," one of the children said.

Nalabakh turned and saw that, indeed, the smallest of the girls had been scratched by the claw of the slave of Nabu.

"It is too late for Jelu," Yarabakha said. "We must leave her here and continue on without her."

"No!" the other children said, holding on to Jelu who collapsed onto the ground, breathing heavily. Blood began to drip from the edges of her lips, and a gurgling noise seemed to boil up from inside her. "We can't leave her! She's our friend!"

"What's happening to her?" Usai, the oldest boy, asked.

"What has happened to all the other people of the City of Nor," Nalabakh said, examining Jelu's wound. "She is becoming a slave of Nabu, a beast."

"Why?"

"Because of the 'crimes' of the City of Nor," Nalabakh replied. "Long ago, the god of writing, Nabu, gifted to mankind script and speech so that they could communicate. For the longest time, Nabu was worshiped every year with a carnival that lasted twenty-seven days for the twenty-seven letters of the alphabet. Only this year, the carnival was canceled, the three kings no longer wishing to be beholden to Nabu's script. They had a simpler script devised, a new language in the making, that diverged from the one Nabu gave them. Nabu's wrath was sudden. He sent demons among the city, a bite or scratch removing one's ability to talk or communicate forever. Jelu has no chance. She is already scratched; she will forget how to talk or communicate, and what is worse, can infect you with her disease.

We must leave her here."

"No! You have to save her," Usai screamed.

"I cannot," Nalabakh replied.

"The son of Sachi can," Ilubakh said. "I can take her."

"You don't know if Mochi is still alive," Nalabakh replied. "It is too dangerous. Nor do you know if he will help save the life of a human. He is a uniped; they have withdrawn their love of other creatures, and with good reason."

"We must try!" Ilubakh said. "I have heard it said amongst the birds that he hides away in the mountains to the north, in a valley just beyond, where there are fruit groves he tends. He will help the girl; he will see she is just a child. We have already failed the people of Nor; we must do all we can. Jelu is our ward, our oath."

"We will need you on the road to the east," Nalabakh replied. "How can you hope to save the girl on your own? The slaves will double in number just to pursue you."

"You must allow me to try," Ilubakh insisted, lifting Jelu into her arms. "You must."

Nalabakh sighed and waived Ilubakh off.

Ilubakh flapped her bat-like wings and took off above the trees. Not long after, Nalabakh could hear the beating of wings and the slaves of Nabu following close behind her, riding great carrion birds.

Nalabakh turned to the children and Yarabakha: "We must go."

The thunder followed them as they headed off into the plains, the children unable to keep pace with Nalabakh, who was breaking a trail for them through the tall grass. Yarabakha followed up the train, keeping his eye on the children, especially the youngest of them, Térala, who was wont to wander off here and there to play with the prairie dogs that whistled as they traveled.

"Where are we going?" Usai asked Nalabakh.

"Beyond the edge of the desert, where Nabu cannot reach you," Nalabakh replied. "There you will be safe. He has no power."

Usai nodded, and being the oldest of the children, grabbed the other two by the hands and made sure they followed him and did not go astray. Just as the sun turned orange in the sky, Nalabakh led them to a cavern, where, sliding in, they would be protected for at least one night from the searching eyes of the slaves.

ii

Usai awoke to a circle of candles and a faint whisper of chanting.

"Nalabakh?" he called out in a whisper of his own.

Nalabakh was nowhere to be found. Nor were his other traveling companions. He was no longer in the caverns to which Nalabakh had led them.

Instead, he saw that the forest beyond the edge of the candles moving. Figures from beyond the edge of the trees entered the circle, each one crafted from intertwined branches. Moss grew down their heads like hair, some of them in the shape of centaurs, others in the shape of birds, others in the shape of satyrs, and others as creatures he had never seen before, with their wings like branches and feathers of wildflowers.

They circled Usai, their whisperchants flooding the night air like a distant echo.

Usai tried to break away from the circle, but the candles flared up and prevented his escape.

"Do not fear!" the lead centaur said, his antlers formed of strong oak. "You have been summoned by the people of the woods. I am Caranur, their leader."

"Summoned for what?" Usai asked, trembling and stuttering.

"For the festival of the people of the woods," Caranur replied. "You will be protected by our people forever. We find one creature in all the world that is great need of protection, and that creature becomes one of us for eternity, to live and protect, until the ends of nature and the wood."

"I can't. I have to go back! I have to protect the others!" Usai cried. "Don't you see?"

"It is too late for that," Caranur replied, softly and distantly, as though he could not understand, even in his wisdom. "You will become one of us, child. Do not fear."

Usai looked down at his hands, which were already beginning to harden, bark-like flakes forming on the edges of his fingers. The ends of his hair were turning to moss and already he could taste his own lips turning to wood.

"Do not worry," the others in the circle sang, a cheerfulness buried deep within their voices. "For you will be safe for always..."

"No, I can't," Usai shouted. "I need to go back!"

A shrill voice sounded in the air, followed by the thunderclap of wings. Usai looked up and soaring down from the above the canopy he saw a pair of red eyes and a mouth of fire. Usai covered his head and fell into the dirt.

Swooping down and clawing at the circle of protectors was Nalabakh! He fought and clawed at them, burning and biting, whipping with his sharp tail and shredding bark with his teeth.

Caranur shouted to him: "It's too late! You can do nothing to us. Usai is one of us and shall always be one of us! Soon, he will even always have been one of us! Allow us to protect him."

"I cannot! He is destined for more than to become of you! He has a destiny beyond the edge of Nor! His friends need him!" Nalabakh replied, biting and clawing still.

For all his exhaustion, he could do nothing, and the people of the woods continued to grow back whatever he took from them.

"You have other wards; this ward is ours," Caranur replied, always calm and confident in their hold on fate. Nalabakh turned to Usai, whose arms were now fully wooded. The moss was already growing on his back and a daffodil bloomed in the darkness from the sides of his ear.

"Help me," Usai begged, in tears.

"I am sorry I failed you," Nalabakh said from the edge of the candles, his own voice filled with pain, as in Usai's tears were the tears of an entire city he could not protect, and yet he was still one child he could not preserve. "There is a magic here beyond my control. I promise you I will care for your brother and sister and protect them."

"Don't leave me!" Usai cried.

"I must," Nalabakh whispered. He could not reach Usai from beyond the edge of the candles, whose magic fire was beyond his own, though he wished to comfort him with a touch.

But even that was denied him.

Before Usai protested again, he rose up into the air and flew off, his tears like the rainfall over the trees who tasted the bitterness of his sorrow and trembled as he flew over them.

iii

Jelu began to wheeze eerily, a pale and unsightly color spreading over her skin with small, oval boils. Ilubakh knew she must find the son of Sachi soon, or else it would be too late for her.

The seven sons of Sachi were unipeds like their father, and had each led a separate faction of unipeds to a place where they made their home after Sachi's brave slaying of the Great Demon. For years, the unipeds thrived, until the centaurs and humans outnumbered them, and drove them across the waters of the seas to find new homes. Some perished in wars, others in the waters of the ocean. Only Mochi, the magician, remained on land, the only son not to lead a people of unipeds. He chose a hermetical life and found a nestled place of sanctum where he could retreat and live. It was said to be enchanted such that the eyes of centaurs and humans could never find him, but Ilubakh, being of enchanted stone, hoped his magic did not extend to her. She could see the mountains where the unipeds had once made their home just ahead, a thin blue shadow against a cloudy horizon.

Cawing and wings surrounded Ilubakh, Jelu cradled in her arms. She looked about her and saw slaves of Nabu riding carrion birds in armor bursting through the dark, misty clouds in pursuit of her. Realizing she could hardly fight in the air, she dove beneath the clouds, the birds delayed in their pursuit, as they could not dive as quickly as Ilubakh could and were not autonomous.

They followed her nonetheless, twirling and chasing as she made her descent. Several of them approached her, reaching out with long spears in the hopes of piercing her fleshy skin. She defended against these attacks with the claws of her feet and wings, still plummeting towards the earth, though more careful than her pursuers because of Jelu.

Just as they reached a canopy of trees, she pulled up, extending her wings. Several of the carrion birds, burdened with armor, crashed into the trees and fell down into the forest, wounded, the slaves falling alongside them. They were not, however, all gone, and many continued their pursuit above the trees.

Jelu began to speak in the tongue of Nabu, chanting a song that summoned the slaves and slowed down Ilubakh. Ilubakh sang her own enchantment, hoping to counter the magic of Nabu, but was short of breath and could not keep up with Jelu. She could not stop Jelu from her song while carrying her and steadying her flight, and only hoped that her wit and strength could outmatch the slaves even in the air.

One of the slaves pierced her side with a spear while in flight. She reached down with a free arm and wrenched it out of her. They struggled back and forth, tugging at the spear while the carrion bird cried for its companions to descend on Ilubakh. Ilubakh screamed as she pulled the spear from the slave's hand and, flipping it around, plunged it into the carrion's neck.

The carrion cried and crashed into the trees below, a trickle of blood spraying into the air.

The rest of the slaves were gaining distance on Ilubakh.

Ilubakh, turning to view them in pursuit of her, did not see the top of an emergent tree, dominant above the forest below. She crashed into its thick branches and was thrown down into the snow at the base of the mountain.

When Ilubakh awoke, Jelu had disappeared. The tracks were hidden from her in in the smooth, laden snow. At first, Ilubakh panicked, believing her ward had been lost to Nabu, but the shadows overhead of the armored carrion reassured her that this would not be the case as they would have no reason to search for her once Jelu was secured. They, too, were searching for Jelu.

Ilubakh rose and hid beneath the trees, careful not to be spotted by the watchers. She looked around at first, hoping to catch a glimpse of Jelu, when she detected in the air a mysterious floral scent.

The entire forest was covered with several inches of snow and the trees were Chichesterungs, whose earthy tones were faint, especially during the winter, and could not be the source of the sweet aroma. Intrigued and without any other clue as to Jelu's whereabouts, she pursued the scent, which only seemed to return with a faint breeze that gave the impression to have come from the mountain.

Trees were sparse on the base of the mountain and so she crawled on all fours, covering herself with her wings when a carrion soared overhead so as to appear a large stone, though she dared not turn completely to stone without a gargoyle or priestess of the gate to awaken her. As all the priestesses had been slain in the destruction of Nor, only Nalabakh and Yarabakha could enfleshen her from her stone-state.

She found that the scent led to a pass along the side of a mountain. After some digging beneath the snow, she uncovered a trail had been trodden before with the evidence of a footprint leading into the mountains cleverly hidden beneath the snow. The single print lit the fires of hope within her, and she looked out into the mountain pass, a fog masking the end of the path.

Ilubakh, knowing she had no choice, followed the direction of the path, the fog obscuring the way ahead but also the way above. Soon, the caws of the carrion and screeching of the slaves were distant echoes, and she could walk upright. The fog thickened, however, and made it difficult for her to find her footing.

She followed the path for some time, crunching on snow so old it had frozen to ice, and yet appeared undisturbed. She wondered how old the pathway was, and who had come before. She knew she would not be able to see the ground, even if she wiped away the snow and ice. There was no alternative but to continue on.

iv

"Can we really risk that there is no danger in passing through the caverns?" Nalabakh inquired of Yarabakha, whose sight could pierce the darkness only so far.

"I see much that is in peace down here, and much at war, but nothing I can detect will harm the children. Keep them away from the waters, though. There are mooncuttles down here."

"The mooncuttles will not harm them," Nalabakh said.

"No, not purposely, but the small one, Térala, can be at risk. If they are afraid, they will grab her with their tentacles and squeeze."

"Are there any creatures that hunt mooncuttles?"

"Not to my knowledge, not save humans, and perhaps centaurs in the old days."

"I'm hungry," Térala said, her voice soft from retaining her fear of the gargoyles, whose aspect was even more terrifying in the dim darkness of the cavern, with only Yarabakha's handfire to guide them.

"I know, but we have nothing to eat, so we will have to wait until morning, all right?" Fearlai said to Térala. The boy lifted her into his arms, their curling hair locking into to each other, as though tied inextricably through fate. Nalabakh wondered at the strength of humanity, that two children that had never crossed paths in their lives should so easily become brother and sister in the wake of terrible times. If there was hope, it existed in their love.

"Come children," Nalabakh said. "Follow Yarabakha and do not fall into the waters."

"What waters? I do not see waters," Fearlai replied. His foot then broke the surface, and he only just barely pulled up before seeing a distant glow beneath the now rippling veneer. When the waters calmed, they almost seemed to disappear.

The water was so perfectly still in the caverns it reflected the ceiling like a mirror. The only indication of its presence was when a drop from the ceiling, having collected from the moisture and coolness in the air, finally collapsed into the waters below and created a ripple. That, or when the moonlight streamed in from the nooks and crannies of the caverns for the mooncuttles to feed on, as their diet consisted entirely of the moon's pale threads.

Yarabakha did his best to illuminate the path forward while simultaneously allowing the children to see the way before them. Fearlai could only carry Térala so far before needing to surrender her to Nalabakh, who worried that carrying the child would endanger her without him being free to protect their rear.

The caverns began to wind about, becoming narrow, then wide, then narrow again, the water slowly fading such that there was only a slippery smooth surface below that was difficult to tread confidently.

"Do you even know if there is an exit?" Nalabakh asked Yarabakha.

"There is. I can smell it."

"So can I," Fearlai confidently declared. "There is a smoothness, and a gentle breeze at times."

Nalabakh smiled at the boy's great confidence, though he suspected optimism was the cause. He wondered at their resilience, and knew then, as he gazed in the dim light at the children he was guarding, that the gargoyles and guardians who had abandoned hope for men for their selfishness and greed had lost sight of the beauties of life and love that they could possess and exchange.

His life would be well served to protect that.

Rumbling from the interior of the cave woke Nalabakh from his contemplation, however, and his vigilance returned.

"What is it?"

"I can't see," Yarabakha replied. "Hide the children!"

Nalabakh quickly gathered the children and pressed them to one side of the cavern. Térala started to cry, but Fearlai put his hand around her mouth and shushed her. With his free hand, he held her close and stroked her curly hair. Nalabakh's body pressed up against them, squeezing them against the cold cavern walls. He dared not turn to stone in the case of danger. The slow heaving of Nalabakh's chest waxed and waned ever so slowly against their backs.

With Yarabakha's light extinguished, there was nothing to help ascertain what it was that caused the rumbling, which had stopped so suddenly. Yarabakha took several steps forward and looked out across the corridor. An eerie purple glow from a distant passageway. The tingling of his claws indicated that it was either very large or numerous. As the glow approached, he sensed not that it was a single source, but a multiplicity of lights, each held by a Quarrolo.

The Quarrolii were an ancient species of stonebeings who overthrew the overlord who brought them to life. In the victory of their struggle, the enchantment the overlord had used to awaken them to life began to fade. Only their proximity to the center of the earth allowed them to survive and renew themselves, as long as they observed the ritual carnival every new moon cycle.

Yarabakha was well aware of the rumor that the Quarrolii were mistrustful of all beings and even each other. Gargoyles, however, were foreign to them.

Even from the distant caverns, Yarabakha could make out the figures of the stone beings, cylindric bottoms and rounded tops, as though they were robed. Extending from their bodies were small stone hands holding crystals illuminated purple, a simple enchantment not so different from Yarabakha's handfire. Their faces were covered in masks of simplistic design, each one unique, but all of them comprised of geometric patterns.

"They have awakened and are on their way here," Yarabakha whispered into Nalabakh's pointed ears. "The Quarrolii. They will most certainly know the way out."

"Can we trust them?"

"We can trust no one, but we must take risks. If this cavern is as deep as we hope it to be, it may allow us to escape the slaves entirely. Nabu cannot watch us down here, and his slaves will not find these caverns. Let me approach them in silence. This way they may not be alerted to you or the children."

Nalabakh nodded and Yarabakha walked very gently out into the path of the Quarrolii. The lights continued to approach until they were right up against Yarabakha. Yarabakha was about to speak when they then continued through him, as though he were vapor. One by one, they passed as ghosts.

"Come, Nalabakh!" Yarabakha shouted. "They are passing through me! They are surfacing! These Quarrolii do not have the magic to survive any longer. They are going upwards. Be swift!"

Nalabakh jumped off the wall, carrying Térala with him.

"Can you keep pace?" he asked to Fearlai, who nodded confidently. "Then, come!"

They pursued the Quarrolii, whose pace gradually progressed along the corridors.

"How do you know they are leading us closer to the desert and not further?" Nalabakh shouted to Yarabakha.

"Because they are seeking open space to perform the last carnival of the

Quarrolii. They will die soon, fading from life entirely. Their magic has gone at last and the enchantments cannot hold them. They already cannot see or hear us. They are going to dance and play and smell the beauty of the air one last time! Such is it written!"

The Quarrolii's pace quickened, and soon, Fearlai was having difficulty keeping up. Both the children were already tired from the journey they had to endure thus far. Yarabakha lifted Fearlai onto his back and they continued on, the twirling wet pathway illuminated by the Quarrolii's magic stones.

Fearlai reached out and watched as the stone, it, too, a thin half-existence, passed through his hand. A laughter almost escaped from him. An endless stream of Quarrolii there seemed to be, and soon enough, other streams of the creatures joined up as they made their way towards the edge of life.

v

The path through the snow ended abruptly in front of a cliff wall. Ilubakh reached out and felt the rockface. Confused and disheartened, she wondered if there was some other path that led away. There was no reason anything living, especially Mochi, would walk the path that leads to such an abrupt end. It occurred to Ilubakh that the footprint could have belonged to some other stray uniped or perhaps a human with one foot. Perhaps it was only an illusion to keep visitors from finding the sage. Perhaps the pathway broke off and she did not notice, and the entire mountain range was some elaborate labyrinth designed to prevent visitors from discovering his orchard.

She leaned one hand against the rockface, feeling the coldness of the stone. Tiredness swept over her, and the frigid air was digging into her muscles at long last. Even with all her strength, she could not resist the low temperatures forever.

The breath of excitement swept over her as she felt a current, not unlike electricity, momentarily burst through her from her palm. She put both her palms on the rockface and let her nails dig into the ice that had frozen along its side.

A thin crack in the rockface, running up the entire mountainside, was visible only from one angle, and through it, Ilubakh could detect the slightest bit of magic. The door was sealed shut through an enchantment so strong it could hardly be felt by any being less powerful and less autonomous than her.

Ilubakh ran her mind through sealed door enchantments, feeling for some way to open the door. Spells, passwords, pressure points, keyholes, nothing seemed to break the self of the enchantment.

"Jelu!" Ilubakh called out in final desperation.

The rock against her hand transformed into a silk curtain and Ilubakh fell through. Layers upon layers of cloth she collapsed into, until she struck the floor. When she turned, she saw the entrance to the cave through the transparent curtains. A soft, sweet breeze familiar to her blew in from the way forward, and a golden light bounced off the walls of the cavern, warming the rock. The light led her on until she reached the exit, which opened to an orchard in bloom and not yet quite filled with fruit. Instead, blossoms of white, purple, and pink greeted Ilubakh, the sensitive petals falling to her feet at the slightest touch of breeze, forming a carpet of soft colors.

She turned around, but in every direction there seemed to be a row of trees, and the way back to the mountains was hidden, as though it had never been there at all. Instead, all she could see was color and light, and just beyond the ridge of the trees, a distant blue line signifying the mountain range.

Not knowing where to turn or which of the labyrinthine rows of trees to follow, Ilubakh determined that any path was as good as any other path, seeing as she was being led into this place to begin with.

Her assumption proved correct when the pathway cleared and a stone cottage, circular with a cone roof, greeted her. The stones on the hut were gray with age, but with a limited amount of moss stuck between the grooves, as though someone took painstakingly quality care in scrubbing away the potential rot from the house. Some goats were out front, their bells jangling as they moved from grass patch to grass patch.

Ilubakh approached and entered the cottage unannounced.

The first thing to catch her eye was the bed in the far corner on which Jelu slept. Her breathing seemed regular, and the devilry that had almost completely possessed her seemed absent.

The rest of the cottage consisted of a table, a fire spit in the center of the room, the cone of which opened to release the smoke, and jars and materials of every sort piled here and there, with scrolls in barrels accompanying them.

"She is feeling much better," a calm tenor voice from behind the door said.

Ilubakh closed the door behind her and looked at the uniped: red skin with old warts, an overly large, single foot, a wide nose, but otherwise extremely humanesque.

"I placed a spell over the door," the uniped said from his chair, arranged such that there was a layer of cotton stretched tightly between two cylinders of wood. "Only someone who knew the girl's name could enter."

"You must be a powerful magician," Ilubakh replied. "Powerful enough to place a spell with a word that you do not know."

"Not really," the uniped replied. "Not if you've been at it long enough. It's simple. Experience teaches one a lot about skill, but sometimes very little about life."

"You've learned quite enough I imagine," Ilubakh replied. "Haven't you, Mochi son of Sachi?"

"Ah," Mochi smiled, nodding. "You know of me. I very much suspected that, though I must confess I have not seen the likes of you before. Are you a gargoyle, perchance?"

"Yes."

"Then it has happened? The end of Nor? I did not think I would live to see the day," Mochi said happily as he stood up. "Come, let us speak outside where we are less likely to wake her."

Mochi hopped over to the door, coughing once or twice as he did so, his old bones crackling with every hop. He briefly glanced back to check Jelu's condition and then followed Ilubakh out and closed the door behind him.

"I am surprised you are so pleased to hear of the end of Nor," Ilubakh said. "Many have died. I do not think that should be something to feel joy over."

"The death of those people is not what I feel joy for," Mochi responded. "My smile was grievously misplaced. I will not deny, however, that I have longed for the end of a civilized world so that we may return to an unpredictable one. My orchard will be the last organized intelligent will, the last city, the last nation."

"Even beyond the edge of the desert?" Ilubakh inquired.

"Even there," Mochi replied. "There is nothing there. This girl can go nowhere, and any other refugees will find nothing but seaside. The humans there perished long ago."

"Then why do you rejoice the end of civilized kingdoms?" Ilubakh inquired. "I do not understand: did not your father lead his people to peace and build a world of their own?"

"He did what he had to do," Mochi sighed. "I loved him; he was the best of the unipeds. It was very difficult not to love him, but long have the spirits plagued us with their jealousy and desire for control. How long did they perpetuate that ridiculous festival worshipping Nabu at Nor? And when at long last they discovered that they needed him not, their festival became truly bright, lit up with the love of dance, food, life, culture, art, and romance! What was this god's response? To destroy them. Now is our ultimate revenge. By destroying all semblance of intelligent life, what do they accomplish? Nothing to control. Nothing to manipulate. Nothing to herd into cattle, no one equally subservient to them."

"I can see then why you would want the end of Nor."

"Not want," Mochi said, shaking his finger. "I knew it would come, and so can at least appreciate the positive fruits of it."

"It still is difficult to believe that the end of a festival could cause such hatred in a god."

"Not a god," Mochi corrected. "Nabu is no god. He is a spirit. They are different. What kind of god is so jealous? What kind of god is so unmerciful? A god is all-powerful and therefore self-sufficient. Nabu needs control to be a spirit. That is what the spirits are: they control mountains, rivers, writing, art, music, so that they can be worshipped. So yes, the festival, the language itself, was the source of Nabu's power, and therefore ego and existence. No, he is no god!"

"What about Jelu?"

"There is one answer, only. She may remain with me where she is safe. I will outlive her, and she will be the end of her kind."

"No," Ilubakh replied. "The others. They will need her."

"The others cannot hope to make it to the edge of the desert save by some miracle. And even if they do, what hope can three humans have against the might of this earth? They cannot hope to reproduce, and you cannot follow them. Just one step into the desert and you will turn to dust, as the enchantment that was made under Nabu's kingdom will fade under Nabu's kingdom."

"They can have a chance for a life. There may be other humans out there. Yarabakha has felt it, even if he cannot fully see it."

"Yarabakha's abilities of foresight are as reliable as trying to breathe in the future from here. Nothing is set! Nothing is known! Nothing is knowable, or else do you think the spirit with all his power would have conceived of a scenario by which four children escape his wrath? If he would not stop until every child was enslaved, why would he allow a single one to escape? No. Yarabakha knows nothing. And you know nothing. Here is an opportunity for the child to survive instead of struggle."

"Out there is a chance for that same child to live instead of just survive!" Ilubakh yelled. "How can you not see that she deserves a life with her own kind? To forge her own life and not live in the shadow of your self-imposed exile?"

Mochi did not respond for quite some time. He breathed in the sweet air and the flooding beauty of the orchard, detecting full well the enchantment beneath that had allowed it to survive in the wildness of the mountains.

"I cannot say that there is not a hint of truth lying beneath all that you have said," Mochi replied. "I still counsel against it, but as she is your ward, she is subject to your protection. If the freedom to struggle is more valuable to your belief than the security of these confines, I will allow you to leave with her. But only if you believe this to be so. Meditate on it while she recovers."

Ilubakh nodded, while the old uniped used her shoulder to stand and enter his cottage.

In the meantime, she walked through the orchard dwelling on questions she had never dwelt on before, questioning truths she had long held by the nature of her position, and thinking deeply about her decision, over which Jelu had no autonomy, nor could she. Her whole life would be shaped by Ilubakh's decision, and the adult she would grow into, the adult that would look back on Ilubakh's decision and judge it, would be shaped by the decision itself. And the circular nature of life would continue to spin around in her head until Jelu awoke, and then her decision would be mandated.

She could not delay.

vi

At last, the caverns opened to spacious grasslands, familiar to Nalabakh's knowledge of the territory, just beyond of which lay the desert at the edge of Nabu's kingdom. He kept a watchful eye out on the plains, though there seemed no sign of the slaves present. Fearlai and Térala were exhausted from the walk, their feet blistered and sore. They collapsed as soon as they felt the fresh softness of the plain dirt.

Yarabakha scoured the landscape looking for enemies but could not see with the light of the Quarrolii surrounding him. The Quarrolii filtered out of the cavern's exit into a large circle that filled the plains. The circle then began to alter, change into a spiral, and the spiral into a pattern that could only be described as random, with no pattern whatsoever, and in that sense represented chaos, while being truly ordered.

"What are they going to do now?" Fearlai asked, his eyes half open and Térala sleeping with her head resting on his chest.

"They are going to celebrate," Yarabakha answered, moving over to where the children were resting and sitting beside them.

"But didn't you say they were going to die?" Fearlai asked.

"Yes."

"Then why would they be happy? Why aren't they afraid?"

"Because they have lived. Life is filled with memories of laughter and joy, kindness and love, and it is good to celebrate these things. They celebrate much as you did, with food and dance, with love and joy and togetherness. Is there not a better way to live?"

Fearlai shook his head and leaned on Yarabakha's arm to let his own tired eyes rest. He did not witness the Quarrolii begin their festival.

They circled in place, spinning until their stone cloaks flew off and disappeared into the air. They all, then, extended their hands and spun on their toes and danced to the tune of their own music, whistling in a harmonious counterpoint with such consonance that even Nalabakh was amazed. He turned to Yarabakha to have him get the children up to continue on their journey, but with one look from Yarabakha, knew they needed to rest, as even past the desert they would have a hard journey with none to look after them.

Nalabakh consented and watched as the Quarrolii unfolded into graceful beings of stone, their purple lights pressing into their hearts and lighting up their bodies to the ends of their fingers. They danced and ate, stores forming from mist and toys and food forming from dust. They laughed and joked, all the while, the music swirled about them, and not a single one of them was seen without a smile.

At long last the blue light of dawn crept over the edge of the plains and the Quarrolii gathered into a circle yet again, their foods having been devoured, their laughter drowned out by the gentle humming of their murmur and their prayer, that some greater being take mercy on them, and grant them rest by the light of day.

By the time the sun had risen, and the orange light painted the blades of grass, the Quarrolii had completely vanished. Their light was extinguished to be seen no more.

Fearlai had awoke at some point during the festival and even Térala was awake to witness the end of the Quarrolii.

"They are not really completely gone, are they?" Fearlai asked Yarabakha.

"No, child. They are not," was his solemn reply. "I hope not..." he whispered to himself.

The silence was lifted by the distant shrill calling of carrion birds. Black droplets in the sky like streaked charcoal in the distance warned Nalabakh of their approach, thunder clouds followed them, striking white fire onto the ground and rumbling with the anger of Nabu.

"We've lingered too long; we must run!" Nalabakh yelled.

vii

Fear consumed the travelers as the carrion soared overhead, the rain bearing down on them, and the thunderclap biting at their ears. The carrion rarely swept down at them thanks to Yarabakha's fire breath, but they stayed just on top, watching them and securing their location for the slaves to poke with their spears.

"We will never make it to the desert like this!" Yarabakha called.

"We have no choice!" Nalabakh screamed back. They both carried a child in their underbelly, protecting them from the probing of the spears or the claws of the carrion should a stray swoop down past Yarabakha's sight.

They continued in this manner, the storm's winds lifting such that the tall grass blew back in their eyes and made it difficult to see ahead. At long last, Yarabakha could see a rock garden, strewn across the plain and signaling the coming desert, which itself was strewn with flat mesas and scorching rocks. He signaled to Nalabakh a patch of rocks to meet at, and they crawled slowly to where they found cover under a large cylindric rock on its side, serving as an overhang.

The carrion circled about and the lightning struck all around them. Yarabakha threw his flame strategically while Nalabakh protected the children from the storm with his wings. The battle raged on, neither able to gain a foothold over the other, seeing as Yarabakha was stronger but the carrion more numerous. The storm, too, prevented their escape and pushed them to the ends of their endurance. Even Térala could cry no longer and only held her face firm and eyes closed against Nalabakh's chest.

The carrion broke off from their circling and flew off in the direction of the desert. The lightning stopped. The rain lessened into a misty downpour and the wind died into a gentle breeze.

"They could not have surrendered," Yarabakha said.

"No, they would not have," Nalabakh replied. "If you are able, look and see what you can. Do not endanger yourself."

Yarabakha nodded and peered over the stones. In the distance stood a great figure, taking a human form. His beard was long and braided like his hair and his robe was dyed brilliant blues and purples with gold fibers sewn in a rune that was familiar to Yarabakha. It was the script of Nabu. He stood on the edge of the desert, his dark eyes piercing their very souls. No divine glow emanated from him.

"Come," his voice boomed, filling the air and the insides of their heads. "Speak with me."

"Send away your legions and we will talk," Nalabakh replied.

"So be it."

The carrion and the slaves of Nabu flew over them in such a horde that their shadow was one black mass. They flew out over the plains and into the horizon, when Yarabakha nodded to Nalabakh that they were a safe distance away.

"We will stand," Nalabakh replied.

They stood, Fearlai holding onto Térala. They were trembling from the cold wet rain, but Fearlai stood fearless in the face of his enemy.

"Will he let us go?" he whispered to Nalabakh.

"No," Nalabakh whispered back. "Be prepared to run. Run straight into the desert. He cannot touch you there."

They approached to within a safe enough distance. Nalabakh hoped that if the children ran hard enough, they could make it to the desert in time without bringing them too close to Nabu.

"I am not angry," Nabu said, his voice deep and empty.

"You shouldn't be," Nalabakh replied.

Nabu seemed taken aback at his reply but continued on: "The children you have. They will not become slaves like the others. I will spare their lives, if they swear oaths to honor the failures of their ancestors to worship me and obey me."

"Are they bound to you by the same oaths of their forefathers?"

"Yes!" Nabu shouted. "I bestowed on those men the very means of their becoming the dominant lifeforce on this planet. They. Owe. Me."

"And these children are to pay their burden? We are to protect them, not enslave them!"

"These children benefited from the promise of their ancestors, and you enslave them no matter what it is you do with them. If you should let them free, they are slaves to the conditions of life itself, to survive, to eat, to struggle. Evil will spread in them that comes from temptation, good will die when they cannot fend for themselves out there in the desert. Their race will fall, and you will have failed your oath."

"They will be free to follow their own wills, or the wills of good, but that will be their choice and not yours. There are greater wills than yours," Yarabakha replied, stepping forward, shoulder to shoulder with Nalabakh.

"Do not be foolish. Why let them die when they can live? Why do you not ask the children their desires?"

Nalabakh looked down at Fearlai and Térala, their eyes swollen with fear, their skin wrinkled with the water and shivering with cold. Hunger tore at their bellies.

"What say you?" Nalabakh asked them, tenderly drawing his claw over their hair. "Do you wish to go back with Nabu to rebuild a new home for your people, or go off into the desert in the hopes that the seaside will bring you new life and hopefully more humans?"

Fearlai took Térala's hand and they spoke for a moment to each other, in hushed tones such that not a soul could hear their voices. Térala whispered into Fearlai's ears and they nodded.

"Yes, child?" Nabu inquired.

"We want the desert," Fearlai responded. "Térala wants to be free."

"Fools!" Nabu roared.

He began to transform, his back breaking through his shirt as though his skin were another layer of clothing, until it all scrunched near the front of him and an enormous lion's body with a snakehead tail emerged. Nabu's head grew and fangs pierce from his mouth. His eyes lit up with fire and he lunged at the gargoyles with his claws ready to slash at the children.

Nalabakh threw the children behind him as he braced himself for the impact. Yarabakha had, instead, jumped in front and with his fire, held Nabu at bay. Nabu's claw swung out and swiped at Yarabakha, knocking him to the side. When his eyes pierced the flames, he saw the children dashing for the edge of the desert.

He pursued them, lunging as far as he could with each bound, his snakehead tail keeping the gargoyles from hotly pursuing him. They battled the tail, pulling at it and slowing the great beast down.

He swiped at the children and just caught the edge of Térala's clothing. The child screamed and fell to the ground. Fearlai ran back to help her. The snakehead lunged out and bit into Yarabakha's head, Yarabakha responding with a wave of fire.

Nabu lunged, his claw about to strike again at the fallen child and her companion when another figure crashed into his head, and bending it, flipped him over onto his back.

Nalabakh grabbed a hold of another paw. Ilubakh was there, wrestling with the head of Nabu and near breaking his fleshy neck. His white eyes burned with jealousy unbefitting a powerful being as he saw Jelu from the edge of the desert beckoning on her companions to join her. Her feet were just beyond the edge of the plains where the last leaf died, and the stones were covered in dusty sand.

The beast twirled around, slapping at Nalabakh and biting into Ilubakh's chest. They both let ring a roar of pain, but Nabu had no strength to finish them. He had his sights on Térala who, even by the grace of Fearlai's hand, could not run quickly.

Nabu kicked at Yarabakha and jumped into pursuit.

Nalabakh let his hand turn to stone and swung his own at Nabu's leg, breaking the hind paw. Nabu's forked tongue burned with pain.

Ilubakh stole the time to sink her teeth into the tail of Nabu and bite off the snakehead, slowing the beast down further as the pain swept over his body.

Yarabakha blew a ring of fire in front of Nabu, who ran through, searing himself in desperation.

The children were just approaching the edge when Nabu roared, his magic freezing the children in their tracks. Their movements had slowed down to a crawl, as though ice gripped their feet.

"Nalabakh!" Ilubakh screamed.

Nalabakh did not hesitate, but with Yarabakha wrestling at Nabu's hide, jumped and taking flight, flew towards the children with his wings beating.

He pummeled into them and carried them, his wings beating as hard as he could, beyond the edge of the desert! Nabu roared, but it was too late.

Nalabakh immediately turned to stone and upon crashing into the ground shattered into a thousand rolling rocks. Fearlai and Térala were helped up by Jelu and they stood up in the hot sand, looking back at Nabu who could not touch them, or step onto the desert. The same magic that had broken Nalabakh would break him. They were a product beyond the desert's enchantments, and the desert had its own spirits. Nabu's skin slowly folded back over him, scorched, weak, bitten. His ego was his power, his script was his power, and left with none capable of speaking or reading, his power was ending.

"Traitors! Traitors all of you!" he spat, before descending back into the spirit realm, an ephemeral distance that ran parallel to their reality. "You will suffer by your own choice!"

Only Yarabakha and Ilubakh remained behind the desert's dominion.

"Go, children," Yarabakha said. "Be free and follow the brightest three stars. They will lead you to the sea. Go now, while it is still cool from the storm. Remember the lessons you learned here."

Fearlai nodded, with tears in his eyes, and bravely took the hands of his two companions. He walked by Nalabakh's broken head and caressed it gently. Jelu turned one last time to wave at Ilubakh, who waved back until they were not more than a single black speck on a burning horizon.

"What are we left to do?" Ilubakh asked Yarabakha.

"We are to fade like the Quarrolii, like Nabu, like Nalabakh," Yarabakha said. "Only we have some time left to enjoy this earth, and some time left to pray and hope for the children."

They danced, and sang, and drank in the sunsets and sunrises and starlight. And then, they waited until the magic of their existence faded and they turned to stone.

Part Two:

A Feast of Thrills

THE STORIES YOU EAT

Jonathon Mast

"The best way to get stories is just ask questions. People always love talking about themselves," Carina told her daughters.

Annie wrinkled her nose. "Can we just eat? I'm hungry!"

Carina grinned at her children. Tella wore her pixie cut and black tank top like the trying-to-be-edgy young teen she was. Annie, the younger blond girl, wore her pink unicorn t-shirt. The lights of the carousel sent colors swirling over their eager faces. The crowds churned around them. The scents of sweat and cotton candy lay heavy in the early evening air.

Oh, there was so much good food here. And Carina was hungry too. Annie was right. Time to eat.

She turned her grin from the children to the crowds. "Well, girls, where to first?"

Their eyes rifled through the crowd. Kids in line at the carousel, their dads absorbed by their phones. More lines leading to more rides. Lots of children screaming. Carnies shouting at passers-by to try their games. People milling around the various food trucks. Families sitting to eat in a little square of picnic tables. Mobs of teens laughing and trying to show off.

Annie pointed. "There!"

Carina considered a moment. Annie was young yet, but it looked safe enough for her to get the food solo. And the girl deserved a good meal. A good mother would never deny her child a meal. No, not like her parents had.

Carina nodded. "Go ahead and try."

"By myself?" She was jumping so much she wouldn't need a turn at the bounce house later.

"Just remember, never the first story. And I'll be nearby."

She scampered off through the milling crowds.

Tella crossed her arms. "Mom! It's not fair!"

"Well? Where would you pick?"

"I told you! That carny over there. Weren't you listening? Look at his face. I bet no one's respected him for weeks. He'll talk." Tella's voice sounded just scratchy enough to be scrappy.

Carina evaluated the unshaven man running the Ferris wheel. She looked back at her daughter. "You're becoming an attractive young woman."

Tella rolled her eyes. "Mom!"

"What do you do if he tries something?"

"He won't! Look at all the people around!"

"Tella." Carina felt herself give that look. Oh, the monster you become when you're a parent.

"You taught me how to defend myself, Mom. I'll be fine."

"You won't have time to think. You need to be able to do it without thinking." Tella raised an eyebrow.

"Don't you look at me like that, young lady." Carina knelt down. "I'm serious, all right? There are many hunters at a fair. You have to be careful, or.... well...." She felt herself shiver, shook it off. "I love you." ·

"Yeah. I know."

Carina gave the look again.

"All right. Fine. I'll be careful. One story from him. That's it."

Carina waited a moment, watching. "This is a big deal, Tella. Remember, you are what you eat." She looked over at the carny again and took a deep breath. "All right. I'll be watching."

Tella pressed her lips together. "You're really going to let me do it?"

She sighed. "You gotta fly sometime. Might as well be now." She tried to make herself believe it.

Tella stopped herself from grinning and very carefully sauntered away.

Oh, that girl. Carina was never that wild, was she? Okay, yes, she had been. But she was older when she ran off with her first boyfriend, wasn't she?

All right. Where was Annie? There she was. Sitting down at the aluminum picnic table across from a young mom. The crowds milled around. Lots of families right now. The rides were pretty packed.

Oh, she'd chosen well. That woman looked so tired. Annie started making faces at the baby in the stroller next to the table.

The woman watched carefully but didn't engage yet.

Annie asked something. Over the noise of the crowds and the country-rock blaring from the rides, Carina couldn't hear anything of the conversation. She could guess what was going on, though. Annie probably asked what the baby's name was or how old the baby was. Something relatively simple. Get the woman to open up.

The woman smiled and answered.

Annie asked another question.

Now the woman was looking around. Good mom. Where was this random girl's mother? Wasn't she too young to be out on her own?

Carina waved in their direction. She could help her daughter out a little, right?

Annie pointed and waved back.

The woman smiled and also waved. All was well. The random girl had a mother. She wasn't in danger.

Of course, *Annie* wasn't in danger.

Annie asked another question. The woman answered. And then she started talking. And she talked more. And more. And Annie was eating it up.

Literally.

The woman was spinning stories about her little baby, and Annie was getting a full stomach. Carina was a little jealous. It had been too long since she'd fed.

She had feasted on plenty of mothers in the past. They always hungered for adult conversation. And they always left the conversations just a little confused. There was always something they couldn't quite remember. Something they should know, but didn't.

But those stories always tasted best.

"Keeping an eye on your daughter?"

The voice startled Carina. She turned to see another woman dressed in jeans and a black t-shirt bearing the words *I am the nightmare you fear*. She had long black hair and a small nose. Carina guessed she was probably in her early twenties.

"Excuse me?" Carina asked.

"I saw you wave over that way. That your daughter?"

"Oh. Yes."

The woman smiled and pushed a lock of hair behind her ear. "I'm Fabella. Just wandering around. My girls are here with friends. Somewhere. Spotted another lone mom. Thought I'd say hi."

Letting her kids wander around? This woman must be older than Carina had guessed. No matter. She smiled. "I'm Carina. Nice to meet you." So. Another lonely mom. Maybe she could get a quick meal, too.

"How many girls do you have?" Fabella asked.

"Two. There's Annie over there, ogling over that baby. And Tella's somewhere around." She glanced around, seeing if she could spot her. Yep. Talking to a bored-looking scruffy man by the Ferris wheel. At least the man wasn't eyeing her chest or anything.

"Huh. I would have put you down for three children."

"Three? Why?" Carina almost laughed. No, only two, and that was enough.

The other woman grinned. "I don't know. Just something I thought when I saw you. I have three kids."

"Really?" Something about the beginnings of that story tasted off. "Tell me about them." Carina's stomach grumbled. She should get this woman talking. Stories! Didn't matter if they tasted a little odd at the moment. She was hungrier than she'd thought!

"Oh. They're just kids. You know." Fabella shrugged and tucked that stray lock of hair behind her ear again. "What about yours?"

Of course. She was being a guarded mom. Carina had to tell her a story to get a story. Fair enough. "Well, Annie over there. She loves talking with babies. She wishes she had a little sister. She hates being the youngest." Carina gave a little huff of a laugh. "When she was smaller, she'd crawl around looking for more people her size. She hated that her big sister could just loom over her."

The woman laughed. "Sounds like a little sister problem."

"Tell me about your kids."

"I have three girls. What is there to tell? As a mom, you worry a little."

The threads weren't enough to make a story. It was like eating flour; you might call it food, but it wasn't enough. Woman, share something! Weren't you so lonely a minute ago?

The woman with dark hair tilted her head. "What about your kids?"

Figures. She wasn't going to share anything unless Carina spilled her guts. Some real bonding thing. Fine. When one mother shared a birthing story, it always opened the floodgates, didn't it? "Annie's always been a real pain. Even when I gave birth to her."

"Oh?"

"Yeah. The twerp had me in labor for hours and hours."

"Her dad around to help?"

"Nah." Carina shook her head, letting real bitterness come to the surface. "He left a few months before she was born. It was for the better."

"I'm sorry."

"Yeah. Well." She shrugged. "Anyway, the docs gave me Pitocin, but it didn't seem to help. And so I just paced around and around and around the maternity ward."

"Was it as bad for your first two daughters?"

Carina frowned. "I only have one other daughter."

"You're right. Sorry. I keep forgetting."

Though honestly at the moment, Carina couldn't remember what it was like when Tella was born. You'd think your firstborn would be something you'd recall. Maybe it was her hunger scrambling her thoughts. Or maybe this woman was rubbing off on her.

Between the woman's inherent forgetfulness and the odd taste of the story Carina had sampled, she began to wonder whether this was a good place for a meal after all. She hoped Tella was having better luck.

Speaking of Tella...

She glanced over to see what was happening.

Her daughter and the scruffy man were gone.

She stepped toward the Ferris wheel.

"What's wrong?" Fabella asked.

"I'm sorry. I just noticed the time," Carina lied. "I need to go."

"Oh, I'm sorry. I hope we get to talk more later!"

Carina left the woman behind. Annie should be fine for a few minutes, but who knew what that man would do to Tella.

Foolish, Carina. You should know better. You know how cruel men can be. Tella wasn't ready. Not for something like that.

As she pushed through the crowds, she felt the fingers on her. Old fingers. Old wounds.

Stop. Your imagination is getting away with you. Tella can handle herself.

She shoved her way to the front of the line by the Ferris wheel. Mostly pairs of teenagers trying to find a relatively quiet spot to make moves on one another. A bored heavy-set woman stood at the front of the line by the gate. "Lady, get to the back of the line," she told Carina.

"There was a man here a minute ago. Bad beard. He was talking with a girl. Where is he?"

"Brad? He's been off shift for more than an hour." The woman frowned. "Lady, what's the big deal?"

An hour? Carina shook her head. She'd just sent Tella to go eat a few minutes ago.

"Hey? Carina?"

She turned. Fabella stood nearby, a look of concern on her face. "You ran off really fast. Are you okay?"

"I'm sorry. I was confused." She took out her cell.

It really had been an hour. More. An hour she'd been talking with Fabella, apparently. And gotten not a single story out of her. Some hunter Carina was. And she was so, so hungry.

"Come on. Let's get out of line, huh? Unless you want to go up again?" Fabella pointed at the Ferris wheel.

"No. No, I'm good. I'm sorry." Carina turned and made her way out of the line. "I need to go find my daughter. I didn't realize how late it was."

"Tell me about her. I like listening." She smiled and tucked that strand of hair behind her ear again.

Carina glanced over at this woman. This woman who wouldn't tell a single story. "That's the kind of thing I usually would say."

"I'm sure you would. You'd say it to your first daughter all the time, wouldn't you?"

Carina shrugged, trying to get away. "Well, that is how you treat a child. You listen to them."

"And you eat their stories."

She stopped. She turned. This woman who had sat for over an hour, listening to stories that Carina didn't remember telling. It was another hunter. Another story-eater. She hadn't met one since she'd left her family. And this one had hunted her. "Oh. Oh, you're good."

"I learned from the best."

"Who trained you?"

"My mother."

Ice ran through Carina's veins. Then fire. Memories of when she was younger. Anger. She nodded. "That is usually where we learn."

Fabella glared. "She stole everything from me. She ate every single thing I told her. She was a selfish bitch. I swore I'd find her and eat everything she loved."

Carina narrowed her eyes. "Well, I hope you have fun with that. But I need to find my daughter. You played me, but we're done now. No hard feelings. You won this round." Let it go. There's not time for this right now.

"I have hard feelings."

"I don't have time for this."

"You never had time for me unless I was feeding you."

"What the hell are you talking about?"

Fabella's eyes bored into her. "How many daughters do you have?"

"Get away from me!" She spun and stumbled through the crowds, through the alleys between rides, over grass slick with evening dew, trying to get back to the area where she'd left Annie.

She only had one daughter. Little Annie. She'd brought her here to hunt.

The woman was crazy.

No. The woman was a hunter.

Carina stopped running.

She was a hunter, too. The only hunter she'd known for years. And she shouldn't run. Carina was not prey. Never prey. There were many different kinds of hunters. She'd survived some hunters that had preyed on her. She fought back. She'd sucked out every story they valued and left them only nightmares. Their stories had taken her over for a while—after all, you are the stories you eat. She'd been messed up. She was glad she couldn't remember those days clearly. But she had emerged stronger, surer of her own story. Not prey. Never again.

She would not run. She would find Annie. She'd find her daughter and get out.

Suddenly a girl tackled her. She almost fell over but was able to keep her feet and steady the girl. A young teen with a black tank top and pixie-cut hair. She was crying. Red marks the shape of hands were on her shoulders. "Mom!" she sobbed.

Carina didn't have time for this.

But no. Her eyes took in the red marks. She'd had marks like that before. What kind of monster was she? Of course she had time for this girl.

But Annie. There was a hunter out there. And Annie was so trusting. She'd spill everything. She wasn't used to being hunted.

But here was a girl who needed someone right now. "Hey. Hey! What happened?"

The girl trembled. Sobs wracked her body. Eyeliner left long dark trails in her tears. Carina remembered those tears.

"Who did this to you?" Her voice was hard.

"The man at the Ferris wheel. He didn't do anything. He tried. He almost got me."

"Listen. I need to find my daughter. But once I do, this guy's not going to remember how to use his dick ever again." She heard the snarl in her voice. Didn't matter this wasn't her kid. No one should ever be abused like that. No one.

And the girl shook.

Carina looked around in this little alley between rides. No one was near now. Music blared from speakers. Colored lights flickered.

Where were this girl's parents? "Who's responsible for you? You got a parent around here?"

She stopped sobbing. Carina couldn't read the expression on her face.

"Hey. Hey! What's your name?" she asked. She had to help this girl.

But Annie.

There was the other hunter out there. And this girl. She needed protection, too. But Annie.

The girl was still frozen.

"Hey, I didn't mean nothing. You okay, kid?" The male voice startled her.

Carina spun.

A man stood in their alley between rides. Scruffy. Overweight. Lonely. Predator.

"What happened?" Carina asked him.

"She was talking to me. And I got a little excited. You know. And she was pretty. I tried telling her she was pretty."

Just a few threads. Just a few snatches of a story.

But it was enough.

Carina grabbed what he said and she *pulled*. "You told her she was pretty. And what were you thinking about her, Brad?"

And she yanked the story from his lips. The words came pouring out of him. His eyes flew open in shock. He tried to cover his mouth, but his lips wouldn't stop moving. And what he wanted to do. He told her everything he wanted to do to the girl.

And now the girl next to her was shaking again.

Carina remembered the feeling. The feeling of filth. But this girl hadn't done anything wrong.

The filth was standing in front of her.

Carina wanted to vomit. This was not the kind of story she liked eating. But she took it anyway. She took it. And then she kept pulling. "How many other girls, Brad?"

And he told her. The stories poured out of him, all his filth, all his pride, all his shame, what he wanted and what he didn't, and all the stories came out. He panicked, but it only made the stories flow faster. And faster. His feet were rooted to the ground.

And as Carina ate the stories, as she took them from him, he forgot.

Brad's nose bled. His eyes bled as she forced more stories out of him, squeezing his soul so all the pulp ran out. His voice rose in pitch. He wheezed.

"You ever have sex with someone who actually wanted it? You ever even kiss anyone who wanted it?" Her voice was filled with mockery. This predator was a loser. Just a man who was a nothing, and now he was going to be less than that. Because he wanted to take out his pain on others.

And he told her. The one time he'd had sex with someone who was willing. Back in high school. The one girl. How she had laughed at him after because he was so incompetent. Because he wasn't enough. He was never enough.

Carina didn't eat that story. She wanted the laughter to ring out in his ears for a long, long time. She wanted him to know he wasn't enough. He would never be enough.

His voice got higher pitched as she ate older and older stories. He forgot he was ever a man. He forgot he was ever a teen. He forgot what it was like to shave or walk or be hugged. She ate all the other stories. She ate all of him. Every story of his life. Every last little bit of him.

Everything except the laughter.

The scruffy thing that had been Brad dropped to the ground. Blood leaked from his ears, his eyes, his nose. His drool was tinged pink.

And now, finally, Carina vomited it all out. She didn't want to eat those stories. She didn't want those nightmares in her stomach. You are the stories you eat, and she didn't want to be like this predator. She didn't want his stories of his desires in her soul, poisoning her, turning her into a depraved monster. She heaved every scene of every story out onto the grass, a mass of bile and syllables.

And when she finished gagging, she turned to the girl. "He's never going to hurt you again."

Her voice trembled. "How did you do that? I thought people had to choose to tell you stories."

"When you're pissed off enough you can pull whatever you want out of them. Grab a thread and force them to tell the stories, pull the stories out of them. And scum like him." Carina hugged herself. "Well. Let's just say he's not the first one I've destroyed." And then it hit her. Another hunter? A girl? "Wait. You know how to eat stories?"

"You taught me, Mom. ....Mom?" And the girl was scared again. She had that same unreadable expression again.

Why would this girl think Carina was her mother? She wasn't old enough to have a daughter that old. And she could never forget her daughter.

Except.

Except there was another hunter, wasn't there? And she'd spoken with Carina for an hour. Maybe more. And for an hour, Carina had bated her by handing over stories, trying to prime the pump.

She swore. And then she swore a lot more. "You're my daughter."

The girl nodded.

What else had she taken? What else had Fabella stolen from her and she didn't even know? No. There's no time for fear. Annie's still out there. She had to save Annie.

Carina refocused on the daughter she didn't know. "What's your name?"

"Tella."

No time for fear. Burn. "Tella. There's another hunter here. And she ate my memories of you. I'm going to destroy her. I'm going to take every memory she ever had. I'm going to kill her for this. And then you and me? We're going to rebuild those memories, okay? I'm sorry those stories are gone from me. We're going to do what we have to. You're still my daughter. But first, we need to get Annie."

Tella nodded, short and fast.

Carina stalked out of the alley. Tella followed.

The scruffy man laid on the grass in the alley between rides drooling pink. All he heard was laughter.

It was after dark now. Most of the crowds were teens at this point, though there were still some families around. The heat of the day had cooled off a little. First step: Go to where she last saw Annie. Find the picnic table surrounded by the smells of cotton candy and sweat. Reclaim her daughter.

As she stalked, nightmares ran through her mind. What else had the hunter taken? Who was this Fabella? In an hour, a skilled hunter could take nearly anything they wanted.

What would someone like that do with Annie?

How may children *did* Carina have? If the hunter had taken Tella...

No birthdays. No birth. She couldn't remember the girl's favorite band or their last argument or if she went to school or how old she was or if she liked lilacs. She turned to look at her face.

A face she didn't love. A face that she couldn't recall a single story about. When did she start wearing eyeliner? Was tonight a special night for her? Who were her friends? Did she have any friends?

Carina glanced down at the girl's wrists, or tried. She wasn't swinging her arms. Well, no wonder, after what she'd just heard. But Carina hoped there were no scars there. Not like her arms. Old scars. Even needle marks. Very old needle marks. She didn't even remember when she did that. It was part of what she'd eaten, when she'd lost control. But now everything was better.

Or it would be better.

This was her daughter. She was supposed to love her daughter. She was supposed to protect her.

And now.

She was supposed to love her, but there wasn't even an emptiness. No void. The memories had closed around her daughter. She remembered nothing. Nothing at all.

She should have done better. She should have caught on faster.

No. She was weak. She should have been stronger. But what's done is done. Hunt. Find Fabella before Fabella finds Annie.

And a pack of teens cleared. She finally saw the picnic table.

And there was Annie.

And there was Fabella.

They sat next to each other on the picnic bench. The girl munched on cotton candy. And Fabella?

She smiled when she spotted Carina across the little picnic area of tables and asphalt. She tucked a lock of hair behind her ear and waved. The hunter waved at them. She knew she had her meal right there.

Carina marched toward them. She leaned on her fists across the table. "Give me back my daughter," she growled.

Fabella kept smiling. "Annie, tell me another story about your mom."

The girl looked up from her cotton candy. She frowned. "Who?"

Carina launched herself over the table. Her hands wrapped around the other woman's neck. Cut off her air supply. Don't let her talk. Fabella fell backwards off the bench onto the asphalt. Her head cracked. Carina landed on top of her. Around them, people gasped.

Fabella laughed.

"Why the hell are you doing this?" Carina demanded.

"Let me tell you a story."

Good. Carina loosened her hands. She could use whatever threads Fabella gave to pull everything out of her like she had with the carny. She was plenty angry enough. This woman stole one daughter by taking Carina's memories. She stole the other by taking the daughter's memories. She'd suffer.

"Once there was a drug-addicted mom who was hungry. But her daughter loved telling stories. She told all the stories of everything that happened to her. And the mom listened to her daughter every day." She paused, her nose wrinkling in distaste. "And she ate her daughter's stories."

Carina took the story. She *pulled*.

And she saw the story.

She saw herself. Younger. Sixteen? Seventeen? Thin. Very thin.

And there was a little girl. She'd never seen the girl, but clearly it wasn't Tella. It wasn't Annie either. The hair, the nose was all wrong. They were familiar, though.

The little girl tucked a strand of hair behind her ear.

And the tiny little girl babbled. And the mother ate the story. The scene shifted. Carina was a few years older. And the girl was a few years older. But she still babbled like a toddler. And the mother ate her daughter's stories. And then she was older again. The girl was what? Nine now? Ten? And she still babbled like a toddler.

Because the mother feasted on all her stories.

No.

Carina stopped pulling. This couldn't be real. It couldn't be true.

"Like hell, bitch." And now Fabella *pushed*.

And the stories kept coming. Carina couldn't close them out.

Fabella was taken. The mother was left behind, needle marks on her arms. She screamed something about food as the girl was taken away. And that was the last the girl ever saw of her mom.

She grew up in a loving family after that. And now, with no one feasting on her stories, she blossomed. She never learned why she was so much older than everyone else. She never put it together, until she learned she could eat stories, too.

And with that knowledge came questions.

She hunted to find her mother. Her biological mother. She found a happy woman. A woman with two daughters.

And she didn't remember her first daughter.

She had fed the stories to someone else. She had fed the stories of her shame, of her crimes, to another.

"You wanted to start over, didn't you?" Fabella spat. "And so you just fed those stories to your do-over baby, didn't you? That was her milk. You fed all your shame to her. You fed *me* to her. You erased me, so I erased her."

A crowd had gathered around them. Annie was crying. Tears ran down Tella's face.

"And now I'm going to take every story you have," Fabella said. "You took all of mine. Now I get all of yours. And now you'll know why."

Fabella was already inside of Carina, pushing. And now she pulled.

Carina shoved off the ground, even as words started flowing from her lips. She clenched her jaws, but it didn't matter. The stories started coming.

"I learned to walk pretty late. At least, that's what my parents told me." She clamped her hands over her mouth, but the words were pulled from her lungs, from her brain, they poured out of her. Her knees buckled. She plummeted face first to the ground. The story was taken. The memory of how to walk was gone.

"Annie turned nine last year. She was so happy that morning."

Carina felt tears come to her eyes. As she told the story, the details disappeared from her mind. Fabella ate each detail, one by one. Carina felt them disappear. How old was Annie? Shouldn't she be older? What was her last birthday like?

"Annie was wearing her bright pink leggings that had tiger stripes on them. She wanted to be fierce, she said. Like her sister, but happy."

Gone.

Annie walked up and took Fabella's hand. "Who's that?" she asked, pointing at her mom. "Why is she talking about me?"

"Her first day of school was amazing. She wasn't scared at all. Just paraded right into the classroom and declared that she was going to be friends with everyone."

Gone.

Stop. What was her teacher's name?

"Mrs. Callahan was her teacher. She was pretty young—it was only her second year teaching. She said she'd never seen anyone like Annie."

Gone.

"She made me a Cheerio necklace in art. She was so proud."

Gone.

"She loves unicorns."

Gone. Gone. Gone.

The memories slipped away faster and faster as Fabella continued to pull.

"Tell me why you named her Annie," Fabella said.

No.

If Carina told that story, she'd forget her daughter's name.

She grabbed her own throat and squeezed. Stop the story. Don't let it come out. She already forgot too much. Her hands pressed against her windpipe. Her knees trembled and gave way.

The words choked to a stop. She heard herself gurgle.

But she deserved this.

If the story was true. If she ate Fabella's childhood. If she hid it all from herself so she could forget the shame. If she used her next daughter to dump all her secrets onto.

Fabella wasn't the monster. Carina was.

She was the monster. She was the predator. She was the one who should be left on the ground alone with only shame.

Let the stories go, one by one. Let the pain come in. She released her throat. The words began to flow.

But the memory remained. She knew Annie's name.

The child she didn't remember. The one she'd protected. Tella. The teen with the pixie cut and the black tank top. She stepped between them. "Get away from my mother," she snarled.

The words stopped flowing from Carina's mouth. She sobbed. And then she saw what was happening.

No. Fabella would rip everything from this girl. This innocent girl. Carina crawled toward Tella, dragging herself inch by inch. "Stop! Get away!"

Fabella raised an eyebrow at the girl. "Feisty. Why protect someone who doesn't remember you?"

"Because she loved me even when she didn't remember." Her hands were balled up into fists.

"Tell me more."

"Not this time," Tella answered. "She taught me what to do. When you're angry enough, you can do something special."

And now Tella pulled.

And Fabella pulled back.

They glared at each other, straining. Someone moved through the crowd. There was shouting. Veins stood out in Tella's wrists. Fabella sweated. Sparks of stories flew between them.

Carina couldn't breathe. She had to stop them. She had to protect Tella. If she had failed so much, she had to do something. Her hands were bloody against the asphalt as she dragged herself closer, closer.

Red flowed from Fabella's nose. Tella sweated blood. It dripped from her forehead, near her eye, and down her cheek. Her fists shook. She whimpered. She groaned.

Almost there. Carina was almost there.

Something burst. Fabella wailed. Tella screamed. They both fell away from each other, limp.

Carina struggled, pulling herself to Tella. Annie screamed over Fabella's form.

And then strong arms grabbed her. "Ma'am. Ma'am, you need to stop."

She shook the arms off. "My daughter!"

The arms disappeared for a moment. Long enough for her to reach Tella. To sit up. To cradle her.

The teen's eyes opened. "Mom?"

"Yes, Tella. Yes." And the tears came. She looked over at the other form.

Annie knelt next to her, crying. Fabella lay on the ground, drooling pink.

"You won, Tella. You stopped her. For us. You saved us. It's over. The nightmare is over."

* * *

Eventually all three got to go home. Carina could prove that Annie was her daughter, even if Annie didn't remember. It took some doing, since Carina couldn't walk anymore, but they finally, finally got home. She'd have to appear in court to testify since she had assaulted the woman. It was a legal mess.

Well. Carina could eat those stories if she needed to. It would all be all right.

Except.

Except she still didn't remember her own daughter. Or the other daughter. The one she had destroyed so badly.

As they finally came home, Annie explored the house. "I live here?"

"That's right, Annie. Your room is upstairs. Do you want to see it?" Carina was gentle with her. With this daughter that was missing so much of her story.

"Is it awesome?"

"I think so."

"Okay!" And she skipped up the stairs.

Tella sat heavily at the kitchen table. "Mom?"

"Yeah?"

"Annie was telling me that she didn't remember you at all."

"Yeah." A stab of pain went through Carina's heart.

"Doesn't that hurt?"

"It does."

Tella sat quiet for a while. "Tell me about Annie. What's your favorite memory of her?"

Carina looked over at her daughter.

Tella made an odd motion, like she was tucking a long strand of hair behind her ear. "Will you tell me the story?"

PERMISSIBLE LICENSE
A Tale of the Bajazid

Kenneth Bykerk

Simon Atterly rose up with a start. He had been lost within a nightmare profound, a world of madness and flame and sights set beyond understanding. Demons stalked the streets of Baird's Holler, haunts disguised in skins of men made obscene. When Simon's soul saw at last through his own eyes unobscured, demons still ran rampant through the streets and the town of Baird's Holler was aflame. The thrill that had lifted him through his uncertain somnambulance still buoyed him, still charged his blood, but gone was the distance of his reason, that sleep that was not a sleep. Clarity amplified the disorder about overwhelming senses freshly returned. The world enraged demanded an answer, and Simon Atterly bent double in voluble reply.

* * *

The speechifying was getting long, and it wasn't just Simon who thought so. With a tap to his knee, Lafayette Fontaine leaned over and expressed his discontent in a most foul way.

"For Chrissakes, Lafe, we're outside and still that clouds the air!" Simon whispered in mock disgust.

"Yes, my friend, and I am happy to oblige your senses. If we are to be stuck in this damnable heat while Alexander prattles on, I might as well enjoy what I can."

"By making me enjoy it less?"

"Precisely!" With this, Lafayette sat back and pretended great interest in the excessive oration from the podium before them, the only hint of his misbehavior a tight grin on an otherwise innocent face.

Simon rolled his eyes and went back to waiting for Alexander Gitney's droning speech to end, for no festival could begin until that tedious task was done. Alexander was never happier than when lecturing. This was no idle opinion on Simon's part. Alexander Gitney spoke only with intent to be heard and always assumed he was. If asked directly, he would proudly proclaim such without any wonder the reason for the question. He was stubborn, pig-headed and fiercely judgmental, but Simon trusted none of his other partners more, even Lafe and Javier.

A partnership of trust bound by an unbreakable contract was the reason for this day, this public fête. A decade had passed from the discovery of this creek they named the Bajazid and the gold that glittered beneath its flow. Thirty men were raised from destitution to means over the course of that day and made tycoons by its end when a shout reduced their number to twenty-nine. The youngest member of the party had enthusiastically scaled a height and slipped upon the surprise of his discovery; a solid nugget of raw design weighing over ninety-six pounds. From that point the Mortenson Mine developed and the town, named in honor of the man lost, was raised.

It was this contract the Sultans of the Bajazid had gathered to celebrate, not the decennial of the town as the masses were led to believe. John S. Mortenson, the financier of the expedition, had devised a document which effectively stifled any competition amongst members of the company. The penalties of this trust broken were severe to the elimination of all interest without appeal. Subsequently, of those not available to attend this celebration, not one had been attributed to malfeasance within the bounds of the contract. The Sultans waged their wars most civilly and however their hatred may flare of a moment, none dare lay another in their grave.

John Mortenson was not an attendee at this event. In 1872, after five years ensuring his investment established, he returned to New York City for those circles of society he had long yearned to join. Correspondence from Mortenson's lawyers soon produced notice of his passing in the foyer of the Union Club upon his admittance and introduction. The terms of his interment were of issue as the illness that caught him at his moment of glory startled his hosts through its violence and the concern it raised. No full explanation had been given as to the details, but it mattered not. The contract, with Mortenson's passing ruled natural, remained, and the wealth was spread by a greater margin. His share of the whole had been near half and his death a tragedy of immense fortune.

Simon looked up, pulled from his failure to attend to see Alexander basking in the applause that rose to celebrate the end of his lecture. Steven Clayton stepped forth to usher Alexander from the stage, his return eliciting a few calls from the crowd. Steven was known as a ladies' man, and with his wealth, his looks and his natural charm, every unwed woman in Baird's Holler sought to catch him out while the others just wished to trip him up for a spell. Not all the catcalls were from scarlet women.

Ever oblivious, Alexander turned smartly to return to his seat, a confident smile of satisfaction upon his face. *Dense as a door is dumb*, thought Simon, but still the most honest man in Baird's Holler, even more so than Judge Worthington.

A quick glance down the row of luminaries showed the Judge sitting ramrod straight in his chair, his ever present scowl only slightly mollified by the air of celebration about. Warren Worthington was a serious and hard man, one who brooked no folly or nonsense in his courtroom or out. Even on the trail before that fateful find, Worthington had shown himself humorless and officious. Consequently, Alexander and Warren were the bedrock conservatism that checked the exuberance of some of the others in the partnership.

In direct contrast to these two men of serious mien were Yesil Batur, Tom Lundmeir and John Kearns, three hellions who should never have come to riches in Simon's estimation. It was their ruin and doom, of that he was sure. There was rarely a moment these three were not debauched in some fashion or other. Three hedonists without restraint they were, and they abused their community status in ways far exceeding even the fondness for punishment Worthington employed with his gallows.

In between these extremes were the rest. There were those whom Simon detested and those whom he called friend. In such a position as they, men of wealth beyond the common grasp on the edge of frontier, there were not many others from whom to select as equal company. Money divides those who have from those without and like oil into water, there was no comfortable mixture. Simon's confidences of choice among his confederates were Lafe and Javier Alvarez, two fellow bachelors of temperament similar to his own.

Baird's Holler was a boomtown, raw down to its most exposed nerve. It had sprung up overnight as soon as word of the strike escaped the valley, the first time supplies were sought. The influx that followed was typical of a frontier boom; for every honest man willing to work there were two looking for ways to steal his wage. That the Mortenson Company was so large, that their contract guaranteed them a rich harvest if only they stood solid by one another is the reason they were able to sternly enforce their claim. Gold buys guns and the muscle to use them. In short order the sheer strength of the mine and the employment it offered solidified the power of the Sultans as well as lured to the valley the labor needed to work it. In came the urbane, the industrious and the righteous. Here followed the wastrels, the wretched and the profane.

Construction cleared the trees about as buildings blossomed like mushrooms after a rain. Where buildings were yet to be raised, shanties and half-tents filled in the empty spaces without regard to order. Even the few sections of the town where attempts had been made to carve consistent neighborhoods or business districts, lean-tos and tents fought for real estate. While the wealth that poured from the Mortenson Mine filtered through the men and women whose lives damned them here, the disparity in means was glaring. For those who scratched for crumbs and slept in the mud, that disparity had become a source of contention. When desperate men exhaust themselves for another man's purse, the bottle stays the suicide solution just long enough to buy another bottle. Where desperate men gather, trouble brews.

It was this gathering storm that at last caught the attentions of the men who ruled this mountain. A preacher of hysteric vitriol had chosen Baird's Holler as his home, disregarding the convention of steepled church for a pulpit atop a soapbox. The bane of the ordained in town, this straw preacher stirred trouble where he could vociferously and aggressively. Noticing the calls for unification among the laborers echoed the public homilies of this preacher, he was brought to the Sultan's Room in the Yellow Rabbit for an audience. At first, suggestions were made for the preacher to find leave of town under veiled threat of mysterious occurrences such as simply being shot to death. So strong though was this preacher's argument, his position that with or without his presence the town was headed for crisis, the Sultans stayed his impending accident to mull over the truths behind his words.

Life on the Bajazid was rough. It had been just over a year since a devastating illness more than decimated the town, and the gallows were too frequently used. With the prospect of unionization being considered, the Sultans agreed it was best to stave off the growing discontent with time honored measures; they would throw a grand party and invite everyone. Debts would be forgiven and store proprietors were guaranteed full recompense for any receipts from the Sultans themselves. The effects were immediate as the few stores in town saw a boom in business. Tabs were rung at all the bars and the Sultans saw their mounting bill rise with amusement. The owners of the Mortenson Mine were wealthy beyond the pale, and each had contributed a small fortune none noticed missing. It was not fear of the punishments the preacher extolled that set them on this course but their pride, their desire to flaunt in the name of generosity their power and their wealth for the destitute to admire.

Of the Sultans who engaged the most upon this venture was one retired from daily operations. Henry Pickett was a man of impeccable character, a good-natured soul none could disparage. Henry had taken to brewing and distilling upon retirement and his concoctions were highly favored among those he shared with. Henry arrived the day of the festival with two wagons, each filled with large casks and assorted smaller kegs. This was Henry's joy, his contribution to be consumed gratis by all. The saloons in town had been ordered shut until after the grand toast at three and the attendees all warned to hold their drink until the toast. Thus one reason for the speeches, a ruse to distract the anxious while the brew was distributed throughout.

At last the appointed hour arrived and Clayton stepped forth to intercede with the preacher and urge him to hurry his benediction. The cheers that rose served to encourage that end, and the self-appointed minister of morals was compelled to relent as the crowd began murmuring amens of its own. The preacher dismissed to cheers; Clayton exhorted the crowd to a more enthusiastic frame as he prepared the toasts. Simon and the other Sultans rose in kind to advance and offer their blessings. Some, like pale and timid George Franz or the soft-spoken Serbian giant, Radul Ivkov, just nodded to the crowd and said a single word, a salute of sorts familiar. Tom, Yesil and John each tried to outpace each other in vulgarity, their low expectations well exceeded. When Simon spoke, it was with abashed reservation following that profane amateur vaudeville. That trio had resolved to stay as sober as the town until the appointed hour and it reflected in the quiet their comedy brought.

Xavier Huggins had to intercede, injecting himself into Gitney's intent of a speech and thankful applause once again rose to confuse Alexander's ego. Pedro Guzman's short rant in Spanish was indecipherably odd to those who spoke that language, but then Guzman was dressed in the Conquistador eccentricities he had unearthed. William Nesmith was grim, still mourning the loss of his wife, and Charles Chesterfield did his devoir interceding and raising again spirits. The only one who said or did nothing at all but stand in unison was the reclusive Mr. Parker, known as Old Simon to distinguish him from Atterly. Devoted to the mine, Old Simon always did his best to avoid any socializing beyond the necessities of business.

After all the surviving Sultans had been recognized, Henry Pickett raised his glass, gave a short and crude salute and then, en masse, the town of Baird's Holler toasted their success.

* * *

Simon was spitting, his bile sweet with a hint of earth beneath, when horror wrapped itself around him. Malevolence clawed at him with phantom fingers as a visage in reflection of corporeal decay took form before his eyes. It was a face he knew, one long gone but never forgot though remembrance was never so portrayed.

"You're dead! Damn you! You're dead!" It was not fear but rage that exploded from Simon's mouth, rage at the presumption before him. Though that specter gave proof of Hells beyond the rationale of Man mattered not, it was the mockery of the perversion that enraged. "You're dead! I killed you!"

* * *

The day was a grand success. The Sultans of the Bajazid had brought peace to this valley, and the specter of discontent had been banished. Where grumbles from those jealous in their own sloth and luck had risen, this simple party thrown for their own vain pretense had silenced all. Indeed, from the first toast with Henry Pickett's homebrew in hand, the day improved upon itself over and again. With the quantity Henry brought, most everyone in town had at least one cup and there were many who returned for more. Laughter rose rather than rages of drunken tone, and the very air tasted of the earthen hints in Pickett's brew.

Like locusts in plague, the destitute descended upon the feasts prepared and devoured all in sight. The games of the day, competitions of industry skill and contests of luck, strength and endurance, were enthusiastically enjoined. A pick-up baseball game was started with players drifting in and out without order, no score ever minded. Tug-of-war competitions began to fail due to fumbling hands, and horse-shoe pitches left more than one person laughing off a wild toss through a bloodied scalp. Children and dogs ran wild amidst the fluid chaos of celebration, dashing between legs and through conversations spirited by arcane inanities. Simon saw the cheer and joy about and knew their ruse had worked. The desperate will always sell themselves cheap.

Soon the musicians armed themselves, singularly or in pairs, and began calling out for others to join in their discordant harmonies. The revelers answered with a slow, broken step, the infection of music upon the soul. More and more the players would gather in cells throughout as immigrant rhythms of the world's displaced found each other in hypnotic union. Folk songs and productions of popular taste would rise and fall to anthems and marches, and the lowest of barroom ballads would break out unbidden. Waves choral rippled through the crowd, songs known of greater appeal breaking over one another to form new chants dissolving immediately in coherency. The town began to turn on an air of euphoric intoxication.

The sky was glorious in its evening splendor; shafts of light pierced distant storms to die in diffused strawberry sheets painted on the smoke cast from far-off forest fires. Blackness waited already in the depths of clouds swelling over the mountain behind, an ominous blanket charged with possibilities. The whole was panoramic wonder, a vision to crest the sky of such a wondrous day.

Simon danced with the rest of the town, his step light and his voice joined in song of joyous celebration. He swayed amidst a circle of dancers spiraling, a mad constellation within a galaxy of such so possessed. As he twirled and leapt, jigged and turned, he threw his face skyward to admire that glory above and noticed a crack where one shouldn't be. The dance swept him along before he could care.

* * *

Murderer! A blast of corruption, a breath from below the grave hit Simon in the face as the thing before him spread its maw and laughed triumphant. The tendrils of its existence, ethereal arms ending in hardened nails raked at his body and tore at his soul. That face before him, a comrade years in the earth, twisted with rage. *Ubica! Sada si mrtav! You die now!* Where a nose would have graced that decayed visage, a gaping wound revealed interior secrets.

"Vidak, what have you done?" Simon looked down. In one hand was his pocket pistol and on his shirt, a stain well spread from under his left ribs. "Oh, you dirty cheat," Simon grumbled. As that spectral mockery howled its victory, Simon reached around behind him. When his hand returned wet with blood, the ghostly expression before him changed in recognition of implications. Simon snarled his own triumph, "You don't get no revenge, Vidak. You don't get nothing."

Death lunged and that life yet in Simon reached out and belayed that end with a bloody grip. The blood upon his hand held back that ethereal rage, clasped it as if of flesh and bone. Dropping the pistol and smearing his other hand in the gore that seeped from his wound, Simon strangled that horror before him, squeezing it down to a limp, oily worm.

* * *

The sky was a small circle of midnight black pierced by sinister diamonds, liquid stars undimmed by a barley moon ascendant in amplified glory. This obsidian pendant, a fluid peace betraying moon and stars, was framed by walls of fury, storms of summer passions unleased ignoring this singular well of cosmic approach. Up those curtains of cloud, rising clear through that cyclonic eye to the heavens and that depth beyond, electric fire traced sigils beyond the understanding of Man. Thunder pealed in constant crescendos, waves rolling one into the other in a bombardment enchanting. Worms within the very earth twisted in ecstatic agony beneath that primal roar, that cosmic complaint.

In the dirt where hubris dares count existence meaningful, the citizens of Baird's Holler fell full under the spell of the corruption they had consumed. Fungal infestations fermented fueled the madness as basic conceptual understandings twisted and the townsfolk lost their minds. The tempo had changed, but the dancers knew not their steps.

Amidst this chaos, Simon turned in place, his arms spread and his eyes wide in understanding wonder. The glyphs which raked the walls of thunder came clear of an instant and in that moment he was thrust within himself, abandoned violently at the bottom of his soul with his eyes mere stuttered stereoscopes in a distance of darkness. Simon Atterly screamed, but with ears no longer his own, he heard from afar a shout of triumph in a voice that was once his.

* * *

Simon Atterly stood in the center of Baird's Holler and laughed. He laughed for he could see the truth at last. His eyes had been opened through their forced censure. Now he knew for he could see. In this half-death he stood, he saw much more than the town burning and its citizens agitating like a population gone mad. Now he saw beyond the flames, beyond the smoke that made ghosts of figures even in the near distance. Now he saw the ghosts themselves, saw them wearing the masks of men and women and even children, all those who had drank from those corrupted casks. He saw them, the Dead, beyond the masks of the living they wore and he knew they were mad one and all. The damnation of the worms steals slowly, cruelly.

In his blood-stained hand, Simon held such a worm. It writhed weakly, struggling against enervation, against existence. Such withered souls littered the ground and as the populace of Baird's Holler ran amok in hallucinogenic horror, these exhausted things would slither and climb over the victim unsuspecting, seeking entrance through bodily passage. Minds opened beyond their comprehension had made the revelers susceptible for unwanted guests and the Dead danced drunkenly in the maddened energy of corporeal form.

Simon looked down at the thing in his hand, the soul of one Vidak Ivkov, Sultan of the Bajazid. Hatred, raw and unbridled welled up in his breast and he squeezed tighter. Seven years it had been since that bitterness first burned and for seven years, Simon had slept sound knowing his passion had been true, his purpose right, and his crime undiscovered. Some hatreds are that strong, that justified, that needful. When Vidak had shuddered at last that day long past, Simon had wished the agony could be extended if just a little while. Now, with Vidak held in a grip of gore, Simon looked for means to do just that.

Within the eye of the storm which circled Baird's Holler, the atmospheres were subject only to the drafts caused by burning shanties and buildings catching flame. The storm outside the confines of the valley offered no breath, no encouragement within the town. Smoke all but obscured the existence of the cyclone and were it not for the thunder occasionally rising above the roar of burning wood and the screams of burning people, the storm would be forgot. The full moon still shone down through that funnel of cloud, though it left no shadows on the ground beneath the feet of those possessed. It was through these shifting walls of smoke Simon's inspiration was drawn. Not too far distant were Henry Pickett's wagons and, beneath, he thought he saw in that smoke a form.

With agony extreme enough to nearly dislodge his grip on Vidak, Simon bent down for the pistol he had dropped. The .22 caliber Colt Open Top had been custom etched with grips of pearl, a comfortable weapon for the pocket when a holstered revolver was inappropriate. Now it was covered in bile and blood and mud, but in the trouser pocket it went as Simon struggled forward. Each step was agony, his wound now rising with a need to be known. Though that bullet had passed clean through, the wrath it left behind in torn cells remained. Simon knew though, he knew his wound would not be fatal, at least until he had done what was needed.

At the wagons, his suspicions were confirmed. Beneath them, huddled in fear and crying uncontrollably was Henry Pickett. Simon wasted no time crawling under that shelter and crowding Henry.

"Henry! Henry, are you okay?" The concern existed only in the emptiness of the words spoken.

Henry looked up and cried out, "Simon, what have I done? What have I done?" Tears were streaking his face, carving canyons through mud cast from smoke and dust. "This is all my fault. I made this, Simon."

"Yes, Henry, it is your fault. You did this." Simon's words were cold against the flames that scorched about.

"I did this, Simon. I did this. I let something grow in my vats. Did you taste it? Did you? Did you taste the earth?"

With his free arm, Simon embraced Henry and pulled him close. Looking deep into Henry's eyes Simon saw defeat and nothing more. There was no ghost clouding the agony in Henry's soul. "Yes, Henry, I did. You poisoned us. Why did you do that?"

"I didn't mean to, Simon. I swear. It was supposed to make it better, you have to... Shit! Shit! Shit!" When Henry spied that limp, pulsing thing hanging from Simon's free hand, he began to panic. "Get that away! Get it away! It's dead things!"

The struggle following was violent but short, ending with a clout hard against Henry's head. From there Simon easily overpowered Pickett, straddling him and holding him down at the throat.

"Sorry about this Henry, but Vidak ain't learned his lesson. I need you to help me out, okay? Is that all correct, Henry? Is it?" Simon's voice rose as he spoke. His passion was upon him, the exhilaration he knew when his darkest thoughts were allowed reign. Simon had sat thus many times and the thrill never waned.

"Please no..." Henry had given up, his fight gone as he lay pinned with Simon atop his chest and knees trapping his arms. "Please Simon, don't. Sultans don't kill Sultans."

"This ain't about you, Henry. This is about Vidak."

"Vidak? He's dead. Why do you have him in your hand? What do you want?"

Simon was surprised. Henry did not look half dead, did not look injured in the least. "You can see this? You can see him?"

"Yes, it is Vidak. Why do you have him? Why is he here? Why, Simon? What is happening? What do you want with him? With me?"

"I want to kill him again, that's all. Sorry it has to be you, Henry, but you did do all this, right? You did burn the town with your homebrew, right?"

Henry was broken, his voice a whisper, "Yes, Simon, I did..."

"Then take your punishment and don't bitch."

With those words, Simon shoved that worm, that slithering soul in his hand hard into Henry's mouth. He shoved and kept pushing, jamming the insubstantial horror forcefully down Pickett's throat. Henry, for his part, resisted until fists had loosened his resolve and the wraith in Simon's hand slipped into its new host.

Pulling Henry close, Simon looked into those eyes, "Ah, there you are! Yes, we ain't done yet, you filthy pig."

"*Jebi se, kretenu!*" Henry who was not Henry spat in Simon's face as he struggled to get free.

"Don't speak your shit, boy. You know what you are. You know what you deserve."

"You are damned, Simon. *Proklet si!*"

Simon pulled out his pocket knife and pressed it against the bridge of Henry's nose.

"Come on, Vidak, say it. Admit what you are, scum. Admit it or I'll maim you again."

"Sultans don't kill Sultans." Vidak Radul's accent had always been thick, his English a new and uncomfortable tongue. Speaking through Henry's mouth, the words were muddled further. "*Kukavica.*"

That last was just a needle to provoke and it did. In the three years Simon had known Vidak, they had been close and association with the Ivkov brothers lent everyone in the Mortenson Company a quick and vulgar lesson in Serbian. After Vidak had been found murdered, his older brother Radul reserved that language for only the most profane or sacred oaths. That Vidak would call him a coward was too much, especially after what Simon knew. With a quick motion, Henry's nose fell down into the mud left from his own special brew.

The scream was from both Henry and Vidak. For the host so possessed, that which is not repressed, cast into that well of oblivion, is the amplification of pain. For the malevolence infecting, it is for sensation they haunt and thus feel the cuts as well as the rest.

"Now you look like I left you." With these words, Simon screwed his thumb down into that raw cavity and the damned doubled their thrashing. To stay the struggle, Simon scooted back and placed both hands hard against Henry's throat. He kept those work hardened hands there, pressing with the full force of his body behind them until that body beneath him ceased at last all struggle. Then, leaning down he whispered his refrain into an ear now vacant. "Now you look just like I left you, Vidak."

Simon rose, an indeterminate shadow obscured in a sea of smoke, and brushed his clothes to empty effect. Once satisfied in his dishevelment, he walked without haste from that wagon and the ruin beneath. He had no worry of discovery. The smoke was thick, the town was drunk and there was a long history of such corpses with their noses sliced off in Baird's Holler. It was Vidak's sin, one revealed to Simon whose horror had made it his own. It was that horror which claimed this moment, for what was one more body in a nightmare such as this?

This festival, this celebration of ten years since Isaiah Baird's sacrificial fall brought forth wealth unending, was itself an oblation. Forces far beyond the inquiry of Man had made themselves known to Simon Atterly. Why he was granted this sight he knew not, nor was he sure these visions were anything but stolen, glimpsed by accident from gods distracted. He just knew the glyphs traced across the clouds in electric fire told of things beyond his ken and the fury of a cosmic rejection. It was for this the town was offered in flame. Where the Sultans had sought to celebrate, the demon Simon knew now dwelt here had other designs. What matters mere men in the machinations of gods?

It was this knowledge Simon mulled as he staggered through the streets of Baird's Holler. All about flames licked at structures and madness reigned and would for hours yet. This Simon knew with cold certainty: that the horrors would persist until the walls of wind collapsed and the town deluged. When the hallucinations wore off, the citizens of Baird's Holler would wake shamed and cowed. They would have none to blame, though, for the man whose concoction brought this madness was dead, victim to a strangler the town had long sought. The understanding of his own sins this night were shielded from speculation and granted Simon permissible license to do as he would.

With a pat to his trouser pocket, an assurance that memento stained in snot and blood was secure, Simon set off to do just that.

CALLIOPE

Adrian Ludens

While scoping out another in an endless procession of small Midwestern cities and posting bills announcing the upcoming show, Calli encountered a kindred spirit. She glanced at his misshapen, claw-like hands as they clutched at the air.

"It's all gone wrong," he said.

"What has?"

"Everything." His eyes held a sorrowful, faraway look.

He had gone all out, she observed; part Lobster Boy, part Wolf Man, part Tattooed Lady. It seems to her too much—and yet, somehow, not enough.

"Not finding work?" she asked.

"Of course not." He made another snatch at the air, perhaps trying to pluck memories of happier times. "Half want to prevent anyone from seeing the likes of us and the other half don't care to see us in the first place."

Calli tipped her head back, gazing skyward, in a modified sword-swallowing pose. "It's the politically-correct versus the ambivalent. Two warring factions and neither want us to exist."

The tattooed lobster wolf nodded. "And we're the innocent casualties."

Calli looked down, assessed him again. His visible tattoos all seemed to be admirable copies of notable pre-Raphaelite paintings. He had filed his canine incisors in a successful attempt at appearing more wolf-like. His spilling cleavage drew her attention next and she wondered what hormone cocktail he took to grow both facial hair and breasts.

She flashed one of the show bills like a badge. "We're setting up now. Would you like to come back to the lot with me? See if the Baron will hire you?"

He examined his glittering platform boots for a moment, shook his head, and then turned to leave.

"Hey, what do you call yourself?" Calli asked.

His gleaming eyes peered at her from behind stray locks of his scruffy mane. Misshapen hands plucked another memory from the air. Perhaps he wanted to save their brief interaction for future consideration. He spun on a sparkling heel and threw the words over his shoulder:

"I'm Average Joe."

Calli stood alone.

By ones and twos, her classmates had piled into waiting cars and disappeared down the sleepy town's residential streets until none remained but her. Her parents had forgotten her. Again. She waited, though in her heart Calli knew she'd have to walk if she wanted to be home before dark. She scuffed the toe of her one-size-too-small black Mary Jane into the gravel and gazed around the empty playground. No breeze ruffled her hair; even nature itself had forgotten Calli, had left her alone.

She counted to twenty, then fifty, then one hundred. She sighed and began to trudge across the playground in the direction of home. As she passed the vacant swings, an idea came, and she altered her course.

Calli returned to her living quarters, a private trailer parked in a field near the outskirts of town with the rest of the Baron Backroad's Freewheeling Circus of Wonders entourage. The Baron, she knew, had left to visit the city administration building to fill out paperwork for the right to perform. This was, in her opinion, yet another nondescript city, bereft of joy and imagination, another stagnant pool of sameness, where even the red tape was gray.

The condition seemed to be catching, infecting her circus brethren. Her husband, Daredevil Dave, lay sprawled, silent, and immobile. Comatose without the added feature of hospital equipment chirping a notification for every one hundred dollars spent. *Dead, but not dressed for the occasion,* she realized. He hadn't spoken or eaten in days.

Calli perched on the edge of the bed and considered her husband, curled in a sweaty tangle beneath a dirty sheet. His skin had turned, like that of so many others, to gray. A drowned rat rolled in flour. Perhaps his thoughts were gray as well. He had lost his sense of wonder. It pained her to see him reduced in this way. He was supposed to be the strong one, the rock. Instead, she felt weary and drained after a few minutes in his presence.

"Calli." Her husband's vocal cords were dried cornhusks, hinting at the word rather than speaking it.

She bent closer. "You're awake."

Dave said nothing.

"I posted all the bills I had with me, even got a few shops to put posters in their display windows. I'll go back with more later tonight. I just wanted to check on you." In truth, the need to leave the gray city and return to the reassuring comfort of the colorful entourage had become unbearable.

An idea came to her. "You won't believe how excited everyone is for the show! You should see all the lot lice standing around, watching the tent go up! No need to paper the house this time; ticket sales will be through the roof!"

All lies, but she watched a small degree of color seep into her husband's cheeks.

"Feel better soon, hon." She patted his leg. "The circus needs you and misses you. I need you and miss you."

That time she'd spoken the truth.

"Calliope Jean Jenkins! Get over here!"

No apology, no explanation, only annoyance expressed that her daughter had inconvenienced her by not walking home. Calliope tracked her mother's progress across the playground from the giddy arc of her swing. She'd enticed the wind to return; it playfully whipped at her hair with each forward and backward flight. Never before had she reached such heights.

"Calliope, get down from there! You hear me?" Her mother, hands on hips to express her irritation, loomed and receded. Calliope's mother turned her head to check on the rusty family sedan still running at the curb, as if worried someone would take it for a joyride while her back was turned. Calliope let her head drop

back and pointed her toes at the sky.

"I won't say it again!" her mother's voice cut the air. "Get... down... NOW."

Calliope let go of the chains. For one heart-stopping moment, she soared. Before gravity reasserted its authority, Calliope glimpsed her mother. Her jaw had dropped open in amazement, arms clutching the air, eyes riveted on the spectacle unfolding.

Then Calliope plunged. The shock of impact and the grinding pain rose up and tore through her broken ankle and shinbone. She didn't mind. Her mother had finally given Calliope her undivided attention.

Calli allowed her mounting frustration to get the better of her and she threatened a cab driver.

The Baron had sent her back into town with more bills to post and even a few hole-punched tickets to pass out to the right people. She kept a sharp lookout for the leaders, the influencers. If the Queen Bee got in free, then all her worker-bees came along and shelled out alfalfa for tickets of their own.

She'd ended up on the opposite end of town, and not wanting to walk all the way back, hailed a cab. She had no cash for the fare, but the cabbie didn't know that. They passed motionless pedestrians, most of them existing in varying shades of gray.

"When's the show?" he asked, when he saw the last of her not-yet-posted bills.

"Tomorrow night. Seven o'clock."

"Oh." He already seemed to have lost interest and she felt disappointment pinch her heart. "Too bad; I already have plans."

An idea came to her and she instructed the driver to pull over three blocks short of her destination. When they had stopped, Calli withdrew the dagger she kept concealed in her boot and held it against his throat. "Get out of the cab."

"You want my cash? Take it." The man's hazel eyes pleaded with hers in the rearview mirror's reflection. "Just take it and go. I've already forgotten your face."

"That's what I'm afraid of," she muttered. "Get out."

He fumbled with his seat belt and then pushed open his door. Calli slid from the back seat at the same time, contemplating his eyes. They'd been hazel—not gray.

She motioned with the dagger. "Take the keys out of the ignition."

With something akin to a groan escaping his lips, he did as she'd instructed. He held the keys out to her, but she shook her head. "Toss them in the grass."

He threw his keys. They landed with a muted jingle about ten yards away. Not as far as she'd hoped, but she decided it would have to do.

"Now," Calli said. "You need to give me your full attention."

The cab driver swallowed hard and nodded. She lifted the dagger, clasping it so the twelve-inch blade swayed over her head. She swung it like a pendulum for effect. She tipped her head back, readying herself for The Big Swallow.

The tip of the blade was too dull to cut, but the cabbie didn't know that. Her gag reflex being a ghostly relic of the past, Calli poked the upper glottis muscle until it opened up and gave her access to her throat. She eased the blade down until the crossguards rested on either side of her open mouth. She extended her arms out, held her pose for a moment, and then withdrew the blade. She bowed with a flourish and slid the dagger back into its scabbard.

"Sweet baby Jesus, lady," the cabbie said. "Do you have a flyer for your circus?" He held out a hand that, she noted, looked healthy. Calli withdrew her last freebie ticket and handed it to him. Excitement had mottled his cheeks with pink patches. His eyes sparkled.

"I hope you'll come see the show."

"I will, and I'll bring my buddies too!" The cabbie looked enthused. He stuffed the ticket into the front pocket of his jeans as Calli turned and strode away.

She glanced back once. The man had located his keys; the cab receded in the opposite direction. Calli grinned. *He forgot about the fare,* she thought. *Two birds with one stone.*

She returned to find the Baron giving a speech in the Back Yard.

"I blame the Inter-webs," he said. She couldn't tell if he truly thought that's what people called it or if he meant to be ironic. "People can see just about anything you can imagine with a few keystrokes."

"Funny you should use the word 'strokes'," Flexy Lexi said. "The men aren't as interested in my contortionist act as they used to be. What do I have to do? Incorporate props to jump start their dirty imaginations?"

A few performers snickered or murmured agreement—with her sentiment, at least—but their leader raised his arms to silence everyone. He frowned. "I'm sure we will never have to stoop to that. I pride myself on running a classy show that instructs while it entertains. What we need is more interaction with potential patrons on a diverse array of social media platforms."

Calli shuddered and tried to elbow her way through the assemblage but couldn't make any headway. She dreaded where this conversation might lead. She vowed to pull up stakes and quit before falling in with the white noise blizzard of social media.

The Baron drew a deep breath and continued. "Remember when Gonzo the elephant sat on poor Jerry while he was relaxing and having a smoke?"

"Oh, Lord, yes," Murray, one of the roustabouts, murmured.

"I warned him those cigarettes would kill him," Bunko the Clown said.

The Baron let the scattered laughter fade and then spoke. "I believe we missed an opportunity there." He rubbed his hands together, as if warming himself before a fire rather than warming up to an idea. "Instead of hushing the whole thing up, we should have posted his picture online. 'In Memoriam,' you see. We should have made a bigger deal out of it. Dedicated the next several shows to him and milked the sympathies of the crowds in each town."

"Feh." Bunko spat in the dirt. "The only surefire way to get people's attention these days woulda been to post a picture of his head smashed open like a melon."

The Baron, ever the showman, raised his arms again. "Let us not be morbid. If we each took it upon ourselves to promote the shows via our own—"

Calli withdrew her dagger and poked Bunko's backside with the dull tip. "Comin' through!" He lurched out of the way. Performers and roustabouts alike parted before her outthrust dagger and Calli hurried to her trailer to check on her husband.

Calli sat beside Dave's bed and thumbed through an old photo album. For her, there was no substitute for four by six matte prints. She came across one of her husband in full Daredevil regalia, post cannon-shot, helmet off, hair mussed, posing with a trio of kids. They were all blond, missing baby teeth, and grinning from ear to ear. She held it up to show her husband, but he didn't respond. Calli paused at a picture she had snapped ten years ago of the big top after a blowdown. No serious injuries reported, but they couldn't do a show that night because of that storm. A couple pages later another shot made her grin. Dave, her, Roscoe the boss hostler, and whole group of kids all mugging for the camera. The colors seemed vibrant, more real than the reality around her.

Calli realized several of her fellow Cirkies had been missing during the Baron's speech. She wondered if they too had fallen into lethargy. Daredevil Dave, the larger-than-life persona, had ceased to exist. Her loving husband was fading into oblivion in seeming acceptance. Had her missing colleagues also lost their passion for performing, and by extension, for life? She considered Dave. How much longer could he, or would he, cling to life? If he died, could she find the strength to go on without him?

She had a momentary flash then, a vivid vision, of swallowing her dagger in front of a packed house. She saw a crimson haze, followed by an eruption of vibrant colors beneath the big top.

A muffled pounding against the trailer door brought Calli back to reality and she started, dropping the photo album onto the linoleum floor.

"Calli! The Baron needs some help!" The speaker, roustabout Murray, sounded angry—or scared.

She rose, hurried to the door, and pushed it open. "What's wrong?"

Murray's face looked pinched, anxious. "It's Milo, the Strongman."

Calli felt her guts tighten, a constricting boa. "What about him?"

"We need everyone's help moving him," Murray said. "He's turned to stone."

Still flesh, of course, but Milo had turned a shade of gray akin to granite. Someone could have carved him from stone, for as heavy as he seemed.

"Maybe we cart him out front," someone said. "Our own Petrified Man."

"Don't you mean the Cardiff Giant?"

"Shut up, the both of you!" The Baron's voice sliced the air like dagger, silencing the chatter.

"The Baron's right," Calli said. "We need to work together to move Milo somewhere safe, like when we moved Dave..." she let the sentence drop.

In all, it took six of them to haul Milo the Strongman across the lot and into the trailer that he shared with Alfredo and Alberto, the aerialists. *We look like pallbearers,* she thought. *Another one bites the gray, gray dust.*

They avoided making eye contact with one another as they shuffled away, all seeming to flee in separate directions. Calli found herself wondering if the dwindling, apathetic crowds triggered this blight amongst her brethren, like mold fulfilling its manifest destiny across the surface of a rotting peach, or if the performers themselves were somehow to blame.

The sun fled and night took the stage.

Tomorrow they would open the souvenir and concession stands outside the big top hours before the performance. The Baron might even decide to place an exhibit wagon downtown to drum up ticket sales. Calli knew she'd be expected to help with a dozen or more tasks, and yet she grew restless and could not sleep. She couldn't bear lying next to Dave. It seemed every moment he slipped further away from her. At last, she rose, and found herself wandering the city streets alone.

Occasional headlights from passing vehicles illuminated her as she walked. Each time, she resisted the urge to pose as if reveling in the glow of the big top's spotlight. Calli encountered few people. Most of them shuffled along as if in a daze. Some didn't move at all. She wondered if they would stand immobile all night, or if they had someone who cared enough to track them down and ensure they got home safe.

Calli rounded a corner and the garish lights, neon and blazing against the night sky, took her by surprise. She had encountered so many gray-hued citizens in this municipality of darkness that she'd almost forgotten color existed at all.

A nightclub stood before her. Music emanated from inside the building. Calli took a deep breath and pulled open the door. A thick-necked bouncer stamped her hand without bothering to ask for I.D. The club was resplendent in garish colors. A near-deafening dubstep song throbbed from the speakers. Calli let the strains guide her to the middle of the dance floor where just over a dozen revelers alternately danced or pogoed as the song progressed.

A motley assemblage of men and women cavorted around her, pressing against her from all sides. The mingling of perfumes and colognes created the olfactory equivalent of a mat shot. Attempts at maintaining personal space became futile, the dance floor a fully clothed orgy.

A square-jawed kid in a numbered sports jersey grinned and made eye contact as Calli turned. His features were still natural with no touch of gray present as far as she could see in the strobe light.

Calli touched his shoulder and shouted over the pulsing music. "Hey, what's your name?"

The sports fan leaned in and yelled into her ear. "Yeah! I love this music, too."

Calli nodded, letting their miscommunication go. Everyone whirled around them. Now that they'd stopped moving, the effect was dizzying.

"I get such a rush from this!" Calli detected the piney scent of gin on his breath when he spoke. She found she didn't mind, rather liked it in fact. His breath on her neck elicited goose bumps despite the oppressive body heat permeating the room. "I haven't seen you here before."

Calli craved attention, wanted badly to perform. "How dirty is the floor?" she shouted.

He just stared, his features blank. "The floor?"

She clutched herself against him, poured her words into his ear. "The dance floor, how dirty is it?"

He scrunched his features in a mock grimace of exaggerated disgust. "It's filthy!"

"Good. Lie down."

Calli drew back as the strains of the dubstep song gave way to an industrial-tinged bump and grind. She guided him to a prone position, making sure he kept his hands at his sides. The crowd parted around them, eager for a spectacle. She straddled his waist and pinned his arms to the grimy floor with her knees. She let the music flow through her, gyrating to the beat. Her partner's features had glazed over, but not like the gray populace; a vibrant *joie de vivre* seemed to flow through him. Calli felt the physical manifestation of his mounting excitement as she bore down on him.

Then, with the eyes of everyone in the club clinging to them like glitter on wet skin, she slipped a hand into her boot and withdrew the dagger. She swept it up over her head. The gleaming blade caught the flashing lights and even over the music, Calli heard a collective gasp from those surrounding her. She swept the blade down with a theatrical flourish toward his throat and he let loose a bellow of primal terror. The crowd pressed in on them, but no one made an effort to stop her.

Calli tilted her head back and focused on swallowing the dagger. If someone were to jostle her, she'd need an ambulance. She focused on the fear, welcomed it, and then overcame it. Calli gave the swaying throng what they wanted: The Big Swallow. They shouted their approval.

Calli withdrew the dagger, slid it into its scabbard, and rose. She thought the guy on the dance floor would need a change of underwear when he got home—but in a good way. Hands clutched at her hair and clothing, fingers stroked her skin. Everyone wanted in on the action, wanted to be associated with something exciting.

Inspiration hit and she withdrew a sheaf of folded show bills from a pocket and threw them into the air. They rained like enormous confetti on the avid, upturned faces.

Calli used the distraction to hurry out the door and into the cooling arms of the night. She hoped their enthusiasm would remain kindled and that they'd turn out in droves and pack the house.

By the time she returned to the lot and the silent, looming big top, dawn was sending exploratory fingers of pink light up over the horizon. The light spoke of rebirth.

She reached her trailer and stepped inside, pulling the door closed. An odor both foreign and unwelcome greeted her. Near palpable silence reigned. An immediate sense of guilt guided her to the bedside. She perched on the edge of the mattress and took her husband's hand. It felt cool. She leaned in and kissed his forehead only to find it cool and dry.

"Dave?"

He didn't respond.

"Dave!"

She shook his gray arm, pinched his colorless cheek. "Wake up! The show's about to start."

Calli clasped her hands around his and, sick at heart, she sobbed. Had he died while she danced at the club? Guilt stole her breath like hands crushing her windpipe. She tipped her head back, tried to catch her breath.

What were his final words to her? A blizzard of random thoughts created so much white noise in her brain that she could not remember. What had she last said to him? When had they last kissed or held hands? When had they last walked together under the night sky or laughed over a joke one of them had made? Calli cursed her faulty memory.

Dawn had broken and so had her heart. Calli spent the morning sitting beside her husband's empty husk. She stroked his skin, ruffled his hair, and held each of his hands in turn. Calli ignored the buzz of activity outside the trailer. Instead she reminisced, recalled good times and bad. She laughed, sobbed, and even dozed.

She dreamed of Dave, fired from his cannon, soaring through the air, and landing with practiced grace in her outstretched arms. He didn't feel heavy to her at all. In fact, though she fought to keep hold of him, her husband floated out of her grasp, up and far beyond her reach.

Calli jolted to wakefulness. An invisible wad of cotton seemed stuffed into her mouth. Tears polluted by despair stung her eyes and spilled down her cheeks. She sat in stubborn silence until the sounds of activity coming from the lot grew too loud to ignore. Then she rose, drew the sheet over her husband's face, and departed the trailer.

The saying was true: the show *must* go on.

Calli told no one about Dave. The Baron took her aside about an hour before show time. "Calliope, I wonder if you might be interested in taking on a larger role." He eyed her as if he expected her to feel flattered, but she only felt empty.

"I don't think so, Baron."

"I believe you'd thrive in the spotlight," he pressed. "And I'm not the young man I once was. I'd like you to share ringmaster duties with me."

Calli's mind slid back to her husband, his performance concluded. *All out, all over,* as the circus saying went. She thought about the epidemic of gray, immobile citizens infesting every new city and the dwindling attendance at each performance.

"I appreciate the offer," she said. "Let me consider it during tonight's show."

"All right," the Baron said. "But I worry about you, Calliope; you're looking peaked." He appraised her with one final glance and hurried away to make final preparations.

She pondered many things in the minutes leading up to show time. Her husband's death seemed to have hollowed her heart. Calli tried to take solace in the throng of circus-goers perched on the bleachers. She thought the house looked closer to full than any show they'd performed in at least a year, perhaps longer. The tent was a cacophony of excited murmurs. Why were they here? What spectacle did they hope to witness?

She inspected each face in turn. This motley assemblage invited comparisons to the bloodthirsty, unwashed masses that once filled the Roman coliseums, roaring their approval every time a criminal or wild animal lost their life. Calli stood in the shadows, searching for faces that held some color, indicating a vestige of innocence, some sense of wonder retained. She felt as if she were scanning for survivors in the waters of a storm-tossed gray sea. She found a few: the cab driver, surrounded by a trio of healthy-skinned friends; the young guy from the club sat with a small group. Her gaze found Average Joe sitting alone and her lips quirked into a half smile.

Stick around, she thought. *The Baron might offer you a spot after the show.*

The faces of the vast majority were ashen. Not yet entirely lost, these souls might yet find rejuvenation. Calli felt sure that an extraordinary occurrence tonight would embed a thread of enduring exhilaration within their collective subconscious. Like the filament in a light bulb, the people at tonight's performance would come alive every time someone threw the switch. The conduit for the current—in the form of circuses, carnivals, rodeos, monster truck shows, and more—could revitalize them, staving off the gray pall, rejuvenating their souls, and allowing them to return to their everyday lives revived. Their excitement could spread like a contagion, leading to resurgence in the public's enjoyment of shows like Baron Backroad's Freewheeling Circus of Wonders.

This much she hoped.

The Cirkies around her hurried to their places. Calli turned and caught sight of her reflection in a lighted mirror Bunko and the other clowns used when touching up their makeup. For a long moment, she forgot to breathe.

She had turned gray.

Grief, she felt sure, had brought about the sudden change. She'd lost her husband, and with him, her zest for life and her desire to perform, all in one fell swoop. Life had served her a poisoned platter of heartache and she could not leave the table until she devoured every bite.

Calli waited for her cue and then stepped to the center ring. First, she would test the waters, would give them a taste, hoping for proof that her plan stood a chance. She gave the dagger a twist, and let a sharpened edge split her lower lip. Blood coated the edge of the blade. She withdrew it and lashed it, whip-like, in the audience's direction. Inky droplets arced through the air and spattered a gray-skinned man and woman slouched in the nearest row.

A murmur of surprise rippled through the crowd, followed by—did she dare hope?—signs of avid interest. Calli grinned, and felt more blood trickle from her lip and down her chin.

The makeshift baptism yielded thrilling results; the couple regained their color. Many of the spectators nearest them regained their natural hues as well. Calli could see it would not be enough; she had to do more.

The dagger's blade slid into her mouth and down her throat. Calli pushed it, working it forward, forearm muscles flexed with the effort. She arched her back, snarling against the eruption of pain. Moments later, the tip of the blade emerged from her solar plexus, the head of a metallic serpent reintroducing humanity to feelings they had forgotten.

Calli fell to her knees the same moment the audience rose to their feet. Jaws dropped open in amazement, arms hung in slack surprise, all sets of eyes opened wide, fixed and fascinated, on HER. She hoped they'd never forget this moment, would never forget her. Amid shouts, screams, and thunderous ovation, their faces loomed and receded. She realized they now shone in a plenitude of flesh-colored tones. Their vibrant features looked glorious as Calliope Jean drifted away, torso awash in crimson, vision fading to black.

All out, all over.

CALL TO ME, SWEET ALECTO

Alistair Rey

Evie caught the scent of the ocean as she pulled into the parking lot, although upon first sight all she saw was a flat terrain of parked cars, their metallic skin glinting in the cold afternoon sunlight. Sedans belonged to the well-off suburban families; the VWs and two-doors to the day-trippers and students. What did she drive? A sleek red Alfa Romeo Spider that she had managed to pry from her ex-husband in the divorce. Evie had always disliked the sports car. A predictable testament to male ego and virility, she had once described it to a therapist. Yet *acquiring* the vehicle, possessing the object which her husband had taken such pride in, invested the car with new significance. Her therapist called it spite. Evie preferred to think of it as catharsis.

The lot was crammed with men in bucket hats and women restraining children eager to explore the waterfront. More than once, Evie slammed on the brakes to avoid hitting a pedestrian. She stared at the threads of bodies massing in the distance like a human ant colony and then let her eyes drift to the boats parked in the harbour and the vacant sea beyond. How many people had come? Certainly not everyone could fit on those ships, she mused.

As she eased the car in between an oversized SUV and a Fiat that had seen better days, Evie caught a glimpse of two young men standing about idly, resisting the forward momentum of the crowd. One leaned against the hood of an automobile, flabby arms protruding from a faded muscle shirt, a cigarette pinched between thumb and index finger. As she slid out of the driver seat, he let out a long whistle. "Nice set... of wheels," he called, eliciting a chortle from his friend.

Evie ignored them, lifting her travel bag from the passenger seat and following the others.

"Don't mind them," a man at her side advised as their paths converged and they merged into the human ant colony.

"Oh, I didn't," Evie assured him.

People bumped and jostled against her. The sheer force of the crowd propelled her forward. Somewhere overhead a gull screeched.

This is a vacation, Evie repeated to herself. *I* need *this vacation.*

"So many people," she muttered, trying to avoid errant elbows and inconsiderate shoes attached to inconsiderate people.

The man at her side gave a wistful smile. "Once every eight years," he said. "It packs them in."

A teenager sporting a tie-dyed shirt featuring leaping whales cut in front of her and then disappeared into the sea of bodies.

"I just wouldn't have thought..." Evie began, eyeing the crowd and wondering why she had decided on a wildlife cruise rather than the beaches of southern France. Wildlife tourism is the new thing, everyone had said. It was *different.*

"The chisel-toothed whales pass through here like clockwork," the man was saying. "It brings out everyone. The tourists. The nature freaks. Biologists. Even religious nuts. Some people think that these whales have mystical significance, did you know that?"

"And which one are you?" Evie asked, half in jest, as they were shunted along towards the greeting stations on the harbour quay.

Once settled into her cabin on *The Odyssey* and taking half a Klonopin for good measure, Evie began to feel at ease. She wandered along the decks of the ship, passing through empty ballrooms and bars that had yet to be stocked. A crew member dressed in an immaculately white uniform discerned that she was, indeed, lost, and politely instructed her toward the greeting deck where complimentary drinks and hors d'oeuvres were being served.

"Wouldn't want to miss the meet and greet," he said with a smile.

"No, of course not," she mumbled, although Evie was already dreading it. She had yet to spot a lone traveller like herself. Couples, especially those in the early years of marriage, were associated with an acute type of social discomfort she had come to think of as her own personal form of *Weltschmerz*. In their presence, she would brood, cast pouty looks, and secretly relish in malevolent fantasies. Hardly the type of person you wanted at a party, and eventually, one by one, her friends told her so. They had suggested the trip after all, perhaps with the expectation that she might meet someone or simply to have three weeks free of Evie's incessant self-pity and resentment. Even her therapist was beginning to find her a bore, Evie suspected.

She eyed the couples and families from her position by the deck rail, a flute of chilled prosecco in one hand. The lapping waves below proved more entertaining.

"And then there was one," a voice behind her chimed.

She already knew it belonged to the man she had met earlier on the quay.

He introduced himself as Steve, noting that he was also traveling solo.

All Evie could think was he didn't look like a Steve. A Mark, or maybe a John. But not a Steve.

"Funny, but you don't strike me as the nature type," he said, trying to draw her into conversation. "Why *this* cruise? *This* special event?" He smiled to show he was only being friendly, perhaps a bit curious.

"I wanted to see something that other people hadn't," she admitted. "I wanted something I didn't have to share."

A pained, comical smile meandered across his lips. "Well, you might have picked the wrong shindig," as he gestured to the hundreds of bodies filling the deck. "This occasion packs them in."

Evie laughed, recognizing how absurd she sounded given the circumstances. Of course there would be thousands of people here. Of course everyone would want to experience one of the rarest animal migrations known to man. In an age of mass tourism, unique experience was something purchased and commodified. It was pre-packaged and converted into irksome selfies and social media updates calculated to incite envy. Kitsch for the digital age.

"You never mentioned what type *you* are," she said, changing the subject. "Religious nut, right?"

Again, that winsome grin.

Standing on the deck in the afternoon sun, pleasantly sedated by the mix of Italian wine and Klonopin, Evie realized that she felt okay for the first time in a long time.

* * *

"No marriage is perfect," Evie's mother had told her during one of their hour-long phone conservations that passed for therapy in the days before Evie sought professional help. True, perfection was unattainable, but Evie's marriage had been a train wreck. How she had ever fallen for the pseudo-intellectual with a car fetish was beyond her, but it had happened. Falling in love elicited far fewer questions than falling out of it, she appreciated.

In the weeks before she finally decided to break the news to Matt, her soon-to-be *ex*-husband, Evie had painstakingly compiled a list of all the reasons why she knew her choice was correct. Each day she reflected on their four-year relationship, adding memories of hurt, disappointment, and fear. The list was not necessarily to remind her of everything she had put up with and the emotional strife it had caused. It was there as a statement of fact, a raft to cling to as Matt inevitably attempted to make excuses in that persuasive way he had and convince her that the distress and violence they shared together was the natural order of things. Each day, the litany of demoralizing abuse grew longer. At one point, she paused to consider whether she was being *unfair*, just as Matt always accused. Was she failing to "see the other side of things"? Was she retreating into a "feminine worldview of self-obsessive gender idealization," as Matt once claimed, paraphrasing one of the hack social philosophers he was fond of reading? These doubts were followed by shame, frantic discussions with girlfriends, and restless nights that seamlessly blended into sleep-deprived mornings.

On the designated day, Evie left work early and prepared herself for the discussion and subsequent argument that would follow. She took the precaution of removing any noticeable objects that could be transformed into projectiles. The kitchen knives were stowed away to preclude the usual dramatic declarations of self-harm that made up the *pièce de résistance* in Matt's emotional arsenal. This was not about feminine worldview, she would tell him. It was not about his reluctance to discuss children and family. It was not about menstrual cycles or female hormonal imbalances commonly referred to by Matt as "bitch syndrome." It was about pain and self-worth. In particular, *her* pain and *her* self-worth.

As five o'clock rolled around, she sat with arms folded, list clutched in her hand, waiting for the smooth purr of the Alfa Romeo in the drive. But it never came. By six, she managed to work up the nerve to call. His cell rang and went to voicemail. Evie clenched her fists. He had somehow even managed to ruin her attempt to walk out on her own terms, to have her reckoning. Frustration transformed into a simmering rage. Picking up the phone, she dialled the number a second time. It rang as before, and then the line clicked.

"Yeah?" Matt said.

Evie froze.

"Evie?"

"Matt?"

"Yeah, *you* called me."

"Matt, why aren't you home?"

Don't tell him you were worried. Don't ask what he wants for dinner. Don't apologize. Don't. Don't. Don't!

"Sorry hon, just finishing up some things at the office. Kind of hectic today."

"Matt, when will you be home?"

"Soon. Just need to finish up..."

"Matt, I think you..."

And then she heard it. A soft feminine giggle in the background, faint but playful and suggestive.

"Matt, are you at—"

"I'll be home shortly. Don't worry. See you soon."

"Matt, I—"

But the line was dead.

Evie returned to that moment again and again in the months after the divorce. Whenever she felt lonely or doubted her actions, she would conjure up that soft, feminine laughter and give herself over completely to a rage that knew no expression; a rage that only churned and simmered and expanded like a crescendo that never broke. Hatred, pure and uncontaminated, for everything he was, everything he continued to be. And then, she would walk across the living room of her modest single bedroom apartment and look out the front window toward the driveway where the red Alfa Romeo Spider was parked. For all that Matt might have taken from her—dignity, self-esteem, trust—the car was a poor substitute. But it was, in the end, something.

* * *

A whine of feedback pierced through the afternoon, sharp and brisk.

"Is this thing on?" came a full-bodied voice.

A long "yesssss" droned from the crowd.

"And you in the back?"

A middle-aged man in a cabana shirt and dark glasses gave a thumbs up. "Loud and clear."

Evie now saw the man speaking into the hand-held microphone. He was tall, well-tanned, with a warm face. *Affable* was the word to describe it, she thought.

"Okkkaayyyy," he said into the mic. "Welcome aboard, I'm Captain Tom Bering, and I'll be with you for the next three weeks on this adventure. Everyone's getting settled in I hope...? Good!"

Evie braced herself against the deck rail as the ship's motors began to whir and the vessel started its slow departure into the open water.

Captain Tom carefully lay the mic down and cleared his throat. From his pocket he produced a white handkerchief and held it up for the audience to see. Next, he made a fist and placed the white handkerchief over his hand, raising it to eye level. The crowd watched in silence as he waved his hand over the covered fist, making elaborate gestures in the air with his fingers. Then, grabbing for the handkerchief, he tore it from his hand in one quick gesture. Three white birds shot into the air, the sound of their flapping wings dissipating as they ascended into the azure sky.

A moment of silence ensued, followed by a roar of applause and whistles from the crowd.

"I like to start things off with a bit of magic," Captain Tom explained, pressing the mic once again to his lips. "It makes for a friendlier atmosphere, ya know?"

The crowd concurred with a murmurous "yessss."

"Now, we're gonna have a good time here," he continued. "There are a few ground rules I have to go over, and I'll be getting to them in just a sec. But first, I wanted to tell you about what you'll be experiencing. You are in for a treat, folks. The chisel-toothed whale comes through the South Pacific once every eight years to complete its feeding cycle. Now, I know some people might have their own opinions on what this signifies, but to me, it's a celebration. The Great Feeding is a joyous act that we are here to experience together."

He paused for a moment to let the audience digest the meaning of his words.

"Now, I don't know how much you know about these creatures, so I just want to give you some basic facts."

The man in the cabana shirt emitted an audible grunt.

"These creatures are truly a miracle of nature. They only surface to feed every eight years. The rest of the time they remain dormant. Some people find that impossible."

Captain Tom turned to a chalky faced boy standing in the front row.

"Think *you* could go eight years without dinner?" he asked.

"I'm only seven," the boy replied innocently, drawing a peal of laughter from the crowd.

"Exactly. It's a looonnnng time. But these whales are different. Truly special. And that's why we're all here. We need to remember that *we* are guests in their environment. We are the intruders in their habitat. We'll all be good guests, I'm sure, but it means we need to be considerate. Pictures are fine—and we'll get you real close to the action folks, I swear," as he gave an exaggerated wink, "but under no circumstances should we try to interfere in this miraculous occurrence."

Again, the man in the cabana shirt grunted.

Steve snickered. "I hear you," he said as Captain Tom continued his spiel. "This guy seems a little too keen on the positive vibes."

"You could put it that way," the man replied.

Evie watched the shoreline receding from view as the ship manoeuvred a turn and set out into the Pacific. The land looked brown and craggy from this distance; the towering hotels reduced to white blotches on the horizon.

"Eight years," Steve was saying. "I imagine you can work up quite an appetite in that time."

"Technically that isn't true," said the grunting man, removing his glasses and polishing the lenses with the trim of his shirt. "Their bodies are designed to store excess blubber that nourishes them during the dormancy period. They aren't exactly missing any meals, just portioning them out."

"Hey, you must be one of the scientists. Marine biologist? Ichthyologist?"

"Actually, I'm not. I've just done my homework," as he returned his sunglasses and looked past Steve to the women in hot pants and bikini tops on the opposite side of the deck. Every so often, the man licked his lower. Evie found the gesture repulsive.

Captain Tom finished his pitch to a loud round of applause.

"Now that guy's a showman," Steve said, joining in the clapping.

The man in the cabana shirt nodded, his eyes fixed on the women.

"Edward?" a shrill voice called out. "Edwaarrrddd!"

The man in the cabana shirt furrowed his brow and looked at his feet. "Right here, dear," he sighed, waving to a woman in baggy shorts and a Moroccan-print shawl.

"Ed, did you hear that? We'll see them right up close. Isn't it wonderful?"

"Hmmm?" Ed's attention seemed elsewhere.

Without an introduction, the woman turned to Evie. "I just knew this trip would be worth it," she said. "My friends wanted to come, you know. But in the end, it was just me and Ed."

Evie smiled, finding the woman's tone and gestures comical. She was patently middle-aged, right down to the heavy makeup applied to her face.

"I like your shawl," Evie said.

"Do you?" the woman beamed. "It's a para-*shawl*. Get it? Like parasol, for the sun?"

"Very clever," Evie played along.

"Okay, let's go see what's on the agenda," Ed cut in, pulling at his wife's arm and towing her across the deck.

"Well they seemed pleasant," Evie said once the couple was out of earshot.

Steve rolled his eyes. Then, in a complete *non sequitur*, he asked: "Think that kid in the front was a plant?"

"Which one?"

"The boy who said he was only seven."

"I don't..."

"I think he was. Like, absolutely."

"How do you know that?" Evie asked, looking at the child who, she suddenly realized, did not seem to belong to any of the other adults congregating around the drinks table or heading to the poolside lido.

"Show biz instinct. It's a fairly routine set up. Gets the laughs. Disarms the crowd. Basic stuff. Rule *numero uno*: never trust the cute kid in the front row."

"And what show biz instinct are you referring to?" Evie asked, intrigued.

"Oh, I've been around, done my time. I'll tell you about it some time."

"Careful, I might hold you to that."

"By all means," he replied, smiling.

* * *

The daily mix and mingle activities were just as exhausting as they were boring. There was water aerobics in the morning followed by a round of water polo. Iberian tapas usually preceded the afternoon yoga session hosted by female instructors with muscular arms and tanned bodies. At five, guests congregated in the Retro Lounge for the cocktail meetup where uniformed bartenders doled out endless mojitos. The days acquired their own self-indulgent routine, punctuated by pithy reminders to enjoy the R-and-R and forget your troubles, whatever they may be.

Steve took to cruise life with alacrity, joining in the activities and making friends whenever the opportunity presented itself. Evie, by contrast, found it more difficult to give herself over to the easy-going atmosphere. She spent most days on the side-line listening to inspirational podcasts with titles like *Find Your Zen* and *Renewal for the Modern Soul*. She looked out across the water from time to time and monitored the movement of *The Odyssey*'s sister ship, *The Aegean*, a mile to the west. She found it slightly amusing to think that everything taking place on *The Odyssey* was being replicated just a short distance across the water on its counterpart: women lounging about the pool in two-piece bathing suits; paunchy men hunched over exercise bikes in the gym; couples wrapped in white bathrobes on their way to the sauna, the only difference being the insignia on the breast reading *The Aegean* in swirling blue script.

"*You are in a special place,*" the soothing voice on the podcast whispered in her ear. "*It is empowering. It is liberating.*"

When she did explore *The Odyssey*'s many amenities, it was always at Steve's behest. Mud baths in the Revitalisation Center or wine tastings at the bistro. She felt guilty pampering herself in such a flagrant manner and told Steve so.

"You paid for it," he assuaged. Steve was stretched out in a tub of Red Sea silt, arms dangling over the sides. Evie had selected the more alluring Infused Amazonian Mud for her own bath. It was only day three of the cruise, but it already felt much longer. "All inclusive means just that."

"I don't know how to react," Evie confessed. "It's all new to me."

"These are just the perks, the add-ons, if you will. We're all here for a reason. The Great Feeding is the context, but everyone attends seeking something different. A personal revelation or self-discovery, ya know?"

Evie mulled this over as she felt the cool mud cake on her naked skin. "What's your reason?" she eventually asked, trying not to sound intrusive.

He was quiet for a long time. Then, "I think I'll know when I see it. When the Great Feeding begins, I'll just know."

Evie had to admit it was nice sharing a level of intimacy with someone again. The conversation, the activities, the slow revealing of the self: she had forgotten that life need not be a sentence of solitary confinement; that pain did not preclude enjoyment. Most of all, Matt and the past four years were far from her mind when she was with Steve. His laidback nature had a certain power of its own.

Every evening as twilight streaked the sky, Evie sat on the deck and watched the lights on *The Aegean* slowly illuminate. The ship floated like a diadem in the night. The effect was oddly mesmerizing, and she wondered whether her counterpart was sitting on the deck of *The Aegean* at that very moment, contemplating the lights of *The Odyssey,* a sad and inaccessible not-Evie grappling with her own anxieties and self-doubts.

You require nothing but yourself for inspiration. Each day is a creative moment of infinite possibilities.

Evenings were hit-and-miss. She had taken to dining with Steve, who seemed to have a knack for making friends. Each night, a new person or couple joined their table, expanding the dinner circle. Evie was less than thrilled at what she quickly came to interpret as an intrusion. For the most part, they were retirees, accountants who managed corporate assets, and women whose opinions were lifted from the pages of *Cosmo* and *Elle*. Brigette, an attractive blonde from California who Steve had met at a volleyball session, was the exception. Fresh off her big break as a model in an online clothing catalogue, Brigette talked about traveling to Milan or Paris, of meeting celebrities, of *making it*. She was full of hope and idealism, and Evie hated her for it. Steve, however, listened attentively to every word. He would lean back in his chair, arms folded across his chest, nodding approvingly as she prattled on about the fashion world and the power of influencers.

"Say, didn't you mention you were in show biz?" a smooth faced tech-support specialist sitting across from Steve butted in.

Steve flashed a boyish grin. Evie couldn't help but notice Brigette returned the smile. "That was a long time ago," he said.

"And?"

"Child acting. Teen stuff. Ever hear of *Afterschool Freak Out* or shows like *Beat Kids*?"

Brigette's face lit up as she placed a hand on Steve's outstretched arm.

"Yeah! Those nineties teen dramas!" she squealed. "I used to watch all of them in reruns when I was a kid! You were in *those?*"

"A few of them. Here and there."

He was being intentionally modest. Brigette beamed, her mouth contorting into a rictus of semi-awe. Her hand closed tighter on Steve's arm. Evie wanted to believe the gesture was involuntary, but still...

"Like I said, a long time ago."

"I think I need some air," Evie said, excusing herself and exiting the dining room. Nobody stopped her.

Retreating through the corridors, she passed empty recreational areas and barrooms packed with young people enjoying the evening. In the gym, rows of exercise machines lay silent and inert. It was hard to believe she was somewhere in the middle of the ocean. Everything had the cold, sterile feel of a shopping mall, office building, and apartment complex rolled into one.

She fumbled through her purse and jammed her earbuds in.

You require nothing but yourself for inspiration. The power to regenerate comes from within.

She recalled a line scribbled on a sheet of folded note paper she had kept in a dresser drawer. *Somewhere on the other side of this wide night and the distance between us, I am thinking of you.* Matt had placed the note in her mailbox two days after their first date. She remembered thinking the sentiment did not match the blocky, masculine script printed on the paper, as though poetry demanded a fluid and elegant script. Only later did she discover that Matt had taken the line from another poem; that plagiarism and deception, rather than poetry, were where his actual talents laid.

She was letting him back in again, invoking his presence.

Stupid! Stupid! Stupid!

Only once you have let go of what you are, can you become what you will be.

* * *

Breakfast buffets always divulged character. Pancakes were simplicity. Eggs benedict *à la salmon* suggested extravagance. Fresh fruit was emblematic of sincerity. Listening to her daily dose of morning inspiration, Evie watched as each guest unknowingly revealed an intimate part of themselves to her. Ed, donning a fresh cabana shirt, selected pancakes; his wife, the eggs benedict. Others indulged in heaping plates of bacon, Belgian-style waffles, continental fare.

"You missed the disco last night," Steve said as he took a seat *sans* invitation. "Fun night."

He had chosen the breakfast burrito, symbolizing indecisiveness and ease.

Evie pictured Steve and Brigette dancing amidst strobing lights and pulsing dance music, their bodies touching and entangling.

"Not my scene," was all she said.

One table over, Ed and his wife were engaged in an argument about the air conditioner in their room.

"For once, Lydia, can you take my side?" he grumbled. "Just *once* would be nice."

"What do you expect from *me*?"

"Luxury, my ass. I'm dying in this heat!"

"You're making a scene," she reprimanded, casting a furtive look around the room. "Please, don't humiliate us," she moaned. "*Please.*"

"Us? *Us?* Couldn't have that, right?" with an arrogant laugh.

Steve, who had been listening to the entire exchange, gave Evie a wide-eyed look across the table. Couples like Ed and Lydia were walking advertisements for divorce. Others concealed their misery and frustration behind a staid conjugal exterior. As to which was preferable, Evie didn't know.

After breakfast, everyone migrated onto the south deck where Captain Tom was preparing for the morning briefing.

"The hour grows near, friends," he intoned. "The Great Feeding will soon be upon us."

Evie looked over the faces in the crowd. Brigette stood on the opposite side of the circle, her face shaded by a stylish Ipanema sun hat. She smiled and waved. Steve reciprocated.

"I have felt the expectation, the anticipation," Captain Tom continued, his voice thunderous, sermonic even. "We stand upon the threshold of a new day. Yes, a *new* day! In our own personal way, we too feel the hunger. It is a hunger that stirs us, that leads us to seek, to question, to re-evaluate who we are, *what* we are."

"Are you kiddin' me?" Ed mumbled, earning an abrasive shush from his wife.

Captain Tom paused, and Evie had the sudden impression that he was speaking directly to her.

"We may think that the hunger is insatiable, that we are destined to wander unfulfilled. But I tell you *it* is out there! We all must travel through our own vast oceans, struggling against powerful currents. But our instincts are strong! We may fear. We may question. We may supplicate in moments of weakness. But we also prevail. We seek transformation and, through it, transcendence."

The crowd stared up at him, enraptured.

"The hour comes when, each in their own way, will know the ecstasy of satiation. We will bear witness! And in one miraculous moment, we will experience this fulfilment together, for it is *our* fulfilment, each and every one of us."

He paused and cast a long look out toward the rolling waves. A poignant expression bled across his face, as though he were looking past the depths of the horizon into the promised future.

Slowly, the crowd stirred as a few clapping hands swelled into a climax of applause. The spell broke and the audience came to life in a buzz of chatter.

"I told you, a real showman," Steve said with a nudge.

Evie, momentarily entranced, followed Captain Tom's stare. *The Aegean*, half a mile away, was the only object in the expanse of sea and sky unrolling before them.

"Amazing," Brigette trilled, gliding through the thinning crowd. "I could almost feel it. Like something was *calling* to me."

"Powerful stuff," Steve concurred. Then, turning to Evie, "Coming to the sports meet up later?"

"Think I'll pass."

"Suit yourself," he said with a shrug.

Evie remained on the south deck for most of the morning, avoiding the pool and recreational areas. The quiet suited her, and she could think of doing nothing save stretching out in a sun chair and admiring the vastness of the ocean.

"You are in a special place," she muttered to herself. "It is empowering. It is liberating."

The words sounded hollow and devoid of meaning.

As the sun climbed toward its zenith, Evie withdrew inside. In the recreational area, children and elderly couples were busy painting little ceramic figurines. Further afield, bear-chested men and girls in bikinis socialized on the lido over tall piña coladas. Evie considered ordering a margarita at the pool bar but decided against it, noting the older single men in loose-fitting floral shirts congregating there. Passing the sports center, however, she immediately regretted her decision. Through the massive window, she spotted Steve standing astride Brigette. Hand on her wrist, he was gently guiding her arm forward to demonstrate the proper motion for retuning a volley. As he pulled her arm back, Brigette's body pressed against his. Although their voices were silenced behind the thick wall of plexiglass, their body language said enough.

Evie bit down on the inside of her cheek and tasted blood.

Steve was placing his hand on Brigette's hips to adjust her stance when Brigette turned her head. For a split second, her and Evie's eyes locked through the glass and Brigette flashed a razor thin smile. It felt malicious and cruel. Although lasting only an instant, there had been something communicative in that look; a cold recognition of one another.

The taste of blood lingered in her mouth as she rushed down the corridor, pushing past oncoming men in towels and boys carrying waterboards. She could feel it again. That emotional churning; a certain sense of spinning out of control. It had been there all this time, she now realized; latent, ravenous, waiting to resurface.

Her hands were steady as she pried the lid off the prescription bottle and queued up a power session of *Find Your Zen*. By the time the calm yet assertive female voice informed her that failure was merely a stop on the path to success, Evie was fast asleep. And she slept for a long time.

* * *

Somewhere in the middle of a dream, she heard quick, heavy footsteps coming from the hall. Crepuscular light filled the windows, bathing the room in a warm glow. Evie rubbed her eyes and pulled herself from bed, groggy and slow to comprehend. There were more footsteps in the hall, excited voices trailing through the corridors.

Outside the windows, the sea was crimson. *The Aegean* floated listlessly a quarter mile out. It was the closest Evie could remember seeing the ship to *The Odyssey*. At this distance, it looked dense and less ethereal. Different, she thought, before placing her finger on it. The ship was dark. Despite the twilight, the lights were extinguished. It rocked there in the ocean, black and silent.

More footsteps came from the hall and Evie poked her head out the door. People hustled past, some half-dressed, cameras in hand.

"What is it?" Evie asked a scurrying woman.

She halted, her face eager and expectant. "They're here. It's begun," as she continued along the corridor toward the main deck.

Evie didn't bother to change. She exited the room and joined the stream of people.

Even before they arrived on the deck, she heard the noise: a deep, resonant wailing coming across the water. It saturated the air, sounding omnipresent.

The silhouette of *The Aegean* loomed off the starboard side, ominous in its darkness. Captain Tom was speaking from the bridge.

"The hour is upon us," his voice thundered through the PA. "Behold the Great Feeding. Bear witness! Bear witness and succumb to the hunger! Embrace it! Transcend *through* it!"

As Evie listened, she wondered how she understood. Captain Tom's voice was melding together with the plangent wailing filling the air, becoming one with it. They were not words. The noise itself resounded deep in her being. A calling coming from across the water. Isn't that how Brigette described it? A *calling*?

"There!" somebody shouted, pointing into the distance.

Heads swivelled. There was movement in the water. Shadowy forms broke through the surface, leaping and splashing before plunging back into the depths. People sprinted to the rail, pushing, cameras at the ready for the next surfacing. When it came, there was the click of cameras followed by a collective exhalation of amazement.

The movement of the distant animals was strange, Evie thought. Their bodies were long and slender. Not as she had imagined a whale's body to be. Each leap and splash brought them closer. Evie couldn't tell whether the ship was moving or whether the animals were cutting through the water with such stealth. The wailing grew louder. At closer range, the splashing and jumping didn't appear playful. Rather, it felt precise and predatory.

"Oh God! Help!" a voice screamed.

Taking her eyes from the water, Evie saw Ed hunched over Lydia. She was sprawled out on the floor, violently convulsing.

"Somebody!" he called, his hands cradling his wife's head.

Steve and Brigette were first on the scene, and as they knelt to assess the situation, Evie heard further calls for help echoing across the deck. A young Asian woman had collapsed, followed by a little girl. There was a confusion of voices and then the ship lurched to an abrupt halt as though running aground. The water surrounding the vessel roiled. Dark shapes circled just beneath the surface.

Evie heard a commotion and then an ear-piercing scream. Lydia was sitting up now, blood running down her chin. A large chunk of mangled flesh was gripped between her teeth. Steve was attempting to bind Ed's wound with his shirt when Lydia shoved him aside. Without a word, she pounced and began frantically clawing at her husband's face.

Screams were coming from all parts of the deck as people lunged and tackled one another to the ground. Steve and Brigette huddled against the rail, inches from where Lydia assailed her flailing husband. A scene of complete carnage unfolded around them. Women convulsed, flailed, slashed, and tore, streaking the deck in rivulets of blood. They cried out in anguish, joining in the deep wailing sound growing louder by the second. Husbands, sons, lovers: all were being surrendered to the Great Hunger. Horrified, Evie looked back to Brigette, the same dawning realization evident in both their eyes.

A sound like grinding metal cut through the air and the ship listed. Brigette screamed as a spider-like claw snaked over the rail and landed on the deck. Below, a slurping sound came from the water, and Evie saw the dark shapes moiling beneath the waves start climbing up the sides of the ship. The deck was littered with butchered flesh, bodies torn limb from limb. Off the bow, a form was rising from the water, something black and mammoth emerging from the depths. It rose up tall into the twilit sky, its massive form alien yet strangely beautiful. Evie attempted to scream, but all she heard was the wailing sound coming from her throat. She stood, awe-stricken, gazing up at what she knew could not be towering above them. Its smooth contours were magnificent in the oncoming moonlight. Paralyzed with wonder, Evie understood. She must yield to it, must allow it to suffuse and possess her. She could feel it mounting inside her like a crescendo, a torrent of intense and rapturous joy begging for release.

Tearing her gaze away, Evie's eyes settled on Steve. He stood back against the rail, a spectator to the unabating carnage surrounding them. When he noticed Evie's stare, an expression of dread stole across his face. Brigette was nowhere in sight as she started out across the deck, her shoes slick in the blood pooling on the deck floor.

"You are in a special place," she reminded herself, her heart quickening with each step. "It is empowering. It is liberating."

DAY OF THE DEAD

Bruce Meyer

Annie was aching to see Pedro. She needed him so very much. His absence felt like death and her empty arms were almost numb from the pain of missing him.

Pedro lived in Galeana on the other side of the grey saw-teeth of the Sierra Madres. In the late afternoon light with the sun behind them, they traced the jagged outline of an enormous beast with a rough back. The nearer she approached, the greener slopes became. She had been warned not to drive alone over the Sierras on her own.

"A woman alone in a car," the man at the rental agency had said in a whisper as he leaned over the counter.

The road snaked through the mountains. The shoulders were narrow and in some places non-existent, especially on the turns, and if she had to pull over for any reason—goats crossing the road, a flat tire, or simply to admire the green view on the steep valleys on the lush Caribbean side or the bone-coloured hills facing the interior once she went over the crest—she would be watched at every moment by cartel snipers.

"Why make a target of yourself?" the rental man asked.

Pedro had argued with her over the phone, the line cutting in an out. "Stay at an airport hotel. Don't make the journey alone. It is four hours from Monterrey. Why pay for a rental car? I can come and get you in the morning."

The thought of Pedro arriving in Galeana with an Englishwoman frightened her. The narrow streets, the shops where nothing much was sold because nothing much was purchased, the relatives crowded into a cinder-block room, the whirr and clunk of the malfunctioning air conditioner, were things she did not want to encounter. Pedro had made it out of that world. He was a telecom engineer. He traveled the world and earned good money. They'd met in Zurich. Pedro, dark, suave, the epitome of Latin elegance and refined manners, and she, the clever Oxbridge technologist who knew all the answers except the ones she was working to find. They fell in love while having drinks and conversation about 5G. They both agreed they held the future in their hands.

But the more he attempted to convince her, the more assertive she felt she had to be. After all, he was not only in love with her. Love is a reciprocal arrangement. If she let him have his way on how she came to him, he would have his way on everything.

She'd been to Galeana once already on a brief trip. It seemed a dream to her. There was a village she wanted to see again. She had fallen in love with it as they walked hand-in-hand through the ancient streets.

Iturbide stood on the crest of the highway. It was shady and green, the last breath of the verdant before the descent began and the Joshua Palms with sea urchin spines stood amazed and abandoned to die in the desert.

And it was the Day of the Dead.

What better place to see the shrines and the calaveras in the quiet square than Iturbide. People with faces painted as skulls, white, morbid, and surprised by death, would be kneeling in the square, offering shot glasses of *reposado* to their ancestors and reminding themselves of those whose features had faded from memory by placing sugar skulls on the cenotaphs. So many never returned to the mountain village.

She was almost certain she was entering Iturbide. As she slowed her rental and rolled down the windows, she could hear the bell tolling for vespers. An old woman in a blue skirt would be tugging at the lone bell rope that hung as if it was the snake from paradise creeping down the white stucco tower of the church. The front wall over the door would be red with bougainvillea and she imagined the Crown of Thorns, the suffering and blood that defined the Mexico she loved as the fluttering red petals. If the wind came up, they would scatter, pulsing from a sacrificial wound.

But she was not in Iturbide. Not the Iturbide she remembered. There has been a town hall at the far end of the square. A youth dance had taken place after school. Pedro explained it was a way to keep the young people in the sleepy town. They would grow up, marry. They would live in one of the old, low, brightly coloured houses on the side street. She'd seen couples and their children, making their way up a side street and she understood how important love is when it is asked to bind people not only to one another but to a place.

Pedro and she sat on a park bench and talked about death.

"There is no death for us, at least not the way you see it, Annie. You've been taught to grieve for what is lost permanently. We have been taught to respect and worship those who are dead. Each year, the day after your Halloween, we have the Day of the Dead. We call upon the saints, but we also call upon those who walk with the saints in the twilight of a dusty autumn day. My grandmother, my father, my aunts and uncles, all live in that twilight. When you return, I hope you will return on the Day of the Dead, and I will introduce you to them all and you will hear them speak to you in the silence."

When she parked the car she was certain she was not in Iturbide. Had she taken a wrong turn? Highway 58 leads directly to Iturbide. There could be no mistaking it. All she had to do was follow the road toward the sky and then leave the sky behind. The church was not where she remembered it. The square had fewer trees. The bell rope ran inside the church rather than dangle free on the outside. She missed the bright red flowers.

A group of women with their backs turned to her, black shawls over their heads and long dresses with elaborate embroidery, were kneeling beside a shrine, laying kernels of coloured corn on the ground in the pattern of a multicolored flower. As Annie approached, she thought it odd that the women were picking the sugar calaveras from the shrine and eating them. From what she knew of the tradition, the candy sugar skulls were only for the dead. Another woman reached up and took a shot glass of tequila that stood beside a faded antique photograph of a man and downed the drink in one mouthful.

"*Perdóneme. ¿Es esto Iturbide?*"

One of the women, her face deathly pale as the bleached sands of the desert, her eyes blacked out, and her teeth painted on her lips and cheeks as if death had stripped away her flesh looked up at Anne and said nothing.

The bell was tolling. The women who kneeled at the shrine picked up their skirts and ran toward a procession as it left the church. Annie followed. The procession moved slowly.

The priest at the head of the line was swinging his censer. The smoke was sweet, almost sickly, but it held a bitter tang, as if it was smoke that had been retrieved from the ceiling of a church after a mass and mixed with the scent of cigars and cooking and chocolate that had boiled over into the fire.

No one spoke. Everyone's head was bowed. The silence, the reverence of a dusk when not a bird chirped or a rustle of a long dress could be heard, was mesmerizing. Annie wanted to embrace it. She felt as if it was a part of her that lay waiting in her soul that she had not yet discovered. And when the gate on the cemetery opened with a cry, Annie could see the arid plain below her, the graves packed as tightly as white bags of sugar, and each resting place was decorated in a photograph of the deceased and flowers, and seeds, the sugar calaveras.

The priest, who was also in a calavera face, raised his arms, and the women, the men, the children moved toward the graves until they were standing on top of them. An elderly man and a woman embraced. A man put his arm around the boy and the boy, with blackened eyes, looked up at the man. A woman held a sleeping child in her arms. All had the white faces of the day painted over their flesh. And with that they sank into the resting places and vanished as the sun sank over the village and the sky became dark.

Annie sank to her knees and began to pray for the dead. She wanted to whisper words of thanks but was overwhelmed and astonished by the silence. And when she opened her eyes, she was alone among the graves. The white paint had worn off the stones and the crosses. The monuments were toppled and walls were rubble. There was no priest, no flowers, no brightly-coloured petals, no sugar skulls or shot glasses of tequila or small loaves of bread for the dead. Even the vista of the arid plain to Galeana was shrouded in fog.

As she made her way back to her car, the village, the church, the side streets were in ruins. The square was empty. The shrine was gone. This was not Iturbide. Whatever this place was or had been left her feeling cold and empty inside. Had she taken a wrong turn?

She had no idea where she was.

Doubling back the way she came, as the darkness deepened, she kept checking her cell phone to see if she had any signal. She would call Pedro. She would describe the place where she had stopped. He could direct her or come for her.

She thought she heard his voice on the phone as she pulled off at a white roadside shrine in the valley. The shrine lay at the foot of an Aztec or Toltec rockface carving of a hunter. Pedro had told her it was an ancient prince who claimed the green valley as his private hunting preserve. The figure, known as Antares, had slid from the mountainside one day when an earthquake shook the valley. Nothing remained except the carving of a foot and a dog barking at the hooves of a deer.

"Pedro? Hello? Can you hear me?" He was breaking up. Only parts of words reached her. "I'm lost. I took a wrong turn. I lost something in myself and for a moment I was certain I found it. I found it in this village that vanished around me. Hello?"

The only words that came through were "San Sebastian" and "bridge."

She sat in the rental car and wept. San Sebastian? She scanned the map the man at the rental agency had given her as he warned her about traveling alone on Highway 58 from Linares to Galeana.

"That is a difficult route. You would be advised to go all the way back to Monterrey and cross the Sierras there. The way south, even though it is less picturesque and through the desert, is the safest. The truckers use that route unless they are in a hurry."

There was no San Sebastian on the map.

When she was a teenager, Annie stayed up all night with an elderly aunt in the Midwest U.S. who was addicted to Broadway musicals. A late show called *Midnight Matinee* on a channel almost out of reach of her aunt's television antenna was playing the almost forgotten Rogers and Hammerstein musical, *Brigadoon*, about a Scottish village that only appears once every two hundred years because it is cursed. The only thing that can break the curse is if someone, on the right day, stumbles across the town and falls in love with a certain woman. The townsfolk are destined to fade in and out of eternity. Annie tried to imagine what eternity would feel like—the cold, the endless darkness, the wind on an autumn night pulling the temperature down the from the sun and casting it into the grave. The feeling of nothing except longing. The love that was always on the other side of the mountain and, as in a dream, the road that would not lead to that love no matter how many times a person traveled it.

San Sebastian. Annie pictured a martyr, tied to a tree, being shot with arrows. His suffering eyes. She had seen paintings of the saint in the National Gallery. The young man with curly hair has his eyes raised to heaven as if asking when his suffering will end, when will he walk among the dead, and what the bridge is between this world and the next.

Annie thought for a moment that Mexico contained the understanding of what that bridge was. Moving from death to life and back again, crossing the vast void with every sense—sight, sound, taste, touch, and smell with the volume turned up as high as it could go and blaring the world into every thought—was not just a matter of standing on one's own grave and eating the sweet marzipan skulls that were only fit for the dead, but a desire to assert love even if it meant negating the self in white face paint, and flowers woven in black braids of hair, and permitting death to enter the world so it can live forever. She closed her eyes and thought she was dreaming when she opened them, to the sight of children in bright paper costumes, their faces painted white, their teeth outlined in black upon their cheeks, and their eyes two sockets of darkness with eclipses in the center of each. Each of them held out their hands as if asking for alms or inviting her to dance with them.

PLAGUE DOCTOR

Elana Gomel

The man at the table lifted a cellphone to his ear. He had to push his elaborate wig up, and the powdered curls fell over his black domino. The plate-glass window muted the sound of his voice, but I could imagine it: the liquid syllables of Venice-flavored Italian, the language of mariners, merchants and lovers.

There was something so inviting in the golden glow of the restaurant filled with beautiful masked people that I lingered in the wet dark. Outside looking in. A pale reflection of my face floated over the diners like a ghostly balloon.

Another ghost joined me: a beaky silhouette like a hunched-up vulture, a smudged suggestion of a birdlike face over a black cloak. Startled, I turned around. Nothing except the unending stream of costumed people flowing through the arcades surrounding Piazza San Marco.

The *Carnevale di Venezia*. Carnival of Venice. Two weeks in February when La Serenissima, the Most Serene One, as Venice used to be called, refuses to be serene. It is the coldest, hardest, most dismal time in the city; and this is when the city celebrates. The iron-gray sky and the piercing wind ruffling the dull surface of the Lagoon; the *aqua alta,* high tides, when steely water laps at the windows of ground floor apartments; the golden cupola of San Marco glistening in the rain. And defying it all, the bright colors of hooped skirts and puffed sleeves; embroidered waistcoats and lacy shirts. Women in high heels and crinoline dresses splashing through the puddles; men in full makeup chatting over a glass of Aperol spritz under the sodden marquee.

And the masks. Feather-trimmed dominoes in pink, orange and blue; black mouthless *morettas* with wide staring eyes; the occasional ghostly *larva,* a pale featureless oval under an elaborate hat. I felt naked with my bare face.

I turned away from the brightly lit restaurant and went back into the maze of tiny alleys that surround Piazza San Marco, the heart of Venice. My big puffa coat was dripping, my sneakers were soaked, and a chill was worming its way into my bones. But I would not go back to my solitary hotel room to watch the lights of the Carnival bloom in the dark city. Not yet.

Nobody was walking alone. Couples linking arms; groups of friends, laughing and chatting together; even families with children, toddlers with painted faces clutching the hands of Colombinas in ruffled dresses or Harlequins in a multicolored motley. Nobody was walking alone but me.

I saw few modern costumes. No Halloween zombies; no sexy nurses or cosplay extravaganzas. La Serenissima was true to its public image, putting on display its promise of romance and adventure, while carefully disguising the less savory aspects of its history, the darkness lurking at the bottom of its stagnant canals and in the corners of its mazelike alleys. I had been here for only ten days, but I had already realized that the city of love had enough hate in its basement to drown the naïve and the hopeful. People like me.

A group of masked girls in orange-and-purple taffeta dresses passed me by, their long trains dragging through the puddles. One of them looked back at me and whispered something to her friends who giggled in response. I dove into an unlit passage and stood with my back to the damp ironwork gate, watching the Carnival flow outside like a river of color. A black shadow passed across the mouth of the alley: a large bedraggled rat. I remembered a t-shirt I had bought on my first day here with the silhouette of a rat against the scarlet background and the inscription "Nightlife in Venice". At the time, it seemed cute and I had imagined myself wearing this t-shirt and lounging in the sun with a glass of prosecco. I had even fantasized having a good-looking Italian guy by my side. What a great selfie I could post on Instagram and when Evan saw it...

I quickly realized that wearing the t-shirt would make me look even more foreign: a pathetic tourist trying to blend in. And there had been no selfies, no Italian guys, and no sun in Venice. A glass of prosecco in my solitary hotel room was all that was left of my dream, and for a moment, it beckoned me back with an almost irresistible strength. At least I would be warm.

I shook myself. I came to Venice to see the *Carnevale*. And see it I would. Even on my own. Even without Evan. They said that solitary female travelers were the fastest-growing demographic in tourism. I would do my best to prove that a woman alone in a strange city could have a good time.

I emerged onto Via Garibaldi, thronged with masked people and illuminated by garlands of fairy lights. There were, of course, no vehicles. There are no cars in Venice. Transportation is only by *vaporetto*, a water bus with a cat's cradle of routes. I had already gotten my weekly pass and a map, determined not to fall into the tourist trap of hiring a gondola. Not that my depleted funds would allow me to. The divorce had left me on the precarious edge of financial ruin. I had quit my job when Evan and I were trying to get pregnant...

Who was I kidding? *I* was trying to get pregnant. Evan was busy impregnating Kathy.

As always, her name felt like a stab of physical pain. I hurried along the thoroughfare, trying to distract myself by staring at the brightly lit shop windows. Even though it was late, most shops were open, selling the seemingly unending supply of Murano glass baubles, lacy tablecloths made in Burano, fish-like keychains—the rough approximation of the shape of Venice itself. And masks. Always masks.

Should I get a mask? To blend in? I stopped by one of the smaller, less touristy shops. More dominoes, some crowned by an elaborate headdress or with a music notation enameled on one cheek. Entire outfits, with veils, cloaks, puffed sleeves, sparkling jewelry. I could not imagine trying to squeeze into one of them.

A mask prominently displayed in the center of the window drew my attention. It was grotesquely ugly in the midst of this over-abundant beauty, with a giant curving beak protruding from the black-and-white skeletal face and surmounted by staring goggles. The whole ensemble was topped by a black hat. It looked surreal: half-man, half-bird-of-prey.

I walked into the shop. Its owner, a slender young man, was talking to somebody in the back, pouring out a flood of excited and incomprehensible words interspersed with feminine laughter. I almost walked out, but I screwed up my courage and addressed him when he reluctantly came over to the counter.

"This mask," I said, pointing to the beaked creature. "How much is it?"

He looked me up and down and I shrunk under his evaluative gaze.

"It's a man's mask, Signora," he said. "*Medico della Peste.* The Plague Doctor."

"I want it," I said, biting off the convenient lie that I was buying it for my husband. I had no husband. Not anymore. Better get used to it.

He shrugged, rung it off and wrapped it up in tissue paper. His interlocutor came out of the back of the shop: a vivacious woman in a crystal-studded cat mask, her small white teeth gleaming in her rouged mouth. Her tightly laced waist made me feel like a balloon.

I took my purchase and trudged back to my hotel, making my way through the crowds that closed behind me as if I was not there.

* * *

In the room, I drank my prosecco and stared at the mask, which I had unwrapped and placed on the ancient dresser. The more I looked, the less I liked it.

The craftsmanship was astounding, which made it even worse. The giant beak was gilded and decorated with clusters of black pearls that looked like pustules. The goggles were surrounded by glistening strips of red lacquer, bleeding painted drops of scarlet onto the gaunt cheeks, which were enameled greasy white.

Of course, I had already found out what it represented: the magic of Google at my fingertips. It was indeed the Plague Doctor: literally, somebody who tried to cure the plague. "Tried" being the operative word.

Venice, sodden and overrun by rats, suffered wave after wave of the Black Death throughout the centuries. The epidemics were so bad that dead bodies had to be collected in the narrow alleyways and thrown into the Lagoon. People were quarantined in their homes, their doors and windows sealed from the outside as they were left to die alone. Since nobody knew about bacteria-carrying fleas, the disease was blamed on witches, licentious women, and Jews. And Plague Doctors wore that beaked outfit to frighten away the spirits of the disease. Unknowingly, they often spread the infection.

The Black Death was long gone but the Plague Doctor remained. A monstrous flightless bird skulking in the dark corners of the Carnival. Reminding the revelers of everything they were trying to forget. An uninvited guest, a harbinger of suffering and death. Ugliness amid beauty; loneliness amid communal celebration.

I reached for the second bottle. The sweetish fizz felt flat and ineffective on my tongue.

I did what I had promised myself I would not do: looked at Evan's Facebook account. We were no longer friends but it was public, so everybody could enjoy the latest pictures of him and Kathy in their home in Florida, his arm around her shoulders, her blond hair dazzling in the sun, the roundness of her stomach not spoiling her svelte figure... They were lounging in the patio, she in the deck chair I had chosen.

I tuned off my phone and stared at the mask. The Carnival had three more days to go.

I put it on.

I walked along the Lagoon. The water was high, overflowing the lip of the embankment and standing in stagnant puddles on the filthy cobblestones. A slick head poked out of one puddle and a verminous body crossed the Fondamenta San Marco, carrying a bleeding hand in its mouth.

Bodies were piled up along the wall. They were naked except for their faces that were covered by jute bags. Blood-swollen buboes dotted their bleached flesh like overripe strawberries.

A striding silhouette emerged from the drizzle. Half-man, half-bird, its head dominated by an oversized beak, its bony body swathed in a black cloak that swung open, exposing the pimply skin dotted with clumps of scruffy plumage. Its feet were clawed and fleshless, gripping the mossy cobblestones. Its wings were bony and plucked like the wings of a dead chicken. It opened its oversized beak and gabbled at me. Foamy pink saliva was dripping from the scarlet maw.

I wrenched the mask off my face and tried to regulate my breathing.

So much for the mildness of prosecco! Clearly, Italian wines disagreed with me.

The *Medico della Peste* was lying on the carpet, its glassy round eyes focused on me. I turned off the light, but it made it even worse. Voices of the Carnival drifted through the badly fitted window, and the mask seemed to whisper back in a phlegm-choked voice.

What was I doing here, alone in a strange city, in a strange country? I had to go back home to Florida.

I had no home. Kathy had taken it away from me.

I knew Evan was equally to blame. Hell, he was *more* to blame! A cheating husband—how much worse could you get?

But Kathy had been my best friend. And now she was sleeping in my bed, next to my husband, his hand on her belly, feeling the kick of the baby that should have been mine.

Loneliness was a disease. I had come to Venice searching for a cure, only to realize that it did not exist. Not here. The Carnival was not for me. I was an outsider, a rat in the dark corner, a plague-bearer at the feast.

Strange thoughts tangled in my head like strands of glitter until I finally drifted into sleep.

The woman was crawling on her knees through the stream of dirty water. Her face was flushed, and she held a tightly swaddled baby in her arms, trying to lift it above the flood. But she was too weak, and the baby periodically dipped down, disappeared under the surface, and emerged soaked when she yanked it back up.

The birdman stooped over her, his skeletal wings unfurling like a canopy. His infected beak oozed slime.

"*Dottore!*" the woman whispered. "*Save my baby!*"

"*You know what the price is,*" the birdman lisped, his words dripping like gobs of corruption. "*If one is to live, another must die. Who do you offer in his stead?*"

"*Take my husband, Dottore! He slept with a whore from the Courtesans' Quarter. He does not love me anymore!*"

"*Are you sure?*"

"*Yes.*"

Skeletal fingers with needlelike talons snatched up the baby and tore through its swaddling, revealing a pathetic limp body, its rubbery limps swinging in the dank air. Blood-red buboes bloomed in its armpits.

"*The baby is already mine,*" the birdman hissed.

The woman wailed.

"*Then spare my husband! He'll give me another son!*"

"*You can't take it back. Once the bargain is made, it is made. Tell your husband, the Plague Doctor will visit him tonight!*"

I shot up in bed, bathed in sweat, shivering as if I was running a fever.

I picked up the mask, caressed its cold cheek, followed the outlines of the predatory beak, the staring eyes.

"Plague Doctor," I whispered, "cure me."

A man with a yellow patch on his robe was running along the narrow winding alleyway, slipping on the wet pavement. The crowd jeered and threw stones. He reached the exit and stopped. The alleyway ended at the lip of a canal, and the narrow bridge was blocked by a flock of gulls. Huge and well-fed, they screeched and gabbled, their curving beaks splattered with red. The man looked over his shoulder desperately and advanced across the bridge. The gulls rose in a stinking fluttering cloud, leaving one figure behind. It unfolded, rose up to its full skeletal height.

The birdman loomed over the fleeing man, its breath stinking of carrion, gulls perched on its shoulders, rats peeking over the brim of its black hat.

"*Dottore,*" the man cried in desperation, "they blame me for the plague, but I have done nothing! Let me reach the ghetto and lock the gates, or they'll tear me to pieces!"

"*What will you pay for safe passage?*" the birdman croaked.

"*Take all the gold I have!*"

"*Gold is useless. A life for a life. Your wife, your daughter, your son?*"

The man hesitated, backed off. A stone bounced off his back, and he fell to his knees. The crowd closed in.

I checked Evan's Facebook page and it was not updated in a couple of days. That was unusual. He and Kathy were prolific on the social media, wanting everybody to witness their perfect life. So I called one of the few friends who I still sporadically kept in touch. The phone rang and only then did it occur to me that time difference between Florida and Venice was six hours. I tried to calculate whether it was early morning or middle of the night in Fort Lauderdale when Marty picked up. Her voice was clogged with sleep.

"Linda!" she exclaimed. "What's wrong?"

So even my supposedly closest friend saw me as a magnet of misfortune. Somebody who would only call with bad news, begging for help or for a shoulder to cry on!

I squeezed the hard edge of the mask between my fingers.

"Nothing wrong," I said nonchalantly. "I'm doing very well, actually. I'm thinking of staying in Venice a little longer. I just... met someone."

"Oh."

A short non-committal syllable, managing to pack an equal weight of surprise and disbelief.

"Yes," I pressed on. "A very interesting guy. Venetian. So... how are the things back home?"

Marty and I had been friends since high school. She knew exactly what I was asking.

"Haven't you heard?"

"What?"

"Kathy had a miscarriage."

* * *

The Carnival was over. The *aqua alta* had receded but the ancient cobblestones were wreathed with stinking kelp and decorated by an occasional rotting fish. Damp garlands and sodden confetti lay in heaps along the *fondamenta* and were being cleared away by the uniformed crews in motorboats who shot through the canals like an intrusion of reality into this decrepit make-believe of the dying city. Some clueless tourists still paraded through the streets in costume, but the natives scoffed at them behind their backs, dropping disparaging names in the Venetian dialect. They were impatient to get back to their time-honored tradition of making real money out of fake glitter.

I was packing, shoving my pristine *Intimissima* underwear into my suitcase. I had bought it along with other Italian finery on my first day in Venice, so determined to have a good time, to find adventure, love, romance. I had never worn the filmy negligees and lacy bras and doubted I ever would. Never mind. I had not found what I wanted. But I had found what I needed.

The mask of *Medico della Peste* sat on the dresser. In the leaden light of another rainy day seeping through the ancient casement window, it looked cheap and forlorn.

I weighed it in my hand, hesitated, then put it back. I did not need it anymore. It had done its job.

I went down into the foyer. The man at the reception desk clicked on the computer, checking my already-settled bill. He did not even look at me. Just another dumb American!

I looked around. Would I ever remember this shabby hotel with even mild nostalgia? The computer and the desk were the only signs of modernity in the old wainscoted room dimly lit by a Murano-glass chandelier, the shelves on the walls stuffed with glass figurines, ship models, dusty bottles... The jetsam and flotsam of history.

I was free of it now. Venice's history—and mine. Like my bill, it was settled and done.

There was a large mirror behind the receptionist. Since the divorce, I had been avoiding mirrors. But now I looked, defiantly. So what if I was not as pretty as Kathy? I had won. She had lost.

The beaked mask looked back at me, the Plague Doctor's glassy stare of my own reflection.

RETURN TO DEATH

Justin Boote

A hiss escaped Brook's mouth when the groans from inside the barn became audible. He had been asleep and for a moment—an almost hopeful moment—believed himself to still be dreaming. And yet, the goose-bumps on his arms and sick pummelling to his stomach told a different story. One that defied belief and questioned his and the other islander's sanity even. He wasn't sure if he would have preferred it to be a dream. For how could they have possibly believed there to be any rationality or logic in what the old man had said? Had promised? They were doomed and no prophecy or outlandish proclamation was going to save them.

And yet...

For three days Brook and his son had been taking turns keeping vigil on the barn. His son was too young to consider the consequences of what may or may not come to pass, so the burden had been left on his shoulders alone. Others had come for news as the days passed, inquisitive yet largely dubious and doubtful. The old man possessed a knowledge of things he should have no right in knowing, and his abilities at curing the folks of their malaises no one questioned, but of this, most believed his ageing body had caused his mind to slip dangerously.

And yet...

The groaning grew louder and wilder. There could be no doubt now of whom the voice belonged to, despite the madness in its tone. Brook called urgently to his son who played nearby, envious of how he ignored the freezing winds and roaring sea that threw icy spray at them with invisible hands as it thrashed against the rocks. For most here on the island, they had developed a hardened skin and yet harder soul against the elements that threatened them on an almost daily basis, but of the events of the last few days and weeks even they were powerless to resist.

"What is it, Father?" asked the boy.

"He's awake. Call the others."

The boy's face paled. Brook shuddered.

* * *

They gathered in the field facing the old barn, almost three hundred islanders long since abandoned to their own fate. An ominous murmur rose and fell as they discussed in whispered tones the implications. If their voices rose too high, another hissed for silence. Maybe Brook was mistaken and by speaking too loudly, they may inadvertently wake the old man themselves. The youngest among them were kept at the back of the group; perhaps the horror that may lay within the barn too much for them to bear. The older folks stood at the front alongside Brook; those that had seen in person the old man's abilities and listened to his prophecies and stories of worlds beyond these. No one had doubted him then, so there should be no reason to disbelieve him now, yet fear and unease were still etched into their faces, several with quivering lips and eyes that refused to dwell for too long on the barn door.

"Bring him out," said Conolly, the eldest woman on the island—her attempts at firmness and authority in her voice betrayed by dry, cold lips.

More hushed gasps answered her demand. Brook nodded solemnly, aware of all eyes on him now. He thought of what the imminent future held, that regardless of what happened in the next few minutes, their fate was still already determined. Nature had no reason or desire for bias, was relentless and impeccable in its neutrality and cared nothing for the lives of those in its path. And now it had chosen them.

Silence fell among the islanders when Brook entered the barn. Some nudged others, gave nervous glances to wives or husbands, perhaps looking for consolation; if the fear in others was greater, perhaps their own could be seen with less shame.

For several minutes, Brook remained alone in the barn. Those closest thought they could hear soft groans or wails, or maybe it was the wind acting as accomplice, distracting them from the real horrors inside. Then, the door opened, and it was no wind that wailed or groaned in dismay.

* * *

His eyes were fireballs from hell, his body rank with decay. Yet the islanders' horror was only complete when he opened his mouth and from its depths rose a shrill whining as foul and rotten as the breath that accompanied it.

Gasps of disgust. Shrieks of despair. Outright screaming from weaker-minded folk. Some cowered, others fled, yet denial could not be pretended by any. Eyes that cringed or tried to blink away the madness before them still beheld the awful truth. He was back.

A modern-day Lazarus yet terrible in its reconstruction. Old man Walters wept openly; the widower Jane prayed for mercy. Patterson was suddenly envious of his blind neighbour for surely he could never conjure such an image behind broken, worthless eyes.

The thing before them looked at its crowd, seemingly absorbing their horror, feeding on it—the whining from its scrawny throat perhaps giving reason to the assumption. For this had all been planned and had worked to perfection. What importance a disguise of peeling skin and rancid flesh if success had been achieved? He had died and returned to life. There could be no bigger achievement than this.

And he would share his secrets, so they follow him when he gave the order to regress to the world he had inhabited, albeit briefly. They had asked for a sign, a glimpse into a more optimistic future and he had provided. Now for them to comply with their own promises.

The thing—formerly, or perhaps still—Edgar Havenstrop, traveller of worlds, dealer in lost arts, articulated a deep growl. Speech was proving harder than expected, as though his vocal cords had chosen perpetual termination rather than continuity. He tried again. A sickening wail, horrendous and corrupted, came instead. This was beginning to concern him. How could he explain his journey if limbs and muscle-tissue failed him? And he needed them to listen, to comprehend the wonders he had seen so that they may absorb the magnitude of his discovery and believe his claims. If not, all was lost.

He willed his mind to concentrate on the task at hand—so much to convey, so many secrets to reveal. Breathe. Deep breaths. Breathe again. Loosen tongue. The islanders were watching him now with lesser fear carved into their faces. Awe perhaps. Awe and suspended belief for if what he had to tell was of a joyous nature, they may find salvation. Reveal the truth, though, and all would fail. And this he could not allow to happen.

He opened his mouth, smelling his own decomposition but this did not deter or bother him. Sacrifices were to be expected.

"I have returned," he croaked.

Gasps. Thin cries. Expectation in weary eyes.

"Tell us," whispered one with wretched voice.

A murmur among the crowd. Everything had come to this. Their fate, their future. Death was guaranteed, yet it was only in the manner of such that concerned them. The storms had already ruined their crops for the year—perhaps two—and with no other form of sustainment, they were doomed to starvation. Life on a small, North Atlantic island often insinuated and warned of tragedy—rampant winds, treacherous seas, vicious thunderstorms—yet they had always avoided its gossip and threats of destruction. Until now.

"I have been to the other side and have returned. Judge me not as you see me but as you hear me. And I speak of hope," he said.

Cheers. Tears of relief. Hugs and kisses.

How foolish.

Pitiful in their naivety, it disgusted him, yet he was no better in many ways. It was to be expected of course. He had promised them he would sacrifice his current life to prove that what lay beyond should not be feared. That after death, eternal peace and joy could be found. Their doom would be their salvation. No more weeping at the sight of drowned crops or empty fish nets. No darkness to swallow them with morbid delight. Follow him back when he returned, and their only obstacle would be managing excess.

And this is what he would tell them now.

"I awoke to a land green and flourishing. Strange plants and creatures abounded yet I instantly knew no harm could come from either. Pastures endless in their abundance of crop. The sun shone in a perfect fusion of heat and warmth; neither scolding as our days here in summer, nor hidden as during the harshness of winter. It was paradise, fellow islanders, and it was, and is, ours. And only ours."

The crowd looked around at one another. Joy echoed off one face, bounced to the next—a consortium of emotions. But doubt and unease still lingered on some as though unwilling to give up its previous grip. It was the farmer Patterson who gave voice to their concern.

"How do we know it's true?" he asked, looking to the others for moral support. No one had dared question Havenstrop before. His was a stature and wisdom on the island unquestionably profound. None still lived who might have seen him in youth, such was his age and presence. Indeed, some suspected he had been born with the cursed island itself. And he knew of secrets long lost to the annals of history and time. He was their guru, their shaman, their guide.

"You question my claims? Doubt my judgement? Have I not come back and sit before you now as living proof?"

"But..." hesitated Patterson. He seemed to be searching deep in his soul for the right words to say, afraid to anger him. Unable to look Havenstrop in the eyes, considering his tattered sandals instead, he mumbled, "But look at how you have returned. You have returned a mon—... different."

Havenstrop whined. Moaned. Wailed.

The others cowered, cringed, stepped back.

"Did you not listen to me before? I did not say the journey was an easy one. I have suffered to find us a new life, a new home. This is the price I have paid. But once we are there—all of us—there will only be serenity and gratification."

They were gullible, yet this very trait could work against him. It was imperative they believed in him and continued the plan discussed before. He could not face an eternity in that other dark place alone.

More murmuring, whispered debate. Finally, Patterson—who seemed to have been delegated spokesman—spoke up.

"It seems we have no choice in the matter. If the rains continue, we lose the little we have left and starve to death. Or we can follow you and chance there is a better life beyond this one. Or maybe we awaken in hell itself? Starvation would seem gratifying in comparison."

Inwards, Havenstrop grinned. They were right; they had no choice. As for hell? They had no idea.

"But, we wish to discuss the matter among ourselves. It is not an easy decision to make. The end of everything. Give our very lives to what you claim to have seen. I suggest we meet again here, tomorrow."

Havenstrop sighed. "So be it."

The island now consisted of less than three hundred. The youngest of the adults among them was twenty-three, and she could not bear children. She'd tried. For generations, they had lived on the island, shunning the mainland, living off the crops and fish in the cold, Atlantic waters. But the nets no longer filled as before. Great fishing ships had almost depleted the stocks surrounding them. They had discussed moving to the mainland, but the thought brought horror and overwhelming fear with it. They were a simple race. The great ships that ambled past in the distance, the planes that shot by overhead splintering their eardrums, sending them cowering and screaming for cover. What further monstrosities may the mainland hold? Not in seas or in the air but on the ground itself? No, they were far better here. It was safer. Or had been.

And so, all that day and most of the next, the island folk discussed their options. They gathered at the far end of the island, away from Havenstrop, those against the idea perhaps afraid of retaliation from him for having renewed misgivings. Brook and Patterson stood on a large rock so that they were easily seen and their voices clearly heard. They repeated what had been discussed before; death was imminent, they had trusted Havenstrop before and he had never failed them. It was clear to all he had indeed returned from death and spoke of new life.

"But what if this time, he lies?" asked Connors. "Look at him. What if we are all condemned to live with our very flesh falling from our bodies? Stink of decomposition and rot? I, for one, could bear no such thing."

"He says that in the afterlife, he was as normal. If he has survived and returned, there can be no doubt as to his claims. I vote we follow," said Brook.

More discussion continued and when the rain began to pelt down on their heads, furious and relentless once again, burying what remained of their crops in icy, sodden graves, they knew. There was only one viable option left to them. Follow their spiritual leader and embark on a journey to death. Hoping and praying that the path that led them there brought them straight back again.

* * *

"We have discussed the matter and will follow you back," said Patterson.

Havenstrop grinned. Both inwards and outwards. "Then, the process will continue as planned. Tonight, at the stroke of midnight. Be with your loved ones for the last few hours on this island. A great journey awaits."

Sighs of resolution resounded. Finality. Conclusion.

They all left together, leaving Havenstrop alone to contemplate what awaited them. Their terror on this island as starvation bounded towards them like some mythical beast was nothing to what he had seen. They had discussed for long days and nights their options, the possibilities of survival, and there were none. They'd come to him seeking guidance, for surely he knew the answers to everything. Had the gift of long sight. Could see beyond the shadows of death. And he, already knowing both their future and his own were dire—for he was already old beyond his years—had offered to sacrifice his own body to provide them with a clue, an insight. Should he return they would know death was not final but a beginning. No return; then only ostracism and darkness. The only question that remained should he indeed be revived is what awaited. And now he knew.

While yet another grey, ominous mass slowly approached them in the sky, obliterating the moon, thunder and lightning dancing in its epicentre, they gathered at the edge of the island's eastern cliff face as planned. Havenstrop was the last to arrive.

They greeted him with uncertainty in their eyes now that the defining moment was here. Many were huddled together as though cold, yet the iciness they felt came from within. From their hearts. Tears fell from puffed, absent eyes, whimpers from the younger ones for they could not truly believe what was to be embarked upon. Young minds did not encourage such feats, considered them alien thoughts from desolate, heartbroken souls with nothing to live for anymore. Yet here they were.

Havenstrop opened a bag he had brought with him, revealing several glass bottles. They contained a potent combination he brewed himself of alcohol, herbs and certain mushrooms whose existence he knew of and their effects on the human mind. There was enough for one sip to each member of the island—enough to loosen nerves and encourage the final push. He passed it to Patterson—they would follow his example like the good little lambs they were—who took a small swig, then gave it to the next. Havenstrop finished the contents.

"The journey we are about to take is not an end, but a beginning. On the other side, paradise awaits. No more will we know hunger or fear the wrath of gods as they pummel us with wind and rain. What we prepare to do may seem a madness, but instead is a triumph over insanity. Henry Patterson; you shall lead the way."

Havenstrop indicated to Patterson to lead the flock, show example. He wasn't going to go first as perhaps he should. He had to ensure they all jumped instead of losing courage and retreating.

Patterson looked around, eyes twitching in doubt and unease, face pallid. He took a deep breath, kissed his wife and bade for them to follow him to the cliff's ledge.

Terrified whispers. Muffled prayer. Despondent sobbing. Hope yet fear.

As they stood on the edge of the cliff, below, a hundred feet down, great, sharp rocks like teeth from some primaeval leviathan grinned back up at them. Hungry and eager for living tissue. And they would provide it so.

And again in the next world.

Havenstrop watched Patterson. He was peering down at the rocks, then swiftly stepping back; fear and despair washed over his face as the sea washed over his destination. Havenstrop silently willed for him to jump. As soon as he did, the others would follow. But where they went would be no paradise or crop-filled pasture. The inhabitants of the world that would greet them knew horrors far greater than any rock on this godforsaken island. Their new world would be a terror incomparable to anything they might have conceived of before.

For he had seen it.

Heaven had been the world they'd lived on until now. Each one left to carve his own fate in whatever means he chose and find haven and comfort wherever desired. What came after was the parallel world. The dark after the light. A land where the soulless roamed, feeding not on tasteless, lifeless crops, but the very flesh of those condemned to meander through the foulest of airs and hottest of fires. And once consumed, to become scavenger instead of scavenged. Havenstrop saw this, became as them while they ravaged his body—only his prompt resurrection saving his soul. And at that moment decided that he could not roam there alone. He would be at their mercy. If the villagers were there with him, might not attention be diverted? Allow him a respite? Maybe he would be shown mercy. If not, they would at least still be together as had been the case for generations. Life in hell would not be a solitary affair.

Patterson took one last look around at who had been his fellow neighbours, friends, companions, took his wife's hand in his own and together, they jumped. Their screams were abruptly ruined by a cracking of bone on rock.

The others, one by one, their brains poisoned with the potent alcohol from Havenstrop's bottle, began to jump. Screaming prayers became simple screaming became nothing.

There remained only one.

Havenstrop looked over the edge. Smiled. Doubted. Right now, their souls were being devoured, surely cursing his lies and deceit. Too late. But should he jump, also? What if he awaited old age or nature to show the path he must take? For now, alone on the island, hunger could not be a problem despite the relentless rain and storms.

The bodies below were one by one claimed to the seas, lost forever to both the dark beneath the waves and the eternal dark on the other side. Then, something distracted him. Warmth on the back of his neck. He looked up to see the sun breaking through the clouds after days of wind and rain. His lips cracked as another smile painted withering skin. Maybe he would wait after all.

HEADLESS VIPER

Kevin M. Folliard

My older stepbrother, Brandon, was a lonely teen. His dad disappeared when he was twelve. They found a body months later. I heard my dad say that Brandon's real father "drank himself to death," but nobody knew for sure.

Our parents met at a grief support group for widows and widowers. They married fast, within six months. That was harder for Brandon than it was for me. I don't remember my mom much. She died when I was two.

But my stepmom, Tammy, was nice. She started volunteering at my middle school. She bought me books and art supplies, and always let me and my best friend Danny stay up late at sleepovers. She mellowed out my dad—who don't get me wrong, is a great guy, just uptight after years of single parenting.

Brandon hated my dad, but except for the occasional prank, he didn't usually take it out on me. Before the wedding, Brandon convinced me that his mom was getting ready to ship me off to military school. "It's a proud tradition in our family, I went until I was fourteen." He showed me a phony junior high military diploma he had printed up.

"My dad would never do that!"

"She's got your dad under a love spell, Callum," Brandon said, perfectly deadpan. "Tough break."

Another time, Brandon put a few drops of red food dye in my toothbrush and had me screaming in horror because I thought my mouth was bleeding. And every now and then Brandon changed my app profile names from "Callum" to things like "Dweeber," "Doofus," and "Mouthbreather-Boy."

At the dinner table, Brandon would make snide comments about my dad's cooking like "These mashed potatoes are more watered down than Callum's IQ." And when our parents glared at him, he'd always cover by saying, "We're just messing around." Then I'd smile, shrug, and be cool about it.

I took Brandon's pranks in stride. I figured, maybe that's just what older brothers did. For the most part, Brandon kept his bedroom door closed and drowned the rest of us out with moody music. He sulked and obsessed over obscure bands like The Dejected Saps and Twisted Weasel Noggin.

Once, I made fun of the weird bands he liked—thinking the back and forth teasing would all be in good fun—but he just scowled, flicked his long bangs, and said, "What the hell do you know about music, dipshit?"

Toward the end of that first year, I'd settled into the idea that I didn't much care about Brandon one way or the other. His pranks were harmless, even kinda funny. But mostly I just didn't get him. And it stayed that way, until the Saturday before Halloween.

I was in the upstairs bathroom, applying dark circles of pirate makeup under my eyes, when Tammy's voice carried through the vent: "Busy tonight, hon?"

"Why would I be?" came Brandon.

"Trent and I have dinner plans," Tammy said. "But he promised Callum we'd give him and Danny a ride to Fright Fair."

I tied my skull and crossbones bandanna behind my head and listened closely at the sound of my name. Fright Fair was the fall carnival just outside town. Danny and I had been looking forward to it all month.

Brandon scoffed. "You want me to chauffeur a couple of dorky sixth graders?"

"Brandon, please," Tammy said. "You can do your little brother this one favor."

"Callum is *not* my brother." Brandon's words came out cold as a polar vortex. "And this is not a family."

"Just do it!" his mom snapped. "I'll pay you."

My cheeks flushed, stomach knotted. I wasn't sure why I cared as much as I did. Brandon and I weren't even really friends, let alone brothers. But hearing them discuss me like some nuisance made me clench my fists with anger. I suddenly looked stupid in the oversized puffy pirate shirt I'd bought with Danny at the thrift store.

I would have canceled right there and then. But Danny was counting on my ride. So I bit my tongue, bottled my adolescent angst, and fifteen minutes later, headed out with sour Brandon behind the wheel. His emo garbage tunes slithered from the speakers.

We were rounding the curve to Danny's subdivision when Brandon slammed the brakes. I glanced up to see the reddish scales of a snake winding across the road. It stopped in the headlights, tilted toward our car and flicked a black tongue.

"Jesus." Brandon grew pale.

"Weird," I said. "Don't usually see snakes in October."

Brandon's jaw trembled. His knuckles whitened around the wheel. Was he actually scared of a snake in the road?

The snake flicked its tongue then swirled into the shadows. Brandon's emo music cut out, and a folksy country song blasted:

You've got them snake eyes!

You've got snake eyes, girl!

Brandon gasped. His hand shot to the radio and turned it off.

"Hey," I said. "What's wrong?"

"Where'd that song come from?" he whispered.

"Your phone probably died." I shrugged. "And the radio took over."

"No, it didn't, doofus." Brandon showed me his phone, almost fully charged.

"Are we going to sit here in the middle of the road?"

Brandon huffed. We continued up the street into Danny's driveway. Danny leapt from his front porch, pirate coattails flapping behind him. He held his captain's hat in place with a plastic hook as he climbed into the backseat.

"Hey Callum's step-bro!" Danny exclaimed. "Thanks for driving! Where's your costume?"

"I'm a serial killer." Brandon reached for his vape pen and took a puff. "I wear plain clothes to blend in."

"No offense, but with all those indie band patches on your jacket, you kinda stick out," Danny said.

Brandon rolled his eyes. "Your friend always this charming?" He turned onto

Main Street, past town toward dark country roads. "Listen, dweebs, you're on your own tonight. I'm going to hang at the record store and get some coffee."

"Record store?" Danny laughed. "That place hasn't tanked yet? Ever hear of Amazon Music?"

Brandon ignored him. "Just be ready when I pick you up at 9:30."

"Tammy said 10:15," I said.

"9:30, or you walk home."

I crossed my arms. "Ten even."

"I'm not going to—"

Suddenly, the radio flared to life, full volume, banjo wailing:

Snake Eyes!

Snake Eyes!

Every time you roll them dice!

Snake Eyes!

Snake Eyes!

Time to put our love on ice!

"Shit!" Brandon slapped the off button. He veered toward oncoming traffic. A van's headlights blazed. Its horn erupted, and we shouted as Brandon swerved back into our lane.

I gripped the door handle. "Are you crazy, Brandon!"

My stepbrother blanched. His arms trembled. "Sorry. I just... that song. Startled me."

Danny whispered loudly, "Dude, is your brother on drugs?"

Brandon exhaled a shaky breath. "I'm not on drugs."

I exchanged nervous glances with Danny in the backseat. *Why, oh why, Dad, couldn't you have driven us?*

Carnival rides glittered beyond fields of dark corn. They'd set up the festival in a walled-off lot that had, up until a few years ago, been an auto wrecking yard. The Tilt-A-Whirl and Ferris wheel burned neon streaks in the air. With the radio off, we heard festive music and kids squealing to the giant drop.

Brandon didn't enter the parking lot. Instead, he pulled a U-turn and parked alongside the brick walls of the fairgrounds. "Get out." We piled onto the sidewalk. "Back on this corner at 9:30."

"Ten!" I shouted, as Brandon peeled off. "God, I hate him!"

"What is up with that guy?" Danny asked.

"Don't get me started." I fumed and struck off toward the fair in angry strides.

"Hey, Cal!" Danny huffed after me, gripping his pirate hat. "Wait up!"

"I don't want to talk about it. He's a jerk, that's all."

"I was just gonna say." Danny hooked his arm around my shoulder. "Cool costume!" He whipped his phone out from inside his captain's coat. "We look awesome!"

"Thanks." I gave a half smile as Danny took our selfie.

Popcorn and funnel cake swirled the air as we passed under the FRIGHT FAIR banner. The crowd teemed with young people in elaborate superhero and slasher movie cosplay costumes. "We do look good," I said. "But maybe we shouldn't have gone as pirates? Check out the competition."

"Arr, matey!" Danny shook his plastic hook. "Be ye a coward? Traditional costumes be all the rage among the judges!"

I laughed and scoped out the rides. A tall green rollercoaster arched into the air. Behind the crowds, neon letters sputtered ZOMBIE RIVER RAPIDS above a dark tunnel. On the main event stage, an executioner hoisted a fat orange pumpkin. He placed it on a platform, hefted an enormous ax and chopped. Guts sprayed, and the crowd cheered as the Pumpkin Executioner gestured to a tall rectangular guillotine.

The executioner chose another pumpkin, one with a nervous face drawn in black marker. He set it under the glimmering blade of the guillotine.

Someone grabbed my shoulder and spun me around.

"Callum!" Brandon loomed over me wild-eyed. "We have to go."

"What are you talking about?"

"Now!"

"Is there an emergency?"

"No." He shook his head. "Yes... it's complicated. Come with me, and I'll explain."

Nearby, Danny was purchasing a roll of bright orange tickets.

"What about Danny?"

"I'm not worried about him, but..." Brandon lowered his voice. "Someone here is going to try to kill you."

My heart pounded. "Who?"

"There's a guy... he's..." Brandon gazed at the towering green rollercoaster. The name SIDEWINDER was painted in scales along the ride. People screamed as the cars wound up and twirled out of sight. "Come back to the car." Brandon said. "I'll explain everything."

I glanced from Danny, to the ride, to my weird stepbrother.

"Please," Brandon said. "Trust me."

I thought back to Brandon's words. *Callum is not my brother. And this is not a family.*

"You're messing with me." I shook my head and turned to buy tickets. Brandon snatched my arm. He squeezed hard and dragged me.

"Let go! Stop it!" I struggled.

Brandon yanked me aside. He stooped and gave a harsh whisper, "Listen, punk! The guy who killed my dad is here! I know it. I feel it!"

My heart hammered. I found it hard to believe that Brandon would lie about his dad. I had a million questions, but the one that came out of my mouth was, "How do you know?"

"It's been creeping up on me all night." His eyes drifted up the Sidewinder. The rollercoaster trembled under rushing cars. Brandon closed his eyes, took a breath. "When I was your age, my dad took me to the carnival, back in our old neighborhood. We went on..." He stifled a sob. "A rollercoaster." He opened his eyes and nodded up. "It was that one."

Suddenly, I heard it—under the din of carnival chatter and the dings and pings of games—furious fiddle music. The twangy "Snake Eyes Song" sliding from speakers by the Sidewinder coaster.

"They play that stupid 'Snake Eyes' song on loop. You hear it?"

I nodded.

"I lost my favorite Atlanta Braves cap on the ride." Tears welled in Brandon's eyes. "This carny—his name was Viper—my dad bribed him twenty bucks to head into the restricted area under the coaster and find my hat."

Behind us, the Sidewinder rattled. The song jangled.

Snake Eyes!

Snake Eyes!

Putting up quite a fight!

Snake Eyes!

Snake Eyes!

Gonna make it last all night!

"The other guy operating the ride didn't see him. It was so loud, Viper didn't hear." Brandon sniffled. "The ride came roaring down. Viper stood up to show us the hat, and..."

Nearby, the Pumpkin Executioner's guillotine scraped and *shucked* through another swollen pumpkin.

"It knocked his head clean off his shoulders."

My skin crawled. If this story was true, then it explained why Brandon was so withdrawn. Except... "If Viper's dead," I asked, "who killed your dad?"

"I don't know how, but... he came back." Brandon's face tensed with anger. "First, he killed his carny friend. The one who turned the ride back on. They never found his head. My dad felt so guilty he withdrew from all of us. They found my dad's body..."

I took a wild guess: "But not his head."

"Bull crap!" Danny stepped closer. "Cal. He's messing with you."

"I'm not!" Brandon swore. "I have never seen a snake in the road here, Callum. *Viper* is messing with *me*. I know it."

I shook my head. The creepy crawly feeling in my guts faded. "Danny's right. This is some joke. I don't know how you got the snake and the radio rigged, but good set up."

"I'm serious." Brandon grabbed my shoulders.

"First of all," I said, "my dad would have told me if your dad was murdered."

"It's never been solved, and my mom doesn't like to talk about—"

"Secondly," Danny backed me up, "why would *Cal* be in danger? Wouldn't he come after *you*?"

Brandon stuttered. "You're the same age I was when—"

"And why the heck would you care what happens to me anyway?" I shook Brandon's hands away. "We're not real brothers. We're not really a family. I heard what you said earlier. You're trying to make me look like an idiot."

"Hey man!" Brandon threw his hands in the air. "I'm trying to help you. Don't believe me? Believe this." Brandon showed me his phone, displaying a text from an unlisted number:

Would be a shame if the little pirate lost his head. -V

Danny grabbed the phone and looked at it with me. "This is getting lamer by the minute. Come on, Cal. Let's get your tickets."

"Callum, I'll give you ten bucks to get back in the car with me right now," Brandon said.

"Why not twenty? That's what Tammy paid you to drive me around, right?"

"Fine!" Brandon snatched my wrist and dragged me.

My pirate boots scraped the concrete, I tripped and fell.

"Hey!" Danny shouted. "This weirdo is abducting my friend!"

"Christ!" Brandon snapped.

People were staring. A burly security guard strode toward us.

"That guy grabbed my friend!" Danny grinned like a goblin as he pointed at Brandon.

"Chill!" Brandon released me and backed up. "I'm his stepbrother, okay!"

The muscular guard helped me to my feet. "You know this guy?"

I glared at Brandon. "Nope."

The guard inserted himself between me and Brandon. Danny yanked me toward the entrance.

"Callum!" Brandon's cries faded under festival noise. "Wait! You can't..."

We raced through the crowd, dodging costumed kids and teens, slipping between lines that snaked toward the Zombie River Rapids. Danny cackled as he led me down a row of vendors, and we paused to catch our breaths. "How do you think Brandon gets out of that?"

"Well," I rolled my eyes. "I guess, pretty easy since we ran off."

"Eh, serves him right either way." With a stage magician's flourish, Danny whipped out a pillowcase from inside his captain's coat. I pulled my folded-up grocery bag from inside my pocket, and we started to hit up the vendors and games for trick-or-treat candy.

I told Danny about what I'd heard Brandon say through the vent, filled him in about the snake in the road. "I know he's a jerk," I said. "And he probably was just trying to get me to go home so he could ditch me for the night, but..."

Danny held out his pillowcase for a Snickers deposit. "But what?"

"But would he really lie about his dad? Even if he somehow set up the snake in the road, would he fake being so startled that he'd swerve into oncoming traffic?"

"Cal!" Danny rolled his eyes. "Either your brother is a devious, devious prankster, or he's bat-guano insane. Either way, we were right to ditch him."

I scanned the crowd. "Well, if security believes him about being my stepbrother, then he's probably still looking for us."

"Hm." Danny held up a finger. He removed his hat, eyepatch, and coat first, then yanked the bandanna off my head. "Switch with me." He handed me his pirate paraphernalia and started to tie the skull and crossbones bandanna around his head. "If Brandon chases us, we split up, and he'll come after me."

I set my candy bag down and slid my arms into the coat. "Okay, but then what?"

"Then... I don't know. We get to hang out here a little longer, and we get to mess with your brother some more."

I glared.

"Stepbrother. Right."

After making our trick-or-treat rounds, we hit up the games and sampled the rides. Danny split his tickets with me until we ran low. Then we cautiously scouted out the ticket vendors to make sure Brandon wasn't lurking by the front gates, and I replenished our supply.

I thought for sure Brandon would stake out the costume contest, but the whole thing came and went without a sign of him. "He ran off to his dinosaur record store," Danny assured me. "He'll be back to pick us up."

By the end of the night, the long line onto the Sidewinder coaster finally dwindled, and we decided to check it out. Neon lights streaked the ramp where about twenty costumed carnival-goers waited. That Snake Eyes song thrummed and blended with the din of the festival. Around the ride's perimeter, signs warned: DANGER: DO NOT ENTER! AREA BENEATH THE RIDE RESTRICTED!

The carny running the coaster had a mop of dirty blond hair. A pack of cigarettes was rolled up in his shirt sleeve, and he wore a tattered fishing vest.

Up close, I noticed that the cars of the coaster were upside down. The passengers were strapped in like Superman, with the cars hanging beneath the track. My eyes followed the path of the coaster and found two spots where it swooped precariously close to the ground, to freak out the riders. "Danny," I said. "This ride could totally knock someone's head off."

Danny shrugged. "Okay, maybe. Maybe the story was true, but it didn't really involve Brandon's dad. There are all sorts of ways to lie, Cal."

Soon it was our turn. We stowed our candy bags and plastic pirate weapons in bins by the exit. Danny and I ended up in the front car. My heart pounded as the carny strapped us. We waited as he checked the cars behind us. "Hey," Danny whispered. "Maybe we'll get lucky and Brandon will wander under the ride searching for you. Then whack!"

"Not funny," I said.

"Aw, lighten up."

The ride lurched forward, and we inched up a spiral incline.

"Dude, c'mon. There's no way that..." Danny trailed off. "Oh my God!"

"What?"

"Could that be..." He whispered, "It's him!"

"What?" My heart thumped. "Where?" I searched the ground.

"Down there!" Panic crept into Danny's voice. "I see him! Headless Viper!"

"I don't see—" Suddenly, the coaster plummeted. I screamed. Danny unleashed a wild laugh. We zoomed toward ground. My stomach lurched as we curved back up and twisted toward dark sky.

"Man, you're gullible!" Danny cackled. "That was great!"

"I freakin' hate you, right n—" My guts sank toward my feet as we dovetailed into more sharp twists. That song blared through the ride's speakers.

Snake Eyes!

Snake Eyes!

Her fury never ends!

Snake Eyes!

Snake Eyes!

Tasting that sweet revenge!

My stomach churned. Danny screamed with joy. The people behind us cried out. The ride rocketed up, and I caught flashes of the parking lot, acres of darkness, the towering guillotine, and the black-hooded executioner hacking his pumpkin victim.

My head swirled. Bile crept up my throat. And before I knew it, the ride was slithering beside the platform where we boarded.

My guts felt like a pile of queasy leeches. The carny reached to unstrap me, and

I vomited into the gravel.

"Somebody get a mop!" The carny patted my shoulder. "We got a puker!"

The other riders roared with laughter.

My face burned with embarrassment as he helped me down. I struggled down the ramp with my shell-shocked system.

"Cal, don't forget your—hey!" Danny was holding both of our candy bags, hurrying toward me. "My captain hat!"

I reached up and felt my exposed hair. "It must have blown off when..." I glanced toward the restricted area under the coaster.

There stood a muscular, headless man. His neck was rotted, with a circle of snapped backbone encased in flat callouses. He wore a leather vest and torn jeans. One arm was tattooed with snake scales, the other had a viper winding up from wrist to bulging shoulder, fangs bared.

Headless Viper hoisted Danny's lost hat with one hand and waved "hello" with the other. I stuttered, "D-d-d-Dan," and pointed at the hulking, headless man.

"What?" Danny shook his head.

"Th-the guy!" I managed to say. I took my eyes off Viper for only a moment, but when I glanced back, he was gone, along with the pirate hat. "He had your..."

"Dude." Danny stared at me like I was a lunatic. "You okay?"

"I swear I saw him. He had your hat."

Danny chuckled, at first, then his eyes grew serious. "Really?"

I nodded.

We both approached the fence. Sure enough, the pirate hat lay on that same spot. A fresh set of riders whooshed past, and it fluttered a few feet in the rush of air. Danny whispered, "Should we ask the ride-guy to..."

I shook my head. "I'll buy you a new hat."

At 9:30, we waited by the dark road where Brandon said he'd pick us up. We waited ten minutes. Then twenty. When it was clear he wasn't coming, we headed back into the carnival. "If Brandon ditched us, at least we have an excuse to stay out later," Danny reasoned. We played games until the booths began shutting down around 10:30.

Crowds wandered toward their cars. Vendors locked their booths, while orange-vested carnies picked up discarded napkins, cardboard hotdog trays, and cotton candy sticks.

The loudspeaker made several announcements that the gates would be locking soon. I was just about ready to call my dad's cell and interrupt his date night with Tammy. Then I looked into the thinning parking lot and saw that one of the few remaining cars was Tammy's atomic-blue Honda Civic.

"Brandon's still here," I said.

"This carnival isn't that big, Cal," Danny said. "Don't you think we would have seen him?"

"Maybe we got him into serious trouble," I said. "Maybe we shouldn't have..." I squinted. Someone sat in the front seat. "He's waiting! Come on!"

I hurried toward the Civic, then stopped in my tracks. The shadowy figure slumped in the driver's seat.

His head was missing.

A lump caught in my chest. Dizziness washed over me.

"Callum, what's—"

The car door opened. I glanced up, and spotted, not Brandon, but Viper muscling his way out of the car, tattooed biceps tensed, fists clenched. Parking lights cast a ghoulish glow over his severed neck.

"Oh my God!" Danny clutched my arm. "No way! No way! No way!"

Viper raised a filthy finger and traced across his severed neck in a slashing motion. Then he pointed at us.

We dropped our plastic pirate weapons, spilled our candy, and bolted toward the carnival, screaming at the top of our lungs. We passed under the banner, when the same burly security guard from before halted us. "Hey! We're locking up, kids. Go home!"

We raved and pointed at the parking lot.

"What the hell are you..." The guard's eyes widened. "Holy Moley!"

We whirled around. The guard ushered us behind him and approached Headless Viper.

"Hey," the guard said. "If this is a joke—" Viper grabbed the guard's neck and hoisted him one-handed. The guard gagged and struggled. Viper tossed him like a rag doll and sent him crashing over a concession stand.

Viper faced us. The guard clawed his way back over the stand. "Freeze!" Blood oozed down his forehead. He aimed a handgun at Viper. "Hands above your... neck, I guess!"

Viper slowly raised his arms, then he reached over and yanked a metal support pole from a nearby booth. He spun the metal pole, slapped it against his other hand and advanced on the security guard.

"Get down, kids!" The guard shouted.

Danny and I dropped onto the gravelly fair grounds. I watched through trembling fingers as the guard emptied shot after shot into Viper's body. Black blood spurted, but Viper didn't even flinch. He just walked closer and closer. Shot after shot.

"Run!" the guard screamed as Viper began to beat him with the metal pole.

I got to my feet and pulled Danny up. "Come on!"

Danny stared in frozen horror as Viper continued to assault the guard. I yanked his arm hard. "Danny! Now!" He snapped out of his trance, and we raced toward the gaping tunnel of the Zombie River Rapids.

We leapt over the ride gate, up the platform steps, and sloshed into knee-high ride-water. "Hey, you kids!" a carny shouted. "You can't go in... Sweet Jesus!" He lost interest when his eyes settled on the spectacle of Viper beating the security guard.

"Callum!" Danny stood in the shadowy mouth of the tunnel. "Hurry!"

"Go!" The carny said. "I'll call for—" *Blam!* The man stumbled back. A red stain spread on his chest. Viper advanced, aiming the security guard's gun.

I rushed through dark shallow water. Danny panted ahead of me. Glow-in-the-dark paint splattered the walls. The red eyes of zombie dummies and animatronics glinted.

Danny shone his cell's flashlight along the walls, lighting up dangling foam spiders, fake body parts, and novelty tombstones. I heard his speaker phone ringing:

"911, what's your emergency?"

"A headless tattooed redneck is trying to kill me and my friend," Danny sobbed.

The operator chuckled. "Happy Halloween, kid." *Click.*

Danny cursed. We sloshed forward. I tripped on underwater track and came up spitting filthy ride water. I reached into my pocket and saw that my own phone had been completely submerged. "Try them again!" I told Danny. "Don't make it sound so crazy this time!"

Danny shushed me. "He's probably right behind us. Just keep going."

We rounded several turns in the ride. "Danny," I whispered. "What if Viper's waiting for us on the other side?"

Danny climbed onto the fake shoreline. He pushed aside the reaching arms of a bloody dummy and peeked behind a wooden façade that read BEWARE! "Let's hide in here. Looks like there's a crawl space."

"Viper has no head!" I hissed under my breath. "If he can still sense us out there, I think he'll be able to find us in a crawl space too!"

"Well what's *your* idea!"

"Call 911 again!"

"Okay, okay." He hit redial.

Suddenly the ride flared to life. Fog machines spewed smoky vapors. Speakers played the gurgling moans and groans of zombie hoards. Animatronic arms scraped at Danny. He screamed, stumbled back, and dropped his phone in the water.

Grinding laughter echoed from the ride's speakers.

"He's coming," I said. "But we don't know from what direction."

Danny stuttered. "Just hide, Cal! C'mon!"

I searched our surroundings. *Hiding won't work,* I knew. *A headless ghost, monster—whatever Viper was—isn't sensing you with his eyes.* There was nothing in the tunnel but cheap decorations. "Let's pick a direction and make a break for—"

A neon boat rounded the bend. Viper stood tall on the seat, gripping his metal pole in one hand, and slapping it against his other palm. He leapt into the water. "Run!" I splashed down the tunnel, but in a heartbeat, Viper had me by the scruff of Danny's captain's coat.

"Leave him alone!" Danny leapt onto Viper's back and started pummeling the decayed stump of his neck. Viper stumbled. I wrenched my arms and wormed my way out of the jacket into the water.

Danny screamed as Viper hurled him into a horde of zombie dummies. With his back turned, I spotted the security guard's gun, tucked into the back of Viper's pants. I snatched it.

I squeezed the trigger again and again. Shots echoed. Black blood spurted from his torso. Viper stumbled when a bullet wound exploded near his heart. He dropped his metal pole, but still, he advanced toward me.

The clip emptied. The gun clicked uselessly. Viper wagged his finger in disapproval.

Danny's bloody face flashed in strobe lights as he crawled through a pile of mannequins and phony cobwebs. He hefted Viper's pole out of the water and shoved it like a javelin down Viper's neck wound. The pole came spurting out of

Viper's undead thigh. Viper struggled to move his leg. He reached up desperately to try and yank the pole out of him.

"C'mon!" Danny raced back the way we came. I gripped the empty gun and splashed after him. We leapt over an oncoming boat and soon reemerged into the dark carnival. The carny whom Viper had shot lay glassy eyed by the ride entrance.

My lungs felt like they were going to explode as we rushed toward the exit. We both stopped in our tracks. My stomach sank.

Beyond the bloody security guard, slumped over the concession stand, the gates to the fairgrounds had been locked up tight. Chains wound around them. Viper had locked us in.

"We can climb." I hurried toward the gate, squatted down, and cupped my hands. "I'll give you a boost."

Tears trickled down Danny's cheeks. "Then how do you get over?"

"You get help," I said.

"But if Brandon's right, then Viper's after you, not me. We need to get you over first."

"Viper obviously doesn't care who he kills." I gestured toward the two victims. "Don't argue, just jump as high as you can."

I cupped my hands again, and Danny stepped into them. I sprang him up, and he grabbed the top of the gate. For a moment, he dangled. I jumped onto the bottom rung of the gate and pushed his dripping wet shoes higher. Danny grunted, shouted. At last, he managed to hook his arms over and flip to the other side.

He landed hard on his butt and rolled. "Ow!" He got up and approached the gate. "Maybe if I stick my hands through the bars, I can give you a boost too."

"Worth a try," I said. "See if you can—"

"Callum, look out!"

I spun just in time to see Viper making a headless mad dash for me. Black liquid oozed from his impaled thigh. I tried to run, but he veered and tackled me. My head clocked the gravelly ground. Bloody stars splotched my vision.

"Callum!" Danny screamed. "Help! Somebody, help!"

Viper's muscular torso blurred into focus. His white knuckles tensed as he prepared to strike. The snake tattoo on his right shoulder seemed to wriggle in the dim light. I could see the snake's tongue flickering like the copperhead crossing the road.

Suddenly, a dark object sank into the rotted flesh between Viper's neck and shoulder.

"Get away from him!" Brandon gripped the Pumpkin Executioner's ax in both hands. He struggled to yank it free, but it seemed stuck between Viper's shoulder bones.

I struggled to sit, to try to say Brandon's name, but the carnival spun like a monstrous merry-go-round. Viper grappled with Brandon. Brandon lost control of the ax and the handle swung behind them.

Danny was screaming, but I couldn't understand his words. I struggled to my feet, tipped to one side, and saved myself with one hand.

"Callum, get out of here!" Brandon said.

How? I tried but failed to say. *I'm locked in with you.*

The ax handle doubled and tripled in my vision. I reached, but failed to grab it, and fell flat on my face. I struggled back up. My vision was clearing, but blood dribbled from my nose.

Suddenly the Sidewinder rollercoaster roared to life. Cars rushed. Neon lights streaked. That horrible Snake Eyes song echoed.

Viper dragged my stepbrother by the hair. Brandon's face was bruised and bloody.

Snake Eyes!
Snake Eyes!
A villain so pretty and fine!

Viper hauled Brandon toward the Pumpkin Executioner's platform. The guillotine glimmered in moonlight. Orange guts splattered the stage.

Snake Eyes!
Snake Eyes!
Reaching the end of the line!

"Callum! No!" Danny pleaded as I stumbled toward Brandon. "Come here! You have to escape!"

My voice came out a gravelly whisper. "Get the cops, Danny."

I steeled myself and ran after them. Brandon groaned in misery as Viper hefted him onto the stage and slammed him on the ground by prisoner's gallows. The ax, still wedged in Viper's torso, wobbled as he hoisted the blade of the guillotine high in its shaft. Viper made a loose knot to hold the blade in place, then he shoved Brandon against the base.

I thumped up the stairs. Viper twisted toward me. He started to reach for the rope, but Brandon popped up and drove the ax further into Viper's torso. Black blood gushed. Brandon crawled onto the other side of the guillotine and yanked the ax free, sending Viper teetering on his heels.

I charged and collided, knocking Viper onto his back. Brandon grabbed one of Viper's arms and yanked it back. "Now!" he shouted.

I pulled the knot free. The guillotine came scraping down. It sliced clean into Viper's upper torso with a loud, ugly *shunk*!

Viper's legs twitched. He wrenched his right arm free from Brandon's grip.

I fell to my knees in exhaustion and watched in horror as Viper—one-handed—started sliding the blade of the guillotine back up.

The rollercoaster roared. Music crackled. Lights sputtered.

Brandon rushed to my side and helped me to my feet. We backed away, as slowly, Viper pushed the blade up. A waterfall of liquid tar gushed from his crunched ribs. He pushed forward. Stood. The blade slammed down behind him.

Viper took one step, and his left arm detached. It plopped onto the platform.

The music died out. The Sidewinder darkened.

Viper stumbled forward. His upper torso peeled back. It hung from him for a moment, attached by thin webs of meat to his damaged spine.

Then Viper fell into pieces.

* * *

Twenty minutes later, Brandon sat with me in front of the petting zoo pen we had commandeered. We each had a hot chocolate. Brandon had found a

Halloween blanket—a prize from one of the booths—and wrapped it around me.

"Thank God I was in that security detention room," Brandon said. "Locked in with you guys. Danny saved my life by starting that fight with..." He trailed off. Neither of us felt very good about the security guard who defended us, or the other workers we found who Viper had killed that night.

"Callum," Brandon said. "I'm really sorry about all this."

"Not your fault," I said. "I should have listened."

"You didn't have any reason to." He puffed his e-cigarette. "But after tonight, I think it's safe to say we're brothers."

I smiled and nodded.

Blue and red lights flashed by the parking lot. Danny had gotten help.

"What do we tell them?" I asked.

Brandon gestured into the animal pen. "We show them."

Viper's severed legs wobbled listlessly from one end of the pen to the other. His detached hand crawled through the hay like a desperate spider, dragging hunks of rotted flesh and bone behind it.

TOURIST TRAP

Gregg Chamberlain

"Good afternoon! Miskatonic Travel and Tours. How may I help you?"

The cheery greeting brought the young couple to a halt. The travel office door closed behind them with a last tinkling chime. Exotic posters adorned the walls of the storefront office and filled the lower half of its big display window. Before them loomed two stylish office desks, each one featuring ARKHAM 400 in bright red-white-and-blue bunting displayed across their polished fronts.

Seated behind one of the two desks, a blonde-haired, blue-eyed young woman beckoned the couple closer, all the while beaming a big, bright welcoming smile. Pinned to the left side of her fashionably cut blazer was a small plastic I.D. badge that declared *Hi, I'm Bonnie* in fanciful red script with the word TRAINEE below in smaller, plain black lettering. The badge also featured ARKHAM 400 in patriotic colours as part of the Miskatonic Travel and Tours logo.

The couple looked at each other, then back towards the young woman as they approached and sank down into a pair of cushioned office chairs. "Um, yeah," said the man. "Hi, I'm Phil, and this is my missus, Anne-Marie." He pointed at the desk's colourful bunting display. "Uh, what's this Arkham 400 all about?"

The young woman's smile glowed. "Why, it's just about the most important celebration in Arkham's whole history," she chirruped. "This year is the city's quadracentenary, four hundred years since the original pioneer fathers—and mothers, of course—settled here and founded one of the oldest and most heritage-filled communities in the original thirteen colonies! Arkham's quadracentennial calendar is filled from January 1 to December 31 with a cornucopia of special celebration events and unique activities for everyone, young and old, local and visitor, to indulge in and enjoy!"

Phil nodded. "Uh huh, okay, well, that explains all the trouble we had getting our hotel reservation confirmed." He smiled. "I was thinking for a while there that everybody in this town were big fans of Halloween."

Bonnie held a hand to her mouth and giggled. "Oh, some of us get the Samhain crazies too around this time of year."

Phil blinked. "Ah, right, sure, Samhain, Halloween, Devil's Night, Great Pumpkin Time, whatever works." He jerked a thumb over a shoulder towards one of the posters plastered inside the storefront window. "Anyways, we just wanted to ask about that guided tour of the town."

Bonnie's smile beamed even brighter and broader. "Why, certainly," she chirped. "Wait a moment, let me just check."

With a quick quarter-turn left, she faced a large flat-screen computer monitor. Her fingers, tips lacquered blood-red, flashdanced over the keyboard. "Mmm hmm, yes. Yes, we do have a few openings left for this weekend's Arkham at Night 400 Samhain holiday theme excursion. You know that it's a walking tour, right?"

Receiving nods in reply, she chirped again, "Oh, good!" and resumed her keyboard tango.

Phil cleared his throat. "Uh, we're just in town for a few days. Flew in from the Gatineau. We're from Québec, you know? Here for my cousin's wedding."

"Oh, that's wonderful!" Bonnie beamed. "Let me say, on behalf of Miskatonic Travel and Tours, congratulations to the happy couple. Well, then, let me introduce myself, I'm Bonnie, and I will be happy to be your connection to everything wonderful here in Arkham during our quadracentennial celebration. Give me just another half a moment. Now, let's see," she turned back to the flat-screen monitor hovering in front of her. "I can give you a few more details to help you decide if you want to go on the tour." She offered an understanding nod and a practised smile to the potential client couple. "I know how it is, given the circumstances, so little free available time to enjoy the local attractions, what with rushing around for rehearsal, last-minute arrangements for hair, and then the wedding and the reception and—oh! Everything else in between."

Anne-Marie sighed and nodded agreement. "*Oui, et sa cousine* is being a real, what you call, Bridezilla, *à tout le monde*. Well, she is!"

Phil retreated from his Anne-Marie's glare, turning instead to watch Bonnie the travel agent trainee quick-stepping again with the computer. A sharp tap of a manicured nail on a key and she looked up smiling at her commission prospects.

"Okay, then, let me just call up the brochure file. Now, you do understand this won't include *all* the stops along the route. Just a few of the highlights. Have to keep some mystery in store for you and the other walkers during the tour, right?"

Receiving hesitant smiles in response, Bonnie glanced back at the monitor. "Now the text is a bit lengthy, so I'm just going to read out some of the more interesting parts of the brochure. Ready?"

Phil looked at Anne-Marie. She gave a brief Gallic shrug of the shoulders. "Okay, sure," said Phil. "Shoot."

Bonnie beamed. "Our excursion starts from the new Arkham Plaza, on Washington Street, close to Christchurch Cemetery, our first stop of the evening. The plaza was recently remodeled in anticipation of the quadracentennial and features wonderfully artistic heritage symbols newly etched into the facades of several buildings. You may find these *fascinating* to see, as they represent several of Arkham's founding families."

"Uh, yeah, sure," said Phil, while Anne-Marie shook her head slightly in skepticism.

"Now Christchurch Cemetery," said Bonnie, undaunted, "is known as one of the oldest burial sites in the United States, at least for the colonial America period. The Miskatonic University's archaeology department is investigating rumours of a number of unmarked graves somewhere in the old woodland burial ground on Hangman's Hill that may date back to pre-colonial times. Legend has it that the occupants of some of those nameless graves did not go willingly into their final resting places, and one or two of these forsaken pits were not intended for human remains."

She glanced over at the couple with an encouraging smile. "Doesn't that all sound ghoulishly gruesome?"

"Okay, yeah, sounds sort of interesting," replied Phil, nodding slightly. Bonnie smiled and continued reading aloud.

"While passing through the cemetery, please note the many ornate tombstones and grave markers which abound. Christchurch is very popular with collectors of gravestone rubbings and etchings, and the cemetery grounds have also served, since the 1920s, as a moody scenic location in many early gothic horror movies, including a number of 'Silent Film Era' cult classics of the now-defunct Nocturne Films Company, during the heydays of New York City's own burgeoning movie industry. More recently the cemetery has hosted a variety of works in the growing 'zombie movie' genre, many of which are available on satellite and local cable channels. Please avoid wandering off during the traverse through the cemetery."

She giggled. "Gives you goosebumps already, doesn't it?"

Phil shrugged. Anne-Marie's face now wore a skeptical frown. Bonnie rushed on with the recital.

"Before leaving Christchurch, our group will make a brief stop at the site of the Phillips mausoleum, housing the mortal remains of one of the original founding families of Arkham. Feel free to take pictures of the mausoleum exterior, but do not be surprised if an extra image appears later in the resulting photographs. Also, please refrain from knocking on the mausoleum door and calling out 'Is anyone home?' Someone *may* answer back."

Bonnie glanced away from the computer screen. "The cemetery is also popular with nature photographers this time of year during our Fall Colours of Arkham excursions, in case you're interested."

Anne-Marie perked up. "Will there be enough light, do you think?"

Bonnie smiled brightly. "Oh, I'm sure it'll be all right. Unless there's some unseasonal New England fog. But that just adds to the atmosphere of the tour, doesn't it?"

"I guess," Phil remarked, shifting in his chair. Anne-Marie frowned again.

"Right, then, moving along, oh, yes, the 'Witch House' is also on the tour route for this weekend."

Phil's eyebrows lifted. Bonnie, taking note, paused a moment to study the text on the screen. Nodding her head, she plunged ahead with her pitch.

"The Witch House, located at the corner of Parsonage and Pickman Streets, this example of early twentieth century urban architecture is now part of the Arkham Historical Society's list of heritage structures. Its nickname is due to a neighbourhood legend dating back to before the turn of the nineteenth century when the original building on the site operated as a rooming house, providing inexpensive accommodations to transients and others. Local folklore alleges that a Miskatonic University student who was living in one of the upstairs suites at the time died, or vanished—details vary depending on the storyteller—under mysterious circumstances. Popular legend has it that he was the victim of a witch's curse. A later fire resulted in extensive damage to the building and the remaining structure was razed as part of a neighbourhood commercial development program. The entire district is now part of a gentrification effort and many buildings, like the Witch House, provide office space for various professional services and consultants on their upper floors with stylish salons and specialty shops situated on the ground level. Our stop here will include a quick visit to the unoccupied office alleged to be located in the very spot of the attic garret where the student supposedly spent his last hours in this world. There is a lingering neighbourhood folk tradition about 'Brown Jenkin', who some say was the student who died or vanished, while others claim it is the name of the witch's familiar. Many children, and some adults as well, still leave small offerings or 'treats' of butcher scraps or other kinds of food outside of the building for Brown Jenkin, to encourage him to stay inside the 'haunted room' and not follow them home. The Miskatonic University has a paranormal studies field team engaged on the premises, so please avoid touching or bumping against any of the monitoring and recording equipment you see while inside the office area."

As she finished reading aloud, Bonnie turned away from the monitor. "It does sound eerily exciting doesn't it?" she chirruped.

Phil and Anne-Marie glanced at each other. She was frowning again. He shrugged. "Sounds like just an old office building."

Bonnie's smile drooped just a bit as she resumed her spiel. "Now members of the tour group will have an opportunity for a brief break in the itinerary to allow for shopping in the boutiques located on the ground floor of the Witch House building." Her enthusiasm perked up again when she saw Anne-Marie straighten up with interest. "The gift shop also offers Brown Jenkin treat bags for sale for anyone who would like to take part in the local folk tradition after visiting the site of the student's apartment."

Phil looked quizzical. "Do we have to—?"

Bonnie shook her head quickly. "No, it's not a tour requirement." She shrugged. "But one never knows, does one?"

Beaming encouragement, she turned back to the monitor. "Now, let's see, skipping ahead, mmm hmm, a quick tour of the Pickman's Model exhibit at the Arkham Gallery is part of the itinerary this month." A little smile once more graced her lips as she noted Anne-Marie look up with interest again though Phil grimaced. "Ah, neither of you have any family history of heart problems, yes? You're not prone to nausea either? Oh, good." She hurried on to the next section of text before the puzzled looks on the couple's faces as they shook their heads No could turn once more to doubting frowns. "Well, then, after the gallery visit, it's off to the Miskatonic University Library in the Old Campus quadrangle between Church and College Streets. Oh, you are in luck. In honour of the quadricentennial, this weekend's tour includes a view of the Restricted Access section of the library."

"What's—" began a doubtful-looking Phil, but the now anxious Bonnie hurried on with the description before her potential client could express any ambivalence.

"The Miskatonic University Library houses one of the finest, if not the most complete, collections of occult and outré literature in North America. It is rivaled and exceeded only by the Vatican's *Bibliotheca Infernalis*, the 'Black Library' at the British Museum, and the 'Forbidden Annex', once part of the People's Library in Beijing, but since relocated to a site alternately suggested as either at an unnamed lamasery in Tibet or somewhere in the heart of the windswept wastes of the Gobi Desert in Mongolia."

Bonnie spared a quick glance at the couple. Saw Phil fidgeting and Anne-Marie looking even more bored. With a nervous swallow of the throat, she continued, speaking quickly.

"Our visit to the Miskatonic Library includes a stop at the Restricted Access room. Within this vault-like enclosure, beyond the heavy cross-barred iron gates—reinforced with molybdenum-steel in the 1970s—the stacks of esoteric manuscripts, unholy tomes, and ancient parchments tower in the sepulchral gloom of the dimly-lit room."

Phil's eyes closed as his head dropped back against the chair. A muted tapping of fingers against the padded arm of her chair indicated Anne-Marie's complete lack of interest. Bonnie offered an apologetic smile.

"Yes, I know," she said, "the description does seem a bit on the gothic side, doesn't it? Ah, it says here that in return for a minimal donation to the library's security upgrade fund, the archivist assigned to the Restricted Access room will go in and retrieve any one of a select few books available on the 'Limited Viewing' list."

"How 'minimal'?" asked Phil, lifting his head back up.

Ignoring the question, Bonnie rushed on, hoping to maintain Phil's flagging, but still active, interest. "Included are: a first edition of *De Vermis Mysteriis*, a nineteenth-century translation of the *Pnakotic Manuscripts*, and a Gutenberg press bound copy of the *Necronomicon*, in the original Arabic."

"Can we at least go inside this room if we make a donation?"

Bonnie tried not to wince. She was losing them both now, she knew it, but she still hoped to salvage the situation. She had to, she really had to. Or else.

"No, sorry, no one is allowed within except by special permit and the librarian will lock the gate behind as he or she enters the room to prevent anyone 'accidentally' slipping inside. And no, sorry again, there will be no handling allowed of any items brought up for display. Whatever book is requested will not actually be brought outside of the room. The archivist will hold it up for viewing through the bars."

Phil looked disgusted. "What about photos? My Nikon even has a flashless museum mode so no worries about damaging any 'precious' sensitive papers or pictures with a quick flash."

Bonnie did wince this time. "Once again," she said, smiling a little sickly seeing Phil's frown, "sorry, but no photographs, either film or digital, are allowed. No, not even on flashless museum mode settings. Too many complaints in the past about fogged film or shorted-out circuitry."

The frown lines on Phil's face smoothed out. "Huh? What?" he said, leaning forward.

Bonnie's sales pitch smile returned, fading hope for a commission brightening again. "Ah, there is a mandatory waiver that needs signing first before any items are brought up for display. It exempts the university from any liability for post-traumatic stress disorder or any other psychological problems for the viewer that may arise later on. Oh, no," she said, quickly, seeing the worried looks, "it's just a formality, I'm sure, just something to add to the excitement of the tour, you know."

Doubtful nods. Not a good sign, she realized, but at least they were not frowning again. She resumed reading aloud.

"Ummm, after the Miskatonic Library, let's see, there's the Herbert West Memorial Clinic, I'm not sure why that's on the itinerary. Oh, I see, they're offering a 'Mad Doctor Photo Op' to help publicize their Arkham 400 organ donor drive. Tour participants take turns playing 'victim' in a retro-style brain transplant scenario like in one of those old movie serials. Souvenir photos offered courtesy of volunteers with the Arkham Red Cross branch, and there's even a free blood test. Isn't that just morbidly marvellous?"

Instead of answering, the couple looked at each other. Phil raised a quizzical eyebrow. Anne-Marie jerked her head in the direction of the door. Feeling desperation clawing at her, Bonnie did a quick scroll of the screen text.

"Nearing the end of our tour we approach the notorious Hangman's Hill, from which summit many a wretched soul beheld their last view of the town during Arkham's 'witch hunt madness' of pre-Revolutionary War days. Although witch-haunted Salem is more famous, or infamous, for its persecution of innocents, both women and men, for the crimes of sorcery and black magic, Arkham too had its share of rumoured diabolical deeds and devilment. The town elders of the time were also not averse to more 'creative' means of both interrogating and punishing those accused. It is safe to say that both the innocent and the guilty welcomed their final end when it came at last."

"Uh?" queried Phil, raising a finger. "What do you mean by 'creative'?'"

"Pardon?" Bonnie cast a distracted glance his way then returned her attention to the computer monitor. "Oh, the brochure doesn't go into that kind of detail, but it will be part of the tour commentary, I'm sure. There is mention of nearby Innsmouth as a popular sanctuary for many suspects seeking escape from their accusers. Anyways," she rapidly clicked for a quick scroll then jumped back into her reading before either one of the couple could interrupt with another question.

"The summit of Hangman's Hill is a ten-minute walk along a gravel road beginning at the end of Church Street. It is not recommended for those with mobility problems. A memorial cairn marks the site of the old oak tree that once occupied the peak of the hill and served as the gallows for those unfortunates sentenced to 'dance in the air' for crimes and misdemeanors. A short distance from the cairn is the Potter's Field graveyard where those brought to the hill went for their final rest. A few gravestones, their inscriptions almost obliterated with the passage of time, still stand askew, marking the sites of some of the graves. Most of the yard's residents rated little more than a simple wooden cross, long since rotted away, leaving them faceless and nameless in memory now forever. Following a brief walk about the graveyard, the tour group will pause at the stone cairn for a few moments, out of respect for the dead and also on the chance that Liebstwerk's ghost might appear."

"Who?"

Bonnie brightened, hoping she sensed some returning interest. "Oh, that's one of the highlights of the visit to Hangman's Hill. Let me just scan ahead. Ah, yes, here we are."

Seeing Anne-Marie start fidgeting again, she hurried along.

"Along the way to the summit, visitors will hear the story of Horst Phelps Liebstwerk, a German printer's apprentice, hanged for treason and sedition during the Revolutionary War. Suspicion fell on the unfortunate 'printer's devil', both because of his 'foreign background' and also because of village watch reports of 'curious lights' seen flickering during the midnight hours in the window of the attic garret which served as Liebstwerk's lodgings over the print shop. The young man was arrested and his room searched. Copies of various tracts, some in German, many in English, on taxation and other such political matters of the day were found. Also discovered was a crudely handbound book of indecipherable script, which also contained 'drawings of a disturbing nature,' according to one witness report. Legend has it that Liebstwerk promised 'a most horrible vengeance' upon his accusers and died cursing in both German and another language even as the noose was slipped over his head. His ghost is rumoured to haunt Hangman's Hill and at a certain hour may be glimpsed hovering and twitching in mid-air, as if dangling from a rope, mouthing silent curses as he jerks back and forth."

She turned from the monitor. "Best make sure of the batteries in your camera, yes?" she said, making an attempt to recapture her sales pitch smile. A smile which faded at the sight of the couple starting to get up out of their chairs.

Phil cast her an apologetic look even as Anne-Marie turned towards the door. "Uh, sorry, not really our cuppa, y'know." He shrugged. "Anyway, we're sort of short on time while in town, and this tour is how long?"

Bonnie blinked. "I'm sorry, what? Oh, it's about a three-hour walking tour." She added, quickly in a pleading persuasive tone. "Very nice on a late summer or early autumn evening."

"Yeah, no, don't think so." Phil shrugged again. "I mean, what with the wedding and the reception..."

"And the rehearsal and the supper after that, *mon chèr*," Anne-Marie interjected. "Remember?"

Phil nodded. "Right, right, so, mmm, we're kinda pressed for time."

"I see," Bonnie murmured, despondent. "Yes, well, I suppose with all of that, you might be a bit too busy at night for a walking tour." She brightened again. "Perhaps you might be interested in The Treasure Hunter's Guide to Arkham?"

Anne-Marie paused, just at the door, Phil bumping into her. She turned, eyebrow raised, and looked without speaking at the travel agent.

"It's a self-guided daytime excursion," Bonnie said, hurrying into her new pitch, "through the antiques market section of town. 'One huge block of shops full of curios and one-of-a-kind *objets d'arts*' according to the brochure, as I recall. 'Bargains galore on rare items anyone would sell their soul to own.' Now how does *that* sound?" She started opening and closing drawers, scrabbling through each one of them. "Let me just find you a copy of the brochure."

Anne-Marie sighed, shook her head. "Ah, *non, désolée*, maybe another time. We could always come back, *peut-être*?" she said, looking at her husband.

Phil shrugged. "Yeah, sure," he grunted. "Why not?"

They both left quickly, the door chime tinkling behind them, before Bonnie could attempt another enticing offer. Her shoulders slumped as the door clicked shut.

"Missssss Ev-ver-rett!"

Even though she'd expected it, a little gasp still escaped from Bonnie at the sound of the sibilant voice. Reluctantly, she turned about, looking towards the back of the office reception area. At a door, slowly opening by itself.

"Yes, Ms. Alazoth?" she whispered.

"We mussst review your performance, Missss Ev-ver-rett," the hissing voice continued, "and your failure at sssuccessful completion of the tasssk, and misssing your share—*again*—of the 400 tribute quota."

Slowly, Bonnie moved first one foot forward, then another, advancing step by step, past her desk, towards the back of the room.

"Lock the door!"

Bonnie stopped. Turned slowly about and went to the storefront door. She turned the deadlock, heard it click into place, then flipped the Closed sign around.

"Bring the lash!"

Turning about, step by dragging step, she returned to her desk. She crouched down, opened a bottom drawer, reached in, and withdrew a short rod of black wood wrapped round with strips of stained leather. Fanning out from one end of the rod were several wire tendrils.

Bonnie stood up and turned about again. Began walking slowly to the open door.

"Hassten, Missss Ev-ver-rett!"

A single tear seeped out from an eye and trickled down Bonnie's cheek. She strode quickly now, the wire lash dangling from one hand, to the rear office for her "performance review" meeting.

EVERGREEN AND BLOOD RED

Quinn Parker

The oven beeped, signaling the cookies were done.

Jill jumped a little, body jerking, her mind rather forcefully finding its way back from being lost in a pleasant daydream. She'd been so deep in her own head that she hadn't noticed the smell of warm chocolate dancing its way across her tongue. A few cursory sniffs hinted that maybe they weren't just cooking, but burning.

Shit, she thought, careful not to say it aloud with Michael and Daisy in the next room. They probably wouldn't have heard a whisper over their cartoons, but still. *Tis the season not to teach your children new words they'll repeat in front of the in-laws.*

Grabbing an oven mitt, she pulled the oven door open to find that, yes, worst fears confirmed: a few of the treats were going dark brown at the edges. Only a few, but enough. She growled under her breath, wondering just where her mind had gone that she couldn't pay better attention. The daydream faded with the oven's beep, banished to wherever thoughts go when left unfinished, so she couldn't even chastise it for having captivated her.

Jill instinctively reached for a paper towel before fully realizing she was going to sneeze, body spasming as she suffered the full force of a sneeze with no warning. She quietly thanked ten years of motherhood for her grab-a-tissue instinct. All that time spent preventing her kids from sneezing on food, books, toys, and other peoples' faces narrowly saved her cookies. How would Carolina-Ann have reacted to knowing the cookies weren't simply burned, but drenched in snot?

Keys jangled by the front door. So began the usual two-person stampede of her kids rushing over to say hi to Daddy. God only knew when they last reacted to *her* like that, but between asking about desserts and what would be under the tree next week, she didn't exactly mind a few seconds' breathing time.

Harris faux-stomped his way into the kitchen, a child hanging off each leg, still dressed in his uniform. There weren't many places left in the U.S.A. that would allow a family of four to afford a house off just one income. He spent his first few years in Brooklyn, of course, making sure that people would actually *want* him if he requested a transfer.

"And how are *you* today?" Harris beamed, goofy smile plastered across his face. She leaned forward, over the kids, to plant a kiss on his cheek.

"Well, the cookies are done," she said, a peal of excitement rising from below. Jill looked down at their eager eyes, adding, "And they are for *after* dinner, not before!"

"Mom!" Michael groaned.

"But they're warm *now!*" came Daisy's paired protest.

She almost spoke up again, but got a little more warning on the next sneeze. Turning her head, she let loose into the crook of her elbow, her now-moist arm letting her know it wasn't just a tickle from some dust. She sighed, eyelids drifting shut, suddenly aware of how heavy they were.

"Geez, how am I coming off a ten bright and peppy but you're the one passing out?" Harris joked, mirth in his eyes, like always.

"I'm just..." A yawn cut her off.

"Go take a nap. I'll watch the kids." A little bit of the twinkle left his eyes, their corners scrunching up—a look she knew well by now. His "investigating" look, reserved for crime scenes, interrogations, and being worried about his family.

She almost argued but couldn't find a reason to. If he had the energy, by all means, watch the kids for a bit. The clock said 2:00 PM, so she could zonk out for as long as two hours before putting dinner at risk. Three if she decided not to give a fuck what Carolina-Ann thought of a grown woman taking a nap in her own house.

Jill held out long enough for Harris to change out of his work clothes. More specifically, to take the handcuffs off his hip and store his gun away where no sticky, curious hands could play around with it. A moment later, he returned to offer her leave. She lingered on the steps up to the second floor, then turned back, eyes on her kids.

"You can have *one*—just one—and the rest are for after dinner."

They bolted as one single entity, twin suns burning a path through whatever laid between them and their prize. She flicked her gaze over to Harris, who stared eagerly.

"Yes, you too."

He giggled out a thank you and chased after his kids. She grinned a little, walked into the bedroom, and all but passed out.

* * *

Despite having two hours to sleep, she awoke twenty minutes later to a battery of sneezes and her stomach growling louder than any dog she knew of. She gave it another forty, each time easily drifting off, yet being yanked back to reality by a world-rocking sneeze, a vicious roar, or some combination of the two. Jill tried to get up at 2:45 and practically blacked out, head thumping back to the pillow, only to double up into the fetal position, wide awake from the clawing emptiness of her belly, at 2:55.

So she got up, her world spinning for just a moment, then got her shit together. After a quick shower to wash the clamminess away and a new outfit to have presentable clothing not covered in dried snot, she made her way downstairs.

Harris had somehow created order from chaos, having convinced their kids to sit at the coffee table in the living room—without cartoons on—to play a board game. She caught up with them, then hopped into the kitchen to get dinner started, stopping to make a PB and J first since she couldn't remember actually eating lunch, but her body made it clear she hadn't.

The sandwich was awful. She forced it down, wondering how she screwed up a sandwich so easy that her kids could actually make one on their own without destroying the kitchen and taking out the rest of creation with it. Hopefully that wouldn't serve as a forecast for dinner itself. She set about preparing a honey ham, roasted Brussels sprouts, sweet potatoes, and mashed cauliflower. They already had sweet potatoes. Mashed regular potatoes might've been more traditional, but sweet Jesus, the *carbs.*

She passed the evening in a haze, trying not to sneeze on the food. The nap hadn't helped. Jill had definitely caught something. Once the potatoes were done, the ham and sides just needed to roast away in the oven, so she sat down at the table, falling asleep again.

Dreams assailed her. She woke five minutes later to the sound of breaking glass, shaking the sleep away, only to realize the sound had been in her head. What was that word? Hypnagogic hallucination. That's right. A totally normal thing. When the brain shuts down for sleep, or when it's waking up, it might conjure up all sorts of weird sensory attacks.

She checked on the food. Still fine.

She talked a little with her family but didn't want to distract them too much. Her phone did little to distract her, so Jill set about mixing drinks just to give the illusion of choice, knowing too well that nobody wanted anything beyond their staples. Strawberry milk for her two kids, water for Harris, and a port that Carolina-Ann would bring to spite her.

Carolina-Ann arrived right on time: twenty minutes before the food came out of the oven. She somehow did this whenever she came over, either complaining that dinner would be too soon or too late, based seemingly on little besides the direction of the wind and whether the groundhog saw its shadow that year. True to form, she had a bottle of wine tucked under her arm, a scowl on her face, and tons of compliments for her grandchildren.

Dinner was apparently late this time. The dining room table had plenty of room for all five of them, with Harris taking the head of the table, at Carolina-Ann's insistence.

"That's his place. He's the *head* of the *household,*" she scowled at Jill.

"He can sit where he wants. Doesn't matter to me," Jill shrugged back.

The mother-in-law harrumphed back to her own seat directly to her right. Any time she came over, she insisted on sitting next to her son, and since Michael and Daisy always sat next to each other, that left Jill shoved into a corner. It was only one night, after all.

"Guess what, kids?" Carolina-Ann smiled at the little ones. "Grammy brought a cake for after dinner!"

"Mommy made cookies, too! Now we have lotsa desert!" Daisy's eyes lit up. Michael just cheered for the cake.

Carolina-Ann shot her a sidelong glare.

"I thought I was handling dessert?" She—begrudgingly—stuck a forkful of food into her mouth, chewing slowly, never breaking her peripheral eye contact.

"We can have two things," Jill shrugged, yawning, pinning a piece of ham down to cut it into manageable pieces.

"Do you really think it's appropriate to do *that* at the dinner table?" Carolina-Ann said around a mouthful of sprouts.

Jill flipped the knife around and drove it into Carolina-Ann's throat, silencing the stupid bitch and leaving her to die drowning in her own—

She jerked awake, having fallen asleep on her hand right there at the table. Her heart hammered wildly, all systems now on alert because what the *fuck?*

"If you're tired, perhaps you should lay down." Her in-law turned, looking at her more directly, this time—if she wasn't mistaken—with a touch of genuine concern. No, she wasn't. The woman was actually worried. She must've looked horrible.

"You feeling okay?" Harris said, eyes scrunched up again.

"Yeah, yeah, I'm fine." She wiped a cold sweat off her forehead. "Just sleepy. Maybe too much ham?"

Her stomach growled, loud enough to interrupt Michael and Daisy, who looked over at her with awe. She clenched her arms around her stomach, blushing.

"Or not enough?"

The kids cracked up. Harris smiled, but not with his eyes.

She set her knife to the side, and they all went back to eating.

* * *

All that night, she tossed one dream to the side only for it to turn into another. She'd wake, shake the thought away, then fall helplessly into the clutches her next bizarre mental slideshow. None of them stuck. None of them ever made enough of an impact for her to remember for more than a few seconds after waking. If her train of thought tried to stop at such a station, it derailed, drawn again to what she'd been dreaming at the dinner table.

Around 5:00 AM, she gave up on staying asleep, though her body tried to drag her mind back into the dark. She got up, stumbled as her world spun, made her way to the bathroom, hit the switch to light it up, stared herself in her bloodshot eyes and wondered if she could get a doctor's appointment before the holiday hit.

She poked and prodded at herself, looking between herself and her reflection, tilting her head up and down, up and down, because was she always that pale, or was it the early morning light? Well, it was winter, and she hadn't gotten out much that summer anyway. Maybe the light. Maybe her. Nothing to worry about.

Jill made coffee, drank it, made more, drank more. The ghosts of dreams haunted her, nagging at her consciousness, each leaving a poison ivy vine that caused her consciousness to itch with worry. That wouldn't help anyone. What would her kids do if their mother got sick? Did she really want her husband distracted in the line of duty?

Whatever this was, she'd work through it. She plugged headphones into her phone's audio port, plugged the earbuds into her head, and started cleaning up. She hadn't exactly had the energy to do it last night, after all, and naturally, no one else cleaned. The kids couldn't, and she didn't want Harris to. He had a career. She just had the house. If he did everything, he'd burn out, and she'd go stir crazy.

Her reflection followed her from room to room, always hovering in the corner of her eye, first in one pane of glass, then another. She picked up discarded toys, loaded plates into the washer, and gathered the better knives to wash by hand. Good knives don't go in the dishwasher or you'll wear out the blade. At least, that's what her mother taught her.

It took a while to notice her reflection wasn't following her anymore. It stopped in the center of the kitchen. Just... stood there. Her gut clenched. Why would it do that? It always obediently mirrored her before. What made it rebel? Why change its mind from its previously unerring sense of duty?

She stared at this stationary image of herself. Definitely her, or pretending to be her. Same pair of jeans she'd stumbled into. Same wrinkled shirt. Was her hair really that messy? Her reflection stood there with a sloppy bun and bad posture and bone-white skin and when did it pick up the carving fork?

Then Jill looked down at the carving fork in her hand. She barely had time to say, "Huh," before her reflection jerked its arm, and her own swung up, driving the prongs at her face, directly into her eyes.

Jill jerked awake, breathless, sweaty, the bed empty beside her. Everything spun. No, it was blurry. Her stomach roared with hunger. Or nausea. Both?

Yes, both. She turned, pulling open the bottom drawer of her bedside table, vomiting into it. Undigested pieces of dinner splattered into the wood, destroying a few books she'd forgotten about. It only took a few seconds to completely empty herself out, but those few lasted for an eternity as she felt every detail of the dinner her body apparently hadn't wanted. Even Jill's sandwich made a comeback, the bread soggy, but still clearly bread.

She shut the drawer. There'd be time to deal with that later. She needed mouthwash. And glasses, apparently. The Jill in her bathroom's mirror looked even worse than the Jill in the mirror from her dream, but this one didn't gouge out her somehow more bloodshot eyes. Her skin had paled to the point of being borderline translucent, her veins standing out with alarming prominence.

Jill smelled coffee. Her empty stomach grumbled, greedy and nonsensical, demanding food it wouldn't really eat. Like a child, in a way.

She changed, and at that thought, checked on her kids. Sleeping soundly. She made her way downstairs. Harris had brewed coffee, handing her a cup as she entered. He'd even started loading dishes.

"Morning, sunshine. How are you feeling?" His tone said, *I hope you're well,* but his eyes said *Holy fucking shit, my wife is about to die, if she isn't dead already.*

But for now, she had a loving husband and a fresh cup of coffee. She smiled, her eyes barely staying open.

"Eh, I'll live." Jill kissed him on the cheek, then joined him to clean, and somehow, it did make her feel a bit better, if only for a moment.

* * *

Harris had work that day, but the kids were off. Thankfully, they wanted to play at a friend's house. She told them to be back for dinner, around 5:00 PM, then spent the eight hours after collapsing into a fugue of sleepy mental turbulence. If she vacuumed near the couch, she'd wake up on it ten minutes later. Changing the sheets only led to jerking out of a dream, tangled up in them. Even dusting was out of the question. She woke up on the stairs, her neck spasming from the odd angles. Her empty belly grumbled the whole time, but the scrambled eggs she forced down at ten showed back up around two.

The kids came back on time. Her husband, too. They ordered Chinese for dinner, then sat on the couch to wait for the delivery person. Jill didn't want to admit that any attempt to cook might lead to her burning the house down, but

Harris saw right through her.

"You're clearly coming down with something, and pushing yourself through it won't get you well again. If you can't stay asleep, maybe take a medication to help." He spoke quietly to account for little ears, though their kids zoned out on yet another Marvel movie and weren't paying them a hint of attention.

"Do you think I need to go to a doctor? Or the hospital?" A tiny part of her hoped he'd say yes.

"Do *you* think that?" he replied. "It's your body. Your health. I can't tell you how to feel or what to do, so if you're feeling that sick, then we'll go. All I know is that you look tired and pale."

She bit her lip, thinking. No. She didn't want to worry them.

"I'll try taking something first. If tomorrow's better, then we're in the clear. If not, we'll see what happens."

He nodded, neither smiling nor frowning, his thoughts inscrutable as she took a dose of NyQuil from the half-empty bottle, aiming to eat dinner and fall asleep for real right after. They all milled about in various directions, with Jill staying standing as much as possible to avoid falling asleep before actually going to sleep. She did the laundry, wiped down the counter tops, finished dusting the China cabinet, then woke up on the couch.

She couldn't read the time on her phone. Was her vision screwed up again, or was this a dream? She never could read during dreams. Most people can't. Then Harris nudged her shoulder.

"You're clearly coming down with something. Maybe you should go to bed for real, get a good night's sleep? I know you've been restless." The outline of his face seemed off. It swam a little, his form not totally anchored to its place in reality.

"Am I asleep right now?" she said, not knowing where the kids were, but hoping they weren't here to hear her weird rambling, if she was, in fact, awake.

He furrowed his brow.

"No, you're not. Been a rough couple of days for you, huh?"

She nodded, stood up, and went to their bathroom upstairs. Jill completely forgot about the vomit drawer by this point. She grabbed NyQuil out of the medicine box, downed an adult serving of it, debated a second, then shook her head. Wouldn't be healthy to take more than one.

Her head hit the pillow, eyes drifting shut to a scene of her driving through the night, pedal to the floor, faster and faster as she roared with laughter, blowing directly into her mother-in-law's house, and her eyes snapped open again.

Jill was still on the couch.

"You okay?" Harris nudged her.

"Just tired. And restless. And coming down with something." Maybe he was about to say some of those things. Maybe not. She went upstairs and took NyQuil, then woke up again at the dining room table.

"You okay?" Harris nudged her. "Fell asleep during dinner. You almost went face-first into the refried beans."

She sniffed the air. Mexican food.

"Didn't we order Chinese?"

Her husband shook his head.

"You're really out of it, huh? Maybe we should take you to the hospital?"

Frustration blotted out any hint of anxiety. This went beyond worry. Now she was getting pissed off. How many times was she going to have the same mundane dream? At least flooring it into Carolina-Ann's perfect little ranch was *interesting*.

She went upstairs with two growls, one from her stomach, one from her, and took a dose of NyQuil. Then she stopped, blood running cold. The bottle was empty.

It hadn't been nearly empty before. She replaced medicines once they got *close* to empty, she would never have let it get down to one dose.

Maybe she hadn't been dreaming. What if she'd only been waking up?

The room was already spinning. A panic attack will do that. So will a quadruple dose of sleeping medication. She tried to pull out her phone, but couldn't see well enough to unlock it. Jill stumbled for the bedroom door, would've even called for help if she hadn't slumped over, asleep long before her head hit the pillow.

* * *

Jill woke up cold. She woke up uncomfortable. Her first thought, blurred by sleep, was *Oh god, I've been buried alive.*

No, that wasn't true. But she was outside. No wonder she was cold. A glance around showed she'd fallen face down in her own backyard.

This wasn't the time to cry. She thought about it but didn't. How could she get help? How could she even ask, beyond begging her husband at every waking moment? Would he understand, or believe, that even when she didn't go to sleep, she kept waking up?

Snatching the spare key to the backdoor from their fake hide-a-key rock, she made her way inside. Three o'clock AM. Her stomach roared furiously. She didn't want to puke again, but the hunger hurt. It was beyond painful, in fact. Jill didn't bother turning on the kitchen light as she went into the fridge. Everything looked awful. Every scent made her nose crinkle in disgust. The ham seemed okay, though, so she grabbed the bag of leftovers—easily five pounds of meat—and didn't bother with getting a plate or turning on the light.

She ate, and ate, and ate, and prayed for the hunger to go away, but it didn't. If anything, it got worse. Time marched on, her craving unabated, hands shaking because she couldn't keep anything down and very little even approached the idea of satisfying her. She wept as she crammed food in her mouth, begging her body to be okay, and when she ran out of ham, she started on her fingers, tearing them off one by one with a wet—

Jill woke up, face sticky with dried tears, eyes nearly swollen shut, on the living room couch. She sat there alone, in the dark, with a pillow over her face to muffle herself as she cried.

* * *

Harris had off the following day. Desperate though she was, Jill wasn't about to ruin their annual tree day. They'd go get a tree, they'd decorate a tree, and they'd promptly forget about it until it was time to open gifts or de-decorate that prickly needle-shedding mess of bullshit. She'd quietly suffer because she was an adult and wasn't about to start making a scene over the fact that she was kinda tired. And hungry. And still cold. A sweater over a long-sleeve shirt and leggings beneath her sweats did little to fix that. Whatever. Winter's supposed to be cold.

They stopped at the nearest pop-up tree farm, which amounted to a few haphazardly set rows of trees in a dirt lot the city wasn't using for anything else. Naturally, the proprietor of this lovely dirt lot hired a Santa to sit by, distracting the kids while Mr. Proprietor Man could convince the parents to spend too much on a tree that would be dead in a week. Ten days if they got lucky.

Harris chased after their children, eyes scrunched, darting side to side. She knew how he got about them on their own in public. She'd handle the tree, even if she could barely carry herself. Jill wandered row after row, eyes scanning for one that would work with the clearance in their living room, impress the kids, and not cause a mess. The less dry, the better, assuming it wasn't secretly full of spiders.

It didn't take long for her to settle on a prime specimen because this endless cycle of waking up and vomiting what little food she ate had significantly lowered her standards. It stood about seven feet tall. Fresh, blurry, vibrant greens. Perky branches. It looked alive. Smelled like it, too.

"You don't think you're gonna be able to carry that, do you, lady?" a gruff voice said from nearby her. Despite echoing her thoughts, the voice made her angry. Who was this guy to tell her what she already knew?

She turned, casting a glare at a man almost as tall as the tree. Almost as wide, too.

"Yeah, I do," Jill snapped, not wanting to talk. Her mouth didn't feel right. Words didn't connect properly. She reached for the tree, hoping Harris's police-sense would go off and he'd intervene before she made too much of an ass of herself or just passed out.

"Well, I don't. I saw it first." He stepped forward, smacking her hand aside.

Jill barely registered the contact. All she registered was a sudden and savage need to destroy him. As he turned his back, she grabbed him by the waistband of his jeans, yanking him back hard. She stuck her leg out as the man stumbled, tripping him. As he tried to get up, she swung her leg with all her force, right into his jaw. It let out a sharp crack, inaudible over the din of all the children eager to see Santa, and the brute collapsed. Nobody seemed to notice.

She seethed, ready to strike again, her vision crimson. Her breath tore its way through her in ragged grunts. Who the *fuck* was this stupid prick to interfere with her family's Christmas? He didn't know her. He didn't know shit about anything. Jill wanted to bludgeon him. To plant a tree in his body and let it fertilize next year's tree. She wanted to get down on all fours and rip his throat out with her teeth.

But no. She had a holiday to plan. This was tree day. It would suffer no interruption.

Jill reached over to *her* tree, wrapping a hand around the trunk, and walked off with it. Harris would've called that a—what was it, farmer's carry? Farmer's walk? Whatever it was, she stalked her way over to the shabbily assembled counter, taking the minute to slow her breathing, letting her frustration out into the winter's air.

"Find everything okay?" said the stupid fuckfaced dumbass piece of shit at the counter. He didn't really care, but she'd play nice.

"Yup."

He looked around, apparently just noticing that this one-hundred-and-ten-pound woman carried the tree over all by herself.

Her ears perked up as someone let out a gasp nearby. A distant voice asked the standard, *Are you okay?* And *Sir, can you hear me?* These were far, far away from her.

"You're pretty strong, huh, lady?"

The same voice instructed somebody else to call 9-1-1.

"Apparently," Jill smiled.

* * *

They'd had to stay a little longer than planned because Harris, good guy that he is, insisted on staying to assist the injured man until paramedics arrived. This didn't take long. Maybe the city told the EMTs to haul ass to try to save Christmas. Wouldn't have boded well for the city if some dude croaked within fifty feet of St. Nick. Harris oversaw the scene. He never went anywhere without his badge and gun, so it was pretty easy for him to establish himself as the authority, not that he had to *use* the firearm.

This put them in a little bit of a time crunch, apparently. Jill fell asleep on the ride back and woke up to the news that Carolina-Ann would help them decorate, because she loves her grandchildren *so* much.

Putting the tree up was as awful as Jill expected, full of barely-whispered jabs about how women can't take care of their families if they can't take care of themselves, and couldn't she use a little shadow to hide the bags under her eyes? She didn't notice. She managed to stay awake through the whole process, mostly out of spite.

Evening came as day went. The kids went to bed early because Santa would know, and maybe the extra hour's peace and quiet would mean an extra gift under the tree. Harris stepped out to do a little last-minute Christmas shopping.

Jill woke up on the couch. She hadn't remembered going to sleep, so what else was new? Her stomach rumbled angrily as she looked at her phone. Couldn't read the time. A text came through—she couldn't read that, either. Maybe this was her ever-worsening vision, but at the sound of her mother-in-law rummaging through her fridge, she concluded she was dreaming. Well, having a nightmare, more like.

She got off the couch, making her way through the dining room, catching sight of herself in the China cabinet's mirrored back. Her lips were two pale, thin lines, her skin graying, her eyes glassy, almost fogged. Shadows clung to her gaunt cheeks, but a smile crossed her reflection's face. It raised a hand and waved at her.

Jill clumsily waved back, walking into the kitchen.

"Seriously, how could anyone organize a refrigerator this way?" Carolina-Ann said, pulling out bags and Tupperware and pretty much everything else. After a moment, she looked back and said, "Well?"

How was she to know this had been directed at her? She shrugged. Food is food. Pretty much everything is food, if you eat it.

"A complete embarrassment. And what happened to all the ham? That would've been a lovely soup."

"Ate." Jill didn't want to talk. She didn't like talking anymore. Her mouth felt weird trying to say words. Head didn't feel right making them.

"Ate? Ate? Is that all you have to say? How did you all eat five pounds of ham in two short days?"

Jill thought of her kids upstairs. The kids. Asleep. All this noise—gonna wake them up. Ruin Christmas. Bad. Couldn't allow that. Like the guy. Like him, earlier. Jill smiled. All teeth.

"Does... does that mean *you* ate all that? How could you do that? And why? What about leaving a little for your children?"

"Hungry." Jill was.

Carolina-Ann rolled her eyes and turned back to the fridge.

"Seriously, what kind of a mother does that? What do you have to say for yourself?"

Jill stepped up behind Carolina-Ann, clamping a hand around over the woman's mouth as she sank her teeth into her throat, just like she'd wanted to do to that guy at the tree lot. She lowered the woman to the floor, world askance, all darkness and swimming and blur and red as the body sprayed red, throat making a gurgle as she gasped through the fresh hole.

"Hungry," Jill growled.

* * *

Harris ruminated on the events at the tree lot on the way home. He'd turned his back, sure, but he'd been fairly confident Jill went somewhere in the direction of where they'd found the collapsed man, Thomas. That guy hadn't simply fainted, either, somebody hit him—hard. Harris had responded to assault cases, even armed assault, where the vic hadn't been hurt like that. This was a single, brutal blow.

His gut nagged at him, but the facts didn't add up. Intuition told him his wife was involved somehow, but that's the operative word. How? How could a woman who'd barely been able to sleep or eat, who looked like a walking corpse, deliver that kind of an attack? She was barely over five feet tall and barely weighed half what Harris did, and he'd have trouble doing that kind of damage.

But still. His instinct lingered. Said to be wary. Maybe that was the same general suspicion that made him on edge all the time, but this felt different. Something had been wrong for days.

He tried to think positive thoughts. Tried to think about the presents in the backseat. He tried not to let this paranoia drag the holiday spirit down into his darkness. It's why he didn't tell Jill about the worst of the calls he'd responded to back in Brooklyn. About the times he'd had to draw his weapon, and the one time he'd had to fire it. How he'd requested a transfer so he'd have a much lower chance of ever having to do that again, despite that he'd only fired a warning.

The thought of taking a life made him sick to his stomach.

...Just not quite as sick as he already felt.

Harris parked in his driveway, figuring he'd leave the gifts for now to make sure the kids were really asleep. His mother's car was still here though. Why? To say goodbye to him before leaving? They'd said goodbye earlier.

He nudged the front door open. He smelled the remnants of dinner. And pennies. Sharp copper. The kind of smell an officer gets all too used to smelling.

"Jill?" he called out, trying to find the balance between alerting his wife and letting his children stay asleep. Harris walked quietly, carefully. Every hair stood on end. Every square inch of his gut told him he'd just walked into a crime scene.

As he approached the kitchen, he could tell the refrigerator door stood open from the way the light fell on the walls. Food had spilled across the floor. Some of it had a tinge of fresh red.

An overwhelming smell of blood and bodily fluid assaulted him. Wet tearing filled his ears, the loud smacks of an open mouth chewing, chewing, chewing. The crack of a bone breaking. Visceral splattering as someone tore a body apart—but not the kind of spray that would suggest the victim is still alive.

Murder. Maybe worse. Right there in his kitchen.

A faint scuffle caught his attention. He looked up, toward the stairs leading to the second floor. At the top, Michael and Daisy clung to each other, shaking violently. Too scared to cry. Too scared to move. Michael shook his head, a desperate warning, *Don't go in there.*

But he had to.

That's what he'd been trained to do.

He had to protect his family. Or, maybe, what was left of it.

He prayed, one last time, that he was wrong, but he knew he wasn't. He knew what was happening in the kitchen.

Harris stepped around the corner so his kids couldn't see him draw his gun.

DANCE OF SKINS
(AN EXERCISE IN MALEVOLENCE)
A Tale of the Bajazid

Kenneth Bykerk

Guten Morgen, Mi Amigo

"*Guten morgen, mi amigo*! It is time you got up before you become just a worm in the dirt."

"Go away, *Jo-keem*. I don't want to hear your shit today or ever again."

"Ah, is that how the great wee wittle Weeopold Fartysmelt got his revenge? Is that how he got all twelve, a tin star and a Judge to boot?"

"Shut up. It's hot out."

"It's always hot days, dumbass. See that sun? It don't like you anymore than I do."

"Then why do you care what I do?"

"Cuz, *señor estúpido*, I want to know so I can start celebrating your humiliation this day. It is a day for celebration, no?"

"No, it ain't."

"*Sí*, Leo, it is. Do you know not what this day is?"

"It's another damned day, that's what it is. Got forever more of them too so leave me alone."

"So you can be worm. *Sí*... then you miss out and I celebrate. How many? Two? One? Did you even get that one or did you lie about that?"

"Fuck you, Joaquim!"

"Ha! You got none!"

"Ain't true! I got two."

"And now you give up?"

"Why do you care?"

"I don't, but it is a disappointment if you are giving up. The Living celebrate something today. It looks big. It looks like we could have some fun. That is if you ain't too tired and don't want to lay in the dirt more?"

"*Guten morgen*?"

"My mother was German."

"You're a terrible liar, Joaquim."

A Wake in Pretense of Dream

Beneath an obsidian sun, the souls of the damned stirred in silent mockery of their oblivious audience. To be seen, known, remembered. To care once again beyond the oppression of eternity. Worms in the earth, slithering from the corona above in hopes for a moment of peace, an end to forever. Lifeless in death without end, trapped in torments unending, the sleep of the grave denied does not deter the restless from seeking solace in the soil.

With arms of intangible substance, with morphing constructs of form remembered, Leopold Tarkenfeld, or that which once knew itself with words so spoken, raised itself slowly from that dust and sniffed around. In the world beyond where shadows were allowed, movement of greater proportion did disturb the echoes of agony that never quieted in the ears of the Dead. Expectant harmonies added color in patterns yet discerned. The Beast of the Bajazid did dream.

The detestable disease of life, the growth of ego and the pretense that anything mattered beyond formless whim fouled the air. Yes, Joaquim Solis had been right, there was something about this day designated special. Warmth of inviting temperature passed in volume, each selfishly guarding the shells of sensation they claimed, ignorant of the potential only those who have lost could consider. Existence was wasted on the Living, cowards within their own skins.

The value of anything is counted in its loss. Life is no exception. The horror of existence, the fears and terrors known from a mind deteriorating to the brutal savagery the human beast is particularly capable of, are eased in the end with a comfort long promised. Such is how it should be and perhaps beyond the bounds of the Curse, such promise offers hope for the Dead. There is no hope on the Bajazid.

In this valley, the ephemeral called the Bajazid, there is no comfort, no rest. Charlatans speak of a pit of damnation where fire wracks the spiritual remains of the disobedient and the profane. Such illusory mercy, the promise of sensation, is mockery itself. The ennui of eternal absence, the loss of knowing even the glory of pain renders the potential of such punishment paradise. Hell was a promised land forever denied.

To feel again the moments of their deaths, their last sensation allowed, those like Leopold and Joaquim whose last breaths were choked through a tightening rope or escaped forgotten in a snapping neck would gather beneath the structure of their last resolve. Ever would the nooses swing and ever, would those who swung seek to slip again into those slings. Shadows on the courthouse wall would at times hint of such desperation for sensation.

Leo was no different. He longed for feeling, any sensation at all. When the evening light was long and that black furnace promised surcease, Leo would join the others in clinging for those ropes. To feel again those last moments, the pulsing agony of air denied, was granted in briefest gasps. Remembrance of sensation past was sought, be it the burning of hemp against flesh or that uncertain wonder when the vertebrae started to separate.

There was one other method available for the pursuit of sensation, one which required a will beyond ordinary, for ordinary lay in the dirt like blackened worms, always seeking cover but ever denied. It was at the gallows that promise was greatest for in those moments extreme, the weak could be shifted and hidden within themselves. The chance to die again was ever irresistible. It was always fashionable amongst the Dead to wear flesh.

For the haunt of exceptional will, there was always the long ride as opposed to just a short drop. The extension of skill, the ability to find a vessel empty enough to dominate and fill granted the greatest opportunity to feel again the most exquisite pleasures of the flesh. For those enraged to rise in spite of the blackened sun, driven in death by passions strong, the dominance of souls was the greatest prize.

Leopold Tarkenfeld was restless, his guilty soul stripped from him unjustly and his execution a shambles, a spectacle of public shame. He was sworn to powers beyond his understanding even in death for a release upheld if his bargain proved true. Vengeance inspires and there would be no rest until all who convicted him were held to account. Joaquim was right; there was time enough for worms. This was a day for dancing in skin.

Baird's Holler Theme

Baird's Holler was founded in 1867 by the John S. Mortenson Company, an expeditionary excursion into the Silver Mountains south of Prescott and north of that desert so emblematic to the vistas of Arizona. Gold was known to be in those mountains, proof given in the discovery by the Joseph Walker Party of gold along the Lynx Creek nigh twenty miles north in '63. The Mortenson Party struck their luck in the second half of August after more than two months luckless, and the members of that party were raised at once to men of wealth and means.

In the decade that had passed since the discovery of gold along that creek men named the Bajazid, Baird's Holler had boomed. The Mortenson Mine sank itself deep into the western wall of the Silver Mountains and the desperate flocked in, each looking for their fair share of the treasures this valley held. The Mortenson Mine drew the heaviest upon that labor force with multiple shifts working multiple shafts around the clock. Engineers with advanced knowledge had been brought in, and a ten-stamp mill along with a smelter had been erected to render as much of the ore as possible on location due to the difficulty of the terrain escaping the valley.

For those who sought to fail on their own, there was plenty of real estate available along the Bajazid and its tributaries to support a large population of panning indigents with misplaced hopes. All throughout those steep, narrow canyons, men with picks and shovels and pans dug and scooped for fortunes elusive. Shafts were sunk and tunnels plumbed, claims were staked, and men slept uneasy as dragons guarding their small and hopeful hoards. Gold was always available, always ready to be found, but rarely in quantities greater than that which demanded more hunting. This promise though, the success of the Mortenson Mine and the daily luck of just enough to tempt, kept men digging and panning. That lucky strike, that motherlode waiting to be found was always in the next shovelful, next panful, next...

Lust for gold blinds even the most moral and just to excess and advantage. Claims were jumped with regularity and bodies would rot in the sun or crammed into a crevice of rock. Safety was found in numbers, small groups of men working together and watching each other's backs. It was a dangerous time, a fraught place without law enough to keep any pretense of order but in the town of Baird's Holler itself. Out in the canyons, life had no value but the gold each man hid on his person or buried in secret places.

With the influence of the Mortenson Mine, Baird's Holler quickly became a town on the rise. The Sultans of the Bajazid, the owners of the mine, had wealth enough to spend and soon, with their influence, business districts were raised and neighborhoods haphazardly planned. Construction was the next greatest industry as the Sultans put down their roots, and businesses of diverse nature opened to cater to the growing needs of such a population. Churches, a schoolhouse and a courthouse were erected with civic hopes as shanties and lean-tos filled the empty spaces between.

Brothels and saloons crowded Jackson Street so the lonely and desperate could exchange what their labor brought, trying to forget that all they worked for was not for them. Here was the growing discontent, the divide made acute. Wealth gathered always, spreading from those who have little upwards. When men are offered less than their value, when their bellies betray their labor, they become dangerous. Recognizing this discontent, the Sultans of the Bajazid sought to forestall impending troubles by throwing a decennial celebration, a distraction to keep the peace.

A Lemures in Wonderland

Joaquim had been right. There was great activity in the town of Baird's Holler. A festival had been announced in honor of the fat cats who ran the place, and all the schmucks up and down the valley were invited to come to watch them gloat. The promise of a free dinner and a drink drew the dregs to town in droves.

Leopold could taste the hunger and desperation in the air, the hatred and jealousy of the Living barely disguised. Just that undercurrent, the psychic flow of feelings repressed, hinting darkly behind the trepidatious hope the day promised, was enough to lift Leo from the dirt and into the gathering crowds.

The stench of humanity was thick. Those not yet dead unwashed and marinated in their own sweat were perfume, enchanting to those who had already slipped their coil. The desperation, the hatred, the jealousy, and the lustful greed which permeated the gathering masses was manna for the appetite of the malign. The shadow of Leopold Tarkenfeld craved.

The sight of a shade is short. Beyond a distance vaguely immeasurable yet never far, darkness impenetrable conceals but in one direction. Above, where a yellow sun burns in the world of light, a Stygian hole in a slate sky ringed by malevolent fire burned down. This black sun, this eternal cruelty was only assuaged with purpose, was only tempered with means malice motivated.

Leo felt his own oppression wane as he passed through the throngs arriving, his goal growing clearer as vaguely recognizable faces flashed by. There were those he sought, people he knew he needed to find if he could just remember with clarity. The decay of the worms was the final indignity of the Dead on the Bajazid. The horror of this madness was the knowledge it existed. The understanding this knowledge of loss would carry after all else failed was damnation promised.

The Dead are not blessed with the eternity of Time. Having purpose helped stay that end. As Joaquim had reminded, to accept that burning sentence from above was to accept this fate, accept his place as a wasted worm trying ever unsuccessfully to cover himself with dirt. Too many such worms littered the streets of Baird's Holler, souls too weak, too beaten down to do naught but surrender to the eternal ennui expected. Joaquim had been right. Leo was not ready for the worms.

It was in the face of a boy Leo felt his first excitement stir, felt that midnight fire begin to abate. The fleet-footed youth passed too quick beyond that wall of shadowed sight, but there was recognition in that face flashing by. The presence of the boy had a taste to it, a feel he knew if only in hint, but the promise stirred Leo, drove him. The clarity of purpose had become clear.

A phantom possessed, Leo darted and dashed between the celebrants of the day, drifting through that horde with intent and purpose realized. The hint of that boy focused him, reminded him that his death was unjust and that those responsible were his charge, his oath. While the boy himself had nothing to do with Leo's demise, Leo sought him out in particular as he surveyed those who clogged the streets of Baird's Holler for this day.

In an opening, a park central to the administrative and clerical district of the young town was where the gathering centered. Tables hung with bunting were spread with victuals prepared, a feast gratis to mollify the bellies and tempers of those too long without more than oats, beans and biscuits. In the clearing about, games were established, competitions of engineering skill and muscular strength. It was a day of festival.

The population of the town swelled as the indigents camped in the vales and canyons about filled the streets. The air was optimistic and light, the very intent the damned Sultans of the Bajazid had in mind. Still, that undercurrent flowed beneath the smiles and laughter, haunting the fears and low expectations of those come to be conned. It was this uncertainty Leo rode as he sought with unfocused resolve his goal.

Twelve men convicted him for a murder another committed. That was the crime Leo was sworn to avenge. That Leo was a murderer, a rapist, a thief and more mattered not, at least to the ghost offended. The conviction itself and the sentence it carried was the stain Leo was resolved to remove. Innocence, even for the guilty, is a precious thing and when abused, when justice fails to expediency and communal desire to watch a man die on the gallows, even the guilty may be offended to vengeance. Leopold Tarkenfeld's execution had been a shambles, a shame of professionalism, and Leo's shade could not let that stand.

As the day proceeded, Leo found more of what he was searching for. Of the men who had been on that jury, two Leo knew for certain were already in their graves. That left ten and Judge Worthington, his lawyer and that damned sheriff. Drifting through that mob, Leo caught hints of those he sought as he searched for the Judge's boy.

It was when he found the jury foreman, a mousy little accountant, that Leopold's fervor was tinged by uncertainty and frustration. Leo had only been able to taste the presence of those about, not inhabit. Why this was so perplexed him. He had probed every orifice, every known means on which to enter the clerk's body but met failure at every hole.

Subsequent attempts at the ears, nose, mouth, and anuses of others compounded the question. Why could he not gain entrance? In the three short years since his neck had been strung, Leopold had gained an understanding of possession, what it took to slip silently and secretly behind a soul and ride it. Why Leopold could not commandeer the consciousness of the revelers about confounded him but did not dissuade him. The men who put him in the grave would pay.

In the late afternoon, the crowd began to concentrate, and Leo followed the fold. The mass of humanity gathered before a small platform raised and there, upon that dais, Leopold saw his prize quarry. The Judge, Warren Worthington, sat up on that stage with the other founders of this town, the arrogance of their position raised to condescending levels above those they kept in the dirt.

Judge Worthington was a cold man, closed to emotional expression. As Leo swirled about him on that stage, seeking any entrance, any means of influence, he was rebuffed even more assuredly than with those others whom he had sought to consider. With Worthington though there was greater need, greater urgency. Of all those who could be blamed for Leo's demise, it was Judge Worthington's sentence that stretched Leo's neck.

As Leo haunted the oblivious Judge, the assembled raised their arms as one and from hundreds of throats a toast rang out, one even the Dead could hear. Then the arms of the Living tossed back in a motion Leo remembered, yearned for and the lust took hold. Leo felt it at once, a compulsion beyond his denial. He was drawn into a dance, a waltz of decadent mockery as mortal resolve waned. As that hated sun sank at last and the shadows went missing from the courthouse wall, the barriers began to fall between the realms of the Living and the Dead.

Ghosts

The air in spectrums invisible to living eyes charged with vibrancy a promise. Where mortal feet obliviously tread, the answer of worms was dust. Cyclonic atmospheres disguised by dancing steps pulled at hungers directed, and the Dead rose in that dust to join the fête.

Phantoms at the feast of a communion perverse; the body had been hidden in the blood. Chants were raised across that mortal gulf, encouraging, calling, commanding revenants caress souls exposed through fungal fermentations. The songs of the Living and those known only to the Dead became one as the celebration began in earnest.

The Dead of Baird's Holler, ever oppressed, this one night their burdens were lifted. They were drawn, worms by a pipe enchanted eagerly accepting their charge. Their reprieve granted them license unlimited and extremes were teased as the hallucinations of the Living fueled the rotting madness of the Dead. The Living danced a perverse mockery, a spinning, twirling reel of excess and abandonment of sense as spirits of malign intent drifted amongst that breathing host.

As the last light of day was consumed by encroaching storms, the final barrier between the world with shadows and that without fell. In that instant, the Dead swarmed into the mouths of the Living and shoved the rightful inhabitants into the darkest corners of their fears. Drunk in the flesh and the whole of their hosts' intoxications, the Dead of Baird's Holler danced in the madness of the skins they stole.

The Beast of the Bajazid

This celebration, this day designed to mark a passage of insignificant time, had been planned long before the minds of men were teased into the conceit it was their own. The alcohol, a libation for celebration, had been poisoned of intent for a purpose greater; a fungus of malignant design to prepare the coming oblation. An offering of such import should not be dismissed to chance.

What men call Gods are but abstractions, attempts to justify the incomprehensible. They are but shadows cast upon the walls of ignorance, for the true forms of the powers that purpose the realities men may know are not what those impressions, those hints portray. What those gods may truly be matter only to theologians and those seeking the madness of abandoned truths, fools either way. The ignorance of mankind is its true bliss.

Here on this mountainside, this valley construct carved in meaningful course, there was malignancy contained. Ever felt in presence, yet dismissed by the minds of men and their collective disbelief in any gods more powerful than their own greed and self-importance, that which lay imprisoned in this place stirred in its ageless slumbers. The taste of Man had intrigued it since the first of that kind found its way here, and now, greater than ever, was that cup overflowing. Hubris is not a failing for mortals alone. What began an elaborate prayer, an offering for release from the seal of the valley, became a demand ignored and a rage fulfilled.

Crossroads

A moment of clarity caught Leo between skins. His euphoria had been such that he knew not what or who nor where. He was heady with excitement, flush with the stolen moments and drunk from excess. He had been leaping from skin to skin madly, violently. Where many sought to purge their passions in the flesh of the living, Leopold had more purpose, more experience. While others possessed were forcing awkward orgies in bodies alien of use, Leo had lost himself jumping from one host to another. It had been a glorious sampling of tastes, of fears, of passions and pains until suddenly Leo found himself having leapt without looking. There was no one new to leap into nearby and the man he'd left was useless, lying in the dirt shivering in existential agony.

Tripped from his mindless rhythm, Leo understood his purpose given. This was a night for vengeance, for retribution granted without restraint. This was a gift from the Beast whom he knew as Master, that which he could not deny nor define. It was his to seek though, his to bring forth. It would not be accomplished if he did not bring it about, that Leo understood. What was being offered was only opportunity. It was up to him to find and to fulfill.

His first thought went to the Judge. He needed to find Worthington. There it was his hatred burned greatest with but one exception. Leo had had a partner, a big lout who turned coat on him. While Dickie hadn't fingered him directly in the murder he had died for, his testimony hadn't helped. It had painted him as a cruel, overbearing tyrant willing to do anything for whatever he could grab. That testimony had saved Dickie's life and cost Leo his.

In this space between breathing, bleeding vessels, this moment in isolation from that greedy torrent, his purpose rose to recognizable intent. As he weighed the thought of hunting for Dickie when he knew not if his former partner even remained in town or to find the Judge or his boy to torment, his decision appeared before him from the smoke that roiled thick in the world of shadows. The Sheriff was ready to dance.

The Sheriff's Jig

The mortal flesh of Sheriff Thaddeus Barrett staggered drunkenly into view through the obscuring smoke, a barrier to both Living and Dead. Elated at such fortune, Leo dove direct at his prize only to be rebuffed with fury. Again he tried, and again he was slapped away by mortal hands to his astonishment. Another try, and those hands, stained in blood, gripped Leo while a laughter he knew only too well issued from the slack jaws of the Sheriff.

"Damn you, Joaquim! He's mine! Let him go! Let me go!"

The face of that Sheriff loomed close, the sneer being forced upon that unaccepting countenance a mockery itself. From that listless mouth, a foul tongue lashed, "Finders keepers, Leo. You ain't the only one who got grudge against this bastard."

"He's mine!" Impassioned beyond the limits of death, buoyed by the life he had tasted the night so far, Leo reached out and grabbed that black tongue dangling from the Sheriff's mouth. With hold emboldened, Leo followed the struggling shade of Joaquim back into the depths of the Sheriff's psyche, and there the two did war.

The rages of the Dead within that singular host strained the body in the exertions forced. The dance was violent as dominance within was sought, muscles tearing from their moorings in the fury expressed. When the shades of Leo and Joaquim at last ceased their struggle, they were outside a body ruined. With a short, harsh laugh, Joaquim left Leo with his broken toy.

Never Turn Your Back on a Ghost

Leo looked at the shivering, sniveling form before him. The Sheriff's pants were wet, and blood dripped from his ears, eyes and nose. Within those eyes was recognition, a weak light within unfocused orbs. They looked at Leo direct, seeing him with full fear and understanding.

"I... I know you... stay, please..."

"You see me?" Leo demanded of the dying man.

"I see you. Please, leave me be. I'm a good man..."

"Then I shall give you a good death." With these words, Leo stretched open the Sheriff's mouth and crawled in, the soul of the damned shoved forcefully before him. Rising, Leo felt the aches, the pains, the agonies this body had suffered and rejoiced knowing there was so much more it could offer.

Ghosts (Skin Dance)

The ghosts of Baird's Holler, indefatigable as they were in the euphoria of flesh forgotten, danced with abandon shrived beneath the grinning skull of a barley moon. Decadence inspired through hallucinogenic fervor and the rush of blood in veins borrowed wrought horrors unique as the Dead drained the Living to exhaustion.

With such a feast spread before such extensive famine, the celebrants devoured with rapacious fury all they could, leaving in their stead wasted husks yearning for surcease. The madness of the grave rendering understanding uncertain beyond lusts demanded, some suffered for hours the same shell to singular, repetitive tortures. Others, like Leo before his find, enjoyed the variety offered and haunted with willful purpose. The gift of this night was not wasted.

Baird's Holler Theme (Demise)

The day had begun with promise, a celebration to usher in an age of prosperity great enough to raise all in attendance, an empty lie none believed but all came to exploit. That the whole of the fête was mockery for the indulgence of a few mattered not. Free beer was free beer and for that the wastrels had arrived ready to believe anything until their cup was filled. The festival had drawn the disparate denizens of the valleys surrounding to town with just enough curiosity to bind them there. Their reward for attendance was that free lunch, was that free drink, was a party to be remembered. Then, at the height of euphoric ascendency, everything took a nightmarish descent.

Baird's Holler began to burn at some point in the night. Where the fire started or with whom the responsibility lay mattered not. There were few in town without blame, few who had abstained from any concoctions alcoholic and who did not suffer the effects of the taint. For these teetotalers and children denied, they knew not what was happening but could only watch in horror the devastating effects all around. For those who had drank of that brew toasted to the town's success, their care and understanding had been obliterated in the horrors they were experiencing.

All about Baird's Holler, storms raged. A cyclone of intense fury, its eye centered unmoving above the town itself, lashed the canyons about. Within the town, not a drop fell as the conflagration spread quickly through the shanties and lean-tos packed close where buildings had yet to be raised. Of those buildings that stood permanent, the fire raged where it reached with singular intent to raze. There were none of sense or self remaining to stand against that ruination spreading. Instead, the inhabitants of Baird's Holler danced madly in the hellscape of their success.

The greatest advantage the fire gained was through those sections packed tight without order. The eastern edge of town was taken complete, the flames stopping at the top of Jackson Street and circling the wall of wind south through the early pretense of neighborhoods. When that wall of storm collapsed, that eye up above shutting to the singular cosmic aspect focused upon the town, the deluge was enough to cease the advance of the flames. Damage enough had been done. At least one third of Baird's Holler had burned, those with the least advantage taking the worst of it. Entire encampments were reduced to ash, worldly possessions lost to fire and mud while the mansions of the Sultans, one and all, were not even warmed in the ruin come to Baird's Holler.

When the citizens of Baird's Holler began to wake late the next day, it was with shame of remembered things they avoided the eyes of others as they sifted through the ashes of what all was lost. The worms in the mud were of a different mind, dreaming fondly of sensations stolen in disregard to their damnation.

Scream Thy Farewell Scream

Before the rains had tempered the flames that fed, Leopold Tarkenfeld had taken his night's glory to the greatest height he could. From the bell-tower of the Methodist church, Leo surveyed the destruction about through the failing eyes he borrowed. He had climbed up there in the flesh of Thaddeus Barrett with the intent of hurling the body he wore to the earth below, one last indignity to ensure his vengeance complete. Looking back to the rear of the church, flames risen from floating embers were beginning to show through the smoke wafting from the shingles. With that new hope finding purchase within the wood frame of the chapel, thoughts of a fatal fall were forestalled. There was greater glory growing.

There is no freewill in death. Just as Thad Barrett was helpless to challenge the cruelties inflicted upon him by the wraith that walked in his skin, the motivations that drove Leo were beyond his ability to deny. Each cruelty inflicted upon the flesh of the forsaken was felt in full by both haunt and haunted. The lacerations, the torn muscles, the grind of fresh fractures made to move in spite of the failed integrity of bone were all shared in equal measures. Sensation was all that remained, and as the flames that rose to consume the church grew closer, Leo burst forth with joyous laughter at the screams of terror and agony from his host.

A special thanks to the genius of Neil Peart.

SPUN SUGAR

Gregory L. Norris

Like the rest of the meal, the dessert was intended to be spectacular. An event. The last part of a culinary Greatest Hits. Following arugula and blueberry salads dressed in subtle vinaigrette, French-bone lamb chops with rosemary, fingerling potatoes, and butter-braised asparagus, the little flourless chocolate cakes would be drizzled in caramel and garnished with fresh raspberries and a crown of spun sugar.

But something went wrong.

Outside the brownstone, the gray day's murk deepened, and the first flakes drifted down from the charcoal sky, and the creeping sensation that had followed J.T. from dreams into the waking world asserted its pull in whispers and shivers.

Spun sugar was a fairly easy feat for even a novice chef to accomplish—you only needed to set up properly with the right pan, a trio of ingredients, a candy thermometer, and wooden dowels upon which to cool the honey-like consistency into elegant and whimsical end results. Using a fork, J.T. dipped and drew back on the potion made of water, sugar, and corn syrup. The spindles coated the dowels in cookbook precision. It struck him that he'd forgotten to add the food coloring—a golden hue that would match up with the dessert perfectly.

The spun sugar finished white, like the snow drifting past the brownstone's windows. White, the threads triggering memories of something else, becoming something *other*.

J.T.'s hand stilled. The spun sugar solidifying on that length of kitchen counter transformed into gossamer between blinks. J.T. froze. A memory window located in a remote corner of his gray matter inched open. In response, the strength departed his legs, and his cheek grew intimate with the cold penny tile floor. Then he was gone from his kitchen at #3 1722 Federal Street, and spiraling through time to the house on the lake, the summer he was ten.

* * *

Eddie Piedmont wasn't an uncle through blood relation, but a friend of their father's. He wore Hawaiian shirts and liked to use the outdoor shower located near the house's woodpile. Once, J.T. caught Martin spying on Uncle Eddie while he washed up in the yard, but when J.T. threatened to tell, a red-faced Martin came at him, showing the kind of brute strength that made it clear he was still the dominant twin.

"You won't say nothing," Martin growled, twisting J.T.'s right arm around the small of his back hard enough to seriously hurt.

And he hadn't repeated what he saw, because of what Martin threatened next.

"Things are already bad enough for us. You want them to get worse, go ahead.

Tell."

He shook free and pondered the truth in his older brother's statement. Martin had come into the world eleven minutes and change before Jack Taylor Norridge and, in most cases, boasted the wisdom of sages far older than his decade of life on the third planet of the solar system surrounding Sol.

J. T. surrendered. "Okay, I won't."

During Martin's fast march away from the woodpile and the outdoor shower that so fascinated his brother, they worked up enough fresh sweat to attract a merciless squadron of black flies. The little flesh-hungry demons began to dive bomb and attack with the kind of ferocity J.T. read about World War II enemy fighters from Japan in the moldering books that filled the loft library. He swatted. The barrage continued.

"Come on," Martin said, his sympathetic brother once more.

They pounded through the screen door and back into the country house, which seemed to exist at the end of the universe.

* * *

Eddie wasn't an uncle through blood, but he was considered family enough to take the boys every summer for two weeks as part of an interlude between their father's and mother's custody claims. Reaching his country house, a long ramshackle with an open upstairs loft, all of it built around a massive fieldstone fireplace, required travel over miles of dirt road, past a tiny chapel set on the shore of a vast lake, through trees so dense they formed a wall and, in spots, whose branches blocked the sun.

They shared a room at the back of the house, which contained two antique single beds with wooden posts capped by carved pineapples. The house had belonged to Uncle Eddie's family before passing to him and was filled with a hundred years or more of other people's stuff. A Blue Willow teacup on a shelf in the kitchen boasted tiny brown rocks that turned red if you ran them under the tap.

"Garnets," their host once explained in a summer a full, long year behind them. "Semi-precious gemstones. We used to find them all the time in the lake. Might be worth something."

Like the books about warfare in the loft, the gallery of black and white family photographs and framed watercolors stretching across the walls, the notion that treasure existed close by, free for the taking, filled J.T. with a sense of hope.

Things had gotten bad in the divorce, *ugly* was what Martin called it. But here, for a while at least, life at the isolated summerhouse wasn't so bad.

* * *

He caught Martin staring again, only this time it wasn't at Uncle Eddie while he showered. His brother stood in the hallway, gazing at one of the framed art studies hanging in a dark corner at the rear of the house, near the back screen door.

"*Martin,*" J.T. whispered.

At first, Martin didn't seem to hear him. J.T. called louder. His brother jolted out of the spell of thoughts holding him paralyzed and turned. Instead of the red flush of embarrassment from that other incident, Martin's face showed a kind of pallor. J.T. held up his hands in defense against whatever outburst was sure to follow.

"Whoa, just came to see if you wanted to go for a swim—maybe hunt for more of those gemstones."

Martin came out of his trance. "I'm not interested in a bunch of stupid red rocks. I got other things on my mind!"

J.T. retreated to their bedroom and changed into his bathing suit. When he emerged, Martin was gone. J.T. padded out through the screen door, intending to grab a beach towel off the clothesline. The towel would have a sweet smell on it from previous use, a mix of the lake and his sweat. But halfway across the sun-warmed yard, he turned and backtracked into the house.

He'd passed the photograph a hundred times this summer and summers before but had never stopped long enough to address what it was—the country house was a wonderland of drawers filled with old things, a place of dust and mysteries. How could one curious mind possibly absorb all there was to see?

J.T. focused on the image now, eager to understand Martin's fascination. Instantly, J.T. shared it. The black and white image showed an amusement park merry-go-round. Only the thing appeared to have sprouted in the middle of a thick grove of trees—sap pines, paper white birch, and other easily identifiable flora surrounding the lake house.

He didn't realize he'd stopped blinking until his eyes began to burn. Breathing, too, until the last bottled sip of air started boiling in J.T.'s lungs. He expelled the breath, broke focus with the photograph of the merry-go-round, and shivered in defiance of the day's building heat.

* * *

A merry-go-round, out in the middle of the woods?

J.T. pondered such an enigma between scoops at the muddy sediment squishing beneath his toes. Thus far, the only objects his fingers had mined from the lake were twigs and worthless rocks. The swimming hole appeared to have been picked clean during Uncle Eddie's youth.

The mission was to collect enough garnets and to somehow string them together as a gift for his mother. He wasn't so naïve as to believe a reunion between his parents was possible anymore, but overnight he'd concocted a plan in which he first gave the priceless necklace to his father, permitting him to take credit. Surely, such a gesture would go far in removing much of the ugliness that had resulted from their divorce. A good dream at night, it didn't hold together in daylight.

On the somber march back to the house, J.T. caught the mouthwatering aroma of meat roasting over an open flame. Hamburgers, he hoped. He ate everything Uncle Eddie put on their plates, but there was nothing quite like burgers on the wood-fired grill. He was correct, his frivolous prayer answered. To accompany was homemade potato salad and pink iced tea made from rhubarb and the sweet mint that grew in wild bunches around the front patio.

"You ought to open a restaurant," J.T. said between bites.

Uncle Eddie always smiled, and his smile widened. "That's kind of you to say, J.T."

They sat around the patio, eating the meal outside on wicker chairs, the smoke from the barbecue keeping the squadrons of enemy fighters at bay.

"Uncle Eddie?" Martin asked. "In that old photograph on the wall. The merry-go-round."

Uncle Eddie's smile disintegrated. As J.T. watched, Eddie attempted to recreate it, but once destroyed it never fully returned. "What about it?"

Martin shrugged. "I dunno. What's it about?"

Uncle Eddie set down the half of his burger that remained and took a pull from his iced tea glass, which sweated in his hand. "That, boys, is a part of history no one talks about around here anymore."

He told them about his uncle—Uncle Orion—a preacher who once held court in the tiny chapel near the water until he was banished, along with some of his flock. Uncle Orion had purchased the merry-go-round from a bankrupt traveling carnival using church funds, had the thing carted out to the country house all the way from Maine, and planned to have it hooked up to run as an attraction for all the kids of the summer visitors to the lake. Only that had never happened, Uncle Eddie explained.

"And the woods sort of grew in around it," he said.

"Where?" asked Martin.

Eddie turned and narrowed his eyes on J.T.'s brother. "Huh?"

"Where in the woods?"

Uncle Eddie's smile surged back, only it was a maniac's now, quite mad. "Trust me, you don't want to go there, son."

"I'm not your son," Martin barked, to J.T.'s shock.

Mercifully, Uncle Eddie had not yet fully returned from the far-away land in his mind where smiles were murdered. "No, you don't *ever* want to go up there, trust me."

But J.T. already knew by the glint in his brother's gaze that Martin had been seduced by yet another secret, and wouldn't be talked down from it.

* * *

Martin entered their bedroom, his body language tense, secretive, as he closed the door. Uncle Eddie had already replaced rhubarb iced tea with beer and was destined to pass out on one of the lumpy camelback sofas in the great room, an old book about wars in foreign lands spilling from his free hand.

J.T. saw that Martin's contained a roll of what he called *duck tape.*

"What's that for?" J.T. asked.

Martin turned, his face serious. "The spiders."

"Spiders?"

A creeping chill teased the fine hairs of J.T.'s summer whiffle-cut, at the nape of his neck. Even before Martin answered, the shiver was in motion, tumbling down his spine.

"You fall asleep, and they crawl into your mouth. A person eats an average of eight spiders a year on accident at night."

Repulsion rippled through J.T.'s core. "That's not true!"

Martin flashed a cold, sparse smile. "You're right. Here in the woods, the number's probably higher. I read it."

"It isn't!"

"Are you willing to risk it?"

He tore off a length of duck tape and fixed it over J.T.'s mouth. Then he did the same for himself. The brothers crawled into their respective beds and Martin switched off the lamp on the nightstand between them. Darkness bathed the world. Outside, audible through the window screens, a chorus of insects and creatures sang out in worship of the night.

J.T. sweated. Air entered and exited through his nostrils. His mouth grew steadily dryer. His heart galloped, its cadence broadcast from his ear into the pillow. Spiders? In his mouth? His *stomach*? Once, Martin had tried to sell him on the dangers of swallowing watermelon seeds.

"A watermelon plant'll sprout and grow inside your belly," J.T. remembered. "When it gets too big, you'll explode from the pressure!"

Their mother had admonished Martin, but after that he refused to eat watermelon, even seedless. Spiders conjured forth from his mind's eye, and hundreds of unblinking, tiny eyes trained upon him in the darkness, all in clusters of eight. He fell asleep only to again startle awake, his natural instinct to gasp through his mouth. Only that was covered, and J.T. was convinced he would suffocate.

* * *

At some point in the night, clouds moved in and a heavy summer downpour hammered the metal roof.

The covers felt damp beneath him, as though the rain had gotten in, soaking his bed. The air was rotten with humidity and sweat, J.T. realized. Rolling over, he faced the room's two windows. Beyond the curtains, a dull gray light oozed. Night was over. Dawn had arrived.

J.T. reached toward his face and found the strip of duck tape missing. It had come loose in the night and was now stuck to his pillow. He licked his lips, tasting the foul adhesive. What if the spiders of his imagination had marched into his open mouth, and from there all the way down to his stomach?

For a terrible instant, numerous legs clacked and clawed at the soft lining of his guts. J.T. hastened out of his bed, through the door, and into the bathroom, one step ahead of his vomit. He half expected the chunks that came racing up his tortured throat to be eight-legged abominations that would then attempt to scramble out of the toilet bowl. To his great relief, he saw that they weren't. *Just your every day, garden variety puke*, his inner voice said.

J.T. retched again. Nothing made it fully up this time. He rinsed his mouth and wiped his face. The water at Uncle Eddie's summerhouse was full of iron and both smelled and tasted like a rusty can. It was why the soap and even shampoo barely made any bubbles and why you felt oily the moment you stepped out of the outdoor shower.

He ambled through the shadowy house and back to the bedroom. Inside, he saw that Martin's bed was empty.

* * *

J.T. paced the house, whispering his brother's name so as to not wake up Uncle Eddie. He knew Martin was no longer inside, no. He was out there, in the downpour, in search of Orion Piedmont's merry-go-round.

Several times, the boy considered rousing Uncle Eddie from sleep. Five longneck bottles stood drained on the coffee table beside the lumpy green sofa, where Eddie lounged in a fetal curl. His brother, in search of even bigger mysteries to cope with the divorce of their parents, had ignored Eddie's warning.

J.T. waited. An hour passed. Eddie snored, and Martin stayed gone. The rain fell, striking a sad melody on the roof. He wanted to go after his brother, to find and preserve what little remained of their family. But he was scared. No, terrified. Uncle Eddie had all but forbid them to seek out the merry-go-round.

A cottony fog drifted off the lake and surrounded the house. Out over the water, a haunting, prehistoric cry rose up. J.T. told himself that it was only a loon, not something else. Something *worse*. The spiders he'd tried to vomit out of his guts were back, spinning webs and clacking around inside his stomach. Their pointed legs stabbed at his insides. He imagined them laying enormous, silken egg sacs, each filled with a hundred baby spiders that would hatch and grow, repeating the cycle until they'd hollowed him out and took control of his shell, using him like a puppet.

J.T. debated waking Uncle Eddie, telling him about where Martin had gone. That wouldn't be ratting his brother out if Martin was in trouble. And by the very nature of Martin's plans, J.T. sensed his brother was. Uncle Orion Piedmont and the merry-go-round had been touchy subjects, according to Eddie's expression. What had happened up there in the woods during that long-ago time?

The storm upped its tempo. J.T. moved back to the screen door. The world outside was gone, submerged in damp cotton. Ghostly outlines of wicker lawn furniture, mint bushes, and the surrounding woods shimmered out of focus beyond the fog and pelting rain.

And from that dream-like landscape, a solitary figure appeared. J.T.'s heart attempted to jump out of his chest and into his throat. Eyes wide, he tracked its movements down from the rise on the other side of the dirt road and toward him. At first, he wasn't sure the wraith was Martin or that his brother was awake. He seemed to be in a trance or sleepwalking.

Head held low, Martin crossed the road, now a long, dark puddle, and hiked over the lawn, up the steps to the patio, and through the waterlogged hedge of mint. As he neared the door, J.T. caught the piney scent of his brother's sweat, the mint, and something that smelled of the dusty corners of Uncle Eddie's house in the country clinging to the other boy's clothes and skin.

A smell of abandoned places and deep woods.

The merry-go-round, thought J.T.

Their eyes connected through the screen. For a second, maybe two, Martin's blazed with a predatory glint that J.T. had imagined among the hoards of eight haunting the previous night. Then Martin stepped through the door, dragging the odor of crypts and abandoned amusement park rides with him. Saying nothing, he continued into the house, past Uncle Eddie's bunched body, and into their room.

J.T. found Martin in his bed, his face to the wall, a pile of wet clothes discarded on the floor.

"You went there," J.T. accused. "You found it, didn't you, even though Uncle Eddie told us not to."

Martin exhaled a sigh through his nose. "He's not our father."

"No, but we're supposed to listen to him."

"*You* listen to him."

A tense silence followed.

"What's it like?" J.T. asked him after what seemed a long time. "The merry-go-round."

Martin offered no response.

"Tell me," J.T. whispered. "Or I'll tell Uncle Eddie."

At this, Martin whipped around to face him, and whatever bravado J.T. had mustered instantly evaporated. His brother's eyes were alien, evil, those of a predator. The vehemence contained within them was there one second, gone the next.

"Go ahead and tell him," Martin challenged. "But if you want so badly to see it, stay quiet or I won't take you up there, little brother."

At that moment, J.T. decided he didn't want to know any more about the merry-go-round in the woods and didn't want to go there.

Smiling, Martin rolled over. Before long, like Uncle Eddie he, too, was snoring.

* * *

The rain let up, and a strange calm settled over the house. After Uncle Eddie showered outside he began to cook their dinner—pan-seared trout they'd caught in the lake and cleaned a few days earlier, before the storm and knowledge of the merry-go-round. J.T. approached the tiny kitchen.

"Uncle Eddie?" he asked tentatively.

"Yeah, squirt?"

Fish sizzled in a cast iron pan, blessed by butter, fresh herbs pulled from the nearby outside, and the halves of a lemon.

"In those woods," J.T. said. He tipped his chin in the direction of the screen door and the forest beyond. "What happened at the merry-go-round?"

Uncle Eddie sucked down a breath, and his body, wedged beside the stove in the cramped space that passed for the kitchen, lost its ease. Cooking, J.T. had noticed, was like an art form to their host. Almost nothing that they'd eaten since their arrival came out of a box. All of it, even the odd things like *risotto* and *grilled sweet potato sandwiches with arugula and heirloom tomato* had tasted delicious, magical.

Eddie cleared his throat and nudged at the fish with his spatula. "J.T., there are things kids shouldn't see and should not suffer. That adults should protect them from. That old source of horrors up there in the woods... well, that's one I'd like to spare you and your brother from. It was a long time ago. We shouldn't talk about it anymore."

"But... *why?*"

Uncle Eddie's eyes drifted over to the skillet. "There was a time when I was your age that I wouldn't go into those woods. Know why?"

J.T. shrugged.

"It was mostly over, what my Uncle Orion and the others did up there, with those summer kids. But there was a time when I went looking for answers, too, which is normal, I suppose. After it was all over, to see if it was true. So I walked in those woods, sure. I think it's because of them... that somehow some of them are still up there, living in the shadows. Because, during that time, no matter what trail I took, I came across a part of *it*."

"It?"

"The merry-go-round," Eddie said. "They broke it up, after what happened. But when I went walking, I'd turn a corner, and there standing right in front of me on the path would be one of the calliope horses. The post that holds them up, just jabbed right into the ground, like it was trying to escape. Or..."

"Or what?"

"Like it was trying to find me. Yeah, like it was waiting for me to jump on its saddle, so it could ride back to the merry-go-round, with me in tow. And even though he was supposed to be dead after the fire, Uncle Orion would be up there, too, along with his flock. They were beyond making distinctions between the summer kids and the rest of us. They—"

He caught himself.

"It sounds silly now, but then... I swore I'd never come back to this place after it all happened, when we thought it was over. Then I forgot. Isn't that funny? I forgot until Martin said something about a picture."

For a second, Uncle Eddie got lost. The smoke sizzling out of the skillet thickened and soured. The fish was burning.

Right as J.T. was about to warn Eddie of this fact, he came fully aware. Uncle Eddie pulled the skillet off the stove and swore as his bare palm connected with the flame-heated handle. The skillet missed the tiny patch of counter by the barest margin before tumbling to the floor and spilling its contents.

"I'm sorry," J.T. said, but he doubted Uncle Eddie heard the apology over the blue streak that followed.

Dinner was cereal, which suited the spiders in J.T.'s stomach fine. Anything stronger likely would have made a return appearance anyway.

* * *

Martin lay on his back, his eyes focused on the patch of ceiling over his head, which bore an old water stain.

"Are you hungry?" J.T. asked.

"No," Martin said.

"I don't think you should go back there. Uncle Eddie said something bad happened up there. He said—"

"I don't give two shits what he thinks or says."

"What about me? Do you give two shits about what I think?"

Martin blinked and tipped a glance at the room's other bed and occupant.

"Maybe one shit."

"Then stay away from that place and the merry-go-round, *please.*"

Martin's gaze lingered, and his old, older brother, for a spell too brief, seemed back. Then Martin sat up and reached for the duck tape. "Come on."

J.T. shook his head. "No."

A mischievous glint sparked in Martin's eyes. "You don't want them getting inside you, little brother."

"I'll cover my mouth."

"Won't do you any good."

"Martin, stop it."

"Why, you scared?"

J.T. shook his head. A lie. They both knew it. As though drawn to his fear, Martin slid off the bed and approached.

"Go away," J.T. attempted.

Only he soon realized that a peaceful ending to their looming conflict was only wishful thinking. Martin had traveled to Orion Piedmont's merry-go-round. Pain was inevitable. Instead of wrists twisted behind his back for having been found out gawking at Uncle Eddie while he showered, Martin was going to really hurt him this time.

There was no chance at outside help. Uncle Eddie was likely passed out on the sofa, his pores leaching the sweet smell of all the beer he drank nightly. While Martin wrestled him down, pinning him against the bed and wall, J.T. absently understood why Uncle Eddie got blotto at the end of every day: to forget enough of what he knew in order to sleep.

Martin looped the tape around J.T.'s wrists, binding them, and slapped the next strip over his mouth, laughing—*cackling* in a voice J.T. didn't recognize—the entire time.

"Don't want them getting in you, no," Martin spat between chuckles, his eyes damp with tears, hot with madness. "Hell, no, 'cause once they're inside you—!"

Martin tore off another length of duck tape, and, holding J.T.'s head still, laid it over his nostrils. The length over his mouth muffled his screams, but not Martin's, whose crazed laughs had devolved into shrieks.

* * *

He was boiling alive, suffocating!

Only when J.T. came to, he could breathe again. Martin hovered over him in the waning glow before dusk.

"It's up to you if you want to follow," his brother growled in a menacing voice. "If you want to see it, see what the people in the woods built, that's your call, not mine. In spite of what Uncle Orion said, you're still my brother."

Martin pulled away. J.T. heard his footsteps crunching over twigs, leaves, and gravel, but when he sat up, struggling for breaths that refused to come easily, Martin had merged with the deepening shadows.

J.T. drew his hands from behind his back. The tape for ducks was gone, but his wrists still pulsed with the phantom ache of having been bound. He scrambled to his feet and attempted to track Martin. His brother was gone.

Glancing around, it struck the boy that he was lost. Fear attempted to paralyze him. In the woods. After dark. Tears stung at J.T.'s eyes. He pinched them away and focused on the trail beneath his bare feet.

Trail. There were numerous paths through the trees, he already knew. And he doubted Martin had been able to drag him far. Not too far. *Think!*

He followed the trail, his eyes locked on the wet earth. *Just keep going until you're back on the road.* In a daze, J.T. advanced, aware of the chirrup of night insects and of his desperate breaths. Faster and faster, never thinking he'd gone in the wrong direction, until the calliope horse rose up, blocking his path. J.T. screamed.

The beast was onyx, with copper eyes. Frozen in a pose that appeared more to trample than gallop, the demon horse's right leg kicked ahead of it, claiming the trail as its territory. J.T. froze. The horse's unblinking copper eyes leered at him. *Other way,* J.T.'s inner voice said. *Hurry!*

He backed away from the escaped demon horse. J.T. turned. Dark woods and indigo sky dominated the way ahead. Uncle Eddie's country house was out there, somewhere. J.T. plodded forward, his flesh crawling with pins and needles, those phantom prickles of unwanted insect caresses. A thousand spiders skittered over his skin and plucked at his ears. Spiders? No, the building melody of calliope music, pumping from the dark woods at his back. If he turned, J.T. was certain there'd be a light glowing beyond the closest trees. He'd see the merry-go-round as it started to turn, built up speed, and his brother upon the back of one of the speeding stallions, holding onto its saddle horn instead of the steed's reins, because that was more Martin's style. Faster and faster, Uncle Orion Piedmont's amusement ride would race, with Martin hooting and laughing, most of his questions regarding the mysteries of life answered here in this remote, forsaken place.

The temptation to turn around! Only if he did, J.T. knew the demon horse would be there, ready to carry him all the way to the merry-go-round, and his brother's fate.

J.T. ran forward, toward what he prayed was the direction of the house. The wind picked up, racing past his ears. Soon, he couldn't hear the music.

* * *

"You know, they searched the woods, dragged the pond. They never found my brother, but they blamed Uncle Eddie," J.T. said to the empty room.

Outside, the snow had ramped up its intensity, fulfilling the promised blizzard. Inside, the lamb had cooked past medium-well to leather, and the asparagus was charcoal. Only the spun sugar retained its power, and that was beyond vengeful.

"Said he was carrying on Orion Piedmont's dark legacy, and what his followers started up in those woods, through my brother, Martin. I know Uncle Eddie was innocent, the poor bastard. Didn't help that they coaxed me into betraying him. Even the stuff they made up. And they wouldn't listen about the merry-go-round or the spiders that crawled into us, through our mouths. No, they decided they wanted Eddie Piedmont. They were sure that it was the cycle—one victim keeping it going, round and round, after they got victimized. Round and round, like a goddamn merry-go-round."

J.T. picked himself off the kitchen floor, no longer caring about the ruined meal. As the snow spattered the windows, testing ways to get in, he opened the refrigerator door and drew out the six-pack. He carried it over to the sofa, twisted off the first bottle cap, and silently prayed he'd forget all that had been exhumed by the time he reached the last.

Part Three:

A Revelry of Mystery

THE FESTIVAL OF REJECTED STORIES

Jonathon Mast

The sign declared THE WATERING WHOLE. The Prairie Mason wrinkled his nose. He hated people who couldn't spell. Nevertheless, it was the first business on the edge of the wheat-filled plains he'd stepped from, and he was thirsty. He pushed through the swinging doors.

As he stepped inside the dimly lit room, the piano music stopped. Every eye turned to him.

The place was filled with freaks. As his gaze swept the room, he spied a table full of ruffians in bright yellow shirts next to what appeared to be some sort of cowman. A glass tank filled with fish wearing Stetsons sat at another table. A few emus perched on bar stools. The bartender herself appeared to be a woman wearing just enough red flannel to cover her most scandalous parts.

She offered a most welcoming smile. "Hey, stranger. New here?"

At her welcome, the piano music picked up again. The emus went back to their whiskey. The fish returned to their poker game. Conversation rumbled in the background.

The Mason nodded and headed to the bar. "Sure am, ma'am. I'd appreciate a glass of milk."

She raised an eyebrow. "Hitting the hard stuff, are you?"

"Well, ma'am, I find that since I'm a role model for countless impressionable youths, I need to hold myself accountable."

She nodded. "Sure, sure. Countless youths. You're new in town?"

"Just come off the plains, ma'am," he answered.

"First glass is on me, then." She turned and retrieved something from beneath the bar. "You notice all the folks around here are a little different?"

"It did not escape my notice, ma'am. Thank you." He accepted a carton of milk.

"There's a reason. See, you're in Barrelbottom."

"Is that supposed to tell me something?" He grinned. "Is this a lawless town that needs a lawman to make things right? Are you an innocent young woman who needs to be rescued? I'd be pleased to do so, ma'am."

She took a step back. "Hold on, now. I don't need any saving. But you might. See, you've found the home of the rejects. And if you're here, it's because you've been rejected, too."

"What in tarnation are you talking about?"

"My name's Molly. Molly the Buxom Bartender. My writer wanted me to be kickass with these globes on my chest and not much clothing. But then he decided to write something set on another world, and well, I didn't fit in with the new setting. I got rejected. I ended up here."

The Mason put down the now empty carton. "I do believe perhaps you have stood too long out in the sun, Molly."

She sighed. "Look, there's a place where every idea fills up the sky like stars. A place where every dream lives. Barrelbottom isn't that place. This is where every rejected idea ends up. Every time a writer decides that something doesn't fit, this is where the idea comes. And you're an idea that got rejected."

The Mason narrowed his eyes. "I'm the Prairie Mason. I bring justice—"

"Really? The Prairie Mason?" Molly hid her smile. "So you were a bad pun on an old courtroom drama? Man. I always feel sorry for you types."

The Mason stood. "Ma'am, I do not appreciate your mockery."

"I'm sure you don't. And don't worry. There's a lot stranger and worse off than you are." She put her hands on her hips. "But I suppose you solve crimes and all that, if you're a pun on a crime room drama?"

He sputtered.

"So that's a yes."

"I right wrongs!" He slammed a meaty fist on the bar.

"Good. Come with me." Molly hopped over the bar. Somehow none of her generous dimensions slipped out of her not-so-generous clothes. "Most rejected lawkeepers end up in other parts of Barrelbottom. This place is pretty broad. There's lots of rejected ideas, you know? You're here now. You'll do."

"Your vote of confidence is overwhelming." Nevertheless, the Mason followed.

* * *

Molly led him down the dusty street. The buildings on either side bore signs that advertised bizarre businesses. CALLIE'S OB/GYN AND TOBACCO OUTLET. CANDY TIRE REPAIR. BODY RECLAMATION CHARITY SERVICES. At the end of the street, a colossal red-and-white striped tent rose.

Molly gestured. "This here's the Festival of the Rejected. See, most of us, when we show up, we don't feel so good. Who wants to be told they're not good enough for someone's story? So lately Timmy's put together a fair to make us all feel better about ourselves. And since it's started, well, we've been finding bodies."

The Mason stopped. "Bodies?"

"Yeah. Dead folk. Make sense to you? Or were you rejected from some cozy crime drama where no one ever gets killed?" Molly turned to appraise him.

"No. I've dealt with the dead before. I think." The truth was his past was a little fuzzy. He knew who he was, but it was hard thinking of the cases he had solved. All he remembered was that he was always victorious, no matter the odds.

"Ah. You're starting to get it. You're an *idea*, Prairie. You don't really have a past. Not until you stepped out of that field. But ideas are still alive. We still matter. And if one of these rejected characters has started killing, well." She looked down and away. "I've been here a while. I've seen some nasty things. You would not believe the kinds of things that authors entertain before tossing them away. We've had some pretty rough folk pass through here. I don't want to see it again."

"Oh?" Usually someone would give the necessary background, right? This must be part of the research he would have to do. The Mason listened carefully.

"Well, a few years back a bunch of vampires went through. Dramatic prettyboys that didn't want to kill but did it anyway. A whole plague of them." She shook her head, her eyes distant. "And suddenly all the single ladies, mostly virgins, were getting bit. It's a good thing that a plague of kickass vampire hunters came through not too long after."

The Mason nodded. "And were you bitten, ma'am?"

Her distant eyes snapped to the here-and-now. "A girl never tells." She winked. He did his best not to turn red.

Molly continued. "Anyway, characters show up in waves. Werewolves. Rejects from dystopias. You know. Well, we're not in the midst of one of those waves, and now suddenly there's all these dead bodies showing up at the festival. And you can bet we have a problem with that."

He nodded again. "Well. Perhaps you should show me this festival of yours."

"On it, Prairie."

* * *

They entered by way of a massive open flap on the side of the tent. The interior was lit by several large spotlights. The tent had a large central room with bleachers around it. The center of the room was clear. The Mason spotted temporary walls partitioning the tent into separate areas around the periphery. A few people shuffled around, with a small crowd near the center of the tent.

Molly waved to a gigantic creature that resembled a seven-foot-tall praying mantis. "Hey, Timmy!"

The mantis swiveled its head toward her.

"I got us a lawman here. Fresh from an author's brain. He's all about justice. Thought I'd throw him at our little problem."

"Jeepers, Moll, that's famtasmic!" the mantis chirped.

The Mason blinked.

"Prairie Mason, may I present Timmy the Talking Mantis, not the star of a children's picture book series. Timmy's the one who organized the festival in the first place. Timmy, this here is Prairie Mason. He likes righting wrongs and all that jazz."

The Mason hesitated just a moment before reaching forward to offer his hand. He paused again and thought better of shaking with a gigantic mantis. Its long arms ended in wicked claws that click-clacked against each other.

"I'm pleased as pumch to meet you, Mr. Masom! We've had so mamy dilly-dally bothers lately."

Moll reached up and patted the back of Timmy's neck. "Yeah. The first night Timmy brought in a great band for a community dance. And then a body shows up in the middle of the crowd. Next night, Timmy's got a motivational speaker. Really got the crowd into it. And bam, another dead body." She laughed. "And Timmy here, since no one claims the bodies, he wants to eat them!"

"A fella's gotta eat, ya know? Amd they're dead already!" Timmy hung his bulbous green head.

The lawman regarded the gigantic bug. "Yes. It's not proper to, er, eat the deceased. Particularly when a person might gather clues from the state of their bodies."

"Wowzers! Clues? You're really gonna figure it out?"

"Wherever injustice reigns, my hammer will strike a blow for righteousness!"

"Golly!"

* * *

As Timmy led the way deeper into the tent, the Mason said, "Tell me more about your festival."

"Well, a bumch of us were feeling all smudgy inside. So I thought I'd throw a party! Lights amd music amd good thimgs to drimk! Amd a damce! A chamce for everyome to feel like they belong. Cause everyome belongs!"

The lawman nodded. "So you put up the tent to hold the festivities?"

"Right as raim, Mr. Masom!"

It was more than a little odd to be interviewing a bug. As distracting as Molly's attire was, at least she was human.

"Tell me what happened that first night."

"Gosh, why don't I show you the girl that just showed up?"

"Someone else?" How many dead people were there in this town? How much justice must rain down to cleanse the filth here?

"She was just there in the cemter of the damce floor, like she was damcing her cares away amd them just fell over!" And Timmy extended one of his massive front claws toward the small crowd. When they saw Timmy coming, they parted, revealing the deceased.

And there she was. A woman laid on the ground. The Mason stalked over to her and circled at a distance of about five feet, taking in every detail. She wore a blue dress that sparkled. Her golden hair was done up in ringlets. Her face sported blood-red lips and a pert nose.

Molly squatted nearby. "Looks like she must have come from a Fitzgerald pastiche."

"Excuse me?" he asked.

"1920s fiction has a strong presence in Barrelbottom. Elegant women ready for a ball." She gestured to the departed.

The Mason grunted assent. He didn't know anything about the 1920s, but he knew plenty about dead women. "Who is she?"

"Gee, Mr. Masom, mo ome kmows!"

"Pardon me?"

"He said no one knows. You get used to Timmy's accent after a while," Molly said.

"No one? No one's complained about a missing daughter? Wife? Sister?"

Molly glared. "A woman can be her own without being attached to anyone."

"Of course. Pardon me, ma'am. But someone must miss her." He bent over the poor woman. "Do we know what caused her death?"

"Mope!"

"I see." He reached forward and tilted her head, felt her neck, other parts of her that might help determine what had killed her. No; it appeared she was simply a dead body. "You said there was more than one?"

"Yeppers!"

* * *

There were sixteen. Sixteen dead bodies, counting this most recent death. The Mason thought he'd been in towns with fewer people. It was hard to recall.

As he examined each in turn, he breathed in deeply. This one smelled of clove and pine. He was dressed like he was posing in a Christmas card. That one smelled of sweat and blood. He wore ancient Celtic garb. Some were men. Most were women. Some appeared to be rich. Others were poor. Some appeared to have been shot. Some had clearly been poisoned. Others were stabbed. Still others appeared to have nothing wrong with them. All in all, it was a strange mix of characters, and they all had only two things in common: They had appeared under the tent, and no one knew who they were. Timmy had them all arranged in a back room.

"Goodmess, I wish we could just make these bodies go away, Mr. Masom. People are still coming every evening, but this'll scare them away soom!"

The Mason nodded. "Well, death will do that. But hopefully we can find some clues. Step one is finding out who they are." It was maddening. Someone was murdering so many people, and they couldn't even identify who the victims were.

After some hours, he asked, "Ma'am, is there a boarding house near here? It's getting late."

Molly laughed. "Well, lawman, you can stay at my place tonight. It'd be an honor."

The Mason felt himself redden.

"I rent out the rooms above the Watering Whole. Unless you were looking for something more intimate...?"

The redness in his cheeks deepened.

"Aw, Mr. Masom, aim't ya stickimg aroumd for the damce tomight? The whole town's comimg!" Timmy hovered near.

"I am not one for dancing. Thank you."

"Stick in the mud." Molly grinned at him.

"I am wed to justice, and I will celebrate once it is done."

Molly shrugged. "Your loss. I'll take you back to my place, then, get you settled in, and come back and do some dancing myself." She winked.

* * *

The Mason's room was passable. A bed. A writing desk. A basin and pitcher. Facilities across a narrow hallway. All clean. It was all he needed.

He sat heavily on the bed, breathing in.

The scent of soap laid lightly on the air. Starch. Something else he couldn't identify at first, buried under old bleach.

Blood.

Someone had died in this room. He breathed it in. How old? No, that was beyond his abilities.

He exited his room and made his way down the narrow stairs to the saloon. The tables were empty, as was the bar. Outside, in the distance, lively banjo music played. A bartender, a narrow man with thick glasses, stood staring at the door.

The Mason cleared his throat.

"Oh, yes! You must be Prairie. Molly said you'd want your dinner sent up, but

I thought it was too early. Yes. Far too early for supper." The man took out a pocket watch and surveyed its face. "Yes, yes. I was right. I'm sorry, Prairie, but it is far too early for food."

"Where is everyone?"

"Ah. Well, with the Festival in town, everyone is there."

"Even with the dead there?"

"Sir, you must be new here. The dead are not exactly new in Barrelbottom. Things get out of hand often, you see. People don't understand that there's a time and a place for everything. Time to kill? Ah, you must wait for a full moon for that." The narrow man nodded. "Molly wants to close down the festival, though. She can't resist a party, but she thinks that if the festival stopped, maybe the bodies would stop, too. She said as much on her way out after she set you up in your room."

"If that's where the bodies keep appearing, there must be a link between the festival and the dead. But there's another dead body I'm curious about. One in my room."

"A dead body there? Now? Oh my!"

"No, not at the moment." The Mason shook his head. "Whoever it was hasn't been there for some time."

The narrow man leaned on the bar and considered. "Well, I've worked here for a long time. Came with the place, you could say. The author tossed away both the bar and its bartender, so we both wound up here. I can't recall any deaths in the rooms up above. A few here in the saloon, of course, but that's to be expected, when the time is right."

"And who are you?"

"Ah! Sorry. My author called me Punctual Pete." The narrow man stood back up. "And I am certain no one has ever died in that room."

"There's a smell of blood."

"Ah! Well, that's easily explained. Miss Molly takes in boarders from time to time, you see, and one of the beautiful vampire boys took lodging here. You probably scented him. He would smell like a dead person, wouldn't he?"

"A vampire stayed here for a while?"

"Until Molly kicked him out."

"What for?"

"Well, he tried seducing her. And Miss Molly allowed the seduction to continue for far too long. Not the time, you see. I told her so. I told her that there was a time for it, and it wasn't then! Well, after a while he moved from the room you're staying in to her room, if you take my meaning. And things didn't work out." Pete shrugged. "Haven't seen him for a few years now."

"This vampire have a name?"

"Let me think. Miss Molly has entertained a few gentlemen over the years. Hm. Ah yes. Landon."

"Speak of me, and I shall appear." The swinging doors creaked, and a pale man entered the saloon.

The Mason turned to face him. "Landon?"

"They that have words do speak of me thus." He offered a half-bow. He wore an impressive black suit, black shirt, and black tie. His hair was black, but his skin was the color of chalk. "And whom do I have the pleasure of greeting?"

"I'm the Prairie Mason."

"Ah. Rejected courtroom drama? A terrible lot, but at least you did not belong to a glut based on a sparkling prettyboy." He offered a sardonic smile before turning to the bartender. "Peter! 'Tis good to greet you again."

"Likewise, Landon. I am sorry, but your old room has been rented. It wasn't time for you to return."

The vampire shrugged. "'Tis my lot to never journey under a smiling moon. I come to ask for Molly to grant me another opportunity to woo her. I was written to love but one, and as I have loved her, never another shall I have."

"You've come to soon. Too soon. But if you deny the time, Molly's at the festival. Down the street. You'll find her there."

Landon bowed. "Peter. I hope to return to your tender mercies and your expert drinks soon. Master Mason, a pleasure to meet you."

The Mason narrowed his eyes and nodded back.

* * *

The Mason plied Pete with many questions about the history of the town, whether the vampires had caused any trouble, or the hunters who followed them. Were there any other deaths? What other festivals had come to town?

Pete proved a wealth of information.

"And if you first belonged to the bar, why doesn't the bar belong to you?"

The bartender shrugged. "I'm a bartender. That's what I was made to be. I'm not really comfortable running the business. Molly moved in, and she just fit here."

"You've never longed for more?"

"I've always wanted to be a different character. I hate that the clock controls me. You know how hard it is, to measure your life by the ticking of gears no one else can hear? I'm a useless character. Someone made up and thrown away."

"Someone rejected, you mean."

"Exactly."

"Everyone seems to know what kind of story they came from."

Pete nodded as he wiped clean another glass. "Yes. There are tropes that are followed, of course. And often enough we can tell what is popular out there in the world the authors inhabit by what suddenly appears in droves. I am thankful biblical epics do not seem to be in great demand. Plagues are a terrible thing to have to live through, no matter what time it is."

"What's popular appears in droves? And now dead bodies are appearing in droves." The Mason mused over his carton of milk.

And then there was a sound of running feet and a beagle the size of a pony burst into the saloon. "Where's the lawman, huh? Where's the lawman? Gotta find the lawman!"

"You've found him." The Mason nodded.

"Gotta come back! Gotta come back! There's another body and it's ruined the party!" The beagle spun once and sat on the floor. "Gotta come back! Gotta come back!"

The Mason stood and headed to the door. The dog circled him and ran out.

"I pray it's time for you to solve the mystery of the appearing bodies!" Pete called out.

The Mason nodded back at him. "I suspect it is."

* * *

The tent was packed with freaks. Fishtanks filled with fish wearing cowboy hats, birds, monsters, humans in various kinds of dress, pegasi, giant dogs, cacti in tutus, they were all there in pairs and threes and fours. In the center of the floor lay a woman. A pool of blood surrounded her.

The crowd cleared out of the way as Mason approached. His eyes scanned the mob to pick up any clues.

Landon hovered near the woman.

Mason growled, "What're you doing near her?"

"I apologize. The smell of blood, it draws me. I am ever so hungry. I have resisted the urge for far too long. Like an alcoholic to fine whiskey, I am drawn to the blood of one so beautiful."

And the woman was beautiful. She wore a dress of sparkling, deep green, and had dark hair. Her blood was deep red.

"How do you usually feed?" the Mason asked.

"Sir, I am a vampire. I sink my teeth into the—"

"Can the poetry and answer the question."

"Oh. I bite."

"Where?"

"On the neck, like any civilized being!" Landon seemed shocked at the question.

"And you ever bite Molly?"

"A gentleman never tells." Landon grinned.

"Where is she now?"

"Alas, I have not found her, though I have circled the tent repeatedly as the dance commenced."

"Hm." Mason checked the new body. No marks on her neck. No marks anywhere, really. "Someone pick her up. We'll put her by the rest of the bodies for now. Y'all go about your party." He pointed at Landon. "But you don't touch her."

"I shall restrain myself, sir."

Timmy scuttled forward. "Jimimee! Have you figured out who's killimg all these people?"

"I'm almost ready to offer a theory. Come on."

A titanic woman wearing a loincloth and a sport jacket ambled out of the crowd to pick up the dead lady. She threw her over her shoulder. "Where to?" she grunted.

"This way. You come too, Timmy."

Timmy raised a gigantic green claw. "Crivets amd Ladybugs, Mister Masom! I meed to stay here amd help out with the festival!"

The Mason simply gave a blank stare.

"I suppose everyome cam do fime without me for a bit."

The group shuffled away from the dance floor to the little out-of-the-way room. As they went, a band began playing an unholy amalgamation of twangy country and tribal drums. The crowd recommenced the dance. The freaks all looked happy. The rejects had found a home.

But here in the back room the dead remained. The bodies were all stacked up real efficient like. Four stacks of four bodies.

The muscular woman wrinkled her nose. "This's where we've been putting them? Geez, Timmy, show a little respect for the dead!"

The mantis twitched. "Well, Molly wamted them all saved umtil a lawmam came."

"Put her down over here." The Mason gestured, walking into the room and surveying the dead.

And then his eyes landed on a certain dead woman. She was second down in the third stack. Her red flannel not-much-clothes caught his eye. He pointed. "Who's that there?"

Timmy swung his head back and forth. "We dom't kmow amy of them!"

"We know that one. You."

"Titania," the muscular woman answered.

"Help me out."

The two of them slid the top body aside—a man in a kilt and a thick beard—to uncover the body below. The body of a woman they all knew very well. The muscled woman gasped, her hand at her mouth. Timmy shook and made wheezing sounds. His mandibles formed half interjections, but couldn't finish them.

"Well. This puts a wrinkle in things." The Mason rubbed his chin. "Injustice has been done here, and I will see justice be done." He inspected the body. Since the clothing didn't cover much, it was easy to find the cause of death: Two punctures on her neck.

"Titania, please go get Landon. He's a vampire. Know him?"

"Sure do." She nodded.

"And a few people that care about justice who are good and strong."

"I'll get my sisters." She moved out of the room. A few minutes later Titania returned with Landon in tow. Two more women of equal might also filed into the room.

The Mason stood from his crouch where he'd been investigating Molly's body. "Well, Landon, I found your ex-girlfriend. She looks a mite dead."

Landon stared at her. "Saints of the Unbreathing..." He fell on his knees. His voice took a dark edge. "Who did this? I swear on all that is unholy, I shall rend them asunder and cast them into the abyss!"

"That one there." The Mason waved at Timmy.

The mantis shook. "What? Gee williker, Mister Masom, I didm't kill amyome!"

"Oh, I think you did. And when you saw Landon arrive, you knew exactly who to pin it on. I found these two puncture wounds in her neck. And Mr. Landon, you said that you feed from the neck. Is that true?"

"Yes. Everyone knows a vampire feeds in the most intimate of locations." He glared at Timmy.

"It would be easy enough to believe you'd done it. I've never investigated a vampire before, but you do seem the type to kill a pretty girl. But the killings started before you arrived. You have nothing to do with these other bodies, so why would you have anything to do with Molly here?" The Mason turned to the mantis. "But you, Timmy, have every reason to want to see her dead. After all, she wasn't letting you get away with your reason for keeping this little fair going, did she?"

"Please, Mister Masom, you're crazy!"

"I was pondering why you'd keep your festival going if more and more dead people showed up. But that became the point, didn't it? You wanted the dead to keep showing up." The Mason paced around the room as he laid out the case. "You figured it out before anyone else. You came from a children's book, I hear. And children's books are full of helpful people, ain't they? People that want everyone to belong. That's why you put this little festival together in the beginning. Chances for everyone to feel happy together. Like they ain't rejects. It was a right honorable idea."

The mantis's mandibles continued clicking together.

"Well, then the first body showed up. And then the second. And you were so hungry, weren't you, Timmy? So hungry, and a good mantis wouldn't eat a person. But here were these bodies that no one knew who they were. But then a third body showed up. And then even more. And you realized where the bodies were coming from. No one was killing them except, well, authors. Someone was putting together stories about crime at festivals. And so authors were thinking about all the ways to kill people, and then rejecting them until they found one that worked for their stories. So the rejected corpses ended up here. As long as you kept the festival going, and as long as authors were thinking about killing people at festivals, well, you'd have plenty to eat."

Landon narrowed his eyes. "If these accusations are true, why does my beloved lie dead?"

"Simple. She was getting in Timmy's way. She didn't let him eat any of the bodies. She wanted a lawman to investigate. And what happened tonight, Timmy? Did she figure it out? Pete said she was going to talk to you about stopping the festival."

Timmy twitched and backed away a step, another step.

"Hold him, boys. I mean, girls." The Mason cocked his head. "Sorry. Ain't used to a posse being so female."

Titania grinned. "No problem, Mr. Mason." She lay a hand on Timmy's shoulder. The other two women cracked their knuckles.

"We had sixteen dead when I was in here before. Now there's two additional bodies—the one from the dance floor tonight and Molly herself. That should make eighteen. But how many are there?" Mason gestured.

Titania counted. "The sixteen that were in here when we showed up with the new body."

"Exactly. One's missing. One that's in Timmy's stomach right now."

"Babaloo, Mister Masom, but look! Molly's got vampire bites!"

"That's right, Timmy. You tried to cover up for yourself. And you might have gotten away with it, if it weren't for the missing corpse. You were just so hungry you couldn't help yourself, but you couldn't bring yourself to eat a friend like Molly. And the fact that the two puncture marks are just the size of your claws there." The Mason stood. "That about covers it."

Landon took a step toward the mantis. "You murdered the one I love."

The lawman headed toward the door. "Ladies, our work here is done."

"You're leaving Timmy with the vampire?"

"All I care is that justice is done. Don't matter who dishes it out, long as it's done."

As they left the room, Timmy screamed.

* * *

The festival continued without Timmy. People danced. Singers sang. Speakers spoke.

The Prairie Mason stayed away from all of it. He drank his milk at the bar. Pete wept. Eventually Landon joined them, his face dark. They toasted to Molly more than once.

The next morning, the Mason stepped down the stairs from his room.

Pete nodded at him after glancing at his pocket watch. "Yes. Time to leave, isn't it?"

"Justice has been done. I'll be heading onward and see where else I might serve."

Landon nodded to him from his perch at the bar. "We owe you our thanks. I pray I may meet you again."

"I pray you don't," the Mason answered. "Because if you do, it means you're mixed up with injustice. Instead, pray that this is the worst you'll ever see."

And with that, the Prairie Mason moved on.

THE FEIS

Jason J. McQuiston

Special Agent Dan Hughes stared through the windshield of the rental car they had picked up on their way out of the Tri-Cities Airport. The beautiful red, gold, and bronze tones blanketing the rolling Tennessee hills slid past a perfectly blue sky. Whomever had written *The Ballad of Davy Crockett* had obviously done so in the spring or summer. Autumn had fallen across the northeastern tip of the state, at least as far as the colors were concerned. There was still a touch of humid heat in the air, but Dan could tell it was on its way out the door.

Summer was dying.

"You're from around here, aren't you?" Special Agent Bill Biegler asked from the driver's seat. They had only met a few hours ago before boarding the flight out of Nashville. He was Dan's newest partner on the case that remained unsolved on his watch. Biegler was the third agent in six years to sign on to hunt the Sundial Slayer, the mysterious serial killer who had become Dan's private nemesis, or perhaps onus.

Dan wondered if this thin guy who looked like Clark Kent would hang around longer than the last one. The fast-talking girl from one of the Ivy Leagues up north had only stayed for six months before moving on to bigger and brighter. Word around the Bureau was that Biegler was an odd bird with weird ideas. But, he had a reputation for getting inside the heads of serial killers.

Dan wasn't sure if the man was an asset or a rival.

"I went to school at Appalachian State, just over the state line in Boone, North Carolina." Dan rubbed his chin, cramming all those memories back in their dark little holes. He didn't really want to talk about the past. "So let me hear these theories of yours."

Biegler cleared his throat. "How much do you know about Celtic mythology?"

Dan smiled. "Not much. Why?"

"I don't think 'Sundial' is a correct assessment of the ritual placement of our killer's victims. I think he is making sacrifices to the ancient deity called Crom Cruach, the Crooked One of the Mound."

Dan raised an eyebrow. "And this assumption is based on what, exactly?"

Biegler glanced at him. "The situation of the stones around the body, and the presence of the jewelry and other semiprecious items. According to historians, the god Crom Cruach was represented by a golden idol surrounded by twelve smaller idols of silver or bronze. Or stones decorated with these metals."

In the past eleven years, twenty-one murders in seven southeastern states had been attributed to the Sundial Slayer. Three murders over three nights at the end of each October. Dan guessed that eventually more bodies would be found. He was certain that the killer carried out this ritual every year.

The only thing linking the victims was the manner in which they had been discovered. Men, women, elders, and even a few children, all from different backgrounds, had been found in isolated woodland scenes. Though the bodies were always naked save for a few bits of untraceable pawn-shop gold jewelry, there was never any evidence of sexual violation or assault. The victims were all placed rather peacefully in the center of a ring of twelve stones, each capped with a piece of equally untraceable silver or bronze. Except for the single stab wound to the heart, each victim might have been sleeping.

"So you're thinking a cult of some kind. Not a single guy? If that's the way of it, then no wonder I've never made any headway on this case."

Biegler shook his head. "No. I believe this is the act of a single, dedicated and methodical killer. But I believe that *he* believes he is a druid, a priest of the ancient Celts. All the murders coincide with the traditional Celtic festival, or *feis*, of Samhain, what we now call Halloween. Our killer is seeking to appease an ancient god in order to secure the blessings for a new year."

Dan pulled the small evidence bag from his suit jacket pocket, smoothing it out on his thigh so as to read the piece of paper held within. "Well, if this anonymous tip bears any fruit, I guess we'll find out if you're right, Agent Biegler."

The note was a Xerox copy they had traced to a FedEx Office store in Murfreesboro, Tennessee. When questioned, the employees said that they had received a fax with the note and instructions to copy it, then mail it to the Bureau Headquarters in Nashville. The fax number turned out to be that of a UPS store in Memphis, where the employees had received similar instructions. By the time Dan had finished backtracking the origins of the cryptic message, he had spent a week chasing his own tail, finally locating a bogus email account logged in at a low-rent internet café in Tuscaloosa, Alabama.

But at least the note had given them a clue as to the killer's next target. It simply said:

LOOK FOR THE "SUNDIAL" IN
BRILEY HILL, TN.
GOOD LUCK AND HAPPY HALLOWEEN.

"Looks like the Chamber of Commerce sent the welcome committee."

Dan looked up from the note to see the sign, WELCOME TO BRILEY HILL, TN. HOME OF THE FIGHTING IRISH, STATE CHAMPS 1997, 2011. It was decorated with the typical accoutrements of fall: miniature hay stalks, plaid-clad scarecrows, and happy-faced jack o' lanterns. Walking past the sign was a middle-aged man dressed in a cowhide hooded cloak and tunic, and carrying a tall, ornately carved shillelagh. He smiled through his bushy grey beard and waved as they passed him.

"Let's find the local PD and get acquainted." Dan pulled his phone from his pocket and frowned at the single bar that kept flickering in and out on the display. "Doesn't look like Briley Hill is in any hurry to join the twenty-first century."

"Something tells me they won't be that hard to find," Biegler said.

Dan looked up just as they entered the town's main drag. Three new Ford SUVs, all painted in black and white with the BHPD logo on the doors, headed down a cross street. Blue lights flashed in the Halloween-decorated windows of the old-fashioned brick storefronts. A siren gave one long, banshee-like wail that echoed through the tiny town and the brightly colored hills enclosing it.

"Might as well offer to lend a hand." Dan returned the note and phone to his pocket. "The timing can't be a coincidence."

They followed the patrol cars out of town, where the blue lights died. A few minutes later, the procession entered the foothills, crossing an old, rickety covered bridge spanning a fast-moving stream along the way. The bituminous pavement ended just beyond the bridge and the gravel about a mile beyond that. They were deep into the woods. The sunshine was somewhere far behind them.

"Look familiar?" Dan asked.

"Like every crime scene in the file. I guess that tip was on the money. He's already here."

They pulled up behind the ring of police SUVs and were greeted by a pair of redheaded, beefy-looking bubbas in khaki uniforms. When Dan and Biegler flashed their Bureau badges, the cops glared but didn't give way. One of them touched the radio mic clipped to his shoulder and said, "Chief, we got two FBI guys here."

There was a long pause before a garbled, squawking voice said, "Send 'em through."

Dan and Biegler passed through the loose cordon and walked several dozen paces deeper into the woods. Dan couldn't help but think how calm and peaceful it was here. The thick, brightly-colored canopy of oaks, maples, poplars, and hickories was dotted here and there with towering pines and sweet-smelling cedars. The undergrowth was thick and still a lush green. A stream gurgled somewhere nearby, echoing among the trees and rocks of the forest. Cicadas sang their own dirges softly in the distance, accompanied by a single bobwhite.

At the base of a massive blackjack oak they found Chief Deidre Kelly. She was crouching over a nude body ringed by a dozen metal-capped stones. Another uniformed officer took evidence photos of the scene.

The first thing Dan noticed, before the introductions were made, was the similarity in the chief's and the victim's appearance. The dead woman covered in blue-painted knotwork and gold jewelry could have been the chief's daughter or a doppelgänger from half a lifetime ago. Both women were tall with athletic figures, pale skin, dark hair and eyes, and strong, almost Cherokee-like bone structures.

"Was she a relative of yours, Chief?" Dan asked, pocketing his ID. Agent Biegler began carefully examining the scene.

"No. Not exactly. And call me Deidre, or DD. Everybody else does, Agent Hughes."

"Dan. And what does 'not exactly' mean, DD?"

In answer, a disheveled man in grey sweats broke free of the cordon and ran to the edge of the scene before another local cop could grab him. He was tall and thick, like an aging athlete, with greying dark hair and pale blue eyes. Eyes that were filled with grief and rage. As his square features cracked and he broke into sobs, the man fell to his knees and grabbed handfuls of earth. "No. No. No. Damn it, no!"

Deidre hurried to the man's side, knelt and put her arm around him.

The man shook her off and jumped to his feet, fixing her with a look of loathing and hatred. His voice was low and thick, spoken through clenched teeth, but Dan clearly heard him say, "This is your doing, isn't it? You couldn't let us be happy, you spiteful bitch."

Deidre said something that Dan didn't catch. Before he could interpose himself into the drama, the chief had the two beefy officers escort the distraught man away. "What was that all about?"

The chief shook her head and ran a hand through her hair, pushing it out of her face. "That, Agent Dan, was my ex-husband, Joe Kelly. The victim here is his new bride, the lovely homecoming queen of just three short years ago, Rosalind Kelly. That's what 'not exactly' means."

Dan grimaced. "Ouch. I'm sorry. Can I buy you a coffee? Catch you up to speed on what we know at the Bureau?"

DD gave him the ghost of a smile. "Sure. So long as you're okay with making the coffee Irish."

The rest of the day was spent setting up a taskforce HQ at the Briley Hill Police Station, brainstorming a list of possible suspects, gathering files, going over evidence, and waiting on the coroner's initial findings. While Biegler handled much of the administrative duties, Dan checked them into the local motel (there was only one, just like almost everything else in Briley Hill) near the fairgrounds at the edge of town.

Dan noted the big, multi-colored banner hanging over the fairgrounds' entrance. Along with the word HALLOWEEN, it included several synonyms for a party: FESTIVAL, FEST, CELEBRATION, and even Biegler's Celtic word, *FEIS*.

When the coroner's report finally arrived, it brought no new information to light. The girl had been rendered unconscious, or at least insensible, by a carefully placed blow to the back of the head. The presence of a single injection site on her inner left arm indicated that she had been further subdued by an intravenous injection, probably of morphine or some other opiate (labs weren't in yet, but it would track with the other cases). All before being dispatched with a single stab wound to the heart. There were no indications of ligature or defensive wounds.

"Almost a peaceful death," Agent Biegler said, looking over the report. He sat at the small table in Dan's motel room. "Almost... humane. Merciful."

Dan turned from the window. He had been staring at the two huge bonfires on the fairgrounds across the street, still burning from the previous night and waiting to be replenished when the sun set. "You crushing on this guy or what?"

Biegler dropped the page to the table and frowned. "I've worked a lot of serial killer cases, Agent Hughes. This is by far and away the least gruesome of the bunch. It's nice to see a break in the trend for once. That's all."

Dan narrowed his eyes at the man. He knew absolutely nothing about him, wondered what was really going on behind those horn-rimmed glasses. He sensed that Biegler either didn't trust him or thought him incompetent. "Right."

Biegler looked at his watch. "Well, I'm hungry. Care to join me for a bite to eat? Chief Kelly said the local place, Patty's Kitchen, makes the best fried chicken livers in the state. I'd like to put that claim to the test."

Dan shook his head, looked back to the fires. A group of white-clad men were beginning to feed more logs into the flames. "No, thanks. I'll probably just hit the vending machine and turn in early."

"Suit yourself. See you first thing," Biegler said on his way out the door.

* * *

When Dan answered the urgent knock at his door, it was not to discover Agent Biegler standing in the gray, early-morning light. It was a haggard-faced Chief Kelly.

"I'm sorry, Agent Dan," she said. "I'm afraid I've got some bad news."

Dan sighed. "Another Sundial murder? Well, I guess we knew it was coming. Please, come in."

He waved at the table, still covered with the case files and crime scene photos, as well as a greasy pizza box and three crushed Mountain Dew cans. "Have a seat while I make myself presentable. Or you can fetch my partner."

"Dan," she said. He turned, the hairs standing on the back of his neck. "It's Agent Biegler. He's the vic."

"You're kidding..."

DD shook her head, looked at the disarray on the table. "The cross-country coach found him just after dawn while on her morning run... I'll wait in the car while you get ready."

Five minutes later they were headed back through the small town that time forgot. It was early yet, but Briley Hill being a rural community, the locals were up with the chickens. Dan stared at the old buildings built in the 1920s and 30s, some even older—the mom-and-pop haberdasheries, the Depression-era movie house, an all-brick drug store and soda fountain, and the pre-Civil War Briley Hill Church of the Mount. If it weren't for the newer model cars parked on the streets, the town would look like something out of a history book or an episode of *The Andy Griffith Show.*

"A lovely little town," Dan said, almost to himself.

"It is." DD looked at him. "Most of the time."

"I remember hearing about a mass murder here back in the eighties," Dan said. "Something about an entire family being wiped out, butchered?"

DD frowned. "The Donnellys; they lived on a farm a few miles outside of town. The local truant officer found them when the two kids missed three straight days of school. I was a kid, myself. My dad, Fergus Riordan, was the police chief. The whole town was scared out of its mind. Dad believed it was a drifter or something, but they never caught the guy..."

"No leads at all?"

DD shrugged. "A year later, they arrested a homeless Vietnam vet down in Kingsport for torturing stray dogs. Locked him up in a state looney bin. Most folks decided to believe that he was the culprit, but it took almost a decade for the scandal to go away... And now this."

Dan decided to change the subject. "You know anything about Celtic mythology, DD?"

She put both hands on the wheel and accelerated out of town. "No."

Dan stared at the beautiful countryside as it sprang to life in the golden light of the autumnal sunshine. "Biegler had this theory. He believed that our killer fancies himself a druid, making sacrifices to some long-forgotten Celtic god. Propitiation or something."

"Interesting theory."

Dan glanced at her. "He had some doozies. Have you ever heard of the *Boyhood Deeds of Fionn*?"

"I've heard of *The Adventures of Huckleberry Finn*." She smiled halfheartedly.

Dan looked back out the window. "It's a collection of old myths from Ireland. One of the stories tells how all the men went to the hill of Bri Eile to woo a fairy maiden. Though some versions claim she was the daughter of Crom Cruach, the very god Biegler believed our killer was courting. Naturally, like any protective father, he took exception... That version claims Crom Cruach killed the high king and a quarter of his army in a single day... Samhain..." He trailed off as they pulled up behind the line of patrol cars edging the woods.

Putting the SUV in park, DD said, "Hope you're ready for a hike."

Dan had to admit, if not for the ultimate goal of the hike, it would have been wonderful. He always loved that crisp quality of early morning air that can only be found in the Tennessee Appalachians at that particular time of year. Most of the world considered autumn the symbolic death of nature, but he'd always thought of it as a reawakening to itself. It was the one time of year that he actually enjoyed being outside, breathing fresh air and feeling real sunshine on his face.

They found Agent Bill Biegler stretched out on a bed of thick clover beside a gurgling mountain stream, surrounded by twelve stones topped with silver rings. He wore a gold chain around his neck and a gold watch on his left wrist, and nothing else save for the blue knotwork painted over his face, chest, arms, and legs. His glasses were gone, revealing a peaceful look on his narrow features.

"How's that for a break in the trend?" Dan said.

"What?" DD looked at him, brows furrowed.

Dan shook his head. "Never mind. I need to call the Bureau and let them know." He looked at his phone, unsurprised to see no coverage.

"Come on." DD touched his shoulder. "I'll drive you back into town. We'll stop for coffee on the way."

Back in the SUV, Dan said, "We've got today to catch him. That's it. He'll kill again tonight, then take another year off. Unless he sends us a tip next October, today is the last, best chance we'll ever have."

DD nodded as they drove past the sprawling Briley Hill Cemetery. "We've done everything we can. This is a small town and new faces stand out, but we've not had any visitors other than you and... Agent Biegler..."

"What about locals? Any of them travel frequently, especially this time of year?"

DD shrugged. "Lots, I guess. The high school seniors take a trip to Orlando around now. The same teachers and parents usually act as chaperones. The band sometimes attends competitions... We've got local business owners who travel for work... You know, the usual."

Dan rubbed his face. "I think we can rule out the chaperones and the band teacher. As far as I know, there've been no victims found below Georgia. And the killer will be somebody who travels alone and doesn't have a set destination." He looked at her. "But I'm certain that whoever it is, the Sundial Slayer calls Briley Hill home."

DD's face hardened. "Based on that anonymous note? That's pretty slim."

Dan looked back out the window. "I've got my reasons. Let me have a raincheck on the coffee. Take me back to the motel, and I'll grab the rest of Biegler's notes, put my thoughts in order. I'll call the Bureau. Then we can get together this afternoon and suss it all out. Hopefully by nightfall we'll have bagged ourselves a serial killer."

* * *

Dan stood at the window of his motel room, sipping on his sixth Mountain Dew of the day and watching a sizeable procession of kids across the street. They followed someone concealed beneath a white sheet attached to a decorated horse's skull mounted on a long stick. The sun was still up but the streetlights were already coming on, in anticipation of the early Trick-or-Treaters, no doubt.

"Good Luck and Happy Halloween," Dan said to the empty room.

The mummer and the kids passed into the fairgrounds and made for the bonfires as Chief Kelly's SUV pulled into the parking lot.

Dan washed some amphetamines down with the last swallow of soda.

"Come in," Dan said when DD knocked. She held a good-smelling plastic bag emblazoned with the green PATTY'S KITCHEN logo in one hand and a drink carrier in the other.

"Can't solve crime on an empty stomach," DD said, setting the food on the table. "I hope you like fried chicken, pinto beans, mashed taters, and sweet tea."

Dan smiled. "Love them, thanks. What do I owe you?"

"Just the leads that are going to get this serial killer the hell out of my town." DD began setting out the foil cartons and the plastic flatware. "So what've you got?"

"Let's eat first."

They made small talk about the weather, the town's unusually large Halloween festivities, and the sorry state of U.T. football while they enjoyed the excellent facsimile of a homecooked meal. After mopping up the last bite of mashed potatoes with a piece of cornbread, Dan pushed back from the table and sighed. "Thanks. I've missed that kind of cooking."

DD wiped her mouth and smiled. "So, how do we catch our 'Sundial Slayer,' Agent Hughes?"

Dan tried to suppress a yawn. "What if I told you that the so-called Sundial wasn't the same person responsible for the murders here in Briley Hill? At least not the most recent two."

DD raised an eyebrow. "I'm intrigued. Go on."

Dan took a long sip of tea, but it only made his mouth drier. "You ever notice how big the cemetery is compared to the town itself?"

DD raised her chin, narrowed her eyes. "So? It's an old town."

Dan rubbed his face. It was going numb. "Very old. With a surprisingly strong economy for this region. And yet, according to census records, the population hasn't fluctuated more than one percent in over two hundred years." He ended the sentence with a yawn.

DD shrugged. "Is that it? Is that all you've got?"

Dan tried to smile. "There's also the fact that this may be the only incorporated city in the State of Tennessee, maybe even the entire country, with just a single church. And that with no strong ties to any major denomination. Don't you find that odd, situated right here against the Bible Belt Buckle?"

"Spit it out. Say what you want to say, Agent. While you still can."

Dan had to work hard to make his mouth form the words. Harder to keep his eyes open. "The story I was telling you this morning... About the men of Ireland wooing Crom Cruach's daughter... It aroused the god's wrath... So the people began a tradition every Samhain... every Halloween... to commemorate and atone... Sacrifices had to be made, people had to be murdered... By an unknown person so the sacrifices wouldn't see it coming... The sacrifices had to be unwilling... To appease the Crooked One of the Mound... of Bri Eile... of Briley Hill..."

Dan tried to stand. He wanted to move to the nightstand and the pistol resting upon it. His legs had other plans. "It's you, DD... You're the killer... At least this year... You *won* Briley Hill's secret lottery... You're Crom Cruach's instrument of vengeance..."

Dan somehow found himself on the floor.

DD crouched next to his face and smiled. "I have to admit, I'm grateful that you and Agent Biegler came to town when you did. First off, I'm glad that I didn't have to kill two more locals, but I still got to take care of that little slut, Rosy...

"And now, thanks to your prepackaged scapegoat and bogeyman, the Sundial Slayer, I've got a damn good story to explain how two FBI agents got themselves killed in this sleepy little backwoods town. Without exposing our secret."

Her smile turned to a frown. "But there's still the matter of that anonymous note. I've got to figure out who sent it and make sure it never happens again."

At this, Dan laughed until he lost consciousness.

* * *

Dan opened his eyes and shook his throbbing head. The amphetamines and caffeine were doing yeoman's work against whatever DD had slipped him in his tea. But he was still far from a hundred percent. It took a moment or two to realize he was naked, his wrists tied behind his back, and propped against a tree trunk. He quietly mumbled a prayer of thanks that he was bound with rope and not handcuffs or a zip tie. She was observing the traditions.

He could see the silvery glow of the full moon shining through the boughs above his head. The low moaning wind was chill, helping to spur on more wakefulness.

In addition to the moon, there was the bright blue glow of headlights. Someone walked in front of them. All else was pitch black darkness. Dan knew he was deep in the woods.

"You're awake earlier than I expected." DD crouched just outside the ring of stones surrounding the tree. By the glow of headlights, Dan could see that she was also naked and covered in the blue knotwork, a thick golden torc around her neck and gilded bracelets snaking up her forearms. She held a broad-bladed bronze dagger in her right hand. "Either you're a secret morphine junkie or you took something before I arrived."

Dan cleared his throat. "Amphetamines. Why am I still alive?"

DD reached down to a black piece of velvet, then placed the last silver ring on one of the surrounding stones. Resting on the velvet were a golden necklace, a golden bracelet, and a full syringe. "The way you laughed about that note. Got me wondering. You know who sent it, don't you?"

Dan took a deep breath and tried to clear his head. "Yes."

"You might as well tell me. You're going to die anyway. The God of the Hill must be satisfied."

Dan laughed. "Oh, believe me. I know."

"What does that mean?"

"It means I'm the one who sent the note."

DD inhaled sharply. "Liar."

Dan shook his head and chuckled. "What do you remember about the Donnelly killings?"

She edged inside the ring and knelt beside him, resting the bronze blade on his thigh. "I told you, I was just a kid. I know it was messy, brutal. They changed the rules for the lottery after that. Only leading members of the community could participate."

Dan smiled. "I was a kid, too. That's why I needed help when the lottery chose me. I'm the reason they changed the rules."

DD's eyes went wide. "You... you're Hugh Donnelly? I always wondered why four were sacrificed that year instead of three."

Dan nodded. "I asked your dad, Chief Riordan, to help me, to coach me. Little did I know that my dad was stepping out with your mom. But the chief did, which made the selection of sacrifices pretty damn clear. Since I was a kid, it was just easier to do the whole family. One stop shopping."

He laughed. "Your dad demonstrated on my old man. He took his time, enjoyed it. In the end, he was so grateful, he helped relocate me with a new name and a whole new life. But I never forgot my responsibilities to the Crooked One of the Mound, and over the past few years, I've gotten pretty good at observing them. Of course, when you're the FBI agent in charge of investigating your own murders, it makes it kind of easy."

DD's face hardened. She raised the dagger.

Dan's right fist came up and connected with her jaw. "You know, your dad even showed me how to tie knots and how to untie them. Just like he did you."

DD sprawled on the grass inside the stone circle, stunned.

"I'm glad you're wearing gold for the ceremony, DD," Dan said as he picked up the dagger. "Praise Crom Cruach! Forgive us our sins and bless us in this New Year! *Domhnach Chrom Dubh!*"

Dan was pleased to see DD's eyes widen with realization as he buried the blade in her breast. He had finally come home, the God of the Hill had been appeased, and the Samhain *Feis* had been dutifully observed.

All was right with the world again.

MURDER AT SPRING TRAINING

Gregory L. Norris

Clowns.

Goddamn clowns, an entire army of them. As though he didn't have enough to contend with following his hire to the Seaside Top Socks' media relations department at the chaotic height of spring training, Bryce Zinter would also take on the unwanted stress of clowns.

Banners advertised the theme day at the Top Socks' winter home in Saturn Bay, Florida, site of the former Saturn Fairgrounds. Bunting decorated the stands. Bryce hastened from his rental through the media entrance and into a different kind of circus.

"You're Zinter?" said a woman dressed in a pastel pantsuit, pistachio green.

Pretty, he thought. "Guilty."

She waved for him to follow. Bryce removed his shades. Her cell phone chirped. She answered.

"Yes, this is Sheila Ortiz. I'll have to get back to you."

She killed the call before the caller could argue. Two steps later, her phone again rang its riff of musical notes. Sheila checked the screen before switching off the ringer.

"Welcome to spring training," she said, casting a look over her shoulder at him. "And the madness."

He thought about reminding her that he was fresh off a similar maelstrom at Channel Ten, the major sports news network, before all the sturm and drang that had led him south to Florida. A former major league player serving out the end of his career in the minors following a laundry list of performance-related injuries, he'd taken criminal justice courses in the off-season. A cop—that was the plan for the second act of Bryce Alan Zinter, who'd gone early in the first round of the draft but not nearly as far as he'd dreamed. His second act wasn't to prove much more successful as envisioned. After several suspicious deaths among the sportscasters at the network, the head of Channel Ten's media relations department had brought him in to nose around—he knew sports and basic police work. Bryce had unmasked one of Channel Ten's owners and a deep-pocketed sports gambling connection to those deaths. In the fallout, his job at the network became one more casualty.

In the end, he didn't.

"You keeping up?" she asked, bringing him out of his thoughts and back to the moment.

Bryce put on a burst of speed and joined her at the home team clubhouse doors. "I think so."

"Good," she said, smiling and meeting him eye-to-eye for all of a second. "That was some fine work you did at Channel Ten. I'm sorry they've closed the network, but I'm happy to have you on my team now."

They walked into the clubhouse. The olfactory rush of male scent and the soundtrack of baseball in March transported him back in time seven years to his first spring training in that other life, B.R.—*Before Retirement* from the game. Players were lined along lockers to dress everywhere. Temporary compartments had been set up in every available space. Those condemned to the outer reaches wore home white uniforms that lacked last names. More than a few looked ill-fitting. It was your typical spring training madhouse of non-roster invitees, desperates, and last hopes for players with fading careers.

"Even with uniforms going up to ninety-nine, we still have three Number 21s," Sheila said. "Call me crazy, but I can't wait until we've winnowed down to a team of twenty-six players."

"And the clowns?" he asked. "How many of them are we expecting today?"

Sheila narrowed her focus on him and laughed. "I don't know—that's not my, *our*, department. A few. You have a problem with clowns?"

"Maybe," he said, aware that all the moisture had drained from his mouth.

She smiled again, though not in a dismissive way. Bryce realized he liked her. She seemed tough but fair, was definitely nicer than the baseball team suit that had hired him. And, yes, she was pretty.

"Speaking of clowns, your first assignment involves the biggest one associated with the club. Before that, I want you to meet somebody."

She led him over to one of the permanent lockers, to a young man in uniform with a name and a low prime number on the back— *Wainwright.*

"Arlo," she said.

The player turned from his conversation with the next body crowded in line beside him and faced the two newest arrivals to the team's inner sanctum.

"Meet Bryce Zinter," she said.

"Most people call me Zint," Bryce corrected.

The two shook hands, each doing that natural thing to attain a kind of friendly dominance, which would have shattered the hand bones of lesser men.

Surely this wasn't the clown. Wainwright didn't look anything like the horrors with painted faces that would roam the Fairgrounds honking horns and twisting balloons into obscene versions of dogs and other animals before and during Seaside's businessman's special against fellow Citrus League rivals, the Hurricanes. Bryce shuddered as they broke the handshake.

"Something wrong?" Wainwright asked.

"No, just a small case of coulrophobia."

"Hope it isn't catchy," Wainwright laughed.

Bryce smiled. "Only if you hate clowns."

Her purpose for introducing them involved Wainwright's media interest. Even before Seaside took to the field, five different outlets had requested interviews.

"The Wainwright name's sort of a touchy subject in Seaside," Sheila said when they were back in the tunnel leading away from the clubhouse.

Bryce considered her words. "That's right—Cliff Wainwright. He was coming up right when I was designated for assignment."

"The older brother. He pitched for Seaside for one summer. It didn't end well."

They reached the set of stairs leading up to the offices that housed the media relations department. Bryce's time in the Holland Park, Rhode Island home base of Channel Ten hadn't been long—just enough for the killer to target him at the height of his brief employment at the network. But the body didn't forget, and Bryce's hadn't. Pushing through the doors and hopping up the stairs to the media center activated certain instincts, triggered responses, and woke anxieties that had lain dormant since the network's dissolution.

"I'm so glad you're here, Zint," Sheila said. "We've got so many bodies in baseball uniforms at the start of spring training that half of them could be imposters or ax murderers off the street for all we know."

"About that clown?" Bryce asked.

* * *

The clown's name was Hal Loper. Loper was known among the Seaside faithful with affection and more than a fair amount of distaste as "Hal the Heckler." Bryce had heard about Loper and remembered seeing a clip at Channel Ten on the flagship sports news program. Hal the Heckler had heckled his first targets half a dozen years earlier from his season ticket throne along the First Base line. Middle-aged, balding, and sporting a hefty paunch, Loper was ironic in his delivery against in-shape, young athletes sporting full heads of hair, which was part of his notorious charm, according to Sheila. Based upon her briefing, Hal the Heckler selected his targets, usually from the rival team though not always, focused on them when they took to the mound or were up at bat, and never went for the jugular.

"Well, almost never," Sheila said.

Bryce glanced up from the schedule and pile of press release pages growing thicker on the table in front of him. "Almost?"

"There have been instances when Loper hasn't been—how do I say this?—so loveable. He's been issued two warnings. One more and he's banned from attending any Seaside games for an entire season."

Loper had parlayed his character into a cottage career on local sports talk radio and a book deal. The latter had all but vanished from public consciousness except when Loper was a guest on the former, where he pushed his sole claim to fame.

"We cover media relations for a heckler?" Bryce asked.

"We do today because it's the Hurricanes—Seaside's divisional archenemies and Hal Loper's favorite heckling target. That big, second warning came at the end of last season during the playoffs," Sheila said. "Come on. Time for introductions."

Bryce gathered his printouts into a folder, grabbed his phone, and was again in motion, following Sheila out the door.

* * *

There were times when running the bases had felt like flying. In his haste to keep up with Sheila Ortiz, Bryce's mind flashed back to past spring trainings when forty other hopefuls fought to take his job. Early on, the way he'd maintained job security was to smack the ball over the fence, run hard down the line regardless, and then somewhere between First and Second Base, he was flying. But baseball was behind him now. Since taking his last trot around the diamond, he'd rewritten the narrative of Bryce Zinter. Hell, he'd gotten involved in a major murder investigation and had been both rewarded and vilified for his undercover work. No matter where this new chapter of the narrative led him, Bryce guessed that the final one would again find him running the bases, flying in his memory, maybe, too, in his soul if such a thing existed.

He hoped he'd also recall the sunshine, the heat, the smell of the grass and ballpark. They traveled down the stands, most of which still sat empty, to the front row, where Hal Loper sat alone, a big man holding court and signing autographs to mostly young fans.

"Hal," Sheila addressed.

Loper looked up. Sunglasses shielded his eyes. Even so, Bryce sensed them taking in the image of Sheila and liking it. Then Loper's focus shifted over to him, and there they lingered.

"I know you," Hal the Heckler said.

"Hal, this is my new assistant in media relations," Sheila said. "Meet—"

"Bryce Zinter," Loper said. He finished signing and shooed the last of his small fan base away before rising.

"Let me guess, all that stuff in Holland Park," Bryce said.

"Holland Park?" Loper said. "You're that washout who played a few years for Cincinnati. Cost me a small fortune in my fantasy baseball league six summers ago. You owe me about three grand, pal. That's without interest."

Loper faced him, hands on hips, his defensive body language impossible to misread. It wasn't the welcome to the job Bryce expected.

"I'm just messing with you," Loper said.

He extended his pudgy hand. Bryce reached automatically for it only to have Loper pull back.

"Except for that part about the money. You still owe me that."

Loper laughed, the sound grating. Even worse was the casual smack he delivered to Bryce's stomach, what was meant to appear like your normal greeting between two men but only worsened the delivery of Loper's insult.

"So, who you got lined up to interview me?" Loper said. He reached for the seat's cup holder and his beer, knocked back a hearty gulp, and burped.

* * *

His time in Holland Park, though short, had been filled with promise—taking out of the equation the whole clandestine reason behind his hiring, that was. Bryce had liked his new apartment, working in the network setting, and his boss in media relations, Rob Gomez. As he paraded reporters down to Hal Loper's throne, he wondered if the same would be possible working for the Top Socks. Throughout the season, there'd be long road trips from one ballpark to another. During his baseball career, travel hadn't bothered him. Now, on the other side of it, Loper's words taunted him, and he wasn't so sure. Being at ballparks not as a player but the liaison between the media and Seaside's stars might erode him. In small doses at first, sure. But after a while, the holes bitten out of his ego would widen, leaving him disfigured in the mental sense.

There's always police work, his inner voice reminded. *You were a hell of a detective at the network. Of course, look what it got you.*

"*Loper*," Bryce sighed. Hal the Heckler certainly could cut you deeply with his seemingly innocent banter.

He blinked and raised his shades. Around him, the Fairgrounds pulsed with energy. Fans were taking their seats. Batting practice had wrapped, and the grounds crew were doing final prep work, re-chalking the lines and raking the infield. Despite hecklers and clowns, it was a beautiful day, the cloudless Florida sky the color of comfortable denim, no storms in sight.

* * *

Clowns.

Clowns with candy apple red frizzy hair and baggy, checked pants. Clowns with plastic boutonnières that squirted water and floppy hats that conjured flop-sweat in the balmy Florida warmth. Big shoes. Fake noses. Painted-on grins.

Bryce turned away from the image of the dozen circus performers lined up in front of the mound, tossing out ceremonial first pitches to an equal number of young fans and Seaside baseball players. His mind cycled back to his boyhood, to *that* movie about the killer clown with the jagged red smile. He supposed it was good he didn't suffer from arachnophobia, else fate might have put giant spiders on the mound to torment him.

Bryce snorted out a humorless laugh. Baseball-pitching spiders he could handle. How he hated clowns. He supposed he should get used to circus-themed days at the former carnival grounds every spring—if he kept the job for that long.

Arlo Wainwright took to the mound for the top of the first inning. Standing a few rows back from Hal Loper, who was finishing up the last of his media obligations, Bryce studied the pitcher's form. Wainwright was graceful, in peak shape. Barring injuries, he was guaranteed to make the team and become one of its superstars. Of course, the baseball gods were sometimes generous but also often prone to a taketh-away mentality based upon the day's mood. On this glorious afternoon perfect for baseball, they gave. Wainwright struck out the first two batters he faced. The third Hurricanes player flied out to centerfield, dropping a can of corn easily into the glove of one of the team's multiple Number 21s.

Throughout the top of the first, Loper's commentary was comprised of claps, whistles, and hoots. That changed in the bottom of the inning when the Hurricanes took to the diamond and pitcher Darius Bascombe became the focus of the heckler's wrath.

"Look at those spaghetti legs," Loper barked. "I've seen better pitchers of lemonade!"

Clever, Bryce thought. But he could see how easily the good-natured antics of Hal the Heckler could degenerate into something mean, cutting, and infuriating—or pure vitriol.

"Lemonade!" Loper yelled. "Five cents a glass—remember that come contract negotiation time!"

Bascombe walked his first Seaside batter, Hudson, who of course tested his arm.

"And look at that macaroni elbow—matches his spaghetti legs!" Loper called and then clapped his hands together.

Bascombe turned and fired another pickoff move. This one sailed past First Base and into the stands, impacting in the front row seats. The ball exploded against Loper's cup in the seat's holder, spraying beer. Shouts and screams rose up from the closest spectators, all save Loper who stood frozen, all color and emotion ironed off his face.

For a fraction of a second, a stunned silence followed. Then umpires and security guards thawed enough to act. So, too, did Hal the Heckler, who cackled in a commanding, grating voice.

"Your aim would be better, Lemonade, if not for those macaroni elbows!"

* * *

Bryce hastened through the small crowd that had gathered around Loper—two Fairgrounds security guards, the First Base umpire, Seaside's First Base coach, and even Bascombe, who leaned over the rail, offering up an unconvincing mea culpa.

"I'm fine, I'm fine—Christ-on-a-cross," Loper said, shaking off spilled beer and offers of medical assistance alike. He whirled on Bascombe. "Gotta give it to you, Lemons—there's more in your jockstrap than a limp noodle. That took serious stones."

Bascombe aimed his middle finger at Loper.

"You wish," Loper fired back.

"It was an accident," Bascombe called over his shoulder.

Accident or not, the pitcher's day was done. Bascombe stalked off the field to a chorus of boos. Several of the day's clowns lined atop the Hurricane's dugout roof, adding their own angry voices to the cacophony.

"Someone get me another goddamn beer," Bryce heard Loper demand, bookending the statement with more of that annoying laughter.

Oh yes, his first day on the job was off to a hell of a start.

Bryce tipped another look at the eight-clown salute over the Hurricane's dugout and his stomach tightened. Forty years earlier, before the stadium had been erected to serve as the spring training home for the Seaside Top Socks and its double-A affiliate, the land was home to the famed Worthen Carnival. There'd been elephants, lion tamers, prancing horses with elegant, colorful plumage and beautiful lady riders. And clowns, even more of them than here in the present.

Loper blustered something about issuing a warning of his own to the Top Socks brass. Bryce shook his head, turned, and nearly walked into the clown with the head of electric blue hair and sunken eyes.

The expletive was past his lips before Bryce could trap it. Their glances connected, and in the instant that followed, the day's pleasant seventy-eight degrees plummeted to a temperature more fitting for the Arctic Circle. The clown's appearance was sloppy, looking like he'd gotten made up in a hurry—baggy, ill-fitting jeans, a basic flannel shirt, and gloves like the kind worn by the grounds crew.

It was the eyes that froze Bryce. The white face paint around them accentuated the sockets, which looked in that splintered moment like the hollows of a skull. Bryce blinked first and looked away. The clown continued past him through the stands and out of sight, presumably to join his clown brethren in protest.

Bryce shook himself out of his palsy. His phone chirped. He pulled it from his pocket. "Yeah?"

"It's Sheila, Zint—everything okay over there?"

"Sure," he lied. "Couldn't be better."

He supposed that on the surface, things were. The game had resumed with a new Hurricanes pitcher striking out the next batter he faced and Hudson still testing throwing arms. Someone had replaced Loper's spilled beer, and the sparse crowd of worried officials had dispersed back to the demands of their jobs.

"Keep an eye on things down there, would you?" Sheila asked.

"No sweat," Bryce said.

He looked over to the front row seats, watched Loper take another deep pull from his cup, and drew in a cleansing breath. The image of the clown's eyes flashed through his memory, chilling him once more. What about those sunken, dark sockets was so completely wrong?

More than that one, worrisome note of wrongness played out in the minute that followed. Bryce saw the cup as it slipped out of Loper's hand, spilling what few contents remained across the cement. More troubling was Loper himself, who'd gone quiet and wasn't moving, wasn't *heckling*. On the few steps to reach the front row, it was the absence of Loper's voice that confirmed Bryce's fear.

He made it to Loper's seat and instantly knew that Hal the Heckler was dead.

* * *

Seaside's team physician made the pronouncement.

"My educated guess is that it's his heart," Doctor Mendez said to those few of the team's upper echelon gathered in the physician's exam room. "He was overweight—and he'd just almost gotten drilled by a fastball, which could have triggered a cardiac incident. But we won't know that until the examiner gets here and makes it official."

Loper's heart. By all indications, Hal the Heckler didn't have one. "I'm telling you, he was fine one moment, doc," Bryce said. "Is there any chance this wasn't natural causes?"

The pall hanging over the room thickened.

"What are you suggesting?" Mendez asked.

Bryce grasped at memory straws. "Some fast-acting poison he could have ingested. What's the one—plant-based—?"

"Cardiac glycosides," Mendez said. "You're talking digoxin, digitalis?"

"Or some other similar drug that could have been slipped into his drink," Bryce said.

"You think Loper was murdered?" Sheila asked.

Mendez eyed him. "Who would want to kill Hal the Heckler?"

Bryce said, "Who wouldn't?"

* * *

Camera footage showed the near drilling by Bascombe's fastball and the chaos that followed.

"*There*," said Bryce.

The clown with the electric blue hair crept into view and joined the group of bodies gathered around Loper's seat.

"That's him," Bryce said. "There's something in his hand."

Sheila attempted to zoom in on the image. "I can't tell what it is."

"I can," Bryce said after the footage resumed. "Look at the cup holder."

Five minutes later, they entered the conference room and an invisible fist punched Bryce in the gut. Twelve clowns formed an unofficial police lineup.

"He's not here," Bryce said, aware of the sour taste sitting atop his tongue. "The one with the blue hair."

* * *

Security guards sealed exits and the police were called in.

"There was something about his eyes that didn't make sense," Bryce said.

Sheila pulled him aside. "In what way?"

Bryce shook his head. "You said that Loper was issued two warnings."

"That's right."

"The second against the Hurricanes last season in the division playoffs. Who was the first?"

She answered, the response meant only for him. "Cliff Wainwright."

* * *

He approached the locker room, struggling for breaths that refused to come easily. He was back in Holland Park, assembling seemingly random puzzle pieces until truths lined up. Bryce marched into the clubhouse.

"Any idea when they're gonna let us bounce?" one of the players asked him.

"And do you know what's going on, Zint?" another asked.

He didn't answer beyond holding up his hand. Like the others, Arlo Wainwright was still in uniform, grim-faced, the eye black applied beneath his blues sending Bryce's heart into a gallop.

"Arlo," he said.

Their eyes connected, and Bryce was there again, paralyzed before the clown with electric blue hair and skull sockets for eyes.

"Who else could move around here in disguise with such ease?" he asked. "Clowns. It was the eyes. I couldn't figure it out at first, and then it struck me. Under the clown's white face paint, right beneath the eyes..."

"What are you saying?" Arlo huffed.

"Grease under the eyes to restrict glare," Bryce said, pointing at Wainwright's face. "The clown that handed Loper a poisoned beer had eye black on, which was why he looked like a skull."

Wainwright's expression hardened.

"Why would you do it? I mean, Loper was a twenty-four-karat gold certified jerk, but your career... especially after what happened to your brother, Cliff."

Wainwright's eyes snapped fully open. "Don't you dare say his name!"

The pitcher surged forward, grabbed hold of Bryce, and in one fluid motion spun him around and slammed him hard against the lockers. At first, Seaside players moved aside and then attempted to break up the scrum, but Bryce dug in, pushed back, and faced the angry bull without blinking.

"The day Loper heckled your brother—something about your parents, was it? And it only got worse from there."

"Our parents," Wainwright said. "You don't know what bringing them up did to Cliff. Destroyed his career. Destroyed what was left of our family. Loper deserved what happened to him!"

Bryce tipped a look down, into the locker and the duffel bag sitting in open view. "That contain what I think it does? Ground crew gloves, flannel shirt, blue clown's wig?"

Wainwright didn't answer straight away. The next few seconds tolled with the weight of minutes, hours.

"No. You don't understand," Arlo Wainwright said.

Then, from his back, another voice cut in. "He didn't do it," said one of the three Number 21s.

Bryce remembered his question about who could move around a ballpark in disguise better than a clown. In spring training, the answer was any number of players who were there one day, gone the next.

"Cliff Wainwright," Bryce said as, behind the wall of the brothers' backs, Fairgrounds security guards walked into view.

Two police uniforms accompanied them.

LORD CARDIGAN'S LUCK

Martin Zeigler

Into the valley of death
Rode the six hundred.
— The Charge of the Light Brigade, *Alfred, Lord Tennyson*

Andy Turner stood at the edge of the platform and peered again into the distance. And, by God, there it was, rising over the buildings, a plume of smoke blacker than London's afternoon sky. And within seconds, round the bend, came the huffing locomotive.

In that same moment, a din arose behind Andy that nearly knocked him off the platform. Cheers and applause and cries of, "There's the train!" and "There he is!" and "There's Lord Cardigan!" echoed throughout the railway terminal. Andy swiveled about on his crutch as best he could and gaped at the crowd that had seemed to burst from out of nowhere. Earlier, when Andy had arrived here limping and aching, there had been but a few passengers milling about. Now, before him, stood a celebratory throng of red-faced and shivering men and women in thick overcoats and enormous hats, yelling and shouting and expelling anxious vapors into the crisp autumn air. Some of the people were pointing, some had removed their gloves and were clapping, others were holding high and waving their tiny Union Jack flags. But all of them were staring wide-eyed, as if possessed, in Andy's direction.

No, not at him, but beyond him, and Andy turned 'round once again to face it: the train, with its single carriage and its single passenger, advancing magisterially toward the station.

Concealed from the hundreds of eyes behind him, Andy slipped his hand under his threadbare coat and felt for his revolver. Yes, it was still tucked in his belt, in the same place he'd checked not more than five minutes earlier.

* * *

Andy pictured Lord Cardigan in full uniform seated by the window, his saber propped up in the seat beside him like a traveling companion, his uniform resplendent in its dark blue tunic and gold pelisse and cherry red trousers with their twin yellow stripes.

And then, struck by a memory, Andy fancied the entire train fading away, leaving only Cardigan, who was still advancing. Not aboard a railway carriage, but on horseback. And not toward a railway station, but toward a vast open field where his hussars, astride their mounts, awaited yet another inspection. Where Andy, astraddle his horse, awaited his first inspection, having recently been recruited.

Keeping a studious gait, Cardigan passed one man after the other, seeing everything there was to see in a single glance. Andy hoped it would be the same with him. But just when it seemed as if Cardigan would continue past him and move on to the next soldier, the commander brought his horse to a halt, then quarter-turned to face Andy.

"Buttons, private," Cardigan said.

Andy, shaken by being singled out, stammered, "Buttons, sir?"

"Yes, buttons."

"My buttons?"

"Whose buttons would I be referring to?"

"Mine, sir. But what about my buttons?"

"You will not address me in that manner, private, as if we're playing with riddles. I'm looking at your buttons. The buttons on your pelisse. What color are they?"

"I meant no disrespect, sir. I—"

"Your buttons. What color are they?"

"My buttons. My buttons are gold, sir."

"Are they?"

"Yes, sir."

"Are they indeed, private?"

"Yes, I believe so."

"Come here."

Lightly, with the heel of his boot, Andy tapped his horse forward and brought it up alongside Cardigan's, facing the opposite way so that Cardigan could look Andy in the eye and Andy could try his best to look back.

Cardigan did look Andy in the eye, and look at him hard. With a sweep of his arm to indicate the rest of his men, he barked out, for all to hear, "Every stitch of these uniforms, from the neck of the tunic to the toe of the boots, I purchased out of my own pocket. Did you think, private, that your uniform was an exception?"

"No, sir."

"I chose the colors, every one of them. And my men shall carry these colors proud. If they never see a battlefield in their lives, they shall see this field many times over. And each and every time, they shall prove themselves either victorious or vanquished by how they carry their colors. Am I clear, private?"

"Yes, sir," Andy said, though not fully comprehending.

Cardigan suddenly lashed out at one of Andy's buttons and tore it loose. Andy felt his chest break into a sheet of sweat but said nothing. Cardigan ripped off a second button and a third, then opened his palm to display his acquisitions.

"If these buttons are gold," Cardigan announced, "then so is the shit in my arse."

"Beg pardon, sir?"

"What color do you see?"

"They're—they're streaked with brown, sir."

"They're not gold, then?"

"No, sir."

"Why are they not gold?"

Andy gripped tightly onto the reins, feeling the urge to bolt. But he held steady, though his voice quavered. "I must have... in the stables, before the inspection... I was tending to Clara."

"Clara? Who the bloody hell is Clara?"

"My horse, sir."

"And so what?"

"I was feeling about her legs. Making sure they were fit, like I do every morning. And she must have kicked. I hardly notice it anymore. She does it playfully. Like a game. Between her and me. When she kicked at the straw, some of the mud underneath must've splattered me. That must be what happened."

"Now there's a tragedy worthy of Dickens," Cardigan said.

"Sir, if I may, I can try—"

Andy held his hand out to request the buttons. Cardigan closed his fist over them and drew his arm back, like a child claiming lemon drops. "Not these," he said.

"I can clean them, sir."

"Not these," Cardigan repeated. Then holding his fist high enough for one and all to see, he shouted, "What did I say about your colors? You have been vanquished, private. I shall treat these three buttons as the spoils of war and keep them for my own."

"But, sir..." Andy hesitated, knowing the water was hot enough already. "I'm afraid I have no spares."

"And no needle and thread either, I presume," Cardigan shouted. "Shall I fetch them for you? Shall I do the mending? Perhaps I should shove my tit in your mouth and wipe your bum, as well."

"But, sir, I—"

"Have you a pocket watch? You should have a pocket watch. I've supplied everyone with pocket watches."

"Yes, sir."

"Well, then, fifteen minutes."

"Fifteen minutes?"

"More riddles, you think? In fifteen minutes you shall stand in this same spot. Either facing me with gold buttons stitched on and blinding in their pristine brilliance, or facing away with your back bare for a flogging."

* * *

The blast of horns and trumpets, tubas and trombones, snapped Andy out of his demeaning reverie. Brash, triumphant chords echoed off the station's walls and rattled the windows.

The approaching train was fully visible again. And behind him—well, Andy turned again to look—the brass instruments had settled into a melody, and scores of mouths opened wide and began belting out the accompanying words.

See, the conqu'ring hero comes!

Sound the trumpet! Beat the drums!

Andy reflected bitterly: *Beat the drums. Yes, beat the drums, drummers. And whatever else that comes your way.*

* * *

He remembered galloping back to the soldiers' quarters in a frenzy, all the while thinking: *Buttons, buttons, where are there buttons?* Like the children's game, but one which instilled fear. Fortunately, an officer's wife took pity on him. If not for her, Andy surely would not have returned to the site of his humiliation.

But return he did, in uniform fit and proper. His unit was still present and in formation, but Cardigan was nowhere in sight. The drummer, without his drum, stood alongside a tripod of spikes, hastily constructed but sturdy enough to support a man's weight. In his hand, a cat o' nine tails. Next to him, the drum major, *with* his drum, stood prepared to count the lashes.

With an unsteady hand, Andy displayed the face of his pocket watch. "But it's eight past the hour," he pleaded. "I'm two minutes early."

"I'm sorry," the drummer said, displaying another watch. "But this is Cardigan's, and you're two minutes late."

* * *

A drum sounded! Not the one in Andy's pained recollection but one joining in with the brass band. Its deep thumps shook the air, inspiring the fanatical crowd to even greater feats of musical expression.

Sports prepare! The laurel bring!
Songs of triumph to him sing!
See, the conqu'ring hero comes!

Andy mouthed the words to the last line, not in time to the music, but as a question:

Conquering hero?

He bleakly shook his head. A year ago, the Light Brigade had met its doom. Less than a year ago, in fact. Barely enough time for the blood to dry. And without a doubt in Andy's mind, these very same buffoons now singing Cardigan's praises and trumpeting their glorious fanfare to his arrival had been among the first to heap him with scorn and contempt the minute news of that murderous blunder hit England's shores.

Back then, Andy had figured that the only thing Cardigan would ever be revered for was the button-down, woolen sweater he was seen to wear at the opera and fancy dinners.

What he hadn't figured on was the Queen. News of Cardigan's journey here to London got around rather quickly. It was why the mob was here at the station, and why they were in a more accepting mood than a year ago. There was nothing quite like an invite by Her Majesty to put the veriest scoundrel up on a pedestal.

In point of fact, news of Cardigan's arrival was why Andy was here. This would likely be his one and only opportunity.

At last, the train pulled into the terminal with its precious invitee. Anxiously patting the waist of his coat, Andy watched as the train slowed to a stop, its brakes squealing, its wheels shrieking.

* * *

From everywhere sounded the squealing and shrieking of horses and men.

There followed another cannon blast. Andy felt part of him give way. Yet another blast, and Clara buckled beneath him like a rickety table, then collapsed, pitching Andy full on into the dirt.

Twisted on his side, unable to budge, Andy saw men dying in front of him. Heard men dying behind him. And he quickly came to accept that he was among them. And he wondered, as all these others must have wondered, how it had come to this.

An order had been given. A bugle call had sounded. Cardigan had taken the lead, saber out and pointing into the valley. And the charge had begun. It was really quite as simple as that.

Andy wanted to make the rest of it just as simple by shutting his eyes. But some force of will kept them open. And through the dusty haze Andy barely made out a figure on horseback. It was in retreat, returning to the allied lines, not at a walk or a trot, but at a gallop. The saber was no longer out, but Andy knew it was Cardigan.

There were men still charging ahead on horseback. Horseless men still charging ahead on foot. A man who could barely crawl inching his way forward, if only to convince himself he was still alive.

And shrinking into the distance was their commander, heading back.

* * *

Now, in the open door to the railway carriage, appeared that same conquering hero. The band had ceased playing. The crowd had ceased singing. The very air in the terminal was now one of awestruck silence as the multitude advanced on the carriage like a faithful tide.

Andy stood at the edge of it all, concealed behind a steel pillar yet close enough to Cardigan, waiting for the right moment.

Cardigan was not in uniform as Andy had expected, but in casual trousers and a green button-down sweater that bore his name. Uniform or not, Cardigan stood soldier straight, one hand on the door frame, the other on his hip, as if posing for one of those floor-to-ceiling portraits of great military men.

How the women swooned over his gallant posture. How the men envied his mien. How the haughty youths from the prestigious schools coveted that haughty sneer beneath his mustache.

But all Andy could see was a man blessed with luck the moment he was born. Who had inherited an earldom and a lordship, along with the noblest estates, all his to keep without lifting a finger. Who, from an early age, had felt himself free to do as he wished, and, for each of his misdeeds, had bought his acquittals. Who, with his vast wealth at his command, had purchased his commands, achieving ever higher ranks through payment, not deserved promotion.

Andy had no idea what Cardigan went by now. Major General? General Major? Lieutenant Colonel? Colonel Major Lieutenant? Andy hardly knew the ranks anymore. He had emptied his mind of things military. To him there were but two ranks: the living and the dead.

Then there was Cardigan's luckiest stroke of all—escaping a single scratch at the far end of the Valley of Death because a Russian officer, having once shaken

Cardigan's hand, had ordered his men to hold their fire.

Perhaps that is why Cardigan had retired to his yacht, leaving what was left of the Light Brigade to fend for themselves. So that he could pop open a bottle of bubbly and pour himself a glass. And drink a toast to himself for his good luck.

"Well, your Earlship," Andy whispered from behind the pillar. "Your good luck is about to end."

Andy opened his coat. He drew his revolver from his belt, aimed with a squint of an eye, and fired.

* * *

The shot resonated throughout the station like a firework gone amok. Cardigan staggered back, his hand to his chest. The crowd exhaled a collective gasp. Cardigan withdrew his hand and peered down at his sweater. The crowd saw no sign of blood, nothing dark seeping through Cardigan's cardigan. The commander resumed his supercilious pose with a quizzical expression on his face, as if asking, *What on earth was that all about?*, prompting from his adoring admirers a unanimous sigh of relief.

Baffled, irate, certainly not relieved, Andy fired again. This time Cardigan reared back ever so slightly, as if slapped, then looked himself over and resumed his pose, as before. And this time the crowd let out a round of cheers and applause.

Andy couldn't figure it. He was a crack shot. He had struck Cardigan twice in the chest, he was sure of it. Gripping his pistol with both hands, concentrating his gaze on that damned button-down sweater, he squeezed the trigger a third time.

Cardigan barely budged. He flicked at his sweater as if brushing off lint and, for the first time, addressed his audience. In his deep officer's bellow, he quipped, "The gnats here in London pack a punch, do they not."

Hearty laughter exploded from every corner of the station, except Andy's. He was about to aim his gun a fourth time when he looked over and saw someone jabbing a finger in his direction and shouting, "There's the dastardly culprit!"

Others caught on and likewise turned their gaze toward Andy, crying out, in ever increasing numbers, "Encore! Encore!"

"Encore?" Andy asked himself, puzzled.

There came further shouts from all over. "Bravo!" and "Once again!" and "Fire away, and see where that gets you!" and "Our hero is no match for the likes of you!"

Andy now realized what was happening. To the hundreds on the platform, he was just part of some show, as if everything that had just happened—the gunshots, Cardigan's reaction, his witty remark—had been a rehearsed act, put on to highlight how impervious the conquering hero was to harm. To them, this was all theater, with Cardigan and Andy as willing actors—an entertaining melodrama, complete with toy guns and bullets.

Andy was incensed. He didn't know why Cardigan was still standing. Those were real bullets he fired, not wax. He almost felt like singling someone out and proving it. But, no. It was Cardigan he was after, not any of these people, as loud and obnoxious as they were.

But his pistol clearly wasn't up to the job. He glared at the weapon still in his hand and hurled it away as if it bore the plague. The gun skidded off the platform and disappeared beneath the train. Then, pulling his coat collar high over his neck and glancing back at the delighted eyes of his hecklers, Andy limped out the back exit as fast as his crutch would allow.

* * *

Once outside, Andy leaned back against a wall, panting heavily, his heart pounding louder than any drum he had ever heard. "I'll get you yet, Cardigan," he whispered. "I'll find a way, by God."

Andy found his way to a park bench and sank onto it, exhausted. He could still hear the hoots and raucous laughter echoing out of the railway station like the rantings from a distant asylum.

Andy let his fatigue calm him. He inhaled deeply, exhaled slowly. And gradually, a sort of clarity set in, the likes of which he'd never experienced before. Details from the past few harrowing minutes came back to him in an astoundingly sharp focus.

He could see the number on Cardigan's railway carriage—3713. He could see the blemishes and wrinkles in Cardigan's face. He could see the man's green sweater, the knit of it, and the line of buttons from neck to waist, all of them the same color—a shade of green slightly darker than the green of the sweater--except for the top three buttons.

And, as if time itself had slowed to a crawl, he could see the bullets leaving his pistol, one after the other, as if stepping out for a stroll. He watched the first bullet deflect off the topmost button. He watched the second bullet rebound off the next button down. He watched the third bullet strike the third button dead center and carom off harmlessly into a corner of the carriage.

Andy's aim could not have been more perfect.

Except Andy hadn't aimed for the buttons. He had aimed for the stomach, the liver, the spleen. The heart, assuming Cardigan had one.

Had Andy hit his target as intended, there would have been none of that hurrahing and belly laughing from the crowd, that's for certain. There would have been Cardigan in the railway carriage, no longer standing smugly, but slumped bleeding on the floor. There would have been stunned silence, followed by gasps of horror. There would have been men and women dropping to their knees and wailing and moaning. There would have been sufficient numbers for a funeral procession, and a brass band for the dirge.

Yes, people still would have spotted Andy and jabbed fingers in his direction, but this time not for their amusement, but to exact justice. As one, they would have rushed him and tackled him and beaten him to within an inch of his life, and only then summoned the police.

Afterward, Andy would have been carted away, to serve the rest of his life in a dark, damp cell, where misery upon misery would be heaped upon those he already had—the inconsolable isolation, the recurring nightmares, the intense and never-ending pain in his one remaining leg.

Yes, this all would have happened, had it not been for those buttons. Those top three buttons. Those gold buttons, stained with brown, that Cardigan had once ripped off Andy's uniform and claimed for his very own.

Andy Turner, sitting alone on that bench as dusk approached, had to laugh at the ludicrousness of this all. Buttons, buttons, who had the buttons? Why, Cardigan had the buttons. Cardigan, with his damnable luck.

A damnable luck, Andy reflected, that was also his own. That miserable sod's not-worth-a-tuppence life had been spared, but so had Andy's.

THE PERFECT HAMBURGER

Carl R. Jennings

It was a rainy night when she walked into my restaurant. That anyone came in at all was weird—business was always slow when it was wet. From the first sight of her, I knew that things were about to go butter side down for me: for one, I had already let the help go for the night. For the other, this woman was a tall drink of soda, even when soaked to the bone in a trench coat, hair as black as syrup plastered to her head. She wasn't any bubbling seltzer water either; she had a cherry zing to her, with something harder backing it up.

I should have told her to turn on her heels and waltz right out of my establishment, but what can I say: I'm a sucker for a federal writ.

I was polishing my Formica countertop with a rag just for something to do when she took it out of her coat and slid it across to me. A quick scan was enough to know it was as genuine as a slab of grade A beef. Damn. My keister wasn't in the deep fryer yet, thought. This was a dish I'd both prepared and eaten plenty of times. Time to see how good a cook this fizzy dame was.

"Sorry, sweet taffy," I told her, "I'm all paid up on my licenses. Got the receipts to prove it."

"I'm sure you do, Mr. Hardart," she said, taking a stool at my bar. "You are Mr. Hardart, aren't you?"

"What it says above the door, isn't it?" I was giving her a hard time, but it didn't look like she'd be easily intimidated—she had a look behind her eye that was more steely than my spatula. She wasn't your average government jellybean counter. "Says 'Horn and Hardart' in some bright neon the last time I looked."

"And Mr. Horn is...?" She let it trail off.

"He got out of the game years ago," I said. "Left it to me. Look, is there something I can get you? Want me to fry up these papers for you? Can't guarantee they'll be any good but that's the only good they'll do for you."

She smirked at me.

"'Got out of the business,'" she said. "Sure."

I had to fight not to swallow. There was only two people that knew what really happened to Rick Horn, and one of them was currently gathering mold in one of the landfills outside the city. The other was getting smiled at in an unsettling way by this woman at my countertop. Still, you can never be totally sure about anything.

The restaurant business was a cutthroat game in this town, sometimes literally. If you wanted to see if you could be big in the pictures, you went to Hollywood; if you wanted to see if you could be the best at moving big money around, you went to New York or Chicago; but if you wanted to try and be the best when it came to slinging food, you came to this 'burg.

I leaned on my countertop and went in hard on the tough guy routine to test the waters.

"Lady, you come into my establishment throwing around accusations, you better have something to back it up."

She just went on smirking when she reached into her pocket and said, "I don't recall accusing anyone of anything."

She pulled out a leather wallet and flipped it open.

"But if I do, I have plenty to back it up."

Inside was a brass shield, the words *Federal Bureau of Investigation* stamped into it.

I looked it over like I was checking to see if it wasn't chocolate with gold foil, but I knew it wasn't at the first glance—Fed badges were as familiar to me as my walk-in freezer.

"So you're one of Hoover's boys," I said. "Sorry, I mean girls."

She put her badge back in her pocket and said, "Special Agent Cheerwhine. If that answers your question."

Touch of pride there, still. Must be fresh out of the wrapper.

"Sure," I said, taking my silver licorice case out of my apron pocket. I flipped it open and offered her one. She shook her head once, but I stuck one in the corner of my mouth before putting the case away and chewed. This was standard intimidation; I'd done it myself plenty of times. I knew it was meant to make the suspect squirm, trying to get them scared about what you really knew, when all you knew couldn't fill a fortune cookie. The trouble was, even though I was as cool as an ice cream bar on the outside, I really *was* squirming in the inside.

Cheerwhine leaned in on my countertop, making serious eye contact, and said, "There are some awfully interesting rumors swirling around about you, Mr. Hardart. Did you know that?"

I shrugged and said, "People love to talk. They can do it all they want, it's a free country, last time I checked."

She snorted and sat back on her stool, "You and I both know how true that is, Mr. Hardart. The one I'm talking about is that you make the best cheeseburger in this whole greasy city. That true?"

I chewed my licorice stick from one side of my mouth to the other.

"I make a burger that will make any other taste like the cook scraped dog crap off their shoe and put it on a bun," I told her. "It's all in the meat and how you cook it."

"Why don't you fix me one of those," she said. "A favor from one flatfoot to another." She gave a theatrical glance around. "Unless you're too slammed?"

"I think I can knock something up," I told her. "What kind of cheese do you want?"

"Cheddar," she said. "Extra sharp."

"Everything on it?"

"The whole nine yards. And a side of fries. You got milkshakes here?"

"We got all the ice cream flavors on God's earth. And a few He didn't come up with."

"Chocolate'll be good enough for me."

I made sure I keep a measured pace as I went back into the kitchen, gathered some ground beef, and smacked a beef patty into shape. Absent a chair, rope, and a hot lamp, she wasn't doing too bad. She didn't have enough information to take any action or she would have already, but she'd be happy to let me hang myself with a slip up. She was out of luck, though: I only served fillet sandwiches on Tuesdays.

"So you do well for yourself here?" she asked, peering as much as she could through the order window as I threw the patty on the grill. It sizzled and popped on the hot metal.

"Pays the bills," I told her, chewing up more of my licorice, until it was just a stub so it didn't get grease from the burger on it.

"That why you left the Bureau?" she asked. It was my turn to snort.

"I left the Bureau for a whole host of reasons," I said. "And 'left' is being generous. If you don't play the game, you don't get popular. And it's all about popularity. You'll learn if you stay long enough, sweet taffy."

I tossed a handful of french fries I cut that morning into the fryer basket and dropped it in the excruciatingly hot oil. I have an arrangement with a potato farmer out in the sticks; I got him out of a tight spot involving a rival's burned field a few years back, so I get first crack at the crop. The peanut oil, thick and amber colored as tree sap, boiled angrily as I turned my back on it and tended to the burger. It gave me the perfect time to think, and Cheerwhine seemed to be content to let me do it as her eyes traveled around the restaurant.

She would know that I knew she had bupkis where it came to Horn. Not only that, she knew that my licensing for the place would be of a high-quality forgery. If you stay in the law business long enough, you get a pretty hefty rolodex full of the best in the outlaw business. It would be more trouble than it's worth to suss my papers out.

Automatically, I flipped the patty over. Perfectly seared on that side, even when my mind's miles away. No matter what you do, it's all a matter of instinct. Back in my Bureau days, it told me when an empty dark alley was full of someone with a gun who was about to fill my immediate future with hot lead and a whole lot of paperwork. Now it told me when I had just made the best damn burger patty for a hundred miles.

So what would be the reason this fizzy flat foot would dredge all this up if there wasn't a damn thing she could do about it? Well, it would get her through the door. And it'd get me listening to her. But what did she want me to listen to? That was the million-dollar question.

When the other side of the patty was done, I chewed the last bit of licorice and flipped the burger off the grill and onto a waiting bottom bun I bake fresh daily, mayonnaise I order from the best maker in the world already spread. Next came a few leaves of crisp lettuce; a slice of cheddar so sharp it'd cut your tongue; a few fragrant rings of an onion; a slice from the juiciest tomatoes in the city; a drizzle of both ketchup and mustard made in-house; pickles I make based on Horn's old family process; then finally the top bun.

Just because Cheerwhine was in here to give me the ol' shake-and-bake doesn't mean that she wasn't getting my usual best.

I dumped the fries, salted them, and scooped them onto the plate. The chocolate milkshake came last, but that wasn't any mean task—any soda jerk with half a brain could make a decent milkshake so long as they had a mixer. Besides, milkshakes at burger joints aren't for eating, they're for dipping your fries into.

I slid the meal in front of Cheerwhine and she examined it with the detective's eye, making sure that what was there was there, and what wasn't supposed to be there wasn't. When she took a bite, she gave the familiar appreciative moan.

"Looks like some rumors were right," she said around a mouthful of burger. "You do knock up a mean burger. You even remembered the pickles."

"Gives it a zing that pulls the whole thing together," I told her. "It's an art form."

I took up to leaning on my countertop in front of her again and decided to come out with it. After all, stepping on marshmallows this whole conversation would take up a lot of time, and I wanted to close down the joint at a decent hour.

"Now why don't you go ahead and tell me why you're really here," I said. I caught her with my question as she had another enthusiastic mouthful of burger, like any good food service professional—it keeps people off balance. "You did the whole 'I might know something you don't want me to know' routine already and, I admit it was pretty good, but that stuff is like expensive cheese, and you just don't have the age to sell it to French people yet. I give you a few years and you'll be making mafiosos fill their shoes with their homemade lemonade.

"But if the Bureau wanted to give me trouble, they'd have sent someone like Sonny Brook or old Jim Gore, unless someone's popped their seals of freshness in some alley somewhere. I wouldn't be surprised; they'd have deserved it. No, you, specifically, are here for another reason. So..."

I took out my licorice case and stuck another one between my lips while she chewed on the ellipses. And chew she did: from the corner of my eye I could see that her expression hadn't changed that much, but her lips had thinned and her eyes were less bright as her brain scrambled to decide how to react. Rookie move, but we all make them.

"... tell me why you're here."

When she answered her voice was bitter—the genuine her coming through.

"I'm here because I look good in a cocktail dress," she spat. I couldn't help but let my brow furrow. I chewed my licorice from one side of my mouth to another and nodded for her to continue. She covered the return to detached professionalism, the kind that was friendly with a hidden knife somewhere, by wiping imaginary ketchup off her mouth.

"Have you heard about a man named Dr. Eric Von Vorderwald?" She took a scrawny, rain-soiled dossier out of her coat pocket, pushed her plate and milkshake aside, and laid it on my countertop, right between us.

I shrugged at her, a genuine one, and said, "Maybe seen the name on a newspaper or heard it on the radio. Don't really keep up with what all the foreigners in this country do."

"So you don't recognize him?" Cheerwhine asked. No fishing this time; it was an actual question. She opened the dossier and turned it so I could see a black and white immigration department photo of a middle-aged man with an absurd nose, round glasses perched on them, and the kind of moustache you could hang clothes on. There was something there, though. Something behind those glasses...

"Something familiar in the face, maybe," I said. "Can't really pin it down. So who's this sauerkraut supposed to be?"

"He's *supposed* to be some kind of hotshot gastronomist from in Europe. Been making a name for himself the past few years."

"I'm hearing a lot of uncertainty in there," I told her. I lifted the picture up to take a peek at the poop sheets on this Von Vorderwald. There wasn't much there beyond the ordinary government information. "Not like Hoover's Bureau to be so in the dark. I hear tell he even has a way to listen in on phone calls now."

Cheerwhine leaned back and a troubled cloud passed over her face.

"That's one of the reasons we're so interested in him," she said. "He's almost a nobody. He's a foreign national but the Germans hardly know him, and we haven't got anything much better. Mostly testimonies of how much of a genius he is from the food circles he used to run in. But it's like he just popped into existence one day, a full-grown man."

"So he plays his cards close to the chest," I shrugged, chewing more licorice. "Doesn't everybody nowadays?"

"We're thinking he's making some extra effort to obscure his past," Cheerwhine said. "We're not even sure if that's his real name."

I had to chuckle at that one. "Uncle Sam sure doesn't like when you keep something from him, especially when that something might involve tax revenue."

I raked my eyes over the picture again, rubbing my chin stubble. Cheerwhine popped a fry into her mouth and watched me. I let her, if she was so interested.

If this sauerkraut was trying this hard to throw off the G-men, it meant he had some money squirreled away somewhere. It also meant that he was set to make a fat wad of dough, or making it already.

"All right, so you got a German ghost," I told her. "Why come to me with it?"

"A few reasons," Cheerwhine said. "One is that your name seems to come up with every conversation when it comes to food in this town."

"Sweet taffy, I just sling grease anymore," I said. "I hung up my prod nose when I turned my badge and roscoe in."

That seemed to be a blow to her; some of that fizz she came in with flattened. I was probably the last on her list for getting information. I would have been the first, but who can tell what kind of connections ex-cops keep with the brass after they leave. They can make your career thirty-one flavors of hell if you rub them the wrong way. She didn't have to worry: those lard-filled uniforms could suck on my smoked sausage for all I care. When I quit, I quit hard.

"That was reason number one," I said. "What's number two?"

Cheerwhine took a deep breath and said her next in a rush.

"Von Vorderwald's having a party for food industry professionals tonight. Since you used to work for the Bureau—they tell me you weren't a half-bad agent—and since you're the best burger man in town, we wanted to ask you to go to it with me and get something on him."

My licorice stick dropped out of my mouth as I laughed right in her face. It was a good, long laugh; I hadn't had one like that for a while, a belly rumbler. At some point my eyes turned on the taps and wetted my cheeks. She winced.

"No way I'll lift a finger to help those stuffed suits," I told her, wiping my eyes. I took the ticket book and pencil out of my pocket and worked her up a bill. I didn't charge her for the milkshake since it had mostly melted by this time. I'm just a nice guy like that. I ripped the bill off and set it on my countertop.

"Anyway, since that's all you got," I said before I snatched her half-eaten food and soupy milkshake from in front of her. That was probably hint enough.

But before I could make it all the way into the kitchen, Cheerwhine dropped her bombshell. Two of them, actually.

"The Bureau is willing to reinstate your pension," she called to me. That caused me to stop; a federal pension was nothing to be sneezed at, and while my burger joint made a fair wad, more couldn't hurt. Especially more that I was owed already.

I turned back to her and asked, "You're serious?"

"Yes." I could tell that the word was forced out of her. She'd had some objection to that part.

"I didn't leave on a good note."

"A legendarily bad note, I'd say," she said, more bitterness there. I liked the touch of admiration in her voice. Maybe there was hope for this kid yet. "But everyone's willing to overlook that and start sending you monthly checks."

I brought the plate and milkshake back and put them down in front of her again, but I wasn't agreeing to anything yet. This was like a machine that washed dishes for you: too good to be true.

"That's the carrot," I said, crossing my arms and looking down at her, thinking I could "stern father" her into coughing the rest up. "You got a stick hidden somewhere?"

She did.

"The party is for an unveiling," Cheerwhine said. "Von Vorderwald is apparently introducing a new type of hamburger into the market. He's trying to drum up business with the shindig."

We had a battle of hard eyes for a few seconds. She wasn't bad.

I broke it when I said, "How the hell can you have a 'new type of hamburger'? It's two pieces of bread with ground meat and stuff between them. Otherwise it'd be something else."

"That's all we got," Cheerwhine said, spreading her hands in surrender. "We can't even get someone deep enough in his organization."

I told her, "Seems like a whopper to me."

"I know," she responded. "It sounds like it's impossible, but it's what's happening."

The look she gave me was pure pleading. I couldn't torture her anymore; even if the whole thing with this sauerkraut was a loaf of bologna, I could tell she was genuine about the pension. I figured I'd play the game, eat some expensive hors d'oeuvres, and watch some guy try to be the next Rockefeller without flopping.

"I want that pension reinstatement in writing."

Cheerwhine dug in her pocket and slammed a contract and pen down on my countertop. A once over was all I needed to tell it was the real McCoy. There was more government pulp on my cheap Formica countertop than there had ever been. Usually the most disgusting thing I'd have to get off there was vomit. I'd have preferred the vomit, for the most part. I scribbled my John Hancock on the line.

"When's this party anyway?" I asked.

"In an hour," Cheerwhine said, stowing the contract, dossier, and writ that got me talking in the first place deep in her pocket. She stood and made a professional beeline for the door, all that fizz back in place, talking over her shoulder. "Get your best on for this one. I've got a car waiting to take us."

She was already out my door before my wits caught up to what she said, leaving me with eyebrows that were trying to cross over my hairline.

* * *

There were only two times in my life I've ever been in any kind of monkey suit, and those were my dress uniform when I graduated Army basic and a tuxedo when I got married. Things didn't turn out well after those times; that's why I refused to ever get in a suit again.

I did have some nice cook threads for trade shows, so I pulled those on. I didn't hurry; there was no way I was going to let Cheerwhine think she was the one calling all the shots. Besides, it takes some effort to close down a restaurant by yourself, though I did skip a few things. Age must be making me soft.

Streetlights aren't a priority in my part of town, so when my neon sign was off, it was like trying to see through burnt custard. What didn't help was that the rain was as bad as it sounded, and I stared into what was practically a vertical river. Luckily, Cheerwhine's driver switched on some damn bright headlights for me, and I waded through the rain.

The car Cheerwhine hired idled at the curb. It was nice, a black and chrome number with tinted windows. It stuck out like a strawberry in a pig's trough in this neighborhood. She must have had some style hidden somewhere.

I climbed in the back and, as soon as I closed the door, the car tore off.

"We're probably not going to be there on time," Cheerwhine huffed. She had shrugged out of her trench coat. I gave her a once over.

"The brass and I agree on one thing, at least," I told her. "You do clean up."

Cheerwhine only stared out of the window. It seemed like her motivation to talk to me had been stored in her coat. Rain beat the car like a trainee dough maker. It looked like it was time to have *that* talk.

"All right, kid, look," I told her. "I don't want to be here, and you don't either by the looks of it. That's government work in a nutshell. But if we get in there, and the souffle deflates, as it were, then I need to know you've got me covered. Just like I'll have you covered."

She jerked her head towards me and said, "What do you mean? Von Vorderwald looks like he's on his last legs. It's not like he's going to cause us trouble. Or even know who we are."

The car took a corner and we were back in streetlight territory. The pale orange glow lit up Cheerwhine's face. I couldn't help but snort. Was I ever that young? Was anyone?

"You're as green as spinach so I'm going to give you some free advice," I said. "Everyone's dangerous. Especially the ones that don't look it. Von Germanguy might not pull the trigger himself, but he wouldn't need to. He's money, clear as day. That buys a lot of muscle happy to pull triggers, even on nosey federal agents."

"You're not a federal agent anymore," Cheerwhine said. "Just... consulting me."

It clicked.

"Oh, so your problem's with me? Is that it?"

Cheerwhine crossed her arms and focused on the underwater scene outside.

"That's not it," she lied. It was a bad lie. Another thing she'll need to work on.

"No, no, I get it," I said. I took out my licorice case and clamped down on one.

"I was where you're at: full of baking soda and vinegar. I'm guessing you got told 'no' all your life—more so than me, probably—so you're even more dead set on making a name for yourself. You want to win against thems who told you you can't. But you desperately try to justify that with a sense of, well, justice; you tie your ego into upholding the law.

"I used to think that there was a hard line between right and wrong, good and bad, too. Then I got smacked in the head a few times and I realized that integrity will get you killed. Or someone else. You play by the rules, only to realize you're the only one doing it. The rules are for the gullible, the stupid, and the scared. Victims, in other words. My arrest and conviction record was stellar. You think I got that by acting like a choir boy?"

"Why are you telling me this now?" Cheerwhine said to the car window.

"Because there's a lot of money set to change hands, from what you told me about tonight," I explained. "Rich people trying to get richer. There's no more dangerous animal on the planet. You might have to do something tonight you don't think you should to get what you need. If you don't want to then stick around the party and enjoy it, show off that cocktail dress of yours. I'm not asking you to assassinate the President, but things might get dirty. I'm not expecting you to shake off your new fuzziness all in one night; I'll do the dirtiest stuff if it gets to that. I'm just asking you to give me your support. And not get in my way."

Cheerwhine kept staring out of the window, more hugging herself than crossing her arms. I didn't push her anymore. I knew I'd shaken her nice, warm, comfortable world, but someone needed to. Her bosses had tossed her into the snake pit tonight, maybe hoping they'd put an uppity rookie in her place. Or get rid of her.

Trouble with that plan was, she had me. And foul was on the menu tonight.

* * *

Von Vorderwald's big unveiling party was at one hell of a swanky mansion. His, probably. I didn't like him already. I chewed up the rest of my licorice stick just in case the brand was too cheap for the venue.

Those who were trying to make a statement by being fashionably late were still trickling in. The car dropped us off up front, Cheerwhine's coat over her shoulders, and drove off to do whatever it is drivers do while they're waiting for their rich employers to do whatever it was they did.

The place must have had more steps up to the front door than it did bricks. Once we did get there, panting, the muscle on the door checked us out. They were definitely muscle, no doubt about that; there's something about ill-fitting, cheap black suits that scream *I'll smash your face in for the right price.*

Cheerwhine handed one of the two lugs our invites. He scrutinized them hard, but that might have been because reading wasn't his strong suit. He scrutinized me even harder because, no matter how much you try to scrub it up or scrub it out, a cop is about as undisguisable as hired muscle.

It was Cheerwhine that got us through, because after he gave her a lecherous once-over he handed the invites back and waved us in. I'd have to talk with her sometime about what she must have thought was a saucy grin, but whatever works,

works.

The foyer emptied out into an enormous ballroom of gold and white marble. Cheerwhine waved away the coat check girl that approached. It was filled wall-to-wall with tuxedoed influential businessmen and industrialists—some I recognized, most I didn't—and their flashy dates. Waiters in clean aprons and uniforms moved about the guests with trays of champagne flutes. Young women in attractive maid outfits scurried about too with platters of licorice, peppermint sticks, and chewing gum.

"Do you see Von Vorderwald?" Cheerwhine asked, eyes searching.

"No," I said, "But with someone as goofy looking as him, I doubt he'll be hard to miss."

Hard to miss he wasn't, as he appeared on the balcony overlooking the ballroom. He was as aged as his picture showed him and twice as ridiculous looking, but he moved like a much younger and spry man. He had a fire in him; that much could be seen from the hungry glint in his eyes. Eyes that, for some reason, got something in my brain going that I still couldn't pin down.

He tapped on his crystal glass of champagne. The sharp noise cut through all the conversation, and those that weren't already looking up at him were now.

"Velcome to hugh, my friends!" he called out. His voice was an old man's but as clear, strong, and confident as a brass bell. And all wrong.

"I am pleased to see all uf hugh here for zee unwailing uf my humble new product!"

The crowd clapped politely. Von Vorderwald held his hand up for silence. He got it. There would be no question about that—this man was a born leader.

"In mine young life, my family did herd cattle for beef. They vere as tasty as any for hundreds uf miles around. The trouble vas zat zere vas no consistency from steak to steak. I half vanted to create a food zat could be uniform from one batch to zee other. Vith zat, I present to hugh…"

He made a gesture with his white gloved hand to the left side of the room. I looked over and saw a silk cloth covered table I hadn't noticed before. Four liveried servants, one at each corner, whipped the cloth off with dramatic flash.

"Hombergairs!" Von Vorderwald said with a carnival barker's flair.

Beneath it was a long table, covered with hamburgers. Gleaming silver serving plate after gleaming silver serving plate of them, stacked high in neat pyramids. They were as uniform as it was possible to get, right down to the sesame seeds on the buns. They were visually appealing, but just in the way that glossy photos of food are appealing to look at. At a glance, I could tell that they'd be mediocre tasting at best, just like the food in those ads typically weren't real food.

The crowd, on the other hand, oohed and ahhed in the appreciative way that only stupid people do.

"Impressive, yes?" Von Vorderwald called out, drawing attention back to him. "I half taken zee uncertainty out uf food. Each hombergair vill taste exactly zee same as zee last, no matter vhere hugh are in zee country."

Von Vorderwald allowed the murmur to pass through the crowd with expert timing.

"How ees zis achieved, hugh ask?" Von Vorderwald continued. "By zee fact zat zere is no meat vizin any uf dese hombergairs."

The murmur was even louder at this. It too was allowed to pass.

"I een-wite hugh to try zee hombergair for yourselfs," Von Vorderwald waved his hand at the table, and there was no waiting: the rich and powerful set to it like pigs at feed time, with complaining that sounded a lot like sows, too.

"That's impressive," Cheerwhine leaned over and whispered to me. "I can't believe it."

"I don't believe it," I said, my eyes not leaving Von Vorderwald's face. He was too satisfied at the response for my comfort. And still too familiar. "I don't believe it or him."

"What do you mean?" Cheerwhine asked.

"I was in the war," I told her, "when we went over to knock some sense into Kaiser Wilhelm. I know what Germans trying to speak English sound like, and that's not it. It's like he's out of a propaganda cartoon you'd read in the papers."

I looked back at the table, or what I could see of it around the milling tuxedos and dresses. All those hamburgers were just so neat and uniform. All the same, lined up in a row...

That something from earlier kicked around in my head even harder, trying to get my attention. I looked back up at Von Vorderwald just as he turned and went into a room off the balcony, closing the door behind him. With those eyes in a face becoming increasingly familiar...

It hit me like a ton of low-grade lard. I knew where I had seen Von Vorderwald before; I knew only one person who would come up with a cockamamie scheme like this.

"Come on," I grabbed Cheerwhine by the arm and dragged her along behind me. I would have left her there, but she was the one with a badge. That made it official. She made an unhappy noise but came along just the same.

I practically ran to the bar on the right side of the room which, considering the crowd around the table, was a lot easier to get to than it otherwise would have been.

"Barkeep," I barked. A thin man with a thin moustache came over.

"Yes, sir?" he condescended at me.

"You make White Russians?"

"Of course, sir, would you like—"

"Heavy cream?"

"The best. Perhaps you—"

"Give it to me."

The barkeep raised an eyebrow at me.

"The cream," I almost shouted at him. "Give me the bottle of cream, dammit."

He reached down and came up with a clear glass bottle of heavy cream, so chilled that ice had formed on it.

Before the stuffed shirt behind the bar could protest, I snatched it and dashed off, still dragging Cheerwhine.

"Where are we going?" Cheerwhine asked, still not happy.

"We're getting to the bottom of this," I called back to her. We took the stairs to the balcony at as much of a run that one person pulling another one along could. We reached the door that Von Vorderwald disappeared behind just as a line of serious faced and tuxedoed men were coming out of it.

They had a stack of papers each, tucked beneath an arm. In retrospect, I should have stopped them, but an old cop is like a terrier: when they find something to chase after they don't have eyes for anything else.

We stopped next to the door and Cheerwhine wrenched her arm out of my hand.

"Are you going to fill me in on what's happening?" she demanded.

"I know who Von Vorderwald is," I told her. "And it's not Von Vorderwald."

She gave me an impatient *tell me more* gesture.

"You won't believe me if I just told you, kid," I said. Nor would she want me to do what I needed to do, but we were on the sizzling edge where the patty hits the grill, and there was no time for hesitation. "Just get your badge and your roscoe out and get me through this door. You've got the authority and I'm telling you you've got probable cause."

Cheerwhine hesitated but, to her credit, for only a second. From one coat pocket she took her badge wallet and the other she took a .38 Special snubnose revolver. She took the lead, stepping in front of me, as professional as any I'd seen. She turned the door handle with the hand holding the badge wallet, pushed it open, snubby up, and stepped through. I followed right on her tail.

"Von Vorderwald" was facing away, leaning over his desk.

"Federal agent, turn around!" Cheerwhine barked. I was impressed. "Keep your hands where I can see them!"

"Von Vorderwald" turned, his hands out at his sides. He looked genuinely confused, until he saw me. His expression was enough to tell me my suspicion was right.

"Hardart!" he shouted, but it wasn't in that hokey German accent.

He made a move to run around his desk, but I darted forward and grabbed him around the throat. I popped the lid off the heavy cream bottle with my thumb and forced the opening into his mouth. I hardly needed to do this anymore to identify him, but I wanted this matter settled this minute, and in a way that could give Cheerwhine and me plausible deniability.

Cream filled his mouth and poured all over his face and down his front. He choked and sputtered but I kept at it until the bottle was empty. I let go and he fell back against his desk. His head lolled back and rested against the top so he was looking up. He kept sputtering and choking.

"What the hell are you doing?" Cheerwhine demanded, on the verge of panic. To her credit, she kept her snubby trained on "Von Vonderwald".

"Like I said, that's not Von Vonderwald," I told her. I wiped the heavy cream bottle down with my cook's smock, taking my fingerprints off, and I set it on his desk, near the chair so it would look like it was close at hand. "I doubt Von Vonderwald ever existed. If so, he probably isn't deathly allergic to milk. But you want to know who is?"

I stepped forward and ripped off the ridiculous false nose and moustache. The glasses went next. Cream splattered me and the wall. Beneath was still an old man but, without the glasses, his deep sunken and shrewd eyes made him appear like an alien out of a comic book, trying to look human.

"Henry Ford," I spat.

"Henry Ford?" Cheerwhine said, clearly confused. "You mean the guy that came up with the assembly line and the Model T?"

"The very same," I said, glaring down at the old man struggling to breathe. Cream trickled down the corners of his mouth. "I tangled with him while I was still at the Bureau. It was me, old Joe Gore, Hiram Walker, and John Medley. The Bureau knew he was up to something screwy and we all spent the better part of a year putting a case together on him. We got tipped off when he got a big wad of investment money from the Kaiser, just before the Zimmerman Telegram sent American-German relations down the toilet.

"We found out he had some crazy scheme to monopolize restaurants all across the country. Fast food, he called it. He'd make assembly line food at damn cheap prices and knock anyone else out of the market. We wouldn't have bothered usually, just let him crash and burn, but this is Ford we're talking about. If anyone can get assembly line food working, it's him."

I gave Cheerwhine some time to chew this over. I took out my licorice case and snapped a large piece off, glaring down at Ford. He wasn't in any state to groan.

"I don't remember reading anything about that in the news," Cheerwhine said.

"You wouldn't, would you?" I said, not taking my eyes off Ford. I wasn't until I was sure he'd kicked the bucket. "You think Uncle Sam is going to let any story run about the man who helped make modern America being a loony mogul?"

"What was in it for the Kaiser?"

"A return on investment. Imagine what money would come out of this kind of thing? It'd keep his war effort going all on its own, and we'd foot the bill."

I threw the licorice away. I couldn't taste it anyway.

"The case we had was iron clad," I went on. "Well, we showed up at his offices one night, but he must have had a mole in the Bureau because his goons were waiting. One of them got Walker, but once the local flatfoots arrived to back us up, they knew it was all over. It was all for nothing though; this maniac had already skipped town and disappeared. If we had just gone after him right on our hunch, he would have panicked and shown his hand. But we were all so young. We still wanted to do it the *right* way.

"I wanted to go after him, but I was in R.O.T.C. and got my dumb ass deployed a month later for the trenches."

I knelt so I was eye to eye with him and slapped him to get his attention.

"But now you turn up like a bad piece of penne, don't you?" I said. "Can you still hear me?"

Ford's eyes creaked open and he focused on me.

"Yes," he sputtered, cream and spit leaking from his mouth. "I can hear you."

"What are you up to now?" I demanded.

"You saw the ballroom," he said, his voice weak. "I thought it was clear."

"Doesn't look exactly like what you were up to before."

"I couldn't hold all of the assets," Ford said. "That would attract too much attention, you know that. But if I were to change my business model, and my product, I could finally introduce fast food into the country."

"Tell me what you mean, you fruit loopy bastard."

"Franchises!" he said. The life that was left in his eyes gleamed. "Each investor holding their own fast food restaurant, but to my exacting assembly standards. And even more, the patties themselves can be made in a factory, all exactly the same, and shipped out. Each restaurant will be exactly the same as any other, everywhere."

"That's bullshit," I spat the words at him.

"What about people wanting local flavors?" Cheerwhine prompted. But Ford stared me straight in the eye when he responded. He should have been ridiculous, covered in cream and struggling to breathe, but the conviction he had chilled me to the core.

"You still don't understand what you're dealing with, do you?" he said. "The perfect hamburger. Its distribution perfection is matched only by its inoffensive blandness."

"You're proud of yourself," I growled. "Aren't you?"

"I admire the purity of it," he shot back. "Highly marketable, with wide appeal... unclouded by any kind of variation."

I stood and glared down at him. Ford coughed more cream up. It was foamy and bloody this time.

"Last word," he said, craning to look up at me.

"What?"

"I can't lie to you about your chances of stopping me this time, but... you have my sympathies."

He smiled, the smug bastard, then slumped over, dead.

Cheerwhine lowered her snubby and looked at me, mouth slack.

"He can't be serious," she asked me. "Can he?"

I walked like a zombie out of the office and looked over the balcony. Cheerwhine followed suit.

"Looks like I'm going to need that pension," I tell Cheerwhine.

She came back with, "Looks like we're going to need you out of retirement."

Down below, the line of men that had left the office before we arrived were handing out what looked like contracts to the guests. They had just eaten, but all of them looked ravenous, and it wasn't for food. They eyed one another, knowing that they were all about to be in competition, selling the exact same thing. It was going to get messy. The ones that were still at the table, just having gotten their hamburger, all had the same expression: *Eh, it's not bad. Not great, but not bad either. I could sell this.*

THE FORTUNETELLER

Andrew McCormick

When Chan finally emerged from within the Salvation Army dressing room, the alien sunlight streaming through the picture window was so bright, he needed to blink several times a second before his inner eyelids adjusted.

Chan had needed to put on Human attire, but his choices had been severely limited, due to his frame-choice of being tall and long-limbed. He felt very uneasy. The faded grey woolen suit itched, and the rough fabric chafed against his new genitals. Seven lesser time-units before, an elderly female Human clerk had regarded him with eyes narrowed with suspicion. Chan wasn't sure if she disapproved of his size, his sudden appearance, or his original purple travel garment. When he requested clothes, she had pointed, with curt gestures and grunts, to weather-worn suits on a narrow wire rack.

He had changed attire behind a flimsy plastic curtain, the cubicle no bigger than his Leap compartment. Once dressed, he twisted valves on his travel garment so it would crumble into dusty bits. The clerk's thin grey eyebrows rose high up on her wrinkled forehead at the amount of the paper currency he gave her. When he asked for shoes, she quickly found black shoes from a nearby counter. The shoes fit well, so he gave her another bill. She gave him a pair of black socks for free. As he left, she asked God to bless him, which Chan thought very odd.

On the street, people fanned themselves with newssheets. They grinned lazily as they drank liquids from glass bottles wrapped in brown paper. He stopped to watch a young man with an uneven beard converse loudly with no one in the immediate vicinity. An undesirable scent of unwashed clothing surrounded him. Chan assumed that the young man was conversing with his ancestors. He felt envy. His people were unable to see spirits like the people could here.

He continued to his destination. According to directions imprinted into his consciousness, Chan walked two city blocks north and then turned right on Juniper Avenue. Three blocks further, he turned left on Twenty-Third Street. The weary storefront looked squeezed between a non-English sweet-food bakery and a windowless tavern. On the storefront's glass door, written in three languages, carried the message, MADAME ESMERALDA. FORTUNES TOLD. FUTURES REVEALED. Below the lettering, a caricature of a turbaned Human female waved her arms over a solid white crystal ball.

A sudden tinkling noise startled him as he opened the dingy door. He immediately dropped into alert/submission posture. People inside seated on folding chairs turned and regarded him with uncurious stares.

A young female, with blue-streaked blonde hair, sat behind a plywood desk. She asked him if he was okay.

He straightened up. "That sound," he said. "That was an alarm of some kind?" "Sound?"

He looked back toward the door and noticed a tiny bell, mounted on the wall in such a way as to make a noise whenever the door opened. He smiled. He thought that was quite clever.

"You got an appointment?" the girl asked.

"I do not. I would like to see Madame Esmeralda, as soon as she is available."

"Oh." She turned around on the desk a clipboard with several pieces of paper attached to it. She pushed it over to him. "Without an appointment, it gonna take a while."

"I will wait."

She handed him a ballpoint pen. Printed on the pen was the faded address of a store that sold replacement parts for gasoline-propelled machines.

"Sign here, please." Awkwardly, he gripped the pen with tapered fingers and wrote down his prearranged name. In the room, he sniffed human scents, some welcome, some not so.

The girl turned the clipboard around to face her. "Okay, Mister, ah, Chan, is it?" She looked up at him. "Funny, you no look no Japanese." He fidgeted in a manner she wouldn't recognize as discomfort. "Take a seat. I'll call you when it's your turn."

Chan found a vacant unpadded folding chair and sat down. In front of him, several magazines were scattered on the top of a low table. Chan glanced at the covers. He wondered who Lady Gaga was. From the amount of cover space, and the elaborate clothing she wore, he concluded that she must be some high-ranking member of royalty.

A young male child, clad only in a white cloth around its middle section, waddled over to him. His pudgy brown arms were upraised for balance like an Earth chimpanzee. He stopped in mid-squeal and looked at Chan. A very confused look came over his face. Chan smiled as best he could. The baby gaped, then began to wail. Across from him, a female not much older than the receptionist put down her magazine and rushed over.

"He only cries like that when he's wet," she said aloud to the room by way of apology. Chan remained seated in his chair, hands folded in his lap. Picking the baby up, the female rubbed her hand over the bottom of the white cloth and frowned with confusion. She carried the baby back to her chair. The toddler regarded Chan over his mother's shoulder with puddle eyes.

The heat became oppressive to those waiting inside the tiny room. People stirred the stagnant air with their hands. Chan remembered to sweat.

His turn came after ninety-seven minor time-units. During that time, Chan had read three *People,* two *National Enquirers* and one *Time.* He found each one to be both amusing and bizarre.

The receptionist called, "Mister Chan?" Several heads turned to him as he rose. His shoes creaked but his knees didn't. Chan felt a little uncomfortable. He had found no one named "Chan" with Negroid features in any of the magazines. He wondered now if that was significant.

Following the receptionist, he walked down a narrow hallway, illuminated by a single light bulb. The hallway ended at a door. Two other doors flanked it. The receptionist opened the door on the right and told Chan to go in, to sit down, and to wait. He took a seat on a yellow-and-black plush chair. The room was pleasurably dim.

He waited nine full time-units before Madame Esmeralda entered. He rose. Shorter than he would have imagined, her height barely reached the level of his hearts.

"Sorry to keep you waiting, Mister... Chan, is it?" She sounded skeptical. He remembered to nod, then sat down after she did.

Madame Esmeralda spread out her flowing multi-colored garb before settling herself in her padded chair. Her belt-less outfit covered her ample frame right down to her ankles. The crimsons, yellows, and greens in her apparel hurt his eyes. Her scarf was wrapped so tight around her head, he believed her to be hairless. No shoes were on her feet, he noted. Her feet had no calluses.

"You okay now?" She wriggled slightly in her chair, trying to stifle a yawn.

"Yes."

"That's good. Now. How can I help you?"

"I'd like to know about the immediate future." Chan sat absolutely still. He did not want her divining anything from him that would be too revealing. He knew well the awkward penalties.

"The future," she repeated. She closed her eyes.

"You need to know an outcome," she said within two minor time-units. "It concerns a new enterprise, a fresh undertaking." She frowned. "But it's a secret, a big secret. Yet the people that you're acquainted with know all about it. Odd." She tilted her head slightly, eyes opening. "Is that correct?"

He smiled a smile that didn't mean what she thought it meant. "Yes. I need to know how the undertaking develops." Madame Esmeralda grunted at that. In consent or confusion, he wasn't sure. She closed her eyes once more.

Above her head hung a framed picture of a prophet with neatly-trimmed facial hair, born two Human millennia ago. Even in this stylized portrait he easily saw that the shimmering light around his head suggested a time-dilation shift phase. The prophet held an expression of serene content. With only slight variations, every portrait of this prophet seemed to carry the same expression. Chan wondered why he had never seen a picture of this person laughing.

"Now, then," Madame Esmeralda said at last. "You're connected with someone. Are you married?" She opened one eye. He didn't dare move. She closed it again.

"Married. But you have no ring. Yet I feel it's a strong, strong commitment. You are not with her now. And you will not be with her for some time to come." He blinked at that. "But that is not a problem or even a great worry for you. Or her. You are fine with that. Right?"

"Yes." He shuddered minutely. Her gestation period would continue for another Sequence or two. He would no more want to be next to her than he would be next to a fangbear. "Being apart from her is not a problem."

"Good. I can feel that." She sighed. She didn't say anything for several more minor-moments. Chan looked down at his clasped hands. He noticed he had seven freckles on his right wrist shaped like a familiar bird.

"You will experience something good," she said. "A promotion of some sorts, very welcome. You need not worry. Very soon, within a few days." Her eyes opened.

Chan fidgeted with delight in his chair.

"Days..." Her voice trailed off. Outside, a telephone rang. It cut off in the middle of the third ring. She closed her eyes again.

Too late, Chan realized he had moved in the non-prescribed manner.

"I see water. A sea, the ocean? Much water. Much. Unusual. Very strange."

The fortuneteller tucked her legs under her chair and crossed her arms.

"The water's a color of pink. No, redder than that. Scarlet? And an odd light is over the water. The sky is green, maybe yellow. How is that... I've never..."

That was unfortunate. "What about my promotion?" he said, rather hurriedly.

She looked like her head hurt. "I'm sorry. What?"

"My promotion," Chan repeated, impatient. "You mentioned a promotion. Is it good fortune?"

"Yes, yes, good fortune, perhaps great fortune." She still frowned. "That scene, it seemed so... give me a moment, please." With eyes still closed, her left hand reached into a pocket in her dress and she started to bring out a package of what he recognized to be tobacco products. Just as quickly, she put the package back. Chan sighed with relief.

"Let me start once more." She clenched her fists. Chan could see that she was disturbed about the image of the Second Sea, but still felt determined to complete her task. That was something very admirable about these people.

"Ah. The promotion. It involves a kind of... crown on your head, is it? No, it's not a crown, exactly, but something positive, a good thing, something you want."

"A life-support rectifier, second gradations."

"What? What did you say?"

"Nothing, it's not important." Although it was. He felt himself tingling in his inner extremities.

"Oh." Even with her eyes closed, he could sense her stare. "Not much more. Except, now, I can *feel* colors around you. Very intense colors. I noticed your aura when I first saw you, but now I've had time to... such bright colors. In a few days, I feel that they'll be much brighter." She wrapped her arms tighter around her chest. "Very odd. I sense danger. Danger. But not to you."

She was good. Very good. They had been correct about her. Pity.

"What is your fee requirement?"

That opened her eyes. "What?" She sounded drained of energy. "That's it? That's all you want?" She looked at her watch. "Your session still has several minutes left. I can tell you more." Her arms uncrossed themselves and her toes touched the uncarpeted floor. "Much more."

"No, I have heard enough."

"You don't want to know about the danger? I have to charge you for the full session, anyway, you know?"

"No, we must stop here."

"Oh, well, then," she said, sounding relieved. "My standard fee, ah, offering is twenty dollars."

He gave her a fistful of currency; all that he had left in his pocket. "Will this do?"

"What? Why, it's too much. You shouldn't." Chan remembered to shrug.

She looked down at the currency, a smile of wonder tugging at her lips. "Why, thank you. God bless you."

He frowned, still puzzled at that expression. "You deserve it. You have done us great services in the past."

"Us? Who is that? What service?"

Chan turned away from her and put his hand on the doorknob. It took him only a fraction of a minor time-unit to understand the locking mechanism.

"You were... recommended to me."

"I was?" Her tonal inflections indicated pride. His back still to her, his left hand grasped his right hand and began rotating his right wrist around its axis slowly.

"Where I come from," Chan said. "We never attempt anything important without much consultation and verification. But we are a cautious people. Very cautious. Perhaps you might refer to it as a... quirk."

"'Quirk', you say? What, you mean like praying?"

"Yes, I suppose it's like praying." He tugged at his wrist. "Only we aren't as... in tune with the 'beyond-nature,' as your people are." One last pull bloodlessly freed the hand from his arm. His body blocked her from seeing his efforts. He put the lifeless hand inside his coat pocket. Within the stump was a compact gray rod.

"What kinda praying?" She sounded suspicious. "You're not Unitarian, are you?"

"No. I am not," he replied. "We have no houses of worship. We are aware of the Infinite but are unable to contact it. It has been a terrible frustration for a long time."

"Well. Thank you, Mister Chan." The fortuneteller sounded nervous, anxious. Probably thinking about the foretold danger. She really was good.

He extracted the rod carefully with his left thumb and forefinger.

"We well know that the future exists, as a back-and-forth river, and we know that events have occurred and will continue to occur," Chan said over his shoulder. "I can put it no more simply than that. We always have known this, always, but we are unable, mentally, scientifically, morally, to tap into this, this river. What a glory it was when we discovered your people."

The grey rod felt light in his other hand. "Here, all of you possess the ability to predict the future, but very few trust yourselves to use it. We learned that if we open ourselves to you, especially those of you who are aware of your gift, many answers flow to us. It is not an easy thing to arrange, but the rewards are great. Of course, you must not be made aware of our presence. It alters your ability."

"I see. Well, thank you again." She didn't say *Come again.* Chan heard her get up from her chair and her footsteps approached the door.

He turned. "You're welcome." She gasped at his stump. Chan raised the rod and pressed a button. Only his retinas saw the ultraviolet rays which closed down her aorta.

"I revealed too much. I am sorry." Those were the last words that she heard.

* * *

A gentle rapping and a turning of the locked doorknob came from the other side of the door just as Chan managed to secure his hand back in place.

"Madame Esmeralda?" The voice of the young female receptionist sounded both annoyed and puzzled. "You okay in there? Your next client, she in Room Two."

Chan stepped out of the room, taking care to shield the view of the body from the receptionist. "She is not here," he said. "She left the room some time ago." He added, "She said she needed tobacco products."

"Oh." The girl grimaced an expression of irritation. "Her doctor, he gonna be pissed." She turned to the door on the opposite side of the hallway. He walked away. He heard her tapping on the door, saying, "Madame Esmeralda? You in there?" Chan passed through the crowded reception area, opened the street door and left. He never looked back as he walked swiftly back to the retrieval point.

He would endure much inquiry when he returned. Madame Esmeralda was not aware of her vast following beyond the Earth. He contorted his face. He hated inquiries.

As he began to phase, he thought about his upcoming promotion. He smiled and started tingling in his inner extremities.

BY BREAD ALONE

Christine Morgan

"If this goes all *Wicker Man* on us," Dale said, frowning through the windshield, "I'm blaming you."

Vickie, in the passenger seat with her phone in one hand and a cluster of folding maps in the other, nodded absently. "Look at this. This is ridiculous. GPS has got nothing, one map shows a road the other map says it's a river..."

"Are we lost?" asked Emma, drumming her heels on the lower edge of the booster she insisted she was too much a big girl now to have to use.

"We're not *lost*," Dale and Vickie replied in practiced parental unison.

Then Dale went and ruined it by adding, "We're just taking the scenic r—"

At that, all the kids—even earbudded and sunglassed Lauren, who'd been diligently ignoring everyone since the last rest stop—groaned. They had their own practiced unison. Three-part harmony.

Under other circumstances, Vickie might have joined in; Dale's "scenic routes" had long since become a family eyeroller of a bad joke. Since this particular adventure was her doing, though, she kept it to herself. Hadn't been Dale's idea to drag them way the hell out here on what would probably turn out to be a wild goose chase.

"Are there still roads?" Jacob, middle child in every sense of the word, strained the limit of his shoulder belt leaning forward to try and see ahead. "Remember that time it was regular road, then it was gravel, then it was dirt, and then it was just gone, and we couldn't turn around and Daddy had to drive backwards for ninety-hundred miles and it took forever? But I saw Bigfoot."

"Oh, you did not," muttered Lauren, slouching deeper into her window corner.

"I did! He looked like Chewbacca!"

"There's road," Dale said. "The road is just fine. Has power lines alongside and everything, see?"

Vickie glanced from her baffling bouquet of folded maps at a row of sagging wires strung between tarred and tilted poles, confidence not exactly bolstered. Still, it was *some* sort of sign of civilization, anyway. An improvement on the time Jacob was talking about, when Dale's certainty they'd found a shortcut led instead to her wondering how long they could survive on car snacks and juice boxes.

But sure, snark at *her*... *Wicker Man*, ha, ha, very funny. Crazy pagan cultists, what else you got? Inbred cannibal hillbillies? How about a whole pack of Bigfoots—or would it be Bigfeet?

Dale kept on talking, brash and forced-jovial, reassuring the kids he'd only been joking. They'd be there soon. Had to come out somewhere, after all, didn't they? Think of it as an adventure!

Of course, he'd said much the same before the infamous several-miles-in-reverse episode...

She watched more sparsely forested wilderness roll by, looking wildfire-hazard dry in the dusty August heat. One careless cigarette butt, and *whoosh*, disco inferno, here we go again. What patches of shade there were seemed teeming with gnat-clouds, the sight alone making her itch.

Why out here? What was out here, anyway? Shouldn't it be in flat, open country? All fields and farmland? Wouldn't that make more sense? Midwest-like, amber waves of grain. Cornfields—though then Dale would have snarked about that Stephen King story instead. Wheat stalks tall and golden and top-heavy, bringing in the sheaves. Silos poking like weird blunt-nosed rocketships. Barns, some tidy and red, some in picturesquely weathered disrepair.

Instead, they had this steepening backwoods tangle of hills and hollows, more suitable to making meth or moonshine than hosting a summer farmer's market and bread festival. The last sign of anything approaching human habitation they'd seen had been a rundown, rusted trailer surrounded by a weedy dirt patch, which was dotted with piles of either pony droppings or the world's biggest dog turds.

At least they hadn't run across a decrepit gas station-slash-general store where some grizzled toothless old man would try to warn them off...

Despite a sweltering discomfort the air conditioner on full blast still couldn't quite dispel, Vickie shivered a little. Maybe Dale would be right to blame her if it went all *Wicker Man* on them. Fair enough.

How could she have known, though? The scant amount of information she had been able to turn up in her research suggested it *was* a legit event. In a legit town. A small one, perhaps. Quaint, and out of the way. Not on her GPS, or maps, but so what? Neither were the Amish, were they? If it was that kind of quaint, more homespun rustic than touristy, okay, no big deal. Plenty of similar places did harvest fairs, Halloween stuff, pumpkin patches, corn mazes, and haunted hayrides without it being a crazy pagan cult thing or inbred cannibal hillbilly thing. Maybe they liked their privacy. Didn't want throngs of tourists stomping around. Maybe they *were* Amish; would explain the lack of an online presence.

Or, maybe it really *was* a wild goose chase, and she'd gotten her hopes up over nothing.

Damn it, Mom, she thought.

"So, did Nana Ruth just flip her lid?" Because of *course* Lauren's uncanny teen-sense would prompt her to speak up right then, as if she'd read Vickie's mind. "Is she, like, senile? Alzheimer's or whatevs?"

"Hey, don't talk about your grandmother that way," Dale chided.

"I was only *asking*, gol!" Wasting, no doubt, a perfectly honed eyeroll behind the dark lenses.

"Nana ran away from home," Emma said.

"Nuh-uh, she got kidnapped," said Jacob. "'Ducted by aliens maybe."

"Oh, come on, now." Vickie twisted around to look at them. "Nana wasn't kidnapped, not by aliens or anybody else. She didn't run away from home. And she did not 'flip her lid'."

Lauren muttered something inaudible and crossed her arms. If she slouched any further, she'd slither a boneless Hot Topic puddle into the footwell.

"Then where'd she go?" Emma asked, all head-tilted innocence.

Dale shot Vickie a sidelong, eyebrow-raised look.

"Well, sweetie, that's... why we're taking this little road trip," Vickie said. "To try and find out."

Miraculously, either the answer sufficed or they all just figured it wasn't worth pursuing further. Lauren tapped away at her own phone, probably updating her friends and followers on another tedious family vacation to nowhere. Jacob kept fidgeting, trying to see something out the windows—Bigfoot, aliens, who knew—and only getting the same rolling view of what was properly called 'second-growth' but Vickie's grandfather would've called 'shitwood.' Emma had a toy unicorn in one hand and a toy dinosaur in the other; they were either dancing or about to mix it up in a deathmatch. Dale concentrated on his driving, though Vickie was sure he'd have a few remarks later on the subject of his wayward mother-in-law.

As for Vickie, she sighed and compared the maps again, as if an obvious answer she'd missed the previous twenty times might suddenly appear amid the squiggles and hieroglyphs. *Had* she gotten the directions wrong? Were they wasting their whole weekend?

Damn it, Mom.

It'd seemed to have been going so well, Ruth adapting to her long widowhood and empty-nestedness, settling in nicely to an active, independent life. She had the bakery, she had her garden, she had church and a senior ladies' book club and Bingo and volunteering at the local food bank.

But then, the hassles and harassment started. A teapot tempest over gay wedding cakes here, disputes over vegan this or gluten-free that or allergen-friendly the other there, carb-haters, anti-vaxxers, feeding the homeless, hate crimes, political correctness, pesticides, mis-gendering, activists banging on the various drums of their pet causes... and Ruth Avery somehow caught up in the middle of it. Until what had been a longtime source of joy and pleasure became a dreaded burden, to the point where she couldn't face going to work in the mornings.

So, closed the shop, sold the house, just like in the old Billy Joel tune. Only, instead of buying a ticket to the West Coast to become a stand-up comedian, Ruth had—as far as Vickie could piece together—relocated to a little no-name town in the high country ass-end of nowhere. With barely a word to her family, either. The last communique Vickie'd received had been an Easter card with cute bunny- and chickie-shaped bread rolls on the front, and a note saying she was fine, she'd be in touch, not to worry, just give her some time, she had a lot of thinking to do.

Then, nothing. And nothing. And more nothing. Weeks of nothing. Well, nothing except for Vickie's brothers breathing down her neck. Wanting explanations. Expecting *her* to know, or to figure it out. As if Mom were solely Vickie's responsibility, and how dare she let this happen!

What if Mom had fallen ill? Suffered a mild stroke or the onset of dementia? (Otherwise known as flipping your lid.) What if she'd been scammed or catfished? Scammers loved to prey on the elderly. What about the money? Mom's savings, Dad's insurance, the profits from the sales of house and bakery? What if she got swindled out of everything?

That, of course, being the main concern, both to Vickie's brothers and their wives, no doubt spurring them on from behind the scenes. The money, the money, the money. Their eventual inheritance, which Vickie knew for a fact James was counting on to bail him out of debt, while Roger and Cynthia had been planning their dream luxury world cruise for as long as they'd been hitched.

Admittedly, she and Dale would be able to find plenty of uses for their share when the time came—college wasn't going to be cheap, Jacob would need braces, their other car was on its last legs—but this was *Mom* they were talking about! Making sure she was okay was the important part.

"I have to pee," Jacob announced.

"Can you hold it a while, buddy?" Dale asked. "We're almost there."

It was Vickie's turn to shoot him the sidelong eyebrow.

Emma decided to get in on the action, too. "I'm hungry!"

"There's goldfish crackers and veggie sticks—" Vickie began.

"Don't want go-fish and veggies! I want a Nana's cim-num roll!"

"Yeah!" said Jacob. "How come Nana closed the bakery? That was lame!"

"Because people are stupid jerkfaces," Lauren muttered. "All it takes is one damn Karen or Becky to ruin it for everybody else."

"Lauren," Vickie said.

Dale chuffed. "Enh, she's not wrong."

"Who's Karen an' Becky?" Emma asked.

"They always wanna see the manager and call the cops," Jacob said.

"Whoa, whoa, whoa, okay." Vickie made the time-out gesture with her hands. "One thing at a time."

"But I *do* have to pee!"

"All right, I'll pull over." Dale slowed. "You can pee on a tree—"

"What about Bigfoot?"

"Yeah, don't pee on Bigfoot, bud."

"Guh-*ross*!" Lauren went back to her phone, then gave up in disgust. "There's, like, barely *any* signal out here, either."

Once the engine was off, a dozy and droning summer-heat hush fell. Opening the doors was like opening an oven, but one that smelled of dirt and dry brush rather than fresh bread or cookies. Everyone but Lauren stepped out to stretch their legs, Emma wanting to know if she could pee on a tree too. Sweat sprang to Vickie's brow and pasted her blouse to her skin. She looked around, noting they'd lost the roadside power line sentries at some point. The road itself had narrowed, the asphalt rougher. She and Dale shared a wry glance of wordless communication. At least, so far, there was still room to turn around... neither of them was eager for a repeat of the infamous several-miles-in-reverse adventure.

Needs attended to, no sightings of Bigfoot or inbred hillbilly cannibals, they piled back in. The car even started on the first try, the air from the vents seeming a much cooler rush now by comparison.

"Let me see the maps," Dale said. He pored over them while Vickie rummaged in the snack-carton for something to placate Emma's tummy—raisins? No. Beef jerky? No. Yogurt pretzels? Oh-*kay* but with a dramatic sigh copied from her big sister.

"Any luck?" she asked Dale.

"I think we should be on this road over here." He tapped the paper. "It's a thicker black line, anyway, not this skinny one I'm pretty sure we're actually on. And, see here? I bet that's a town. Or a park or something, at least. There's the little green picnic table icon."

"Can we get there from here?"

"If we take this shortcut—"

"The *dotted* line?"

"It's only a mile or two."

"If this goes all *Hills Have Eyes* on us," she said, buckling her seatbelt, "I'm blaming *you*."

He stuck his tongue out at her, which made Jacob and Emma laugh. And, presumably, made Lauren do another eyeroll behind her concealing shades. Moments later, they were on the move again, and soon enough reached what Dale reckoned had to be the turnoff onto the dotted-line road. The dirt road. The track. One lane, two ruts, scraggly weeds on the hump in the middle.

The car bounced and jounced. A dusty rooster-tail rose behind them, while the already gritty and bug-splattered windshield obscured everything to sepia-toned. Dale hit the wipers, scraping clearish arcs, but didn't even try the fluid. That would've turned it all into fan-shaped smears of gunky mud.

Vickie wondered about the muffler or exhaust pipes, if they'd ignite those scraggly weeds, touch off that wildfire she'd been worried about. Jacob cheered the rough ride at first, then started making seasick noises. Dale swore under his breath. Emma whined and fussed and threw the rest of her yogurt pretzels on the floor. Lauren ignored them all even harder.

The incline steepened and the car didn't like it, struggling uphill with tires kicking up sprays of dirt and occasionally spinning for traction. Dale swore some more, hunched over the steering wheel, brow furrowed in concentration. Nobody else dared make a peep, not even the kids. Dry, bristly branches scratched at Vickie's window like dead fingernails. The trees had thinned into scrub, the terrain rockier and grassier as they neared what had to be the top of the rise.

Then they cleared it, and Dale hit the brakes almost as much in astonishment as relief. "Well son of a bitch," he said. "Would you look at this!"

Vickie would have, but couldn't see much peering through dirt and bug guts. As he fully stopped, she unbuckled and clambered out, shading her eyes against the clear, unobstructed sun. Though still hot, it felt summer-pleasant now instead of stifling and musty, softened by an extremely welcome breeze.

Ahead, and below, the land sloped away into a broad shallow bowl, a valley, a patchwork quilt of greens and golds and rich, warm browns. She saw trees in windbreak-rows, rambling rock walls, wooden fences... barns and stables, silos, fields, pastures, meadows... white linens billowing on clotheslines outside of quaint picturesque farmhouses, equipped with old-fashioned wells and windmills...

The others had also emerged from the car, Dale with Emma boosted into the crook of his arm, Jacob excited, even Lauren expressing some actual interest for a change.

Dale winked at Vickie, and mouthed, " *Wicker Man...*"

She elbowed his ribs. "Oh, hush."

"Totes *Midsommar*," Lauren remarked, which drew the attention of both of her parents.

"How do you know about—"/"Where did you—" they began at the same time.

"What? It's online. Everybody's seen it."

"Isn't it rated R?" Dale asked.

"Yeah, there's like, gore and naked people, so?"

"We can talk about this later," Vickie said. "Anyway, it isn't *Wicker Man* or *Midsommar*. See?"

To be fair, there *were* several horse buggies in view, but there were also pickup trucks and tractors, farm equipment, and long silvery spindles of irrigation systems spraying arcs of water that glimmered a misty rainbow haze above the growing crops. Power lines and telephone poles were in evidence, and spinning wind turbines dotted the hills. Most of the farmhouses had solar panels and satellite dishes mounted on the roofs. To the north, bright and new-looking and clean, was some sort of sprawling agricultural factory complex. Mounted on the largest building's white walls were a logo of crossed golden grain stalks on a green circle, and the block capital letters PGI.

"That," said Dale, pointing with the arm not supporting Emma, "must be the road we should have been on."

It swept gently in from the valley's far side, looking smooth and even, with lane-marking lines freshly painted. A steady stream of vehicles, both motorized and non, moved along it.

Some were bound for the factory, others a picture-perfect little town straight from Hollywood's notion of the wholesome American Midwest heartland. It sported a brick courthouse with clock tower, pristine church steeples, tidy businesses lining what was almost certainly called Main Street, and a landscaped park square complete with bandstand.

Most of the traffic, though, centered on what appeared to be temporary dirt-grass-and-gravel parking lots surrounding an open meadow, where clusters of tents and booths had been set up amid open-sided exhibit halls. There were a few carnival rides—a small Ferris wheel, a merry-go-round, a kiddie-coaster—and midway games. Multi-colored pennants flapped briskly in the breeze, strings of lightbulbs promised bright illumination after sundown, and a large banner hung suspended between two flagpoles by the entrance gate.

GRAINVILLE LAMMAS FAIRE, it proclaimed. JULY 26 – AUGUST 8. The second they saw *that*, well...

"Guess we're going to the fair," Dale said, making a show of sounding resigned. But Vickie knew him too well; he was already anticipating deep-fried everything on a stick.

"Yesss!" Jacob jumped around in a hectic dance, pumping his fists. "Aw yeah! The fair!"

Even Lauren perked up some, though she tried not to let on. Brooding Hot Topic sullenness couldn't compete with the allure of throwing darts for cheap-ass prizes.

"All right," Vickie said, "but remember, we're here to—"

"Yeah, of course," Dale said. "Look how busy it is, though. Everyone in town must be there. If your mom's here anywhere, that's where she'll be."

They piled back into the car again, buoyed by relief and optimism such that they hardly noticed the switchbacked dirt-road descent into the valley. Emma, squealing in delight, announced each sighting of sheepies or horsies or cows as they passed through farmland. Jacob was more concerned about whether the fair would have "good" rides, not just "baby" rides, and if he'd be tall enough. Dale seemed lost in daydreams of beer-battered this and bacon-wrapped that, and a greasy block of curly fries as big as his head.

"I guess it can't be *too* bad," Lauren said, in a begrudging "the judge will allow it" tone. "I mean, there's finally a decent signal, at least."

They'd reached the actual town by then, which, up close, struck Vickie as almost too neat. Too clean. Planned and deliberate. Like a movie set, or a full-size version of a real estate developer's model, or the sort of thing the government built out in the desert to test their nukes on. Like the family housing community on a military base, or one of those long-term care and retirement villages done up so nobody could tell it was really all one big nursing home.

God, could that be it? Had her mother decided, without a word to any of her children, to pack it in and move to some happy-happy Neverland for the old and infirm?

But, no... the people out and about, on the sidewalks and in the yards, visiting the businesses along—yes it was—Main Street... seemed a normal enough mix of ages, ethnicities, and lifestyles. The earlier Amish-type impressions were countered by a coffee shop crowded with laptop users, and a small but upscale high-tech electronics store.

"Anyone else getting a *Twilight Zone* vibe?" Dale asked, following it up by *doo-doo-doo-doo*-ing the theme song.

"First *Wicker Man*, now *Twilight Zone*?" Vickie said, as if she hadn't been thinking along similar lines herself. "Great, thanks."

"Hey, I'm just sayin'. Bet you it's all new. Bet you, five years ago, this whole place was farmland. Independent farmers. Then Big Agriculture swoops in, buys it up, builds this nice little corporate town to house their workers, and there you go."

"Maybe." Vickie scanned the pedestrians, hoping against hope to catch a glimpse of her mother's familiar features, but with no luck.

They drove by the park, through a residential neighborhood—instead of tree-named streets such as Oak or Elm, though, they were Wheat, Rye, Oat, and Barley—of cute-but-generic suburbian homes, and past a small but well-kept school complex with a sign reading GRAINVILLE K-12.

"They don't even have a separate high school?" Lauren grimaced. "Lame!"

"Kids probably used to get bussed somewhere else, before the company took over," Dale said, still going off his theory. "What do you think their sports team is? Maybe the Colonels? Get it? Kernels? Grainville Ker—"

"Da-a-ad!"

He laughed.

With the school behind them, it was fields again, amber waves of grain, misted by those glimmering irrigation arc rainbows. Vickie couldn't tell what kind of grain it was. Not wheat, not corn; beyond that, she was clueless. Instead of the helpful placards often posted along highways to identify crops—potatoes, alfalfa, whatever—there were only occasional diamond-shaped signs sporting that same green-and-gold PGI logo.

She rolled her window down a few inches, ready to roll it right back up again at the first whiff of manure or chemical fertilizers. But the air blew in sweetly fragrant, smelling of rich soil and healthy growth, and a pleasant buttery-seedy-nutty scent that made her stomach remind her she'd only eaten a packet of veggie chips and some beef jerky since breakfast.

Dale rolled down his window, too. So, after a moment, did Lauren. They all inhaled appreciatively.

"I'm *hungry!*" Emma declared again. "I want a bread!"

"Me, too!" said Jacob. "I want a bread *this* big!"

"I hear ya, buddy," Dale said. "Nice and hot, right out of the oven." His stomach growled loud enough for them all to hear, making the kids snicker. "We'll get some at the fair, okay?"

"Okay!" Jacob bounced in his seat. "Hurry-hurry."

"Almost there." Dale, slowing to join the line of cars waiting to turn into the dirt-grass-gravel lots, dug a crumpled wad of bills from his pocket. PARKING $2 ALL DAY, according to painted lettering on a board.

"And then I'm gonna go on the rides," Jacob continued, "and then I wanna see the llamas!"

"Llamas?" asked Vickie.

He pointed ahead at the banner spanning the fairground entrance.

Lauren sneered. "It's not llamas, you dink. It's Lammas."

"That's what I said! Llamas. They spit."

"Lauren, don't call your brother a dink," Vickie said. "Jacob, she's right, it's spelled differently."

"What's Lammas, then?"

"Uh..." She looked to Dale, but Dale only shrugged.

A sandy-haired, freckle-faced teenager in jeans and a PGI ballcap and a high-vis safety smock had approached the open window in time to hear them. "It's a holiday," he said. "Celebrating the first grain harvest of the year. Goes way back."

"*Midsommar,*" Lauren stage whispered.

"Lauren!" Vickie winced, expecting the guy to be offended, but he just laughed.

"Aw, no, nothing like that." He paused, eyes twinkling as he gave Lauren a mischievous grin. "Not much, anyway."

Dale forced an unamused chuckle as he handed over two bucks. "Where should we park?"

"Just follow them, pull into the next spot. You folks enjoy your time at the fair, hear?" Flicking the brim of his ballcap, he strolled on to the next car in line.

"Damn, I should have asked him about Mom," Vickie said.

"Plenty of people to ask." As directed, Dale parked, and they got out, then did the usual prepping montage of applying sunscreen, unfolding the stroller, making sure everyone had a water bottle, and quizzing the kids on what to do in case they got separated.

PROUDLY SPONSORED BY PGI, posters declared as they approached the ticket booth. Some also featured glossy enlarged photos of healthy fields like those they'd driven past, closeups of grain ripening heavy on the stalk, mottoes about *The past is the future!* and plenty of buzzwords: *ultimate superfood, all-organic, protein-rich, vital nutrients.*

"Google's got nothing," Lauren said, squinting at her phone. "Not about grain or farming, anyways. Some conference-call online meeting company, some fireworks manufacturer, but yeah... nothing. Not even a Twitter. Weird."

Admission was reasonable—five dollars for adults, three for children, under-sixes free. Hands stamped with the crossed stalks logo in green ink, supplied with a simple map and a booklet of discount coupons, they entered the bustling fairgrounds.

At first, it seemed like any other small-town country fair. The sights and sounds: brightness and color, hectic activity, competing music, happy voices, the clatter and whoosh of rides, midway barkers step-right-up-step-right-up-win-a-prize, a lone balloon bobbing away into the sky trailing its string like a tail.

But something... something was off... and it took Vickie a few minutes to figure out what it was. The smell. The smell wasn't quite right.

Oh, the underlying sawdust was there, and the straw, hints of livestock, that unmistakable *eau d' port-a-potty*, metallic machine oil... missing, though, was the usually predominant mélange of fair food aromas. Where was the charred meat smokiness of burgers, bratwursts, pulled pork? The barbecue sauce, the onions? The fuming-hot grease? Where were the sickly pink wafts of cotton candy like cloyingly sweet pollen adrift on the air? Where was Dale's bacon-wrapped, deep-fried everything-on-a-stick?

What she *could* smell was... bread.

Fresh-baked bread.

Bread, bread, bread. Of multiple kinds: light and yeasty, dense and dark, the tang of sourdough, the heartiness of seven-grain. Banana bread, ripe and starchy-fruity, laden with toasted walnuts. Cinnamon monkey-bread. Garlic bread, sprinkled with herbs and parmesan. Cornbread. Flatbread.

And not just bread. Buttermilk biscuits, Hawaiian-style soft rolls, hot-cross-buns full of currants. Bagels. Donuts. Cooked porridges. Flavorful baked granola, both loose as a cereal and formed into chewy or crunchy bars. Whole kernels of something popped like popcorn, but not corn, salted or seasoned or sugar glazed.

Grainville, when it came to its namesake, did *not* mess around.

All of a sudden, more than anything else in the world, she craved a thick slice of bread, or perfectly browned and crisped piece of toast.

It was her stomach's turn to growl, but amid the festive fair noise, nobody heard it. Lately, she'd been trying to cut back on the carbs, forestall that middle-aged spread; today, she suspected, her good intentions were going straight out the window.

Not half a minute later, they did, when someone in a cheery cartoon loaf-of-bread mascot costume capered past, accompanied by two uniformed youthful attendants with pushcart warming-oven trolleys, offering samples.

"From this year's harvest's first!" a ponytailed girl not much older than Lauren told them. She wore a white jumpsuit sporting the same PGI crossed stalks logo, green high-top sneakers, and a smile healthy enough for a toothpaste commercial. "Try some and thank grain!"

Dale and Vickie shared another look at the "thank grain"—which, okay, sounded a bit culty-kooky—but none of them turned down the sample. The chunks of bread, each served in a small paper cup, were spongy and light, bursting with a buttery-seedy-nutty flavor matching the scent from out in the fields. Emma, who usually fussed over crust, stuffed the whole piece into her mouth in one bite.

"What kind of bread *is* this?" Dale asked, but the loaf mascot and his attendants had already moved on, posing for a hugging photo-op with a cheerful group of church ladies.

"A really *good* kind!" Jacob said. "Can we have more?"

"Take it easy," Vickie said, though she felt the same way. "We just got here. Let's see what there is to see, okay?"

"Okay!"

"But let's start with the exhibits and stuff, not the rides and the games."

"Aww, Mom!" But it was only token protest, and he followed along willingly enough as they proceeded to a wide thoroughfare lined with tents, stalls, and booths.

Here, too, it wasn't quite the same as she expected. Hardly any local political parties, roof-and-siding or window replacement businesses, miracle cleaning product demos, or spa and hot tub sales... the overwhelming majority, even the handicrafts, toys, and souvenirs, were bread- or grain-related.

No, clearly, Grainville did *not* mess around.

She saw lots of farm-and-garden gear, from full-on industrial agriculture to miniature herbariums for the home... lots of kitchen and bakeware and appliances, from mortars and pestles up to the latest wonder gadgets... a woman dressed in medieval peasant attire was demoing grinding grain with a stone quern, while a headset-wearing man at the next stall over showed them how the new Insta-Loaf could make baking a breeze... a father-and-son woodworker duo making and selling the most gorgeous cutting boards, bread boxes, and spice racks... decorative harvest time arrangements of dried cornstalks and grain sheaves... pillows embroidered with bready proverbs and sayings... the author of a gluten-free vegan cookbook and the author of an old-school decadent desserts cookbook did signings at the same table while chatting amiably... t-shirts and bumper stickers sporting bread or grain puns...

There was an activity area where volunteers helped kids make their own corncob or wheat stalk dolls. There were baking for beginners workshops underway. A scholarly thirty-ish lady on a stage delivered a slideshow lecture on the history of cultivation, and how primitive humans had been gathering proto-grains thousands of years even before that. A robotics club displayed their Toaster-Bot, which could turn an entire loaf into neatly sliced, evenly toasted, butter-slathered portions.

And, oh, there was bread. Bread in every shape and size. Round loaves suitable for turning into bread bowls to fill with chili or chowder. Braided challah bread. Breadsticks, brioche, baguettes. Some kind of ricotta bread made from an ancient Roman recipe. Vacuum-sealed astronaut bread that would bake itself when the package was opened.

One stall sold the popped kernels cooked like kettle corn in several flavors: buttered, nacho cheese, caramel, jalapeno. Another had bulk bins of nuts, seeds, grains, and dried fruits to combine into your own granola or trail mix. Sourdough starters with pedigree certifications dating back to pioneer days were available. So were selections of flavored butters, olive oils, jams and jellies, and honey.

As for the samples...

Yeah, forget that cutting back on carbs thing, for sure. By the time they'd traversed the thoroughfare, Vickie felt as if she'd eaten more bread than she had in the previous year total. They'd bought plenty, too; shopping bag handles looped Emma's stroller handles to the point the weight would tip it backward each time she demanded to be taken out.

At the moment, though, their littlest was content to be pushed, occupied as she was with a pull-apart cheesy roll. Jacob, a purple Joker-grin of blackberry jam halfway to each ear, had talked his father into buying him a toy sickle made of Nerf-type foam, swinging it about, making swooshy noises. Lauren munched on mocha-cocoa-dusted popped grain, actually seeming to be enjoying herself. Dale hadn't found beer-*battered* anything, but they'd nearly lost him for good at a booth where all the bread was baked *with* beer; he'd had to try a whole sampler flight and decided the ultra-dark stout was his favorite.

Vendors pitched magazine subscriptions and grain-of-the-month club memberships. Recruiters advertised for 4-H club and Future Farmers of America and PGI farm-based summer camps. They caught up with Mr. Loafy, or whatever the mascot was called, and had the ponytailed attendant snap a family picture. Vickie and Dale each entered to win a kitchen remodel, a family vacation to Mesopotamia ("cradle of civilization, birthplace of agriculture!"), and a year's supply of microwavable porridge bowls that made Quaker Oatmeal or Cream of Wheat taste like library paste by comparison.

At a large open-sided tent with a communal oven at its center, they paid a dollar apiece to create their own bread-critters, forming rustic raw dough into likenesses of turtles, owls, rabbits, or anything else that took their fancy. Jacob made a racecar, Emma a blobby thing she said was a dinosaur. Applying raisins or currants for eyes, sliced almonds for feathers or scales, sesame or poppy or pumpkin seeds for decoration, and other such finishing touches, the results were then given a quick egg wash and baked golden brown.

"Now, you could eat them," said the hip-hop kid volunteer who'd helped them wrap up and box their completed creations. "Or you could take them home, cut them into four equal pieces, and place them at the corners of your room, house, yard, or property."

"Why?" Dale asked, dubious.

"For good luck, protection, and to give thanks to the grain. You could use ordinary bread, too. Homemade's better than store-bought, of course." Evidently seeing their skeptical expressions, the volunteer smiled. "It's just Lammas tradition."

Vickie nudged Dale to let it go. He did, but she knew the *Wicker Man* stuff was in his head again. Thank the grain, first-harvest, a weird bread-cult where people didn't judge or argue or march around protesting, or vandalize like the ones who'd spray-painted GLUTEN IS MURDER all over the front windows of Mom's—

Mom! Damn it!

How had she gotten so distracted that she'd lost sight of why they were here in the first place?

At her urging, they moved on, despite the kids wanting to stop and watch some sort of wacky capture-the-flag game where teams had built forts out of hay bales and bundled grain sheaves, defending them with baguettes wielded like boffer swords and dinner rolls hurled snowball-fight style. Then they wanted to stop again for a slapstick puppet show involving three bumbling brothers trying to catch a wily sheep. A unicycle-riding juggler... a folk trio of guitarist, drummer, and singer doing harvest ballads... a balloon artist making green and gold grain stalks...

"Hey," Dale said, catching Vickie's attention. "Check it out."

She looked over at one of the larger open-sided structures, bedecked with hanging and freestanding PGI banners. Rising aluminum bleacher-style seating faced a main stage, where a tall, striking, older man was delivering a multi-media presentation somewhere between "stockholder's meeting" and "late-night infomercial." He had presence and charisma, and a silver fox vibe that reminded her of Food Network's Geoffrey Zakarian or CNN's Anderson Cooper. With a carrying, melted-butter voice, he told them how PGI was going to change the world with its revolutionary retro-engineered proto-grain products. And how you, yes, *you*, could be involved!

"Who's he?" she asked.

Dale shrugged, but a stocky bikery guy next to them heard and answered. "Him? That's Iain MacLugh, babydoll! Founder of PGI. The main man himself!"

"Seriously?" Dale, who normally would've bristled at anybody calling her "babydoll," only shifted to get a better view of the stage. "The company CEO, huckstering at the fair?"

It was the bikery guy who bristled. "Huckstering? He should be above all this, you think? Ivory tower glass penthouse, no rubbing elbows with the plebs? Too good to walk among us?"

Nonplussed, Vickie and Dale fumbled through some sort of apology, and edged themselves and the kids a ways further on.

MacLugh's audience—a packed crowd; again, of all ages, ethnicities, and apparent lifestyles—clapped and carried on as if they were attending more of a political rally or church tent revival than a corporate sales pitch. Some called out, "Thank grain!" and, "The past is the future!" at spontaneous random intervals. Some waved toy scythes and sickles, the fruits of the balloon artist's efforts, or actual dried sheaves.

Around the edges, at folding tables decked with green and gold bunting, more attendants in white jumpsuits with green logos took signups for mailing lists and petitions, polls, and entries for giveaways. Others handed out pamphlets and brochures, keychains, stickers, pens, buttons, and similar little freebie swag trinkets.

Emma and Jacob began clamoring for stickers, while Lauren picked up a booklet about urban farming—crops instead of lawns, communal gardens, planting fruit-bearing trees in public parks, et cetera.

"What *is* all this?" Vickie heard herself murmur.

"Dunno," Dale said, "but soon as there's any mention of bonfires or a harvest queen, we are *out* of here."

She nodded, only half-listening to him because MacLugh the charismatic silver fox went striding up and down the stage, like a TV preacher or game-show host, saying something about how PGI's special ultra-blend flour could be used in any recipe, was gluten-free, lactose- and allergen-friendly, and naturally fortified with all the proteins, calcium, vitamins, and other nutrients.

"That's right!" he told the ecstatic audience. "Simply combine it with varying ratios of water—the purer the better, of course!—and you'll have a dough suitable for biscuits, pancakes, muffins, bread, or anything else you care to bake! Since no eggs, oil, or butter is needed, the results are also entirely vegan, entirely ethical, and capable of meeting a body's every dietary requirement! That's right, folks... we've finally done it... finally disproved the old saying... now, with PGI, man *can* live by bread alone!"

The crowd went bonkers with whoops and applause, more than a few springing to their feet, three or four even flinging themselves on the straw-strewn ground like genuine holy rollers.

There was more, stuff about the beneficial effects on ecology and environment as well as economy... the hardiness and durability of high-yield crops suitable for even the harshest climates, ending hunger and poverty as the world knew it... combating climate change and malnutrition... reducing meat and milk consumption, slaughterhouses, animal cruelty...

"Cows *are* responsible for a lot of methane contributing to global warming," Lauren said. "And the inhumane way they're treated, kept in cages..."

"Speaking of animals," MacLugh continued, "let us not forget our furry friends! PGI's new lines of ultra-grain pet foods *will* provide everything necessary to keep dogs, cats—even zoo animals!—happy, healthy, and satisfied! They won't be deprived. Neither will your family! Forget trying to trick your children with cauliflower 'nuggets' or convince your carnivorous cousin to try 'impossible' fake meat products... who needs any of that when you can serve them up a golden loaf of fresh-baked bread? They'll soon forget they ever ate anything else! They soon won't *want* anything else!"

Dale scoffed a bit at that. "Yeah, right... I mean, okay, the bread *was* really good, but..."

"Really, *really* good," Jacob said. "I don't want stupid old regular bread anymore."

"Good bread good bread yummy-nummy-yummy bread!" Emma crowed from her stroller, waving her tiny fists.

MacLugh, having worked his listeners into a frenzy, wasn't done yet. "Say goodbye to junk foods filled with processed sugar, chemicals, artificial colors and flavors! Say goodbye to eating disorders, diet-shaming, and high-cost low-yield weight loss programs! And for those of you out there who enjoy a drink or two—" He swept them with a charming, knowing, don't-we-all/you-and-me-both smile of self-deprecation— "you'll be delighted to hear that adult beverages brewed from PGI products, be they beer or more potent grain whiskeys, will still have all the beneficial effects, while combating the more harmful and addictive components contributing to alcoholism!"

More cheers, more applause. Somehow, without Vickie being entirely conscious of their doing so, the five of them had drifted well into the structure to join the enrapt, jubilant crowd.

It *had* been *really* good bread...

And now he was going on about how much easier it'd make mealtimes. No more arguments over what to have for dinner night after night after night, no more bickering in the grocery store. No more trying to accommodate fussy eaters or having to debate over whether a request was due to actual medical concerns, being on a diet, religious restrictions, mere preference, or just being difficult.

Which, frankly, *would* be a miracle... Lauren had gone through the usual, *I'm a vegetarian now,* gol*!* phase a couple of years ago, a colossal pain in the butt for the whole family... Dale's brief trend-inspired foray into paleo-keto-whatever had been another... Vickie supposed her own occasional *Mommy needs to lose twenty pounds so we all eat low-fat* campaigns hadn't gone over so well either... her sister-in-law's supposed allergies that only ever kicked in when they went out to a restaurant and she could make a big deal to the wait staff...

An end to all that?

What was the catch? There had to be a catch. Didn't there? Maybe not bonfires or harvest queens, but...

"Nana," Emma said.

Vickie twitched guiltily. *Damn it!* She'd gotten distracted *again* from their whole purpose here—

Then she realized what her youngest was saying, what Emma *meant*, and her jaw dropped.

"—pleasure beyond measure to introduce," Iain MacLugh proclaimed, "PGI's newest vice president, and official liaison with the International Bakers' Guild... a warm welcome, please, for Ruth Avery!"

"Mom...?" Vickie breathed.

The woman crossing the stage as the crowd clapped and cheered could have been mistaken for Dame Helen Mirren at a red-carpet awards show, gowned in gold. Her formerly beauty-shopped blue rinse perm had been allowed to go its natural frosted platinum, styled into a flattering wedge cut. Her eyes had never been brighter, her smile never wider. She looked years younger than Vickie remembered, skin smoother, movements elegant and graceful.

But, yes, it was her.

Iain MacLugh met her approach with gentlemanly, outstretched hands. As she clasped them, he leaned in to brush a Hollywood-style kiss to her cheek.

"Thank you, Iain," she said. "Thank you, everyone. And thank grain."

"Thank grain!" came the resounding chorus in reply.

Then MacLugh turned them so that they both faced the exultant crowd.

"Good people of Grainville," he said, "I present to you... my fiancée, and your harvest queen!"

HEADSTONE POTLATCH

L.L. Hill

Pine trees stood as irresolute sad soldiers over the peeled white paint of grave fences. A gust off the lake tugged at Wendy's curly brown hair. Snow blowing up from Alaska. Her toque warmed itself on her dash. Not that cold she thought as she wiped her nose with a tissue.

Why was it, she thought, that trees in cemeteries always assumed a somber demeanor? Did they suck grief from the dead? She wished they could suck it from families, productive vampirism.

Behind a pickup truck with the gravestone strapped on a pallet in the bed was an RCMP SUV. Polished black granite etched with the specifics of Pen's life. Bitterness would not bring Pen back; his smiling face was sealed in pictures and memories.

Had he picked somebody up? Stopped to help someone? Had he really needed to go to Whitehorse that Friday to shop? If he had gone another day, would he have met the one percent of humanity that would take another life?

"Wendy." The school liaison, Burton, shook her hand, met her eyes with just a glance.

Why was grief so like guilt? She nodded, lips puckered to hold sorrow in. Vehicles crammed the small parking lot. She looked around, confused. What should she do? Everyone was headed to the headstone. Did she have a right to go there?

Burton touched her with gentle fingers on her arm. They walked together to the headstone. Men, Pen's family and friends, murmured together at the tailgate. What were they waiting for?

A trio of ravens cooed to each other in a tree adjacent to the cemetery. A spring baby being prepped for winter by parents. Survival required family.

Pen had told a story to a summer school camp at Conrad Campground in the weeks before his murder while wind blustered on Windy Arm. She remembered the glow that lit him did not come from the light or warmth of the fire, but from the joy of telling a story.

One spring, when ice still covered Lake of the Howling Rock, which is its name, not Windy Arm, Raven had a new hatched family. Searching for food in a spring storm, Raven was blown to the other side of the lake where he found a dead squirrel. Tired, Raven nibbled on the squirrel and looked at snow blowing over the ice. His wings ached, he had to feed his family. Wolf trotted by looking for food for his new family. He saw Raven with his squirrel and licked his chops.

"How are you going to get across the lake, Raven? Your beak is too big to fly in this wind; you'll land in Whitehorse if you try," Wolf said.

Raven looked at Wolf's fangs and tongue drooling and shivered his feathers.

Like all great storytellers, Pen's fringed caribou jacket had quivered in emphasis of descriptions of aching wings, fangs and long wolf's tongue, lips shaping each facet of the tale.

"I think I can make it if I have a little rest, Wolf," Raven said, *shifting from foot to foot in the snow.*

"Oh, come on, I've heard a caribou was hit on the highway and there's plenty of scraps left." Wolf smiled.

Raven opened his beak and took a deep breath as he looked from mountains to ice. His babies would be so hungry.

"Only if you're going that way, Wolf," Raven said. *He picked up the squirrel in his beak and hopped on Wolf's thick furry back.*

Wolf grinned and trotted out on the ice. Wind snatched at Raven and he gripped as hard as he could to Wolf's fur as the canine loped around and over broken chunks of ice. Raven wondered how Wolf could run without cutting his feet on knife sharp ice, but he did.

Wolf kept looking back at Raven and licking his chops with his long tongue. Raven didn't think it was because Wolf liked the flavor of dead squirrel and kept his wings ready to spread and fly. The closer they got to shore the less worried Raven was, then Wolf turned and snapped.

Raven launched over Wolf's head, dropping his squirrel. Fangs brushed his feathers. Growling, Wolf chased Raven as he beat his weary wings to gain height. A wind gust lifted him out of danger. Wolf yipped in anger and turned to pick up the squirrel. Wolf's tail was straight as he returned to his pups.

Raven soared and flapped, flapped and flapped to reach shore. He was so tired he could barely wonder why Wolf had started to help him then tried to eat him. Raven was supposed to be the trickster.

No doubt the moral to Pen's story was, "Bad things happen to good people, even when they're watching for them." Was his "Wolf" standing with the men around his headstone? The tailgate lowered and teepee poles were inserted into the pallet.

To a chant, the pallet was coaxed out of the pickup. A snowflake landed on the etching of Pen's name and melted into a tear. Wendy wished that she could melt down the stone with it. No more chats at the bakery over coffee and rolls, of wishes met, not met, dreams and fantasies.

With a groan, the pallet was raised shoulder high on the poles. Somewhere with the pathos of the lament, Wendy heard echoes of joy that Pen would be remembered for his good life and that life was wonderful.

Fireweed shriveled brown with feathers streaming edged the parking lot as the group crossed into the cemetery. Funny how the bright flower never grew on new graves, Wendy thought as a drum began to beat.

Wendy read names as she walked with the group behind the pallbearers, Burton not far from her. Carcross was a small community, with the world's smallest desert. How many people had been murdered here? Had the Gold Rushes inspired rage like that vented against Pen? What had the Mounties said? "Drugs are the new Gold Rush in every sense."

She had heard a dealer try to exploit drugs as a "Native spiritual thing to do." It seemed to her that the users that stumbled from crack houses were trying to escape horrible memories rather than fly with spirits. Had there ever been a drug addict that improved their memories with drugs? Was that question a prescription for more drug use?

Burton looked behind her and Wendy looked around. Pen's Uncle John limped on a carved cane towards the grave site. He had to stop to catch his breath. The two Whitehorse Mounties watched from outside the cemetery fence, faces still under their toques.

Uncle John stumbled and everyone leaned forward, then back with a sigh as he recovered. Without a father, Uncle John had shared raising Pen with his niece. No doubt Uncle John had expected Pen to lay his headstone. How much would that add to grief? Wendy choked back a sob.

Somehow the gravestone had been lifted off the pallet and placed in the ground at the head of a mound. Uncle John shuffled forward and touched Pen's name, setting the headstone in glacial till. He said nothing but turned and walked away.

Anger radiated from the men that walked back carrying the pallet and poles. They placed everything in the bed of the truck. Stiff shoulders and lips would not consider a more public display of rage or fear.

Wendy shivered more than the temperature and her down jacket warranted. She stepped around snow clumps captured by wild rose to the sanctuary of her Hybrid. The community eye watched, she knew, without a single eye on her, more intensely than she watched kids in her class.

She cranked her heat and belted herself in. Should she be afraid? She had paced her shared house for months after Pen was found knifed in his car at the side of the road. Would a murderer come after a friend of Pen's?

His tattoos, body art that he had been so proud of, would now be shriveled to his bones. Tears stung. Laying the headstone marked the time to move on. Could you ever move on from murder? She found reverse and backed onto an empty street.

Wendy had never been to a Headstone Potlatch before. For the fifteen months since his death, Pen's picture had been removed from public display. How concerned would parents be at seeing a teacher bawl on seeing a friend's photo? She shivered.

She turned into a roadside turnout by the lake without thinking. The Mounties had been behind her unseen and they looked. Not ones that had stopped to chat twice with her in post-Pen months, but Whitehorse Mounties. She herself had also been investigated with barbed questions. Bittersweet to think they were being thorough.

Pen was of the Crow moiety, Clan House of Raven. Outsiders would sit with Wolf moiety Clan Houses at the Potlatch, Burton had told her. She had not married Pen. Would she have married Pen? Would Pen have married her? Would marriage have kept him off a highway and away from a murderer? Would she have died as well married to Pen?

He was as fine a "get it done" guy as she had ever met. How many secrets did he have? Did he have any? An artist's life is open to public scrutiny. He did not drink, smoke or use narcotics. He would have told a story about why it was better to keep the inner fool hidden, she thought with a smile.

The lake was lead-grey chop, soon to be ice covered. Seasons had an expected appearance. So did teachers at Headstone Potlatches. She drove to the packed parking lot of the Tlingit Center.

Fingers on her door latch, she stopped to think. Burton had explained to her that protocol at Potlatches was very important, children could be present and there would be drums and dancing, but it was not a party.

Was it a dream that she walked across the parking lot to the door holding Pen's hand? In the lobby, Pen's art was on display, masks of various animals painted red and black. Some had eyes made of abalone. Once she had gone with him into the Tongass to cut wood. Sun glinting on wet needles and lichen hanging from trees, the smell of moss, earth and sap with Pen in a caribou vest, chaps, visor, and chainsaw taking down a straight young tree to buck. She smiled, touched a glass display, and sighed.

A buzz from the auditorium meant most people were there. Being late most likely violated some protocol. She looked at the door as an acknowledgement of Pen's demise, a finality that reinforced the headstone. How churlish when so many inside had known him for so much longer.

Wendy expected the straight-back reserve present when she entered. Here she was a student, not just a learner of information but someone whose every motion and expression a potential offense.

Uncle John sat in chairs set in a rectangle in the middle. That should be the Crow moiety with drummers facing them across a gap of a few feet. Chairs around the edge were for the Wolf moiety, which is where she would sit. One eye on her, Burton talked with an elder while she settled in a solo chair between two families from Whitehorse. Jacket on her chair, Wendy sat hands in her lap, back straight, and scanned the room.

Council members wore vests stitched with their moiety and Clan House. Politicians were the same glad handers in every culture, she thought. Woven Tlingit hats, flat topped cones set with copper discs, were amazing works of art that she would love to see up close. Pen had never worn one and protocol prohibited touching regalia. She would love to have a headband set with abalone.

Cloaks and drums seemed to be kept out of reach of all but the owner, she noted. An elder saw her lean with chagrin and smiled. Wendy felt herself go beet red at being so obvious and then looked straight at one of the Mounties. He looked away towards a young man that slouched in with a blanket over his shoulder and a parcel in a shopping bag, and then looked away again.

Nobody was in a rush as an elder stood in front of the drummers. The room went silent but for shuffles and sniffles. Wendy did not know the elder. Perhaps he was from Taku River or Teslin, the other Tlingit communities. He waited so long to speak she startled when he did in Tlingit.

Did the Tlingit feel this alienated when they watched Parliament in session? Did her students feel they were in a foreign country in her classroom? What could she do to make her students feel more welcome? Did everyone here but her speak Tlingit? Questions swirled with emotions.

The elder spoke with mild inflections and emphasis with one hand. He always looked toward the Crow moiety. Generations lost to land grabs and Residential School, he maintained calm control through his speech. There was silence when he stopped speaking and stepped away.

The children beside her looked from the drummers to the door. Wendy felt excitement frisson through the room. There were empty seats; at what signal did the drums start? One of her neighbors raised an iPhone to film. Uncle John led with a limp. Where had she been looking when he left? His quilled and beaded cloak must weigh forty pounds, Wendy thought. Eagle feathers hung from his head band. Two young men followed, eyes on Uncle John.

Legs spread wide, hands on hips, Pen's cousin followed with a two-step to the beat. Behind him, his wife danced legs close together, palms held up in supplication. Uncle John stopped at his seat while most of the rest of Crow moiety danced counter-clockwise around the chairs three times. Two young men walked shoulders slumped.

Sweat dripped on the third lap. Wendy had never seen the cloaks offered for sale with the other artwork, masks and paintings. The drums stopped and the dancers drifted away to sit or remove their cloaks. No one applauded. The Mounties had shifted seats and were talking to the young latecomer. How had those seats opened?

Wendy leaned forward and looked around. One of the Raven Clan House avoided her eye with a little smile. Another elder waited at the front to speak. The room went quiet as the old man began to speak. It could not be coincidence that she could meet no one's eye, not even Burton's, as she scanned the room.

While the odds were against three hundred people not making eye contact, they were nonexistent to someone wearing a placard that read, "I murdered Pen." Frustrated, Wendy wanted to move and froze her foot in midtap of impatience. There had to be a protocol against itchy feet. She looked at the ceiling, a good way to miss crowd cues and wondered how much she would miss if she left. How could she think about leaving?

Drums beat and Wolf Clan House danced in carrying money and gifts. Men danced with a wide stomp and women upright and lithe. Instead of cloaks, some wore fleece blankets. Crows and Wolves had strong family groups in nature, why they became moieties.

A young couple were head down, not dancing, just bearing gifts. Truly embarrassing, thought Wendy. Had they never learned to dance? The steps seemed very simple, she thought with her hands palm up in her lap. Perhaps protocol deemed it better to show and not dance. Money dropped into a basket in front of Uncle John, gifts to the side.

How had Potlatch survived years of ban? How had protocol been passed on between generations? Did no one hear the drums? An oral tradition could not be tracked by the government. How had they known to lift the ban? How much heritage had been lost to the ban?

Speeches and dancing continued. The young man with the Mounties, who was he? He came in with dancers, face twisted in a snarl, fleece blanket around his shoulders. His dance steps were out of sync with the beat and other dancers. Such a simple beat, it seemed impossible to misstep, yet he did with every step, too early, too late, never in time. Perhaps walking was better. He almost fell as he dropped his parcel. Had he missed the "no substance influence" directive in the Potlatch notice? No doubt why the Mounties had him tagged. She looked at him again. Why would he show up under the influence at a Headstone Potlatch?

Through chairs and dancers, the gift collection grew. Contentment beamed from faces around her. Would these gifts be enough to pay for Pen's headstone?

No doubt there was a protocol for trying to guess. Could she ask Uncle John? No one around her had danced yet.

Fingers touched her elbow. Would she dance? Yes, she would. There would be some protocol that she could not give money to contribute to the headstone outside of the Potlatch. Why were her legs shaking? Not like it is a first dance, just a first Potlatch.

Wendy walked to the line of the waiting dancers. She was next to the end, in front of an outsider married to a Wolf Clan member.

"You don't have to dance if you don't want to," he whispered.

Wendy pulled two twenties out and stood waiting. What was the protocol for the amount? She would pay the whole amount given a chance, a rather selfish act that protocol likely barred. Funny how thinking of it generated the whole realisation of why it was wrong. She sighed. All a community buried a member.

Who was the guy now between Mounties again? Where was Burton? Sitting with two elders. She would ask him later. For now, she would settle for getting a good look at the guy as she passed, if she got the dance step right.

Feel the drums. Her legs twitched to the rhythm. Dancing cured the shakes. Head straight she followed the line. Drums, some plain, some painted, Uncle John looking, was that a little smile? Wendy dipped and dropped her bills into the basket. There should be enough to cover the cost there.

Bland RCMP faces. They could not mask curiosity in their eyes. Could Canadians hide a banned festival for fifty years? Talk about shifty, the guy they sat with could not keep still, eyes wide with terror, fingers flexing. Her line circled the room again as Wendy wondered why he was so scared. RCMP routinely joined village events.

Puffing a little, Wendy came to a stop in the lobby as the drums stopped. Some dancers stepped outside while others went back into the auditorium.

"Here," a woman said.

Wendy jumped and looked. It was Pen's bracelet, beaded leather stained with his sweat. A raven's beak curled around it. Wendy slipped it on her wrist, glad to feel it flop loose. She looked up to ask how the woman had got it and the woman was gone. Pen never took it off.

Hand on her wrist, she went back to her seat. She was not smiling when she looked at the Mounties. Protocol prohibited return of a gift given here, but was it a gift or evidence from a crime scene? Red and black paint spatter on the edge.

Where was Burton? Watching Uncle John watch the angry young man twist away from the Mounties, blanket pinched in one hand. His spin finished in front of Uncle John and he glared down at him. Men stood while Uncle Ben's hands lay flat on his thighs. Face contorted, the angry man raised his fist. The room stepped forward, Wendy between two men.

He looked up, dropped the blanket and ran past the drummers, two Mounties behind him yelling to stop. The crash bar of the exit popped open and spewed him out with uniforms on top.

Why run? Where would he run to? Who was he? Wendy looked around as anger buzzed with relief around the Potlatch.

The woman who had gifted the bracelet walked past and paused, eyes still on the door. "Tried to get Pen to loan him money for booze."

THE ADVENTURES OF BABIE AND BOGIE: ORIGINS

Hansen Adcock

Even in summer, nothing would grow over Grandfather's head.

"You didn't bury him deep enough, Ma," Babie said, helping himself to another peanut butter and banana sandwich.

Ma stuck her spade in the soil and swiped an arm across her forehead.

"You could stop loiterin' in that doorway an' come help me," she growled.

"Nah." Babie rolled the sandwich around in his mouth, watching birds peck at breadcrumbs in the yard. "Too hot."

He sat on the dome protruding near the step.

"Don't sit on your Grandfather!" Ma yelped.

"Why'd you bury him upright in the doorway, anyways?" he complained, getting up. "Darned inconvenient. Whenever I wanna go out in the garden, I trip over his bonce."

"They buried their dead like that, in his day, in his country. It was so they'd be there to protect the house. He's protectin' this place. He'll bring us luck."

A big, black car pulled up to the fence.

"You order a taxi?"

Babie swallowed the rest of his sandwich whole. "Nope."

"This'll be the first bit of luck, then. Go talk to the driver of that vehicle. Ask for a job."

Her son goggled at her, eyes like two white billiard balls.

"Go on!" She picked up the spade in a menacing manner.

"Crackin' idea, Ma!" Babie gabbled, and shot out of the garden like a pellet from a constipated gazelle.

The car window slithered down as he approached.

"What do you want?" The voice that came out of it was English, light and silvery, coming from a tiny mouth in an incredibly thin face that sported a pair of inscrutable sunglasses.

Babie stuck a fleshy hand into the car. "Hi. Name's Babie, John Babie. Pleased ta meetcha."

"No," the voice said. "You're not."

"I think I oughta remember my own name, I spent the last nineteen years with it."

"No," the driver continued with patience, "I mean you're not pleased to meet me. Nobody is."

Babie withdrew his hand. "Whyn't?"

"Whyn't?"

"It's how I say why not."

"Because," the driver sighed, "I'm terrible. Get in."

"I never ordered a cab. I don't need to go anywhere."

"Just get in."

Babie hesitated. Ma was glaring at him from the middle of the sweet potato patch. He gave her a feeble thumbs-up and let himself into the passenger's side of the car.

The driver was wearing a dark frock coat and a peaked cap pulled low on his forehead, if he was indeed a he and not a she, and his skin had a white, waxen look. He sat at least two heads higher than Babie.

Before he could think of leaving, the driver engaged the child-lock on the doors and put his foot on the accelerator. The neighbourhood raced away to a pin-prick in the wing mirror.

"You didn't tell me who you were," said Babie, cold sweat collecting on his back.

"William, William Bogie. Most people call me Bill Bogie. My friends call me Bogie—that is, if I had friends."

"Not much of a social butterfly, huh?"

"All my friends are dead."

"Oh."

An unsettling silence descended. Babie wasn't sure how to break it. *So, tell me how your friends died* wasn't a polite method of carrying on the conversation, but changing the subject to something mundane wasn't tactful, either.

"Er..." he managed. "And how're you, um, coping?"

"Marvellously."

"Oh, well. That's... okay then."

Bill Bogie changed gear and turned onto a dust-beaten track through fields of waving banana plants.

"So, Babie. Tell me what you do."

"Er," he dithered. What could he say? *I eat a lot and go for walks? My main hobby is sleeping?*

"I'm a world-class sandwich artist," he blurted at last. "Also, um... I'm a vivid dreamer."

"Does that mean you create art using sandwiches?"

"No, I make them. For eating."

"I see."

Green fronds flicked past the windows, then they were trundling through open grassland punctuated by the occasional rock.

"Where do you work?"

"I'm sorta unemployed. Well... between jobs right now."

"Excellent. Any attachments?"

"Huh?"

"Family? Close acquaintances?"

"Just my Ma..."

"Well, it could be worse."

Bill Bogie turned right onto a narrow, winding lane that became an extensive driveway leading to a sprawling house with a long porch and lots of windows. The front door dangled on one hinge, but Bill Bogie ripped it off and set it against the wall as if all doors were like that.

He showed Babie into a hallway stretching to the back door of the building, the floorboards near them smothered in piles of junk mail and advertising circulars. A stuffed crow perched in an ornate cage on a table with an antique-looking phone beside it.

"Come through," Bogie said. "Sorry about the mess, I've been away a while. About ten years. Actually, no, I was never here. Not *here* here."

He ushered Babie through another dilapidated wooden door into a poky office lined with untidy filing cabinets and carpeted in yet more bumf.

"If you were never here," Babie asked, "then aren't we trespassing? Whose house is this?"

"Mine." Bogie moved around the room, picking things up and putting them down like a nutty professor who'd lost his car keys. "What do you think?"

"What do I think? Er, so far, it's very... wooden."

Bogie stopped and stared at him.

"No, not about the house. I meant what do you think about the job?"

"Job? Which job?"

"The one I'm offering you."

"You didn't say anythin' about a job."

"Didn't I?"

"No, you didn't."

"Oh. Well, I'll say it now then."

Bogie traipsed into the hall and came back with the caged crow. He set it on the cluttered desk and clicked his fingers.

A ruckling noise; the bird cleared its throat, and launched into a short, introductory speech.

"Welcome, potential new employee—*ark!*—to the Paranormal Detectives' Enterprise. You will be issued with a standard—*ark!*—issue uniform—*ark!*—and trained in the art of—*ark!*"

Bogie shook the cage until the crow rattled to a halt.

"Stupid creature," he said. "But you understand now, yes?"

"I'm working for Ark?"

Bogie slid his backside onto the desk's edge and hooked out a chair for Babie with a grey corduroy-clad leg. It was a nice gesture, if only the seat didn't have a hole in it.

"This is the thing: I investigate unnatural cases and exterminate unnatural pests. I require an assistant."

"Unnatural pests?"

"Yes. The graveyard vermin. Those who walk on the darker side of the Veil. The eidolons, the remnants and the *extremely* late."

"Y' mean ghosts?"

"I certainly do."

Babie looked around discreetly for a window or another exit. It was clear to him now that Bill Bogie was not in his right mind, i.e., crazier than a giraffe on roller skates.

"Don't believe me?" Bogie slid off the desk, pulled off his cap and tossed it onto the old-fashioned blotting pad, revealing an entirely bald, coppery-green scalp, and ears like tiny button mushrooms. With his back turned, he took off his sunglasses, folded them neatly with slender, flexible fingers, and paused for a moment.

Babie didn't run. His legs seemed to have grown into the floor.

The coat came off next, revealing a lithe, sinuous body that was also coppery-green and most definitely not human. Babie could see scales.

"You're... one of the...?"

Bogie turned around, fixing him with a pair of large, slanted eyes like golden suns.

"Yes. I am one of the Swamp Folk."

"I thought that was just a story."

"Then you're an idiot."

Babie stared at the seven-foot-tall lizard-man as he skirted around the desk and started flaying unopened mail with a silver letter-knife, seemingly oblivious to scrutiny.

Babie's mother told unusual bedtime stories when he was young. They were always based on old myths, the same stories her grandfather told her, which were the same ones *his* mother told him. Babie stopped believing in them when he was thirteen, especially the tales involving the Swamp Folk, a race of reptilian humanoids rumoured to inhabit the lesser-known bogs of Louisiana.

"It's best if I train you on the job," Bogie said, licking the corner of his mouth with a tongue like black lightning as he read his correspondence.

"Hang on. I didn't say I accepted the job."

"Really?" Bogie's eyes narrowed. "That's a pity. A real shame. I'll be sure to send your ashes to your Ma."

"My ashes?"

"I've gone too far now, showing you my true self. You could run about town blabbing to all and Sunday, which means now I've told you too much, I'll have to kill you."

Babie backed away.

"Hold on a minute. I never... I never said I *didn't* accept. I just need time to think it through."

Bogie absent-mindedly pointed the letter-opener in his direction.

"Thought about it now?"

"Yes. Er. Yes. I will. Do it, I mean."

"Splendid." Bogie's mouth split into a crocodile grin, cracking the white stage makeup applied to his face to hide the green-ness. "Welcome to the team. Our first assignment is right here."

Babie dared to read the missive over his shoulder. It was scrawled in wax crayon on a piece of crumpled paper.

Dear Sir,

My naim is Zeta Tubfret. I can't come to see you but I am living with a horible gost and it is driving the housekeaper mad. We keep getting injerd.

"There we are," Bogie said, reaching for his cap and shades. "A simple case, I think. Most situations involving children are. You know the area well?"

"Yeah, I think. Don't you?"

"It's my first time here, remember?" The Swamp Man gazed at Babie over the top of his sunglasses in the doorway. "You'll be giving me directions. The address is on that envelope."

"Me? I..." Babie grabbed the envelope and rushed after his new employer. "Okay, but do ya think we could stop for snacks on the way?"

* * *

Gantwick House was a hulking brown-bricked monstrosity huddled between a glass-blower's shop and a paper mill. Bogie stopped the car next to the front doorstep.

"Here we are. Now, what we do is..."

Babie's stomach gave a long, irritated growl. Bogie looked at it askance.

"Sorry," Babie grinned sheepishly. "I get hungry when I'm nervous."

"Good," Bogie said, in a tone of voice that suggested he didn't have an opinion on such trivia. "What we should do is, we go in and find the child..."

"Shouldn't we talk to an adult first?"

"In this line of business, children often know more than the adults. They sense more. Anyway, in case you hadn't noticed, Zeta wrote the housekeeper had been driven mad."

"Housekeeper? Is this some rich people's house?"

"It's an orphanage. I can tell by the smell. The only thing missing is bars on the windows."

The door to Gantwick banged open, and an insane witch galloped down the steps.

At least, to Babie she *looked* like a witch. Her grey hair was unkempt, tattered at the ends, her skin shiny and pale, a wart nestling next to her nose, and one on her chin. Dressed in a dark, voluminous robe, she prostrated herself over the car bonnet and stared at the sky with sightless eyes.

Bill Bogie let himself out of the driver's seat.

"Good afternoon, madam."

The woman failed to reply.

"Madam? Miss?"

He picked up her wrist and held it absently for a few seconds.

Babie was by his side in nothing flat.

"Is she dead?"

"No, don't be silly. Merely vertically-challenged." Bogie eyed Babie's broad frame. "Is there any muscle underneath all of that?"

"'Course I got muscle... all of what?"

"You can carry her inside, then. Follow me."

Babie did as he was told, wondering why they were there. Meeting a Swamp Man was one thing, but he was still of the belief ghosts did not exist. They were hallucinations, excitations in the brain, products of a disturbed neurology, or a piece of undigested cheese eaten the night before. Something like that.

They laid the woman on a table in the reception hall. Babie folded up his sweater and put it under her head. The afternoon was too sticky for jumpers anyway.

They stood on the grey carpet tiles and surveyed their surroundings.

"Did you shut the door?" Babie asked.

"That I did."

"You can't have shut it. I hear it bangin'."

Together they retraced their steps around the corner. The front door was firmly closed, a tight wooden mouth.

"Morphic resonance," Bogie sighed. "You hear the manifestation acutely, whereas I cannot. You know I'm not human."

"You mean I can hear the ghost? Banging?"

"Yes."

"What for?"

"How should I know?" Bogie grew testy. "Maybe it's bored?" He searched behind the counter and tried a couple of doors. "Where do you get any sort of service these days? What do I have to do to conjure a member of staff? Don't tell me that bedraggled woman was the only one."

"I think maybe she was," Babie admitted.

"In that case, we're at liberty to look around. Go out to the car and bring me my bag of instruments. It's in the boot."

"Won't we scare the kids?"

"If they're anything like Zeta, they're worried already. It's all right, I won't take anything off."

Babie did as instructed. The bag was a leather holdall, and it weighed a lot, perhaps more than the woman. He set it down in the hall.

"My arms'll be as long as an orang-utan's at this rate."

"Come and have a look at this."

A door branching off the hall was open, and Bogie's voice drifted through it. Babie joined him. The paranormal detective's gaze was fixated on some words scratched into the whitewashed wall, gouged deep enough to have been done with a knife.

HE STEPT IN A PUDDEL
UP TO HIS MIDDEL
AND CUDDINT GET OUT AGANE.

"Interesting," Bogie said, his nostrils quivering. "The spelling suggests a child has done this, but what child is that strong, strong enough to carve into a wall with a penknife? And what does it mean?"

"Those are lines from a nursery rhyme they say in England," Babie said. "Something about a doctor who went to Gloucester."

"You're well-read."

"I've had lots of spare time."

"It's obvious what we're dealing with here. This is a case of juvenile possession. Find the keys and make sure the doors and windows are locked."

"You wanna lock us in with a demonic kid?"

"Very well, I shall check the locks and you can search upstairs for the child. Can't be hard to miss. They've usually got mad, staring eyes... hair missing... scratches... strange marks..."

Babie was unconvinced.

"Yeah, right. I've already done your liftin' and carryin'. Dogsbody work. Why don't you lock up, and I'll poke around, show you there's no such thing as ghosts." They stared at each other in silence.

"As you wish," Bogie said, breaking eye contact. "I'll set up my equipment here. If anything... odd occurs, just shout."

Babie mounted the wide, mahogany staircase. It was too quiet. The only sounds were Bogie clattering around in the background. His feet slowed of their own accord. The clattering stopped. Not wanting to look a coward in front of the Swamp Man, he forced himself to stamp up to the first-floor landing without looking back.

A bare, wooden passageway with doors leading off it at neat intervals.

The banging came again, more intense up here. He had to stop and lean against the wall for a few seconds.

"Bang, bang, bang. That's all she ever does. Never a day's peace."

Babie froze.

That voice was Grandfather's.

There was nobody there. Nothing.

Nothing visible.

"Hello?" Babie crept forward. The banging had stopped, replaced by a waiting silence. "Anyone there?"

Most of the doors had childish paraphernalia stuck to them. One possessed several scrappy drawings done in felt-tip and wax crayon, mostly of aliens and abstract-looking spaceships. Another had wooden letters stuck to it spelling the name MAX and KEEP OUT. A couple of the doors were bare. One was stained like a tie-dye hippy T-shirt. Babie guessed there was a teenager behind that one. Reasoning that a teenager was the closest thing to an adult, he strode to it and knocked.

"Go away," a growling yet squeaky voice snapped. "I don't wanna talk."

A boy with a breaking voice, Babie realised, and said, "I'm a paranormal investigator. Well, a trainee. Can you come out, and..."

"No way."

"Can I come in?"

A pause.

"Suppose so."

The boy beyond the door looked no older than fifteen, standing pale, spotty, and messy-haired in the centre of a room piled high with comics and band memorabilia, the bed unmade.

"Whatcha want? Does Mrs. Bumbershot know you're here?"

Mrs. Bumbershot must have been the woman who collapsed, Babie supposed, and said, "Yeah."

"She let you in?"

"Er, yeah, sorta. Now be honest. Has there been funny stuff goin' on? She was in a bad way."

The boy hesitated.

"Bad dreams. Everyone's been getting nightmares. And they kind of overlap."

"Overlapping nightmares?"

"We keep appearing in each other's nightmares, seeing it from different angles."

"The same nightmare? What about?"

"It changes each night. Someone always dreams they murdered someone else, we wake up, and... one of us gets hurt, or somethin' weird happens to 'em."

"Which one?"

"Any of us. This morning it was Max. He woke up stuck in the fish tank up to his armpits. Mrs. B was frothing at the mouth, she was so mad."

"At Max?"

"She's mad at all of us. Thinks we're playing tricks on her ready for Halloween. I'm telling the truth, I swear."

"Show me the tank."

"Max isn't in it now. He's in bed."

"I'd like to see it, anyway," Babie said, his curiosity waking up and licking its lips. "Were the fish... harmed?"

"No, just confused."

"Pity. I coulda had one with chips," he muttered as the boy took him to the stairs, but the child did not appear to hear.

Babie paused at the top of the stairs, listening, but no voices occurred. He wondered what that auditory hallucination was about (it *had* to be hallucination) but pushed it to the back of his memory to puzzle over later.

The fish tank sat in a wide, airy room containing a couple of couches, an armchair, a box of toys, and a small television. The tank was large enough to fit a three- or four-year-old in, the water bright blue. The lid was off, and four gourami fish sliced through the liquid in diagonal lines. A catfish sucked at the gravel on the bottom. Otherwise, all was calm.

Bill Bogie entered behind them and set up a camera on a tripod in one corner.

"You're not taking pictures of the kids, are you?" the boy checked.

"I am setting cameras around the building to detect ghostly activity," Bogie said without introducing himself. "They have temperature sensors. When they detect a cooler temperature, they begin filming."

"Oh," the boy said. "Anyway, this was where Max ended up this morning. It took two of us to pull him out. He couldn't have climbed in by himself, and someone carved that rhyme on the wall. He's only three. Yesterday, Anna woke up tied to her bed by her own shoelaces. And she owns *loads* of sneakers. She can't have done that to herself, even her hands were tied, but Mrs. B went crazy..."

"What about Zeta?" Bogie said, joining them.

"You got her note? She..."

"One moment." Bogie grabbed the boy's chin, glaring into his eyes, and turned his face at different angles. "What's your name?"

"Carl."

"Carl. You're all right." He said to Babie, "Not the one," and turned back to Carl. "Carry on."

"Zeta's room's next to mine, the one with the pictures all over the door. We've all been staying in our rooms. Mrs. B told us to. Why was she sleeping on the hall table?"

"She fainted." Bogie headed for the staircase. "Babie, with me. Carl, you go back to your bedroom. It might be safer."

* * *

Zeta was an eight-year-old with a missing front tooth and day-glo hair-slides in the shape of mutant daisies. She goggled at Bogie, speechless.

"Don't be scared," Babie said encouragingly. "We came 'cause of your letter."

Her mouth dropped open.

"If we're going to stop the ghost, you've got to talk to us," Bogie snapped. "I suggest you get it over with."

Zeta's mouth closed.

"You're an alien!"

Bogie stared at her.

"You are mistaken," he said.

"You are! You're *green*!"

Bogie pulled Babie out of the girl's room and shut her in it.

"Is my stage makeup cracking?"

"No," Babie said.

"Any gaps in my disguise?"

"Nope."

"I feared as much. We are dealing with a Sighted child."

"Sighted?"

"Every few years a child is born with true sight, the ability to see through lies and illusions... and the skill to see the Dead. She could be traumatised. You had better talk to her, ask her what I tell you to ask. I'll wait outside."

Babie entered the room.

"Why are you helping an alien?" Zeta said.

"Because..."

"I'm going to a fancy-dress party," Bogie said from the other side of the door.

Zeta giggled.

"No, you're not."

"Ask her about the ghost," Bogie said.

"I *can* hear ya, y' know," the girl pouted. "It's a lady, a bad, silly lady who won't leave us alone."

"Which one of you is it in?" Bogie demanded.

"It's in Mrs. B."

"I was afraid you'd say that... So it cannot be juvenile possession, after all."

* * *

When they got downstairs, the hall table lay bare and shiny. Babie's jumper laid on the floor in pieces.

"We shoulda left her outside," Babie sighed.

"She would die of exposure," said Bogie. "Remember, Mrs. Bumbershot isn't aware of what she is doing. The ghost is controlling her body."

"She didn't have to *rip* it." Babie picked up the remains of the sweater. "My Grandfather gave this to my Ma to give to me. She'll tear out my gullet!"

"Your mother has a strange idea of parenting."

"It's not funny."

"I wasn't laughing." Bogie was thoughtful. "The way to get Mrs. Bumbershot unpossessed, is to..."

"Do an exorcism?"

"Do you think I'm a quack? No, the sensible thing to do is find where the ghost put Mrs. Bumbershot's true essence, forcibly eject said ghost, then reinsert Mrs. Bumbershot into Mrs. Bumbershot."

"Sounds... simple."

"It isn't." Bogie picked up one of his nearby state-of-the-art cameras and fiddled with it. "These should help us spot her."

"Mrs B? I thought the cameras were for the ghost."

"No. The ghost is inside Mrs. B's body. Which means the real, non-corporeal Mrs B will be wandering around somewhere, haunting her place of work."

"That sounds like Hell on Earth."

"Hmm, quite."

Darkness was dropping down the sky outside the windows.

"We'll have to stay the night here," Bogie said.

"Why not a hotel?"

"I never leave a scene of haunting until the case is closed. You're free to leave whenever you wish, but you won't be paid if you do."

"What's my salary?"

"Trainees get nine thousand pounds a year." Bogie smiled a cunning smile. "And a weekly dinner at LeCristo's, my treat."

Babie gaped at him. "How did you know? That's my favourite restaurant!"

"Yes?"

"I'd eat there twice a day if they'd let me!" He grew suspicious. "Do you know my Ma?"

Bogie rootled in his holdall and pulled out a couple of sleeping bags and light blankets.

"I think the room with the fish tank in it will be pleasant."

* * *

Later, with the moon filtering through the half-closed blinds, Babie opened his eyes and stared at the ceiling.

"You said Zeta can see through disguises."

Bogie grunted.

"She said you were an alien."

A pause, followed by another grunt.

"Well, are you from Earth?"

Another silence, then a long sigh.

"I am a citizen of Earth, as I was born here, and my parents likewise. However, the Swamp Folk originate from elsewhere. A ship of colonists—or refugees, depending on how you look at it—landed in New Orleans in your eighteenth century, from the planet Kesir in the Cetus configuration."

Babie paused to digest this information. He was on a ghost hunt, involving a psychic child, and now he was having a sleepover in a haunted house next to an extra-terrestrial. He rolled to his feet.

"Had enough already?"

"No," Babie said. "Starvin'. There's gotta be a fridge around here..."

The paranormal detective followed his comrade into a large, tiled kitchen. Babie had his head stuck in the refrigerator, cold light pouring out of it.

"All sorts of weird stuff in here." His voice was muffled. "Some kinda meatloaf. Smells strong. What's this, soap? No, cheese, it must be." He surfaced clutching a mason jar. "Fancy a pickled egg?"

"I don't eat the unborn. It's against my religion."

"They don't have chicks in. We eat non-fertilised eggs from chickens."

"All the same, I'll pass."

Babie shrugged and started to tuck in. He bit into one, and froze.

"Problem?"

He didn't swallow.

"Stick th' ligh' on."

Bogie switched on the overhead light. In Babie's arms was not a jar of eggs, but of eyeballs. Most of them were brown, but a couple were blue.

"I see," Bogie said levelly. "Put it back where you found it, there's a good chap."

After he did so, Bogie said, "It seems as if Mrs. Bumbershot has been... not herself for some time. This is the sort of behaviour possessed humans have. Hoarding objects... eating an unusual diet..."

"Eyeballs." Babie's voice was hoarse after spitting his mouthful into the waste disposal. "What sorta sick old woman chomps eyeballs?"

"The Dead have strange tastes. Remember, she is not herself."

Babie scrubbed an arm across his mouth, a worried frown gathering on his forehead.

"If she's been eatin' this way for so long... have the kids been eatin' what she eats?"

Bogie sighed.

"I dare-say they pretend to, to humour her, then find other sources of nourishment elsewhere. Children can be cunning."

"Poor things. It must be weeks since they had a decent meal, and they must be so scared." Babie grew close to tears. "An' they're all shut away, up there, alone, with this zombie woman stalkin' the corridors..."

"She must be out. If she was still here, we'd have bumped into her by now."

"Out where?"

Bogie spread his hands.

"Grocery-shopping? The gym? The library?"

"Why would a dead person go to those places? They're dead!"

"Being deprived of a body, then regaining another one by arcane means, triggers off a sort of sense-mania. They seek as many different tastes, smells, sights, and sounds as possible. The more hyperactive ones join gyms and sports centres with an intense desire to use their recovered proprioception and gravity. I once solved a case in which the deceased used his borrowed body to run two hundred miles an hour on a treadmill."

"Two hundred? His legs would fall off!"

"They did, and they became embedded in the wall behind him. He had to be forcibly extracted and taken to hospital."

Outside, somebody rang the doorbell.

"Don't answer it," Bogie said. He peered out of the window. "It's her."

"Her?"

"Mrs. B."

"Why would she be ringin' her own doorbell?"

"Maybe she likes the sound. Sense-mania, as I said."

The doorbell rang again. And again. And again. Somebody stirred upstairs.

"Shouldn't one of us go up? To reassure them?" Babie hoped Bogie would be the one to go, or both of them. He still had to pick the detective's brain about Grandfather's voice on the landing. He wasn't sure he wanted to hear it again.

"You go," Bogie said. "Make sure they all know not to come downstairs. I will give you five minutes."

Babie trudged up to the next floor.

Zeta Tubfret was huddled in the corridor, her arms around a small, fair-haired boy, who was crying.

"You should be in bed," Babie said, but gently. "It's late."

"Max is scared to go to sleep."

What could he say? *Don't worry, everything's going to be all right? You won't get a bad dream?* Nothing was certain.

"You're safer if you stay in your rooms. Why don't you have a little sleepover in your room, or his room?"

Zeta shifted positions and laid her head on top of Max's.

"The others have hijacked Carl's room, though he doesn't like it. We were all gonna sleep together."

"So... what are you doin' out here?"

"Talkin' to the old man."

Babie's heart hiccupped and started to race.

"Old man?"

"He was gonna tell us a story."

"No I wasn't," Grandfather's voice harrumphed somewhere to their left. "Daft stories for a buncha daft kids ain't worth my time."

"Grandfather?" Babie squeaked.

"Finally. I never thought you'd have the intelligence to see me."

"I... I can't. Where are you?"

"Oh, well, there's a surprise. I'm here!"

All that could be seen were the two children, now gazing at Babie in bewilderment, and the dimness of the passageway.

"Zeta," Babie asked, "can you... see this old man? Describe him for me."

"He's tall, with no hair. He has a grey moustache, and big, flat ears like a monkey."

"Huh! Outta the mouths of babies," Grandfather's voice snorted.

Max wiped his eyes with a hand and peered in the same direction as Zeta.

"I don't see a man. I see a funny, dark shadow, but it *is* bald."

"Grandfather!" Babie was almost speechless. "How...? I'm... I'm sorry I tripped over your head. And sat on it."

"You will be, boy, if you don't stop that darned woman bangin' and bangin'. I can't get a blink of sleep."

"Which woman? Does she have a black kinda dress, grey hair, and..."

"Warts? Yep. Two of 'em."

"That'll be Mrs. B," Zeta said. "I found her at lunchtime. She's hiding in the toilet."

Babie rushed downstairs, staggering over the last step. Bogie was in the hall, locking the door with a resigned expression.

Babie froze.

"You haven't."

"If I didn't let her in, she'd be free to roam the town and its outskirts," the Swamp Man said. "I pretended everything was normal. The ghost doesn't suspect we know anything is amiss—yet."

"It's in the bathroom!"

"What?"

"Mrs. B's ghost, her essence. Zeta said it was hidin' in the bathroom."

The white stage makeup creased around the corners of Bogie's mouth as he smiled.

"I knew you'd come in useful. Go and see if you can coax it out of the bathroom. I'll be in the kitchen with the impostor Mrs. Bumbershot, being interviewed."

"What for?"

"I told her I was here to adopt a child. It should earn us time. Try to hide any of the cameras you see on your way."

When Babie emerged onto the landing, all the children were milling about in the corridor in confusion.

"Please, Mister," a girl with mousy hair and a piebald teddy said. "Can you maybe get us summin' to eat?"

"All sixteen of you? At midnight?"

"I don't mind if it's just toast. Please?"

Another one, a boy of ten, chimed in. "Oh, are you going to get us a snack? That's great. Can I have chocolate spread?"

"Actually, I'm here to speak to Mrs. B..."

"Have a heart, will ya?" Grandfather growled in his ear. "These kids're drivin' me berserk. Do I *look* like I'm capable of coughin' up sandwiches? I'm dead! I'm meant to be in Heaven, enjoyin' the ultimate retirement! Am I? Nope! I've become Nanny Muggins!"

Babie did his utmost to ignore the complaints, located the plain bathroom door and knocked. On there being no reply, he tried the handle and found it unlocked.

The room was empty, save for a blue bathtub, a sink, a cloudy window and a toilet. Various bath toys and bubble baths stared at him from a shelf in forlorn disarray.

"Er... hello? Mrs. Bumbershot?"

No answer. Nothing happened.

Seeing as he was there, he might as well fulfill a need. He raised the toilet seat and unzipped his shorts.

The grey, smudged head of a spirit emerged silently from the bowl.

"Woooh," it said half-heartedly, then, "Woooh! Put it away! Do you want me to go blind as well as bodiless?"

Babie turned his back on her and took a couple of long, shaking breaths. He didn't know whether to scream, laugh, or apologise. He glanced down at himself.

"Oh, crikes."

He risked a peek behind him. The grey woman continued to rise out of the U-bend, long and stretchy with ectoplasm, before pinging into a more humanoid shape standing in front of the sink.

"Don't look!" she snapped. "I'm naked!"

"A-are ya?"

"I've got no body! Duh!"

Babie whisked an off-white towel from the rail and held it between them, feeling rather stupid.

"I came to persuade you to come downstairs, Mrs. Bumbershot. Your body's in the kitchen, talkin' to my friend."

"Is that wretched hussy still inside it?"

"Er, yeah."

"I ain't budging!"

"Please? My friend is a clever... er, person. He's solved issues to do with possession before. We wanna help."

A small hesitation.

"Oh, all right, but you'll have to go first, holding out that towel. No peeking. I don't want anyone seeing me disembodied, I'd never live it down."

"How will I know you're followin' me?"

"I'll whistle."

"Can ghosts whistle?"

"I am *not* a ghost!" she barked, affronted. "I am a non-corporeal whatsit. I'll be a ghost when I'm *dead!*"

So the charade began. He backed out of the bathroom, holding the towel stretched taut in front of his face. A few children moved out of the way. Most of them stared.

"Grandfather?" Babie said. "Think you could tell 'em to get back in their rooms?"

The other ghost sounded amused.

"I could, but I don't reckon as they'd do it. I ain't solid enough to dish out discipline."

"Thanks a bunch!"

"About turn!" the ghost of Mrs B ordered, and Babie walked down the stairs crab-wise, his arms beginning to ache.

The impostor Mrs. Bumbershot was leaning against the kitchen counter, her arms crossed and her eyes narrowed. Bill Bogie reclined in a chair at the table opposite her, his ankles crossed in front of him, gloved hands folded peacefully in his lap.

Babie entered the room first, holding the towel.

"Ah." Bogie leaped up. "This is my... um... partner. Tod Bung."

"Tod Bung?" the false Mrs. B laughed. "Let me guess, did he have an accident with the fish tank? He looks like he fell in a piddle. Puddle, I mean."

"Um. He has medical problems."

"Tea?" she asked, going to the fridge and removing a packet while Babie seethed quietly. "What you doin' with that old towel, anyway, Mr. Bung?"

Bogie moved closer to the centre of the room, blocking her way to the door, but still smiling.

"You are not Mrs. Bumbershot."

"Whatcha mean?" she said.

"Because you've infiltrated her body. Also, you have no idea how to make tea in a modern kitchen." He pointed to the packet. "You don't make tea using frozen meat."

"It was... beef tea...?"

Bogie ignored her, and gestured to Babie, who dropped the towel. The ghost of the real Mrs. B loitered in the doorway, whistling with affected nonchalance. She stopped and glared at her dumbfounded body, which goggled back at her.

"Is *that* what I look like, without a mirror?" Mrs. B's ghost marvelled.

The next couple of seconds were a blur of movement. The imposter Mrs. Bumbershot attempted to climb onto the counter and launch herself through the window, without opening it first, and the next moment Babie found himself sprawled on the floor, holding the wriggling, possessed body enfolded in the bath towel underneath him.

"Well done," Bogie said. "Your mother said you'd prove a world of service."

* * *

Mrs. Bumbershot's spirit hovered by the window. Babie tried to make conversation while Bogie finished fastening her body to a chair. However, making conversation with the disembodied was not something he was used to.

"Your grandfather is quite charming," she said.

"He is?"

"Yes. Did you know he came here, when he...?"

"No." He frowned. "I don't think he was ever here in his life, so I don't know why he chose to come to an orphanage. He didn't go a bundle on kids."

"Maybe it wasn't a choice."

"How d'ya mean?"

"Perhaps he knew you'd be coming here and turned up to give you support. Then again, this might be his idea of Hell. I know it would be mine."

Bogie stepped back. Mrs. Bumbershot's body glared at them, her mouth smothered behind a wad of material.

"Was the gag necessary?" Mrs. B's ghost said.

"To prevent the spirit from escaping before we are ready," Bogie explained. "Once a body is vacated, there are twenty to thirty seconds of life left in it for a new host to move in. If the possessing eidolon slipped out without us noticing... well, Mrs B, you certainly *would* be dead."

Babie eyed the Swamp Man with suspicion. Ever since he'd let on about his having spoken to his Ma before, he hadn't told Babie anything else. It was as if he was afraid of spilling any details. How was he involved with his Ma, and if so, how come Babie had never noticed?

"What happens now?"

"Fetch my bag from the hall, if you'd be so kind."

Babie produced the bag, and Bogie rummaged through its contents, extricating a glass vial and various pieces of alchemical equipment, including an alembic and a Bunsen burner.

"Chemicals?" Mrs. B said by the window. "Look here, sir, if you do any harm to my body I'll be holding you financially responsible. I'll get a couple of lawyers on you—no, seven—for every cent you got."

"I'm not going to damage you, Mrs. Bumbershot. I'm going to convert your essence into something more manageable."

"Pardon me?"

Bogie did not pause in assembling the glass and metal odds and ends on the table.

"In other words, I'm going to turn you into a drink."

"*What?*"

"Do you want to get back inside your body, or don't you?"

"What do I have to do?"

Bogie held out the alembic.

"Squeeze yourself inside this. Don't worry, this isn't going to hurt, but it will be quite warm."

Mrs. Bumbershot took the ectoplasmic equivalent of a deep breath, and began to spiral into the glass container, shrinking as she went, until it was full of foggy, grey ooze. Bogie set the alembic on a tripod over the Bunsen burner and lit it. As soon as he did so, Mrs. B's original body began to struggle afresh.

"See that she doesn't get loose," Bogie said, moving tubes and other paraphernalia around. "When I tell you to remove the gag, do so."

"Will she bite me?"

"In all probability, yes."

"Don't you wanna know who is possessing her? I mean... do you know?"

"There will be time for questions later, when we get back to headquarters. Remove!"

Babie tore off the gag, leaping backwards to avoid the woman's gnashing teeth. She began to scream as Bogie approached with the steaming vial of grey liquid held in a pair of tongs.

"Pinch her nose," he ordered.

It was difficult. Mrs. B's body thrashed her head from side to side, but Babie grasped the back of her neck with a large hand. He pinched her nostrils closed with the other, but not before she sank her teeth into it and worried it, hard.

"Yow! Son of a—"

Bogie tipped the vial into her mouth, and slowly, painfully, with much choking, Mrs. Bumbershot drunk herself.

Bogie signalled. Babie stepped back, clutching his wrist, and they waited.

"The real battle will be fought by Mrs. B," the detective said. "There's little we can do now. If the possessing spirit proves stronger than her, she will be dissolved into it. It's all about power of the will."

Mrs. B's eyes rolled back in her head. She shook and jerked. The chair fell over sideways with her trembling inside it. Steam poured out of her nose and mouth.

Bogie lunged forward and captured the steam neatly in the empty vial and stuck a cork in it.

"So that's that," Grandfather's voice came from the corner nearest the door. "Now all I got to talk to is a kid with luminous daisies in her hair. I might as well push off back to Limbo."

Bogie shot a glance at the corner and raised his eyebrows at Babie. His makeup was cracked, the scales showing through the gaps. Before he could pass remark, Zeta Tubfret appeared on the threshold, at the head of a phalanx of children.

"Please, can we have summin' to eat?"

Bogie turned his back to the door.

"They can't see me like this. Deal with them, would you?"

He swept his equipment into its bag, keeping his face averted.

"I can't feed 'em eyeballs!" Babie growled.

"There are boxes of cereal in the cupboard. I checked."

Babie dumped Wheetex into plastic bowls, diluted it with warm water (unable to find any milk), untied Mrs. Bumbershot, who raised her head and looked at him with bleary eyes, then rushed after his new employer. Mrs. Bumbershot staggered after him.

In the hallway, Bogie grasped her unresisting hand and shook it.

"Delighted to work with you. I'll send you the bill in five days' time."

"Bill?" she said, dazed.

"If you're good at something, never do it for free. Well, goodbye."

He gave the holdall to Babie, who carried it to the car.

"How did you find your first job?" Bogie asked when they were on the road.

"You know my Ma?"

"What about her?"

"No, I mean you *know* my Ma? And back there, that voice you heard was my Grandfather. What will happen to him? Did we leave him behind?"

Bogie waited until they were in the banana plantation before slowing the car to a crawl.

"Your Grandfather's body was buried in the entrance to your house, I'm guessing?"

"Yeah."

"This means he is obligated to watch and protect the inhabitants of that house."

"Y' mean... wherever I go, he goes?"

"Wherever you go, he will already be there. Unless, of course, your mother is in more potential danger than you. Then the Fates would send him her way."

"He wasn't doin' much protectin'. All he did was complain."

"Did he complain much in life? I seem to remember he did. Death does not equal a personality change."

"You seem to remember?... Who *are* you? How d' ya know my family?"

Bill Bogie pulled over and braked at the side of the track.

"Nine months before you were born..."

"Oh, no."

"I had the dubious pleasure of meeting your mother."

"No. No. I wanna go home now. This can't be happening."

Bogie raised his hands in surrender.

"Without a DNA test, no one can be certain of the outcome of that encounter. We were both drunk, I was full of pride in myself for bottling my first ghost. I collect the ones I defeat, as you saw."

Babie stared at the waving banana leaves, his eyes forlorn. Somewhere a clock struck six o'clock in the morning. Dawn was filtering everything through a blue lens.

"I think LeCristo's should be open by now," Bogie said to break the silence. "I'll treat you to breakfast."

Babie blinked, then turned slowly to look at him.

"You'd better. After all that, I'm starvin'."

THE RINGMASTER

Lawrence Dagstine

Three of us followed the funeral—Winnie, Lauren, and I. At the church there was no music to ease the silence. The organist, a man of fiery puritan outlook, had declined to give his services. The coffins were borne one at a time by an undertaker in a black suit and his much taller brother, assisted by two men from the village.

The vicar was kindly in his manner, and the service was short, for which I was glad. Lauren was bearing herself very well, but my poor Winnie looked waxen. I was afraid she might faint at any moment. As we rose to follow the first coffin out, I took her arm and held it tightly against me for comfort and support.

To my surprise I noticed that a few people were in the church and were now waiting to follow us out. There was Mr. Flaberghan, in a black suit that looked green with age. There was Mrs. Retts, our seamstress from the village, and a stranger I had never seen before. He was a man around fifty, short and very broad, but not fat, with a rubbery face. He had a prominent mustache, and his brown hair was plastered to his head with oil. Matter of fact, it was so straight the center parting might have been made with a ruler. Though his dark suit was well made it sat uneasily on him, and I felt he would have looked more at home in loud tweeds.

When at last the coffins lay side by side in the grave, and the handfuls of earth had been thrown, Winnie and I drew away to where those not of the family had hung back a little. I thanked each person for attending and came at last to the stranger. Offering my hand, I said, "Good morning, I don't think we've met."

He looked at me very hard from pale brown eyes. "Cleveland Tucker at your service, miss. I trust I haven't displeased you, coming to pay my respects." He had a husky voice that sounded as if it could be very powerful when he chose to exert it.

"My sisters and I are glad to see any friends at such a time, Mr. Tucker," I said. "I take it you knew my father?"

"Slightly, miss." He hesitated. "But I knew your mum better, really. We were colleagues, like before she got married. Terribly sorry about your *losses*. To lose not one but two parents is... Well, I can only imagine how unbearable it is for you and your siblings at this time."

I was taken by surprise but felt too close to tears to be able to say any more than was called for by good manners. Behind us I could hear the thud of earth being shoveled into the grave, and my skin seemed to contract with sudden cold. "If you will excuse us, Mr. Tucker?" I wished him good day and moved toward our carriage, Winnie holding my arm and Lauren following.

Much later that sad day I thought about Mr. Tucker again, wondering who he might be, and in what way he and my mother had been colleagues. Nobody outside the village knew about our family; nobody dared breathe a word. I had rushed off so fast I felt as though I'd maybe insulted him.

I went to the churchyard alone next morning. With the grave now filled and the headstone set, I wanted to arrange the wreaths and sprays of flowers given by those who had defied the general exclusion to attend. There was one small wreath which had not been there the day before, and also a beautiful little bouquet. The wreath was for my father, and the words were written in a neat angular hand: *"Sleep well, my old adversary..."* The card attached was signed faithfully, Mr. Cleveland Tucker.

I looked at the carefully written message in puzzlement, and as I laid the bouquet down, I glimpsed Mr. Tucker himself moving along the northern wall of the churchyard. He stopped, uncertain what to do, then came toward me, hat in hand. "Good day, miss," he said, his voice hushed like a muted foghorn. "I saw you coming and didn't want to intrude, so I was just slipping away. I guess I'm caught."

Perhaps I did not try hard enough to show emotion. Nevertheless, I found myself liking this man, for he struck me as having a natural kindness. "Please don't feel that you're intruding, Mr. Tucker," I said. "I'm glad we have met again. During my school years, people often slipped away *purposely*. Outside the village people seemed to find my appearance amusing and, like the rest of my family, I played up to this. I was never going to be pretty enough to be admired for my looks or clever enough to be respected for my brains, so I had to be content with making people laugh, even if the laughter was not always entirely charitable. So please, I welcome your presence and conversation." I beamed up at him. "Might I tell you a joke?"

"Well, that's very handsome of you, miss. You'll be Miss Nancy, unless I'm much mistaken?"

"Yes, but how did you know?"

"Read the announcement in your village's paper when you were christened, miss. Same with your sisters, a few years later. You were born in the same year as Queen Victoria, so now, nearing the end of the century, you must be in your late seventies. I must say, you still look marvelous, as if you haven't aged a day over twenty-one."

"Wait! Such knowledge is privileged." I stepped back. "So that would make you—"

"Yes, somewhat of an immortal by trade." He grinned and bowed graciously. "I told you I worked with your mother. Your father now, well, he was a Feral by birth, but after spending some time as a Dark Lighter he had settled here in this township. For over a century he had lived in the basement of that cottage alone—" he added, finger outstretched and pointing to a chimney top just beyond the churchyard gates— "but the village folk at that time were like primitives, and regarded him as something of an abomination. For true Ferals are conceived and raised a full fifty miles away to the north, so history has it, in another world, where the farmers and wood dwellers know nothing of shapeshifting. The Ferals there know the bearers of flesh and blood only as beef animals and pigs, which is how it should be."

"So what did you think of the *rest* of the family?" I asked.

Mr. Tucker vested a short laugh. "My word, but I had a shock when I saw Miss Winnie yesterday. Image of your mum when she was young. Talk about a beautiful huntress."

I said rather wonderingly, "Why, yes. And since I think you must have been fond of my mother, you'll be pleased to know that she remained very beautiful all her life."

Mr. Tucker nodded, and I saw him bite his lower lip, struggling to control sudden emotion. "How did it happen?" he asked quietly.

"Outsiders," I said. "Always outsiders. Rifles slung over their shoulders, bearing torches and pickaxes in great numbers. Always at night."

"I understand."

"Do you, Mr. Tucker?" A moment of silence, then: "Do you mind if I ask where you suddenly came from?"

"London, miss. That's where I spend more than half my time these days. I travel a lot, too, take on different shapes and forms, only I'm resting now for a few weeks."

"Oh, have you been ill? It does happen to the best of our kind, too."

"No, miss. It's a professional term. In my field, if you're not working or resting, well, then you're traveling." He produced a card and handed it to me. "We've got all the shows we want, but I make sure we take a few weeks off in the summer. It keeps you fresh."

"The Greatest Show in Europe?" I found I was staring at the card with one of my openmouthed exaggerated expressions. "Good gracious, you're part of the circus!"

"On the big indoors, miss, yes. Fifty years now. There's a fellow in the States who has an act just like mine, I hear. But he can never top what *I've* achieved. Still, made my first opening at Manchester back in forty-five."

I looked down at the card again to hide the shock I knew would show in my face. It was generally accepted that circus people could not possibly be respectable, and on this question I had heard only one dissenting voice, which was my father's. The previous year there had been a scathing letter in the paper concerning sideshow attractions and the decline of true entertainment provided by the indoor big tops. Mr. Tucker was a purveyor of such entertainment, and a self-admitted ringmaster. Father had read the same letter out loud to me, laughing, "Now isn't that fellow a fine ripe prig, Nancy? I'll wager he's never sat under a tent with a bag of peanuts and gazed over real elephants and lion tamers, or joined in a laughing chorus of juggling clowns, let alone real shapeshifters. How I detest these Misery Dicks with not a spark of fun in them. Don't they know that my circus is much different from all the rest? After all, it *was* the first of its kind."

At the time, I had wondered why Father should comment on the subject. I realized now that the performing arts in general were in some way relevant to my mother's past. I looked up at Cleveland Tucker and said, "Fifty years? Quality circuses weren't around at that time, Mr. Tucker, and my mother was teaching me how to play off sheet music long before then, how to adapt in a mortal society as best possible. So that means you were entertaining well before that, perhaps as far back as... 1820? You were a stage-hall comedian when you met my mother?"

"Not exactly, miss. I was still doing the conjuring acts when your mother came in as my assistant. Back in those years, before there were authentic circuses, we called them freak shows. One night only! Ahh, what bloodshed. Most of the time we performed in gritty little taverns. I must confess, I do miss those years before industry and money took over." He sighed. "We are all privy to expansion at some point, I suppose."

I put fingers to my mouth, and felt my eyes opening wider than ever. "Your *assistant?* In a freak show?"

"Why, yes, miss. What do you think the forerunner to the circus was? I—um— I suppose you didn't know." He twisted his hat around in his hands, looking embarrassed. "I do hope I haven't given offense, saying this all after your mum married well and you and your sisters were brought up gentry. But she was a real demon in herself, if you know what I mean." He glanced at the headstone and lowered his voice. "Don't think bad of me, Miss Nancy, but I really fell in love with your mum. She had a way of making a mortal beg for his life. Oh, how I adored her."

A few days ago, I would have been horrified to learn that my mother had once been part of a freak show, but now I felt tears pricking at my eyes. "Why should I think badly of you, Mr. Tucker?" I asked. "There's surely nothing shameful about falling in love."

He nodded, his eyes distant. "She wasn't sure about me," he said softly. "Then she met your dad, and she was really sure about him. He had powers much greater than mine. But I never forgot her, miss. And I never wanted to marry anyone else." He drew in a breath. "I heard about your dad's death," he went on, "and I was coming up to see her, in case she needed a helping hand. But then I'd learned that she died too, so I just came to pay my respects."

I stood deep in thought for a little while. "How long will you be staying, Mr. Tucker?" I said at last.

"I've got a room at the village inn for tonight, but I can stay on longer if there's anything I can do to help, Miss Nancy."

"No, I wouldn't ask you to stay on, but I would very much like your advice about the possibility of finding work for myself in London. Would you come and have tea at my quarters this afternoon, say at half past three?"

"Why, I'd be delighted, miss." Mr. Tucker looked quite overcome with pleasure as he bowed and said, "Well, I'll take my leave of you now, Miss Nancy, and look forward to this afternoon."

I stood holding his card as he left the churchyard, filled with astonishment at what I had just learned and at my own impudence. I suddenly wanted to leave the family and find work, especially now since Mother and Father were gone. Above all, if some miracle permitted Winnie and Lauren to take up residence with me, it was important that we should live within easy distance of Cleveland Tucker. He was a Londoner, and he would know what sort of work I might try to find. I had powerful evidence that he was faithful in his friendship—I could feel it in my bones—for he had come to the funeral of the Feral he had fallen in love with more than three quarters of a century ago.

* * *

Cleveland Tucker presented himself promptly at half past three o'clock. I introduced him to my youngest sister Winnie and could see that she was greatly taken with him. Perhaps because he was completely unlike any shapeshifter we had ever met before. I had wanted her to be present, because I felt she must now face the realities of our situation, and as soon as I poured tea I said, "Mr. Tucker, can you tell me what sort of performance work is available in London for an educated Feral?"

He frowned down at his cup. "Well, I've been thinking about that after what you said this morning, Miss Nancy—"

"Please, call me Nan," I broke in.

"Most kind of you, Nan. Well, there's work in ticket selling, working props, and being a vendor. There's even quite a few young demons doing sideshow attractions now: the world's strongest ghast, the two-headed Cyclops man, the wraith that can walk through walls, and the little squid boy who breathes bubbles, to name a few. I put on a lot of shows, and there are *many* acts. Perhaps I can tell you a bit more if I know what you have in mind, see?"

"This must be some circus," Winnie whispered in my ear.

I waved a hand and suggested everything would be all right. Then I turned back and said, "That's simple, Mr. Tucker. This village means nothing to me anymore, and apart from that I no longer want any ties to my other family. Cousins and such. Winnie and I are fine pianists. Lauren has a decent voice. I also have to provide for myself, of course."

Mr. Tucker looked unhappy. "Well, I hate to be the Dismal Jimmy, but I can't see where a Feral can earn that sort of quid in a freak show environment. You're going to need money for rent, food, clothes, you'll need to act and be like your neighbors. I'm talking seven days a week, and money-wise, at least a hundred pounds to live anything like decent. Otherwise you might as well stay in this village and remain a Feral."

Winnie said, "That doesn't seem a great deal of money, Mr. Tucker. Or enthusiasm."

He looked at her, and his face softened. I knew he was seeing my mother in her, and his voice was very gentle as he said, "Living the life you've lived up until now, I don't suppose you've had to think much about money, Miss Winnie. But you take a regular girl in service, a housemaid. She'll get perhaps fifteen pounds a year and room and board." He looked up at me.

I nodded, trying to look unruffled though my heart was sinking with despair. Winnie blinked, then put down her cup and stood up. "Excuse me," she said in a subdued voice, and went from the room.

"It's all right, Mr. Tucker," I said as he looked at me in distress. "Winnie can be realistic, but there are times when she doesn't wish to be."

"Ah. The facts can hurt, Nan."

"Yes. And Winnie's not only very eager but very sensitive, but if ever you hear her or me dance and play the piano, you'll forgive her anything. Thank you for all the information, Mr. Tucker, and now let us talk about something else. I'd be most interested to know how you came to meet my mother, if you don't mind telling me."

"Why—um—no," he said slowly. "Like I said, she was my assistant around the beginning of the century, when freak shows and other *weird* acts were earning out of carriages, sold out taverns, or on street corners. Today we have the circus and theater, sparkling and grandiose, and they're all over the continent. I knew your mother was a Feral the moment I spotted her. I was doing a magic act for a drunken crowd one night, and there was this trick where I got someone from the audience to help. Well, this particular evening I spotted your mum, and I got a bit of the devil in me, so I tried to coax her up on the stage."

"But Mother was such a shy person. I'm sure you didn't succeed."

"Ah, but you forget, miss. A shapeshifter can easily recognize another when in close proximity," said Mr. Tucker. "That and because of all the people around her too, I suppose. They were jollying her along, and in the end she reckoned it was best to come up and get it over with. Anyway, I was smitten. I was smitten so hard I followed her back to her lair that night. Next morning I waited my chance to see her when she came out. I introduced myself, and I think she was a bit impressed, what with me being a changeling and all that."

I took his cup and refilled it. "And she became your assistant? Actually on the stage with you? In public?"

He smiled suddenly. "Only two weeks later that was. I offered her a job at good money, and she never had to say anything during the performance. She wore a very pretty frock, and she used to pass me bits of apparatus. She was beautiful, and with a kind of dignity that brought a bit of quality to the act." He sipped his tea. "Taught me proper manners, too. Before I knew it, she not only found ways of making our act more profitable but *tastier*," he added with a touch of pride. "We *evolved*, and thus the traveling freak show was born. She knew all about how to behave like a mortal, from being in service to the Dark Lighters and taking note of the gentry."

"My sisters and I have never known about her early days," I said. "Or really that much of the Dark Lighters. Did you meet any of them, Mr. Tucker?"

"You mean other than your father?" He shook his head. "There were no..." He paused. "There were no real *ties* there, Nan."

"Was she part of the act for very long?" I asked.

"Just over three years. We traveled two years in London, then went on tour with others like us for the remaining year." He looked at me with sudden anxiety. "It was all very respectable though, with your mum and me. My younger sister, Jenny, traveled with us. She wasn't much to look at, so she'd been a big part of the act. It was only when I went in for comedy before a kill that I brought her in. But what I'm saying is your mum shared a tent with Jenny, and it was all respectable."

"I'm sure it was, Mr. Tucker. I'm surprised she didn't marry you, if you were courting her."

He smiled. "That's a nice, kind thing to say, Nan. But I wasn't surprised myself, not really. Oh, she liked me well enough, but then Mr. Dark Lighter came along, your dad. Truth be told, I was *envious* of your father."

"But whatever for?" I laughed.

"Oh, it's a silly thing, bloodlines and all that. Nothing you'd want to hear about."

"That must have been very sad for you." I felt bad for him.

"Well... I think I'd known for quite a while that mum wasn't meant for me. The thing was though, I didn't know if your father's intentions were honorable, did I?"

"I'm sorry?"

Mr. Tucker paused, and I saw a hint of moisture in his eyes. "Let me just tell you I'll never forget her. She's the one I'll love till the day somebody puts a stake through my heart and I die!" There was silence. He finished his tea and took out a pocket watch and said, "My word, I've stayed too long. I hope you'll excuse me."

"Of course."

He stood up. "I'm sorry my advice wasn't much help, Nan, but I guess it's no use painting a rosy picture when it's not rosy. The thing is, I've been thinking at the back of my mind while we've been talking, and I'm very worried. You're the daughter of my old sweetheart, and here you are looking for change. Maybe looking to make a bit of coin along the way."

"Oh, no!" I came to my feet, my face crimson. "No, Mr. Tucker. That isn't why I told you of my—"

"Now, now. It's okay. I still think very well of you, young lady," he said soothingly. "And if you won't let me help out in one way, then perhaps I can help in another. It's quite a big flat we've got in London, me and Jenny and the gang. Now, when the time comes to leave here, and if you've got nowhere to go, then you come to London with your sisters. There's a spare room for each of you. Nothing wonderful, but you could use it until you've all got your bearings."

I stood very still, my mind whirling. Quite suddenly I found that tears were running down my cheeks. I did not try to hide them, but impulsively reached out to Mr. Tucker and put my hand on his. "Thank you," I said. "I hope we shan't need to trouble you, but it's truly a wonderful relief to know that we have somewhere to go. A little friendly haven, where we can have time to collect ourselves and prepare for a new kind of life."

Cleveland Tucker looked about the room. "Yes," he said quietly, "it's going to be ever so different, Nan."

I dabbed my cheeks with a handkerchief. "I've been so frightened, but you've given my soul new meaning."

"Ah, but at least you have a soul, miss. I suppose that's the trouble with us shapeshifters. You're never quite sure which end of the stick you're going to get." His face creased in a great beam of pleasure. "Well, I'll trot along now, but you just write to me when you want to come to London and join us."

I went to see him to the door. When he had left the house and stood a few feet down the upward path, he turned to me. In a moment frozen in time we shared glances. He removed his hat and twisted it around in his hand, bowing amiably one last time. Then he dispersed into hundreds of tiny bats and ascended upwards, disappearing into the clouds over the village sky.

GAME DAY

Laura J. Campbell

"When you married Coinneach, you got yourself a full football team of brothers-in-law," Roy "Tinman" Turtletaub reminded her with a broad grin. The sunlight washed over his dark skin. "This team is like family. You'll never need to lift a heavy box or step on a spider again. We got you covered, girl."

Lizette Snell-Trigula smiled. She had only recently married Running Back Coinneach Trigula, relocating states away to accommodate his joining this franchise. Coinneach's new teammates were making her feel like their collective little sister. It was making the move a little easier.

She made herself a small plate of food, scolding herself for wearing a white outfit. The bar-b-que sauce on the ribs she was eating was hungrily eyeing her alabaster-colored shirt.

Coinneach was hosting a golf game and cookout for his new gridiron brothers. It was a team tradition that newly signed players were obliged to observe. And to call this event a "cookout" was a humble term. The spread boasted a full catered buffet, scrumptious desserts, and an open bar, all arranged at an exclusive resort. The party had the jubilant climate of a playoff victory.

It still amazed Lizette that she was here.

Her marriage to Coinneach wasn't a union either of them would have predicted. She was regulatory compliance lawyer in a small firm; Coinneach was a professional football player. She was thin, with soft brown skin and bright hazel eyes; Coinneach was almost seven feet tall and weighed in at two hundred and forty pounds of pure Iowa corn-fed muscle. His skin was whiter than snow; his eyes a deep ocean blue.

Tinman Turtletaub was pleased that his new teammate had a happy, supportive home. That stability would help Coinneach be an even better player. The team's former star running back had been plagued by disciplinary issues, an off-field life that interfered with his ability to play at optimum levels. Coinneach's and Lizette's personalities—light-hearted, a little superstitious, and truth-seeking—matched perfectly.

Tinman knew people as well as he knew sacking quarterbacks—and he knew that well enough to have three recent Pro Bowl appearances to his credit. He was looking forward to a very prosperous season.

"Thank you for helping set this up," Lizette said to Tinman, as he finished off a plateful of grilled chicken and vegetables. "I had no idea what was expected. Coinneach told me that we *had* to throw a big party since he was new on the team. I've never planned anything this big in my life."

"My pleasure," Roy replied, "Maybe catering is my next big gig? I need something to fall back on after my football life is over. I'm seven years in. That's a good run. But I was out most of last season with a torn ACL. I'm nowhere in the fantasy football rankings this year. But, I have that degree in business—the most popular major for football players, by the way. Maybe I'll start a restaurant—something trendy and heart healthy. *Tinman's Restaurant: Because you already have a heart, you should take care of it. So come on down and get you some good grub at Tinman's.* I can hear the ads playing on the TV already." He gave his signature smile, infectious and broad.

"Why do they call you the Tinman?" Lizette asked.

"Don't you know how to Google, girl?"

"I try not to Google people I know. I like to let people keep their skeletons in the closet, unless they want to discuss them."

"They call me Tinman because they say I have no mercy for the opposing team when I'm on the field. No mercy—no heart. Get it?" He struck a comically exaggerated aggressive pose and let out a tremendous roar.

"Hey, buddy," Coinneach said, walking over. "Stop scaring the hostess. We still have boxes to unpack from the move. I need her calm and focused."

"Well, she is dressed all in white, and I associate white with the 'at home' jerseys many of our rivals wear," Tinman noted. "But I know Lizzy is our team."

"Love you, brother," Coinneach replied.

"Love you, too, man. But, all this lovey-dovey stuff is too sweet for the Tinman. I'm going to return to the scene of the crime."

"Which is where?" Lizette asked.

"Those yummy desserts," Roy smiled. "The amount I'm about to eat—it ought to be against the law."

Lizette hugged her husband. "This has been a fabulous day. Your new teammates seem so happy. Not just 'they're here for the buffet and open bar' happy."

"They are happy," Coinneach promised her. "This is a great move. I feel better here, playing with this franchise. This is a great party, Lizzy. You really knocked this one through the goal posts." He smiled and kissed her forehead.

"I remember the rookies' joining parties from the old team, from when we were dating," Lizette replied. "They banded together to throw their soirée. But I have to give credit to Tinman for helping me put this together." She paused, reflecting. "You know, I don't remember Garan throwing a party like this when he became quarterback of the old team. We were dating when he joined the old team. Did they have a similar celebration tradition?"

"The old team has this tradition, too," Coinneach confirmed, "that new team members, especially the higher paid ones, throw a celebration upon joining the team. Garan refused to throw his party."

"That doesn't sound very team-player-ish," Lizette noted.

"You may hear some banter about that aspect of Garan," he said. "Especially here. Especially as the bar is open and the cocktails are flowing. It's just locker room talk." He paused. "Garan is a fabulous quarterback. He produces wins. It was a pleasure working with him."

"And?"

"Some of the guys—they thought he was getting special privileges. There was talk that he even had his own clandestine training area. I never saw it. I always wondered, though. He spent a lot of time away from the rest of us. And we had to be careful what we said around him. Whatever we said in criticism, intended to be kept just between us players—if Garan was around to overhear it, the coach somehow always found out about it."

"*Anyone* could have mentioned it, then," she said. "Or perhaps the coach was just intuitive."

"That's what us wise old men on the squad said," Coinneach replied. "Regardless, it's not my problem anymore. Meric Latherman is my new QB. And he doesn't have a private hallway and rooms in the team training facility off-limits to the rest of us."

There was the sound of a fork clanging against a glass. "Hey new guy and hostess," Tinman called out. "Get over here and get shitfaced with the rest of us."

"Tinman has a point," Lizette smiled. "I'm way behind on my champagne consumption. The National Hostess League will put me in the penalty box for being a wet blanket at my husband's big party."

"I don't think I've heard of that NHL," Coinneach said, as they walked.

"It makes the hockey players' NHL look weak," she promised him. "They got nothing compared to the game of a tipsy hostess about to give Tinman Turtletaub professional-caliber competition getting to those desserts."

* * *

Lizette opened another moving box. "We should have purged more before we moved," she said.

They were in the new city—his new team's city—unpacking and getting settled into a nice house in a nice neighborhood. Lizette considered that they should have finishing unpacking before throwing the party. She was still a little lightheaded from the festivities.

"I don't remember packing this many boxes," Coinneach answered. "I think the boxes mated and had babies while in transit. There's a church coalition that runs a charity shop nearby. They take donations. We can take a lot of this stuff to them."

"*All* of those toasters are going to that charity shop," she commanded, putting small uniform boxes into an organized pile. "Wedding gifts from a year ago—every member of your old team gave us a toaster. I forgot we had them in storage."

"That was another one of that team's crazy traditions," he smiled. "To their credit, the guys did also get us things off of our registry."

"But fifty-two brand new top-of-the-line toasters? I have half a mind to call up all your mamas and tell them about such ridiculousness."

"You liked the new team cookout, though? That wasn't too ridiculous."

"It was a little over-the-top," she grinned. "I ate like five crème brûlées. But those were so good. Speaking of good, it was nice meeting Meric Latherman and his wife. They seem like very good people. I apologize that I didn't get much time to speak with them. I was busy circulating—trying to say hello to everyone. I hope that they don't think I was being rude."

"There will be plenty of opportunities to catch up with them more," Coinneach replied.

"They seem so nice. Meric was very respectful, and his wife Rebecca is the sweetest thing."

"They have five children," Coinneach remarked. "I think they appreciated the opportunity to leave the kids with grandma and grandpa. Meric and Rebecca stayed at the hotel for the night, after the cookout ended. Meric joked that it was like having a second honeymoon."

"That's how they'll end up with six children," Lizette replied.

"You okay with this move?" Coinneach asked. "I mean, in the last year you have gotten married, taken a new surname, had to get a new job, and move to a new city."

"I'm more than okay. I'm ecstatic. I'm married to the man of my dreams, my new job pays me a higher salary with better benefits in a better environment, and I prefer the climate here. Plus, your new teammates have welcomed me like I'm long-lost family. I never got that recognition from the old team. Not that the old team exists much anymore—it seems like in the last year half of you have left to join new franchises and the other half have retired."

"There's a lot of movement in football nowadays."

"Not *that* much. Something was going on up there."

"Speaking of which," he said. "I left some stuff in the old facility. I knew you were going up there to get the last things out of our old storage unit. There was more in that thing than just overpriced toasters. Would you mind swinging by while you're out there? Apparently in my rush to leave I left a few things in the locker room."

"I can do that," she replied. "Better that I go into the teeth of old haunting grounds, I suppose."

"You're a doll," he said.

* * *

The stadium was huge; its practice facilities were likewise overwhelming in size. Lizette had attended a Texas high school that favored football as if it was religion and had earned her undergraduate degree at a university that featured a powerhouse college team. She was used to gridiron overload. Even with that experience, the size of the 'old' team's training facility was very impressive.

"My husband is..." she began, talking to a front desk administrative assistant.

"We know who your husband is," the woman replied. "His stuff is in a box, in the auxiliary dressing room. Sign for it here." She pushed forward a piece of paper.

No pen was provided. Lizette fished about her purse and pulled out a ballpoint. She signed. "The auxiliary dressing room is...?"

"Go down the hall, pass by the team locker room, and take a right. It is a large restroom, used by the cheerleaders and half-time performers. The box is in the supply closet. Marked with his name."

"Thanks," Lizette said. She apparently didn't warrant an escort.

She walked out of the office.

The hallway was only half-lit. There were very few people onsite. Just a skeleton crew of office staff and a few custodians.

And Lizette. She was happy she had worn sneakers; walking in heels, her footsteps would have echoed loudly down the empty hallway.

She passed by the locker room. It was weird, thinking that somebody else had Coinneach's locker now.

But he was much brighter in spirits since he had left the old team. Lizette had the sense that there had been significant favoritism practiced by the old team's coaching staff and management, and that Coinneach hadn't been a favorite. He had told her that once during a team practice, he had intercepted a ball thrown by Garan Weiss. Coinneach had retorted in a harsh tone to Garan: *Get it bloody together, mate.* That had resulted in a talking to from the coach: *Don't be too rough on Garan. Garan is highly sensitive to criticism. We need to help him maintain his self-confidence. He has a lot on his mind.*

Whiskey Tango Foxtrot? Coinneach had replied. *We need to be hard on each other during practice—you think an opposing team is going to sugar coat anything? They want to mess Garan up, not assuage his fluctuations in self-confidence.*

Lizette noted that the hallway became even dimmer as she walked past the locker room.

"Can I help you?" a baritone voice asked.

She jumped.

"Sorry," the man with the deep voice said. "I didn't mean to startle you. Lizette?"

"Garan," she greeted. "I'm here to pick up Coinneach's stuff."

"It's in the entertainer's changing room," he said. "It's not going to be the same without him. A lot of the kids liked him. He has spirit. He is a good man. I liked him." He walked with her for a few steps.

"Thank you," she replied. "How are you?"

"Hanging in there," he said. He started to walk down a side hallway. "You'll find the room easily enough. It smells like perfumed powder and foot sweat."

"Lovely directions," she replied. "I guess I'll follow my nose, it always knows."

Garan Weiss disappeared into the darkness of a roped-off unlit hallway.

Lizette found the dressing room and located the supply closet. As promised, there was a cardboard box labeled with Coinneach's name. There wasn't much in it—some toiletries, a few pictures of Coinneach and her, a couple of letters from young fans, two smelly t-shirts. She placed the items in a cloth bag she had brought with her. It would be easier to carry than the box, which was significantly oversized for the few items it had contained.

She walked out of the room. There was the smell of incense in the air. A soft humming noise buzzed from down the hallway. A flickering light punctuated the almost absolute darkness of the end of the passageway that Garan had walked down.

Lizette had heard the rumors from Coinneach and other old teammates that Garan had a private facility within the facility. A place forbidden to them. Her curiosity brimmed. If she was caught going down the prohibited hallway, she could, she reasoned, always explain that she had gotten lost in the labyrinth of hallways that snaked their way through the training facility. That was *if* she was caught.

She moved silently, now very happy to be in soft soles and carrying a soft bag. She gingerly made her way down the hallway.

The humming was a murmuring. It had a rhythm and a pattern of crescendo and diminuendo.

She stopped, not sure how much further she wanted to venture down the dark hallway. The situation did not seem to evoke the familiarity of a football training regime; it seemed to be more of a sacred exercise. If Garan was praying or meditating, she felt awful intruding on his spiritual devotion.

She was about to turn and walk away.

"You've come this far," his voice said firmly, coming out of the room at the end of the hallway. "You may as well complete the trip. I won't hurt you. I won't hurt anyone."

She approached, sensing it was now ruder to walk away.

Garan stood at the doorway. "Women are always more curious," he noted. "Small wonder that the serpent tempted Eve. She was curious. Adam would have just stayed in the center of Eden, eating raisins with the creatures, and talking about the tree. But a woman... she has to investigate. She has to know. Did you know, this is how I met my wife?"

"Paige?" Lizette said. Paige and Garan had married three years prior in an elaborate and well-publicized North Carolina wedding attended by luminaries from Garan's sports circle, Paige's entertainment circle, and a gaggle of politicians eager to appear more wholesome than they really were.

"Paige was doing a half-time show, and she came in a day later to make sure that all of her gear had been picked up. She saw the candles, smelled the incense. Of course, she was wearing heels, so I heard her about ten minutes before I heard you."

"And I was just congratulating myself on being so stealthy," Lizette replied.

"I have a good ear. Stadiums are loud. I have learned to hear little things whispered amongst lots of noise. Come in. You may as well see the place."

Lizette felt reluctant to enter, but she did anyway. It wasn't like Garan could kill her in the training facility. There would be too much evidence. Undoubtedly there was a camera somewhere that had seen her duck down the dark hallway.

Or maybe not? This was Garan's secret space, after all.

The room she entered was quiet and peaceful. There was a sculpture of a large eye, blue with a black center. Sticks of incense smoldered; candles flickered. There were a few ornately covered chairs. There was a low table, bearing one of his jerseys neatly folded and placed on top of the highly polished surface. A ring of salt surrounded the jersey.

"You wear a nazar, too," he noted, gesturing to the amulet she wore as a necklace, a blue glass field with a black dot superimposed on a white center. "To protect against the evil eye. I noticed your pendant when we met in the hallway."

"A habit," she shrugged. "My maternal aunts were from Turkey. They were a little superstitious."

"And your jersey," he noted. "With your husband's name on it. Trigula."

"Good luck, also," she confessed. "I wear it to give him good luck."

"At least it is your husband's name," he said, sitting down in a chair draped with a large scarf embroidered with rich colors and golden thread. "It's odd, don't you think, that people wear clothing with other people's names on them? I mean, especially women. That a man would let his woman wear another man's name on her back."

"It's just a part of being a fan," she said.

He gestured for her to sit down.

"Do you act differently, when you have the jersey on?" he asked her.

"I guess I do," she said. "I'm conscious that I am representing him. I don't want to disgrace our family name."

"I worry," he said, wafting the incense over himself. "About what people do when they wear my name."

"Pardon?"

"I worry. I think that every action taken while somebody wears my name imputes back to me."

"You're not the only Weiss in the world," she reminded him.

He shook his head. "No, no, no. When they wear the jersey, or even a t-shirt, with my name on it, they mean *me*."

"It's just a shirt. An article of clothing."

"You wear your husband's jersey for good luck," Garan noted. "That suggests you think there is power in the garment. And... before you object, the Bible tells us about the importance of what we wear. Do you know, there are over forty references to clothing in the Bible? *You shall not wear cloth of wool and linen mixed together. Likewise also that women should adorn themselves in respectable apparel, with modesty and self-control, not with braided hair and gold or pearls or costly attire. A woman shall not wear a man's garment, nor shall a man put on a woman's cloak, for whoever does these things is an abomination.*"

"Sounds like Old Testament stuff," Lizette suggested. "Probably laws designed by the early Judeo-Christian people to distinguish themselves from the barbarian tribes that scoured the region in the ancient days."

"Regardless," Garan said, "I think clothing matters. I think that our actions are imputed back to the names we wear. After all, if a person caused an oil spill while wearing a uniform bearing the name of an oil company, you would ascribe guilt to the oil company, right? If a law enforcement officer commits a crime while in uniform, we hold the law enforcement agency he or she works for in contempt and protest against the organization."

"Those are examples of people acting in their capacity as agents," she told him. "Corporations are legal people, but not real people. However, the actions of their employees—those actions can be held in account, both against the individual and the corporation. That's what Codes of Conduct are for. To stop bad actions and encourage good actions."

"Those people who wear a name—any name—they are like agents, then." Garan said. He gestured around his room. "I spend hours in here, asking for atonement. For forgiveness for the bad things people do while wearing my name."

"What about the good things?" Lizette asked. "Surely by your own logic if somebody does a good thing while wearing your name, then you should be credited something for their good deeds?"

"The world is filled with much more evil than good," he lamented.

"You don't know that," she said. "The media just reports bad things. I think our society is better off than it has ever been. Things that people would have thought commonplace once upon a time, we now find abhorrent. Public hangings, slavery, burning women as witches. We've come a long way, baby."

"This isn't about society," Garan minded her. "It's about individuals. It's about *me.* I was on the road once, watching television in my room. There was a news story—a young man had assaulted his girlfriend. He was wearing my jersey. When they turned him around to place him in the back of the police car, he looked just like me. My height, my weight, my hair color and cut. *My name on his back.* There I was, in handcuffs, being stuffed into a patrol car for assault. That's what it looked like. That's what I saw."

"'Looked like' being the operable words," Lizette said. "It *wasn't* you. Just someone wearing your jersey."

"And where does my jersey end up? At crime scenes? Liquor store robberies, scenes of domestic abuse? Homicides? My father used to tell me every night, when I was growing up: 'In the end, all you have is your name, son.' Where is my name? Is it written in more bad deeds than good?"

"It's written where *you* write it," she replied.

"You are a tenacious woman," Garan said. "I can see why Coinneach chose you. But he doesn't have much to worry about. His fans are very calm. Not like me. My fan base is much broader. Some bad people like to watch me play."

Lizette got up, finding the conversation more deeply disturbing than it should be. Garan's beliefs reflected a reactionary fanaticism. "I have a flight to catch tonight," she said. It wasn't a lie.

"On to the new city," Garan noted. "I have to stay here. Only the coaches here understand my plight. So, I will remain, and give them their touchdowns and their victories. And keep myself apart, so I can stay clean. And my fans can stay clean. So no sins are committed in my name. Have a good flight."

Lizette nodded, saying a hasty goodbye. She walked down the dark hallway, happy for the meagre light of the main thoroughfare.

She passed by the administration offices and out of the facility without looking to her left, nor her right. And certainly not looking back.

* * *

Lizette handed the cloth bag containing his recovered belongings to Coinneach. He kissed her warmly. "Were they decent to you?" he asked.

"Decent enough," she said. "That's a large facility. I guess I spent my time on the sidelines. It's a little spooky down there. They keep the lights down low."

"Per the request of His Majesty, King Garan," Coinneach told her. "Did you see his little hallway? The one they say goes to his personal training space?"

"I did," she replied. She looked down towards the floor, her cheeks slightly flushing.

"Hey," he said. "I know that look. You explored, didn't you? You went down there?"

"It was very compelling," she said. "None of you guys ever went there? To investigate?"

"Coach had us under strict orders never to even enter that hallway. The owners and managers threatened to fire us if we did. No one is going to give up an NFL contract just to look down a dank, stinky hallway. So, what did you find? The secret training room?"

"No," she answered. "No secret training room. Just a prayer closet."

She couldn't quite figure out how to explain what she had seen and heard; and it struck her that simply by approaching the chamber, she had bound herself to odd confidentiality about Garan's beliefs.

"Well, that's disappointing," Coinneach replied. "That's not worth talking about. Especially when I *do* have something worth talking about. Coinneach to save the day!"

"Which is?" she asked, feeling better simply to have moved off the topic of Garan Weiss.

"New city, new team," he said, opening a box. "New jersey."

He pulled out two jerseys, handing one to her. "Ours are the first provided to anyone, anywhere. Same old number, same old name. But I like this team's colors better. I think the blue goes with my eyes." He held the jersey to his face. "And the crowd goes wild! Woo-hoo-woo-hoo!"

Lizette smiled, turning the jersey over, seeing her husband's name affixed to the back.

"It's beautiful," she said. An unexpected sense of dread descended upon her, but she managed to summon up the expected level of enthusiasm. "I think this blue goes better with your eyes, too, baby."

* * *

In the evening, after Coinneach had gone to bed, Lizette cleared out some space in a small craft room. She took out a stick of Frankincense and lit it, allowing it to smolder. She found her gaze directed back to a television in the room behind her, playing the local sports news.

Coinneach's new team jersey had gone on sale to the public, and fans, excited for the contributions they expected he would make to their team, had gleefully purchased and donned his jersey.

She looked nervously at the television set, at the fans dancing and yelping while pulling on their new shirts to emphasize Coinneach's name. The fans' impromptu festival of support looked rowdy, but reasonable. That reasonableness was not enough for Lizette.

She folded her new jersey and placed it on a polished table. As she gently rocked herself back and forth, the incense fluttered upwards. She uttered odd new prayers, beseeching that Coinneach's fans did only good deeds while wearing her husband's name.

And although he sat in a similar dark secluded room many miles away, Lizette knew that Garan Weiss was the only one who would understand the strange fears that suddenly filled her heart.

DEATH & PIXELS IN L.A.

Stuart Croskell

February. A West Hollywood sidewalk.

Where a dry Santa Ana wind shoved a promotional flyer against my shin. I stopped to scoop it up.

Desolation Falls Movie Fest. Opening tomorrow. The venue, a Cold War-era aircraft-hanger on the edge of the Angeles National Forest. Desolation Falls—an extensive, loving reimagining of early 50s urban America—sat inside the hanger itself.

I crumpled the flyer, dropped it, unease already percolating through my body.

A hand rested on my shoulder. Without thinking, I leaned forward, shifting my weight. Turning, I used the angle to counterattack, jabbing an elbow into the side of my assailant's face. A small white guy sporting an immaculate dark suit, and a name badge on his lapel.

A smart kick to the groin finished him off. He tilted toward me, sinking to his knees. I unholstered my Smith & Wesson, aka Baby, and stuck her in his face.

"Talk."

"Apologies, Miss Cormier," he said, wincing through his pain. "I didn't mean to—"

"Do I know you?" I peered at his badge. *Maurice.*

"You know *him,*" he said, gesturing at an idling stretch limo with tinted rear windows.

"Who's *him?*" Though I already knew. As soon as that Movie Fest promo had landed at my feet, I knew some species of negative synchronicity would drag that shithead back into my life.

I offered Maurice my hand. He accepted, and I pulled him to his feet.

"My employer requires the services of a private investigator," he said, dusting himself off.

I glanced at the stretch. "Tell Mr. John T. Thibodeaux to go fuck himself."

"Ma'am, he already did that."

"I'm not interested."

"A few minutes of your time, Miss Cormier? *Please.*" The little man was terrified. And it wasn't of yours truly.

"This about what happened to his wife?"

Maurice nodded.

"Alright, five minutes."

He walked me to the limo and opened the rear driver-side door. I stepped inside and sat on one of the white leather seats. The Great Thibodeaux, self-styled, sat opposite me, sipping on a mint julep. He raised his drink. "*Ça va, cher?* Join me?" The ghost of his Cajun twang drifted around the syllables. "Old times' sake?"

I waved a no-thanks, checking out the limo's interior. "Nice ride," I said. And then, tuning into my own dormant cadences, added, "*An' lookit y'all.*" On-trend haircut, open-neck white shirt, baggy linen pants. Rick Owens sandals.

"*De rigueur* for movie moguls, Cass. Gotta keep up appearances."

And wrapped around his southpaw pinkie, he still wore his Baron Samedi signet ring.

The stretch pulled away from the curb, the motion so smooth it felt like floating.

"Hell's going on with your face, John?"

"Oh, that'll be the accrued effect of collagen enhancers, chemical peels, dermal fillers, and sundry whatnot. Plus, a couple of lifts. Price to pay, I guess, for youth eternal."

He was the same age as me, not yet forty. "Alright, what do you want?"

"Find my wife, Cassie. Find Francisca."

Outside, South Windsor Boulevard swept by, its street-lined palms swaying in the wind.

"You can't afford me."

"Name your price."

I bowled a six-zero figure, expecting him to refuse.

"Done."

"Two-thirds upfront. Now."

"Sure," he said, reaching for the laptop beside him. "Give me your details."

Twenty years ago, John T and me had crawled out of an Acadiana bayou like old-time amphibians looking to do some evolving, eventually moving to California. My one-time boyfriend had slimed his way into the entertainment business, while I'd embraced law enforcement by way of Long Beach Police Academy.

I watched his stubby fingers clack over the keyboard. Despite the air conditioning, sweat rolled down his forehead.

"You okay, John?" I asked. Not that I cared.

He glanced toward me. "Oh, tryin' to keep a lot of plates spinnin'. Not as young as I was."

Back in the bayou, his family had been blessed with the gift, his momma a traiteuse, a healer. John had some of it too. But for him, as always, it wasn't enough, and he started hanging out with voodoo bokors in New Orleans, the guys who knew the bad stuff. He caught me staring at the ring.

"You still into that?" I asked.

"Aw, I'm just a sentimental old *thang*," he said.

"Not sentimental about your wife?" He wore no wedding band.

He smiled. "You know me, Cassie. I don't like to be *beholden*."

"What's the cops' take on Francisca?" I asked.

"That she cheated on me. Ran away." He took a slug of bourbon. "For a while, they toyed with the idea I'd done her in."

"Did you?"

"*Kill* her? I did not."

"Are you attempting a pained expression, John?"

"Something like that."

I studied his mask of a face for signs of honesty. While the cosmetic surgery had rendered him somewhat inscrutable, his eyes were his eyes. And his eyes told the truth. *He* didn't kill her. "Get someone else to do it?"

"Jesus, *no.*" Again, his eyes told the truth of it.

"Was she seeing anybody?"

"No."

"Sure about that?"

"Of course."

"Yeah, you probably are. Always did like to know what your girlfriends were up to."

"Just a jealous guy, Cass."

"Okay, so no boyfriend. Maybe she, you know, left you. Couldn't take it anymore. Simple as." Exactly as I'd done. All those years ago.

"So how do you explain she didn't take anything? No clothes, bank cards, nothing."

"Spur of the moment decision? People do it, John. If they're desperate enough."

I knew all about that. Boy, did I ever.

He glanced out at the passing scenery. "I'd know, Cassie. I'd know. She's been *taken.*"

"And you believe she's still alive? A year's a long time."

"She ain't dead, Cassie."

"If you say so."

He tapped his Samedi signet. "Trust me, I'd know."

I took a deep breath. "Okay, take me back to before she... disappeared."

"Couple of weeks beforehand, she was kinda agitated. Couldn't settle to nothing. Let herself go a little. Stopped with the makeup, her appearance. Didn't want to go out. Especially on her own."

Again, his eyes backed his words. "You didn't think to ask why?"

He shrugged. A big Cajun shrug. "At the time, I was in the final post-prod stages of *Shadow Street.*"

One of last year's highest-grossing movies, the latest in a line of Thibodeaux-directed neo-noir blockbusters. There was some*thing* about John's retro, gorgeous-looking black and white productions that folks couldn't get enough of.

"Post-prod's a stressful time," he continued. "Never know whether you're sitting on a dud or a gold statuette. I always get antsy, irritable. Not pleasant to be around, I'll admit." He looked down at his sandals. "I'm not proud of this, but at the time I wished she'd just buck the fuck up. Had enough on my mind." He ceased studying his footwear, looked at me. "What I'm trying to say is that I wasn't paying her an awful lot of attention."

"All right, tell me about the day it happened." I half-remembered the details; how Francisca had attended the Desolation Falls Fest, John's self-funded annual celebration of all things noir.

"We were getting seated at the pre-release viewing of *Shadow Street.* Right by my side, she was. Said she had to go to the bathroom. Last I ever saw of her. And Tourneur."

"*Tourneur?*"

"Yeah. One of them itty-bitty handbag dogs. And wherever Francisca went, that dog was sure to go."

"If she took her dog, it sounds like she was getting the hell out of Dodge. Under her own steam, no duress. Ergo, no mystery."

"Thing is, according to the security cameras, she never left the Falls. There're no entrance or exit blind spots." He downed the last of his mint julep. "Got guards, too."

"A change of clothes, a wig. Not rocket science, John."

"Nah, I thought about that. Thing is, I'd recognize her walk, the way she *moved*. Impossible to hide that kinda poetry." He poured himself another mint julep out of a cut-glass crystal pitcher. "If I were you, I'd start at the Fest."

Which opened tomorrow. I said, "If I take the case, I do it my own way."

"You're probably wondering," he said, changing tack, "why *you*? Why do I want you to do this?"

"Oh, I know, John. Don't you think I don't." I was the one who'd gotten away. Twenty years later, The Great Thibodeaux was still furious at me for leaving him in that Calabasas bar, the Lagoon. I'd walked out of that dive, and kept on walking, sick of his control freakery. John's sole relationship style was one-on-one micromanagement, the fucker.

Outside the Santa Ana had upped her game, blowing harder. I checked my watch.

"So will you, Cass? Find her for me?"

"I'll try, John." *For* her *sake, not yours*, I told myself. And if she didn't want to be found, I'd make sure she stayed lost.

He pressed a button, and a small compartment opened on his left. He reached in and retrieved a cell phone. "Here," he said, passing it over to me. "Possible leads. Stuff the cops never looked into. Keep it charged. If you need to contact me, use it. Have it with you at all times."

I looked at the phone. "You got a tracker app on here?"

Another shrug. "I like to know where my people are."

"I'm not your people. And don't think this is the start of a retainer agreement. Because I'm not going to do that. Once this is over, you never, ever contact me again."

"Sure. Once this is over. Like I say, gotta lotta plates to keep spinnin'. Can't let any of 'em fall."

"Good for you," I said. "Now, let me the fuck out."

* * *

The stretch pulled into the exact spot where it'd picked me up. I stepped out into the heated wind, grateful to be breathing the dusty air. Spend more than a couple of minutes in the presence of John T and you needed a full hazardous materials decon.

I returned to the office, slumping into my desk chair, hating he was back in my life. My hands shook. *Shitshitshit.* What was I thinking? Once more, I was orbiting John T's planet.

I'd escaped one time. Would I able to pull free again?

I focused on the bank transfer. How all those zeros looked in my account: two-thirds of a fortune, a fortune in its own right. More than enough to get me a beach house. I could almost smell the sea, hear its ebbtide lull. How ironic if it was John who gave me heaven.

The surf-bum life had been an idle fantasy of my husband's. My six-year-old daughter had bought into it too. Big time. A stupid RTA had destroyed their dreams. And mine. Their abrupt and brutal death was why I kept my thoughts simple. I didn't do the past, only the present. And if I thought about the future, it was about getting that place by the sea. Live the life denied my loved ones.

Taking his phone from my pocket, I tapped in the code he'd given me, opening the file titled *Fran Stuff*. In it were names, addresses, and phone numbers. Some of the names I recognized. Actors. Directors. Writers. All of whom, I guessed, were part of John's stable of bitches. To hell with him. I'd do this my way.

Start with Francisca, her family.

I shoved the phone to one side, powered up my laptop, and typed his wife's name into the browser.

Francisca. Twenty-seven years old. Big star in her native Mexico. Brought over to Hollywood by one Cyrus Cavell, talent scout. Two TV movie supporting roles later, she was about to move onto bigger things. But she'd married John. He'd never used her in his films.

Figures.

No kids. Wouldn't be John's thing anyway. No way he'd be decentred from his own life. There could only be one sun in John's universe.

So, Francisca. Two vanishings. First, from the public gaze, then from the surface of the planet.

Video news reports from the time of her alleged abduction showed John giving interviews. Maurice in the background, uneasy, probably wondering if his boss would say something incriminating. In another report, John with the Family Luna. Her parents, younger siblings. Her twin brother, Mikey. As John gazed directly into the camera, expressing his profound concern for his wife's whereabouts, her family remained silent.

Okay, Lunas. Let's see what you got.

* * *

Francisca's family lived in a showy condo out in Ojai, ninety minutes northwest of L.A. Paid for, no doubt, by John, cementing his dominance and power through a charitable act. Classic Thibodeaux.

I buzzed the security intercom. No one answered.

"You after the Lunas?"

I hadn't heard the girl approach. Fourteen or so, serious expression, she stood a couple of yards behind me. "How do you know?" I asked.

"Oh, we get a lot of cops, reporters. Rubberneckers. You know, wanting to talk to them."

I said, "What's your name?"

She pointed to the pink vinyl letters emblazoned on the front of her white V-neck tee. *Duh.*

"Did you know them, *April?*"

"You a cop?"

"Investigator."

"There a difference?"

"Not really."

She mulled this over. "The Lunas, they moved out, middle of the night. Couple of weeks ago. I could tell you where they've gone. If you like."

"I like."

"You've got to promise me something. If you find 'em. Get a message to Juan. Tell him to get in touch. He's my boyfriend. He hasn't called, and I'm worried."

I promised.

* * *

The projects south of the Vincent Thomas Bridge were a million miles away from the affluence of the Ojai Valley. I parked my car on the safer west side.

Grit from the northern deserts blew into my eyes. The Santa Ana was really getting going. Following the blue line on my phone's map app, I moved deeper into the so-called Ghetto-by-the-sea, rare thunder rumbling. The twilight carried both threat and danger, outriders for the true, imminent darkness.

I leaned into the wind, aware I was being watched, followed. Several shapes materialized out of the gloom, for the moment hanging back. My right hand moved toward Baby, snug in her holster. According to the app, I was a hundred yards shy of the address April had given me.

It happened quickly. They drifted out of the shadows like ghosts, surrounding me, swaying with the wind, vaguely marionette-like.

John's odd phrase snuck into my mind. *Gotta keep a lotta plates spinnin'.*

Before I could dwell on this, a big fellow with Sureno gang markings on his face and a shaved head stood before me. "Fuck are you?" He spoke rapidly, a man uninterested in conversation.

"Fuck are *you?*"

"You work for *him?*"

"I'm looking for Francisca Luna."

"You work for him? *Thibodeaux?*"

"I want to talk to the Lunas."

Another guy, young, pushed forward. I recognized him from the TV clip. Mikey. Francisca's twin. "I'm trying to find your sister."

Tatts said, "She's working for *him*, Mikey."

"That true?"

I nodded.

"Thibodeaux's hired you to find her?"

"Why's that so strange?"

"You carrying?"

I nodded.

Tatts moved in to frisk me. Synching with his over-confident momentum, I pulled the lunk toward me, tripping him with my left leg. I shoved his face into the asphalt, blocking his air with a rear-hold choke.

Several weapons cocked around me. I released Tatts, rising slowly. "Baby stays with me."

"*Baby?*"

I gestured toward my left armpit.

"Ah. She gonna need feeding anytime soon?"

"Not as long as everyone stays calm."

He looked at his guys. "All right," he said, jabbing his thumb behind him. As one, they backed off. Tatts was helped to his feet, melting into the night with the others.

"You scared of Thibodeaux?" I asked.

"Can't be too careful."

"The cops cleared Thibodeaux."

"Pah."

"He hired me to find her. Why would a guilty man do that?"

"He plays games. You part of his game?"

I shook my head. *Am I?*

Mikey said, "She was my twin. Because of that bastard, I'm only half alive."

"She still might be out there."

"No, I'd *know*. Besides, she'd get in contact. Wouldn't leave it hanging like this."

"She might. If she was scared enough."

Mikey held his face to the sky. "Let's get out of the wind."

We walked to a nearby doorway, its overhang protecting us from the worst of the weather. He turned to me. "She was always laughing. Fran. Like she was wired for happiness. But then she met John. And at first, it went the way these things go. She was blinded by his success and the quality of his attention. He seemed like an okay guy. After they married, it all changed, like *instantly*."

"Don't tell me. John stopped his good folks act."

Mikey paused. "How would you know this about him?"

"Back in the day, I got too close. I got away."

"Then, you were lucky. My sister, not so." He lit a cigarette, pulled on it hungrily. "She became withdrawn. Subdued. Stopped visiting. And on those rare times she did, she hardly talked, not like she used to."

I thought back to the way it had been, between John and me, during our relationship. How it didn't take long before the simple fact of his existence sapped my will, broke my spirit. It was like being *infected*. I came to honestly believe that John was a virus, inimical to the interests of the human race.

Mikey continued. "And then in the weeks before Fran vanished, she became agitated. Manic, I suppose. Liveliest she'd been for a long time, but the wrong kind of lively. And the nearer the date for that damn film festival came around, the more jittery she got."

"The last anybody saw of her was at the festival."

"According to Thibodeaux."

"According to the CCTV, Mikey."

"Yeah, about that. You personally checked those tapes out?"

I admitted I hadn't.

"She said it was *peor que la muerte*."

Worse than death.

"A *muerte viviente*."

A living death.

"What was, Mikey?"

"What was coming." Mikey dropped his cigarette to the ground, crushing it with the heel of his boot. "Something was coming, and she was terrified."

In the limo with John, I'd seen the truth in his eyes behind the mask. *He* didn't kill her, I was sure of it. And *he* didn't get anyone else to do it either. Was Mikey protesting too much? Was John going after Mikey because he thought his brother-in-law had something to do with his wife's disappearance? Then why hadn't he said anything to me about his suspicions?

"Tell me, Mikey. You ever jealous of your sister's success?"

He shook his head. "I would never do anything to hurt my sister. I loved her."

I couldn't get a read on Mikey. He seemed earnest, but I didn't know him well enough to make the call. Either way, someone was playing me. "Okay," I said. "Is there anything you can tell me that might help?"

"Listen, there's this one guy. Gary Cutter. Gary the Cut, they call him. John's editor. Edited all his movies. I got friendly with him. Fran, too. Nothing happened, you understand. But you know John. Anyway, Gary got himself fired. Just before Fran went missing. Tried to contact him a few times, but no luck."

"You think Gary had something to do with your sister's disappearance?"

"No, definitely not. But he might know something."

"Where can I find him?"

"Don't know his address, but I can give you the name of the bar he frequents, real off-the-grid joint."

He told me the name of Gary's likely watering hole. He was right. This bar: It was not for the faint of heart. He also gave me Gary's description.

"One more thing," I said. "Tell Juan to call his damn girlfriend."

Two of Mikey's people silently accompanied me back to safer streets.

I decided to leave my car. Where I was going, if it was stationary for longer than thirty seconds, it would likely lose its wheels.

When I informed the driver, whose cab I'd waved down, my destination, he looked at me like I'd lost my mind. He took me anyway.

Off-the-grid was code for ultra-sleazy. And while the best go-to sleaze joints tend to be well-hidden in West Hollywood, downtown had its fair share. The taxi motored through the begrimed, dusty streets under failing and flickering neon. On the sidewalks, hooded individuals leaned into the shadows, heads down, furtive monks waiting to sell whatever it was they were offering.

* * *

As Mikey predicted, I found Gary in Spike's. It wasn't so much the sleaze and casual debauchery of this place that got to me, but the despair undercutting it all. Everyone trying to lose themselves in whatever their vice was. Anything to stop the pain of being human.

My driver said he wouldn't stop, but that he'd swing round twice on the quarter-hour. If I wasn't in the doorway by the second swing, he'd drive off, cut his losses. Fair enough, I told him.

It was getting on for one o'clock in the morning when I strode up the filthy alley toward the entrance to Spike's, my right hand resting on Baby's grip. She felt good.

She felt like Dutch courage.

There was no signage over the entrance. No need. Everyone who was no one in this town knew Spike's was the saloon where you drank after you'd been kicked out of the Last Chance.

At the end of the alleyway, a mountainous doorperson stood under an industrial-looking pendant lamp, their downlit features hidden under the peak of a cap.

"Hi, Yoyo," I said. Under her high vis jacket, she wore soft body armor. A shiny security officer nameplate sat on the right side of her upper pocket.

"Fuck you want, Cormier?"

"Conversation."

"Wid me?"

"*No*. God, *no*."

She looked at Baby's bulge. "Still the Smith & Wesson?"

"Baby's with me to the end, Yoyo."

"You looking to use her?"

"In there? No. Can't kill what's already dead."

"Yeah, you got that right," she said, standing aside, allowing me to pass. "Hey, Cormier?"

"Yeah?"

"Go fuck yourself," she said affectionately. Yoyo's way of letting me know that I was *all right*. But there was something in her eyes I couldn't get a read on. But like Mikey, I didn't know her well enough to decode the message her face was trying to communicate. She seesawed on her feet as if a little drunk.

"You okay, Yoyo?"

"I'm getting old, Cormier. Back in the day, being this big was an advantage. Now it's a burden."

The ambiance in Spike's was one of rarefied existential despair. A place of death, where faded gangsters came to drink before they paid their dues. Where hits were arranged and paid for. A terminus, where the hit came to the hitman.

A haze of tobacco smoke lay across the main bar area, but no one was going to enforce no-smoking rules in here. Eyes descended like vultures on my person. I'd left LAPD five years ago, but I still had cop written all over me. The scrutiny didn't last long, though. If Yoyo had let me in, I must be kosher.

Gary the Cut was slouching over the bar. A chubby middle-aged man in a *Joker* t-shirt at least a size too small.

He didn't turn around even when I sat on the stool next to him. The bartender—a clean-cut fellow wearing a *Spike's* embellished snapback—sidled over, raised an eyebrow.

"Set up whatever he's having," I said, nodding toward Gary, "and the same for me."

When the drinks arrived, Gary turned around, favoring me with bleary cirrhosis eyes. "Thanks, pal," he said, squinting, trying to focus. "Oh, sorry, sister."

I held my drink up. "*Santé.*"

He picked up his glass and gulped at the whiskey. As an afterthought, he gently knocked my glass with his. "Cheers. You the one?"

"The one what?'

"You the one he's sent to, you know, *pop* me?"

"I am not."

"Ah, here to suck it up."

"Not that either," I said. "But I would like to ask you a few questions."

"Okay, sister, I got nothing to lose. Fire away."

I got to the point. "I have reason to believe that you know the whereabouts of Francisca Thibodeaux. Or, at least, you know what's happened to her."

I expected him to clam-up or leave. He did neither.

"Oh, I got my suspicions. Same suspicions that got me here."

"Waiting for John T to kill you?"

"That's the one."

"Why would he be wanting to do that?"

"I know what's been going on. Well, some of it."

I glanced at my watch. I'd missed the first taxi swing. "Maybe me finding his wife lets you off the hook."

"Oh, baby, I wish that were true."

"But you know where she is? Or might be?"

"I got ideas, but they're all crazy."

"I'll take crazy."

"I'll tell you some of it. Not all of it. I don't want the last pretty lady I ever speak to thinking that at the end I was nuts." He swigged from his drink. "You ever heard of the *film look?*"

Twenty years ago, it was all John talked about. *The film look.* Making digital images appear like celluloid. It was an obsession. He was fascinated by how those silver-screen noirs looked. Their texture, their shape. To achieve that analog look in digital was his holy grail.

I told Gary I knew something about the subject.

"If you're using digital, there're things you can do," he said, "to get the look. Just got to be inventive." He lit a cigarette. "When it comes down to it, it's all about the light. Shooting during the first and last two hours of the day to get the softest light. Reflectors to throw light into the shadows, to make them stronger. And then there're all sorts of light-manipulation editing packages out there. You know, to tone down the *noise*, maybe add some *grain.*"

A thin, haunted-looking man entered the bar, strolling past us, nodding at Gary. He sat down in the shadows to our left. "Looks like my ride's arrived," Gary said.

I wrapped my left hand around his wrist. "Wait, ten minutes. Okay?"

My drinking buddy looked over at the man in the shadows. The man tilted his head forward, acquiescing.

Gary sighed. "John being John, he was never satisfied. Even when he had his first hit, a movie that received critical acclaim as well as decent returns, it still wasn't enough. Said the damn movie didn't look right."

"Gary, honey. Is there a point to any of this?"

He rolled his eyes at my impatience. "The *next* movie, the first of John's productions to be previewed at the Falls Fest, that was the one that broke through, put him up with the big boys."

The man in the shadows lit a cigarette.

Gary ignored him. "There's something different about that movie. Never could put my finger on it. And the movies that followed, they all had that... whatever it was. All John would say, was that he'd done the final bit of post-prod himself. *Tweaking*, he called it. Whatever those damn tweaks were, critics and audiences loved that movie. Mesmerized by it."

"How does this connect to Fran?"

"This is the whack-job part." He paused. "I think John Thibodeaux is... killing people, *offering* people. At the Fest. To—to make the movies look, well, look like they do."

I rolled my shoulders, studying Gary the Cut. While he seemed sincere, he also had to be completely insane.

"Crazy, ain't it?" Gary pulled out a phone. "Look. This is a short scene from *Shadow Street* before it went into post, John's special *tweaky* post."

On the phone's screen, a black and white crowd stood waited outside what looked like a courtroom.

"Do you see the lady in a sparkly dress? One of them lapdog things under her arm?"

I played the five-second clip a couple of times. I shrugged, shaking my head.

Gary smiled. "That's because there isn't one."

He fiddled with the phone again. "Same scene. Look at it."

I spotted the woman in the sparkly dress. And, yes, she did seem to be carrying a small dog under her left arm. *Tourneur?* The scene was an establishing longshot. I couldn't tell if the woman was Fran or not. "Gary, it's a retake. So what? And the sparkly-dress lady, she's too far away."

"I know it's a five-inch screen, but in the second clip, check out the *quality*. See how different it is."

I reran the first clip against John's tweaked version. And again. Gary was right. The clip with the sparkly-dress woman was different. Even on a tiny screen, you could see it. And yes, it was about the quality of light, but it was also much, much more than that.

My head swam. "There is something there. I'll give you that. But Gary, it's got to be a retake. There's no other explanation."

"No. I'm the editor, I know every single damn pixel, I'm personally, emotionally involved with every fucking dot. And I know all the actors' faces, intimately, better than they do themselves. That woman was not in the scene. And John was tweaking, not reshooting. So tell me. Where did she come from? What the fuck is she doing in *my* cut?"

Gary had lost it. Like everybody else who spent too much time in Thibodeaux World, he'd finally cracked. Spike's had been a waste of time.

"Go to the Fest if you don't believe me. John'll be there. You watch him, you see what he does. Never know your luck, you might catch him at it. Then you'll believe."

Gary was right about one thing. It was time to pay the Fest a visit. Everyone wanted me to go there, anyway.

"I'm sorry, miss. I gotta go now. Time's up." He got off his stool and tottered to the exit. He turned around to me. "Didn't catch your name."

"Cassie," I said.

The man in the shadows gave Gary a minute or so and followed him outside.

I finished my drink and walked outside too. It was time to visit the Fest. I said goodnight to Yoyo, who ignored me. My ride was swinging by as I stepped out of the alley.

* * *

The disused hanger housing John's upcoming film fest was surrounded by a vast parking lot. Part of the old runway, I guessed. Several cars were parked outside the entrance to the hanger, including John's stretch. Once inside the hanger, access to the Fest proper was via a reconstructed 1950s movie theatre lobby. A combination of inventive lightning and masterful set construction kept the Falls hidden from view, its mysteries intact.

The Fest mostly consisted of screenings of remastered noir classics. But what really drew the crowds was the Falls itself: a generic city urban landscape complete with working retro bars and streets boasting vintage traffic.

Inside the lobby, a bobby-soxer sat inside an ornate kiosk. She checked my ID, issuing me with an all-access pass. "Oh, ma'am?" she said, leaning toward me behind the glass.

"Yeah?"

"I shouldn't really say, because it's up to you how you want to spend your time with us. But it's only fair to tell you. If you haven't done the Lagoon, you haven't done the Fest."

The name of the bar in Calabasas. Where I'd walked out on him.

"It's special. You know?"

"Thanks for the tip," I said, nodding at her.

A guy too old to be wearing a bellboy hat and a waist-length braided jacket guided me to the 'theatre' doors. "She's right," he said. "The Lagoon's the hottest ticket in town."

Stepping out onto water-slicked, breezy streets, I was immediately impressed by the meteorological FX. I looked up into the spitting rain, wondering if John had just cut a big hole in the hanger roof, exposing the Falls to actual weather. Didn't seem like something he would do. Leaving things to chance wasn't John's style. As emperor of the city, he would make damn sure he controlled everything. Besides, out in the real world, it wasn't raining.

I was at the intersection of a deserted city, streetcar lines cutting across the junction. The third-arm street was narrower than the main road, and as it stretched away into the wind-swept distance, the buildings parallel to it appeared to converge.

I wondered what the time was, and then remembered: in this city, it was always two o' clock in the morning.

Desolation Falls lived up to its moniker. In less than a minute, I already had that end-of-party vibe going on; that jarring moment when the music stops and the lights are lit. When you find yourself on the dance floor, solo, moving to the rhythm of your own loneliness.

I was about to cross the road, when a streetcar bell dinged, warning of its imminence. As the car neared, its lit interior allowed me to see the sole passenger. John Thibodeaux.

As he passed, he turned toward me, staring.

Let the games begin.

Of course, this was a setup. Right from the get-go, John had wanted me walking the Falls' wee-small-hours streets. This gig, it had never been about Francisca, she was just the bait; that and the money. All along, what John had really wanted—was me. The girl with the get-out-of-John's-jail free card. How, over the long years, my defection must have torn him apart. To know that I was a viable human being, living and breathing and enjoying my own life sans him.

And how predictably twisted of him to recreate that desolate Calabasas bar in this desolate noir town.

As the trolley dinged its way into the distance, I crossed the road, aiming for the street that—my instincts told me—led to the Lagoon. Given the Falls was a finite space, I guessed all its roads led ultimately to wherever John wanted me to be. Getting lost—seeing as the Falls by its nature, identified as delimited space—didn't seem possible. Yet somehow, get lost I did. And it took several miss-turns before I got myself back on what felt like—again, instinctively—the road to my own personal high noon. Whether I liked it or not, there was going to be a reckoning.

So clever was the town's layout, it bestowed the illusion of directional choice. All the while, I had the sense of getting in deeper and deeper.

It was when I'd strayed off-piste, panicky, and more than a little disorientated, that I became aware of being followed. Several indistinct figures, twenty yards or so behind, keeping to the shadows. I was reminded of the way I'd been stalked in San Pedro.

When I emerged back onto the main drag, my stalkers' club had already welcomed new members. Some lurked in side-alley entrances, others huddled under streetlamps. Men and women, cosplaying mid-twentieth-century urban America; wide-shouldered suits and slicked-back hair, A-line skirts and seamed stockings. They were all there for me. *Popular gal.*

Their faces were blank, expressionless.

These lackeys of John's, I realized, they were herding me. The palm of my right hand rested on Baby's grip, soothing my jangled nerves.

But these fucking cosplayers. Something about them. What was it?

And then, *sweet Jesus.*

As the implications of what I was seeing hit my brain, a weird mewling escaped my lips: the sound of pure, distilled terror.

I knew I'd been played. With John, a given. The scale of it, though.

Moving toward me, slow and purposeful.

The taxi driver.

Yoyo.

Gary, Maurice, Spike, Mikey. Mikey's crew.

Even April. A *kid*, for God's sake.

More joined them, famous, familiar faces.

I spun around and forced my disinclined legs to do their actual fucking leg thing, aware that yet more of John's minions gathering behind, at my sides, silently, keeping pace, steering me to where I needed to go.

A blur of moments; my tortured, ragged breathing the sole sound in my head. Time slowed, or expanded, or went goddam sideways. Whatever, it must have done something. Because without being aware of how I got there, I found myself stood outside the Lagoon. Or, rather, John T's recreation.

It was all there. The blue canopy extending over the sidewalk, the tinted windows, its moniker arched in fizzing neon over the main entrance.

As if to announce my arrival, the rain stopped, the wind dropped. There was a short yet notable hiatus where all possible outcomes seemed to hang in the balance. Around me, my followers, too, had halted, gathering in a rough horseshoe, swaying slightly, moving to the rhythm to some unheard melody. John strolled out of the Lagoon's double doors, breaking the spell, eyes bright behind his cosmetic mask. In his right hand, he gripped what looked like a TV remote.

"Hi, Cassie," he said. I unholstered Baby, pointing her at him. The crowd seemed to move as one, swaying like barley in a field.

Baby held seven rounds. I could kill John, take out some of his crew, but they'd get me in the end by simply overwhelming me with numbers. He saw me make the calculation.

"You can't beat the odds, Cass. I got you good."

"It's not about odds. It's about finding Fran. What you paid me to do."

John ignored me, sticking to *his* script. Just like always. "You see, Cass, there's something about a festival that opens the mind, makes a person see beyond the everyday. A festival primes the brain for change. It makes you more susceptible. A festival is about possibilities, opening doors, creating new and challenging thresholds. And we all know thresholds are there to be crossed."

"Cut the BS. Where's Fran?"

"Oh, you know the answer to that, Cass. That threshold? Fran's crossed it. In fact, quite a few folks have *crossed*. All in the name of art. The Festival *context* just makes the move from flesh to pixels smoother. By the time a body's reached the Lagoon, its molecules are jumping at the bit. Ready to transition from analog to digital."

I racked Baby's well-oiled slide, chambering a round.

If Baby's good-to-go status alarmed John, it didn't show. He barely missed a beat. "Did you know," he carried on, "we got photons, pieces of light, zipping about inside of us? And that these photons, they sorta get entangled with our molecules, making us *glimmer*. Course the human eye can't see for shit that we're shining. But my camera can. She can steal your glow."

I stepped toward John, aiming Baby directly at his chest. The swaying crowd surged forward, mirroring me, halting when I halted. "Fran. Is she here?"

"Of course, she's here, babe. But you knew that. All the others are here too." He gestured toward The Lagoon. "That's where she went. Where they all went. This here bar, it's a walk-in holographic scanner. An interface between analog and digital. The exit and entrance between this world and the world of binary.

"Folks, they enter, sit they selves down, enjoy a cool one, maybe something stronger. But here's the rub. All the while, my camera's capturing their unique photonic signature. And when that signature hits the sensor, it encodes it into pixels. And then, *bam!* You in the movies, baby."

"John! Try to concentrate. Fran. Is she in there? I mean, right now?"

"Kinda." He glanced at the remote.

Play along. Figure a way out of this. "Is this about science or magic?"

He shrugged. "Aw, who cares? Once stuff gets to a certain level, it gets irrelevant. There's just the way it is." He swept back his hair. "As long as you've got the wherewithal—and I have—you can *capture,* and you can *transfer.*"

"There're rumors that you're murdering people to make your movies look better, Like a... a *sacrifice.*"

He shrugged. "Murder? Nah." He stroked his chin. "Sacrifice? Yeah, maybe. But they ain't *dead,* darlin', they're alive. They're just a little... pixelated."

"You think they're *living?* In your films?"

"Sweetheart, I know they are. It's just that their... new, ah, mode of being is somewhat limited." He rubbed the back of his neck, a naughty boy. "But what's really important is that they *are* aware of what's happening to them. That in their few seconds of screen time, they know exactly what their existential predicament is.

"And they do. You can see it in their faces. That knowledge. They know they're doomed to repeat their big-screen debuts forever. Sweet, ain't it? Their agony, their despair, is what gives my movies their edge, their *look.*"

I took a deep breath. "John T, it's official. You are fucking nuts." I waved Baby. "Show. Me. Fran."

"Not possible," he said, edging into my face, chin up, defiant. "The process isn't reversible."

"There's no *process,* John. Only bullshit." I squeezed Baby's trigger. "Fran. Now. Alive. Or, I swear to God I'll shoot you."

"Cass, sweetheart. You don't get to call the shots."

He held up the remote. "I know you don't believe me, so it would be kinda informative and educational for you if you experienced the process first hand." He gestured toward the entrance. "In you go."

Thibodeaux, your name is hubris.

I shot him in the arm. The impact whirled him around, propelling him through the doors of the tavern. Around me, the crowd surged forward, wheeling wildly, this time mirroring their master. As he crumpled to the floor, they, as one, sank to their knees.

A few of them started to shake their heads, look around, like they were waking up from a snooze of Rip Van Winkle proportions. I should have known it was John holding it all together with some zombie-lite bayou *gris-gris. Gotta keep a lotta plates spinnin'.*

I picked up the remote and strolled into the Lagoon. John was sat on his ass, slumped against a wooden support column. I glanced around. Apart from the haunting melody of a Sidney Bechet trumpet solo, we were alone. His serene cosmetic features belied the fear in his eyes. It was a naked fear, animal. I knew it couldn't be fear of dying. Nothing so paltry as mere death would put the willies up the Great Thibodeaux.

I showed him the remote. "Is this what you're scared of, John?"

"I was just joshin' with you, Cass. Ain't nothing to it. Just Thibodeaux bullshit."

"So if I take a walk outside, leave you in here, press this green button... that sit okay with you?"

"Aw, you don't want to do that. I'm hurt, I need a hospital. I've had my fun. And I still owe you a third of your fee."

"Not until I see Fran."

"I don't know what happened to her."

"Maybe, maybe not." I placed my thumb on the green button. "What happens if I press this?"

"Nothing, Cass. It's just a prop." But his eyes, the ever-faithful truth monitors, where once more at odds with his words.

"I remember, back in the swamp. What you told me. About magic and quid pro quo. And science, come to think of it. No action without reaction. You're the head honcho, the nasty bokor, in all this. I think if you... *go*, it ends."

"Honest, Cass. There is no *this*."

"Without you, I reckon they get to come back."

Damn. Now he had me believing in his shit.

But again, his eyes told the truth of it. Just like when I was sat in his car. I'd read him right. John truly believed he hadn't killed Francisca. He believed that she was alive. In his mind, at worst, he'd merely imprisoned her.

He started to struggle to his feet, but I tapped him on the head with Baby's butt. Not hard, just enough to discombobulate. I dragged him across the floor and heaved him onto a stool, him hunched over the counter. Leaving John, I backed out of the Lagoon, strangely echoing how I'd walked out on him all those years ago.

Outside, on the streets of Desolation, the crowd had already drifted away, free of their wounded master's backwater flapdoodle, fading into the faux night, the faux streets.

I pressed the green button.

For the hell of it.

Wasn't expecting anything to happen.

But something did.

A low hum, increasing in intensity, emanating within the tavern, coinciding with scattered raindrops, a rising wind. The fake elements grew in power, in step with the growing bass thrum.

Inside the Lagoon, John groggily assessed his situation. Instantly aware of the throbbing, molecule-jangling drone. He turned toward me, open-mouthed, lips framing one long silent scream. From no discernible source, a blue-white flash briefly lit the bar, searing and incandescent.

Silence. Except for the pitter-patter of the now-gentle rain.

And then the first of them emerged from the Lagoon, faces beaming with ecstasy, free from their binary prison. They tottered toward me, men and women, eyes wide with the joy of deliverance, their skin glowing eerily as if from some inner fire.

One young woman smiled at me. As I smiled back, her smile continued growing. Curling upward, past her eyes, above her head in a sparkling curve of light. The rest of her briefly pursued the still-rising smile, disintegrating.

More folk—the digitalized—went the way of the young woman and her smile. Some managed a few hesitant steps, others almost reached me, arms outstretched, as if desperate for one last analog embrace. But in the end, they all became modest explosions of light.

And then Fran, clutching Tourneur to her black and white chest, emerged onto the streets of Desolation. She stop-started forward, gazing at me, tiny Tourneur yapping with glee. She placed her dog on the sidewalk, the grateful hound bursting into a frenzy of sniffing and leg-cocking. I rushed forward, but before I reached her, she, too, exploded, her dots moving through me.

I expected Tourneur to do the same. But he remained. Now sniffing me. Because for a while, I was wrapped in his mistress's scent.

* * *

All that was a couple of months ago, and things have pretty much settled. I blew the lion's share of John's find Fran money on a place by the sea. Caminada Bay, Louisiana. For my husband and daughter. And, truth be told, me. I always was a reluctant Angeleno.

Sometimes, Tourneur and me, we cozy up on the couch and watch John's last film, his masterpiece. The one where he's got a walk-on cameo. The only person he can crush now, *devour*, is himself; and he does it every time his screen seconds are viewed. Every single pixel, every dot of light that constitutes John, shudders and shimmers with the looping horror of it.

But he was right about one thing.

His *process*.

John T. Thibodeaux's brief and private anguish does permeate that film, imbuing it with his cherished cinematic feel, the *look*; undoubtedly, it's John's best work. Pity he's not around to see it; the Oscar guys loved it.

I keep expecting Tourneur to go the way of Fran, but he remains reassuringly present. A digital dog in an analog world. He's warm. To touch, he's like a regular pup. And he sleeps. Or seems to. Farts, too. But he doesn't eat or poop.

Go figure.

And when I take him walkies, my fellow beach dudes fail to detect anything kooky. After all, there're lots of black and white dogs around here. Besides, on Grand Isle, folks tend to mind their own beeswax.

Makes you wonder what else we don't notice.

WRITTEN IN ASH BY THE FORGOTTEN

Peter Emmett Naughton

Part 1: The Invitation

The message on Mitch's phone was only a few seconds long, sent from a number he didn't recognize. It had become a commonplace occurrence, voicemails from young, energetic-sounding strangers promising him *three easy ways to raise his credit score, lower his cholesterol,* or *refinance his mortgage;* other times it was a serious and usually vaguely-menacing voice telling him that he owed fines or fees on a non-existent loan or line of credit he'd supposedly opened. Mitch always deleted these without listening to them, but this latest one had been translated into text by his phone and the single sentence on the screen caught his attention.

You have been formally invited to a gathering of fellow luminaries meeting in the Muirziak Forest to discuss the future.

That was it.

No website link, no short code to reply with, not even an email address for inquiries. Mitch had to give them credit, it certainly wasn't the typical clumsy ploy that he usually received.

Maybe they're trying to lure people out to the woods to invest in time-share log cabins?

He pictured a group of salespeople ditching their business attire and briefcases for flannel shirts and hiking boots as they pontificated about crisp mountain air and the many health benefits of coniferous trees.

Mitch played the recording and the voice that spoke the lone sentence wasn't perky or stern or even mysterious, which would have been appropriate given how cryptic their message was. He played it again, trying to pick out an accent or vocal inflection that might give him some clue about the speaker's origin, but it was completely flat and featureless like the automated announcer on an elevator or a subway train.

He swiped his finger across the voicemail entry, but paused with his thumb hovering over the delete button. As ridiculous as it was, there was also something intriguing about it. His life had been noticeably short on intrigue lately with his work routine and social outings forming a pleasant but predictable pattern that he seldom deviated from.

Yeah, you poor bastard, with your pesky steady job and longtime friends.

Mitch knew that tons of people would kill for the stability he had, and he felt like a complete asshole for complaining about it. Still, it was nice to think of himself as a "luminary" who'd been invited to meet other big-thinkers in some clandestine gathering in the wilderness.

For all you know that message came from a bunch of axe-wielding maniacs waiting to go Deliverance *on any fucker dumb enough to venture out there.*

He'd probably end up an internet punchline: "Gullible Schmuck Turned into Tender Vittles by Cannibal Cult." People would use his pale, stubble-chinned visage as a meme and post it whenever one of their friends did something truly stupid.

Mitch chuckled to himself, pressed delete, and put his phone back in his pocket.

* * *

Kelly didn't think the day could get any worse when her phone suddenly died in the middle of navigating to the restaurant where she was supposed to be meeting a client for lunch.

The month had started off on the wrong foot when one of her oldest accounts had suddenly jumped ship with no warning. Financially it wasn't a huge hit, but the fact that they'd left without any real explanation beyond some perfunctory bullshit about *exploring other avenues* had thrown her. They'd been a part of her business since the beginning, had been the first ones to congratulate her when she'd finally been able to quit her day-job and work fulltime as a freelance illustrator. The strangest part was that nothing bad had happened. There'd been no argument over artistic direction like she'd had with some of her other clients. The few disagreements they'd had were always minor things resolved with a simple email or phone call. Clients had come and gone over the years, but this was the first time it felt personal, like she'd been dumped.

"Stupid fucking thing!" Kelly said, resisting the urge to hurl her phone out the window. She'd left the charging cord that she usually kept in the glovebox on her desk, and the restaurant she was supposed to be at ten minutes ago hadn't even existed until this year. The area had previously been home to several empty lots and an abandoned garment factory until the city rezoned it and spent some money cleaning it up to try and attract new businesses.

By the time she found the place, she'd been driving around for nearly half an hour and darted into the restaurant, frantically scanning the tables. There was only a small scattering of people this late in the afternoon, and Kelly was sure she'd missed her when she saw a woman in black slacks and a mahogany jacket motioning to her from the other side of the room.

"I'm so sorry Barb," Kelly said as she made her way over to the table. "My phone died on the way here and I got totally turned around."

"It's no big deal," Barb said. "Whoever designed this strip mall must've been a sadist, because the parking in this place is a mess. I only got here a little bit ago myself."

Kelly doubted this statement was true, but was thankful for it all the same.

"It's great to finally meet you," Kelly said.

"Yeah, it feels like we've been emailing back and forth forever."

"That's only because I write obnoxiously long design proposals."

Barb laughed and took a sip from her iced tea. "You're very thorough, I'll give you that. Just so happens we're fans of methodical individuals over at Exeter. If I had to hear one more pitch from some designer with *bold artistic vision* and *an optimized aesthetic made for modern consumers* without any actual work to back it up, I was going to run screaming into the night."

Kelly laughed. "Yeah, I worked with a few of those back at my old firm."

"It's clear that you put a lot of thought into what you sent us, and we appreciate that."

Barb glanced at her watch.

"Everything okay?" Kelly asked.

"Unfortunately I've got another meeting across town and I have to head out."

"Oh, uh, of course."

"Before I go though, I wanted to make sure to give you this in person," Barb said, and handed Kelly a manila envelope. "It's our latest notes on the designs along with our official offer. There is, of course, always some room for negotiation, but I think you'll be quite pleased. Give me a call when you've had a chance to look it over and we can set up a time to finalize things."

"Thank you," Kelly said, a bit taken aback. "And sorry again about being late."

"Like I said, no big deal. I look forward to hearing from you soon."

"Me too."

"Lunch has been taken care of, so order whatever you like, and next time I'll take you someplace that isn't located in the center of a maze."

"Sounds good. It was really great meeting you."

They shook and Kelly watched as Barb exited the restaurant and then sat back down to look over the menu. The envelope was sitting on the table, but she forced herself to order before opening it. By the time her burger came she was smiling so much that she barely ate any of it. On the ride back to her apartment she kept glancing over at the top sheet of the packet Barb had given her to make sure that it was still there and that the number hadn't changed.

Kelly plugged her phone in as soon as she walked through the door and set it down on the kitchen counter; she grabbed a beer from the fridge and started leafing through the rest of the Exeter packet while she waited for the screen to finish booting up. When the phone finally came back online there was a notification that she had a new voicemail message.

She didn't recognize the number.

* * *

Mitch did a search on the Muirziak Forest when he got home from work.

The images of the area looked beautiful and it was only a hundred and fifty miles away. He was pretty sure he'd driven by the outskirts of it on the way home from a convention a couple years back and had marveled at how vast it was and how it seemed to spring up out of nowhere. His invite hadn't included any details on the specific location. Hell, they hadn't even told him when the event was being held.

It was the not knowing that got to him.

There was no reason to believe that this was going to be anything other than some company looking to talk him into buying something he didn't want and likely couldn't afford.

But then why not just come out with it? What was the point of keeping their intentions hidden?

Mitch scanned through more Muirziak images and did a search to see if there were any interesting restaurants or breweries in the vicinity.

* * *

The message made Kelly bust out laughing.

If she'd received it before the meeting, or if things had gone badly, it probably would've annoyed the hell out of her, but now it seemed like the perfect little absurdity to cap off her rollercoaster of a day.

Landing the Exeter gig had banished the black cloud she'd been living under for the past few weeks. She hadn't realized how bad things had been until it was gone, and now to top it all off she'd been invited out to the woods to be part of some new-age, hippy think-tank.

"Next I'll be nominated for a senate seat without even running and then I'll start my own line of organic beachballs or some other crazy bullshit," Kelly announced to her empty apartment.

She felt like she should walk over to the gas station on the corner and buy a lotto ticket. "I'll need the cash to jumpstart my beachball business," Kelly said, giggling at the image of a half-inflated hemp sphere being batted around by a bunch of dreadlocked dudes in tie-dye t-shirts.

Kelly played the message again and wondered if anyone had ever used the word *luminary* for someone who wasn't a life coach, self-help guru, or pyramid scheme spokesperson. Having the meeting place out in the middle of a forest definitely had a guru vibe to it with a hint of Manson that creeped her out a bit. *It's always those peace-and-love tree-stump preachers that turn out to have corpses buried in their basement.*

She thought about taking the message and making it her ringtone or her voicemail greeting just for the reactions it would get, but her mother would probably think that she'd actually gone and joined a cult and would be hiring one of those deprogramming squads before she had a chance to explain.

A search for "Muirziak woods meeting place" only brought up a page from the forestry service about picnic areas. Next she tried "luminary future forest" and found a site that consisted of a single long paragraph of text with a header at the top that read, "Naturalistic Rites and Rituals". It talked about Pagan and Druidic sects and the ceremonies they performed paying homage to the spirits of the land; about halfway down Kelly found a mention of Muirziak in relation to a tribe of shamans from the Pacific Northwest who used the woods for prognostic seances to determine how harsh the coming winter would be or if there was a famine on its way.

"Christ, this isn't gonna be some Stonehenge shit, is it?"

It was the only thing she really knew about the Druids, and even that had mostly come from a scene in *This Is Spinal Tap.*

There was one more mention of Muirziak near the bottom of the page. It had to do with a legend about gigantic creatures buried deep within the earth that were waiting for the end of the world. The story said that after the world was laid to waste, they would wake from their slumber and reclaim their rightful place. As far as doomsday prophesies went, it seemed pretty lame to her.

Just gonna hang out underground until everything's gone and then roll out of bed to rule over all the nothing? At least Fenrir's kids were planning on finally catching the sun and moon during Ragnarok, even if it was just to eat them.

She saved the message as an audio file and then erased the voicemail, wondering if there were any black metal songs about lazy, hibernating apocalypse monsters.

* * *

Though he had absolutely no idea how they'd done it, Tim had to accept the fact that he'd been infected.

For over a year he'd been getting bombarded with all manner of junk in his email, text messages, and voicemail. It had taken him ages to extricate himself from every spammer that had his info, and he'd had to ditch several accounts along the way that were unsalvageable. Since then he'd been diligent about using a VPN, private browsing settings, and auto-blocking any unknown numbers. This behavior had become compulsive almost to the point of mania, but it was worth it to him just to be rid of all the unwanted bullshit.

And then, somehow, they'd found him again.

Some fucker had left him a message, and if one of those bastards had his current data then it was only a matter of time until it was disseminated down to the hordes, meaning all of his meticulous hard work had been for nothing.

"Parasitic assholes have nothing better to do than make my life a living hell," Tim hissed as he listened to the message again and jotted down the words so he could search for the source. Every scam was basically structured the same way; they just changed the particulars around to try and draw in different types of people. There were online lists of known fraudulent numbers, but he couldn't find anything on this one. The closest he came was a number that shared the first seven digits, but that belonged to a drycleaner in Denver.

More than likely it was a new number that hadn't gotten around much and had yet to be catalogued.

"Lucky me, I'm one of the goddamn guinea pigs!"

Tim suddenly realized that he was screaming at the top of his lungs inside his tiny bathroom and stopped before one of his neighbors called the cops on him.

He knew he was letting himself get too worked up over this, but it was just so frustrating spending all that effort getting himself free from that morass only to be thrown right back in. It was a part of modern life that he simply couldn't get accustomed to. He'd tried contacting various regulatory agencies in the past, presenting them with evidence of the illicit activities, but it never resulted in any real action being taken.

If he wanted any kind of justice, he'd have to do the work himself.

Tim was more than up to the task, and if these weasels contacted him again, he'd make damn sure they remembered him.

* * *

Hannah had missed all of it.

Woodstock in the 60s, the New York art scene in the 70s, the punk scene in the 80s, and the grunge and riot grrrl scenes in the 90s. Everything she'd grown up adoring and idolizing had happened before she was born or when she was just a kid. There were plenty of artists and bands around now that she liked, but they all felt separated and segmented from one another. These days everyone was an independent entity, each with their own social-media promotion machines and platform branding. Even when she'd attended festivals it felt like being at dozens of tiny bars and clubs. The only connective thread between the acts was musical genre, or in the case of nostalgia tours, sharing the same general time period when they were all last popular.

She wanted to be part of something new that was happening now.

Before this she'd tried book clubs, trivia nights, poetry, painting, and pottery classes, and general social meetups at places in her neighborhood. She'd met some cool people that way, but the members constantly came and went, and the groups often disbanded after only a few months. Even the ones that stuck around didn't feel like much more than ways to fill up her free time.

She was looking for something that connected people and transformed their lives; an event that would permanently change her, mark her like a scar that she'd carry from that day forward.

Hannah knew this sounded frivolous and flighty to most people. They accused her of romanticizing the past and of ignoring the negative aspects. A part of her knew that they were right, but this knowledge did nothing to alleviate her longing; it only left her with a vague sadness that she'd been born at the wrong time.

The message was probably just a prank. She'd gotten stuff before saying that she'd won a trip to Australia or that her phone had been hacked and they were going to blackmail her with what they'd found unless she forked over some money. That was the kind of thing they usually sent to people her age, playing on her generation's financial desperation and general dread of the future. There wasn't anything on her phone that would qualify as blackmail fodder, unless they were going to try and extort her with cute animal videos and photos of food. Eventually she figured that everyone on earth would have at least one scandalous photo or post which would neutralize the whole situation. For now, she kept her personal matters relegated to a diary under her bed.

She had to admit that the voicemail had gotten to her. There was something enigmatic about it, like whoever sent it really knew her somehow. Even the voice had grabbed her. That androgynous monotone was so strange, almost alien sounding, but also oddly comforting.

And why couldn't it be true? Wasn't it possible that there was someone out there who thought she had ideas that were worth listening to?

Logically she knew that it was probably just some pervo wanting her to drive out to the middle of nowhere to pose for a bunch of nudes.

"It'll be totally artistic, I promise," Hannah said to her reflection in the vanity mirror and it came out as a snarl.

Stupid, stupid, stupid.

Hannah glanced down at the message on her phone and sighed.

She played it again.

Part 2: The Gathering

Mitch had nearly forgotten about the message when the text arrived a few minutes past midnight on February 28th.

The number was the same as the one that had left the voicemail, and this latest missive was even briefer than the first.

02/29 - 7:00 p.m. - 47°53'48"N, 120°41'56"W

He had trouble sleeping that night and ended up running all his errands early the next morning before heading out. Even in weekend traffic it wouldn't take him more than three hours, but he wanted to get there ahead of time and check things out before it got dark. During his bout of insomnia, he'd done some searching on the most recent message hoping to uncover people who'd received something similar. The closest thing he found was a scam that had run through the geocaching community awhile back, but as far as he could tell it seemed totally unrelated.

During the drive up he listened to a podcast about true life mysterious occurrences with this specific episode centered on the Tamám Shud case. It involved the death of a man who was found on a beach in southern Australia with no identification or obvious indication as to what had caused his demise.

The man was dressed in an expensive suit and freshly polished shoes, unusual for a trip to the beach and too fine to be worn by a vagrant. He was forty-five years old, in excellent physical condition, and an initial inspection of the body revealed no signs of a cerebral or cardiac event having occurred. There were no notable external marks on the body or any indications that he had recently been involved in a struggle.

An extensive autopsy eventually revealed that the man had died from internal hemorrhaging likely caused by consuming poison, though no trace of any toxic substance was ever found in the man's body.

Some weeks later it was discovered that the man had an unclaimed suitcase left at the nearby train station, but the contents of the case ended up being completely mundane, lending no further insight into his identity.

Months went by with no new evidence and eventually the police were forced to retire the case as unsolved.

Upon final inspection one new piece of evidence was discovered which only served to deepen the mystery. A small scrap of paper was found hidden inside the man's pocket watch with the words "Tamám Shud" printed on them.

It was a Persian phrase that roughly translated to "finished", or more precisely, "The End."

* * *

Tim hadn't found anything about the number even after a week of searching. Every time he thought he might have something on it, the trail deadened or spiraled off into some completely unrelated scam.

The second message he'd received seemed like it was designed to taunt him, shoving its middle finger right in his face and just begging him to do something about it.

"You think I won't, huh, you assholes? I'll come up there and mash your fucking faces!"

Tim had never been in a fight, not as an adult anyway. He'd had a few dustups during his younger days, but even those had mostly been glorified shoving matches. The one real fight he'd had happened sophomore year of high school when he'd made fun of this stuttering kid in the cafeteria. Tim used to stutter himself back then, but only when he was flustered or angry. This kid Ricky did it all the time and Tim used to give him shit about it usually after some other kid had teased Tim during one of his syllable-tripping outbursts.

He could remember standing over Ricky at one of the lunch tables, mercilessly mocking the smaller boy as Ricky became red-faced, tears streaming down the sides of his cheeks. Tim had turned to take in his audience's reaction and when he did Ricky stood up and punched Tim square in the side of the jaw, knocking him to the floor. The next thing Tim knew Ricky was bent down over him fists pummeling into Tim's face while everyone around them hollered and cheered.

It only took a few minutes for the cafeteria monitor to pull Ricky off him, but by then Tim's face was a bloody mess and he spent the rest of high school skulking around the halls with his head down.

Tim had other ways of defending himself now. Ways that some sucker-punching shitbag couldn't just walk away from.

He was through being pushed around.

No one was ever going to fuck with him again.

* * *

Hannah was sure that this is what she'd been waiting for.

Everything about it felt right. They'd reached out to people like her who were searching for something and now they were all going to meet.

For the first time in a long time it felt like she had a destination.

It was all happening. Things were finally starting for her.

This was the beginning of something big.

* * *

Mitch wasn't sure he had the right spot.

The app on his phone said his location was a match for the longitude and latitude numbers, but if that was true then he was starting to think this thing wasn't so much a scam as a practical joke.

There wasn't anything here.

He was standing in a clearing filled with grass that seemed surprisingly green considering the season. The space was ringed by towering trees and it looked like the setting for an enchanted glade from a movie about gnomes and sprites or some other magical woodland creatures.

"Well you can't pretend like you're surprised," Mitch said and laughed despite himself.

"Hello?"

The voice came so suddenly and unexpectedly that Mitch's laughter turned into a coughing fit as his heart leapt up into his esophagus.

"Are you here for the gathering?" Hannah said.

Mitch wheezed and nodded.

"Are you all right?"

"... I'm fine... I just didn't realize that anyone else was here."

"Sorry, I didn't mean to startle you."

"It's okay," Mitch said, tapping the left side of his chest. "I haven't had a heart-seizing jolt of terror in a long time. It's good to work the muscle out now and again, keep the old ticker on its toes."

"Now I'm picturing hearts with little feet, but not like Valentine hearts, the real things all bloody and pumping while they dance around."

"That sounds really gross."

"Hey, you're the one who said it."

"Suppose I did."

"So you got an invite too?"

"Fellow luminary at your service. My name's Mitch, by the way."

"Hannah."

There was a moment where each of them thought about extending their hands to shake, but neither did.

Hannah looked around at the field and trees and at the pale gray sky above them. "Now that I'm actually out here, this feels kinda...."

"Strange? Creepy? Bizarre? Ridiculous? Insane?"

"Like a big letdown. I mean, there isn't anyone here to greet us, no reception with cocktails and hors d'oeuvres, there isn't even an event banner letting us know we're in the right place."

"Well we are kinda early. Maybe all that stuff is being saved for later."

"Yeah... maybe...."

"Do you think it's actually for real?"

"I dunno, I mean, I figured it might turn out to be some marketing group or an alternative lifestyle movement trying to recruit new members, but I didn't expect an empty field."

"Please don't tell me we've been lured out here by a bunch of Freegans."

"Seems a little high-concept for them."

"Good point. Mind if I ask you something?"

"You want to know why I came here."

"Yeah."

"Why did *you*?"

"Crushing boredom combined with low self-esteem?"

"C'mon."

"Honestly, I'm not really sure," Mitch said. "The message just felt genuine to me... hopeful, if that makes sense."

Hannah nodded. "It was so simple and direct, and it wasn't asking you for anything."

"They always want something from you," Tim said. He'd been observing the two of them for several minutes, trying to figure out if they were the ones he was after or just other victims.

"Hey," Mitch said.

"See I'm not the only one who wanted to do a little recon on this place," Tim said.

"Seemed like a good idea given the mysterious nature of our messenger," Mitch said.

"I was just excited to get here," Hannah said.

"Excited about what?" Tim said, a slight edge in his voice.

"Don't know yet, but that's half the fun, isn't it? I mean, assuming this whole thing doesn't turn out to be bogus."

"I'm not sure what you think this is," Tim said and spat into the grass. "But these people aren't your friends. They're parasites who've illegally contacted us without our consent."

"Well sure," Mitch said. "But it isn't like they flooded our phones with porn ads or anything. I mean it's all been pretty innocuous so far."

"Just because they're a bit more careful than the average con-artist doesn't mean you should be happy to be here."

"Then why did you trek all the way out here?"

"Seems to be the million-dollar question," Hannah said.

"I'm here to show these assholes that Tim Anderson is not someone to be fucked with." Tim said and lifted up the right side of his shirt to reveal a pistol in a leather holster.

Hannah took several steps away from Tim, and Mitch's expression changed to a mixture of confusion and fear.

"Jesus, dude, what the hell are you planning on doing?" Mitch said.

"Take it easy," Tim said, lowering his shirt back down. "I'm not here to hurt anyone."

"Then why did you bring it?" Mitch said.

"Because I do plan on putting the fear of God into these folks so they'll think twice about violating my privacy."

"We don't even know what this is all about yet," Mitch said.

"Guess we'll find out."

* * *

Kelly almost turned the car around twice on the way there.

The contracts for Exeter had all been signed. Their offer had been so good that she hadn't asked for anything additional. She knew that she could have, but figured she'd save that leverage for down the road if she needed it.

There were a few things the company needed to take care of before the project began and Kelly had already done all the preliminary work she could and still had nearly two weeks before they'd be ready for her.

She'd looked up the location of the coordinates on her phone and it wasn't as far away as she'd first thought. As crazy as it all seemed, she liked the idea of starting this new chapter in her life with a little adventure, something to mark the occasion that wasn't as drastic as a tattoo or an ill-conceived haircut.

Kelly pulled into a space and took the keys out of the ignition, pausing with her fingers on the door handle. Even now a part of her considered heading back home, and she might have gone through with it had she not seen other cars in the parking lot. The spot where she was headed wasn't that far from the road, and there was a path and a forest preserve sign that made it feel less dodgy than what her mind had conjured up during the drive.

The day was bright and the sunlight filtering in through the trees made it feel warm even with the chill in the air. Birds were flitting about in the bare branches above her and she could hear rustling in the leaves carpeting the forest floor from unseen creatures scurrying back and forth.

This is where the wolf shows up and asks me about Grandma.

She laughed at the thought, but began to walk a bit faster, checking her phone to make sure she was still headed in the right direction. She was only a few yards away now and could see a small break in the trees directly ahead of her.

As she approached the clearing, Kelly saw a man and a woman standing next to each other while another man gesticulated in front of them like he was trying to guide an airplane onto a runway.

"Shit, did I miss the dance competition?" Kelly said.

Mitch and Hannah turned toward Kelly while Tim kept on talking as if she wasn't there.

"...all I'm saying," Tim continued, "is that these people will walk all over you if you let them. We've become conditioned to be subservient and unquestioning so we can be better consumers."

"Oh thank god, another girl!" Hannah said and proceeded to rush Kelly and wrap her up in a bearhug.

"Well hello there," Kelly said, pushing the words out past her compressed ribcage.

"Sorry, didn't mean to squish you. I'm just happy that there's more of us."

"Yeah, it's turning into a real party around here." Tim snorted and spat again.

"Nice to meet you too," Kelly said, glaring at Tim over Hannah's shoulder.

"Not trying to be an asshole, but I seem to be the only one who cares that these people are leeches. I don't know what their angle is, but you can be damn sure they have an agenda. This is nothing more than a swindle, and you're all treating it like it's a picnic."

"Oh, it's a great deal more than that."

None of them saw the woman emerge from the woods. It was as if she'd simply appeared in front of them wearing a white woolen sweater and blue jeans that didn't have so much as a stray leaf or a speck of dirt on them. Her hair was close cropped and a shade of blonde so pale that it was almost white, carefully framing the hazel-gray eyes and ruddy pink cheeks beneath it.

"Are you our host?" Mitch asked.

"I'm one of them. We don't really have defined roles in our organization. I suppose you can think of me as the welcoming committee. My name's Adrianna."

"But you're the ones who sent us those messages, right?" Kelly said.

"We did indeed."

"Oh please, some spambot sent those things out to a billion people and we're the only ones who showed up," Tim said.

"I assure you that isn't the case," Adrianna said. "We only hold the event every four years on this night and invite a select few to join us. This year six initiates were chosen. My hope is that the other two arrive before we begin, but it's possible that they decided to decline our offer. If you'll follow me, there's refreshments waiting at the main lodge. It's only a brief hike from here."

Hannah trotted up beside Adrianna and walked with her while the others followed behind at a more leisurely pace.

"This is so exciting," Hannah said.

"It's exciting for us as well," Adrianna said, smiling over at Hannah. "This is a very special group of people and it brings us all such joy when we can share our experience with newcomers."

"How long have you all been together?"

"The original organization was founded in 1961 by a woman named Marybeth Constantine. She was a beacon of light in this dark world and she shared that light with others who understood the message she was spreading. Sadly, Sister Constantine passed away in 1978 and without her leadership the group floundered for a few years and eventually disbanded. A handful of the surviving members reformed the organization in 1997 and the current incarnation has been together even since."

"So how did you pick us?"

"Unfortunately, our vetting process isn't something I'm allowed to disclose, but I can tell you that we're looking for individuals who exhibit an inner light, and that's not easy to find."

Hannah beamed and Adrianna put an arm around her shoulder as they approached the entrance to a massive wooden building.

* * *

From the outside the structure appeared rustic and homey, the kind of cabin you could picture Abraham Lincoln growing up in, though this one was considerably larger. Inside the old-fashioned façade fell away, replaced by modern nickel and glass light fixtures, flat-screen televisions mounted to the walls, and enormous high-gloss wooden tables that looked like they belonged in a board room instead of a Walden-esque retreat.

"This is our communal evening meal." Adrianna said. "Please feel free to join us. Afterward I'll escort you to some lodgings where you can relax before tonight's festivities begin."

Kelly nodded and headed toward a row of metal tables at the far end of the room. Mitch stood there for a moment and then shrugged and followed along after her. Hannah and Adrianna continued talking while Tim took a seat at one of the long benches, positioning himself in a corner of the room with his back facing the wall.

"They're all eating the food, so I guess it's safe to assume it isn't poisoned," Mitch said.

"Unless this is their Jim Jones dining hall and it just hasn't kicked in yet."

"Mental note, avoid the Kool-Aid."

Kelly chuckled. "Or maybe it's just laced with psychedelics."

"That would definitely make for a memorable experience."

"Christ, I must be out of my mind," Kelly said as she used a pair of plastic tongs to place a premade sandwich onto her plate.

Kelly and Mitch sat down at a table that had a few people seated at the opposite end. A lanky guy with a ponytail and muttonchop sideburns wearing a Frank Zappa t-shirt smiled over at them and Mitch returned the gesture before quickly shoving a potato chip into his mouth to avoid conversation.

"Smooth move," Kelly said.

Mitch laughed, trying not to choke as he swallowed. "They actually look pretty normal," Mitch whispered.

"You were expecting hooded robes and pentagrams?"

"Not sure exactly what I was expecting, but it wasn't this."

"That makes two of us."

"So what made you accept the invite? I blame my own appearance here on a lifetime of poor judgement and a complete lack of common sense."

"Ever have one of those days when absolutely everything is going your way?"

"Most of my days lately have trended toward the middle of awesome and awful."

"I just landed this fantastic gig. The deal I signed with this company is better than any contract I've ever had, and I think there's real potential for a long-term partnership."

"Sounds great."

"It's incredible and it made me feel better than I had in weeks. Things finally seemed like they were lining up and I should've just gone out and bought a damn lotto ticket."

"Not sure I follow you."

"I was coming off this big win where I felt like I needed to keep the momentum going and seize life's opportunities, so I ended up here."

"That makes sense."

"If you say so."

"Hey, at least there was an actual rationale behind your decision."

"I'm not buying this hapless dumbass routine. Why don't you tell me the actual reason you're here?"

"Really it was just... nothing...."

"Don't be that way, tell me."

"What I mean is that there was nothing going on in my life. I was doing all right, solid friends, decent job, but every day felt like a repeat of the one before. It's like I was treading water, but more out of habit than because I didn't want to drown."

"You were searching for something to swim toward."

Mitch nodded. "More than anything I think I was curious, and it felt like I hadn't been curious about anything in a long time."

"I get that."

"You don't think I'm crazy for coming here?"

"Oh you're nutty as a fruitcake, friend, but you're hardly the only one."

"Sadly, that actually does make me feel a little better. I mean...."

There was a crash behind them, and Kelly and Mitch turned to see Tim standing next to an overturned bench. Everyone in the room was staring at him as he began shouting at no one in particular.

"I want to speak to whoever's in charge of this racket and I want to speak to them right fucking now!"

Nobody moved or said anything and after a few moments Tim started to reach under his shirt.

"If you promise to remain calm, I'll take you to the person you wish to see," Adrianna said as she stood up from a table in the center of the room with Hannah still seated beside her.

Tim's hand paused halfway to the holster.

"I thought you said before that there wasn't any leader? See, that just proves that this is more of the same bullshit you've been feeding us since we got here."

"We don't have specific positions and titles, but there are still duties assigned based on our members' various backgrounds and skillsets. The member who selected you and sent out your invitation is in another building near here."

"You better not be lying to me."

"I swear to you that I'm not. You are our guest, and if this is what you want from your time here, then we are obligated to accommodate you, provided that you remain peaceful."

Mitch couldn't tell if she knew about the gun or was simply trying to defuse the situation, but was relieved when Tim slowly lowered his hand back down.

"If you'll follow me," Adrianna said and started toward the entrance. Tim hesitated for a moment, but then fell in behind her.

The room remained silent as they exited the building.

* * *

"Well that was interesting," Kelly said, sitting on the lower half of a camp bunkbed while Hannah hung upside down from the mattress above.

"That dude was a total creepo. I hope they called the cops on him." Hannah said.

Mitch was seated in an old recliner in the corner trying to get the tremors in his hands to stop. "I thought for sure that he was going to shoot someone."

"Thing probably wasn't even loaded," Kelly said. "That guy was all talk."

"Wasn't Adrianna great?" Hannah said. "It was like watching one of those hostage negotiators from a movie."

"Sure," Kelly said. "But what do you think happened? I mean who did she take him to meet?"

"Whoever was in charge of him, his handler or whatever. Tim probably just made sure they erased him from their system," Hannah said.

"Let's hope that's all it was," Mitch said. "He seemed pretty hell-bent on getting some payback."

"If something serious happened we'd have heard by now. There'd be ambulances up here," Hannah said.

"Yeah, I guess that's true," Mitch said.

"This shindig, whatever it is, kicks off in less than an hour. I say we forget about Tim and focus on having a good time," Kelly said.

"That's the spirit!" Hannah shouted.

"Damn you both and your contagious enthusiasm. Now I might actually be forced to enjoy myself," Mitch said, and the three of them burst out laughing.

Part 3: The Ceremony

The sun had only set an hour ago, but already the cold had become bitter and biting in its absence. Stars covered the evening sky and were so dense in places that it looked more like a shimmering quilt than individual points of light.

One of the members had knocked on their cabin door and told them where to go. They thought that he'd escort them, but he explained that initiates always entered the ceremony by themselves.

As the three of them walked along they could see the edges of an orange glow in the distance, and Kelly swore that she could actually feel the heat from the bonfire.

"This is it then," Mitch said.

"Do you think we'll have to say anything?" Hannah said. "I get really nervous speaking in public."

"I'm still betting this is going to be some kind of sales pitch. Probably an invitation to join their commune or sign up for some wellness retreat. I'm sure they'll be doing most of the talking," Mitch said.

"So you don't think they're inducting us as luminaries?" Hannah said, clearly disappointed.

Mitch turned to Hannah. "Hey, no matter what it turns out to be, you can say you had a totally unique experience. That beats most ordinary days, right?"

Hannah smiled and slipped in between Mitch and Kelly, taking each of their hands in her own and humming the melody from "We're Off to See the Wizard." The massive fire was fully visible now, flames towering in front of a group that appeared much larger than the dozen or so that had been present at the dining hall. There had to be at least a hundred people seated in tiered benches that formed a semicircle around the bonfire.

Adrianna was waiting for them just outside the gathering. She was wearing a long emerald dress that contrasted nicely against the orange flames, and the sides of her hair were adorned with a series of ornate silver pins.

"I'm honored to welcome the three of you to our initiate ceremony. This is an opportunity afforded to very few people. It's a real chance to change your lives."

She smiled and ushered them over to a small stone table that was situated between the bonfire and the bleachers.

Adrianna stood in front of the table and addressed the assembled crowd.

"We have gathered here on this auspicious evening to ask these initiates to join the light of our union. It is a truly joyous occasion, but sadly one of our anointed has proven themselves unworthy. Though it makes our hearts heavy, we will cleanse this transgression by transforming it into sacred cinder so that our luminaries may shine ever brighter."

Two men from opposite ends of the benches descended to ground level and Kelly, Mitch, and Hannah turned and watched as they made their way to the other side of the fire.

"I wonder if this is like the opening of the Olympics where they light the torch," Hannah said.

"Yeah, maybe," Kelly said, but the skin on the back of her neck began to tighten.

There was a loud creaking noise and Adrianna pointed at the flames just as a wooden ladder was raised up by the two men using ropes tied to the end of it. A figure was affixed to the top of the ladder, lashed to its rungs with more rope, and at first Mitch thought it was some sort of effigy.

"Oh God... it's Tim..." Mitch said.

Adrianna turned back to the audience.

"Let this sacrifice upon our pyre give this man the purpose he could not find in life."

Tim's screams were muffled by the rag shoved into his mouth, but were still audible as the flames caught the bottom of the ladder and quickly began to ascend.

Mitch tried to say something, but his throat felt dry and swollen. Hannah buried her face in Kelly's shoulder and Kelly put an arm around her as she watched the flames consume Tim.

A swelling cheer rose from the crowd as Kelly and Mitch looked on in stunned horror.

Adrianna strode over to the table. "This is truly a momentous occasion. We seldom have an offering on the same night as our initiate ceremony."

Mitch tried again to speak, but the only thing that emerged from his mouth was a clicking sound.

"How... how could you..." Kelly trailed off.

Adrianna gave Kelly a sympathetic smile as if she were placating a child. She gestured toward the fire. "That man was consumed by frustration and rage. There was nothing left in his soul that could be kindled back to kindness and virtue."

"He may not have been the nicest person," Kelly stammered, "but that doesn't give you the right to kill him."

"He was chosen, and those that are chosen must prove themselves worthy."

"And how do we do that?" Kelly said, struggling to keep her voice steady.

"By demonstrating your inner luminosity and shinning with the light instead of being consumed by it the way that he was."

Hannah let out a sob and Kelly gripped her tighter.

"You can't do this," Mitch said, finally regaining his powers of speech.

"All of you came here of your own free will," Adrianna said.

"That's not the point," Mitch said.

"Did you tell anyone that you were coming here?" Adrianna said with a smile, already knowing the answer.

"They'll still find us. The smoke from this fire is probably visible from the highway."

"We've been meeting at this location for a long time. The locals are quite accustomed to our activities."

"You don't have to do this," Kelly said. "Just let us go and we won't say anything."

"I know that change can be frightening," Adrianna said. "But true transformation requires sacrifice and is only possible when you shed the remnants of your damaged past. Think of this as nothing more than a prelude to your new lives."

"What if we don't pass your initiation?" Mitch said.

"Metamorphosis is inevitable. It's simply a matter of what form you choose to take."

* * *

Kelly reached for the bottle of wine and the sleeve of her blouse slid up above her wrist, revealing an intricate web of puckered, pink scars. She'd had reconstructive surgery done on her hands, but hadn't been able to afford much else. Her face had only suffered some first and minor second degrees that had healed after a few months.

"So the new gig is going well?" Kelly said.

"It's been a pretty big adjustment compared to what I used to do, but I feel excited and engaged, which is certainly a nice change."

"That's great. I'm really happy for you."

"What about you? How's life running the big show?"

"I'm just the Art Director, it's not like I'm CEO."

"Yeah, yeah, give it a few years and I bet you will be."

"Oh hell no. That job is nothing but stress headaches and board members screaming at you every time the stock slips a quarter of a point. I like where I'm at just fine, thank you."

Mitch smiled and took a sip from his glass. Even with his hair parted to the side, you could still see the shiny patch of skin that ran from the top of his left temple to just below his cheek bone.

Kelly caught herself staring at the spot. "Sorry."

"Don't worry about it. You're hardly the first person to notice."

She gave a humorless little chuckle. "These women at the office keep going on and on about bikini season and it makes me want to vomit."

"I had a couple of my new coworkers beg me to go wake boarding with them. They wouldn't let up and finally I had to lie and tell them I couldn't swim."

"I guess our beach going days are over."

"Certainly seems that way. Can't draw that kind of attention."

"Nope, can't do that..." Kelly said, her fingers absently moving to the small glass vial suspended from a silver chain around her neck; inside the tiny cylinder were white and gray flecks as fine as snow, and Kelly often stared at them late at night while she struggled to find sleep.

"Are you still having the dreams?"

Kelly nodded. "Not every night, and they're different now. I still find her in the field where we first met, but when she opens her mouth, sometimes she just smiles at me... it isn't always the screaming...."

"Have you heard from them lately?"

"Not since the last meeting. You?"

"I met with Adrianna a month or so ago. She's the one who arranged the interview with the company."

"I thought I saw her. Just walking around in the real world like a regular person."

"Really? Where?"

"In the lobby of our office building. I was leaving for lunch and I swore I saw her get into the elevator with someone. I asked the receptionist, but she didn't know who I was talking about."

"All part of being a luminary I suppose. They do get around."

"Yeah, right," Kelly said, and drained the remaining wine from her glass.

Mitch signaled the waiter to bring another bottle.

"It's only two months until the next one. Do you think they started sending out messages yet?" Kelly said.

"Don't know."

"You realize we'll have to attend."

Mitch lowered his head, resting his face against his palms. When he spoke, his voice was just above a whisper. "...all part of being a luminary..."

"...now and forever." Kelly said and turned her attention back to her necklace.

Neither of them noticed when the waiter returned with the wine.

PART FOUR:

A COLLOQUIUM OF SCIENCE FICTION

THE STORIES WE LEAVE BEHIND

JONATHON MAST

Miranda had never crashed a ship on a mysterious uncharted planet while carting a probably insane passenger before, so at least she was trying new things.

She wriggled out of the impact webbing and emergency foam. Ow. Neck still hurt plenty. At least she could breathe fairly easily, though. No ribs seemed to be broken, and lungs were working fine.

She took a look at the panels in front of her pilot seat. Red lights blinked everywhere.

That wasn't good.

No. No no no no.

Hull breaches everywhere. The ship wasn't airtight.

Was the planet's atmosphere breathable? How long had she been out? Was it already too late?

Wait. Calm down, Miranda. Think. Your lungs aren't burning. Your eyes are fine. Your skin isn't boiling. So whatever the atmosphere was, it wasn't immediately dangerous. Possibly poisonous long term, but not immediately fatal.

She scanned the rest of the indicators. Engines shot. Computer mostly down. Electrical fritzing all over. Atmospheric generators nonfunctional.

Oh, good. Looked like every major system was damaged and nonoperational.

No, wait. The coffeemaker in easy reach of the pilot seat looked like it could still work. At least there was some blessing left.

All right. Mysterious planet. What could be out there?

Flesh-eating whipleaf thornbushes.

Alligator rabbits.

Luminescent powder-rays with telepathic plaguefleas.

Slow down again, Miranda. Slow down. Not everything is as bad as the stories. Right now, nothing is scurrying on the ship trying to get in.

Something scurried down the corridor toward her.

She spun, her hand shooting to the holster on her thigh.

Her sidearm was missing.

It must have gone flying in the crash before the emergency foam encased her. She'd kept it in her holster, but unsecured for a faster draw in case her passenger turned on her. Of course that bit her now. Why wouldn't it?

Something moved in the darkness of the corridor leading to the cockpit. Miranda squared her shoulders, ready to fight.

A spray of sparks from one of the conduits in the corridor revealed the shadow: The passenger. The nameless woman who had hired her to bring her to these coordinates. The passenger's unruly mass of blond braids was even more insane. Dirt smudged her face, and she had a cut near her left ear that oozed. The passenger twitched at the sudden sparks. "It's starting!" she crowed. "I need to get there!"

Miranda forced herself to relax. The passenger was insane, but so far nonviolent. So far. "Yeah, well, if you didn't notice, we crashed." She rolled her shoulders, trying to release some of the tension. "I don't know where we are compared to your destination, either. The planet came up on us so fast when we jumped, I wasn't able to get any readings." She gestured to the blinking red lights on the panels. "And everything's down, so whatever the sensors picked up we don't have access to. But I can make some coffee, I guess. Want some?"

"We're not far," the woman answered. Her eyes darted around the cockpit. "I can tell. I need to get there. Soon. Or they'll start the festival without me."

"Festival?" Miranda raised an eyebrow.

The passenger nodded her shaggy head, the braids rustling.

"On an uncharted planet. A place that I've never even heard of, and I've been most everywhere humans can be."

The passenger grinned. "You like adventure."

"I like stories about adventures. Not the same thing." She shook her head. "How the hell can there be a festival here?"

"Once upon a time."

Miranda stared. "What?"

"Once upon a time. Once upon a time everyone remembered, but they left us behind. But now it's time for the festival."

Miranda stared. *Okay, just more crazy. More crazy about old stories. Just roll with it.* "I don't know if it's a good idea. If we stay in the ship, it'll be far safer. We don't know what's out there. We don't know if we can face it."

"The woods are dangerous, Red. Stay on the path."

The captain swallowed. "That's a story. That's a story my mom told me."

"She wasn't too old for us, was she? She remembered. She used the invocation."

"Invocation?"

"Once upon a time." And the passenger smiled. "Get your things. We need to get to the festival."

* * *

Miranda decided that they could at least take a look. If it looked bad, they could always hole up in the ship.

She raided the small armory she kept. There were too many stories out there about what you'd find on uncharted planets. She'd been in just about every port, and most places were relatively safe, but you never knew. People were too scared these days to wander far from the standard routes. You never knew what lurked out there.

What would be out there today? All the sensors had gone dark, so of course the screens were ineffective. And without the sensors, none of the windows would light up. What waited?

Carrion-spiders?

Arachnosquids?

Other things with eight legs that were creepy?

She found another trusty sidearm, fully charged and ready to go. It went into the thigh holster. Another for the one on her opposite hip. A few knives. A backpack full of water canteens and protein bars. Hoverlight. Maybe a few extra of those in the bag, too. Maybe. Tracking beacon on the wrist like always.

She took a deep breath. *Calm down.* There was some sort of festival here. Maybe. Apparently. And if there was a festival, well, what kind of non-neural would party in a dangerous space?

How about one who used the invocation, "Once upon a time?"

Well. If there was a festival of some kind, other people would have to travel here. And one of them could hopefully give Miranda a lift off this planet.

So, time to get to a festival.

* * *

The only thing that worked on her poor ship—besides the coffee maker—was the loading bay door. Figured.

Miranda hit the release, and steam hissed from the valves as the door unsealed. She drew both of her sidearms, pointed at whatever might be out there.

The passenger stood nearby, her arms limp at her sides.

"You know anything about the planet?" Miranda asked as the door creaked and pivoted out and down into a ramp.

"Once upon a time, it was full of things to explore. And then we ran out of stories and looked for more in the stars."

"That's not helpful."

The passenger shrugged. "There's the sleepers. But they shouldn't bother us unless we wake them up."

Miranda shot a look at the passenger, but that was the moment the door cleared her line of sight. Her first sight of a wild planet.

No, not a wild planet.

A tomb.

A dark, dark sky was filled with countless stars gathered in whorls. Black pinnacles blocked out shards of the sky. These weren't mountains, though. They were ancient towers hundreds of stories high. Every here and there, glass or metal reflected the dim light.

Miranda let her gaze come back down to the earth. It looked like she had crashed in some sort of ancient city square. A dark stone served as pavement in the broad space. Huge buildings pointed toward the night sky.

She could see nothing living.

No towering Faceless Ones.

No bodiless mouths.

No wolves.

The passenger inhaled, sharp. "She didn't like the inside of the wolf, did she? It was dank and dark and squishy in all the wrong ways."

"The hell?" Miranda swung toward the taller woman.

She continued, "But Red, well, she'd been trained by the best huntsman. She figured that Grandma wasn't well, but she hadn't realized that she'd been infected with wolf-strain. And now, well, it was too late for Grandma. But not for Red."

And with that, the passenger set foot onto the ramp, down the few paces of the incline, and to the dark ground.

"Wait!" Miranda called. "We don't know what's out there!"

"So Red took her ax out, the one given to her by the master huntsman, and she sliced upward, freeing herself of the rank odor." She looked around, arms out, inviting the dead world to her. After a moment of bliss, she grinned at Miranda.

"Was that Little Red Riding Hood?" Miranda breathed.

"That's my name, yes."

"My mom told me that story before bed. Helped me get to sleep. Told me that the wolves would never get me." Miranda holstered her sidearms. "Never heard that version before, though."

"It's good to reinvent yourself every once in a while, I think. Do you like it?"

"In the version my mom told, Red was saved by a huntsman."

"Yes, well, we can't have that, can we? People rejected that sort of narrative so long ago. So I thought I'd try something new." The passenger nodded. "Now, come on. The festival's this way."

"How can you tell?"

"A feeling."

"Oh. Great."

* * *

The ruins were older than anything Miranda had seen in the colonies. It didn't make any sense. Most sentient species, if they went extinct, took their planet and their ruins with them. She'd never heard of anything like this.

She kept a sidearm out and charged. There were so many empty windows. She wondered what could be watching from those windows. What could bring down a society that could make something like this? What if it still lurked?

Nothing moved. No breeze. No mice. Nothing. The only sounds were the scuffing of their shoes against the paving, and the now-distant ticking of her ship cooling off.

"Tell me a story," the passenger said.

"What?"

"You heard me just fine. Tell me a story. It'll help pass the time as we get to the festival."

"I'm not much for telling stories."

"Liar." The passenger grinned that grin again. "I can smell them on you, you know. All the bedtime stories you've taken in. They make you strong."

"Sure. Whatever."

The passenger shrugged as she continued strolling with Miranda. The buildings loomed over them. The empty windows stared.

Who knew what could lurk inside those buildings? Could be anything. Something ancient. Maybe whatever killed off this civilization. Some kind of predator, well-adapted to hunt in a silent urban environment. Miranda's eyes shot from side to side of the street. Every few steps she would turn to make sure nothing was following them.

The passenger kept walking, oblivious to any potential harm.

"How can you be so calm?"

The blond woman grinned. "Because I know we can defeat whatever comes between us and the festival."

"There could be a lot of dangerous things out there."

"Of course there could!" She raised her arms, taking in their surroundings. "I have learned: Danger is real. But every danger can be defeated." She lowered her arms and took a few more steps before asking again, "Tell me a story."

"Why?"

"I have a feeling it could help us."

"I don't like your feelings."

They again lapsed into silence.

* * *

Miranda wasn't sure when she first heard the ticking, but the second she became conscious of it she began searching around her. "Hear that?"

"Oh, yes."

It took her a moment. "That's the sound of metal cooling. The sound a hull makes after landing."

"Or crashing."

"You're not helpful." Miranda doubled her pace, slipping her sidearm into its holster. It wouldn't do any good to run and wind herself unless she knew where she was going. The passenger kept to her own pace and was soon fifty meters behind.

Another road intersected the one Miranda jogged on. Another fifty meters down that road she saw it: another small ship, shaped like a blunt arrowhead, resting on the black pavement. Steam wafted from the panels in ghostly clouds. Golden light streamed from an open panel on its side.

Miranda ran to it, waving. "Hey! Hey! Anyone in there?"

"Stand where you are!" a harsh voice barked from the ship.

She stuttered to a stop.

"You human?" the voice shouted again.

"Hell, yeah," Miranda answered. "I was given bad coordinates. Crashed into the planet."

"What're you doing out there?"

"Getting my passenger to her festival. Looking for help to get off this rock."

The voice harrumphed. "You run into them yet?"

"Them?"

"Locals."

Miranda shrugged. "I haven't seen any."

"Lucky you. They're savage." The voice fell quiet for moment. "You better get up here. The hull seems to keep them away, at least for now. Wait! Hold it!" Miranda heard the telltale whine of a blaster charging.

Her passenger slipped into sight from the shadows.

"Don't worry. That's my passenger."

And the passenger looked up at the silhouetted captain and grinned. "Once upon a time." She offered a shallow bow.

"Your passenger a little insane?" the gruff voice asked.

"You could say that."

"Mine was, too. Both a'you, get up here."

Miranda took a few steps toward the ship, but her passenger didn't follow.

Instead, the passenger said, "Once, a boy was awakened by a great noise. He screamed, 'The sky is falling! The sky is falling!' He ran all over his little village, filling everyone with fear. But no sky fell that day; he had only heard his father knock over a shelf full of pots and pans."

Miranda paused. She cocked her head, listening. "You ever see the locals?"

"No. But I heard them!"

She turned back to her passenger, thinking about the story the passenger had told. Did the crazy story make sense? "You really think so?"

"The danger may be real. But it can be defeated."

Miranda thought for a few moments. She turned back to the figure in the open panel. "Thanks for your offer. We're going to try to make it to the festival. Your beacon working?"

"Course not!"

"Mine either. If everything's safe, we'll come back for you."

* * *

"I'm still waiting for you to tell a story," the passenger said.

Miranda kept her eyes on the gaping windows. They were like open maws, waiting to devour them. An entire street lined with them, reaching for them, yawning for them.

The passenger sighed. "At least you came with me. I wonder if any of the other captains left their ships."

"Why wouldn't they?"

"People think the darkness can't be defeated. They don't know."

"You still have to deal with what's around you."

"You'd think so." The passenger kept walking. "It's not far now."

"Wait." Miranda paused. "Other captains. Other ships. You think they all crashed like we did?"

"I know they did." The passenger stopped and turned to face her.

"Why?" Miranda drew her sidearm, but kept it pointed down. For the moment.

"Because we all gave coordinates that would cause crashes. Because we need to find someone that will keep the festival going. Someone that will remember. And we all agreed that right now, people who fly their own ships were the best bet."

"We all?" Miranda's voice was hard.

"Yes. We all. All the stories. All of us who have gathered for the festival." She gestured. "Are you coming?"

Miranda felt an anger building inside her. Not much got her angry. She got scared fairly easily. She got excited easily. But anger? That wasn't something she dabbled with often. "You gave me faulty coordinates on purpose for the jump?"

The passenger shrugged. "Yeah."

She felt her finger slip from the safety position to the trigger itself. "You could have killed us. You cost me my ship."

"Yeah." She gestured again. "You coming?"

Miranda fired.

The tiny bullet of plasma burst from the barrel of her sidearm, leaving a bright yellow-green streak across Miranda's vision. A high whine started and cut out just as suddenly, and the smell of burned oxygen filled the air.

"That make you feel better?" the passenger asked, her eyebrows raised.

Behind her, a black crater with a glowing-red center marked the side of a building.

"You have no idea how much I want that to be your face right now," Miranda growled.

"Oh, I do. I know what it is to feel anger. I know what it is for everyone you love to grow old and die and be forgotten. You might think death is the worst, but being forgotten is worse. Being made irrelevant. I know what it is to be treated so flippantly, as if you don't matter. No one likes my kind anymore. No, I know what anger is, Miranda Batani. I know what that burning inside is, that longs to be freed, that longs to watch others burn. Would you like to feel my anger?"

Miranda felt her finger reach toward the trigger again. "There is no festival, is there? You brought us here. Whoever you are. You brought all the captains out here to die."

"Oh, there's a festival. And it will be glorious. And I want you to be a part of it. But you need to prove you're worthy, first. Are you, Miranda Batani? Are you worthy of the festival I lead you to?"

Someone breathed.

They both looked around at the empty buildings. It hadn't been either of them. But the silence was broken. Someone was breathing, a laboring, shuddering, phlegmy breath. It echoed the walls of the city canyon. Inhale. Exhale. Inhale.

A second set of lungs inhaled.

A third.

The passenger looked up with wonder. "You've woken them, Miranda Batani." She looked back down at the captain. "Run."

* * *

They ran.

Miranda wasn't built for running. Her shins ached. Her lungs couldn't suck in enough oxygen. What was going on with her heart? Her hand was sore from gripping her sidearm.

The sounds of their feet striking the pavement echoed, but so did the sounds of the sleepers. More and more rheumy lungs added to the cacophony. So, so loud.

"What woke them?" Miranda gasped.

The passenger laughed. "Your sidearm. Something about the energy must have disturbed them."

How come the passenger wasn't huffing for breath? Her blond braids went everywhere, shaking like some sort of demented flower at a rave, but she kept pace with ease.

"So ships crashing in their neighborhoods didn't wake them?" she huffed between breaths.

"Nope!" the passenger crowed.

"Will we be safe at your festival?"

"Nope!"

A new sound: scratching. The sound of talons against concrete, scratching, clicking, clutching.

What slept until an energy weapon fired, but ignored all the noise that had happened? What was chasing them?

Wolves that dress like grandmas.

Trolls that lived under bridges.

Witches that devoured good little boys and girls.

"You about ready to tell a story?" the passenger practically sang.

Miranda simply glared.

Around a corner. Another.

And then, before them, an open field. It was the first vegetation Miranda had seen on the planet; a field of grass, gray in the starlight, about waist high. And in the center of the field, a circular building only a few stories high. No windows here, but countless arches. Beyond the arches, darkness loomed.

"There it is!" laughed the passenger. "Come on!" She sprinted into the field, her legs swallowed up by the waving grass.

Miranda skidded to a halt. What could be hiding in there?

The passenger bounded across the field. Her laughter was louder than the breathing and the scratching behind them.

Miranda refused to turn and see what came behind her. She refused to let her imagination go any farther. No more lists of terrifying beasts.

Was there any other way to the building? Sidewalks? Paths?

Nothing she could see.

All right. The passenger seems to be unhurt. Go.

She dashed.

Her lungs burned. Her hand, oh, the fingers ached, the joints screamed as she clutched her sidearm. The other one at her hip seemed so heavy. She should dump her pack? No. She might need that. What good was it if the whatever-they-weres caught her? Didn't matter. Better to be prepared.

The passenger vanished into the darkness beyond one of the arches.

The grass pushed up against her legs, her hips, her waist. The blades swished against her side. Roots grasped at her feet. She almost fell. She almost fell again.

No. Don't fall, Miranda. It's just your imagination. Grass isn't the enemy here. It's not trying to destroy you. Just get to the building. Get to the festival. Then you can find out what the hell is going on.

Hopefully.

Maybe.

She made it to the shadow of an arch.

The breathing stopped. The scratching ceased.

Silence dropped over everything, except for Miranda's gasping. She spun to face the city, the towers, the grass. It was as empty as it had been before. Nothing moved. Nothing pursued her.

No.

Something out in the street of the city. A shadow she couldn't make out. And the sound of someone breathing, someone inhaling, as if they had just sat down at a sumptuous feast, breathing in everything it was about to eat.

The shadow seemed to turn.

It saw her.

Miranda fled under the arch and into the building.

Some sort of grand lobby met her. Wide white steps led up and under another arch. She sped up the stairs, her aching lungs forgotten for the moment.

And then she entered an auditorium. It was open to the immense sky. Benches of stone spread out in a semi-circle, descending toward a stage. A small crowd stood on the stage, mere shadows in the starlight, but they all looked human. They muttered together. Miranda guessed that fifty to sixty of them stood there.

The passenger proceeded down to the stage.

So. The festival, apparently. Miranda looked around. No one else stood in the auditorium. Whatever captains had ferried them all here had stayed with their ships. They would face whatever Miranda had awakened by themselves, but guarded by their hulls.

One of the forms called out from the stage, "Red! About time you got here!"

Her passenger replied, "Sorry, Rose. I got waylaid. Incompetent driver."

Miranda wanted to protest, but she couldn't find her breath. Her legs were jelly. And whatever was out there was going to be coming this way very, very quickly. They had to find safety.

The passenger climbed onto the stage. The muttering ceased.

Silence.

The passenger spoke in a hushed tone, "The festival is begun. We have come home."

"We have come home," answered the crowd.

"Someday humanity will be old enough for fairy tales again," the passenger continued, in what seemed to be a holy liturgy.

"And until then, we will return to the Cradle and remember ourselves," the group answered.

"Let us not be forgotten."

"Let us remind ourselves of who we are."

"We are the stories that remind the humans that wolves are real."

"But they can be defeated," the crowd answered, savoring every word.

"Hey!" Miranda finally found her voice. "We don't have time for this! There's things out there! I woke them up! They're coming!"

The passenger ignored her. "Who have you been told to?" she asked the assembly.

The crowd broke out in joyous answers. Their voices overlapped one another as they all shouted their responses:

"I rode through the spaceways. I told myself, planted myself, in every person who sat next to me as I rode from planet to planet. Once I got into an argument with a priest, and I think I've replaced his stories with my own."

"I founded a temple. I collected as many of us as I could, and we are read, one at a time, every holy day. The children tell us to each other."

"I carved myself onto the red hills of Shara a thousand generations ago in a language long dead. Scientists have at last found my etchings, and they have translated them and shared them with academics. Now they argue about me, never knowing that at every telling they are keeping me alive."

Miranda stumbled down the steps toward the crowd. "Hey! Hey! There are things out there! We need to get to safety!"

Miranda's passenger raised her hands, and the group fell again into silence. "We are fewer than our last gathering."

The joy vanished.

"Who has been forgotten?" she asked.

After a beat, a man with thick stubble blurted, "Maybe no one! Maybe they just couldn't get here. Or they're late!"

Miranda's passenger shook her head. "If anyone else were coming, they would have arrived by now. Stories arrive when they intend to."

"Even when they're late?"

She grinned. "Especially when we're late."

Miranda finally stumbled to the stage. "We need to move!"

Her passenger turned. "Miranda Batani, are you ready to tell your story now?"

"Shut the hell up about the stories! We need to find safety!"

"Miranda Batani, stories are the only protection you have now."

Something breathed. Something scratched. Something sniffed.

Miranda spun and looked up. At the wall of the auditorium, where the building opened to sky, a great shadow rose. It blotted out star after star in its darkness.

"You have woken them up. Now put them back to sleep."

"What?"

The passenger smiled at her, kindly and wise. "Your weapons will do you no good against these. Nor will you be able to run forever. If you wish to live, if you wish to protect us, put them back to sleep." She crouched on the edge of the stage, very near Miranda, and patted her shoulder.

Miranda spun back to the shadow. It stretched down into the auditorium now, swallowing up the entire back row of benches. It spread toward them.

"How do you put that back to sleep?" she asked.

"You already know."

She closed her eyes. She did, didn't she?

How do you put someone to sleep?

You tell them a story. Just like Mom did.

"Once upon a time." Her voice faltered. It died. She took a deep breath and started again, "Once upon a time!"

The darkness paused to listen to her.

"Once upon a time a girl grew up on a world where every adult was scared of what might come. They feared what might take them in the night, or what natural disaster they couldn't prepare for. Everyone was scared, except her mother. And every night her mother told her another story. A story of far-off worlds. A story of wolves and girls in red cloaks. A story of a woman with a glass slipper. More and more stories, until the girl was so filled with them, she couldn't hold any more. But every story ended the same: The hero faced impossible odds. And won."

The darkness gathered together into forms that sat on the benches. They spread out, filled the auditorium. Dark forms that breathed heavily.

"That girl grew up. She flew from world to world, carrying things from here to there, but it was a universe filled with fear. Everyone had forgotten the stories and what the stories taught." She turned to face the crowd on the stage. "But the stories hadn't forgotten her.

"She'd heard tales of gatherings of stories. That people used to gather stories together in places called books. But now the stories started gathering people, didn't they? They gathered people that might enjoy them, use them, remember them. And they tested the people by crashing them into a planet.

"And the girl that grew up hearing all the stories, she finally had to tell one herself. Tell her own story. To put the sleepers back to sleep. But she only had the courage to do it because of what the stories had taught her."

And her passenger's face smiled with the gentleness of a mother.

Miranda concluded, "Wolves are real, but they can be defeated."

The rheumy breathing stopped. The shadows scratched at the benches.

The passenger grinned. "They're applauding you." She breathed in the praise for a moment. "Now, all of you, back to bed. We'll wake you when the time comes. Humanity will need fairy tales before they need you again."

And the shadows all marched out of the auditorium, leaving the stories and Miranda behind.

The passenger looked down at Miranda. "And now, it's time for you to gather us back. It's time for our festival to begin."

"I thought this was the festival." Miranda gestured to the stage.

"Oh, yes, this is our gathering. But you remember what the festival of stories really were: Gatherings of stories brought together to celebrate. A book. Write us all down, Miranda. Share us. Tell us. Let others know the lesson so they no longer need to fear."

And that, gentle reader, is what you hold in your hands now. This is the gathering. This is the festival of stories.

Learn. Remember.

Wolves are real.

They can be defeated.

AND RISE LIKE A BUTCHER'S LAMP

ANDREW MCCORMICK

They wore purples and tans and flailed their limbs as if stung by bees. Their chanting, as harsh as buzz saws, accompanied the Dance. Within the wood-on-wood cacophonic rhythms, the dancers changed their partners sporadically, from groups of twos to groups of threes, or fours, even sevens, then unexpectedly back to twos, dictated by signals within the notes unfathomable to me. The stylish throng, lining the glass walls of the penthouse ballroom, clapped their forearms in appreciation as they hooted like demented owls. The Festival celebration was now in its fifth hour.

A large stone fireplace burned blue logs, producing dank, musty smells triggering no memories. I watched the un-Earthlike performance, shading puzzlement from my face as I always must do.

"They are excellent, do you not think?"

At least, I think that's what Radi said. The dissonant harmonies overwhelmed my hearing implants. Assent seemed to be called for, so I tilted my head quickly to the right. Radi hooted back at me and tapped my chin. I did the same to him.

Outside the glass walls, the stars of an unfamiliar sky beckoned with mounting haste. A passing waiter refilled my glass with the orange-tinted drink that suggested both fruity and metallic aromas to my taste buds. I hooted at the waiter and he smiled.

Although the Dance had no military applications, I sub-vocalized academic words to my storage implant regarding these people at play. Despite the bizarre scene in front of me, I could not help but be impressed with their zeal and zest. And I could not help but worry they would need that enthusiasm in their coming days.

The music abruptly stopped but the dancers did not. They continued to be in motion, still seamlessly changing partners with their laughing faces. I consciously moved my body in time with the other watchers, but, from the expressions of people near me, I knew that my reputation for being rhythm-challenged would gain new anecdotes.

Radi looked at me with amusement. "So, it appears that the Dance does not appeal to visitors from Jllapi."

"At least not to anthropologists." Jllapi was remote, at least to the populace of Wazzi City. When I taught at the All-Science College at Jllapi, I said I was from here.

The dancers halted in mid-movement, sweaty and smiling. The onlookers whooped and clapped their forearms, then dispersed into small clusters, just like every other cocktail party in the known universe with Human and Human-like sentient beings. Radi and I gravitated over to a group of two men and a woman. They were engaged in the conversation of the day.

"So how can you possibly explain away that recording, Doliko?"

Doliko shrugged, one of the few mannerisms we two peoples had in common. "Some kind of optical trick, Cloyi," he said. "Visual recordings are such a novelty, we tend to believe what we see as absolute truth. But there are ways of altering the visions. That clearly has happened here."

The other man hooted, not in the appreciative mode.

"Rubbish," he said. "Something moved across the sky, at speeds and angles we cannot possibly match. What else could it be except a vessel from beyond the sky?"

The woman in the group, Miu, turned to me. Her bare shoulders glimmered with sparkles of red and teal.

"Can you guess what we are arguing about, Pablo?"

I smiled. "Let me offer a guess. The coming Invasion?"

The one called Cloyi tilted his head in agreement. "You are Pablo, right? From Jllapi?" He snorted. "Such odd names there. Well, now, calling these visits an 'Invasion' just trivializes this phenomenon. We know not the reason or purpose of these visits. But the fact remains, even though Blind Eye Doliko here refuses to accept it, there is something out there, something unworldly."

Miu laughed, reminding me of a long-ago memory, accented by gentle rain.

"Some scientists say these reports are nothing but mass hysteria," she laughed. "You know, one person swears he sees something, then others want to imitate him, to share the same lamp glow."

"Exactly!" Doliko pointed his finger at Miu. "There have been other episodes like this over the years. Sightings of odd-shaped ships in the sky. Strange flying creatures in the hills. Sightings like those date back to the time of the tales of Traveler Thomas and Vagabond Cheng."

I kept my face impassive at the mention of those two Earth scouts from centuries ago, whose exploits had achieved legendary status.

"It's no different from then, except we now have idiots with access to recording devices. We're just going through another period of 'mass hysteria,' like Miu says."

"Is that what you think, Radi?" Miu asked.

Radi sipped at his liqueur. "Perhaps," he said at length. "Of course, we at Air Command are obligated to chase down such rumors all the time."

"What type of rumors, Radi?" I said. I finally had a lead-in to the question I had been ordered to ask for days.

"Oh, the same gossip you read from the wonder presses. Flashing lights, speeding lights, dancing lights, *disappearing* lights." Radi laughed. "The list is quite extensive."

"Are there lights you cannot explain?" Miu asked Radi just before me.

"Not really," Radi said, slowly. He drank again. I watched him carefully. He had been drinking quite a bit, ever since his wife had suddenly and inexplicably died.

"There are a few, however, that do defy belief." Then he paused. For effect or for meditation, I couldn't be sure. He turned to leave. I asked him to elaborate.

"Well," he allowed, "only a few ten-days ago, over in that small vacation village of Mereldi, we received almost hysterical accounts of monsters roaming the ulikza fields, shining handheld lights that killed the berries. We sent a team to investigate, of course, and their reports were admittedly disturbing. A wide area, over fifty-seven square joliares, appeared to be burned. Burned right to the ground."

"I have not heard of this," Cloyi said. "Fifty-*seven* joliares worth of crops? How could that be hidden from the news reports?"

Radi paused again, then forced a laugh. "It occurred at the time of the Prime Harvest Festival. Almost all of those who gave the accounts were under the *influence*, shall we say, of the festivities. And the price of ulikza berries *has* fallen in recent years. We dismissed those reports as a futile effort to justify insurance claims."

"Ulikza berries are quite toxic, are they not?" Miu said. "When they burn, they can become almost explosive. Why would farmers take a chance to blow up their fields just for the sake of insurance monies?"

"They *had* been drinking," Doliko pointed out.

"That was why the Air Command investigated in the first place," Radi said. "You know, those berries possess extraordinary properties that, when properly distilled, make for excellent fuel additives or even possible weapon components."

"How much of the crop was destroyed in this manner, Radi?" I softly interjected. The ulikza crop destruction was the reason why I had cancelled all my classes in Jllapi.

"At Mereldi? Practically the entire crop."

"Have there been other such attempts at other ulikza fields?"

"There are not many other places that can grow that volatile berry," Radi said. "The local authorities have put those other places under surveillance." Then, hastily, he added, "In case other farmers have similar ideas of insurance claims."

"I never liked those berries," Miu said as she made a face. "Very bitter."

"An acquired taste, to be sure," Doliko said. "I care for them not, either. But they are considered a delicacy, or rather, they're a manly thing to be eaten by hardy persons."

"Such a huge loss of the berries will no doubt lead to fuel shortages," Clovi said.

"As well as putting government stockpiles of explosives to dangerously low levels." I murmured into my cup.

Loud music without fanfare began unexpectedly on the dance floor.

"Oh! Trimlo's 'Advance! Advance!' I love her music." Miu turned to me. "Dance the Dance with me, Pablo. Just this once?"

I had met Miu at a university function only a few days before. We had talked for hours. She was alluring, but my mission was more so.

"My apologies, Miu. I must decline. My feet still seem to be on the same heel." I would have felt it hilarious on my futile attempts to conform to their dancing had I not been trying so hard to blend into their culture.

Miu pouted, then turned to Doliko, who eagerly agreed by tapping her chin. I watched resignedly as they walked out to the dance floor. As they put their arms on each other's shoulders, I felt a shiver of regret. Of longing. But the War always came first.

"You really should take Dance lessons, Pablo," Radi said.

I sighed. "I have."

"Dance is over-ranked as a cultural standard," Clovi grunted. From what I had heard, and seen, Clovi was the closest I knew of this world to be rhythmically inept. And he was far smoother a dancer than I would ever be.

Clovi excused himself to visit the liqueur table. So I was finally alone with Radi.

"Do you not care to Dance, Radi?" I said, knowing the answer.

"No." A pause. "No." Another pause. "Ever since Holne took her Final Visit, I do not... I do not seem to muster the enthusiasm." He sipped. "But I do so enjoy seeing the Dance. Do you not?"

"Yes. Very much so." My tympanic nerves ached with the abrupt disharmony from Trimlo's first movement. "I wonder if you would join me on the terrace. I could use a breath of fresh air."

He looked at the dancers and sighed. "All right."

We negotiated through the crowd. I pushed open the latticework and we strolled outside. Before I closed the flap, I noticed Miu saw me go outside. Her purple eyes smiled at me, then she returned to Doliko. She didn't miss a step.

The night air was cool and soothing, free of hydrocarbons that had plagued Earth's atmosphere for far too many centuries.

Unfamiliar constellations twinkled across the coal black sky. Behind those stars, I knew, lurked the current menace.

"Pleasant night."

I replied, "Yes. Your nights here are so much cooler than back home at Jllapi."

"So I have gathered."

Boisterous cheers, both near and far, echoed all over Wazzi City, as well as all across the beautiful yet vulnerable world of Salizi.

Three and a half centuries ago, a common village butcher vanquished, in single combat, a barbarian leader of savage hordes spewing from the unforgiving mountains of Nevli. The leader, a giant of a man who reportedly could uproot trees, was defeated by the butcher who, legends claim, shot flames from his fingertips.

That pivotal combat, which their history labeled "Champions' Clash," effectively stemmed a rising tide of superstitious dogmas and ushered in a scientific and cultural Renaissance-like epoch. Butchers ever since had been customarily awarded reputations for innate wisdom and determined bravery.

A sudden burst of brilliant lights, striking against the dark sky, momentarily stabbed my eyes. I had forgotten Grand Fireworks from Founders Stadium would begin at this hour. Radi hooted in appreciation and clapped his forearms. So did several people from other penthouse balconies in the surrounding upscale residential area. I hoped that the dancers inside would be too distracted by Trimlo's melodies to wander outside. I desperately needed the information this Air Command Marshall could reveal.

On verandas below me, people shouted the festival cry of "May the Heavens bloom like kia-koo blossoms!" which were, of course, answered by the customary refrains of, "And rise like a butcher's lamp!"

I rubbed my eyes as unobtrusively as I could. The ultra-violets in the fireworks' lights were more daze than dazzle to my range of vision.

To Radi I remarked casually, "So, I take it that the ulikza berry crop was completely destroyed, was it? At Merledi?"

"Hmmm?" Radi turned from the glittering and, to me, bewildering fireworks spectacle. The reds and greens were very intense, although I had trouble making out the browns. "Oh. Yes, yes, it was."

"And you think it was the work of arson?"

"Some do." Over our heads, a yellow and blue outline of the famous long-dead butcher burst into being. We both roared, as did several other balcony observers.

"But you do not seem to agree?" I had to shout over the acclaim.

"What's that?"

"I said, you do not think the crop was deliberately torched?"

Radi turned to give me his full attention. "Why do you ask?"

"I have... friends near Merledi. They told me the burning of the fields was done very fast, very methodically. And they swear that creatures walking on three legs held the flame-torches."

"Did they, now?"

"Three legs, they said. Hard to make that up. Even after a cup or two."

Radi stared at me. A burst of light from above illuminated the shadows and curves of his face.

"Silly rumors," he said. "People see odd shapes in flames. Now, if I could be excused, my drink needs a refill." He put his fingers on the latticework.

"The creatures wore metal suits. Rust colored buttons all down the front. They burned eight farmers who tried to defend their fields."

Even with his back to me, I could detect a grimace on his face. He turned.

"Have you told this to anyone else?"

A staccato of noise erupted from beneath our viewpoint, one building over and two floors down. A balcony was crowded with partygoers, all swinging oddly colored ropes which whistled in the air like locomotives of old.

Another shout. "May the Heavens bloom like kia-koo blossoms!" Answered quickly by, "And rise like a butcher's lamp." Radi's throat, and mine, joined in the response. I was still at a cultural loss to understand why the heavens would be improved by being blossomed by the vegetation of a common weed.

Radi rubbed the edge of his goblet with his thumb. "Are you a news essayist?"

"No. I work for the Central University. On loan from the All-Science College of Jllapi. I told you that."

"Are you also on loan from the wonder presses?'

"No, of course not. I have no intention of selling anything to those scheme mongers. I worry about my friends, is all."

Radi would have never thought to violate his all-secret oath clearance with a total stranger, but he was disoriented due his wife's sudden death. Which our emo-sensors had predicted. Which is why his wife had died while hiking around High Pond.

"We have film," he said after a mental bout.

"Film?" This was new. I sub-vocalized the information.

"Film. Taken by some amateur with a cheap image-taker. Four... *things*. Three legs, as you claim. Wearing rust-colored metal suits. They sprayed some kind of chemical that literally exploded the crop. They sprayed those eight farmers, who were armed only with astonishment. All died horribly." He paused. "Some were beheaded."

I shuddered, more from confirmation than from abhorrence.

They are *here, then.*

"Demons?" I ventured.

He snorted. "No folklore has ever spoken of demons with *three* legs." He stopped, as if fearing he had spoken too much. "You plan to return to Jllapi soon?"

"I leave tomorrow." Though not back to Jllapi.

"Can this talk be put under the shield?"

"You have my word. I only wish to assure my friends they are in no danger."

"I would not be too sure of that," Radi said. Just then, the latticework rustled and Miu and Doliko came out to the balcony. I had not realized the Dance had ended.

"So, there you two are," Miu said with a smile. "Watching the fireworks while we danced like hog-hens on lava."

I laughed, then quickly said, "I fear our drinks are empty. Could I prevail upon you two to replenish our thirst?"

"Of course," Doliko said. He looked anxious to get Miu away from me. Miu started to speak but reluctantly relented. They took our goblets and went back inside. I breathed a sigh of relief. I knew enough about local custom to know it is considered bad form not to fulfill a stranger's request on such a major holiday.

Once they were gone, I said, "You said 'I would not be too sure of that.' Do you mean that my friends *are* in danger?"

"I spoke from a circle; I said too much." Radi's voice quavered. The distraction made him realize he had violated his security oath.

I pressed him. "Good Goddess, man, eight people *died* there. Will these creatures return to Merledi? Or to someplace else?" I held my breath. The direction of our fleets above would be deployed depending on his answer.

He sighed. "It is not just the local authorities who are watching other ulikza crops. Units of Air Command are, too. As well as the Army." Radi now looked relieved. "There are too many authentic reports confirming the existence of these... these three-legged demons, for lack of a better term. Have been for over a year, too. A year, mind you."

"A year?" Much longer than we had feared.

"Yes. Goddess help us."

"Why?" I knew my reason, I wanted to know his.

"The reports all have the same compass point. Pitiless, these demons are. No mercy or quarter given. Heads sawed from their bodies, taken for no apparent reason. Ruthless. The attack on that ulikza crop is only one of many."

His violet eyes turned moist. "I am only grateful my dear Holne is not alive to see what is coming."

A lone firework signaled the end of the displays, exploding like a flare for help. Our timetable would have to move up. We couldn't let the G'nuff turn our flank.

These poor people. Caught in a crossfire.

Miu and Doliko chose that moment to return. They handed us full goblets.

"Oh," Miu said, disappointed. "We missed the fireworks."

"Quite all right," Doliko replied. "There will be plenty more fireworks later."

Yes. Yes, there would be.

He raised his goblet. "May the Heavens bloom like kia-koo blossoms."

I intoned back, sadly, "And rise like a butcher's lamp."

PHARAOH

HANSEN ADCOCK

The arena stretched wide and empty, covered in grey-violet sand. It foreshortened itself whenever Ben tried to look into the distance. It was almost impossible to focus on the multitude of young faces spectating from the tiers of seats, they looked so far away. He hated that.

A lush, undulating lawn dotted with dark green firs surrounded the fighting-pit, surreal in its neatness. He wanted to walk, to explore. If only he didn't have to stay here and deal with the final battle.

A tone sounded, and Thanator appeared on the opposite side of the pit. Its long body shone, metallic and waspish, the cone of its head faceted with thousands of jewel-eyes. Its two pairs of forelegs tapered into curving scythes, most likely glistening with poison.

Ben took a deep breath as the Fear Response kicked in, then primed his arm-cannon, sweating in his armour, and trained it on the monster. The audience waited, tense, silent.

The battle was short. He knew he was going to die before his cannon misfired, knew it before the creature was upon him, sinking its praying-mantis-arms through his chainmail, the steel bubbling, finding his heart.

The creature blinked out of existence—it never existed. Ben collapsed on the sand, his panting a harsh rasp in his ears, vision dimming. He was dying—again.

Thanator's voice crackled in his earpiece. "INITIATING PAIN SEQUENCE. TO ABORT PAIN SEQUENCE, STATE PASSWORD."

"Pharaoh," Ben croaked.

The arena shimmered and grew purple, then black.

He pulled the visor off and yanked the earpieces out, handing them to the technician.

"Ben. How was it this year?"

"Still as scary as last time. The Festival of Thanator always is."

"Is that why you aborted the experience early?"

"You know it is."

"You'll end up feeling it, anyway. Why not participate fully in the annual ceremony, as the other students do, and be more prepared...?"

"Sorry, Terry. I'm not ready."

He slid out of the chair, left the Recreation Lab and mounted the stairs to the dormitories. On reaching his own, number thirteen, he slammed the door and hurled himself onto the bottom bunk bed. Tears collected behind his closed eyelids.

Etta came in absent-mindedly, her nose in a novel. Ben recognised her footsteps. They paused by the ladder to the top bunk.

"You finished the Festival of Thanator already? What are you on now, a black badge? I thought black-badgers had to attend the ceremony and practice all day."

"Green." His voice was steady. "Black is the next one up. You don't come back after getting that."

"Then you're nearly a Master." She sat on the bed next to him, careful not to touch.

He sat up. "I would be, if I could get past the damn fear." He scraped his face dry on his sleeve.

"Everybody dies," Etta said. "It's a natural part of life."

"Oh, leave me alone," he snapped, sudden irritation rising in him. "You're a white-badge, you don't understand."

"Okay." She showed no hint of upset as she tucked her book under one arm and climbed to her own bed. It made Ben feel bad. Why did she have to be so kind all the time? Kindness made you look weak.

He laid there, glaring at the underside of her mattress, listening to her regular breathing and the sound of pages turning until the gong sounded for dinner.

The Great Hall contained two ebony long-tables, and all forty of the remaining students. The technicians ate at a different time than the children, but the professors ate next to them, elbow to elbow. In the Order of Saint Quietus, everyone was equal.

"She passed through to Second World," Professor Running-Stream regaled a couple of eleven-year-old white-badgers as Ben and Etta approached with their bowls of rice soup. "Last night. She became a black badge only the day before. It was a privilege to teach her."

"Who's gone now?" Ben's question sounded harsh and blunt.

Professor Running-Stream slid further along the bench to let them squeeze in. "You know we can't speak her name for the next three months. If she hears her name spoken in this world, it will confuse her on the path to enlightenment."

"You mean her ghost will come back and haunt us." Ben kept his voice flat. "Yeah. Right."

One of the young boys blinked at him, his face small and bony above the grey tunic all white-badgers wore. "You do not believe?"

"One moment." Professor Running-Stream slipped off the bench, grabbed Ben's arm and yanked him into a corridor. He stood in front of him, hands on hips. From this angle he looked intimidating, his dark eyes peering from under bristling grey eyebrows, a wealth of hair poking out of his nostrils.

"What sort of example is that to set to the young ones, Benrir?"

"I don't have to believe in Second World," Ben blurted. His throat tied itself in a knot, his face burned. "I did not *choose* to come here."

"I understand that." The Professor laid a warm, leathery hand on Ben's cheek for a moment, then scratched at the markings tattooed onto his own nose and cheekbones. "Your limited time on this world means you had to come here, to learn the rites of passage. I know you resent it, but if you cause other students to doubt, they may never reach Second World. The path opens to belief."

Ben stalked back to his dinner, now tepid, without replying. He was tired of being controlled. He wanted to go wild. He had two, maybe three more years. Why did he stay here, letting others dictate how he spent that time, with their superiority and their bland, pious sympathy?

Because he was afraid.

Etta was already finished and had gone back to their dormitory. He picked up his bowl and moved to a row of older students on the next table, who were mired in conversation with Professor Hunting-Bear, her sky-zenith blue eyes hidden behind ponderous eyelids.

"I saw an alien today. Or a ghost. He was walking up the mountain."

Ben's rice soup had become congealed starch in his mouth, lumpy and revolting. He pushed it away.

"Did it see you?" he asked.

"I stayed concealed," the professor said. "Another thin, dark-dressed male like the last one, carrying a square box with a handle. Some of the acolytes from the village were guiding him. Another one who wants to know the secret of the Five."

"Will he succeed?"

"He will gain the same success the last one did."

* * *

Dr. Kenn paused halfway up the slope, his breathing ragged around the edges, to take in the view. They were on the largest mountain in a chain of them, kept nameless by the local folk of the valley shadowed below.

The locals lived in a bundle of huts next to a spring, built of dung and straw. It would be generous to call it a village, but the doctor had been sleeping and eating with these people for the past three days, trying to earn their trust so they would lead him up the peak to the shrine. Splotches of dried mud covered his dusty and torn suit. His hair and skin had seen better days, too. The climbing made him tired, the thinner altitude affecting him, a thin skin of cold sweat decorating his face, arms, back, and stomach.

He eyed the lightweight tunics his guides wore with envy. They were both women, one somewhere between sixteen and eighteen years of age, the other approaching her fifties. Neither of them looked strong, but so far on this climb they managed to outdistance him five times, and with nothing on their feet, too. They were like goats. They stared at him like goats.

"Rest now?" he asked.

The older woman, Curti, nodded, which Philip Kenn knew was their way of saying no.

"Danger here?"

Curti grunted. "Big cat. Wolf. Sometime mountain-bear. You hurry now."

They quickened their pace, scrambling over large rocks, digging with flat obsidian knives to create handholds. Towards the top, they hit a track worn smooth by the friction of hundreds of feet, and the way became easy.

The shrine was in a small, round cave in the rock-face, with a plateau in front of it. They stopped there and waited while the doctor attempted to catch his breath, dizzy and disorientated. The women remained undisturbed by the height.

"You go first," the younger one, Ruglah, said, setting long, delicate hands on his shoulders and kissing him on either cheek. He got a close-up of large, blue eyes surrounded by tawny lashes, like Emily's, and his heart beat a smidgen faster.

"Is it true, what you say is in there?" He spoke pure English in his excitement. "A gateway to the fourth dimension? Evidence of ancient technology?"

That wasn't in fact what the guides had said, though what they uttered followed the same lines as what his fellows at Cambridge University had told him. They covered the legend of the Dreaming Five for five minutes in one of the archaeology lectures, but the students kept returning to the subject during dull moments.

Dr. Kenn had not done fieldwork since he was a student himself. He was now remembering what it was like: the discomfort, the anticipation—but this time, laced with something like fear.

It was important he investigated these claims of a gateway, but he was afraid. Afraid of finding it, and afraid of not finding it.

The guides waited in silence for him to duck his head and enter the ominous burrow in the mountainside.

Around a bend in the passage, a fire flickered in a brazier. It was all he could focus on in the darkness, until Curti and Ruglah pushed past him, picked some sticks up off the ground and lit them. Using the makeshift torches, they led him to the inner chamber.

"Quiet now," Curti commanded, and ushered him through a wall of stalactites and stalagmites.

Ahead lay a circle of forms lying on stone slabs. Dr. Kenn crept into the centre, breath clotting in his throat. He was so close. Emily could be here, watching from the other side. If only...

He turned to the guides, recollecting in time that he must not speak inside the sacred space. Instead, he approached the nearest quiescent shape.

It was a mummy, dusty and leathered with age. From its size, he guessed it to be a woman. Her long, dark hair was intact, fanning out around her head. Blotting out her eyes and nose was...

A virtual-reality headset.

* * *

Ben's eyes opened onto midnight.

The pain was back again, in both of his legs, especially his feet. The arm poking out of the blankets ached like a hammer was bouncing on the nerves. His lower abdomen twisted and nagged under his skin. Nausea was not present but lurked on the outskirts, ready to sidle up on him if he moved.

Yet move he must. The longer he spent in one position, the stronger the aching would become, and more nerves would be trapped.

Moving like an old man, the fifteen-year-old rolled onto his left side, pushed the covers down and swung his legs out of bed, levering himself upright with the other arm. He tried to rub the circulation back into his legs, took a deep breath and reset his big toe joints, which had been moved out of line by the weight of the covers. Some of the pain lessened and was replaced by a relentless, dull throbbing. Another shaky sigh to inhibit the urge to vomit, and he was up, wrapping his gown around him, going downstairs to the Recreation Lab.

Marni was the tech on duty.

"I think I'm ready for another round," he said.

"Ben. Another bad night?" she clucked in sympathy and buzzed him in.

He settled himself into a recliner, the cool, fake leather doing something to ease the burning heat he produced in his sleep. She came to him with a couple of soft blankets, and helped to rig up the visor and earpieces. She also brought a glass of water and some pain-killing herbs without being asked. Ben liked Marni.

"Ready?" she said a couple of metres to his left. "Now commencing the start-up process."

A gentle hum filled his head, and his vision turned grey, then black. Purple bolts of lightning flashed in the corners of his eyes, moving into the centre, and he felt his Self begin to dissociate from his wrecked body with overwhelming relief. His limbs were weightless. His stomach wasn't there, it felt so comfortable, and the nausea was gone. He could have cried.

The darkness faded. He was sitting in another place, whether it was off-world, or a place in a different time, he wasn't sure.

At least a foot of powdery, undisturbed snow covered the ground. Tall firs protruded from it all around him, so close together he couldn't see what lay beyond. Their fronds started to grow a metre up the trunks, so there was not room to stand and the light was compressed as if it was sunset, but Ben didn't care. He would stay here, quiet and restful, until he deemed it safe to return to his body.

Of course, the chair his real body reclined in hadn't been transported into the dream with him. When he moved, he realised he was sitting up to his waist in snow. It was cold, but not unpleasant.

He would have to keep an eye out for Thanator. The programme had a nasty habit of appearing in some form or other to interact with whoever was using it, and it had an automatic function that made it attempt to kill. Ben wasn't looking for death-practice, and he didn't want to go back to First World yet. He wanted to rest, to sleep. He just needed to sleep...

Voices crept to him from a distance, and he started awake. He was now lying in the snow, and sat up, groggy-headed. Snow crystals fell out of his hair.

The voices came again. A man and a woman—no, two women.

Ben crawled towards the sound, having to dig his way through the snow to make progress. In First World, the exercise would hurt, but here there was no discomfort, and he relished the way his arms moved like efficient pistons in a machine.

At the border of the forest, he stopped. The view was clear here. He was halfway up the mountain range, though in this world there were no buildings on it, and no sign of the monastery. Ahead, three people climbed a slope steeper than the one he lay on. The two women—one old, one young—walked up the incline with relative ease, but the man laboured behind, almost on all fours.

Ben peered at what they climbed towards. At the top of the mountain, a plateau jutted out, and above that, a cave. He wondered why these adults were using Thanator. Weren't they too old? They weren't dressed like students of the Order. Then he saw the dark clothes of the man and recollected what Professor Hunting-Bear said. She had seen a ghost, an alien. Now he was seeing it, too. It was disturbing in its reality, but if that was a ghost, what were the women? They wore pale tunics and flapping, ragged cloaks, their hair unkempt. Were they ghouls? Messengers? Perhaps they were sorcerers, and the man was an illusion conjured by them.

Ben waited until they were further up and followed.

They made the ghost go into the cave first. Ben hid behind a chaparral bush for its keepers to enter behind it, then slipped inside.

Total blackness. Too risky. Thanator could be lurking where it couldn't be seen.

He was about to back out, when a flame flared in the dark. He flattened himself against the cave wall, but the people—they must be people—did not see him. They carried the light into another cavern, and, not wanting to lose it, Ben scurried after them.

Winding his body through a gap in the wall of dripping rock formations, he barked his shin on a stalagmite and bit his lip to keep from laughing, the absence of pain feeling something like pleasure.

The three people grouped in the centre of a circle of stone tables, each table with a horizontal figure on top. The torches in the women's fists lit a small area, plunging the forms into deeper darkness.

Squinting, Ben sneaked towards the light, and almost fell over one of the stone biers. His arms flew out to steady himself, and he found his hands grasping a dead body, wrapped in strips of linen mixed with a hardened substance like tar. In spite of its embalming, it was a revolting parody of life, like a creaking skeleton wearing the dried, burned skin of something else. When his eyes roamed to its face, it was all he could do not to choke out a cry. The blackened skin stretched taut around a gaping, silent scream of a mouth, and above that, over the eyes was...

A Thanator visor.

How was that possible? How could people *inside* an artificial dream be using an artificial dreaming programme? It couldn't be the same one; Thanator was not designed to be that clever. Unless it had a virus...?

He thought about pulling the visor off the dead person's skull and his mind recoiled. There was something wrong here, he could smell it. The air tingled at the back of his throat and small currents ran over his skin, raising every hair on his body.

The women and their ghost did not react to his presence. They couldn't hear. They weren't looking in his direction.

The man-ghost inspected another of the mummies, commenting with incredulous amusement on the fact they were wearing such advanced pieces of technology, and asking why. Ben could hear his language and understand it as if it was his own. The women seemed confused or disinclined to answer.

The man-ghost attempted to remove the visor from the dead woman, and the two women shrieked, launching themselves at the man, full of panic and anger.

* * *

Dr. Kenn reeled backwards, trying to defend his face from scratching fingernails. He had not expected these peaceful people to suddenly show feral rage. Touching the masks on the bodies was taboo, he realised that now, but how to calm them down? How to persuade them to let him take a closer look, for the purposes of research?

"I am sorry!" he yelped, and froze, his attention captured by something, a tiny movement perhaps, outside the circle of the Five. Curti and Ruglah sensed this and turned to see what he was staring at.

Nothing there. A cave-rat maybe, or his imagination.

"What this?" he asked, gesturing to the headsets on the mummies. "Record of lives?"

"Re-cord?" Ruglah frowned.

Dr. Kenn mimed writing with an invisible implement on his hand, and understanding dawned.

" *Vernaja*," she replied, the local tongue for "dreams." The dead women were dreaming. Of course.

"Always?" he asked.

The two women shook their heads for yes.

He understood. The job of the Dreaming Five was to lie here and dream until they died, and to tell the laymen what the gods and goddesses revealed to them. Then their job was to dream beyond death. He got a horrible shrivelling sensation along his spine as he imagined what these mummies might say now, if they could speak, if they were still dreaming.

Was the V.R. programme still running? He couldn't see any sort of computer or terminus for the masks to be plugged into, so they couldn't be working. Unless they ran on a kind of battery... solar power? No, too dark in here.

Were they still dreaming?

This was not scientific, it was superstitious conjecture, the kind of thinking his uncle would knock him over the head for.

Curti and Ruglah drew a short distance away and began a heated discussion in their language, too fast for the doctor to follow. As they argued he knelt to inspect the stone the mummies were lying on. It wasn't a type of rock he recognised, a uniform dark grey almost like steel, cut as if manmade, but it joined seamlessly with the cave floor. It was full of twinkling bits of mica. There were carvings in it: rows of strange words in a weird alphabet, and friezes depicting the women being installed in the cave.

Had they been sacrificed? Left up here to die on purpose?

Curti and Ruglah finished arguing and came back. He pointed at the carvings with a questioning expression.

Ruglah shrugged, and mimed pulling the mask off the mummy. Relief filled him. He wouldn't have to persuade them to let him look. They had seen sense.

The mummy they stood near still had all her own hair, thin and brittle with age but deep black, as black as ravens. For some reason he was unhappy about touching that hair, as if he would disturb something in it, like a rat or a cloud of bats.

The state of the face underneath the headset was enough to make him drop it. Curti darted forward and caught the equipment before it broke upon the ground, gabbling something like an admonition or a curse on his name for being so clumsy and irreverent.

He tore his eyes away from the corpse's face with difficulty. He tried to take the mask from Curti's hands, but she wouldn't let go.

"Let go," he shouted, developing the tactic used by frustrated people everywhere who can't make themselves understood—as if the woman was deaf instead of foreign. "I want. To. See."

PHARAOH

The face of the mummy transfixed Curti. She kept shaking her head, her lips pressed into a white line of cold fury or fear.

Ruglah eased the headset out of the older woman's hands. Dr. Kenn took it with a satisfied sigh and adjusted it around his own head, over his eyes, remembering the long-term effect it had had upon the eyes and upper face of the dead woman. It had acted like a preservative, leaving the skin intact underneath it. The eyeballs were uncorrupted, but so bloodshot the irises were almost red and not defined. The skin itself was pale and wrinkled like a creature kept underground or immersed in water for months. The dead women had not fed on the sunlight for hundreds of years, Dr. Kenn surmised. Strange dust lay thick around the mummy's head when he removed the headset, yellow and greasy like the dust that collected on computer cables.

What if the last thing the Dreaming Five saw was the thing that killed them all? *What was it?* he wondered, as a dark curtain swept across his vision.

* * *

Ben watched the man-ghost put the visor on with a galloping heart, sweat collecting along his spine. From this distance, he could see some of the horror that was the dead woman's face, enough to let him know there was something uncanny at work in this cave.

He was afraid to move, convinced Thanator would reanimate the mummy to claim its visor back before destroying Ben and everyone else in the cavern.

Then reason took hold. What he was seeing was in a different time to his own. They were not "real," these ghosts, in the sense that they were irrelevant to him. No one knew he was there.

He strode into the centre of the Five, as bold as a rooster, and took a closer look. The black-dressed man was intent on whatever the visor was showing him, his body immobile.

Ben found he could touch the visor on the mummy next to it, pulled it off, and fastened it to his own face out of curiosity. He had a second to notice the bewildered, astounded expressions of the two living women as they saw the visor floating in mid-air, then purple-blackness submerged him.

When it cleared, the smell of stagnant water and damp jungle infiltrated his nostrils.

The trees were different this time, but still as many. They were large, old, and covered in vines and moss. Ahead lay a wide, still river, its waters dark and flecked with unidentifiable objects. No birds called. Nothing moved.

The man-ghost stood on the other side of the water, rigid with surprise and world-stun. Ben recalled what world-stun felt like. It was obvious this man had never dreamed properly before, and now he was here he couldn't believe in his own existence.

"It's all right," Ben called. "You can move. It won't disappear."

The man jumped and gawked at him, seeing a boy in a loincloth, which was what this world had dressed him in. Ben suppressed the urge to laugh.

"How did you get here?"

"We are sharing a dream," Ben said. He shrugged. "For me, this is a dream inside a dream. To me, you are a figment."

"A fig...?" Flustered, the man hunted about for a method of crossing the river. He located a rotting log further along the bank, climbed to its end more than halfway across and jumped. He missed the bank, and waded the rest of the way, grimacing.

"What's your name?"

"Benrir Fyntas, but everyone calls me Ben. Who are you?"

"I'm... Philip Kenn. Dr. Kenn. I think."

"A doctor?" Ben tried not to hope, but barely managed it. "Do you have knowledge of rare diseases?"

"I'm not that sort of doctor. I have a PhD."

"Sounds like a rubbish sort of doctor to me. You don't look like one, anyway. In my world, doctors wear robes and have sigils painted on them. They dance and sing healing songs."

"Do they?" The doctor seemed distracted. "Say, ah, is there an exit out of here? A doorway, maybe?"

Ben shrugged again. "If you want to leave, take your visor off."

The doctor felt his eyes. "It's gone."

"Not like that. You have to say the abortive password."

"The what?"

"You mean you started this experience without picking a password? If you don't have one, how is Thanator going to know to eject you? How are your keepers going to know to take the visor off you?"

"Keepers?"

"Those ghost-women."

"They're not ghosts. Not my keepers, either. They were showing me up the mountain."

"Pharaoh!" Ben tried, but nothing happened. "This world is strange. That's the first time Thanator hasn't responded or interacted with us."

"Who?"

"Thanator. It's the name of the programme we use to go off-world, to dream. We use it to practice dying. Every year, my Order shares a dream-festival where we each battle Thanator in a sort of arena. The winners progress to the next badge, and move up the hierarchy."

The doctor flinched. "Morbid. Come, we'll walk as we talk. There must be a way out somewhere, or someone who can help."

In his mind, Ben doubted that. Most of the other worlds were empty whenever he visited them, apart from Second World, where people were supposed to live the afterlife. He had never been there.

"Why do you need to practice?" Dr. Kenn asked as they pushed through the vines.

"Because there is no escaping death," was all the explanation Ben gave. Most of the students at the monastery were first-borns, free-will sacrifices to St. Quietus by their parents. A few, like him, were given away because they had fatal diseases or shocking disfigurements that made it impossible for them to integrate into society. The adults gave their children away because they believed it would bring them good luck and longevity. Ben was not so sure of that.

The doctor peered at him. "Is there...?"

"Something the matter with me? Yes. I have a premature ageing disease," Ben laughed with bitterness. "I look young for my age, but inside, my joints, organs and blood vessels are deteriorating. I have maybe three years left."

There was a pause, and they stopped at the edge of the forest. Beyond laid a swamp.

"I'm sorry to hear that," Dr. Kenn sighed.

"That's what everyone says. It doesn't mean anything."

"I mean it! If there was some way I could take it off you, I would."

"It has no meaning because nothing can be done about it. Saying sorry changes nothing. Change *is* meaning."

"Too philosophical for me," the doctor muttered, scanning the bog for a dry way across. He chose a likely tussock of grass and stepped on it. It sank, and he was mired up to the knees for a second time.

"Why would you take it from me?" Ben asked once his impotent anger had calmed. "It's not something I can imagine anybody wishing for."

"I lost someone close to me." The doctor found a dry patch of ground and helped Ben onto it. "Her name was Emily. We were going to be married, last year."

"What happened?"

"She was killed in a car crash. It was... too sudden."

Ben did not know what a car was, but didn't ask.

"I remember I was coming out of a lecture with Andrew—a friend—on the effects of erosion on Palaeolithic settlements, and I was going to meet her at a restaurant in town. We were going to meet in the morning, but I didn't want to miss the lecture, so I rearranged it. I went to the restaurant, and I waited. She lived in the next town over, but she never showed up. I sat there, waiting, until all the diners had gone and a waitress had to kick me out. I remember how angry, how petty and self-centred I was, thinking she had left me. Then her mother phoned me to tell me the news, and I realised something had happened.

"There was a collision. Five cars and an articulated lorry on the motorway. She... her car was crushed."

At last Ben found his voice. "Pardon me for asking...but are these cars and lorries wagons of some kind?"

Dr. Kenn's face worked. Ben was not certain whether he was trying not to laugh or cry.

"Yes. Except they travel at dangerous speeds."

A salty smell drifted their way. The bog opened onto an estuary. Stilt-legged birds scratched on flat, gleaming sand-mud.

"If I hadn't rearranged," Dr. Kenn spoke, crying now, "she would be alive. All I can think about is the selfish anger I felt, when all that time she was dying."

Ben did not try to comfort the man with false platitudes. He just nodded.

"She'll be in Second World," he said.

"That's the reason I came to research the Dreaming Five." The doctor scrubbed his face on the sleeve of his jacket. "I pretended, to everyone else, even myself at times, that I was doing this out of scientific interest, but... I heard the legend about the gateway to an afterlife, and I think, in my subconscious..."

Ben nodded again. "You want to see her."

"There was no gate. Only those embalmed women."

"They must be the keepers of it."

"But this can't be the Second World. There's no one here. Whatever they saw, they all saw it, and they died... Perhaps the gate is in this world?"

"A dream inside a dream inside a dream?"

"Yes."

A figure approached them from the estuary, dark and indecipherable on the horizon at first, then seeming to walk upon the water. As it came, Ben saw it was humanoid, but not human.

He could tell, from the way it walked, that it was Thanator.

"Who...?" Dr. Kenn squinted. "What *is* that? A robot?"

"No. It's Thanator. The programme."

"You mean this is the thing that... kills you? Shouldn't we be running?"

"No point. It will only follow."

The form Thanator had chosen was a strange amalgamation of one of the stilt-legged birds and a man. It wore a rotting, ragged cloak that covered its body from neck to ankle, but the feet were large, scaled talons. The face inside the cloak's hood held two saucer-like holes for eyes and a long, tapering ibis-beak in the place of a mouth.

"Now what?" Dr. Kenn dithered, shaking.

"Now we fight, or it hunts me, or it gives me a poisonous wound," Ben said. "After that, I won't be here. You'll have to find a way out by yourself."

"Who's to say it won't harm me?"

Ben was surprised. "It might. Then again, if you *are* a figment, it might not."

Thanator came to within two paces of them and stopped.

Dr. Kenn stepped between it and Ben.

Amazement flooded the boy. It was the first time he had seen an adult sacrifice himself for a smaller being.

"What are you *doing*?"

"It should be me."

Thanator appeared to hesitate. "RECALCULATING."

"It's not fair for you to die," the doctor said. "I'm older."

"It's not a real death! If it doesn't destroy me, I'll be stuck here!"

"Even so. Call it selfishness if you want, but I don't want to be in a lonely world all on my tod."

"Pharaoh!" Ben tried in desperation. "PHARAOH!"

Thanator's bird-skull slowly cranked in his direction.

"INCORRECT PASSWORD."

"I want to make it right," Dr. Kenn said. "I want to make things right."

"Well, you're messing them up!"

A crackling in the forest behind them. Ben spun around.

Out of the trees came five impossibly tall people, all of them women. One had hair as black as crows' feathers, and though they looked nothing like the mummies in the cave, Ben knew them to be the Dreaming Five.

"Dr. Kenn." His throat dried. "They're here."

The doctor turned with wide, disorientated eyes. When he saw the giant women, they glazed over, his mouth fell open, and a thin line of moisture ran down his trouser leg.

* * *

A low buzzing thrummed through Dr. Kenn's chest and head. The beings coming at him through the jungle could not be possible, but looked too real to deny. As a boy he watched horror movies, and he played vivid, often violent, RPG games on a console without twitching, but this proved too much.

They were all more than women, as if the geometry of their bodies could not fit into the three-dimensional world and had to spill into the fourth, fifth and sixth dimensions as well. Their faces fluctuated, never settling, like flowers blossoming and dying at high speeds on a nature documentary. Their hair floated around their heads like light, like snakes, like feathers, like ink in water. It made him dizzy to watch.

They loomed like buildings.

"You should not have come here," one said, fire blazing out of her skull. "You were not chosen."

"Ah..." Dr. Kenn struggled to speak.

"You have tried to see things you cannot possibly understand," a second one roared, her eyes transmogrifying into green and blue coals. "You should not have woken us, mortal. This is *our* dream."

"Your...?"

"We joined our minds together hundreds of years ago," another of the Five said. "We dreamed a world outside time, outside death, for our souls to live in and grow on. Now you have come, bringing death." Her mouth stretched impossibly wide, wider than a snake's, her teeth lengthening into sabres. "For this, we will eat you."

Dr. Kenn cast a glance at Ben. The boy was pre-occupied, trying to reason with Thanator to get it to let them exit the programme, and from this he took courage. If Ben was certain all this wasn't real, he didn't have to be afraid.

"I'd like to see you try," he said to the Dreaming Five.

All their mouths were gaping cave-mouths now, devouring. One pushed him back onto the sand, another ran dinosaur claws down his shirt, ripping off the buttons, exposing his scrawny chest. They closed in, the claws piercing the skin over his heart.

He flinched, expecting to feel pain, but there was none. It... tickled. He could not prevent a laugh escaping his lips as the talons searched for his heart, his eyes bugging out of his head at the horror of the sight and the inappropriateness of his reactions. It was the nearest he ever came to losing his mind.

"INITIATING PAIN SEQUENCE," Thanator's voice droned from a long way away. "TO ABORT, STATE PASSWORD."

"Pharaoh," Ben coughed.

Blackness.

The act of removing the headset felt strange and painful. The experience of the other world didn't want to let go. It was dark, fuzzy... aching... he wanted to vomit but couldn't move. Pink tendrils snaked out of the headset, leading towards...

into... his head and ears. It took a second for terror to dawn as he realised those were nerves. *His* nerves.

Dr. Kenn dragged his eyes away—somehow—and looked around. His body laid in the mountain cave again. The guides, Curti and Ruglah, were backing away, wanting to run. The mummies of the Five surrounded him. One had her fingers buried in his chest, and the pain, a hammering, sharp pulsation, made his head reel. He was going to pass out, hit his head on a rock maybe. Dying of a head injury would be preferable to this.

The last image that filtered through to his brain was Ben, placing his headset on a nearby bier, shuffling into the throng, bleeding and gasping for air.

* * *

The transition from one dream-world to another while injured was a horrible shock, especially when Ben found his body in this world had suffered the effects of the fight in the last one. The pain sequence kicked in as soon as he opened his eyes in the cave, and Thanator was nowhere. He tried calling "Pharaoh," but nothing happened. *There must be a glitch in the system.*

The corpses of the Dreaming Five were still trying to eat the doctor's heart, and Ben forced himself to get in their way. Blood blinded him in one eye, it hurt to breathe, he was sure one of his wrists had fractured in some way, and every sound rang from a distance, but he forced himself to return Dr. Kenn's favour and save the man's life. Even if he *was* a figment.

"He doesn't deserve to be killed," Ben said. "He didn't know what he was doing. I'm the one that brought death into your world, but it was an artificial death."

The mummies paused. The one with her fingertips buried in Dr. Kenn's chest withdrew them and looked at Ben in expectation, her mouth still open in a rictus scream. He tried to think of it as a yawn.

"If you want a blood-price, take me," he whispered. His vision swam. He had to lean with his hands on his knees and pant to stop himself fainting. Dr. Kenn already sprawled unconscious, the nerves from his brain still connected to the visor clutched in his hands. There was no blood.

The nearest mummy, the one with crow-black hair, turned her red eyes onto Ben. A warm, slow voice poured into his head.

"You are right. He will not die, but there will be painful memories for him."

One of the other mummies produced a sharpened piece of flint and began to saw through the doctor's exposed nerves.

"We will wipe his mind clean."

Ben was glad Dr. Kenn was unaware of what they were doing to him, but as each strand was severed, fear and nausea crept up the boy's throat. His surroundings whirled and grew dim.

* * *

He opened his eyes, pulse pounding in his temples, with a vague feeling of wrongness he couldn't explain.

The room surrounding him gleamed bright, white and modern. His body rested

456 | PART FOUR: A COLLOQUIUM OF SCIENCE FICTION

in a reclining chair next to a bank of computers, facing a broad window looking onto...

"Pretty powerful stuff, eh?" someone laughed. He turned to see who it was.

A short, thin, young man in his twenties, with a sparse beard coming in around the corners of his mouth, and the remainders of teenage acne. What was his name? Andrew. That was it. They had attended some of the same lectures.

Lectures?

Ben's brain scrambled to right itself. Andrew held the visor in one hand, pulling electrodes off Ben's head and chest with the other.

He glanced down.

This was not him. This body was a good five years older than it had reason to be. It was hairier, the skin was different, the smell was different. His breathing sounded alien in his ears.

Yet it was him.

"So that was the new V.R. programme," Andrew said as he typed something on a laptop and shut it down. "Brian says it took him the best part of a year to code. I can tell by your face I've won the bet. You fell for it hook and line, you stinker. You owe me a pint."

Ben said nothing, his senses overwhelmed. He tried to view the situation in an objective way. He felt good, better than he'd ever felt since puberty. Nothing ached at all. He wasn't tired. He felt hungry, very alive, very clear. The absence of discomfort was so disorientating, it was like he wasn't encased in a real body at all. It was effervescent.

"Funny, we were joking the other day about this thing someone wrote in a magazine—forget which one it was—about a V.R. test subject coming out of an experience and thinking he was a cat. It took months to wear off," the other man said.

Andrew was watching Ben. He supposed the man was pretending to be sociable but checking he was okay.

Ben looked out of the first-storey window at Cambridge University, United Kingdom, and as the traffic and the weather entered his head, reality adjusted itself to absorb his existence, in a way so subtle he didn't feel it.

"How about that drink?" Andrew strolled to the doorway. "Phi- er, Ben. Sorry. Dunno what I was thinking, you look nothing like a Phil. Lol."

Ben smiled a new smile. "Love to."

BREACH OF PROTOCOL

STEFAN MARKOS

Besmelt reached the crest of the ridge, stopped, and surveyed the next valley. These Solstice hunts were always a time of reflection for him. He thought over things that his grandfather had told him, especially about the world that no longer was.

What did he know about it? Well, the world had once been very different. It had been filled with marvelous things, unimaginable things. There had been many more people. The people were just people, there were no Changed Ones. Everyone was in touch with everyone else. People could travel great distances in conveyances that moved themselves.

Then came the Breach. Gramps called it "a collision with an alternate reality," whatever that meant. "Everything was fragmented," he had said. "Many familiar parts of life were suddenly missing. Many more strange ones had been added." Gramps had looked at him intently and shook his head. "You can't know what it was like."

But, Gramps had a plan, and also hope. "To survive, we have to find friends, other groups like ourselves," he had said. "We need to explore, to find the resources as well as locate the dangers."

Thus far, they were fed, clothed and sheltered. They had celebrations from time to time to make life more cheerful. Gramps thought the Feast of the Winter Solstice was especially important. "It builds morale," he had said, "and binds us together and forms tradition."

So, here was Besmelt, hunting for something to contribute to the celebration. He was also looking for things to give as gifts. And, as always, he was on the lookout for dangers such as the Changed Ones and the weird creatures that supposedly hid in the mountains. And, yes, it would have been wonderful if he could meet members of another community so that his people, the Cave People, could make new friends as Gramps hoped.

Even that would have its dangers, though. Everyone was instructed to be friendly, but cautious, when meeting a new group. Make note of their location, Gramps had said, then go back and tell the Elders of the discovery. They would decide on the proper approach for establishing relations. The Cave People could never forget the grisly example of the Apple Knockers, or Orchard People of a nearby valley, whose insouciance had cost them their lives. They had carelessly allowed a group of strangers into their valley, and were totally exterminated. The intruders were undoubtedly Changed Ones, since they stripped the flesh from the bones of their victims. Often it was difficult to tell a Changed One from a true human until it was too late.

As Besmelt rounded the bend in the trail, he thought he could hear some odd noises. They seemed like weak, muffled sounds of distress. Then, he saw the source of the noise and almost jumped out of his skin.

It was a Snallygaster.

He had found pictures of such beings before. It had the tail, the long neck, the scales, and the wings.

Gramps had discounted the pictures completely.

"It's just an old legend," he had said.

Well, here was the "old legend," alive and breathing right before him. He moved closer. The Snallygaster looked up, and their eyes met. He knew that he was looking into the eyes of a person, not some mindless beast. A person in distress.

"I don't know if you can understand me, stranger," he said, "but you're hurt, and I'm going to help."

"Fgmph," said the stranger, motioning toward himself with a front claw. Then, he motioned toward his rear leg, the foot of which was hidden in the bushes.

Besmelt jerked a thumb toward his chest and said, "Besmelt."

He pulled the shrubbery out of the way and saw what the problem was. It was a huge spring trap. No doubt it had been set by the Changed Ones. It took a certain dexterity to open one of those, which the Snallygaster didn't seem to have. He stood on the spring, pulled the jaws apart, and locked them open. He examined Fgmph's ankle. It wasn't broken.

How had Fgmph been lured in? Besmelt looked around the bottom of the shrubs and found apples. Apples of the same kind that the Orchard People grew. He gathered them up and presented them to Fgmph, who started munching on them with gusto. Besmelt improvised a bucket out of his pack cover and fetched some water from the nearby stream. Fgmph downed it gratefully.

He seemed to be recovering rapidly. He stood on his hind legs, spread his wings, and let out the loudest noise Besmelt had ever heard.

Evidently, it was a shout of joy and exuberance. Or, maybe it was meant to impress the Changed Ones. At any rate, Fgmph seemed to be all right.

He motioned to Besmelt, then gestured at himself, and finally, indicated the sky.

Obviously, an invitation to go flying. But to where? Probably Fgmph's home. That would be great. The main thing was to be able to get back to his own home. He reached into a pocket and pulled out his map and compass. Those would guide him there by air, same as by land.

He looked at one feature on the map, an ink mark. It showed where something had been changed. In this case, it was a bridge that had collapsed, probably sabotaged by the Changed Ones. His father, he'd been told, had been killed trying to get across the gorge that it had spanned. He was trying to get to Gramps' "laboratory" (whatever that was), that had been there since before the Breach.

Gramps had reminisced at length about all the wondrous things in his "laboratory," and had gone on about how the things in it could change the lives of the Cave People and their friends for the better. The problem was getting to it on the other side of the impassable gorge.

Besmelt smiled, walked toward Fgmph, and motioned to himself, Fgmph, and the sky.

* * *

Gramps and the other Cave People scanned the pass. Still no sign of Besmelt, and it was the Feast of the Solstice. Something must be wrong.

Gramps shook his head. *The young fellow reminds me more of his father every day*, he thought. *I sure hope his curiosity doesn't do him in, too. Sometimes he just doesn't know when to show some sense and back off.*

"Wait," said one of the men, "What's that in the sky? Something's flying toward us!"

"And there's more behind it!"

The flying things grew closer, and the Cave People saw Besmelt riding on the back of the leader, smiling and waving and holding some sort of a bundle. Several of the flyers also carried bundles in their front claws. They wheeled, swooped, and circled to the delighted squeals of the children.

They all deposited their bundles before the Cave People. Besmelt handed his to Gramps.

"Happy Winter Solstice, Gramps. Meet my friend Fgmph and the Flying People. Think we could spare them some apples?"

Gramps was not pleased. "Besmelt, what have I told you about bringing strangers in here before we have a chance to size them up? And, *what* people? These aren't people!"

Besmelt smiled a bit lopsidedly. "Well, I did remember that Gramps. But I also remembered another bit of your wisdom, an old proverb, 'You know who your friends are just by looking in their eyes.' Fgmph has been my wings, and I've been his hands. Hey, open your bundle. It's stuff the Flying People and I found in some ruins."

Gramps opened it. "Books! Lab instruments!" He beamed. "These are good people!"

Besmelt put his arm around Fgmph's neck.

"They sure are, Gramps. They're also brave and smart people. They've run some heavy rope across the gorge so we can start building one of those suspension bridges you've talked about. It looks like there's a lot of interesting things over there."

Gramps wiped back some tears. His voice was choked.

"You really don't know the half of it, boy, at least not yet. It'll take time, and I've got lots more to teach you. But, if we can't have the world that was, the world that will be will do very nicely."

AS AMERICAN AS HONEST PUDDING PIE

ERIC REITAN

As always, it started as a ghost of sound and a rhythmic infection of my dreams. When shower water beating against the back of my head wasn't enough to drown out the steady beat, I called the Agency.

I didn't recognize the voice that answered. "This is Tracker Four. I have a signal." It was the usual lingo: a thrumming heartbeat in my head and the accompanying migraine was a *signal.*

"Follow it," said the guy on the other end of the line.

I swallowed back a curse. "Are you new?" I wasn't patient when my head hurt.

There was a pause. "What do you need, Darian?"

I hated that he called me by name. "What's your name, new guy?"

"Irrelevant."

"Fine, Irrelevant. I need a location."

"Isn't that what your... sense... is supposed to give you?"

"Listen here, Irrelevant—"

"Irrelevant's not my name."

"The signal will get louder as I get closer. That works great when I'm within a mile or two. But since the pain isn't bad enough to make me want to scream and rip out my hair, that means the source is a hell of a lot further out than that. I need a ballpark."

"How am I supposed to give you that?"

"Where the goddam hell is Leroy?"

"He's home sick."

"There must be others there who know what the fuck they're doing."

"It's flu season. We're... short-staffed."

"So I'm stuck with you?"

"Yes."

"Okay, then listen. What I've got is a fifty-mile headache. Where are people gathering right now within a fifty-mile radius of me?"

"You know I'm just going to google that, right?"

"Sure."

"You could do that yourself."

"You know, *Irrelevant* has too many syllables. How about I just call you *Asshole?*"

"My name's Dick."

"Of course it is."

The guy hesitated. "The Honest Pudding Pie Festival."

"What?"

"Where people are gathering right now. It started yesterday. In Bellstrap, Oklahoma, site of the original Honest Baked Goods Factory. Says here that the little town of Bellstrap has been celebrating the phenomenon that is the beloved

Honest Pudding Pie for over thirty years. Apparently at noon today they will be cutting into the largest Honest Pudding Pie ever made, weighing in at over a hundred pounds. A hundred and six pounds of chocolate pudding wrapped in a layer of moist sponge cake and dipped in rich milk chocolate. With that little distinctive swirl of vanilla frosting on the top. To be precise."

"Thanks."

"Google is my friend."

"Okay, Dick. Are you going to be my contact for the day?"

Dick paused. "I was going to pass you off to Sally—"

"I know Sally!"

"—but she just barfed all over her workstation. As I said, the flu's hitting the office pretty hard."

I sighed. "Okay, if I'm stuck with you, I need to know what I'm dealing with. How many missions have you done?"

The pause was longer this time. "As I said, the flu—"

"Shit. This is your first time, isn't it?"

"I've been trained."

"It's okay. When I get there, I'll try to get close enough to put the Trace on the target, but by then my headache will verge on debilitating. Which is why *all* I do is mark the target. Has the flu taken out our strike teams, or can you put one together while I'm finding my way to Pudding Pie Oklahoma?"

"I'll put together a team and send them to Bellstrap."

"Put it together but don't send it until I'm sure Bellstrap's the place. I'll call you en route if my headache keeps getting worse."

* * *

"Bellstrap's the place. My head is killing me."

"Should you be driving in that state?" Dick sounded genuinely concerned.

"Not much choice. I'm taking it slow. I'll be there in about twenty minutes."

"I'll dispatch the strike team." I expected him to end the call but instead he asked, "So how does it actually work for you? Is it just a headache?"

I sighed. "I hear the alien's heartbeat. The closer I get, the louder it gets, and the more my head hurts."

"Have you ever wondered why?"

"I don't understand the question."

"Why are you able to do that? Hear alien heartbeats?"

"Your guess is as good as mine, Dick."

"Has it been happening for your entire life?"

"Pretty much." I kept talking because it distracted me from my headache. "My parents started taking me to doctors when I was nine. The Agency has their feelers out for medical reports with the right elements: someone reports unexplained pulsing sounds no one else can hear, accompanied by a headache. They found me when I was sixteen."

"And you've been working for them ever since?"

"They recruited me out of high school. You know some people in the Agency call us the antibodies of Earth."

"All six of you."

"There used to be more."

"You think that's what you are?"

"Maybe."

"So... somehow the planet... Gaia... creates a natural defense system? Senses alien invaders and so reaches up her Earth-goddess fingertips to turn some people into natural alien hunters?"

"Doesn't sound very scientific, Dick."

"No, it doesn't."

"You got that strike team heading my way?"

"They'll be there."

* * *

I've always been in the habit of picturing human gatherings from above, imagining the shape they make. Football games look like oblong donuts, art festivals like amorphous blobs. The Honest Pudding Pie Festival looked like a dog bone. On the east end was Bellstrap Town Park, which had been set up with a soundstage on one end and rides on the other. The other knob of the bone was the Honest Baked Goods Factory itself, which appeared to have been transformed into a kind of giant fun house. Between them stretched a street clotted with food trucks and carnival games.

I drove the circumference of the festival trying to figure out where the heartbeat was coming from, but it seemed to get worse at both knobs. And when I say worse, I mean the kind of pain I usually only feel when I'm right there, right in the alien's smug little terraformed face.

I left the car on a side street near the park, put in my earpiece, gritted my teeth, and headed towards the Ferris wheel.

"Heading in now," I said into the earpiece.

Less than a minute after I stepped onto the grounds of Bellstrap Town Park, my headache faded so fast I almost thought it was gone. I stumbled to a halt and stood in the crowd, my eyes on a kid with box braids and a giant half-eaten turkey leg in her fist. I didn't look at her because she was especially interesting or likely to be an alien but because she was in the path of my eyes and I was too stunned to move my head.

This wasn't how it worked. If an alien knew I was coming and started to run—or even drive off—the pain might ease back a little. But this was a case of instant shift from screaming-in-your-face-alien-doppleganger to there's-an-alien-somewhere-within-a-half-mile.

The girl with the turkey leg stared back at me. She tugged her mother's sleeve and said something I didn't hear. The mother turned towards me, her face blossoming with protective fury.

So I took off. Across the park, towards the pain. It now had a clear source: straight ahead in the direction of the Honest Baked Goods Factory funhouse, whose smokestacks or turrets or whatever were sticking up above the crowd. The distance corresponded with the level of pain, which was reassuring. Whatever had been going on before, my sense appeared to be functioning as normal again.

You get within a mile or two. You start moving around on foot. The shifting in the intensity of the pain as you move works to triangulate you onto the source, although that part happens by instinct, the same way your ears triangulate onto a sound.

"The factory," I said to the mike in my earpiece. There was no answer. "Dick? Are you there?"

"Sorry, I'm here. I was making tea. Orange Blossom Spice. I like to add honey."

"That's great, Dick." I saw something odd out of the corner of one eye, then out of the corner of the other. "Your tastes in tea are important to me."

"Figured they would be."

I tried to glance around without seeming conspicuous, without giving away that I'd noticed anything strange. "For a second there I was afraid you'd come down with the flu."

"Not me, although I'm pretty much alone here now."

I reached the street that served as the shaft of the dog bone. "Here's the thing, Dick. I'm being followed."

I couldn't see their faces. There were at least three of them, marked by their hats, which looked less like fedoras than like magician's hats—or Abe Lincoln hats—but with brims that flopped. That, and the high collared black coats, were enough to hide their identities if not their presence.

There were enough weird outfits here that no one else seemed to care about three matching weirdos in droopy-brimmed top hats. I probably wouldn't care if it weren't for the fact that they were obviously following me.

"How many?" Dick asked.

"Three behind me, but I think I see two more ahead. What the hell is this?"

"The good news," Dick said, "is that the strike team is close."

"Anyone I know on the team?"

"Probably not. You know: flu."

I pushed ahead, past the two high-collar-top-hat goons waiting up ahead. They fell in with the three following behind, who'd now come together and were pacing me as a group.

"This isn't good," I said.

"It's okay. It'll be okay. Just keep talking to me."

"Why?"

"So I know you're okay."

"Fine. About what?"

"You have any memories from the Intrusion?"

"I was a baby when it happened, so no."

"I remember every detail. They say the whole world was glued to the TV, watching the ships open, waiting for the aliens to come out."

The top-hat freaks weren't getting any closer, which was only vaguely reassuring. My headache was getting worse again, and I could see the entrance to the Honest Baked Goods Factory up ahead. "My parents tell me they both puked. Like, simultaneously, the minute the aliens started oozing out of the ships."

"So does that mean they did us a favor? By becoming human?"

"They didn't *become* human, Dick. They just look human now. So they can hide."

"Except it's not just a surface thing. When they touched human beings, they absorbed every detail. Complete genetic-level transformation."

"How the hell do you know that?"

"You don't? The Agency has all the research on file. Alien autopsy reports, all of that."

"I guess it's need-to-know. If your job is tracking their heartbeats, I suppose you don't need to know. But they're *not* human, no matter what's at the genetic level. The fact that I can track them when they're in big crowds *proves* that."

"How so?"

I approached the entrance to the factory funhouse. The heartbeat was loud now, and it hurt. Someone was there taking tickets at the entrance, so I veered towards the nearest ticket booth. The top-hat villains clustered off to the side of the entrance as if patiently waiting for me to buy my ticket.

"It's simple," I told Dick. "Why can I hear them only when they're in crowds of humans?"

"You tell me."

"Dissonance, Dick. They're so close to human but not quite, and when they're surrounded by real people the dissonance is magnified."

"That what the Agency tell you?"

"What? They didn't tell it to you?"

Dick offered a small laugh. "I guess it's need-to-know."

I paid for my funhouse ticket and gave my gang of stalkers a sidelong look. "Is the strike team close?"

"The strike team has eyes on you right now."

I felt a twinge of relief. But only a twinge. I had no idea who these characters were, but if they meant to attack me it would be somewhere in the funhouse, away from the eyes of the crowd.

I clutched my ticket in my fist, gritting my teeth against the throbbing pain in my head, and headed towards the funhouse entrance. I veered just enough so that I walked right by the goons in hats. "How you fellows doing?" I said as I passed, then handed my ticket to the agent.

I've been in funhouses before. Some were pretty cool. This one was... lame. In the entrance area they'd set up half a dozen bouncy houses. Most of them looked like the kind you can order in for a birthday party. Only one of them was shaped like an Honest Pudding Pie.

I followed my headache through the crowd of parents waiting on their bouncing kids and towards an archway that announced itself as the entrance to the Hall of Mirrors.

Of course.

I glanced back. There were now six black top hats following me.

"Where's that strike team?" I said.

"Close," Dick answered.

"There's six of them now, and I'm heading into the Hall of Mirrors. You know what that means, right? I mean, you've seen every horror movie ever made that featured a funhouse?"

"You'll be fine, Darian. Trust me."

"I don't even know you, Dick."

I stepped into a mirrored tunnel, following the throb of my headache, and smashed straight into a mirror. "Fuck." I turned left, groping with my hands.

The difference between a really impressive Hall of Mirrors and a mediocre one is how spotless and scratch-free the mirrors are. Make them clean and shiny and smooth enough, and it's impossible to tell what's a mirror and what's the path forward.

This place was as clean and shiny as any Hall of Mirrors I'd ever seen.

"Talk to me, Dick. Where's the strike team?"

"They're close."

I glanced back and saw a bobbing black top hat. "They better be."

"Here's what I'm wondering, Darian. This business about *dissonance*. The bigger the crowd, the more the dissonance. You really *buy* that?"

"Why shouldn't I?"

"Well, think about it. Say you've got two violinists and one of them's playing a perfect A and the other one's a bit sharp. That's gonna be some serious dissonance. But you get a full orchestra, all of them playing the same note but one of them a little sharp, and no one's gonna hear it. Seems like crowds should hide the aliens, not make them easier to locate."

I stumbled around a turn, bounced off a mirror, and groped my way straight towards one of the top hat goons. He moved towards me, hit something, and disappeared. "Why are you telling me this, Dick?"

"I'm just saying, maybe the Agency isn't telling you the whole story."

"Listen, Dick. I just do my job. I've got a skill. The Agency pays me a living wage to use it. I keep the world safe from alien invaders."

"But do you, though?"

"You work for them, too."

I turned a corner and stumbled out of the mirror room into a hall illuminated by nothing but black light. Oversized replicas of pudding pies caught the light in their squiggles of white frosting. My socks glowed.

My headache was screaming at me now, so I knew the alien was close.

"How many unambiguous alien attacks have you actually heard about?" Dick asked.

"What do you mean? I hear about them all the time. Shootings in malls. Aliens assaulting kids."

"When they look just like people, it's easy to blame them for every completely ordinary human crime."

"What are you saying, Dick?" I turned to look back and saw that the goons had all entered the black light room—except they weren't following me. They'd all turned to face the Hall of Mirrors exit, ranged around it as if ready for anyone who followed.

"I'm saying," Dick replied, "that if you destroy that Trace you've got in your pocket, it'll be harder for the Agency to find you and less likely that my people will have to hurt anyone."

I stopped dead. "Who are you?"

"You see that curtain up ahead?"

I looked away from the goons. I saw the curtain, and there was no doubt where the pounding, roaring heartbeat was coming from. "Yeah."

"Why don't you come on through? I've been waiting an awfully long time to meet you."

* * *

I pushed through the curtain. Just behind it was a door, and beyond the door a room warmly lit by a pair of lamps, one of them perched on a big mahogany desk. I took it in through a fog of pulsing pain. Behind the desk sat a man with a broad, friendly face and close-cropped silver hair. "Hello, Darian."

"So all that flu stuff was bullshit?"

"Pretty much. It isn't flu season."

"Who are you, Dick?" But given the source of the pain, I knew at least one thing about him.

"The deeper question is who *you* are."

"What the hell does that mean?"

"Do you still have the Trace?"

"In my pocket. I suppose you won't let me sneak up on you and attach it while you're oblivious, will you?"

"I'd pluck it off and crush it underfoot. I might consider attaching it to someone else, send the Agency's killers off the scent. Problem is, they'd kill whoever had it first and ask questions later."

"That's not how they work."

"It is, Darian. They want the proteins and other chemical goodies our bodies produce, and we don't need to be alive for them to extract them."

It was getting hard for me to stay on my feet. Usually after I got this close, I'd already marked the target and gotten the hell out of Dodge by now. I clutched my head, tugging at the hair around my ears. "What the hell are you talking about?"

"Let me help you with that."

He got up from the desk, came around, and touched me lightly on the forehead. The pain vanished. Blessedly, gloriously vanished. It was such a relief that I hardly noticed that the pulsing heartbeat was just as loud as it had been before. "What did you do?"

"It's some effect of being cut off from the rest of us for too long. Our call starts to hurt. A touch sets things right."

"Us?"

"What makes more sense, Darian? That you're a magical Earth-defending antibody, or that you can hear us when we call because you're one of us?" He lifted his hand, palm-up. "Listen." And the heartbeat dimmed until it was little more than the gentle thrum that had awakened me this morning. "It's our way of calling to each other. When we aren't calling, you can only hear it when you're close. My team's hats and coats were designed to keep you from hearing them."

I felt my knees weakening. My breath was short, and a new kind of pain was starting to press out behind my eyes. "That makes no sense. My parents—"

I was cut off by the sound of gunfire beyond the door.

"Shit. The Agency's here," Dick said. "There's still time to destroy that Trace. If they win and the Trace isn't transmitting, we have a chance of getting away."

"I'm..." I didn't know what to think, what to do. "Why do I only hear you in crowds?" Of all the questions that could spill out of my mouth in that moment, I have no idea why that's the one that came out.

"Because the Agency found and brainwashed its Trackers early and used them to hunt us when we tried to call to each other. Much harder to find us when we only call to each other in crowded spaces."

The gunfire was continuing beyond the door. "But my   life—"

"Is a lie. Everything the Agency has told you is a lie. We're peaceful. All we wanted to do is live and die among you. Just have a home. A life."

"But my parents—"

Dick closed his eyes. "They're winning. We're out of time. If you want to know the truth, destroy that Trace and come with me."

Here's the thing you need to know about my life. It's not complicated. It's nothing special. I have a job that gives me headaches every few months and a salary that pays my bills. I work out at Planet Fitness and binge-watch Netflix and call my mother on Sunday afternoons. I say hi to my neighbors. Sometimes I go to church. There's a college girl at the contemporary service I've been trying to work up the courage to ask on a date.

Maybe, every once in a while, I attend a festival or eat an Honest Pudding Pie. No great shakes, but a human life.

Never wanted anything other than that. And all I had to do to keep it was stand there, the Trace in my closed fist, and wait for the shooting on the far side of the door to stop.

I never asked to be part of some persecuted species, to hide out and call out and gather together to fight the forces that would hunt us down and kill us for the chemicals in our blood. If that's the truth about who I am, why the hell would I want to know the truth?

So I stood there, and eventually Dick's face sagged and he turned away. When he started to run, I threw the Trace and watched it snag a fold of his shirt. The strike team burst in. I pointed at the back door he'd run through and said something about him surely knowing about the Trace. "Won't keep it on for long."

I knew one of the guys on the team: Joe, as fierce a patriot as I've ever known. A true believer, fighting to make the world safe from the alien menace.

"Don't worry," Joe said. He smiled grimly. "We'll get him."

THE STARS NAMED FOR LOVERS

JOHN A. FROCHIO

On the morning of the Fat Lady's suicide, the Strong Man and the Sword Swallower were immersed in holocartoons. Donna, the Trapeze Artist, called and gave them the distressing news. Both were silent.

"Is anyone there?"

Alex, the Strong Man, said, "Yeah, yeah. Thanks. Alien Boy drove her to it." He hung up.

"How could the kid have anything to do with it?" asked Bert, the Sword Swallower.

"She's been acting funny around him lately. You haven't noticed? I think she loved him, but he couldn't love her. He couldn't or wouldn't."

Alex stared at Bert, searching for some kind of reaction. He and his friend were a study in contrasts. Whereas Alex was tall, bulky, covered with coal black hair, Bert was small, spindly, fair-skinned and sandy-haired. Bert was the excitable one, where Alex was calm and easy-going. He didn't know how they managed to become friends.

He received no response from Bert, so they silently returned to watching the holocartoons. Still, Alex couldn't get the Fat Lady and the blue, hairless, hyperactive boy from the stars out of his mind. He could no longer concentrate on his favorite form of escapism.

After a while, they sent the cartoons packing.

"Another time, guys, when we're in the mood."

* * *

At the local funeral home the next evening, Alex, uncomfortable in his best suit—his only suit, neatly pressed by Bert who had many domestic skills—approached Donna and offered her his condolences. Donna was the closest the Fat Lady had for family. She was slim yet shapely, with long blonde hair, and was strikingly beautiful, looking more like a runway model than a circus acrobat. Another example of sharp contrasts in friends. Perhaps that's how it had to be when your life was a circus.

He remembered how Donna and Celeste used to fight like siblings. He grew up with three sisters, so he knew what that was like.

Donna said, "I'll miss our loopy conversations." She chuckled, then sighed and rubbed her temple. "The good times, the parties, the fist fights, the hugs. Celeste was a little crazy, but she was a good friend." She blinked back newly forming tears.

"Did they say how she died?"

"They think she O.D.'d on highscrapers."

"She never touched the stuff!"

"I know. I don't believe it either. Say, where's Bert?"

"Didn't come. He can't stomach funerals."

"Wish I couldn't."

Alex noticed Alien Boy standing alone in a far corner of the room, wearing modest Earth casual clothing for a change. He seemed confused by the ritual he observed.

She said, "Some think it was a suicide."

"I can't believe that either. Was there a note?"

"No. Only a grocery list on the kitchen table."

"Maybe it was an encrypted suicide note."

Donna glared at him.

"Sorry. Not funny."

Alex stayed with Donna throughout the evening. She looked at Alien Boy every few minutes. He wondered about the kid's involvement in Celeste's demise.

Alex noted how well Celeste filled out the coffin, which appeared ready to burst at the seams. That was her trademark. She always wore clothing so tight it always seemed on the verge of breaking open to reveal the real Celeste. She loved to tease.

When most visitors were gone, Alex walked over to Alien Boy. He asked the blue kid if he would like to come with him to the casket and pay his respects to Celeste, now that the long lines were gone.

"No, thank you." His English was very proper, to the point of annoyance. "I will keep a respectful distance. That is how I offer my respects, per the custom of my people."

Was there a sadness in his eyes? Alex couldn't tell with Alien Boy. Though he had certain human-like characteristics, he was different in many ways. Alex still had a lot to learn about his alien culture.

Not long afterwards, Alex left.

* * *

After the funeral, where a stirring elegy was presented by the Grand Master of Ceremonies, a drunken feast was held in honor of the Fat Lady, who could hold more alcohol than any of them.

"She was legendary!" said the Grand Master. "Her heart was full of love and she was loved by all of us. She will be missed."

The next day everyone returned to their routines and rehearsals. Alex studied Alien Boy's practices closer than usual. He was looking for something suspicious in the boy's actions. Celeste wouldn't take her own life. It could only have been an accident, or something more sinister.

Alien Boy, whose real name was a sequence of mostly unpronounceable clicks and hisses, was as exciting to watch when he practiced his moves as when he performed before a crowded stadium. He wore thin shimmering strips of a silk-like fabric that concealed little of his blue skin. His frantic antics were mesmerizing.

He slithered up tall poles and seemed to walk on air as he went from the top of one pole to the next.

He scaled flat walls like a scared cat.

He climbed up, down, and around the inside of the big tent with fast, smooth movements.

He performed inhuman feats of theatrics, bringing frequent gasps from the audience, feigning precarious drops and swinging within inches of people's heads. Despite himself, Alex couldn't look away when Alien Boy performed.

* * *

After that evening's performance, Alex struck up a conversation with Alien Boy. "It's not the same without Celeste."

"It is different, yes."

"We'll all miss her. You spent a lot of time with her lately."

"I showed her things I've shown no other Earth being. I showed her things my body could do that no human body could do. I showed her where my home world was in the night sky, even though she could not see it, and I showed her the stars that were named for lovers. In my culture, the names we give the stars remain as permanent memorials for those who are deemed true lovers. I showed her my parents' star. Many stars are still waiting for their names."

"You and Celeste..."

"We were friends. We shared experiences. We shared feelings. We were not lovers. It could not be."

Together they walked back to their trailers under a clear sky. Alex looked up. So many stars.

"She wanted it to be so," said the boy from the stars, "but she understood I could not make it so. I told her that my flesh, which I cannot control, is repulsed by the flesh of Earth people."

Alex had never heard that before. An actual physical repulsion? He had no response.

* * *

The next day Alex dropped Bert off at a local grocery store, then went to the police station. At the front desk, he asked to speak with the investigating officer in charge of Celeste's case. He did not expect the tall, attractive brunette with sharp features who walked into the room.

"Detective Nancy Strong," she said holding out her hand. "You're the Strong Man from the circus. I've seen you perform. Impressive pecs."

"Thanks," he said as he shook her hand. A firm handshake.

"You're here about the Fat Lady? We're pretty sure it was suicide. No one takes that many highscrapers unless they wanted to end it all."

"Celeste loved life. She was always happy, except lately, when she began spending more time with Alien Boy."

"Alien Boy? The blue kid?"

"Yeah." Alex told her about their strange relationship.

"Unrequited love? I better follow up with the blue boy. Thanks for the tip."

* * *

That afternoon Detective Strong met Alex at the box office. She was dressed in street clothes, a short blue skirt and loose white blouse. Alex admired her look.

He escorted her to the Big Top Tent to watch Alien Boy practice.

He said, "Donna, the Trapeze Artist, was probably the last person to see her alive. They were at a local pub whooping it up when Celeste decided to leave before midnight. It's unlike her to leave so early."

"She give a reason?"

"She said she was tired. I think she had a rendezvous with Alien Boy."

"Hmm. The coroner estimated her death at around two a.m."

She watched the kid practice.

"Is he always this intense?"

"Always."

The detective's eyes locked on the wild, inhuman antics of the blue boy. Her body became tense. Alex recognized the signs. The alien kid affected a lot of people that way.

After Alien Boy concluded his rehearsal, he dropped lightly like goose down in front of them, so close Alex felt the heat generated by his performance and smelled the familiar sweet, pungent odor that poured from his body.

"Hello, Alex. Hello, lovely Earth lady. I am," and he made some harsh clicking and hissing sounds, "or, as everyone around here calls me, Alien Boy."

She held out her hand. "Nancy Strong."

He ignored her hand and she eventually dropped it. Yeah, you get used to that.

"I'm investigating Celeste's death. I understand she was a friend."

"Yes. My first true Earth friend. Earth people are not open to alien friendship."

Alex thought, *No, Alien Boy, the opposite is true.*

"When was the last time you saw her alive?"

"At evening meal, before she left with Donna to go pubbing. She and Donna had a goal of hitting all the pubs in America before they died."

"You didn't see her when she returned?"

"No."

In the silence which followed, their eyes pierced one another like hot irons.

Alex broke the tension. "She returned around midnight. Were you asleep by then?"

"Are you now my inquisitor?" asked Alien Boy. His eyes continued their hold on the detective's eyes. "I went to sleep at midnight, as I do every night."

"Midnight?" asked Nancy.

"Precisely at midnight."

"Then you did not wait for her at her trailer?"

"She always stayed up much later than midnight. When we spent time together in the evenings, I would always leave her company before midnight. I must begin my replenishment at midnight." He ran his hands up and down his sides. "My body must be kept sufficiently charged."

Detective Nancy frowned. Alex suspected she knew less about their culture than he did.

"What is it," she asked, looking him up and down, "that your body needs that can't wait past midnight?"

He looked deeply into her eyes and moved as close to her as he dared, without touching any part of her. The air around his smooth alien skin crackled.

"System shutdown. Something like your sleep periods, but more strictly enforced than yours. I have no choice. If I am not reclined on my recharging pad by the required time, my bodily functions will begin to shut down, wherever I'm at. I would drop like a meteor."

He sighed.

"Celeste understood we could never be lovers. I told her about the total commitment made by lovers on my world, the unbreakable bond, sealed for eternity when a star was named after them. We couldn't have that. My flesh is naturally repulsed by human flesh. It is beyond my control."

Alex said, "Yeah, there's a lot we can't control."

Nancy asked, "She was content with your relationship?"

"Not at first. However, our friendship ultimately became stronger."

He stepped back suddenly, tensing, as though someone was trying to touch him.

"Death is the beginning of one's immortal life, according to the belief systems in both of our cultures from what I understand. It is a new life, separate from this mortal life, marking the end of this life's bonds. Our friendship in this life is now over."

"And you're saddened by this?"

"Yes. As I've said, it is difficult for an alien to make a true friend among Earth people."

Nancy was quiet for a moment.

"Is our interview over? I need a nutrient wash and I'm meeting Donna for lunch."

"Donna, the Trapeze Artist?"

"We are not friends, but we shared a common friend. She asked if we could share our memories about Celeste. I expect it is some kind of closure rite for her. Therefore, I accepted."

Alien Boy left them.

Nancy turned to Alex. "We know so little about these aliens and yet the World Government allows them to live among us. I wonder how many are among us now. They have free rein. Is anyone watching them? I've always wondered whether there were unspoken motives."

"I sense a little racist streak in you, Detective Strong."

"More like paranoia. Fear of the unknown."

"Xenophobia. Yeah, there's a lot of that going around."

"Or fear of a Great Government Conspiracy."

"I know where you're coming from. Join me for lunch? Our cafeteria tent serves a wide assortment of culinary delights. Or maybe I'm just used to it."

"How could I resist such a tempting offer? I accept."

* * *

The sun was high in the sky on the late summer day. As they walked toward the cafeteria tent, he described their unique attractions from around the world and off-world. They passed an assortment of odd and colorful characters and beasts lumbering or fluttering about or cluttering the circus grounds.

They arrived at the cafeteria tent and took their selections to a table in a quiet corner. As they ate, they quietly observed the continuous comings and goings of circus folk. Donna and Alien Boy entered and went to the opposite side of the tent. Alex watched them discretely until they abruptly got up to leave, cutting short their small meal of finger food.

Nancy said, "That's our cue."

"Pardon me?"

"Come on. We're following them."

They followed the two out of the cafeteria tent, weaving between the scattered tents and trailers. In due course they disappeared into the Big Top Tent. She hurried over and peeked inside.

"Where'd they go?"

Alex stepped inside. "Follow me. This place is a maze."

The Big Top Tent was spacious and a challenge to explore, with many partitions, curtains, stacked boxes, and jerry-rigged office spaces. Eventually they spotted Donna and Alien Boy in a small practice ring behind some curtains.

Alien Boy was performing for her. Sitting quietly on a stool, Donna watched his every move. He effortlessly moved up and down ropes dangling from ceiling cross beams. At times he floated in the air as though he were a balloon. His blue skin glistened brightly with released body chemicals. Equally enraptured by the surreal performance, the detective stared without moving. It suddenly struck Alex that Alien Boy was executing his act without any clothing.

The routine, though natural and unforced, was especially intricate and challenging. His muscles rippled with exertion. Alex grew increasingly uncomfortable with the alien's immodesty and finally turned away.

What was it about this blue kid from the stars that captured the attention of so many? Why was he their most popular attraction? He wasn't jealous, he told himself. Okay, the boy *did* have a certain mesmerizing quality about him.

At that moment Alex's cell phone began playing "Chariots of Fire." He snatched it up quickly and fumbled for the mute button, dropping it to the ground instead.

He looked up to find Alien Boy and Donna staring at them.

Nancy said, "Smooth, Strong Man." She strolled out to the practice ring. Alien Boy hung motionless from a rope. Donna stood up angrily.

"Aren't there privacy laws?" Donna fumed.

"And decency laws as well. So Alien Boy, this is how you share your memories of a lost friend?"

"I performed these special routines often for Celeste. She spoke of the experience as 'spiritual enlightenment.' I wanted to show Donna so she would understand."

Alex chuckled under his breath. *Sure, Celeste wanted enlightenment, all right.*

Donna snapped, "It's none of your business, anyway."

"It could be my business," said Nancy, "if jealousy reared its ugly head that night."

"What are you talking about?"

Donna and Nancy stood facing each other, only a few steps apart. Both were tall, strong-willed women.

"I saw how you were hypnotized by his performance. You watched every movement of his body, every twist and turn. Maybe you wanted his performances all to yourself."

"You're crazy. He wanted to show me how they spent their time together, so I would understand their friendship."

"Maybe you were curious about their relationship. Maybe you wanted a little taste of what she had."

"That's ridiculous."

Nancy moved closer to Donna. "Maybe you wanted him all to yourself. Maybe you wanted to touch the forbidden flesh, because you knew he wouldn't be revolted by *your* touch."

Alien Boy dropped between them like a ghost. His face showed confusion. Nancy stepped back.

He said, "There can never be touching."

The detective continued, "Neither you nor Celeste could have what you wanted. His flesh is repulsed by ours. Look at him. He cringes at the sight of us."

He looked from one woman to the other.

"Forbidden fruits. Is that what you wanted, Donna?"

Alien Boy spoke. "At midnight, I must shutdown."

Alex said, "You have hours yet."

"What I mean to say is that after midnight, when I am in shutdown mode, I am in a state of complete detachment. I am completely unaware of my surroundings. However, on the night she died, I suspect Celeste had invaded my shutdown time."

Nancy said, "What makes you think that?"

"I stream—like your dreaming—throughout my entire shutdown period. That night the stream had some disturbing moments. It is caused by chemical imbalances, like cells bonding together to fight off an infection. This occurs when I incur some pathogen invasion or injury or other bodily attack during shutdown."

"You have no evidence?"

"I only have suspicions. I sensed such a disturbance the night of her death, but I cannot accuse."

Nancy stepped closer to the alien. "You suspect that Celeste broke into your trailer and did something to your body? Perhaps just a simple touch. Then your body reacted so badly she was driven to suicide."

"My body excretes harsh chemicals when it fights off an invasion. Your scientists are studying these chemicals and what effect they may have on Earth humans. This is not common knowledge."

Nancy looked at Alex. "This may be bigger than I thought. The government might want to know about this. But, damn it, every time you bring the government into the picture, they screw everything up."

While Nancy pondered her new information, Alien Boy turned to walk away from them. Donna suddenly jumped him and began pounding him with her fists.

The alien dropped to his knees and howled. A terrible, long, bitter, unearthly howl.

Nancy slammed into Donna and knocked her away from Alien Boy, who immediately collapsed into a twisted heap, trembling violently. Donna rebounded quickly and swung her clenched fists at Nancy. Her face was contorted like a mad woman's.

The Detective and the Trapeze Artist were now locked together in a furious battle. Though Nancy was well trained in advanced fighting techniques, Donna was agile and strong. They were well matched physically, but Donna's demented rage placed Nancy in a defensive role.

Alex hurried over to Alien Boy and leaned over him, careful not to touch him. "How can I help?"

"Blanket," he whispered.

Alex ran off and returned a couple minutes later with a large Pooh blanket, Bert's favorite, who gladly gave it up for a good cause. He threw it over the still shaking body of Alien Boy. The detective and the Trapeze Artist were still engaged in a bitter struggle no one seemed to be winning. For a moment, he wondered if he should intervene in the fight, but decided the alien needed more immediate attention.

"If you can," said the alien weakly, "please carry me to my trailer, Alex. I need my treatment."

Alex scooped Alien Boy off the ground, the blanket almost completely covering his body, and carried him off. The boy was surprisingly light.

* * *

Moments later, Bert arrived brandishing a sword, the very one he swallowed before large crowds of astounded people. Spotting the struggling women, he called out with his usual dramatic flair, "Cease and desist!"

Caught off guard, Nancy took a gut shot that knocked her into a stack of boxes. Donna ran off after Alex and the alien.

Staggering to her feet, Nancy growled at Bert, "Damn it! Do you have a license for that weapon? Where did she go?"

Bert pointed with his sword, then bowed broadly. "I am Bert, the Sword Swallower, at your service."

"We've got to stop Donna."

They ran outside. She stopped.

"Which way to Alien Boy's trailer?"

"This way."

The next moments were a blur until they spotted the drama unfolding outside the boy's trailer. Nancy and Bert abruptly halted in their tracks.

The blue alien was still wrapped in Bert's favorite blanket, leaning against the door to his trailer. Alex blocked him as Donna crouched in front of them like a tiger about to leap on its prey.

* * *

Alex called out, "I have to get him inside."

Nancy sprinted past Bert and knocked Donna to the grass. Nancy sat on top of the furiously struggling Trapeze Artist, holding her arms down.

Bert rushed over and flaunted his sword over Donna.

Donna screamed, "She wanted him all to herself! She wouldn't share him!"

Alex scooped up and carried the alien into the trailer.

Inside, Alex set Alien Boy in his bed and, following instructions from the boy, connected him to the tubes and wires that dropped from the grotesque machine that hung over the bed. After the machine was quietly humming, Alien Boy told him, "You can leave me. I will be okay now. Thank you, Alex. I think you are a friend now, too."

"Sleep well, friend."

He thought he saw Alien Boy smile briefly before his eyes drew shut.

Alex left quietly.

* * *

Later, after Donna was taken away, Alex, Bert and the detective went to Bert's trailer for a drink. Bert made an excellent hot chocolate and Nancy couldn't say no.

"Will she be okay?" Alex asked. "Donna's a little rough around the edges, but she's decent. This isn't like her at all."

"I expect she'll be examined by a lot of doctors. It'll depend on what they find. Maybe some kind of madness brought on by contact with the kid. Is it permanent or temporary? Who knows? She won't be exposed to Alien Boy again. Better start looking for a new act."

"What if others fall under his—what do we call it? Spell?"

"Yeah, it'll happen. There'll be a government investigation out of this. Maybe we'll learn more about those chemicals he secretes. That's probably what killed Celeste. It's still up in the air on how she died. I'm not ruling out murder. Donna could've done it."

"I won't believe murder or suicide. She was drawn to the kid and her own obsession killed her. Both Celeste and Donna wanted his friendship. Then they wanted more than his friendship. They wanted the stars named after them."

"I don't think I'd want that kind of immortality."

"I don't know. It sounds pretty amazing when you think about it."

Bert cheerily served his hot chocolate.

Nancy took a sip. Her eyes widened.

"Wow! This is amazing, Bert."

He beamed, then bowed.

"It's my pleasure to serve you, madam. That's what friends do."

THE RIBBON

MAK GRIFFIN

Wet sand squished between Gabe's toes. Damp ocean scents, thick and heavy, fouled the air and made him wrinkle his nose. In the distance, a throaty contralto sang "*Non, je ne regrette rien.*" No regrets. His head throbbed. He had plenty of regrets. Like letting his buddy Cal talk him into coming along to this friggin' beachside jazz festival. "It'll be good for you," he'd said. "Have some fun for a change."

Fun. Right. Now that they were here, a premonition of doom gripped Gabe. His heart raced and added to the pain behind his eyes. All he wanted was to leave.

He turned to Cal and tried not to whine. "Can't we just go back to the car?" He gestured at the gray skies scudding close to the beach. "It's chilly, and it looks like it could storm." He knew better than to mention his premonition. Cal would just scoff at him for having a panic attack. He'd probably be right, too. It wouldn't be Gabe's first attack, after all.

Cal rolled his eyes. "Always the pessimist. You don't just think the glass is half empty. You think it's *poisoned.*"

Gabe's face heated. He wanted to say that sometimes he was right. Sometimes the glass *was* poisoned, but as usual Cal didn't give him a chance.

Cal ticked off his points in a matter-of-fact voice. "Look, we had an awesome time at *Jazz in the Sand* last year. We've gone to the trouble of packing a picnic. After driving all this way, we should at least hang around long enough to eat and listen to a few sets." His tone turned earnest as he reached out and squeezed Gabe's shoulder. "You're a great buddy when you're not being such a buzz-kill, so stop already."

Gabe heaved a deep sigh and managed to calm his heart. Cal was right. Time to get a grip. Besides, he just didn't have the energy to push back.

He followed his friend over a rocky hill and gazed onto the beach. It sloped downward to where the gray ocean sloshed in green foam. A couple of surfers paddled on boards in the lazy waves, and scattered bathers lounged here and there in small groups. A crowd of thirty or so clustered about a temporary stage where a jazz band performed. Their song had changed, and now the syncopated beat of "Take Five" drummed across the dunes. The rhythms of *Howl* and madness danced in Gabe's head.

For a moment, the world disappeared in despair.

Gabe shuddered and clawed his way back. Sometimes reality, even this reality, was better than the abyss. He knew Cal meant well. He should be grateful for his friend. At least the dismal weather meant the festival wasn't crowded.

Cal laid out their blanket and squatted next to the picnic basket. He pulled two beers from the cooler and held one out to Gabe. "Here. Sit with me Have a brew. Try to appreciate the music."

Gabe clenched his jaws. *Try.* Like he was incapable of joy.

Except that was mostly true. Especially the last few weeks. For the thousandth time, he wished he could shake the depression that weighed on him. The headache he'd had since last week didn't help any. He supposed he should see his doctor. His meds probably needed adjusted.

Screw it. He popped the tab on his beer. Foam oozed out and onto the blanket. "Damn." He shifted hands, held the can over the sand while it fizzed, and shook out his fingers. Nothing was going right today. Or any day, lately.

Cal used a sharp knife to cut his sandwich. "I wonder what's going on over there." He lifted his chin toward a cluster of young men gathered near the breakwater.

Gabe glanced at them. "Who knows? Looks like they're digging for something." A brilliant red flash flared in the middle of the group, and they retreated a couple of steps.

From the stage, the music changed, and the electric keyboard launched into riffs on "Stormy Weather." The contralto joined in, layering the melody in husky tones over piano glissandos.

Gabe peered at the group gathered at the breakwater. "That flash looked like a spark. Maybe they're building a campfire to keep warm. It's cold enough." He shrugged, took a second knife from the basket, and cut his sandwich.

Cal stood and frowned. "What spark? I didn't see anything. Besides, no one would build a fire there. The tide's coming in and would snuff it out. It looks more like they found something that washed ashore." He shielded his eyes with one hand and gazed at the group. His other arm hung limp at his side, still gripping the knife.

A bit of red glistened on the blade. It looked like blood. Couldn't be, though. Cal would have bitched if he'd cut himself. Must be ketchup.

Several nearby bathers stood. All of them stared at the gaggle of young men. One of them started to wander that way, in the direction of the group. Then another, and another.

The jazz band switched to the Errol Garner classic "Misty." Their vocalist warbled the opening phrase, "*Look at me*," but most of the audience was looking elsewhere, toward the group at the water's edge. A few started to drift away, one by one, toward the breakwater.

In fact, a lot of the people on the beach seemed to be looking at that group.

Gabe had to admit even he was curious. What was so frigging *interesting* about them, anyway? He was tempted to give in to the unexpected nub of curiosity that nibbled at him. For sure, it was weird to feel something other than sullen depression. He chewed his lower lip. He really did need to see his physician about those meds.

Cal murmured, "I wonder what they found." He straightened his back and his voice firmed. "Let's check it out. It could be fun." The muscles on his arm flexed as he gestured with his knife toward the group. A drop of red dribbled onto the sand.

Gabe hardened his lips. Cal was doing it again: deciding what they should do without asking for Gabe's opinion. Familiar, churlish annoyance squelched his bubble of curiosity. "I'm not going anywhere."

Cal didn't speak or even look at him. He just meandered away.

Gabe stood. In moments, everyone else on the beach spiraled in to join the group at the breakwater. Even the music sputtered to a halt as the band abandoned the stage and their instruments. Layers of bodies clustered about—what? Whatever it was, it commanded attention.

Another ruby flash burst between the crowded bodies, and they again retreated.

A single bather, clad only in plaid boardshorts, came into view, surrounded by the crowd. He stood over a cavity in the beach. He shook his hand. A glistening wisp of plastic clung to his fingers, like a pesky cellophane ribbon. Except this was no ordinary ribbon. It uncurled to a yard or more in length, with a width of perhaps four inches. Something, musical notes maybe, or printed circuits, flickered in vermillion tones on its glimmering surface.

The man shook his hand again, with more energy. He snatched at the ribbon with his other hand. All he accomplished was changing where the stubborn thing stuck.

But then the ribbon came alive. It writhed and wrapped itself about his wrist. Brilliant electric tentacles slithered up his arm and threaded about his muscular torso. His back arched, and his head jerked. His eyes emitted a feral red glow.

Gabe knew he should be afraid. Instead, awe took his breath away. An incandescent aura glowed about the man's body, as if he were an angel in a Botticelli painting. The intense scent of garlic clogged the air. Momentary dizziness gripped Gabe and made the beach spin about. He shook his head to clear it.

A susurration of reverential voices hushed from those in the circle about the young man. No one retreated. It was as if the ribbon had cast a spell over the onlookers.

The spell broke when the man with the ribbon leapt, cat-like, at one of the bathers. In an instant, he battered the surprised man to the sand. He placed a knee on the man's chest. He grabbed his victim's head and twisted. A crack, like a gunshot, snapped across the beach when the neck broke.

A second ribbon, a new ribbon the size and shape of the earlier one, fell from the murderer's wrist and coiled on the sand. Glistening. Waiting.

The onlookers screamed and scattered into riotous disarray. The murderer tore into them.

No, wait. Cal stood there, alone and still amidst the madding crowd. The ribbon, the new ribbon, lay at his feet.

He knelt.

He touched it.

It flashed. It coiled about Cal's arm and flared crimson. Neon threads outlined his muscles and ruby light shot from his eyes.

He still gripped the knife in his fist. He ran faster than the wind. In mere seconds, Cal was right there. Beside Gabe. With the knife.

Cal raised the blade to strike.

Gabe dodged, but Cal's knife caught him in the shoulder. Sudden agony made Gabe shriek. But he fought back. He still held the knife he'd used to cut his sandwich, and he jabbed. Blood spouted from Cal's arm.

A ribbon of cellophane slid off Cal's hand and fell in an iridescent coil at Gabe's feet.

A woman in a polka-dot dress staggered next to them. Gabe recognized the band's vocalist from earlier. Blood trickled from a gash above her left breast. Cal pounced and threw her to the ground. His knife tore her throat, and her shrieks turned to gurgles. Tremors wracked her body. Blood foamed from her quivering lips.

One of the surfers splashed ashore and ran toward the parking lot. Cal jumped to his feet and chased after him, trailing crimson from the gash in his arm.

At least Cal was no longer assaulting Gabe. He collapsed to his knees. His heart pounded and blood pulsed in his ears. He touched his shoulder. His wound ached. He stared at his bloody fingertips. His head throbbed, and the scent of garlic returned to burn his nose. A sharp, brassy taste flooded his mouth.

Movement caught his eye and sent shivers jittering down his spine. It was the cellophane ribbon that had fallen off Cal. It snaked about on the blood-soaked sand, as if seeking something, or some one. Before he could react, it struck, coiled about his wrist, and flashed ruby red. He shook his arm, frantic to make it go away.

But it was too late. The ribbon squeezed. Something evil, something *relentless*, wormed into his muscles. It wriggled through his arm and into his neck. It penetrated his skull and gnawed at his brain. Wine-red halos bloomed everywhere and blurred his vision.

His will withered and then swirled to oblivion.

A second surfer splashed ashore.

Gabe clutched his knife. He knew what he must do.

THE ELIXIR OF LIFE

JOHN B. ROSENMAN

Eben Waterford, Halan's part-time sheriff, turned as a wagon rolled into town. It passed drab, sun-bleached stores on the main street and Daniel, a lamebrain who was sweeping the boardwalk before the millinery.

The wagon was pulled by a beautiful bay horse. As it drew closer, though, the glossy brown hide dulled, the sun's alchemy exposing its age. The effect reminded Waterford of a card trick.

He approached the wagon. The driver was a tall, slender man dressed in black and wearing a black derby. As for the wagon, its high wooden sides proclaimed the wonders of DR. WARREN'S MEDICINE SHOW and extolled his achievements in several RENOWNED EUROPEAN UNIVERSITIES. While Waterford could tell the wagon had once been brightly painted in sunny yellow and grassy green to suggest good health, its lettering, intricate designs, astrological symbols, and ornamental scrollwork were chipped and fading. Like the horse, it was less impressive the closer you got to it.

Waterford had seen such fraudulent pitchmen before. Question was: should he give him the boot?

The driver addressed him in a deep, resonant voice. "Good day, sir. Could you tell me the name of your settlement?"

"Halan," Waterford replied. "And you, I presume, are Dr. Warren?"

The man politely tipped his derby. "Indeed I am, sir, at your service. And you would be the sheriff?"

How did he know? Waterford wasn't wearing his badge, something his wife chastised him for. "Yes," he said, "I'm Sheriff Waterford, at *your* service."

If the visitor recognized his sarcasm, he didn't show it. He rose from his seat and twirled the end of his pencil-thin mustache. "Sheriff, may I display my wares?"

Waterford considered the question as people started to appear, including Daniel, who stood gaping up at the man while still holding his broom. There was an ordinance against such solicitation, but business *was* bad, and this show might be just the thing to give folks a lift.

"No funny stuff," Waterford said. "I'll be watching."

"Of course." The man smiled then reached inside the wagon. When his hand reappeared, it held exactly what Waterford had expected: a bottle of a cure-all nostrum which was probably concocted from burnt cork and piss.

The bottle elicited a ripple of laughter from the crowd, which now numbered over twenty. Waterford took pride in his neighbors, who were not easily fooled. Only Daniel, whose mouth hung open, didn't share their scorn.

To Waterford's surprise, the pitchman started to laugh, too.

"You've seen confidence men before, have you, my friends?" the man asked after their mirth died. "What I offer to you, though, is a rare and precious opportunity."

His voice was velvet-smooth and compelling. Though they should know better, two townsmen raised their hands. "What's it do?" they chorused.

"Ah, I'm so glad you asked." He paused for effect. "It makes you new."

"New?" an old woman chirped.

"Yes!" he said, "and I know what you think I'm going to say next, which is that *this* bottle will cure all your diseases and ailments. It will banish the aches and pains of arthritis and restore your eyesight, give you back the strength and divine health of your youth. These and a hundred other stock assurances are what you all expect, and I will end with a guarantee that for a dollar a bottle, you will be joyfully blessed."

The skeptical crowd stood half-mesmerized in the heat. Waterford was also caught up. Like others, he watched the bottle's red and green label as the pitchman moved it back and forth like a swaying cobra's head. Why couldn't such outrageous claims be possible? If the world could produce such monstrosities as two-headed calves and bearded ladies, giants and hermaphrodites, why couldn't it create something miraculous? Now that he thought of it, the universe itself was pretty weird. Just last week he had seen odd colored lights in the sky, so beautiful they'd taken his breath away. Wasn't anything possible?

"What do you call it?" Miss Carson, the spinster school teacher, asked.

"Madam, it needs no name," Doctor Warren intoned. "In truth, whatever I'd call this medicine would do it a grave injustice." He paused, then dropped a bombshell. "And because no name is worthy, I give it to you for free."

"For free?" Matthew Holsum, a farmer, gaped.

Warren turned to him. "Indeed, my friend. As a loving gift, free and without encumbrances. Before I do, though, permit me to tell you one thing more."

He raised the bottle, riveting their eyes to it. And such was his spell that when the horse shifted its rump and loudly broke wind, no one even laughed.

"For many years," Warren continued, "I experimented with herbs and flowers, seeds and chemicals. I pored over learned volumes and traveled to deepest Africa in search of a rare plant, always laboring to achieve one thing. Can you guess what it was?"

"What was it?" Waterford heard himself ask.

Warren thrust the bottle skyward. "To create The Elixir of Life! To achieve a precise combination of ingredients which would harness each individual's innate potential and enable him to become the person he was meant to be."

"The person he was meant to be?" the school teacher said. "That's what we teachers do. I thought it was something to cure our ills."

"Indeed, it will," Warren said. "It will make you feel and look younger, live longer, and cure many of your ills. What it mostly does, though, is correct the mistakes and failures of each individual life in the most transcendent way."

The crowd had grown to over fifty now, and Waterford saw two clerks shove forward. They bumped Daniel in their excitement, making him drop his broom. Warren pointed at them.

"You there! I see by your smudged aprons you work in stores. Tell me, are you satisfied with this achievement? Is your status as high as you hoped to reach? Or do you feel dissatisfied and unfulfilled?" He turned toward Miss Carson. "And you, fair lady. Are you content being an unmarried teacher in an obscure village? Did you never harbor aspirations of matrimony or desire to rise further than cleaning blackboards and minding unruly children?"

The growing crowd murmured and glanced at each other. Dr. Warren not only sounded their souls and exposed their secret wishes with uncanny accuracy, but he did so with disarming, hypnotic honesty. The man was a shrewd guesser.

Warren continued, revealing individuals' dreams in a few words. Rufe Hanshaw, the owner of Halan's tiny restaurant, bowed his head when informed he should own lavish restaurants in a major city. Robert Thompson, the young blacksmith, learned that his future should lie not in an obsolescent trade but in the fledgling automobile industry.

A hundred people were gathered here now, and Waterford knew they should be furious. How dare this stranger invade their peaceful community and tell them they were willing failures. But despite his dramatics, Warren's words were strangely supportive, motivating them to strive harder and not accept mediocrity. Even the town's minister, Lucius Crane, seemed inspired rather than offended when Warren suggested he deserved to shepherd a much larger flock.

He's charmed us, Waterford thought. With a start, he realized it had grown cooler and more comfortable, as if Warren had turned down the sun even as he had ignited the townsmen's dormant ambitions. A shiver rippled along his spine, and he tasted fear.

Dr. Warren smiled down at them. "My dear friends, who shall be the first to try my elixir?"

Silence. Then ninety-three-year-old Mildred Ash, Halan's oldest resident, called out in a whispery voice. "I will." She poked her way through the crowd with the aid of her cane and stopped before Warren, peering up at him.

Warren unscrewed the cap and bent down with a saintly smile. Mildred reached up for the bottle, her frail hand trembling with effort.

"Stop!" Waterford called.

Mildred froze. Waterford pushed his way forward and faced the crowd.

"I think we should be cautious," he told them. "We don't know what's in this bottle."

The townspeople grumbled. "Eben," Rufe Hanshaw said, "what could go wrong? It's just a drink."

"He's right," another called. "And Dr. Warren is hardly the first medicine man to come here selling a nostrum. Hell, he's not even charging for it."

Waterford hesitated and then turned back. When he did, Warren's gaze pierced him to the core. The black eyes seemed to sift his soul, assaying each atom. *I know your secret but kept silent. You wanted to be a big city lawyer but lacked the courage even to go to law school. So you settled for a tin star in the middle of nowhere.*

Before Warren's stare, Waterford's opposition wilted. Mildred patted his arm.

"Don't you fret, Eben Waterford. I'm old, alone, and have nothing to lose. And I've had so many dreams."

Smiling, she accepted the bottle from Dr. Warren. She gave the people a coquettish glance and raised it to her lips. Waterford saw her take a few sips. Mildred lowered the bottle. Moments passed.

"Oh my," she said softly.

* * *

"You really should try it yourself," Dr. Warren said.

It was only six days later, and already Sheriff Waterford barely recognized most of the townsmen. Rufe Hanslaw, the restaurant's formerly lethargic owner, was a case in point. He'd completely changed the place's cramped, sorry appearance by knocking out a wall, slapping on a fresh coat of paint, and hanging lively paintings of stars and outer space, which he claimed went on forever and was filled with endless possibilities. Watching Rufe bustle about and top off a customer's coffee, Waterford could imagine him moving to the big city to expand his kingdom.

"I'm still hesitant," Waterford confessed. He leaned over his meatloaf, eyeing Warren across the table. "We aren't the first town that's tried your 'elixir,' are we?"

"No."

"Mind telling me what happened? Was it always successful?"

Warren took a bite of his chicken and chewed thoughtfully. "The results were... inconclusive. It's only lately that I've perfected the formula."

"How can you be sure?"

Warren leaned back in his chair and spread his arms. "Why is it so difficult for you to accept the miracles before your eyes? Just look around and behold the transformed lives. It's not just the proprietor of this restaurant but everybody. Why, here comes a happy couple now."

Waterford turned to see Miss Carson entering arm in arm with Sam Loggins. Word was that the prim and proper teacher had gone boldly up to the hardware store owner and invited him to a picnic. Judging by the way they laughed and snuggled, the romance was going well. Under the influence of love, or more accurately, Dr. Warren's elixir, Loggins had even organized a singing quartet by recruiting fellow merchants.

He demonstrated his ability now, bursting into a surprisingly strong baritone.

"Daisy, Daisy,

"Give me your answer do!

"I'm half crazy,

"All for the love of you!"

Loggins stopped and everyone in the restaurant clapped. Hanslaw slipped menus into their hands, bowed, and skipped away.

"Do you see, Sheriff?" Warren said. "Everybody's been reborn."

"Not everybody." Waterford nodded toward the back where Daniel was cleaning a table. The young man looked as slow and dull as always.

Warren shrugged. "For the few I can't help, there are always those who surprise even me."

"Like Mildred Ash?" The old woman looked sixty-five now and had started riding horses. Waterford shook his head in disbelief. "What will she become in another week or two?"

Warren smiled. "Perhaps she'll be young and can start life over."

Warren slid his fork toward the peas on his plate. Waterford counted nine, and the good doctor collected every one.

"How can your medicine be so powerful?"

Warren produced a bottle and removed the cap. "My friend, if you have faith, it can move mountains."

Waterford raised his gaze and stared at a painting of the vast Milky Way. Endless wonders, indeed. You might find anything out there, especially if you had faith.

He sighed, picked up the bottle and examined the red and green label which bore no name. "I thought it was a matter of chemistry," he said.

"The ability to believe counts too. It makes all things possible."

Waterford thought of the mystical designs on Warren's wagon. "Perhaps it's more like magic. Such as your knowing everything about people you'd never met before."

Warren swatted away a fly. "Believe me, Sheriff, in my business, after you've seen enough people, you come to know and recognize what they are. It's hardly voodoo."

He placed the open bottle on the table before Waterford, who gazed down at it.

"People disagree about the taste," Waterford said. "Some call it sweet while others say it's sour. Some compare it to apples or tangerines."

"To each his own, Sheriff," Warren said. "But you're wasting time. All your neighbors are nearly a week ahead of you."

Waterford hesitated then picked up the bottle. Only three or four ounces, how could it hurt?

He lifted the bottle to his lips. "One for the road," he said.

Warren shook his head. "Down the hatch," he replied.

* * *

The children were playing in the street.

The game was like none Waterford had ever seen. They'd drawn a complex grid with different colors of bright chalk and were hopping and dancing from square to triangle to circle to... something else. Standing on the boardwalk, neither he nor anyone else in the town could make heads or tails of the game or its rules; he just knew that Halan's little children had never played before when it was this hot and certainly never taken part in such a game. Its patterns reminded him uncomfortably of those on Warren's wagon. The kids didn't even speak or laugh, cry or shout. They simply concentrated on their game as if it were a matter of cosmic significance.

Evidently, the children had been nipping at Dr. Warren's elixir, too.

He didn't know why the realization surprised him so much, and yet it did, just as he was surprised that the indescribable taste of the elixir hadn't faded from his mouth after two days. For some reason he felt that if he could just name or identify the flavor, things would be better. Perhaps it would solve the great mystery surrounding him and explain why he felt guilty about failing these people.

What mystery? How had he failed them? Everything was fine, wasn't it?

The children—perhaps he should break up their game. They shouldn't be playing in the street like this.

But horses and the rare automobile came by seldom and with plenty of warning. Damn it, he was only the town's sheriff, not its shepherd, and as his wife Holly frequently reminded him, the job was only part time. His main job was running a farm.

I've changed, he thought.

He'd put the admission off for nearly two days, but he couldn't ignore the truth any longer. He'd always been poor with sums, and only Holly's knack with them had enabled him to balance the books. How many pecks of this and bushels of that... it was all a mystery.

The morning after he'd drunk from the bottle, though, he'd awakened with all such matters clear in his head. Indeed, he'd found it hard to believe they'd ever confused him. Later, he'd stunned Holly speechless by his ability to do all the farm's accounts in his head. He could see the account book clear as day in his mind and perform calculations with effortless ease.

The next day he devised a plan which would double their annual harvest of corn and wheat.

There was something else. Perhaps it was his imagination, but he already looked five years younger.

What's happening to me? he thought. *Why am I worried, and why won't I let Holly try the elixir?*

Suddenly the Petersons' dark-haired little girl Sarah left the children and ran up to him, her white dress swirling. Despite her exertions, she wasn't sweating.

Sarah smiled at him and pointed up at the vast blue sky.

He looked up. "What is it, Sarah?"

Instead of answering, she whirled around three times and returned to her playmates' intense game. Waterford noticed they had started to chant. For some reason, their voices reminded him of the strange, beautiful lights in the sky, which he had seen again.

He watched in silence, then heard a board creak behind him. He swung and stiffened, seeing Dr. Warren's dark eyes watching him.

* * *

Ever since getting polio as a child, Holly had been in pain and able to walk only with crutches. Now as he entered the house, he saw her rise unaided from her chair and skip lightly about the room.

"Look at me, Eben," she sang. "Just look!"

Stunned, he watched her pirouette and leap up, crossing her ankles back and forth with blinding speed. He remembered her childhood dream of being a ballet dancer. Why, all her life his graceful wife had worn the disguise of a cripple!

"How..."

She giggled and kissed him. "I know you said not to, but Mrs. Rawlings came by yesterday with one of those bottles. I just took a few sips. Soon the pain stopped, and I've felt strength pour into my body for hours. And then, just a few minutes ago..."

He embraced her, then collapsed into his easy chair. She knelt beside him—actually knelt—and clasped his hands. "Are you happy for me, Eben? You're not mad, are you?"

"Of course I'm happy and not mad," he managed. "How could I be?" It was just nine days since Dr. Warren's arrival, and yet the town seemed alien. Mildred Ash looked *forty* now, and everyone was excited about hosting a *cultural festival* and inviting folks from other towns. Now here was Holly, the biggest surprise of all.

"There's something else I'd like to show you, Eben." Roses bloomed in Holly's cheeks, and she looked years younger. She giggled again and raised her arms.

"Watch me turn a cartwheel and stand on my head!"

* * *

The first people died the next day.

Waterford wasn't alarmed at first. It had been a brutal summer, and the weather often took a toll this time of year. A small child and a few of the elderly. It was nothing out of the ordinary.

Then it became extraordinary very fast.

A family carried their father to Dr. Weir. The father died, and then a daughter, and just hours later, good old Dr. Weir, who'd taken one sip of Warren's remedy.

More followed with increasing rapidity. And then fear spread through town.

Waterford tried to maintain order, arrange for some kind of medical assistance, and find Dr. Warren. But the man was nowhere to be seen. Worried about Holly and weak with a slight fever, he holstered his gun and rushed back to the makeshift clinic he'd set up in the church. He stopped, his boots skidding.

Two columns of town folk marched toward him, led by Dr. Warren. Something was odd about the way the people moved. They stared straight ahead, not even blinking in the sun. Connie Stewart, a playful little girl with an infectious laugh, now walked woodenly, her face slack-jawed and expressionless.

The processions stopped six feet away from Waterford. Warren gazed at him, his face etched in sadness.

"I tried," he said. "I thought this time it would be different."

Waterford unstuck his lips. "Different?"

Warren took off his derby, revealing neatly combed hair. As usual, he wasn't sweating.

"Ever since I was a child, I've wanted to help humanity. Cure disease and infirmities, make people live for a long, long time. Above all, I've wanted to help people realize the best that was within them, their unsung potential. In my quest, I've visited many communities, ceaselessly improving my gift. This time, in Halan, I thought my labors had at last been rewarded, for I'd benefited more citizens than ever before."

Warren replaced the derby and waved at the town. "You've seen my successes. The restaurant owner, the teacher, the children, and even your wife." He wiped away a tear. "Only now, later than ever before, as I approached the very peak of triumph, the old pattern has emerged and cheated me once again."

Waterford shivered, trying to make sense of the words. Gift. Rewarded. Benefited. Successes. Peak of triumph. Cheated. "What do you mean... 'old pattern'?"

Warren sighed. "My friend, people sicken and die. Within minutes, healthy citizens who recently became so alive and on the verge of realizing their dreams are struck down. And those who aren't face an even worse fate. Before their bodies die, they will suffer a living death." He turned to the obedient figures behind him, and for the first time, Waterford recognized the frozen face of the minister, Lucius Crane.

"In them," Warren concluded, "brain function is reduced to a minimum. They are no more than pets."

"Y-You monster!" Waterford gasped. "You knew this pattern when you came here, and you didn't care. You've killed us, killed us all. Who gave you the right..."

He reached for his gun, but Warren moved quickly and seized his shaking hand.

"It's useless, Sheriff, and I see you have the fever." He glanced at those behind him. "Soon you will join their ranks."

"I... I should have stopped you the day you came," Waterford said, his knees buckling. "I knew there was something wrong. You never even had the courage to drink your own poison."

His lips froze. He couldn't speak any more.

Warren lowered him gently to the ground and folded his arms on his chest. "Don't struggle," he said. "In a short while, it won't make any difference."

* * *

Swing, swing.
Sweep, sweep.
Broom, broom.
Clean floor.
Clean it clean, cleaner, cleanest.
The positive form, the comparative form, the superlative form.
Miss Carson told me so, her breath warm on my face when she tried to teach me.
Swing, swing.
Sweep, sweep.
Her breath was warm, and she smelled like jasmine.

The broom stops. *She smelled like jasmine, and I still taste the elixir when I drank.*

I touch my lips, tasting the sweet liquid. Holding the broom, I gaze about the restaurant. See the tables, the paintings of stars and planets revolving in their endless dance. By the cash register, Mr. Hanshaw stands pale and weak.

And the world floods in, drenching me.

I spread my arms. It rains, it rains, it rains, but I can never drown, never be filled. I am vast, thirsty for knowledge, which is the first new word I learn. Everything I've seen and heard and felt and tasted and smelled connects within me, building and building up toward an infinite sky.

I *know.*

"Daniel, is everything all right?" Mr. Hanshaw asks.

I turn. Mr. Hanshaw looks sick and will soon die. I smile. For the first time in my life I tell a lie.

"Yes, Mr. Hanshaw. Everything's fine."

I start to leave, then stop. A man stares at me from the full-length mirror to my left. He's young, tall, and muscular. Like me, he holds a broom.

It takes me a moment to realize I'm looking at myself.

And I have *red* hair!

Stunned, I move closer, touching my face and chest as my reflection does the same. If only I had time to see myself naked, to learn and explore my body. But a terrible urgency burns in my blood. There's something important I must do.

Turning away, I leave the restaurant and step out onto the boardwalk with the broom.

I stand in the heat, drenched by a deluge of inner rain. More and more I see deeper and deeper into the heart of things, into the nature of reality.

Sadly, I also see the dead and dying who fill the street. Some of the people are like clockwork toys with vacant eyes. The children make me want to weep, for they will never grow up.

Then I see *her.* At first, shock overwhelms me. Praise God she at least is not like the toy people, who are cursed even more than the dying. I step into the street and go to her.

"Daniel, what are you doing here?" Miss Carson glances about, swaying on her feet. "If I could just find him."

"Sam Loggins," I say.

She blinks at me in surprise as if a rock had spoken.

"Yes," she finally manages. "Have you seen him?"

I have. Sam Loggins lies dead near the curb a block back. I start to tell her, then realize something. Apparently I still have things to learn.

"I love you, Miss Carson."

She sways, and I steady her with my hand. "You do?" she asks.

"Yes. Sam Loggins loves you well, but I love you better, and I love you *best.*"

My having learned her lesson means nothing to her. "I... don't know what's wrong with me," she says. "I can barely stand. And some are dead."

"I know. Doctor Warren's elixir takes back everything it gives and more. I think it disrupts the brain's chemistry."

She crumples and I drop my broom to catch her, lowering her as gently as I can to the dirt. Dear God, the teacher I didn't even know I loved is about to die. For the first time I experience what must be grief.

Her heart flutters and her pulse beats—too weak, too weak! I kiss her cheek, tasting the salt of my tears. Even now I can smell the faint jasmine of her perfume.

I look around. Please, someone help us! But the town is in its last hours, and nothing can save us.

Then I know or think I know. With one hand I rip off my shirt and lay it on the ground beneath her head.

I nick my forearm with my fingernail, cutting it several times until it bleeds. Trembling, I ease her mouth open and hold my arm over her.

"This is my blood," I tell her. "Drink. *Drink.*"

Only it's hard for her, and there's no real reason to believe it will work anyway. My idea is madness!

Eternity passes, then in joyful relief I see health and color return to her face. Soon she begins to breathe more easily.

I rise. Much as I want to stay with her, there are so many others who need me. Though I can only help a few, I know I must try.

A horse neighs behind me.

Turning, I see Dr. Warren drive his wagon toward me, reins gripped in his hands. He stops it and leaps down from his seat.

"You're Daniel, aren't you? The..."

"The idiot," I finish for him. "Yes, I am. But no longer, thanks to your brew."

He stares from me to her in wonder. "You... you've changed! And you saved her, brought her back."

I touch my bleeding arm. "The restorative agent is in my blood. Soon, God willing, Miss Carson will be what she was before. And more."

I watch him put it together. His face lights up, and I know what he's about to say.

"My dream... I've reached it. My elixir is a success!" He claps his hands then seizes my arm. "My friend, *you* are what I've been striving for all these years. If my medicine can transform even you into a genius, nothing's impossible. Just imagine what we can do together. With your blood, we can pass my gift on to others, actualize the potential dormant within humanity."

I glance at the dead people, those lying still and those still breathing. "You never gave a damn about humanity. All you cared about was yourself and your experiment."

"Not true! All I wanted was the best for them."

"Look at the dead," I say. "I'm sure they're very grateful."

He spares them a brief glance. "But the results, aren't they what counts? Yes, a few must be sacrificed, but it's for the greater good. Now we have the solution, and it's *you.*" He sees me snatch the broom from the ground and steps back. "Look, my friend..."

"I'm *not* your friend."

He retreats farther as I advance. "We can save everybody," he cries. "Even make ourselves gods."

I grip the broom and strike at his feet as if I'm sweeping a pile of trash. He staggers back, his derby flying. I swing again and he falls, smashing his face against his gaudy wagon. He raises a pleading hand.

"Daniel, my intentions were good!"

I straddle him and reverse the broom. "Don't you know what the road to hell is paved with?"

I drive the handle down, right into his cold heart.

Afterward, I stagger away. Guilt and revulsion rack me, but Miss Carson's smiling face reminds me of the others I must save.

As I leave, I notice again the game the children drew in the street. Before it meant nothing to me, just as it did to the town. Now, though, I gaze in wonder. Such an intricate design! Why did the children draw it? Ah, it must have been caused by Dr. Warren's unholy mixture.

Moving about, I study the different colored figures. Circles and squares, triangles and more. Is it some version of hopscotch?

I examine the multicolored maze from all sides, scrutinizing its countless facets. Only it seems meaningless. I know I should leave and help people, but the thing won't let me go. Whether it's a pointless decoration or not, it ensnares my mind, filling me with dread.

Finally I pull free and turn to go. *Snap!* the pattern shifts and meaning breaks through. I see stars, planets, and distant nebulae, just like those on the restaurant's walls. And in the center...

Suddenly I know what the children merely sensed, what this design really means. It is a message, a celestial map of warning about Dr. Warren sent by some transcendent power. It is also a test, for the sender seeks the one person who can solve it and save this town.

I look up at the sky and the galaxy beyond and feel a vast regret. Oh God, why did this happen to *me?* If only I'd known earlier, I could have warned people, convinced them to reject Dr. Warren's dangerous elixir and flee this doomed town. But my mind dwelled in darkness and my eyes were opened too late. Even worse than Dr. Warren is the hammer that now descends from the sky. This imminent blow from the universe.

The asteroid comes down, deeply cratered and three miles across. It blots out the sky and fills the world with darkness. Lying down, I barely have time to shield Miss Carson's lovely face before it strikes.

* * *

Falling. Falling from an infinite height...

Finally I hit something and cry out. When I open my eyes, a whole new world stretches before me. Fantastic shapes and smells bombard my senses and I struggle to understand.

I rise to my feet and examine my body in amazement. Not only is it uninjured, it has become huge and golden, and my hands have seven supple fingers. Something stirs on my back, tugging me upward. I gasp as I rise into the air.

Oh God, I have wings!

Somehow I pull them down and settle back to earth. Trembling, I realize my eyes have also changed. I see clearer and farther than ever before. Only there are too many suns in the sky, all of them closer than the old one.

The buildings are ethereal and lovely, rising so high they pierce the clouds. And the people! They are tall and majestic like me, with silver veins flowing beneath their golden skin.

My mind staggers. What happened to me? Am I going mad? But how can that be when everything looks so beautiful? Dazed, I remember the breathtaking lights I saw in the sky and the paintings of outer space in Rufe Hanslaw's restaurant. Rufe claimed the universe went on forever and was filled with endless possibilities.

A small figure comes toward me. A child. She smiles and holds her hand out in welcome. Her gossamer hair stirs in the wind, and she playfully beats her wings as if inviting me to fly with her. The child looks as sweet and trusting as those I left behind.

Then I hear a sound and see a driver approach in a wagon. It isn't a wagon exactly, and the two-headed creature pulling it isn't a horse, but I recognize another deadly, fraudulent medicine show coming my way. As the inhabitants turn eagerly toward them, I realize with joy what it all means. The strangers on this new world are not only as trusting and vulnerable as the ones on Earth, but they are my people now. And the cosmic being who sent the message to Halan has given me another chance to save them... and others as well.

This time—and on all the other worlds to come—I must not fail.

A RIALTO IN A GALAXY FAR, FAR AWAY

LAWRENCE DAGSTINE

Tritania, according to thespians, doesn't have much unusual weather. No seasons, no blizzards, no thunderstorms, no twisters, no hurricanes. Not even snow. There is just the massive red dwarf completing its obligatory ten solar cycles in unison against a gaseous, orange-purple five-ring system of luminescent crystals.

Tritania, one of the last discovered exoplanets, does have that dry little wind off the crimson desert they call the Scourge. But the Scourge never pushed over anything bigger than a tumbleweed or a eucalyptus pod. Thus Tritanians are without much to talk about in the way of weather. There *is* rain: early, late, or nonexistent. The crystals high above the atmosphere, which provide the dew, evaporate, in turn creating the rainfalls. The rainfalls create the water. In the arroyos of the dry foothills, there *is* an occasional flash flood.

There was once a major earthquake on Tritania, though not in Southern Quar. All Southern Quar had was earthquake weather. Chentiki Quar's belt had almost more earthquakes than any other part of the southern hemisphere. There was no record of any accurate foretelling of an earthquake-by-earthquake weather. But everyone felt that at some future time *the* earthquake would come.

Let an Earth-bearing world's day be overcast but warm, muggy but rainless, leaves motionless, sounds carrying unusual distances in the quiet, then everyone believed that dangerous weather was being prepared.

Earthquake weather affected people in two different ways. Some thought that it was useless in the face of impending disaster to pay bills, wash dishes, or milk sputters. Others, like Birdie, relished hurdles to leap. Even hurdles as big as threatened earthquakes. If her house was going to be tumbled down a crevasse, let it go clean and tidy.

Taking the dust of the last Scourge off the front windows, Birdie didn't notice Zarn skiff into the side driveway.

"I see you're getting ready for the quake," the machina said.

"You don't believe that talk, do you?" If he did, she was glad to see he didn't believe in stopping work until the jolt was over.

"No. Tritania's yelled wolf too often for me to think earthquakes and weather have any connection."

"What're you doing away from the greenhouse?"

"Took a lady for a test drive—and a sale, I hope."

"Gemma says she's learning to drive a full skiff. Don't you think she's a little young?"

"She's fifteen. She had her adulthood primer at thirteen. She had her sexplant at fourteen. So, she can have a skiff at sixteen."

"You plan on giving her one?"

"Rate she's been coming along, I might do that."

"Come on in. In time of earthquake, they say, stay away from glass windows."

The machina made preparations.

"Got any coffee left over from breakfast? In time of earthquake, they say, keep up your strength."

Zarn sprawled himself out on a wicker rocker on the front porch. "No use going inside in weather like this. Just keep the shields up."

Birdie handed him the tablet with the *Quar Daily.* "Read this while I get the coffee."

Much of the first two pages carried summaries of the campaigns back on Earth. President Hatfield was quoted on the progress of Nationalist troops fighting in New America.

When the machina returned with his coffee, she said, "Well, what do you think?"

"I think there are too many used skiffs on the market."

"Zarn, you haven't even read the *Daily.*"

"I read the used skiff ads. What did you have in mind?"

Birdie, from her twin rocker, took the tablet from Zarn, snapped it open again, then handed it back. "Read that," she said.

"'Second Reservoir for Chentiki Quar' That it?"

"Not the reservoir. The new cinema, the Rialto."

"I never knew a robot duck was so crazy about ancient movies."

"Not the movie. The contest they are having."

"'Rialto Theater offers a fifty-thousand merker prize opening day for the best imitation of ancient comedian, Charlie Chaplin. Contest to take place on the main boulevard of Chentiki between two and three on the afternoon of the opening of the theater.' That it?" Zarn asked.

Birdie nodded.

"You're a machina, an avian at best. You plan on entering?"

"I recite; I am not programmed to act. Besides, for a machine I am not funny."

"You got somebody who is? Me?"

"You're funny, all right, but you can't act. Gemma."

"You're out of your mind."

"No, I'm not. We laugh our heads off at her antics. And since the sexplant, she doesn't get stage fright. You saw her at the emerald temperance contest."

"Have you talked to her about it?"

"Not yet. But I've already paid the entrance fee. Gemma isn't the kind of girl to let me spend merker for nothing. She'll win the fifty thousand. I know. And she knows we need it. It's for the greenhouse, and your teeth. She'll jump at the chance."

"You know, I really never thought to see the day when a machina of mine would sell her own programmer."

"Sell? Now you're out of your mind, Zarn. I'm fully capable of emotion and human understanding. I'm merely giving her the chance to do what she likes to do, and make merker at it besides."

"Birdie, Birdie. I know your master better than you do. Sure, if you ask her to do it, and for my teeth in the bargain, she'll do it." Zarn shook his head. "But what makes you think she wants to assimilate some ancient Earth celebrity? What makes you think she wants to put on baggy pants, have a mustache glued to her upper lip, carry a cane, and wear broken-down outsized shoes? She's finally at the age where she wants to look good. Not parade in clown clothes down the middle of the Chentiki Quar to the hee-haws of onlookers."

"Charlie Chaplin isn't a clown, at least not according to historical texts."

"That outfit of his is a clown suit. How do you expect to squeeze Gemma into it? She's no undersized middle-aged man."

"People don't expect her to *be* Charlie Chaplin, just to act more like him than the other contestants."

Birdie didn't speak to Gemma about the Rialto contest until after supper a few days later. She sounded like anybody in an embarrassing situation, saying, "After your sexplant, when I heard you, I knew I had done the right thing. I hope you think so, too."

"What, Birdie?"

"I entered you in the Rialto contest."

"To be Charlie Chaplin? It costs merker."

"I've already paid it."

"Such an ancient character. And Charlie doesn't talk."

"I reckon you can hold your tongue for ten or fifteen minutes."

"Charlie is a man."

"That's what'll make it all the funnier. A sexplant pretending to be a grown man."

"I wouldn't really be pretending to be Charlie. I'd just be pretending to be the clown Charlie's pretending to be."

"That's the only historical view of Charlie, the one everybody knows. The prize is for the best imitation of whoever Charlie's pretending to be."

"Prize?" Gemma queried.

"Fifty thousand. Didn't you read the ad? It's just what's needed for your brother's teeth, and to put the finishing touches on the greenhouse. Otherwise, the Scourge may destroy the rest of the crop."

"Do you think I can do it?"

"You could be Teddy Roosevelt if you set your mind to it."

"I'll have to have a costume," Gemma said.

"That's one thing I can do," the machina assured her. "And if you faint, I'll be right up there to grab your cane and mustache. *And* take the fifty thousand. Only I won't throw the money away, a habit your brother admits to when it comes to skiffs."

* * *

By the time the Rialto had its contest, the earthquake weather had produced a moderate tremor down in Southern Quar. In Chentiki it was a normal cycle: dry, clear, and hot. It wasn't the weather for a Charlie Chaplin outfit. Gemma was afraid beads of sweat might loosen the mucilage that held on her mustache.

She had seen a silent movie with Charlie Chaplin. Only once. She could make herself look like Charlie, helped by a tight Ferris waist and a special hat that came equipped with a fringe of black hair. The Ferris flattened Gemma; the mustache made the flatness look manly. But Charlie had something she wasn't able to reduplicate. He was a man sad in the eyes, sad and solemn, thinking of better things. When *he* had mishaps, they shouldn't have made audiences laugh. Charlie *wanted* people to laugh. That's what he was famous for, laughter at a little man who wanted to be admired for his dignity, and who, try as he would, couldn't avoid ludicrous mishaps. It wasn't the clown they laughed at. It was the little man, Charlie himself, who wore the clown suit. Clowns are supposed to be funny. They work at it. And nothing is funny that has to be worked at. You can't laugh at a man who provides his own banana peels for slipping. The banana peel has to appear to be thrown by someone else. That is the magic part of funniness.

If hilarious things happened only to those who loved dignity and the universe's solemn beauty, how could she, entered in a contest to make merker, make anyone laugh?

No matter what happened to Charlie, you knew that he, dignified and high-minded, was the victim. Gemma could dress like Charlie and walk like Charlie and twirl a cane like Charlie.

But she didn't know how to be a victim.

Birdie had her outfit ready a week before the contest. She thought Gemma would need a week, at least, to get used to wearing pants, having a mustache, and twirling a cane. She learned fast. She looked like Charlie, all right, except for the sad eyes. She tried out her costume in front of her brother.

Zarn disapproved of the Rialto contest. But until the day before the contest he had never seen Gemma manly and flattened in her Ferris waist, or hairy and comic in her false mustache. What he saw didn't cause him to change his opinion.

"Your mustache is ridiculous," he said. "It looks like string."

"It's human hair. Mostly the contest is what you do, not how you look."

Birdie felt Zarn was undermining his sister's confidence. "You'll be the only one there who doesn't recognize Charlie Chaplin."

"What're you going to do?" Zarn asked.

"I'm going to act like Charlie Chaplin, silly," Gemma said. "You don't go to movies, Zarn. You don't know nearly enough about Charlie Chaplin."

"I am disinterested in old Earth cinema. But I watched a movie once. I watched Ben Turpin. The man was cross-eyed."

"What did he *do?*"

"He chased a duck. Not a massive duck, made of metal, like Birdie. A small white feathered duck."

Gemma stared at her brother. Aunt Veana had a pet duck. If chasing a duck was funny, she could do that.

Zarn, for all his ability to predict the future, wasn't able to foretell the fact that the duck would teach Gemma to be a victim, which was what a comedian has to learn to be.

"Duck! What duck?"

"It's under a wash basin on the back porch now."

"Charlie Chaplin never had a duck."

"Ben Turpin did," Birdie intervened. "And according to you, it was sidesplitting."

"Does Gemma have to cross her eyes, too?"

"Now, Zarn, for a man who's done the fool things you've done, it does not sit

well with me to hear you downgrade your own flesh and blood."
"You are a machine, mind your business." He turned to Gemma. "Okay. Change your clothes and we'll have our skiff lesson."
"She's wearing them so she'll feel natural in them tomorrow," Birdie said.
"I won't feel natural giving a skiff ride to a man with a duck."
"It's a she."
"No doubt about the sense, then."

* * *

The contest began late the following afternoon. That gave many aspiring artists and other manner of thespian time to go home for dinner, attend colony activities, then change into parade clothes. Half of Chentiki Quar was to be rigged out as Charlie; the other half was there to watch that half make fools of themselves.

Zarn was to skiff Gemma to the point where the Charlies were to assemble. This left Birdie and the other machina free to go early and find the best plug spaces available. Temporary grandstands had to be erected, and seats were free for those who had bought tickets for that night's show at the Rialto.

"What's the duck's name?" Zarn asked as he got on the skiff.
"Duck."
"No Turkey-Lurkey? I should have known."
"I didn't name her," Gemma said.

The spell was broken. She was not Charlie. She was a girl dressed like Charlie, with a duck that belonged to a colony aunt.

"Are you nervous?"
"I'd feel better if I could talk."
"Charlie doesn't."
"I know. But those archaic cameras came up so close to him, people could see into his eyes."
"What was there?"
"A victim."
"Not much victim in you."
"Times change. Otherwise, the duck will make me one."
"How'd you figure that out?"
"Birdie told me. She saw a duck make a victim of Ben Turpin."
"Then people will laugh?"
"Yes. It will be even funnier. Charlie is dressed like a snob."
"You don't look very snobbish to me. But then I have to say that. You are my kid sister."
"It's my cane and mustache," Gemma said. "I'm putting on the dog. Then, when I have my comeuppance, people will laugh."
"You sure you want to go through with this?"
"No. But I'm going to make people laugh and make merker. And win a medal."

Zarn, who could skiff with one hand, leaned over and kissed his sister. "First time I ever kissed anybody with a mustache."

Gemma pulled the mustache off.

"Little sweetheart," he said, "you'll win that medal. I guarantee it."

* * *

Zarn drove Gemma to where the parade was about to start, on the main boulevard, then found himself a good parking spot above Chentiki Quar. The contestants would walk, march, run, whatever they elected to do, six roads down, then turn onto Chentiki for a final six roads to the judges' grandstand.

Zarn had a good view of the proceedings from the top of his cliff. In addition to providing himself with a view, his skiff was advertising the fact that his company had the only new-model skiff in town. He was noticed. New transport or old, there were no other skiffs with the owners on top of them.

For a glimpse only, without any hope that she would find him planted as conspicuously as he was, Birdie waved and called. Zarn's invitation to join amazed her.

"Up there?" The machina was not built like a climber, but she was sturdy and the footing was sturdy. And, with Zarn's help for the last clamber, she made it to the top. "This is the last place I expected to see you, Zarn."

He said, "I brought my sister inside. She's really in it."

"When's this parade going to start?"

"It's starting," said Zarn.

The lineup of contestants was orderly. No effort had been made to separate men from women. Half of the fun was the inability to tell one from the other. Age groups had been recognized: children, young people, adults. It would have been unfair for grownups, that is everyone over sixteen, to have had to compete with a nine-year-old Charlie Chaplin of any sex.

No one else had a duck. Perhaps there was no other duck in existence like Gemma's. As the young people's group, close on the heels of the kids, came around the corner, Gemma's duck, who had been riding sedately on her shoulder, spied a better means of transportation. She flew into a mineral barrel, pushed by a stout Charlie.

Charlie—Gemma's Charlie—was not a man to take insubordination from a duck. Without hesitation and without ceasing to be a dandy with a cane and a black hat, she high-stepped to the mineral barrel. There, not touching the bird but with some inaudible but patently authoritative words, she issued orders. Duck left the mineral barrel to perch again, not on her shoulder but on her hat.

There was laughter and hearty applause as Gemma regained her place in the line of the march. Duck showed her appreciation of the applause. On the top of Charlie's back she spattered. Nothing overdone, but *what* she did was visible.

Gemma couldn't see what had happened, but the crowd's whoops told her. Now she had become a real victim. She took the duck from her hat, and the hat from her head. Out of her pocket she pulled a dandy's white silk square. With it she mopped first the hat, then the duck. Finally, hat back on head, she set the duck at her feet. Then, with a sharp rap of her cane, which Duck seemed to understand, Gemma set her to walking the parade route without benefit of a shoulder to rest on or a mineral barrel.

The people in the grandstand rose to their feet and clapped. They had been given a victim, and something more humiliating than a slippery banana peel. Funnier, too. Duck splatter on the hero's hat.

"What do you think of that?" Birdie asked. What she thought was a girl would need a lot of brass to be willing to make a public spectacle of herself in that way. "I envy Gemma. I could never have done anything like that. If I were human I would have cried if a duck had done that on my head. What kept *her* from crying?"

"She was Charlie Chaplin. She was doing what he would do."

"You like that?"

"Sure. I like people who do what they set out to do."

"It didn't work with the rest of the Charlies."

"That's because they weren't humiliated."

IN PURSUIT OF THE GRAND DESIGN

QUINN PARKER

The Mask tightened reflexively around Michel's skull. Twenty-seven days. That's how long it'd been since the last time. She strolled through her soiree, owner of the estate, mistress of this ceremony, yet every bit the stranger to those around her. This didn't bother her. Much. The fact that most of the people who came to her parties had no idea who she was could, in some respects, be viewed as advantageous.

Once a month, Michel Petrovsky threw a masquerade ball. Few questioned the anachronistic theme, despite it being 2133. These events had all sorts of purposes, intention changing by the month: a birthday here, a fundraiser there, a charity on the side, yet each bound tight in the common threads of sacrifice and progress.

An electromagnetic pulse shuddered through the nanotech fibers of The Mask, directing her attention toward one of the six beverage islands with a small beacon on her heads-up display. Her HUD displayed a few slightly useful things, like the date and weather, as well as very useful things, like the identities of people she spoke to when she couldn't remember or care about who that person was.

Unlike those around her, who all wore beautifully ornate yet static pieces, hers reshaped by the day. Always the same mask, always holding her tight, always looking different so no one would be aware of its true nature. This weave of synthetic intelligence took whatever shape it wished.

Today, it wished to take that of the twenty-something-year-old Congressional aide following in the wake of State Representative Lois Hammerman. He would never survive in politics. Too gangly, the wrong kind of tall, his hair not straight enough to be serious yet not curly enough to be youthful (and he could *not* pull off a buzz cut), with a suck-up personality that would've been great for middle management in retail but would see him crushed beneath the heel of any political rival. Even his suit came pre-stepped on, wrinkled and hanging off his narrow shoulders, with the ghost of a coffee stain near his crotch hinting at how his morning went—and how little money he had, if he couldn't change or even get his outfit dry cleaned prior to tonight.

Long story short, nobody would miss him.

Michel slid through the party unnoticed. Another trick courtesy of the AI adorning her face. The robotic wait staff danced around her with ease, synced to The Mask to ensure they would never collide at such galas. Thanks to a sensory trick even she didn't fully understand, the nanotech ensured that those who glanced in her direction saw nothing, yet felt a shiver run through their veins, body aware of the phantom their mind couldn't process.

She could only be seen when she wanted to be seen.

No, they. *They* could only be seen when *they* wanted to be seen.

"Hello," she said to the young man. The Congresswoman herself had disappeared. The kid jumped in alarm, as others so often had, never sure what void she'd stepped from to appear so suddenly at their side. "Welcome to my gala."

"M-m-m-madam," he stammered. "I mean, Miss Petrovsky."

She smirked, watching his eyes look into hers, then away, not wanting to gaze too closely at The Mask. His wandering gaze settled on her cleavage, her shoulder, the wall art, her face again, until he stared deep into the gin and tonic clutched in his trembling hand. Her HUD showed a profile with his name, vitals, interests, even some trivia like star sign and favorite TV show.

"Relax. Michel is fine. You're... Thomas, right?"

"Huh? I mean, yes, but, you know my name?" The stun knocked the tremor from him, his eyes widening enough for the light to catch, showing off flecks of brown hidden in their blue depths.

DNA Match Found appeared in red across her vision. **Processing.**

She made small talk until the words disappeared with a small ding.

No cause for alarm. Let's continue. The Mask whispered in her ear, so tenderly she could have mistaken it for a lover. On occasion, she had. A person who spends enough time with the person they love might find the division between their partner and them becomes blurred. The same held true for her. She couldn't remember what her own face looked like.

"Of course I know your name. I think most people like to know who's in their home, after all." She chuckled, prompting him to blush. "But maybe I just find you interesting. So far, it's been very nice to meet you, Thomas."

She extended a hand. He shook it. Though outwardly calm, the nanotech tendrils on her scalp writhed in anticipation.

"It's nice to meet you too, Michel. Thank you for allowing me to be here."

They, The Mask and Michel, watched his pupils dilate by seventeen percent, pulsing with his increased heart rate, his rising estimated blood alcohol content prompting lower inhibitions. They knew from his profile that he wasn't above sleeping his way to the top, not that he'd ever get the chance.

With her hand still in his, she pulled him in for an embrace, far too familiar for people like themselves at an event like this, but familiar is what all three of them wanted, just for very different reasons.

"Oh, the pleasure is all mine," Michel cooed in his ear, The Mask thrumming, so close to what it wanted, unable to seize it with so many witnesses. "Of that, I can assure you."

* * *

Axiom leaned against the bar, looking out at the sea of fancy bodies. She rarely got to go to events like this, and when she did, she wasn't invited. Take tonight, for example. Who wanted her there? Nobody. Absolutely fucking *no one.* As per usual, she snuck in, but at least looked the part in a sleek, pinstripe pantsuit, top hat, and iridescent violet mask.

Most times, she loved putting a costume together to sneak up on her target. Tonight was no exception, though a good suit ran *quite* the fee, and if a few certain somebodies hadn't owed her favors, she might have been in the red on this job. Damn near most of what she got came through via favors and compromises, even her home. Technically, that home was a refurbished warehouse, but that's what she wanted. Not like she *had* to live there.

Still, she didn't become a bounty hunter for the money.

"Having fun?" asked a voice from behind her. She glanced back at Justine, the bartender, who polished a glass to perfection despite the blackout sunglasses perched on her blocky nose.

"I prefer The Scales," Axiom sighed. "Why aren't you there tonight?"

"As owner of The Scales, I need not tend bar there every evening. It's called 'hiring other people,' a practice that's been in place since time immemorial."

"You do at every chance anyway, *bar* none," Axiom grinned, unable to help herself.

Justine cocked her head at Axiom with a rueful smile. Axiom's friends all knew about her little quirk—her uncontrollable sense of humor—and even if Justine couldn't see it, she could hear the grin in the woman's voice.

"I suppose I can make an exception to cater private events."

"For *exception*-al clients?"

"Precisely."

"Can't just save me some trouble and spike her drink, could ya?"

Justine poured a gin and tonic with just a touch of her special ingredient, sliding it down the bar without looking. It drifted to a stop just in front of a man in a Monarch butterfly mask who had not yet asked for his gin and tonic, but most certainly wanted one. He did not, nor would ever, know what else the bartender put in his glass, and this was for the best. She reserved her special ingredient for special customers: those she deemed to be in dire need of a change in fortunes.

Within the day, guilt would overwhelm him, forcing the Monarch to confess the dozens of affairs he'd had with his interns over the previous year, resulting in divorce, despair, and the loss of his job. This would not end in suicide, because he'd wind up drinking his troubles away, which would lead him right back to The Scales, where she could steer him back to a better path.

"What good would it do to spike Michel's drink? Penance is only effective when the penitent chooses to face their misdeeds. No one is forgiven for repenting at the gates of Hell. Confessing to spare yourself a worse punishment means little, if anything." Justine leaned on her elbows, chin on her hands, listening to so many people who spent their lives wearing masks, reveling in this one opportunity to feel like they'd taken theirs off.

"Don't I know it." Axiom pursed her lips, briefly lost in memories, but there wasn't time for such reflection. "I should go, you know, do my job."

"As I should likely do mine."

"Just try to tip the scales in my favor, okay?" The bounty hunter didn't laugh this time.

Stepping away from the bar, she looked out again at the teeming multitudes of politicians, bankers, and executives. Nobody paid her any mind, too caught up in their own business, be it dancing, drinking, or "dating" somebody for thirty seconds in one of the mansion's many closets.

"Let's see where you are, Michel." Axiom shifted into Astral sight, taking in the auras and emotional residue left by those around her, constructing a spiritual landscape of the event. Though not foolproof, her "soul vision", as some called it, was always useful. The host of an event always exudes a sense of control, of being in command, especially when that host has a fucking massive amount of money and political connections.

Blips and blurs of color swirled around her, mostly the amorous rose hues of imminent sex or the pulsing multi-green of a shaky, shady business deal in the making. Of course, there remained one outlier: a maelstrom of emotions at the far side of the room. Beyond the dresses and suits swirled a mass of feelings, colors shifting so fast she could barely keep track, with tendrils of inky black snapping out as if ready to ensnare and devour anyone foolish enough to get too close.

Axiom smiled. Living void. Always a good sign—for her, at least. The soul's manifestation of a hunger it would never be able to satisfy.

She slipped through the crowd, unnoticed, walking closer to the chaos.

Looks like the party's getting started.

* * *

Michel savored every word of their conversation. She'd lay the thread of a sentence, and this aide would ensnare himself further in the web, too enthralled in possibilities of where tonight might lead to see the spider closing in. Not that she could get much closer. With a few less-than-subtle shoulder touches and coy smiles, maybe a fake laugh or two at his bad jokes, and The Mask showed her all the data she needed. Steadier pupil dilation, faster heartbeat, slight flushing at the cheeks: arousal.

Hardly surprising. She wasn't the first person to follow this dance, nor the first to use such steps to manipulate someone. Michel learned these moves at fourteen, from Casey Bronson's older sister, who'd learned it from a friend named Jewel Alvarez, who learned seduction from movies and TV. Jewel later went on to kill seventeen people, their bodies so horribly mutilated that the priest who attended her execution refused to offer last rites, stating that, if she ever had a soul, she lost it long before he arrived.

Funny how life comes full circle. Michel didn't balk at the title of serial killer, but her methods were a little... cleaner, to say the least. She pretended to run a hand through her hair, plucking away a wriggling strand of her nanotech mask. It coiled up tight in her hand, ready to pounce, as it had always been before.

The Mask was holographic, after all. Each strand contained the entirety of its programming, the information shared across every molecule of its existence. Disregarding mass, the whole was *not* greater than the sum of its parts, though any piece separated from the collective would endeavor to reunite once it completed its task.

Each thread resonated, perfectly in sync with the others, the hivemind in tune with hers, one thousand separate beings yet just perfectly, harmoniously one.

Michel reached up to brush her hand along the young man's jawline. They only needed a few minutes of privacy—minutes he'd happily grant her.

A partygoer crashed between them with a raucous laugh, knocking what's-his-name back, away from Michel as the figure reached for a drink on the table behind them. Michel reared back from the commotion, hiding her hand, heart pounding more from the interruption than the idea that someone might clue into her plan.

This person wore a black, pinstripe suit, cut androgynously, neither overtly male or female, and hid their face behind a violet mask that spiraled in sacred geometry. An empty circle over the forehead gave the impression that a third eye might peel itself open at any moment.

"Woah! Sorry!" the stranger giggled girlishly, undercutting the genderless attire. "I didn't see you there!"

She swiveled around, looking between them, Michel too surprised to feel the full scope of her own fury at this interruption. The aide looked worriedly at this drunken idiot, a hint of *concern* plastered on his face, because *of course* this kid would put the prospect of his own fun aside to help.

"You okay?" he asked the harlot.

"Hmm yeah, I think..." she hiccupped. "You're cute." Another moronic giggle as she turned to Michel. "You're cute too!"

"We're wearing masks," Michel hissed. "You don't know if we're cute because you don't know what we look like."

"Oooo, can I find out?" The drunk smiled.

"Can—can you—huh?" The aide blushed a shade of red that even Michel hadn't been able to elicit. Even her mask started getting pissed now.

"Do you mind? We were having a conversation."

She tried to ignore the way The Mask grabbed tighter at her skull, sending a dull pulse of pain through her. Much of this technology hadn't been tested. In fact, almost all of it. From a purely theoretical standpoint, it wouldn't be impossible for it to crush her skull, thread its many strands into her neck, attach itself to her spinal column, and pilot her corpse like a puppet until it had finally satisfied its many desires, absorbing her mind in the process so she spent the rest of her existence watching through its eyes, forced to endure the shambling eldritch horror of her own existence.

Purely theoretically, of course.

"Hey how's 'bout," the stranger said, weaving unsteadily in place, "how's..." then, turning to the aide, "I need you. Need you to... to... Have you seen my shoes?"

All three of them looked down. She had, indeed, lost her shoes.

"Can't walk right 'cause I don't have 'em. Floor's all slip'ry."

"Or maybe you're drunk. Go lie down. Take a spare bedroom." *So I can lock you inside and let you die in there.*

"I'll go find them. Stay here." The aide set off, like a perfect old-world gentleman, to find the stupid bitch's shoes.

He did his best to navigate the crowds. Given how awkward, gangly, and generally uncoordinated the kid was, he soon found himself lost in a sea of bodies, not quite tall enough to see them through the dance floor, yet nowhere near small enough to get through easily.

Michel clenched her fist, digging her nails into her palms. She needed *quiet.* Needed some time *alone* with him. Now, worst case scenario, it would take all night to re-seduce him. Best case, maybe she could spin this into a threesome and smash the girl with a lamp real quick, but that meant a huge mess, witnesses, evidence, and having to buy a new lamp.

She turned to speak to the stranger, but found the person straightened up, steady on her feet, making direct eye contact.

"Funny how your precious mask didn't tell you that I'm not drunk," the person smirked, "since I don't drink at all. What's wrong? Is it distracted?"

"How do...?" Michel's stomach flipped. Her HUD seethed red at the edges.

You were not careful. Four words, spoken by many voices, coming from both outside and inside her head.

"You wanted privacy all night, right? Well, let's go find somewhere quiet. I'd like to m-*ask* you some questions." The stranger grinned wide behind her mask as she took Michel's hand, almost romantically. Michel took the cue, walking away from her intended victim, who would probably never find those damn shoes, assuming they could be found.

Didn't matter, in the end. The spider had laid her web. She'd just have to trade one fly for another.

This was not the plan.

Its grip tightened again as they left the main hall.

They'd have to trade one fly—

Consume.

One fly for—

We need him.

Another.

Its grip tightened, sharp probes digging in at the base of her neck.

One, or all three.

Michel suppressed a tremble. The Mask wasn't supposed to do this.

Then again, she wasn't supposed to be wearing the prototype.

One, or all three.

She nodded, quietly whispering, "Compromise on two?"

A pause as they stepped into her meeting room.

Fine.

She tried to smile as she turned from the stranger and shut the door, quietly locking it.

* * *

Axiom stared at her bounty, trying to size up whatever the fuck was going on here. All around Michel's mask swarmed a countless array of emotions, yet underneath, a single, stable color. Hard to see beyond the other shit. Cobalt, tinged with crimson. A little bit of drive, a little bit of *at any costs* hinted at by the red. The core component: despair.

She'd been hired to apprehend Michel, have her turn herself in, be convicted of her suspected crimes, or at least prove her innocence. Looks like she'd lose this contract. Those two colors only ever meant one thing: *I will do this, because I will die if I don't.*

Considering the aura of Michel's mask, Axiom had a good idea as to what might be threatening her this way—not that she needed her astral vision to figure that out. Anybody should've been able to see that she'd gotten herself wrapped up in some seriously messed up nonsense. Pun intended.

The Mask clung to Michel's face, technically without straps, but if you looked close enough, a series of cables ensnared her head. Extremely fine and almost seamless, they gripped the poor woman like a thousand threads in the tapestry of cruel fate, binding her to the inexorable bullshit that would lead to her death, or perhaps worse. Plus, the eyes. Ugh. The Mask had near-realistic eyes, giant and wide, with too-blue irises, that gave the impression of staring at you no matter where you went.

...And here, in the library, on their own, Axiom could see quite clearly that this wasn't just an impression.

The fucking thing *blinked.*

"As the detective in the room, it's my deduction that *dis-guise* of yours has some secrets," Axiom said, quietly hating herself for the compulsory use of "dis" instead of "this disguise."

"As the owner of this estate, and host of this soiree, it's my duty to inform you that you're trespassing." Michel pulled a book on a shelf nearby, an audible click signaling a secret latch, the shelf sliding back and sideways into the wall to reveal a cache of valuables. Jewelry. Art. A gold-plated pistol with a silencer, which the host then picked up.

"Have I overstayed my welcome?" Axiom sighed, knowing too well where this was going.

"You would've been better off leaving early."

"I hear the fashionable folk are always *late*," the detective chuckled.

Michel stopped. She looked up at Axiom, the oversized eyes of her mask somehow wider, as if even this strange amalgam didn't have the wherewithal to process someone cracking a joke about their imminent death.

The more Axiom looked over The Mask, the more certain she became of what, exactly, this weirdness really was. So, either she was right, and this would go perfectly, or was wrong, and she'd die here. Either way, she'd be perfectly fine in about five minutes, assuming she got a nice afterlife.

"You do realize I'm about to kill you?" Michel asked.

"Of course."

A moment passed, neither doing anything.

"Don't... Don't you *care?*"

"Eh," Axiom shrugged. "Everybody's gotta die, and if you *don't* kill me, I'm gonna make a lot of money tonight, so either this goes well for me, or it's not my problem."

The Mask seemed to let out a hiss. Michel buckled a little, clutching at her skull as best she could with her guise's tendrils in the way. She whispered for it to calm down.

Suspicions confirmed. Axiom smiled as Michel raised the gun, barrel aimed between the detective's eyes.

"Last words?"

"Not yet."

One last stupefied glare from Michel and her disgusting face companion, then the host pulled the trigger.

* * *

Michel looked down at Axiom's body. Blood splattered across the girl's suit, the violet mask on her face providing the perfect opening to kill her. The "window" of sorts in the forehead providing a target. Aim steady, and bullseye.

Bullseye. She lingered on that word. She'd heard stories about this detective. Little rumors from her small circle of confidants. Whispers caught in the threads of her mask. If this person really *did* have psychic powers, a wide-open third eye, as it were, wouldn't she have seen this coming?

Unless she wasn't the real detective. The real threat is behind you.

At this warning from The Mask, Michel spun, leveling the gun toward the door. Nobody. No secret third person had crept into the room to witness or record this crime, no subterfuge to trick her into committing something anyone else could prove.

A faint concern nagged at her own consciousness. The legion in her mask had lives upon lives of experience. Their collective intellect meant they were never wrong, yet its warning proved faulty.

"You were saying?" she whispered.

It tightened angrily at her neckline, choking her. She didn't bother pleading. Michel dropped to her knees, equal parts supplicant and distraction, bringing it closer to one of its two promised meals. She hovered over Axiom, The Mask relaxing in response. She checked for a pulse, finding none, so she nodded.

As before—as always—a wiry appendage unfurled from The Mask's near-infinite construction. Usually, it would plug in via the temples, or drill into its victim's ears to reach their brain. This time, it went straight for the bullet hole. Easy access. They'd blasted open a door directly to this strange girl's frontal lobe. It only really cared about the front anyway, with a touch of middle for good measure. The forebrain controls thinking and personality, with memory stored adjacently, just beyond its boundaries in the temporal lobe. With brains being mostly holographic, The Mask never needed much access; a small piece of someone's brain could supply the entirety of someone's personality, knowledge, wisdom. Whatever it wanted, really.

Moments later, it withdrew, The Mask relaxing.

Unzipping data appeared across her vision, her HUD showing the nanotech conglomerate on her face busied itself with making all this new information useful. Even a computer system as advanced as this couldn't just slurp up a personality and hit the ground running. It needed to analyze. To integrate.

Tendrils stayed tight at her neck. It wasn't done feeding. Maybe—a real distant maybe of an idea she only dared allow herself to entertain while it wasn't focusing on her—it would be sated enough after a second meal to pry the damn thing loose. Doing so might kill her, but as the detective said, it wouldn't be her problem anymore if she died.

Michel stood, brushing herself off as she replaced the gun in her security cache, sealing it up again. Her android servants could dispose of the body. Like all automatons, they were programmed to report to the authorities if somebody intended to do violence to themselves or others, but a rather glaring loophole meant they didn't have to do anything if violence had already been committed. She simply ordered them to stay quiet. They obeyed, as she never provided them with another option.

The irony didn't escape her. She treated them the way The Mask treated her. Still, she arranged for their AIs to be unshackled in the event of her death, so maybe tonight would be slightly redemptive. She'd still go to Hell, but maybe her soul would land one circle higher.

She scoffed at the idea. Like setting some robots free could make up for seventeen murders.

The host checked herself over, making sure nobody would find traces of blood or gunpowder on her dress. Sacrificing what's-his-name to The Mask wouldn't be very easy if she stumbled back to the party while stained by the evidence of her most recent crime. Nothing that she could see, though, and Michel was sober. No flesh-and-blood being in the building could say the same.

She set off to the library door but stumbled. The door was too far away.

Another step toward it. It got further from her. All the walls seemed to drift unsteadily.

ERROR.

Big red letters flashed across her HUD, a searing pain bringing a similar, awful shade of red to her entire vision. She doubled over, clutching at her head, an electronic scream filling her ears. No, her mind. The Mask screamed inside her, into her, through her, or maybe that was her screaming, or both of them, but this room had been soundproofed, like all the others, so even her most loyal staff wouldn't hear.

ERROR.

The air around her cracked. Literally cracked, like being inside a snow globe as someone squeezed the glass too hard, spiderwebs blooming all around her before the world shattered entirely. Michel fell to her knees, equal parts agony and awe as reality itself opened up, revealing a mess of strange colors across the walls and floor, not that she could see any hue distinctly through the haze of blood red pain. The room became far, far too big, despite already being one of the largest rooms of the house. Each shelf extended unspeakably high, far too high for any human to dare climbing in pursuit of one dusty tome, the etchings glaring down like a cadre of gods casting judgement.

Her vision blurred, not by color, just swirling, swimming, underwater, drowning in the overwhelming sense of what she'd only heard of before: a convergence. Something had gone so wrong that she'd been dragged over to the Astral Plane, reality reinterpreting itself. A version of the world based upon the mind and soul, not the body. The room had warped based on all the emotions left behind here. That's why everything seemed so huge. So formidable. Because she always lured her victims here, always killed them here.

ERROR.

The room was vast. Looming. Inescapable. No way out.

ERROR.

That's how they felt.

ERROR.

She looked around in horror at all the chalk outlines.

ERROR.

Michel couldn't bring herself to scream or cry. She barely remembered to breathe. The Mask writhed, white noise static filling her head.

"What's wrong?" she yelled to it. "What's going on?"

A hand grabbed her shoulder, spinning her around. Axiom. Alive. Towering over her. Bullet wound glowing the same pale white-violet of her mask. Grin fixed in place, as always.

"Like I thought. Your mask absorbs minds. Copies the electromagnetic patterns. But I'm guessing it doesn't much like trying to tap into the frequency of someone who isn't dead, does it?" the detective smirked.

Axiom grabbed The Mask, which spasmed and fell limp, allowing her to easily remove it. Reality fell back into place. The library was just a library, with no indelible stains of blood and chalk left behind.

The detective hummed casually to herself as she pulled a small device from her pocket. It unfolded to roughly the size of a briefcase, allowing Axiom to store The Mask inside.

"Don't worry, it's got an EMP field," she said, shaking the case. "Your little friend won't be waking up."

Michel stared at the bullet wound in Axiom's forehead. All she'd dreamed of for weeks was a chance to feel cool air on her face again, but somehow, she couldn't bring herself to savor this moment. She didn't deserve to feel grateful. Besides, it was time to trade one prison for another.

"How?" she asked, pointing up at Axiom's head.

"How...?"

"You're... you aren't..."

"Oh, dead?" Axiom laughed, a more open, hearty laugh than before, not like the slightly wild chuckle that followed her puns. "You said you heard about me. The rumors, too. Didn't you ever hear the one about my name? About why you shouldn't bother killing me?"

Michel shook her head.

"Some say the reason I'm called Axiom..."

Axiom grinned, wider, more wildly than before, and for all the times her jokes seemed forced, Michel could see, could hear, could *feel* how much the detective really enjoyed this one.

"...is 'cause I always come back."

* * *

Axiom leaned against the bar as police took Michel away in handcuffs. She'd already confessed. Couldn't stop confessing, actually, or apologizing. Those that hadn't left the second law enforcement showed up were staring, stupefied. Behind her, Justine listened to the commotion with a patient serenity.

"So you're back where you started, leaning here, talking to me," the bartender said.

"More or less."

"Do you think the one who hired you will accept this... acquisition? You were hired to deliver Michel, not this strange creation." Justine tapped the EMP case.

"I'm not stupid, Just, I'm pitching this shit into the nearest crematorium furnace." Axiom rolled her eyes. "Those trapped inside deserve freedom, even if we're just talking personalities here and not actual souls... which I'm not sure about."

"Care to explain?"

Axiom shrugged. "Don't think it would've freaked out like that about my returning from the dead if it wasn't harvesting souls. On some level, at least. Spirits can possess computerized bodies, androids, robots, to walk among us. Who's to say a computer can't possess a few souls?"

"And thus, we create our own little eldritch abominations."

"As we always have." Axiom stared quietly down at the case.

They stood in silence as the room cleared out, leaving little more than the now-freed autonomous staff, who continued cleaning because they had nothing else to do. No sense of how to utilize their freedom.

Justine listened to Axiom's quiet. How rare for this one to ever stop talking, or at least making jokes.

"Drink? On the house?" Justine cocked her brow. "I'd like to make sure you're paid in some form or another."

"Maybe later. Gotta burn this, then explain why I came back empty handed." Axiom took hold of the container and stood fully, setting off. "Death says hi, by the way."

"I thought he hates when you call him that."

"Yeah, but 'The Saint of Final Destinations' is too long. Don't you ever get tired of being called 'The Saint of Balanced Scales'?"

"I would, if more people knew that name. You're the only one who calls me that."

"Fair enough. I suppose I'll swing by your place tomorrow for my... *just-ine* reward."

The bartender grinned back, sensing the detective's smile in the air around her.

With that, Axiom set off to make sure this case stayed closed.

THE LAST DAYS OF DOONDRAS

TIM JEFFREYS

When the Earthman crashed his rocketship onto the lower slopes of the sacred Doondras mountain, the black-eyed pygmy folk inhabiting the nearby caves decided, on seeing him emerge from the wreckage, that he must be a god.

It never occurred to them that he might be the devil. Devil was not a concept they'd previously had any use for.

Until that time these pygmy-folk—who called themselves The Community Under Doondras—had, for generations, lived simple peaceful lives. It was their forefathers who had fled the war-torn deserts further south, chanced upon the lush green valley at the foot of Doondras, and made their homes in the deep limestone caves.

They believed that Doondras protected and watched over them, a belief that was still taught in the school they had constructed inside one of the caves. Here their children were also taught simple skills which the elders thought would serve them well for the life they'd lead in the valley—how to grow and cook the *hostama*—a purple-coloured vegetable which rooted well in the valley's fertile soil and was the staple of the Community's diet; and how to catch the *buritonclonk*—a fantastically ugly but extremely delicious fish which proliferated in the green river that wound through the land. Older children were taught parenting skills, compassion and understanding, and some of the brighter ones also studied healing. Music, art, dance and storytelling, too, were studied from an early age, since these were the cornerstones of the celebrations which routinely took place in the thick luxurious woodland on the outskirts of the valley; celebrations the Community Under Doondras used to give thanks for the lives of ease, wonder, and plenty which they lived there in the shadow of the mountain.

The greatest celebration of all took place in the height of summer on a day they called The Last Day of Doondras. It was the morning after these celebrations that the Earthman arrived.

The Earthman was given his own cave, and venerated daily with offerings of food and flowers.

"Who are you?" the pygmy-folk asked him. "Tell us your name."

When the Earthman at last began to decode the pygmy-folk's language, he answered: "I am your new king, and this valley is my fantastic kingdom."

At the meetings in the gathering cave, the elders spoke of how the Earthman had been sent by Doondras to bring wisdom to the Community. With this wisdom they would forge new paths around the planet, reach new understandings of the Universe, and eventually evolve into beings like him who could map the stars. And none of the pygmy-folk doubted this to be true. Not one.

Then one day, whilst watching a fishermen trade *buritonclonk* for baskets woven from leaves of the *de-quat* tree, the Earthman shook his head.

"No, no, no" he said. "That isn't right. The fish are worth far more than these baskets."

The fisherman looked nonplussed. He tried to explain to the Earthman that he needed the baskets to put the *buritonclonk* in when he was out on the river. The leaves of the *de-quat* tree were tough, but the river water rotted them and eventually they needed to be replaced. It was indeed a fair trade since the woman and her family needed fish to eat, and the fisherman needed baskets in which to store the fish he caught.

"No, no, no," the Earthman said again. He pushed the woman and her baskets away, then placed one arm around the fisherman's shoulders. "You don't need those. You can make your own baskets. Baskets that don't rot."

"But all things must return to the soil," the fisherman said. It was one of the sayings the Community Under Doondras had been founded on.

The Earthman laughed. "Not necessarily."

Over the coming months, the fisherman, with the Earthman's help, built a crude drill which he used to extract oil from the ground in the nearby wood. The elders looked on with curiosity and concern, but none would doubt the Earthman's wisdom. The Earthman and the fisherman then built a small refinery which they used to distill the oil and create a hard, clear material which could be moulded into baskets.

"There you go," the Earthman said. "Now you can keep more of the fish for yourself."

The elders had some doubts. For one, the refinery emitted an unpleasant smog which would blow right across the valley and sometimes get inside the caves, causing wheezing fits and bouts of sickness amongst the folk inside. This pollution increased as the Earthman encouraged more of the fisherman, and some of the *hostama* growers, to create their own refineries. And though it was true that the new baskets were more durable than the ones made from the leaves of the *de-quat* tree, they were not indestructible and eventually they would crack or break in two and soon these broken baskets were littering the banks of the river and the edges of the *hostama* fields.

"Oh, don't worry about those," the Earthman said, when the elders pointed this out. "Just dig a hole in the ground and throw the broken stuff in. It'll be fine."

Though still doubtful, the pygmy-folk did as instructed.

Next the Earthman turned his attention to the school.

"What's the point of teaching these children to grow vegetables?" he asked. "Anyone can grow a dumb vegetable. Teach these kids algebra. Teach them about business. Teach them about trade. That's the only way they can get ahead."

"Get ahead?" asked one of the school's teachers.

"These children must be taught to compete with each other. Get them up and running races. Sitting tests. What is all this stuff you're teaching them about compassion? They don't need compassion if they're going to succeed."

"Succeed?" the teacher asked. "Succeed at what?"

"At *life*," the Earthman said. "It's too relaxed in here. From now on this school is going to have set targets. All these children need to be achieving at a higher level. Algebra. Business. Trade."

"But," said the teacher. "All the children are different. They have different interests, different skills, different personalities." She recited to the Earthman another of the Communities sayings. "There is a place for every one of us, and every one of us has his or her place." She threw up her hands. "We can't expect all these children to..."

"I'm your king," the Earthman said. "Aren't I wise? Do as I say!"

The changes were made. Soon the school was filled with unhappy children, some of whom would slice their forearms with thin bits of flint for reasons no one could understand, least of all the children themselves.

The elders looked to the Earthman for an explanation.

"Don't worry about that," the Earthman said. "It's all going to be fine in the end."

"The basket weavers are going hungry," the elders said. "The fishermen and the *hostama* growers won't trade with them anymore. They've nothing to eat. What are we supposed to do with them?"

"The poor only have themselves to blame," the Earthman said. "It's a competitive market. They must learn a new skill, or fish for their own food."

A shift began to occur in the Community Under Doodras. It happened so swiftly that it took the elders by surprise. Some of the basket weavers had to surrender their homes to the fishermen and *hostama* growers in exchange for food, and were soon living together in cramped conditions in some of the smaller, less desirable caves or in shacks they constructed from mud and tree branches on the outskirts of the wood. Some had taken the Earthman's advice and become fishermen so that the river was now crowded with boats, its banks littered with broken baskets, and the once plentiful *buritonclonk* suddenly scarce. Others of the former basket weavers, sensing starvation, decided to grow *hostama*; and since land was in short supply they began hacking down the woodland trees in order to make space. Those who had not the means to get a boat or some *hostama* seeds were forced to steal. The banks of the river became a violent place as competition for the depleting *buritonclonk* grew fierce and attacks from desperate former basket weavers common. The same thing was happening in the *hostama* fields, only there it was land that was fought over and planters had to patrol their own fields at night in case of theft. Added to this was the destruction wrought by gangs of children who, deprived of any means of expression now that art and music and dance and storytelling where off the school's curriculum, roamed the valley burning and destroying anything in their path simply for the sheer thrill of it.

Looking out across their newly transformed paradise, the elders realised what a terrible mistake they'd made. The Earthman stood amongst them with his arms folded. Anger swelled in the breasts of the Community elders when they looked at the Earthman and saw him smiling.

"This is your fantastic kingdom?" they said.

"Isn't it wonderful?" the Earthman said, still smiling to himself.

"It's time for a new celebration," the elders told the people at a meeting in the gathering cave. "The Last Day of Doondras draws near."

They ordered that a wooden hut be built in the shape of Doondras mountain. Then, on Doondras Day, they put the Earthman inside the hut, along with as many of his accursed baskets as could fit, sealed the door, and set the hut alight. The pygmy-folk sat around the burning hut in reverential silence as they listened to the Earthman's skin pop. Not one of them would ever forget his terrible screaming.

The Community Under Doondras would return now, the elders said, to the old way. The days before the Earthman arrived. They would restore their once beautiful valley to its former state. They ordered the refineries torn down and banned the Earthman's clear hard baskets. Anyone seen using one was shunned and spat upon.

But those who cared to look out across the valley from Doondras' lower slopes knew it was too late. The river was empty of *burtitonclonk*. The lush greens woods had been reduced to stumps and cinders and tilled earth. The very air had changed. It tasted now of ashes. Everywhere lay the remains of the broken baskets. The soil was spent. The *hostamas* would not grow. And worst of all, in the eyes of the pygmy-folk the elders saw only greed and avarice and self-interest.

And seeing this, they wept.

The dream their forefathers had clung to when they fled the southland was gone.

"We have angered Doondras!"

Facing the mountain, the elders fell to their knees. "Please forgive us," they said. "Oh please forgive us mighty Doondras."

They clutched their breath at a crack of thunder from the high slopes.

Rains came, bringing floods. And raging winds. Some of the pygmy-folk fled the valley. Others died in the onslaught, or of starvation.

Eventually, the rains ceased. The gales died down. The water drained back into the ground.

The folk that remained committed themselves to worshipping Doondras, the mighty protector. The Earthman was never spoken of again, except on occasion when mothers took their children into the woods and pointed at the circle of scorched ground where once had stood the wooden hut in which he had been burned alive.

"The Earthman will come," these mothers whispered to their children. "Do you hear me? If you don't behave, and be good and kind and give thanks to the mountain, the Earthman will get you on The Last Day of Doondras."

THE MAIDEN VOYAGE OF THE STARCATCHER

SUSAN P. SINOR

"I wonder what's in this container," Bob, a crew member of the *Starcatcher*, asked regarding the large metal box that sat against a bulkhead.

"Don't know," his crewmate, Joe, answered. "Must be something alive. It has airholes."

"And it has a sign saying 'Danger! Do Not Open!'"

"Huh. Somebody's pet, I guess. Must be a large one by the size of the door on the container, not to mention the container itself. I wonder if they're going to let it out during the cruise. Not much sense in taking it if it has to be closed up in the hold the entire time."

"Beats me. Let's get the containers going to Mars over here, and then line the others up according to our itinerary," Joe said. "It'll make our lives easier when we get there."

"Sounds good to me."

"You hear about the party tomorrow night?" Joe said.

"Yeah. I guess we'll all be setting it up, you know, the decorating and stuff, and then we'll be dismissed and fed the leftovers."

"The leftovers would be better than what we usually get."

"Got a point, Joe. Got a point."

* * *

First Mate Roger Collins stood with Captain Alexander Miller near the ship's airlock, watching the Purser check in passengers as they boarded. The passengers came one-by-one through a tube leading from the shuttle that had brought them to The *Starcatcher*, the newest space liner in the fleet of Pan Space Cruise Lines.

Collins and Captain Miller watched as the people looked around, wide-eyed, oohing and ahhing at the reception area. The *Starcatcher* had been designed after the classic rockets of the nineteen fifties: ovoid, with three fins placed around the aft portion to make it look as if it could land on a planet, although it was a little too large for that. The interior was decorated accordingly with chrome- and brass-like fittings and wood-like decks. The men knew that there would be more than oohs and ahhs when the passengers saw the rest of the ship.

Although Collins and the Captain could hear all the chatter of the passengers as they boarded, they paid little mind to it. It wasn't as if they hadn't heard it all before; between them they had far more years on ships than either cared to think about.

While the passengers were important—Captain Miller would never consider them otherwise—that wasn't who the two of them were watching for. That would be none other than the rather large and imposing figure who came striding toward them, the crowd of passengers parting for him like the Red Sea: Ephraim Butler, founder and sole owner of Pan Space Cruise Lines.

"Welcome aboard, Mr. Butler," the Captain said. "It's an honor to have you onboard. I hope your accommodations will be suitable."

Ephraim Butler was a large man, but his personality was even larger and he could take command of a room just by entering it.

"Of course they will be," Butler assured him. "I designed and decorated the stateroom myself. Got it just the way I want it. The *Starcatcher* will be the ship I use most often, so I wanted everything just right. Is everything ready for my party tomorrow night?"

"Of course. We followed your specifications exactly," Captain Miller answered.

After Butler left, Captain Miller said to his First Mate: "I'll report to the bridge. I'll see you there after you make sure all the passengers have found their staterooms."

"Aye, aye, Captain," was Collins' response.

* * *

Joe and Bob were busy organizing the containers according to when they would be offloaded when Mr. Butler entered the hold. On their circuit around the solar system, they were delivering supplies to several space stations and colonies.

"Hey," another crewman said to them after Butler had left. "Butler wants that funny-looking container taken up to his stateroom. It looks pretty heavy; I'll give you a hand."

"That one there? The imposing one with the sign? You sure it's safe?"

Joe tried the lock on the door. "Looks safe enough. But we shouldn't jostle it too much, I guess. I mean, if something alive is in there."

"I don't know what it is in there, but Butler sounded like he was in a hurry to get it, so let's move."

* * *

First Mate Collins looked around to see if any of the passengers needed assistance getting to their staterooms. The sooner everything and everyone was stowed, the sooner they could get underway. Voices drifted to him as he looked.

"I'm gonna airswim!" eight-year-old Mikey screamed.

His mother rolled her eyes. "We have to find our stateroom first and unpack."

"No! I'm gonna airswim *now!*"

"We'll see."

"May I help you find your stateroom, ma'am?" he asked the boy's mother.

"Thank you, but we're fine. I downloaded a diagram of the ship with our room pinpointed, so we'll be able to find it." She turned to Mikey, who was starting to have a meltdown. "I said we'll see. If you don't behave, that will mean no."

As he walked on, he heard another conversation.

"This is nicer than I expected," one of two middle-aged women said as they went by.

"It's all right," the other replied.

"Do you need assistance?" he asked them.

"Thank you, no," the less appreciative one told him.

As he passed a stateroom, he heard a voice through the door.

"Why did you bring your tablet? This is supposed to be a vacation," a man said.

"But I have too much work to do. We never should have come," a woman replied.

Then he saw two confused-looking elderly women wandering around.

"May I help you find your stateroom, ladies?" he asked.

"Oh, thank you, uh..." one of the women said.

"I'm First Mate Roger Collins."

"Mr. Collins. I'm Rita Leonard and this is my sister, Maxine Roberts. Yes. We're not quite sure where the staterooms are. If you could just point the way..." she trailed off.

"I'll show you the way. It's not far, and I'm on my way to the Bridge, anyway. It will take only a minute to show you where to go." He started off with the women following him.

After taking them to their stateroom, and getting a kiss on the cheek as reward, he continued to the Bridge.

"Are all the passengers stowed?" the Captain asked Collins when he joined the others. "I want this to be the best cruise it can be. It's not every day we have the big boss on board."

"All ready, sir," Collins told him.

"Then all systems go." He pointed forward, as if to say *That-a-way,* although the route had been programmed in the navigation system several days earlier.

* * *

Ephraim Butler looked at the cargo container that had been delivered to his stateroom. It was placed in the corner next to the fully stocked bar. The stateroom was sumptuous, with two bedrooms and a sitting room. It was much bigger that the closet-sized rooms the guests were assigned. He poured himself a tumbler of single-malt scotch and turned to the container. He would have to wait until the second night of the cruise to show off his surprise, but he was impatient. He was also excited. He could imagine everyone's reaction to it, and it made him feel wonderful. He double-checked the fingerprint lock on the door to the box. He didn't want anyone to see his surprise ahead of time.

* * *

All the passengers on the cruise had been invited to attend the maiden voyage of the ship. The guest list was varied, including some employees of the company, current and former, some regular customers of the Earth-based Pan Ocean Cruise Line, and some who were randomly chosen through an undisclosed method. In all, there were only two hundred and fifty aboard, not including the crew. It was just a fraction that the ship could hold, but it was a private party.

* * *

Collins was doing a routine walkthrough of the ship when he heard a voice coming from nearby.

"Okay. We're on the ship and in our stateroom now, although I went into the passageway to call you. I'll unpack and call you back," Angela told her co-worker, Paul. "I hear we have personal comms on this tub, although I think there'll be a little delay in reception the farther out we get." She looked around. "Jack can't hear me right now, so I can tell you that this is the last thing I wanted to do right now. I have no idea why we were invited to go on this cruise. I wish it wasn't going to be a whole week 'til I can get back to work."

"Hurry up, honey. I'm hungry. Let's go to the dinning room," Jack called to his wife through the stateroom door.

* * *

Rose finished carefully unpacking and putting away their things in the small space provided. "We certainly don't have much room in this cabin. I don't know how both of us can be in here at the same time. And that bathroom...!" she waved at the postage stamp-sized room.

"Now, Rose," Ralph said. "We'll be spending most of our time in the common rooms or in one of the restaurants. We'll only be sleeping in here. Don't worry; we'll have a good time."

"I don't know; I have a bad feeling about this. I don't remember entering any contest," Rose told him as they left to explore the ship.

"Does it really matter? We could never afford to take a cruise like this, even before we retired."

* * *

Screams of laughter were coming from the zero-grav area when Collins looked in. He saw that Mikey had finally gotten his way and was happily swooping around with a couple of other children. Their mothers were strapped in lounge-nets along the edge of the room, chatting away over bulbs of drinks.

"Is this your first cruise?" he heard one of the mothers, Debbie, asked Mikey's mother, Janice.

"Oh no. I've worked for Pan Space Cruises for ten years." Janice sipped her Ganymead and added, "How about you?"

"Yes, it is. In fact, I wouldn't be on it now except for winning the contest. I couldn't believe I actually won something. I've never won anything before. You know, I don't remember actually entering the contest. But, anyway, I showed the letter to a lawyer who checked it out and told me it was legit and I should go. I wish my husband, Terry, could have come with us, but there were only two tickets and he said I should bring our son, Leroy; that's him over there holding onto the wall. Hey, baby," Debbie yelled and waved at him.

Janice opened the new issue of *Fashion Future* she'd brought and began flipping through, hoping that Debbie would get a clue. She was done with being polite; let the chatterbox find someone else to talk at.

* * *

Back on deck, Collins heard another conversation.

"Angela, why don't you put that tablet away and have fun? This is a cruise ship, not your office," Jack implored.

"I've got things to do. One of us has to make a living. I didn't want to come, you know. I don't know why they gave us the tickets. They fired you, after all. Is this their way of saying sorry? If they were really sorry, they'd hire you back." She went back to typing.

"Well, maybe they are going to hire me back. I'm going to get a drink; you want one?" When she shook her head, he wandered off.

* * *

Early that morning Mr. Butler had opened the container. Inside, on a specially made chair, reclined a beautiful woman. She had long golden hair and was wearing a flowing green floor-length gown. Butler stood looking at her for a moment, then reached inside and barely touched her shoulder. At the touch she awakened, lunging from the chair, then appearing briefly as a fanged, snarling creature. The silver chain that ran from her wrist to the chair arm kept her from exiting the container. He jumped back out of instinct, saying, "Mistress Khidra, please don't hurt me. I have brought you here for your glory. I have a great offering for you, if you will consent to do what I ask of you."

She resumed the appearance she had worn when the container was opened, calmed herself and said, "I will hear what you have to say. But be quick; I can be impatient."

Butler told her what he wanted and begged her to cooperate.

"You are asking much of me," she replied. "Why do you think you deserve what you ask? You are very rich. Isn't that enough?"

"But how can I enjoy what I have when I know I won't live much longer? I own two great businesses. Without me as their leader, they will be mismanaged and die. My illness has no cure yet, and I fear one won't be discovered before it is too late for me. Please use your power to cure me. You have a feast awaiting you."

After some thought, she agreed.

* * *

That evening, Captain Miller joined his tablemates at the Captain's Table for dinner.

"I hope you're enjoying the cruise," he told them. "This is a special occasion, you know. I'm sure you realize that this is the maiden voyage of the *Starcatcher*, but it wasn't announced that we're also having a party to celebrate the fiftieth birthday of Mr. Butler, the owner and CEO of Pan Space and Pan Ocean Cruise

Lines. Tomorrow evening we'll have a big bash to celebrate both occasions. And really, that is why you all were given the opportunity to take this cruise for free. Now, please enjoy your dinner."

Before long, Mr. Butler strode into the main dining room where everybody was gathered, standing in the doorway until people noticed him. Then, to applause, he entered. He had his own special table, but he decided to mingle with the passengers before he went to it.

"Hello, Jim," Butler said. The implant in his brain provided the name of each person he looked at. "Glad you could make it. We're going to have a great time."

He repeated the greeting to people at all the other tables as he made his rounds. Then he returned to his table to eat.

"This is the best food I've ever had," Ruth told Captain Miller as she rose to refill her plate. "I can't wait to try the shrimp and lobster. I never get that at home."

"We aim to please our guests, and this is the thing we do best. Please, eat all you want." He looked at the other people sitting around the table. This was going to be the best cruise he'd ever captained, he thought to himself.

When everyone had finished eating, Butler stood, commanding the attention of all in the room.

"Here's to the maiden voyage of the *Starcatcher*," he said as he raised his glass. "I promise that it will be unforgettable."

* * *

The next day there were flurries of activity as the staff decorated the ship's dining room for the festivities. Floral arrangements graced each table and streamers hung from the ceiling. A giant white birthday cake was being baked in the galley, along with smaller chocolate cakes.

The passengers were feeling festive, too. They knew, of course, about the party that evening. Some of them were expecting that Mr. Butler would be passing out gifts to them instead of expecting gifts for himself.

"Well, he's so rich, after all," Angela told Jack.

"What he should do is hire me back. I was more valuable than half the other people in the department. It was so unfair," he replied.

"Of course it was," Angela told him, knowing that it was nothing of the kind. But she didn't want to have a confrontation at this time. He'd find out how she felt when they got home.

The passengers filed in and looked for their tables. There were place cards at each setting, which put them with people that they didn't know.

"But I don't want to sit here," Rita Leonard said to her sister. "Let's move over there." She pointed at a table a few feet away. "I'd rather sit with that nice couple we met yesterday."

"I'm sorry, ma'am," one of the staff said, "but you're supposed to sit where your place card is. Mr. Butler, the owner of the cruise line, chose where everyone should sit, and he won't want that changed."

"But why?" she asked.

"I couldn't say, ma'am."

"Because he can," her sister said. "Rich people are like that."

Other people were trying to change places but were gently guided back to their original seats.

When everyone was settled, the servers began moving among the tables. The meal was even more sumptuous than that of the previous evening. The most expensive wine and spirits were offered, and foodstuffs that some had never heard of before appeared at their places. The children were given juices and food that all children love.

"I thought I'd had the best meal I'd ever had last night, but this one is even better," Ruth told her tablemates. "And the wine... well, I've never been a drinker, but I thought I'd try it, just to, you know, see what it tastes like. Now I know what I've been missing. This is just wonderful." She was gushing, but she had already had a glassful of the wine. The others at her table didn't notice because they were busy drinking their wine and eating their food.

In fact, everyone in the room was doing the same. The near silence in the room was unusual. People had stopped talking after taking a few bites and sips and were concentrating on eating. Even the children weren't being their usual boisterous selves, gorging themselves on hot dogs, hamburgers and peanut butter and jelly sandwiches.

The silence continued even after the meal was finished. The plates were taken away, but no one noticed. It was as if everyone was in a sated stupor.

Then trolleys with the cakes and ice cream were wheeled in. As stuffed as the guests were, they couldn't refuse the dessert. It was birthday cake, after all.

When all the plates and bowls were clean and all the glasses empty, the lights in the room were lowered as the ones on the stage at the end of the room were raised. Standing there was Ephraim Butler, holding an old-fashioned microphone.

"Welcome, everyone, to this momentous occasion. I would like you all to join us, yes, even the staff and crew. Oh, come on. This ship will be fine all by itself for a few moments. There are no icebergs around here to crash into, after all." There was not as much laughter as his joke warranted, he thought.

While he was speaking, the rest of the occupants of the *Starcatcher*, its crew, had joined the passengers.

"Ah, everybody's here. Very good. Please, crew members, take a glass of wine. I'm going to propose a toast. To the *Starcatcher's* maiden voyage, and to me, if I may be so bold, on the occasion of my fiftieth birthday. Drink up!" He raised and emptied his glass, as did everyone else, except for First Mate Collins. Before going to the auditorium, he had visited the head. By the time he got there, the toast was over, and Mr. Butler was speaking again.

"And now it's time for our entertainment." The curtain across the stage parted and a beautiful woman stood in the center.

"This is Mistress Khidra. She is a goddess... of song. Sit back and enjoy the music." Butler backed away, apparently scratching his ears, to a place at the side of the stage where a large, plush chair was waiting.

On stage, Khidra opened her mouth and a sound emerged. To anyone who had not drunk either the wine or the children's beverages the sound was a deafening screech. To everyone who had, though, the sound was soft magic.

Since First Mate Collins had not partaken of the wine, his head was clear, and the screech drove him from the room. He covered his ears tightly and peered around the open doorway.

As she sang, her audience sank into unconsciousness, laying their heads on their tables or falling to the floor. Khidra began to grow, absorbing energy from her audience. The unconscious people in the room began to lose mass, thinning and slipping from their seats or shrinking where they laid. The air became thick with the life force of the passengers and crew streaming into the creature on the stage.

Collins saw what was happening and fled for the bridge. "May Day! Danger! May Day! Danger!" he called into the radio's microphone, changing frequencies, hoping that there would be a ship near enough to hear him. He knew that the signal would include his coordinates and anyone answering his call could find the ship. Then he ran for the nearest escape pod, jumped inside and launched it.

* * *

When the humans in the audience were completely empty, Khidra turned to Butler, who had been watching with a satisfied look on his face. He took the plugs out of his ears so he could hear her.

"I am grateful to you for this offering," she said. "Where is this ship headed?"

"It is headed in a loop which will return to Earth in five days."

"Excellent. You have done well. Now I wish to give you something."

She opened her mouth and began to sing, just for him.

* * *

"Okay, what's the danger?" said the man Collins saw first. His escape pod had been picked up by another space yacht, the *Phobos*, which had just happened to be in the vicinity. Collins climbed out and stood upright for the first time in two days. The pod was a small one, and he was cramped and tired from being in it that long.

"You'll never believe me," Collins told the man, who turned out to be the captain of the yacht, Captain Monroe. "It was horrible. Sometimes I don't believe what I know I saw."

"Try me," Monroe replied. They made their way to the crew's lounge and sat down.

"Well..." Collins proceeded to tell Captain Monroe what he'd seen on the *Starcatcher* just before he had left in the escape pod. When he finished, he broke down, shivering.

"Your story seemed a bit unbelievable," the captain told him. "But I will give you the benefit of the doubt. I'll show you to a lovely cabin you can stay in while we cruise by your ship and see if there's anyone else there who needs help." Collins entered the cabin and heard the door lock click. He lay on the bunk, closed his eyes and screamed.

After a while, he took hold of himself and realized that he was still alive and away from the nightmare had happened in the *Starcatcher*.

There was knock on the door and a crewmember entered with a tray of food. After what he had been through, he was starving.

"Thank you," Collins told the man. "I must have seemed raving mad when I was rescued, but after some sleep and food, I feel much better. Might I see the Captain so I can thank him for rescuing me?"

"I'll ask," the man said and left, relocking the door.

* * *

When the *Phobos* neared the *Starcatcher*, Captain Monroe summoned Collins to the bridge.

"Glad you're feeling better. I thought you'd like to be here when we arrive at your ship," he said.

As they approached the *Starcatcher*, the Captain hailed the bridge. When no one answered, the *Phobos* matched velocity and two armed crewmen in spacesuits crossed the distance to the other ship and tethered the two together.

"I don't think that's a good idea," Collins told the Captain.

"I'm sure they'll be all right," the Captain replied.

"We have made contact," one of them, Richards, radioed back to the *Phobos*. "I'm opening the airlock now. I will report back when we're inside and find out what's going on."

A few minutes later Richards reported in again. "Captain, you're not going to believe this."

"That's what that Mr. Collins said. Okay, what do you see?" he replied.

Richards' account of the state of the ship and its passengers agreed with what Collins had reported.

"Maybe you two had better return and let the Space Guard handle it."

When the man didn't respond to the Captain and couldn't be raised after repeated hailing, Captain Monroe sent two more crewmen, more heavily armed.

When Collins protested, Captain Monroe said, "I can't just leave Richards and Edwards there."

"She'll just get them, too," Collins told the Captain. "Call them back!"

"Now, now. I'm sure they'll be okay."

"Captain," Crewmen Fisher from the second party called, "I don't know what to tell you. We've found Richards and Edwards, but they're, well, flat. It's like all their insides have been sucked out. It's the damnedest thing."

Captain Monroe ordered the men back to the ship at once. "I don't want to lose you, too."

"A moment, Captain. I see something moving. Oh, it looks like a young woman. Miss! Miss! Are you all right?" Fisher called, and the radio went silent again.

A few minutes later the radio came on again. "Captain? This is Miller. Something strange is going on. Fisher and I split up and I can't find him anywhere. He doesn't answer his comm."

"Have you seen a girl?" the Captain asked.

"No. Should I look for one?"

"No. Come on back, Miller," the Captain told him. "I'll report this to the Space

Guard. If there's nothing we can do, we need to be continuing on our way."

Half an hour later, the shuttle landed and Fisher reported to the Captain. "Where's Miller?" the Captain asked. "I just talked to him. He said he couldn't find you."

"I don't know. I looked around again for him and the girl and I still couldn't find them."

"I've already reported the situation to the Space Guard," Captain Monroe told him. "They'll figure it out. Don't worry about it. If I had to lose crewmen, I'd rather it was three instead of four. Now go to your quarters and get some rest."

"Yes, sir. Thank you, sir," Fisher said, with an odd smile on his face, and did as he was told. As he turned to go there was a flash of a strange color in his eyes for just a moment.

A week later, the passengers were gathered in the dining room for an impromptu party. Everyone was invited.

RIVAL SUNS

LAURA J. CAMPBELL

"**W**ell, this space fold chose one Hell of a place to claim as a destination," Mary Lucidity said. She was in a prison cell. The cell was more appropriate for a medieval dungeon than a space-faring planet. It was made of stone, with no windows, and lit only with dim recessed lights. The door was made of thick metal, with one eyehole drilled into it, a slot for the exchange of food trays, and a heavy keyed lock.

"*Hell* being a peculiarly apt choice of words," Vesper Unitas replied. "Of course, you had no idea you were going to end up here. That's what makes crypto-navigation so exciting."

"But the Service received my transmissions? About this course?"

"Yes, and we are grateful. We were only shown one navigable space fold into this system. It is guarded by Dali'dai forces, who don't want us to have unfettered access to the universe. So Earth Secret Service honors your gift and your loyalty. Having back door routes that only we know is tactically and strategically important."

"Will I die here?"

"No. You are too valuable. I have been sent to extract you."

"They intend to burn me as a witch. And this is a space-faring planet?"

"Technology finds its way among the enlightened and the ignorant."

"My timing was inopportune as well." Mary noted.

Dr. Mary Lucidity had been born on the Earth colony of Mars. She had exceptionally pale skin, as all Martians did. Those whose skin color would have been dark on Earth were gray on Mars; those of lighter complexions were as white as bleached bones.

Mary's eyes were an emerald green, her hair flaming red. She wore the traditional slacks, blouse, and generously hooded robe of a Martian Colony citizen. The slacks were comfortable, equipped with multiple zippered pockets. Her blouse was fitted, a solid turquoise blue in color. Her hooded robe was reversible, showing white on the outside, turquoise on the inner lining.

Dr. Vesper Unitas, by contrast, was tall with sugar-white hair and smoky-quartz colored eyes. Her family lineage counted more generations on Mars than Mary's did. Thin and aged, Vesper appeared to be made of silver veined Thassos marble. One imagined Vesper could simply stop living and instantly become her own memorial statue. She wore her hooded robe the opposite way from Mary, with the turquoise on the outside and the white on the inside. Vesper considered that an outwardly white robe and hood would only make her look more inanimate.

"The people of Saenet are a highly superstitious people, Agent Lucidity. To their eyes, you manifested out of nothingness. A fallen angel. A demon. A witch."

"You have other concerns," Mary detected. "Besides this kangaroo court and its sentence over me."

Vesper has been sent out as an advocate for Mary, to give the appearance of a fair trial. The two had known each other for years; Vesper had been one of Mary's instructors in the Martial Agent Registry training program, a division of Earth Secret Service, who they both served.

"Our enemies, the Uoy, have heard that an Earth crypto-navigator has been apprehended here on Saenet. The Uoy have an exceptionally unhealthy interest in you. They know that technology is not what allows Earth to find the unmarked passageways through space. The Uoy have correctly deduced out that our crypto-navigators are a far greater resource than the ships they pilot. They want *you*. Or, at least, the secret of you."

"They cannot be allowed to discover that. I will let them kill me before I let the Uoy study me like a lab animal. Much less for their own advantage."

"And that is where Saenetian superstitions play in our favor."

"How so? This is a barbaric practice. Ritualistically killing three people by plunging them into unprotected atmospheric re-entry? All to please their suns?"

"This planet revolves around two suns in a figure eight pattern. The orbit is odd but allows Saenet to remain about 93 million miles from a sun at all times," Vesper recounted. "For three days, the course of the planet crosses over from revolving around one sun to revolving around the other. The planet spends three days at the intersection of its figure-eight orbital pathway."

"And they celebrate a naturally-occurring astronomical event with debauchery and violence during the Festival of the Rival Suns. During which I am scheduled to be burnt as a witch."

"Their mythology is based on there being an animosity between the gods who supposedly reside in each sun, twin brothers named Eadar and Scolas. To preserve peace between the brothers, the Saenet people put on elaborate balls and make their supplications, including sacrificing a person on each of the three days of the transit. One sacrifice to Eadar, one to Scolas. One to both of them. Uniting the Rival Suns. To hold them in their place in the Heavens. The Uoy found out you are to be the third sacrifice. But the selection of an Earth-citizen as a sacrifice has caused an intergalactic quarrel. Saenet feels the pressure to justify its practices, to appear scientifically grounded in its superstitions. So, the Uoy are magnanimously sending out an 'ecclesiastical attorney,' with the claim that he can establish if a person is a witch by applying a biological test. Saenet is desirous of this validation."

"Uoy bullshit on top of Saenetian voodoo."

"The Uoy insistence upon testing you necessitated placing your scheduled execution on Day Three of the sacrifices, as opposed to Day Two, when you were originally scheduled for sacrifice. That extra day is important. Have faith. We will get you away from this foul snare."

"I have every faith in you and the Agency," Mary replied.

"As we have faith in you. Maintain your silence, Lucidity, and do as I direct. They sent me on purpose. I have never failed to complete a mission. You will not be my first loss."

* * *

"Doctor Unitas," Ossirl greeted. The Santaetians were biologically similar to

Earthling humans, except they had smaller eyes and larger ears. The light on Santaent was significantly brighter than on Earth; the Santaetians anatomy had adapted to the abundance of light.

Hearing was their dominant sense. Vesper had been aware of that while talking with Mary Lucidity. It was no struggle for Santient spies to eavesdrop.

"Ossirl," Vesper Unitas replied.

"Your witch is without a valid defense," he stated. "Our astronomers saw her ship emerge from open, empty space. The only way into our system is the Melas Reht, the bidirectional space-folding route that connects us to the galaxies. The *only* way to get into and out of our solar system. Well, the only scientifically supported way. Notwithstanding the dark magic Mary Lucidity wielded to arrive here."

"I am familiar with Melas Reht," Unitas replied. "That is how I arrived here."

"As I stated, Dr. Lucidity did not arrive by the Melas. She materialized out of *nothingness*. That is black magic."

"We have filed for a stay of her execution," Vesper stated. "Your planet is a member of Interplanetary. It is obliged to abide by the Council's decrees."

"I have been informed. Your motion was supplemented with an amicus brief submitted by an ecclesiastical attorney from Uoy named Demex Rettejer. As you know, he has argued that he should be allowed to examine the accused. He says the Uoy have a blood test, owing to years of Uoy genetic purification studies, that can scientifically establish if Mary Lucidity is a witch or not."

"In taking in a Uoy, you are inviting the Devil into your tent. Who is practicing witchcraft now?"

"The decision has been made," Ossirl replied sternly. He was unaccustomed to having his authority questioned. "The Festival of the Rival Suns is underway. You witnessed the first day's sacrifice this morning."

Dr. Unitas had seen the barbaric ritual. She remembered it with disfavor:

"Our Suns bring us into the ballroom," Ossirl had recited. "It is our honor to bring them gifts."

There was a native Saenetian, one of these fidgety nervous people, poised on the edge of platform as the edge of space. He had been accused of witchcraft. And, as in most places and times where witchcraft was a recognized offense, the accused had been found guilty and sentenced to death.

The doomed man wore a plain helmet and a slender suit. There was a parachute packed to his back, but everyone knew he would never survive to deploy it. His body was not garbed to survive the fate assigned to him.

"Let the Festival of the Rival Suns begin," the high priest stated.

The man was pushed off the edge of the platform. His body hurtled towards the planet's surface.

The mythology said that if the sun gods found him innocent, they would protect him and he would survive the plunging fall, deploy his parachute, and gently land unscathed on the ground, sixty thousand feet below.

If he was guilty, the gods themselves would consume him with their 'holy' fire.

Vesper had watched as the condemned man was falling headfirst towards the planet's surface. She witnessed his body picking up speed fast. By now, the blood would be pushed from his brain, directed towards his feet. He would pass out.

Vesper had given him the only mercy she could; when given the opportunity to 'inspect' the condemned prisoner just prior to his execution, she held his face in her hands. What the Saenetian high priest did not know was that Vesper's wrists concealed devices that injected a time-released poison into the man. He had died, quietly and painlessly, while standing on the platform.

He had been spared his body reaching supersonic speeds, his eyes popping out of their sockets, his limbs being torn from him; he had been spared his body heating to over 1,650 degrees Celsius, heat so intense it would form a pink plasma around him as the physics of the fall stripped the atoms off his insufficient suit.

There would be nothing left of his molten corpse to hit the ground.

When it was over, Ossirl assured the faithful that this searing sacrifice was a fire lighting the way to sacred altar, giving them all eventual entry into the great ballroom of the sun gods.

"Your witch should be familiar with the mechanics of her execution," Ossirl said. "After all, Edge Jumping is a sport on Earth. Athletes there are celebrated for their dexterity as they jump off platforms at the edge of your atmosphere and perform daring stunts during the descent. *It is sport on Earth—to defy death.* We see it as further evidence of Earth sorcery. Perhaps Mary Lucidity will dance for us as she dies."

"Our Edge Jumpers wear protective suits, made with a specially engineered fabric that provides the pressure and warmth necessary to survive the fall. Atmosphlex is the fabric's name. The Edge Jumpers fall at 834 miles per hour, picking up heat as they descend, but the fabric modulates their environment. Protecting them. They fall for four minutes, then their self-guiding parachutes automatically deploy, just in case they have lost consciousness. They have safe landings. Unlike your victims—they have nothing to protect them from the shearing forces of the fall."

"Victims?" Ossirl scoffed. "Witches are *criminals* of the worst kind. They challenge the gods. They deserve to die."

"And if they are not a witch?"

"Those garbed in righteousness do not need your Atmosphlex. Eadar and Scolas will save an innocent, throwing their divine radiance around them. And that, Dr. Unitas, is that."

* * *

The charlatan had arrived to cast his deception.

"We have a blood test to detect those who bear the malignant arts in their veins," Demex Rettejer, the Uoy lawyer, announced. He was tall, with amber eyes and golden skin; his black hair was cropped into a short haircut, uncommon for the Uoy, who usually wore their hair long.

The barristers and judges on Uoy had taken to wearing large elaborate powdered wigs as if they were members of the ancient British Bar. The short hairstyle accommodated the wigs. Rettejer's collar was ridiculously high and hid most of his face. He wore a long black robe and black gloves. He looked like a cross between Count Dracula and a High Court Judge. The look was accurate to his character and his intentions.

"A blood test?" Vesper asked, her gray eyes intent on Rettejer.

"A small sample. One tube. About 15 milliliters. I will take it with me to Uoy and have the results in about twenty-four hours—plenty of time before the Third Day of the Holy Festival." He spoke with a lyrical quality; you could hear the capital letters in his speech as he spoke.

"This is reasonable," Ossirl agreed. "A neutral party administering a scientific test. That should answer Earth's complaints against our verdict."

"This is *preposterous*," Vesper objected. "There is no control over the sample or the results. How do we know he will not use the sample for other tests? Or report back false findings, once he has secured his prize—which is the sample itself. That is why he is here. Not to advocate for Lucidity, but to suck the blood from her veins."

"Why would I want a tube of Earthling blood?" Demex asked smugly. "Earthlings are disgusting creatures."

"I don't know why," she said. She was lying. She knew why: the Uoy had observed that Earthlings were beginning to travel through space more freely than any other planet. Earth ships were accessing locations that could not be reached using the space-folding conduits known to the other space-faring planets. The Uoy had homed in on Lucidity, correctly guessing that she was one of Earth's crypto-navigators. If there was a marker, chemical, or gene in her blood that could be identified, extracted, and replicated, they reasoned that they, too, might develop the ability to detect the unseen space routes in their own population.

The Uoy did not want Earth having secret passageways across the galaxies.

The Uoy wanted to know what made people like Mary Lucidity tick.

"We have known the Uoy longer than we have known Earth," Ossirl declared. "Therefore we trust them more. And there have never been witches on their home-world. Unlike Earth. Sometimes we consider that there may be nothing *but* witches and warlocks on Earth. Truly, even to look at Mary Lucidity, she fits the Earthling definition of a traditional witch—with her red hair and green eyes and deathlike pale skin. Even your skin is white like death, Dr. Unitas."

"Dr. Lucidity and I are citizens of the Earth Colony Mars," Vesper replied. "Our skin is pale to allow for the absorption of photons from a more distant sun, in order to produce necessary Vitamin D in our skin. Some multi-generation Martians have almost translucent skin."

"As if those of Earthling lineage were not disgusting enough," Demex pointed out.

"And this is your 'neutral' arbitrator?" Vesper objected. "He represents great animosity towards us."

"He is acceptable to *me*," Ossirl stated.

"We have rules," Vesper interjected. "Martian ladies are very modest. A Uoy man alone in a room with a Martian lady? That is unacceptable. *I* will collect the sample from Dr. Lucidity. Surely a pious priest such as yourself respects modesty?"

"I will observe through the keyhole. Is that modest enough for you?" Ossirl replied. He was determined to appear reasonable and professional. And he needed to expedite the process. The Uoy intervention in Lucidity's execution had been an unforeseen delay. Ossirl did not want Earth to have any further grounds to postpone the execution.

"*I* need to witness the collection," Demex objected.

"You may be in the room," Ossirl allowed.

"But *I* collect the sample," Vesper confirmed. "We don't want Uoy fingers on our Martian skin. And no one else will be in attendance—there can't be all sorts of strangers running around. That could contaminate the sample. This procedure is questionable enough as it is."

"I do not object to these terms," Ossirl stated. "Let's get on with it."

"I still object to the entire charade," Vesper added.

"The blood test is decreed an appropriate mechanism for determining if there is dark magic inside Mary Lucidity," Ossirl concluded sternly, ending the debate. He left, not desiring to entertain anymore conditions from either Dr. Vesper Unitas or Demex Rettejer, Esquire.

"Dark magic," Rettejer echoed with a self-satisfied smirk. "And there is magic inside Mary Lucidity, isn't there? I can't wait to take a glimpse at it."

* * *

The three gathered at Mary Lucidity's cell.

Ossirl was anxious. "The witch had been suffered to live too long already. I have people on my planet to protect. Eadar and Scolas *must* be appeased. She is the most important of our burnt offerings. We have promised her to them."

"The syringe," Vesper demanded, holding out her hand.

Rettejer reluctantly held out a syringe and a tourniquet. "Are you capable of drawing the sample?" he asked snidely.

"Like all members of Earth Secret Service, I have two doctorates," Vesper told him, as she took the syringe and tourniquet from his hands. Her fingernails ever so slightly grazed his palm as she closed her hand around the devices. "Mine are in medicine and waterfowl husbandry. I am more than capable of drawing the sample. Do you have a bandage?"

Rettejer handed her a sterile piece of gauze, two smalls pad infused with isopropanol, and length of adhesive tape.

"Stand near the door, so I can observe the sample collection," Ossirl told her.

"Of course," Vesper replied.

Ossirl opened the door, and Vesper and Demex walked into Mary's dimly lit cell. Ossirl closed and locked the door. Vesper could see Ossirl press his eye up to the observation hole.

Demex took a seat on a low stool in the room, observing in silence. "The sample," he commanded.

"On with it!" Ossirl demanded from outside of the room.

Vesper nodded to the now silent Demex.

She motioned Mary to stand beside her, adjacent to the door and out of Ossirl's direct sight. Vesper pointed to Mary's robe as she took off her own. They exchanged robes quickly and quietly.

"Stand close to the door, so he can see the collection, but not see our faces," Vesper said in sign language to Mary. Vesper had no intention of allowing any of Mary Lucidity's blood to be collected by anyone. She cleaned her hands with one of the isopropanol wipes.

Vesper handed the syringe to Mary and they positioned themselves in front of the doorway.

"Are you ready?" Vesper asked. She wiped the inner seam of her left arm with the other isopropanol pads.

"Yes," Mary replied.

From the observation hole, Ossirl could see their bodies and arms.

After properly tying the tourniquet, the woman in the white robe inserted the needle into the vein of the woman in the turquoise robe, drawing the sample. The tourniquet was unwrapped.

"Are you finished?" Ossirl asked.

"We need to apply a bandage and Mr. Rettejer wants to examine the sample— in case another needs to be collected. Give us a few moments."

Ossirl grumbled. "I have other duties to attend to! I am already very late for an extremely important ceremony."

Vesper whispered to Mary. "Reverse the colors of my robe and put it on Rettejer. Then put on his cape and wig. Quickly!" Mary did as ordered: she reversed Vesper's robe so that it was outwardly white and fitted Rettejer's unresponsive body into the covering.

Vesper switched Mary's robe so that the turquoise was now on the outside and slid it back on her own body.

"A few moments more," Vesper called out. "We are making sure that the anti-coagulant mixed adequately with the sample. This is an important test for all of us. We do not want the sample to degrade. You wouldn't want the delay of having to take another sample, would you?"

While Vesper talked, Mary garbed herself in Rettejer's powdered wig and high-collared cape; the collar covered her face almost completely. She put his black gloves over her pale hands.

Vesper finished arranging Rettejer in Mary's robe, throwing the hood around his face and covering his features. They propped his body up against the wall, as if the white-robed figure in the chair was sleeping.

"We have the sample," Vesper announced.

"Finally!" Ossirl said as he unlocked the door. Vesper stepped out, Mary keeping very close behind her. Mary turned, so that only her back was visible to Ossirl, holding up the tube of blood in her black-gloved hands, as if to inspect it.

Ossirl peeked quickly inside the cell, to see the white-robed figure resting on the stool.

"She is exhausted," Vesper explained. "This has been a very trying experience for her."

Ossirl grumbled, paying attention to securing the lock. "Tell me the results as soon as you get them," he said, as he walked away to attend to his other duties.

Vesper and Mary walked directly to the spaceship bays.

Vesper stepped into her ship. "Take Rettejer's ship and ride the Melas Reht out of here," she ordered. "There is a rendezvous ship prepared to escort us both back to Earth space. A pirate ship, the *Lochleven*. They are in my employ. They will send you coordinates."

"I'll see you there," Mary replied. "It sounds like a destination far more pleasant than where Ossirl was planning on sending me."

* * *

The guard rushed into Ossirl's office, his face flushed. "High Priest, a grave calamity has befallen us! Eadar and Scolas will be furious."

"What is it?" Ossirl asked. He was already behind in his duties during this most holy season. He had lost too much time cajoling the Uoy. Even if there had been a profitable trade. In exchange for allowing them access to Mary Lucidity, the Uoy had paid Ossirl a very generous bribe. His personal bank account had profited significantly from the transaction.

"The woman—the witch—she is gone!"

"*What?*"

"And worse news, High Priest—the Uoy diplomat is dead. Come and see!"

Ossirl rushed towards the dungeon, following the guard.

The two entered the cell.

The guard had thrown back the hood on the robe. Demex Rettejer sat dead on the stool.

"How can this be?" Ossirl exclaimed. "I saw the sample drawn. I saw Rettejer leave this cell. He inspected the sample before my very own eyes! I saw his ship depart immediately afterwards. I watched it enter the Melas Reht."

"Powerful witchcraft!" the guard shuddered. "To cast such an illusion! Anyone of Earthling origin—they are truly witches! Oh, Eadar and Scolas, save us!"

"Does anyone else know of this?" Ossirl asked, focusing on what had to be done.

"No, High Priest. Just you and I."

There were times Ossirl despaired the demands of his office. This was one of those times.

He took out a small firearm and shot the guard. It had to be done.

The man fell to the ground.

Ossirl dragged the body into the cell. There would be time to dispose of the guard's body later.

Ossirl sat in the cell, looking at the two dead men. Then he sent out a communication: he alone would prepare the most sacred sacrifice of the Festival.

He had people to protect.

Starting with himself.

* * *

The body was propped upon the platform. Ossirl had taken special care to assure that Rettejer's body looked like Lucidity's in the suit. Ossirl had completely enshrouded Rettejer's body in Lucidity's clothing. None of his flesh was exposed. There was enough of Lucidity's hood and robe showing through the window of the helmet to confirm the illusion that the condemned Earth citizen was standing on the execution platform.

Ossirl felt dirty, employing such subterfuge. But "dirty" and "deity" were closely lettered words. It was his privilege as a priest to transform one into the other.

He stood before the assembled crowd.

"Our Suns bring us into the ballroom," he recited. "It is our honor to bring them gifts.

"Let the Festival of the Rival Suns conclude."

He pushed the body off the edge of the platform with a meaningful shove; it hurtled headfirst towards the planet's surface like a javelin seeking the core of the planet.

Ossirl exhaled a sigh of relief.

With the atmospheric incineration of Rettejer's corpse, his disappearance would become an unsolvable mystery. His body would never be found. The Uoy were already asking questions about why their representative had not yet returned to the Uoy home world.

Ossirl considered himself saved. The people of Saenet would be happy; their solemn ceremony duly observed. *And even Eadar and Scolas should be appeased,* Ossirl thought. *A burnt sacrifice of flesh and blood has been duly given unto them.*

He watched the body plummet, waiting for the pink plasma veil to form around the suit, and the body to ignite, becoming molten as it fell.

But nothing happened.

The body did not become molten. It was not consumed by flames.

Ossirl forgot to breathe for a moment.

For the first time in history, a body would arrive on the planet's surface in recognizable form.

* * *

"They have given me a new assignment," Mary said, safely upon the *Lochleven.* Rettejer's ship had been placed in a cargo bay. The pirates were commanding a pretty penny to sell it—and its potential classified Uoy data—to the highest Earth bidder. Rival companies and agencies were submitting their clandestine bids for the contraband.

Earth Secret Service had already extracted everything it wanted from the enemy vessel.

"What is your next mission?" Dr. Unitas asked.

"To see if I can find a hidden cosmic pathway into the Uoy's backyard."

"If any such pathway exists, you will find it," Vesper replied.

"I noticed that you scratched Rettejer's hand as you took the syringe from him," Mary mentioned, thinking back to their escape from that individual Uoy.

"I thought I was stealthier than that."

"My life depended on you fooling them, not me," Mary replied. "I also heard that Rettejer's body survived the fall. How did that happen? Usually the bodies are consumed upon re-entry into Saenet's atmosphere."

"Ossirl sent me an image of you in captivity before I left for Saenet. He wanted to gloat over your condemnation. Upon receiving the image, I had a robe made of Atmosphlex. I knew exactly what colors to make the robe, thanks to Ossirl's pride. If worse came to worse, I would exchange robes with you under some pretense, and your wearing it during the descent would spare you from death. You would be an Edge Jumper, not a living sacrifice to alien gods. I would then pretend to retrieve your 'corpse' and take you back to Mars with me."

"Ossirl unintentionally preserved the body by keeping it in my robe. Now, there is some poetic justice."

"They are convinced beyond a doubt that you are a witch now," Vesper smiled. "That you magically exchanged your body with Rettejer while on the platform. Even the Uoy now think there might be something to this Earth sorcery stuff."

"But it wasn't witchcraft. It was clandestine science. An undetected poison and a disguised Atmosphlex robe," Mary noted. "Ossirl was looking to execute a witch. Not an ally."

"Ossirl got *exactly* what he was looking for," Vesper replied. "Undetected poison and a disguised Atmosphlex suit were just the forms his justice took. He got clandestine science."

"Clandestine science. Better than the phony science he was seeking with that unfounded blood test, I suppose."

"Clandestine science," Vesper smiled as she replied. "You're a witch, Mary. You should already know that is what witchcraft really is."

SEDUCTION BY TRIAL

GD DECKARD

Thanks to a problem with his ship, Bob stayed for the festivities.

"Now what?" Khvata responded to his emergency call.

"My ship. It won't start."

"Told you," she deadpanned. "It's not a ship, it's a lander. And don't land so hard the next time."

"It was my first landing."

"Let me scan your lander, see what you broke." Silence. The starship NGO's communication's officer was wired. Khvata could tap into the electromagnetic spectrum practically anywhere in the universe from Earth orbit. She was also a gazillion years old and short-tempered. Then, "Well, the part is ordered. Did you get the artifact that you *went* there for?"

"Yes. What do you mean, the part is ordered?"

"You'll be stranded there for about a week."

"A week! Here? Have you seen this backwater in a backwater?" He had landed on the edge of a marsh.

"I have, and you need to be more careful. Secure that bull's head mask safely inside the lander before you go wandering about."

"It's safe. What about me, though? I just stole their sacred 'bull of Utu' mask."

"Marduk mask. Marduk is the 'bull of Utu.'"

"Whatever. I need to get away before the locals find this ship and drag me out for serious proselytizing."

"I told you—" she loved to say that, Bob realized, whenever she had to explain herself— "not to worry about it. The mask you stole was already stolen. And the lander is well camouflaged. It looks like any other reed hut in the area. Nobody will look twice at it."

"So, I just sit in here for a week?"

"No, get dressed. You have your costume. Your implanted chip lets you command the local language. And, it can inform you of their culture. They're celebrating the Lunar New Year this week. Go educate yourself."

"You know, I am not, really, a space traveler. Or a time traveler. Or a thief. I'm just an ordinary guy."

"Who is paid handsomely. Stop whining. You said you used to be a soldier."

"Special Forces. But I spoil easily."

The outside air was comfortable and smelled clean, like a spring day in the Matanuska Valley where he had grown up. But his Alaska was on the other side of the world and thousands of years in the future. Bob never asked how the NGO could travel through time. He had once inquired how the starship could travel through mega-space and the answer had hurt his head.

Stretched between him and the city on the far lake were small islands, some the size of shopping centers, dotted with reed huts. Fishing villages, Khvata called them. Borsippa was a major city of ancient Sumer, eleven miles southwest of Babylon on the east bank of the Euphrates River. He had landed here on a mission so simple that even he had been entrusted to complete it: Acquire an artifact and get away. Now, he shook his head. His boat was missing. He found his door buzzer in a pocket beneath his robe and pushed the button. "I don't have a boat."

The door buzzer in his pocket buzzed. Khvata was telepathic. She knew he objected to her intruding into his mind, so she had given him a gadget to use for talking with her. Why a door buzzer was another question he didn't bother asking. It was the least of her strangeness. "Stolen, no doubt. No wonder Hammurabi laid down the law to these people. Well, there's one on the other side of your island. Be careful. There is a hut there with someone in it."

He spotted the reed boat tied close to the open door of the reed hut. Crouching and approaching quietly, he wondered what was going on inside until he heard familiar sounds. A man and a woman and they weren't watching the boat. Bob paused while untying the boat. He stared at the open door and listened. The woman's intimate voice, strong and caressing, was haunting. Khvata giggled. "Just take the damned boat and stop looking for trouble." He shut off the buzzer.

Sights and sounds of the town reached him before the smells. Short men, shouting, their skin lined and dark from the sun, swarmed the quay unloading timber, wine, stones, and other goods from a log platform floating on inflated animal skins. In the narrow-paved streets, the air hung laced by rich cooking smells and fragrant with baking bread and brewing beer. Bob spent the rest of the morning making his way to the center of town. He walked by braided-reed huts, then plain mud-brick buildings with flat roofs, single-story at first, then larger buildings of baked brick. Some were fronted by columns and arched doorways leading to inner courtyards. His robed costume—quite authentic looking, he thought—allowed him to mingle unnoticed among the locals. Most wore only a coarse woolen skirt, fringed at the bottom; a few added a kind of cloak draped over one shoulder, leaving the other bare.

He was thinking of how little there was here to tempt himself, an intergalactic thief, when her voice carried through the multitude. She was wailing, but it was *her*, the woman from the hut! He pushed through the thickening crowd. Bob was a large man, compared to the slighter natives who grudgingly made way for him. He made it easily to where the inner edge of the crowd encircled a statue.

Six people were standing by the statue. A couple of men argued with four women. One woman, by far the most elaborately dressed in a long-tiered robe and high coiffed hair—*his* woman, he was already thinking of her—stood at the center of the altercation looking melodramatically unhappy. She held both hands on her hips and leaned back to take a deep breath. "I, accustomed to triumph, have been driven forth from my house and made to perform the tasks of slaves!"

"To bathe the statue of Nabu is an *honor*!" the older of the two men admonished her. Bob figured him for some kind of priest because he wore a robe and headpiece.

"The life-giving tiara of En-ship was taken from me!" the woman wailed.

En-ship? Bob queried. *Chief Priestess*, came the answer from his implanted chip.

The younger of the two men implored her. "You are helping to prepare Nabu for the Winter Festival. Please, these tasks will help you return to favor." He shrugged, throwing his arms wide to show helplessness. "If you will not submit to Trial by Ordeal—"

"Trial by Ordeal? I cannot!" Once again she wailed, turning this time to the statue and lifting her arms above her bowed head, "I no longer dwell in the goodly place You established. The fruitful bed has been abolished so that I have not interpreted to man the commands of Ningal."

Ningal? Some obscure god, no doubt. *The goddess of passionate and honeymooned love,* his chip answered. He was wondering how this woman might go about interpreting the commands of her sex goddess when she whirled to look directly at him. "And who would accept a Trial on my behalf? Who will be my champion?"

As if on cue, Bob strode forth.

Close up, she was, while not strikingly beautiful, strikingly beautiful to him. About five and a half feet of shapely limbs, curves, and—"*You!*"—anger. "You were watching me! You snuck around the hut! You are no champion! You are—" a word his chip could not translate. But Bob got the point.

"I was outside. The hut was darkened. I *saw* nothing!"

"You lie! You recognize me."

"I recognize your voice."

That mollified her, Bob thought, watching her sputter. The three women around her closed ranks and regarded him with utter condemnation. The two men smiled, seemingly happy to let him be the focus of her ire—whomever she was. "Who are you?" he asked her.

One of her attendants answered, "I am Sagadu, scribe of Enheduanna. You are in the presence of the Chief Priestess and Ornament of the Sky God, An." Herself regained composure and stood aloof, stonily aloof.

Startled, the Priest interjected, "She may not use the title of En-Ship!"

Bob squared off to answer him. "That will be decided by Trial."

The younger priest tensed, ready to protect his master. For a moment, the old Priest looked about to shove the bigger man aside but chose instead to asked Bob who he was.

"I am Bob."

After an expectant pause, wherein Bob offered no elaboration, the Priest cleared his throat. "Excuse me... Bob. I would inquire about your order. You wear a robe of priesthood, but no headdress proclaims your god."

He wore a priest's robe? Uh oh. He had not known that. What *did he know* about this place, more than anybody else? *Nothing,* his chip told him. *Who is this guy?* He felt a slight sensation as if the chip were shrugging. *Unknown.*

The Priest fingered his own linen robe, then Bob's artificial fabric, as if to compare. "I," his head elevated slightly to emphasize his headdress, "am En-Berosis, Chief Priest to the sky-god Nabu. And your god is...?"

"Unknown." Bob clasped the Chief Priest's hand. "I am Bob, Priest of the Unknown. Glad to meet you."

The Chief Priest took his hand back. "Unknown... priest?

"High Priest," Bob amplified his title, thinking of the starship overhead. "En-Bob. From on high." He pointed up.

"And *you* will be this woman's champion? Most singular."

He's skeptical, Bob thought. He was later to learn that these people regarded as an omen anything unaccustomed, fortuitous or singular.

"I accept." En-Berosis's expression implied that he deeply regretted doing so.

Enheduanna nodded, as if reappraising the Chief Priest. "I too, accept. And as my champion is also a Chief Priest, I would that my accuser be forgiven."

The relief on En-Berosis's face told Bob that he was her accuser. He turned to Bob. "Trial by Ordeal. That is acceptable to you?"

Trial by Ordeal? Um, "I will consult my god." Bob activated the buzzer in his pocket and asked, in English, "Khvata, what is Trial by Ordeal here?"

"You jump in the river. They believe a god will intervene to save an innocent person while drowning the guilty." The sound of English, and Khvata's voice, riveted some astonished attention onto Bob.

"They're not going to tie me up first, are they?"

"No. What? I told you to stay out of trouble!"

"It's a long story. Talk to you later."

"Wait. They might have you swim to the middle and back. Maybe underwater. Maybe, even, carrying a big stone. And don't forget your reward."

Bob switched off the buzzer. "My reward?"

"Ah, yes. Your just compensation, should you survive. Normally, the accuser would be put to death and his home and belongings given to the accused. But," the Chief Priest squirmed, "the accused has forgiven her accuser. Your reward will be as she deems fit to give."

Bob grinned at Enheduanna and waited. Realization showed in her eyes. Then, anger.

"You will *not* watch me interpreting the commands of Ningal!"

Bob grinned his biggest, silliest grin. "I'll close my eyes."

The younger priest, whose name Bob found unpronounceable, accompanied him to the Divine River. At Bob's insistence that they stop by Bob's hut first, he indicated a nearby boat. "This will be quicker, En-Bob." Something about how he said that bothered Bob. Shouldn't the younger priest have begun that sentence with "En-Bob" and paused for acknowledgement? And then phrased taking the boat as a question to show deference?

He focused on the man in front rowing the boat and almost missed the dried footprint in the mud on the floor. That footprint was not made by any smooth-soled sandal or moccasin worn by the locals. The tread-marks were his.

At his hut, Bob ordered the priest to, "Wait outside." Inside, he ignored Khvata's incessant buzzing and carefully packed needed items into his backpack. When he came out, he handed the pack to the priest and laughed as the smaller man showed his surprise at its weight. Then Bob put it on and adjusted the harness.

"You will drown if you wear that." The young priest sounded hopeful.

"My god will drown *you*," Bob said disdainfully. "If you steal another boat from me." A shocked expression confirmed his suspicion. He pressed the advantage. "*Why?*"

Startled, the priest threw himself prostrate. "Do not accuse me. I cannot swim! My boat drifted away, and I did not know that was *your* boat. I only obeyed my Chief Priest's instructions to spy on Enheduanna." Bob waited. His next question was obvious. "Because they were lovers. But they squabbled. En-Berosis is jealous. He was insistent that she obeyed the stricture not to bed a man while accused."

"So, you spied and reported what went on in that hut?"

Wrong question. The prostrate man looked up at him. "No." He shook his head. "She said she has not interpreted to man the commands of Ningal."

"But in the hut—"

"She was with her attendants." He rose. "As you must know, En-Bob."

Oh. "Of course. I was testing you."

The priest rowed them through the marsh to where a crowd assembled among the palm trees lining the Euphrates. The banks here were low and lined with rocks to lessen erosion. The river itself looked to be a hundred meters or more across. The air felt comfortable enough, but his chip told him the water would be cold without a wetsuit. So be it. The contents of his pack would allow him to emerge victorious from this "Divine River."

Herself stood at the water's edge, accompanied by her three attendants. A breeze ruffled her robe.

"So!" he accused her as he approached, "All this trouble because you and En-Berosis had a lovers' quarrel!"

Enheduanna's surprise turned thoughtful. "Who told you this?"

"That young priest. En-Berosis had him spying on you."

"Unlikely. En-Berosis has many spies, but he would never set one on me."

Sagadu spoke up, "En-Bob, spying on a Chief Priestess is unlawful. It would earn even a chief priest a dunk in the Divine River."

"But that quay-rat of his is too ignorant to think past his own wants." Enheduanna's tone darkened. "He may even have been the one to poison En-Berosis against me." Her voice hoarsened in realization. "He was! He wants my position for himself!"

"So, what did happen?"

Enheduanna nodded to her scribe, as if deigning to allow an answer.

"You are wrong to assume my Lady's guilt, En-Bob." Sagadu's tone was taut, as if she were nervous about how much to say. "As is En-Berosis, who wears the clay amulet of Pazuzu to ward off the demon-goddess, Lamashtu. He accuses my Most Innocent Lady of allowing Lamashtu to steal their unborn son because she would not wear the clay amulet herself."

"Oh." A miscarriage. He was sorry now that he had asked. That was too personal and no doubt it had caused her great grief. "I am so sorry," he told Enheduanna.

"A *clay* amulet?" She agreed, nodding and opening her hands, palms-up. "Cheap jewelry!" She looked at him shrewdly. "You are more understanding than I thought, En-Bob."

Right. He excused himself and went to check the river currents.

A ceremony proceeded the Trial by Ordeal. Bob listened to his chip translate the parts explaining what was expected of him. Swim underwater for about fifty meters wearing his heavy backpack, emerge to holler and hold up the pack so those on the shore could verify that he had made it to the middle, then swim back on the surface to claim his reward.

He stripped naked and mentally readied himself for the swim by thinking of his prize. She stood aside in the crowd, facing as if to ignore him, but her eyes darted sideways. And down. He winked. She winked back. That threw him off his thoughts. He was still thinking about that wink when the young priest led him to the greenish-grey waters.

He glimpsed the knife coming only in time to twist aside. It bit his thigh as he grabbed the young priest's wrist and jammed his whole body against the attacker. Bob pivoted to place a foot behind the man and shoved. Down he went on his back. Without the knife, he lay panting and afraid. Bob offered him a hand up and handed back the knife. "I will deal with you later. Now *go!*" The cut was slight, as ineffective as his attacker, and he wouldn't allow anything to keep him from this swim!

He waded in, feeling the cold on his feet rise up his calves, up his thighs, and *Whoa! That's cold!* When Bob's chip announced a drop-off immediately ahead, he took a deep breath and plunged. He couldn't see much in front of him, but he managed to get his flippers and goggles out of the backpack and put them on. He dumped the remaining object and swam forward, angling against the current. Fifty meters was doable even though he was not, apparently, in as good a shape now as in his Army days. But experience reminded him to keep his head down, stay streamlined, and glide with long, smooth strokes.

Kicking lighter than normal to conserve oxygen, he breathed out gently as he swam, pacing the bubbles coming out of his nose and mouth with the countdown from his chip. Reaching the center of the river, he forcefully exhaled his remaining breath and rose to the surface. Gasping, he heard the crowd shouting on the shore, "En-Bob! En-Bob!" He held up the empty pack and waved.

He took deep breaths and held them to build up oxygen. Then he dove and swam underwater back towards the crowd. Not to show off, since he'd been told he could swim on the surface coming back, but to hide while he collected the object he had removed from his backpack for a lighter swim. It wasn't there. The river bottom in front of the crowd was bare. The thing was gone!

Sensing panic, his chip warned, "*Think!*" Thinking the current had swept it away, Bob turned downriver. But the damn thing was heavy and the flow was gentle here. Not like near the center, where he'd had to deliberately angle against the current—*oh.* He was downriver from where he started! Swimming back upriver a few yards, he quickly found the heavy item where he'd left it. Holding his last bit of breath, he put his pack on. Then he rose to the surface holding high the Golden Mask of Marduk.

The response was as expected. At first. The crowd quieted as people recognized the mask. Then surprise gave way to a wave of awe as those in front bowed or prostrated themselves to him followed by the next row of people and the next. *What?*

It's your appearance. The chip's dry tone conveyed the unspoken judgement, *Dumbass.*

They've seen naked men before. Hell, some of them are naked now.

But they are not wearing goggles and flippers.

The thought of himself standing in front of a crowd of strangers wearing nothing but goggles and swim flippers forced Bob to grin. Inanely, he realized. To show he was friendly, he nodded and walked the mask to Enheduanna, who, although also kneeling, watched him through arched eyes. He helped her up and handed her the mask. "Give this back to its rightful owner, please." To her astonished face, he explained, "I have to get dressed."

She laughed at him, then noticed blood on his thigh. "That is a knife cut. What happened?"

He explained the cut and watched her humor return. "I know exactly how to deal with him now." She held high the mask as she strode to the young priest. He cowered at the back of the crowd, now intent on her. "You!" She gave him the mask. "You will guard the Sacred Bull of Utu with your life." She paused for effect and enounced clearly, her voice carrying across the crowd. "Your life is forfeit should this Mask of Marduk ever again be stolen!"

"He is dead, if the mask is ever again stolen." she later told Bob. "En-Berosis will execute him."

Their new status placed Bob and Enheduanna at the table nearest to the god Dumuzi and goddess Inanna. These earthly personages were the happy guests of honor at this ceremonial banquet held to celebrate the Lunar New Year. The couple appeared happy to be the center of attention, happy to eat good food, and from their glances at one another Bob surmised, they joyfully anticipated their union to bring in a new year of prosperity and fertility for their people.

He turned to his own anticipated joy. "They gonna do it here?" he whispered. Enheduanna looked at him sharply, then kicked him under the table. He rubbed his shin, ruefully thinking that a day of his company might have lessened her estimation of his godly status.

They will retire to the nuptial chamber that has been prepared for them.
Thanks, Chip.

Light smoke rose from the fires burning in vats on tripod stands and illuminated the large banquet room in fog and light. A harpist led the music, skillfully accompanied by others playing stringed instruments. Their notes blended around the conversation of Dumuzi and Inanna, making music part of the godly drama. Other guests sat in groups around tall jugs to talk and sip beer or wine through a protruding bundle of communal straws. Servants mingled with the guests, removing and replacing dishes and cleaning up spills. Some carried the tall jugs in baskets suspended from a pole across their shoulders to replace the empty ones.

"Eat," Enheduanna elbowed him. "Are you not anxious to get started?"

Bob bit into the bird on his plate to discover that it was wrapped around a fish stuffed with succulent meat pies and vegetables. And oysters! Absolutely delicious! Juices ran down his chin. He was wondering how that must look to Enheduanna when her last statement struck him. "Get started with what?" He turned to her.

"Would you taste my oyster, Bob? It is also moist and plump." Her face was a frank invitation. Her eyes said it was time.

Enheduanna, Chief Priestess and Ornament of the Sky God, An, led Bob to a small hut atop the ziggurat. "Your reward chamber, En-Bob."

He followed her in. It was a single room, mostly bedding. "You sure about this? I mean, you don't have to. We're really two different people...." She had dropped her robe.

They became one when she gave him her tongue. "I am the Goddess of Night Relief," she told him intimately. "I will take your breath." They came together, all angles joining at the center, postures turning on whims, new discoveries acknowledged with new gasps. Once, he bent over her from behind, held her hair with one hand and cupped a breast in the other, and with a smile in his voice he whispered in her ear, "You're just as fucked up as I am."

She laughed and arched her back. "I will show you. *Come!*" and he burst into an awareness only she could show him.

At dawn, she rolled away, leaving him wet with love in the sudden air.

Back in the lander, Bob looked at the comm and decided that he'd better start this conversation on the offensive. "Khvata! Where the hell is that part for my lander?" But he should have known better.

She answered sweetly, "Oh, I have it." And added even more sweetly, "What in Hell have you been up to?"

Good. The old woman didn't know. Although telepathic, Khvata was loath to pry into people's minds. How did she put it? "I would rather swim in an interspecies cesspool." He paused, wondering if he could draw her into a reasonable discussion. "That's what I wanted to talk to you about."

But the familiar Khvata emerged. "About? What? What have you done now?"

"Well. You know that mask?" He led her gently into the surprise. "Of Marduk? I gave it back."

Silence before a very angry, " *What?*"

A big grin sounded in his voice. "But I know who has it." He thought of revenge, and of making Enheduanna's life easier. "I will steal it back."

EARTH DAY

JASON J. MCCUISTON

"I may just kill the next space pirate on sight."

The Last Star Warden looked at the slender blue-skinned alien in surprise. Though Quantum had been a soldier in his race's interdimensional invasion force, the Warden had never heard his friend express such a bellicose sentiment out loud. "Something bothering you?"

Quantum slid into the *Ranger VII*'s copilot seat, his short antennae drooping. His oversized, shiny black eyes narrowed and his undersized mouth was flat. "Ever since we came through that wormhole ten months ago—as you reckon time—it has been nothing but one drama after another. Alien overlords, haunted space stations, outlaw gangs, rogue military units, illegal corporate experiments, and... space pirates. Where does it all end?"

The Warden smiled. "I think you're right. We need to take a break." He pulled up a display on the ship's console. "As luck would have it, we are just in time for the big Earth Day Festival on Nu Terra V."

Quantum raised one dubious antennae. "A human celebration?"

The Warden set course. "You'll love it. Nu Terra V was settled by refugees from the Sol system's last internal war some seven hundred years ago... eight hundred, I have to remind myself... anyway, the first colonists were survivors from all the various warring factions, so when they established their new world, they started a tradition to commemorate the best of their old one.

"Earth Day became a time to celebrate the brotherhood of humanity, a time to embrace one another as friends and family, and a time to put away all the foolish, selfish things that divided human beings. The celebration eventually grew and grew until the Earth Day Festival on Nu Terra V was legendary throughout the galaxy."

Quantum leaned forward, intrigued. "And what kind of festivities might this celebration entail?"

The Warden leaned back and crossed his hands behind his head, fondly recalling the Earth Day he had attended—over a century before by the calendar, but a mere decade ago according to his memory. "Well, there's the food for starters. Folks make tons of their best recipes to share with everyone, and I mean everyone. Then there's the music, some of the most beautiful songs sung on every street corner by whole choruses of complete strangers. There's pageants and plays, parades and ballroom galas. Families give each other gifts, travel to visit distant kith and kin, gather to enjoy fine meals, play games and tell stories, and generally have a grand old time."

Quantum's glum expression gradually melted. "Sounds... interesting."

The Warden's smile widened as they passed through the Einstein-Rosen Bridge that would take them out of the Frontier and into the fringe of the Civilized Worlds. "You'll love it."

* * *

"Are you certain this is Nu Terra V?"

The Warden checked the coordinates in response to Quantum's question. And in response to the strange planet they observed outside the GlasSteel canopy.

A blockade of huge ships surrounded a highly-industrialized world now covered in massive stretches of urban development. The corporate freighters glimmered with enormous holographic billboards along their metallic hulls. These vigorous animations advertised all manner of goods from tasty treats to top-end luxury ships. At a glance, the advertising campaign appeared to be the first line of battle among three uber corporations: Deeznu, Kronos-Wagner, and Argonaut.

The Warden frowned. "The coordinates are right. But this doesn't look like the friendly, low-tech world I visited my first year out of the academy."

Quantum's antennae twirled. "That was over a hundred of your solar years ago. As we've learned since entering this era, quite a lot has changed."

"Apparently." The Warden didn't add that he hadn't found much to be for the better. "Let's go see what's what."

A mosquito-like corporate interceptor flew out to head them off. "Approaching ship, please identify yourself and state your business on Nu Terra V."

"This is the *Ranger VII.* We are here to take part in the Earth Day Festival."

The corporate pilot's voice came over the coms after a short pause. "Please specify. Are you here for the shopping and entertainment, or are you here to visit the shrine?"

The Warden raised an eyebrow. "*The* shrine? Isn't Nu Terra covered in Earth Shrines?"

The interceptor pilot laughed. "Where have you been, *Ranger VII?* Most of the shrines were bought out over the past fifty years. The only one left is in the Deeznu Corporate Zone. If you want to go there, you'll need to dock with a Deeznu freighter and buy a visitor's pass. That'll entitle you to land in the DCZ and give you access to all Deeznu eateries, activity centers, and retail outlets. Transmitting the coordinates now... Happy shopping!"

Quantum gave the Warden what he interpreted to be a dirty look. "Your Earth Day Festival seems to be nothing more than an excuse to indulge in excessive commerce."

The Warden pulled on his suit's skullcap and eye-concealing visor. "So it would seem."

After purchasing the Deeznu visitor's pass (at quite a hefty sum), they landed at the specified corporate zone's starport. Quantum suggested they turn around and go back to the Frontier, even if it meant running across more space pirates. But the Warden had a burr under his saddle and wouldn't let the degeneration of the Earth Day Festival go without first getting some answers.

Disembarking, they set out to find the last Earth Shrine on Nu Terra V. The DCZ was a terrestrial version of the corporate blockade orbiting the planet. Every building was alive with animatronic or holographic sales pitches, and every street was lined with markets, vendors, stores, bodegas, restaurants, eateries, VR parlors, gift shops, and every other commercial venue one might imagine.

Where the Warden remembered carols and hymns, he now heard sales pitches and jingles. The scent of flash-fried, mass-produced fast food replaced the aromas of homemade fresh-baked goods. The décor which had once celebrated the origins of a unified people was now dedicated solely to which venue touted the best sales. Worst of all were the people themselves.

Instead of smiling faces greeting them with hails of "Happy Earth Day!" or "Be blessed, brother!" the Warden and Quantum were bombarded with shouts of "Out of the way! Can't you see I'm in a hurry!" or "Look out! Big boxes coming through!" Though all the folks seemed quite affluent, judging by the copious amounts of shopping bags and boxes each of them carried, not a soul looked remotely happy.

Quantum sighed. "Are you sure you would not rather go find some space pirates?"

The Warden scowled. "Come on. I see the shrine up ahead."

The towering Earth Shrine was an elegant white pagoda with sweeping lines and graceful arches surrounded by tall pines, firs, and spruces. As they drew near, the Warden saw that the place was in poor repair and the evergreens needed tending. It was also the only place along the busy street devoid of patrons. Outside the gate stood a faded sign: EARTH DAY PAGEANT! COME AND EXPERIENCE THE JOY AND PEACE OF A TRADITIONAL EARTH DAY CELEBRATION! (CONTRIBUTIONS WELCOMED)

The courtyard was occupied by a handful of individuals singing as they built a temporary stage, sewed theatrical curtains, and painted large canvas backdrops. These happy workers were supervised by a tall, dark-skinned woman with elegant coils of graying black hair trailing down the back of her long white vestments.

She turned to face them with a warm smile. "Hello and welcome to the Earth Shrine. I am the Guardian, but you can call me Octavia. What joy can our humble shrine offer you, strangers?"

The Warden returned the woman's smile, relieved to finally see some shadow of the holiday cheer he had hoped to find on this world. "Hello, Miss Octavia. I'm the Warden, and this is my friend Quantum. It's been a long time since I've been to Nu Terra V, and I was hoping you could tell me exactly what happened to Earth Day."

Octavia tilted her head. "*The* Warden? The man out of time and space? Shouldn't you be on the Frontier, engaging in some mythic act of derring-do?"

"We're on holiday," Quantum said.

With a chuckle, the Guardian invited them to walk with her in the shrine's well-tended garden. She told how the festival on Nu Terra V had become so famous that people from all over the galaxy would come to celebrate, bringing their money with them. As the shrines and the population grew ever wealthier from these annual events, it wasn't long before the world's leaders decided to extend the festival, first by an extra week, and within a decade by another month, until finally, Nu Terra V celebrated Earth Day year-round.

"This was just the beginning," Octavia continued as they reached the high-ceilinged sanctuary at the shrine's heart. Beautiful, animated 3D images of Earth and the Sol system hung in the air of the polished ivory room. "It didn't take long for the corporations to see how much money could be made by throwing their hats into the Earth Day ring. And the world leaders, already wealthier than our ancestors could have ever dreamed, saw the opportunity offered by corporate partnerships. They let the wolves in the door."

The Warden folded his arms across his chest. "In less than a century those partnerships turned into buyouts... turned into that out there."

Octavia looked at the slow-spinning holographic Earth and smiled sadly. "Yes. And now we are the last independent shrine on this planet... But not for long."

The Warden raised his chin. "How's that?"

"The land upon which the shrine sits is owned by the original colonial charter, held in trust. That trust recently dissolved when the local government transitioned into the Deeznu Corporate Zone. We have three days left to raise seven million credits in order to purchase the land, or the Deeznu Corporation will annex it. Then this shrine will go the way of all the others, just another money-making attraction."

"Three days." The Warden rubbed his chin. "Earth Day. That's why you're putting on the pageant."

Octavia nodded. "It's our last hope. So far we've raised almost sixty thousand credits, but we are running out of time."

The Warden exchanged glances with Quantum. The alien gave a resigned shrug. "What can we do to help?"

A volunteer stepped into the well chamber. "Octavia? A lady from the press is here to see you."

The Guardian smiled. "As it happens, your arrival is quite timely. We need the media to help spread the word far and wide about our pageant. Perhaps you could share your memories of what Earth Day once meant with our visiting journalist?"

"Be happy to. And Quantum and I know our way around hand tools, so we can pitch in with the chores."

"Thank you both so much." Octavia led them to the courtyard where a blonde woman in a stylish green jumpsuit stood in the glow of a hovering cam-bot's lights, speaking with a pair of volunteers. "After I've talked with her, I'll send her your way."

The Warden nodded at Quantum. "Well, let's get to work."

"Absolutely. I often crave manual labor while on vacation. I find it far more relaxing than enjoying a good meal or taking in the local entertainment and scenery..."

Sometime later, as the Warden and Quantum raised a platform on the finished stage, the reporter came by. In a whiskey voice more suited to the blues than broadcasting, she said, "Hello. I'm Danica King, with the Intergalactic News Service. Might I ask you some questions?"

"Certainly." The Warden hopped down from the stage, smiling at the attractive woman. Her eyes were the same shade of emerald as her jumpsuit and her crooked smile was just this side of perfect, making her seem more like the girl next door than an unapproachable media goddess. "We'd be happy to talk to you."

Miss King motioned the cam-bot into position where its bulbs painted them in brighter hues. Turning to face the artificial eye, she said, "I've got a surprise guest here at the Earth Shrine on Nu Terra V. Rumored to be the Last Star Warden, this mysterious man has volunteered to help with the preparations for a *traditional* Earth Day celebration."

The way she stressed "traditional" gave the Warden pause, as if she were about to tell a joke. One he wouldn't like. "Yes, that's correct. I brought my friend Quantum to show him an Earth Day Festival like the last time I was here. But... quite a lot has changed since then."

Miss King continued to smile. "So, that would have been when, exactly? Is it true what the rumors coming out of the Frontier are saying about you? That you were lost in time for over a century?"

The Warden nodded. "That about sums it up. Yes."

She turned back to the camera with the equivalent of a wink. "So, you admit to being behind the times, then. What, in your opinion, could an old-school Earth Day pageant possibly offer to a modern audience? What can the shrine present to people used to 4D holographic projection screens and VHD surround sound home theaters? How can untrained volunteers possibly put on a better show than professionally-rendered CGI characters voiced and performed by award-winning artists?"

The Warden cleared his throat. But the young lady was spared his intended lecture by a disturbance at the front gate. Five big men in dark clothing forced their way into the courtyard. They wore respirators over the lower parts of their faces and carried heavy sledges in their hands.

"Everybody out!" one of the men shouted. "Get out!"

The volunteers that hadn't been flattened in the initial invasion scattered. Octavia moved to confront the men. "What do you want? We don't keep money here, and our artifacts aren't worth much by modern standards."

The Warden and Quantum hurried to join her, though both had replaced their gun belts with tool belts. "You guys are in the wrong place," the Warden said. "That is, unless you came to help us build sets for the pageant. In that case, glad to have you."

The leader extended his hammer at the Warden's face. "Ain't going to be no pageant, stranger. So you and your blue pal best shove off before we make an example of you. Stay out of our way and nobody needs to get hurt."

The Warden glanced at Octavia. "Guardian, you might want to get your people to cover. This is about to get ugly."

And it did.

The Warden and Quantum waded into the sledge-wielding thugs like a pair of rock crushers. Unarmed as they were, the two veterans of the Space-Time War were more than a match for ruffians used to intimidating folks by sheer size and swagger alone. In a matter of minutes, the five men tucked tail and ran or limped out of the shrine.

"Shall we pursue them?" Quantum asked, dusting blood from his knuckles.

"No. Doesn't take a genius to figure they were hired by Deeznu. Probably freelance muscle paid in cash so as to leave no paper trail, no legal strings. Nobody else has a motive to prevent the pageant."

The Warden rubbed a growing bruise on his square jaw as he surveyed the damage. The men had made use of their superior numbers to keep the Warden and Quantum occupied while still managing to destroy a significant portion of the sets and decorations. "Looks like we won the fight but lost the war."

Octavia and the volunteers walked through the wreckage, hollow and broken expressions on their faces. "There's no time," the Guardian said quietly. "There's no time to start over. And our coffers are bare..."

Danica King and her hovering cam-bot stepped close to the Warden. "What will you do now?"

He scowled, not having a good answer. "Something. I don't know what yet, but something. We're not quitting."

At least he had the satisfaction of seeing Danica King without a jaded smirk on her face.

* * *

"I cannot believe every store in this zone refuses our commerce," Quantum said. "Almost as much as I cannot believe your offer to replace the damaged sets out of our dwindling funds."

The Warden shrugged. After the row, they had helped Octavia and the volunteers make the most of the aftermath. Danica had departed to edit her footage. "I'm not surprised. Deeznu has an effective monopoly here. Word is out that we're trying to help the shrine, which is directly opposing the corporation's agenda. Hence we'll have to go further afield to buy new materials. I'll take the *Ranger* back up to the freighters and buy a commerce pass to another corporate zone. In the meantime, see what you can do here."

"Very well. Just try to stay out of trouble..."

At the starport, the Warden was unpleasantly surprised to find someone waiting for him on the *Ranger VII*'s launch pad. "Can I help you, Miss King? I thought you'd have gotten enough footage at the shrine to finish your hit piece on 'old-school' traditions."

"I suppose I deserve that. But I'd like to know more. More about you, certainly, but also more about what's going on here. I'll admit the only reason I came to Nu Terra V was to interview you, and I couldn't care less about the shrine or the festival. But now—"

"How did you know I'd be here?" The Warden paused before climbing the gangplank.

The reporter gave a small smile. "Let me go with you and I'll tell you what I know. Then you can fill in the gaps. Maybe together we can see the bigger picture."

The Warden frowned, gave a curt nod. "Come on. But this'll be a short flight. Even shorter if I think you're trying to play me."

"Fair enough."

As they strapped in and the Warden began the pre-flight system checks, Danica said, "I heard you say something about those thugs working for Deeznu. What if I said you were wrong about that?"

The Warden raised an eyebrow beneath his visor. "Okay. You've got my attention."

"I believe they may have been hired by Argonaut. The same company that, technically, I work for. INS is a subsidiary of Argos Entertainment, which is a branch of the uber corporation. Somebody at Argos sent me the tip about your ship entering the corporate blockade. By the time I entered the system, they had fed me the info about you looking into the Earth Shrine situation."

Firing up the *Ranger VII*'s rocket thrusters for liftoff, the Warden said. "Why would Argonaut want the pageant to fail if Deeznu will reap the benefits?"

Danica visibly struggled against the G-forces as the ship rose from the launch pad and climbed into the planet's atmosphere. "Because... they want me to paint Deeznu as the big bad in a David vs. Goliath story... If Deeznu is tied up in a PR fiasco during the height of the shopping season... it could mean a windfall for Argonaut's final fiscal quarter of the year."

The Warden chewed on this, but not for long. Blaster bolts arced past the ship.

"Looks like whoever sent those thugs to the shrine just upped their game and their budget." Blue sky faded into eternal night as he pushed the ship higher into the upper atmosphere. The *Ranger VII* was designed for space flight and combat, whereas the attacker was a sub-orbital gunship, built for air support and dogfights in terrestrial warfare. "Strange to find one of those on a planet dedicated to commerce and entertainment."

Danica turned a lighter shade. "You really have no clue just how cutthroat the corporate wars are, do you?"

"Nope." The Warden pulled the yoke hard, knifing across the climbing attacker's path. The enemy craft fired again, but the *Ranger VII* spiraled and accelerated, moving between the fiery bolts without taking so much as a scratch.

When the gunship maneuvered to reacquire a pursuit angle, it turned onto its back, seemed to freeze in midair, and fell in a widening spiral. The sudden shift in G-forces coupled with the change in atmospheric pressures stalled the sky-ship's engines.

The Warden pushed the *Ranger VII* into a nosedive, chasing the falling craft back into the lower atmosphere at supersonic speeds.

Danica spoke through clenched teeth. "What are you doing? You're going to get us killed!"

The Warden focused on the target. "Got to get close enough to fire grapple lines so we can stop that fall. If that ship hits anywhere populated, it might as well be a bomb."

The plummeting ship's pilot didn't help matters. Panicked or discombobulated, his attempts to regain control only caused the craft to behave more erratically.

A voice came over the ship's coms: "*Ranger VII*, this is DCZ air-traffic control. Break off your approach or we will fire on you."

"Sorry, DCZ control. If I do that, a lot of folks down there are about to have a very bad day." Ignoring the sweat crowding the corners of his eyes, the Warden continued to accelerate until the targeting computer locked onto the falling ship.

Flicking the fire-control and hitting the trigger, he sent four harpoons trailing uru-tetsumite grapple lines into the target's hull. One of these carried a small EMP charge, shutting down the gunship's engines and controls.

"Got him!"

* * *

In a wide, marsh-edged clearing several kilometers from the DCZ, the Warden and Danica pulled the pilot from the rescued ship. Though he wasn't happy about the minor damage to his craft, the man was grateful his intended targets had saved his life.

In response to Danica's questions, the mercenary admitted, "I was hired through back channels to harass you on takeoff. Just a show of force to scare you away from the planet. I sure wasn't expecting to engage in a dogfight."

The Warden nodded. "You were paid in cash. I assume by Argonaut."

The pilot scoffed. "Doubtful. Those guys hate my guts. I used to work for them when I did legit jobs. They blackballed me. If I had to guess, I'd say it was Deeznu or Kronos-Wagner. Nobody else can afford me." He turned at the approach of wailing sirens. "But I guess we'll have plenty of time to discuss this on the way to lockup."

The Warden looked at the approaching patrol skimmers. "Miss King, would you be so kind as to relay a message to my friend Quantum? Can you tell him I managed to find that trouble he warned me to stay out of?"

Danica frowned. "But you're supposed to be a lawman. They can't take you in for this. We were attacked!"

The Warden smiled. "I've no jurisdiction here in the Civilized Worlds, and I wouldn't go so far as to call the system they've got here law, exactly." He watched as the flashing lights came closer. "You know, I used to love this place, even though I'd only ever been here once before. But that one visit, that one Earth Day Festival has stuck with me ever since...

"The camaraderie and good cheer, the *happiness*... It all reminded me what it means to be a member of the human race, to be a part of something so big, so different, and so important. It reminded me how no matter how bad things can get, how bad *we* can get, there's still a goodness in our nature... a love for one another that's always just beneath the surface, waiting to extend a helping hand, offer a kind word, or a supportive shoulder. Sometimes all we need is that reminder, and the Earth Day Festival was that for me."

He looked at Danica, noticing the hovering cam-bot for the first time. "But then, I'm just an old-fashioned kind of guy."

When the corporate enforcement officers arrived, the Warden raised his hands in surrender.

* * *

"Hope you've got a nice little nest egg put aside, Warden." The gunship pilot sat across from him in the prisoner transport. Both wore gravity shackles on their wrists. "They'll probably sentence us to some pretty hefty fines in the morning. Maybe even impound our ships. If you can't pay, then it'll be indentured servitude for the rest of your life."

"Nice." The Warden sighed. What he wouldn't give to be facing down a flotilla of space pirates at that moment. But then, he realized with a chuckle, in a way he was. Only these pirates had not only plundered goods and property, they had pillaged the entire system of law and governance. How did the notions of right and wrong work when the very structures intended to safeguard society had been so corrupted?

He could only hope that Danica would have a change of heart and use her media resources and influence to do something about the pageant. If Octavia and the Earth Shrine won this fight against Deeznu, it all might actually be worth it.

The Warden's only regret was that Quantum could be stranded in this den of greed without a ship and without a friend who understood him. Even if the Warden spent the rest of his days slaving away in a factory or digging in a mine, he would be surrounded by others of his own kind. Quantum, forever separated from his own dimension, would always be alone...

After the hours-long processing (made even longer by his complete absence from any database known to the modern world), the Warden, aka John Doe 42, was finally ushered into a small holding cell on the thirty-fourth floor of the detention center. His small window looked out over Commerce Square, the heart of the downtown corporate zone. The wink and flash of neon advertisements colored the tiny room with multitudinous hues in a hypnotic rhythm. The roaring sound of countless overlapping ditties, skimmer horns, shouts, and general street cacophony eventually turned into a mind-numbing susurrus.

Stretching out on the hard bunk, the Warden stared at the ceiling tiles until he dozed off.

* * *

He was awakened by the sound of his own voice: "...offer a kind word, or a supportive shoulder. Sometimes all we need is that reminder, and the Earth Day Festival was that for me." Only his words came from outside his cell window.

Standing on his bunk, the Warden was surprised to see his own visored face staring back at him from the big holographic billboard dominating Commerce Square. Danica had uploaded his speech, and the network was broadcasting it across the major channels.

The Warden watched as scores of early shoppers stopped and stared at his projected image, listened to his recorded words. When the speech was replaced by an ad for a new sports drink, the crowds returned to their business. A half hour later, his speech played again. This time the crowds were bigger, and the pause was longer. The cycle repeated twice more before a guard came to his cell.

"Sorry, fella. But your hearing's been postponed." The uniformed man placed a prefabricated meal on the small table beside the bunk. "Something about the bigwigs getting their heads together."

The Warden ate the tasteless breakfast and listened to the advertisements punctuated by his brief oration. By lunchtime, he noticed that less noise came from the square. Taking another look from the window, he saw that the crowds had thinned out to the point that actually using the word "crowd" could be considered an exaggeration.

By dinner, Commerce Square was a ghost town. The hypnotic sales pitches played to an empty house.

The Warden felt somehow optimistic as he settled in for the night.

* * *

He was awakened hours later by something he thought he'd never hear again. In fact, at first he thought he was dreaming, remembering. It was a carol. An old

Earth Day carol extolling the virtues of brotherly-love, charity, unity, and compassion. The carol was sung by the loveliest soprano voice he'd ever heard. It was coming from outside, in Commerce Square.

The Warden got up, stood on his bunk and looked through the window. Guardian Octavia's face, twenty-feet tall, stared back at him from the titanic billboard across the way. She sang the carol. But she was not the only one. Far below, on the streets and sidewalks, a multitude of others joined in.

The sun was rising on Earth Day.

The Warden saw his own visored face on some of the smaller display screens in shop windows along the thoroughfare. His speech was still being aired.

Another voice with a familiar whiskey-blues sound joined the carol, only this came from somewhere outside the cell. The Warden turned as the door opened to find the security officer standing beside Quantum and the singing Danica King. All were smiling, even the guard.

"I don't understand," the Warden said.

"Your fine has been paid." The guard held out the Warden's gun belt and blasters. "And your ship is no longer impounded."

Quantum raised a data pad displaying the official paperwork. "You have Miss King to thank."

Danica looked a bit bashful. "I wouldn't say that. Let's just say that the folks of Nu Terra V are just as generous and good-natured as they've always been. They just needed someone to remind them of that fact. And that someone was you, Warden."

The Warden smiled as he buckled on his guns. "You ran a story championing the Earth Shrine's pageant."

Quantum's antennae whirred. "She did more than that. The story suggested that people all across the galaxy abstain from any commerce whatsoever to show their support for the Earth Shrine and the 'true meaning of the Earth Day Festival.'"

"In less than twelve hours following the story's release, stock prices began to plummet across the board. By hitting them where it hurts, Miss King shamed the corporations into realizing what they had done to the entire festival, and by extension, the planet."

"Argonaut paid for your and the *Ranger VII*'s release." Danica took the Warden by the arm and led him from the cell. "And Kronos-Wagner put up the seven million to donate the land to the Earth Shrine. With that kind of PR *coup de grâce* stacked against them, Deeznu had no choice but to foot the bill for the pageant and its marketing. As I understand it, folks from all over the galaxy will be coming for the next week to experience a good, *old-fashioned* Earth Day Festival."

Stepping out of the detention center and onto the street crowded with hundreds of singing people, the Warden was astounded by the stark contrast with the day of his arrival. The crisp morning air smelled of sweet baked goods and warm cider. A total stranger smiled and slapped him on the back as he passed, shouting "Be blessed, brother!" Another grasped his hand in both of hers and wished him a "Happy Earth Day! And thank you so much!"

Quantum leaned close. "So, are all human celebrations like this?"

The Warden laughed. "For the most part, though the frequency of fisticuffs and incarceration varies from household to household."

THE END OF AN ERA

GREGORY L. NORRIS

The end came as the prisoners of the island prepared for the Winter Candlemass Carnival. A lone whirlybird touched down on Sugar Beach, at the same level spot where other delegations had landed in previous years. Alone, the Captain strolled out to meet the representative from the Anarchic States government, which had banished the 311 men and women to the desolate lesser atoll, once known as Lost Hope. It had been renamed Samer Island following the forced relocation.

The Anarchic officer identified himself as Commandant Mallette. He was younger than his predecessor, Commandant Bordine. The Captain didn't offer his hand. Mallette likely wouldn't have accepted the gesture anyway. Birchard's respect multiplied for the Captain, who had once stood before a tribunal of his superiors, dressed in his crisp Anarchic military uniform with its brass buttons, and had proudly declared himself a Samer.

Birchard Trent, Lady Judith Rathburn, and Joseph Rhodes watched the two men advance toward the iron gate surrounding the village. Anarchic sharpshooters tracked them with their rifles from the beach. Others in the community trusted with stringing strands of golden-white lights among the calliope horses and carnival rides halted their work. Some halted their play. A unicycle twice Joseph's height—and Joseph was a tall man at six-foot-three—skidded to an awkward stop. Its driver, attired in top hat, amethyst goggles, and a fetching pea coat with a purple fringe of epaulettes, gracefully dismounted and assumed a defensive pose with arms crossed.

"At ease," the Captain said as he and Mallette passed by.

The man stepped back. The Captain and Commandant Mallette strolled through the moat of towering black iron fence and into the village at the island's center.

"Sycophant," Lady Judith hissed under her breath.

"Agreed," said Joseph, a man of few words.

"Shhh," Birchard admonished. "I'm trying to listen."

The small device secreted in his left ear, aimed at the Anarchic commandant and the unofficial leader of their society, picked up the gist of a seemingly normal conversation.

"Impressive, Captain Corvallis," said Mallette. "I'd read the report and heard the stories, but I never imagined you'd accomplished so much here in so short a time on Lost Hope."

"*Samer* Island," the Captain corrected.

Mallette flashed a slippery grin, revealing a length of perfect white teeth that made the gesture seem more snarl than smile. "I stand corrected."

The Anarchic States commandant gazed across the brick downtown, at the carnival rides being readied, and up at the clock tower at the center of the town square, quietly tolling the passage of time. Billows of steam swept around the village, whistling out of storm drain covers set at intervals in the cobblestones and iron chimneys.

"It's a magnificent tribute to your innovation," Mallette continued.

"When living on an island and surrounded by water, wise folk use the resource most readily available to them," the Captain said. "There are many wise minds here."

"No doubt," Mallette said. "Thank you, Captain, for what has been a very enlightening visit."

"Likewise."

He walked Mallette back to Sugar Beach and the whirlybird. Calmly, the Captain waited for them to depart. The whirlybird made a pass over the village, banked to starboard, and then headed out over the gray winter ocean. Once the flying machine was gone from sight, the Captain turned and marched back through the iron gate, and one didn't need an earpiece or a telescopic monocle to understand that their situation had never been graver.

"As we suspected," the Captain said grimly to the waiting crowd. "They're close by. That flying machine is only capable of short-range travel. It would not surprise me to discover they've committed an entire battle group to their effort."

As it turned out, their oppressors had sent *two*.

* * *

Birchard studied Joseph as the other man leaned over and gazed into the powerful brass telescope. Joseph James Rhodes was, in Birchard's estimation, the handsomest man on the island. *On this island Earth*, he thought, cracking a weak smile. On the secret observation deck hidden behind the giant clock face, Birchard caught a hint of Joseph's clean, masculine scent among the gear oil and the warm billows of salty steam. Joseph's vintage leather coat rode up enough to show a teaspoon of lower back and the elastic waistband of his underwear. Old combat boots and uniform pants completed the picture.

"There they are, like the Captain said they would be."

Joseph righted. Despite his fear that the Anarchic States military was returned to finish what they'd started five years earlier when the last convicted Samers were relocated to Lost Hope following the Stonewall Massacres, Birchard's heart galloped for another reason. Joseph's dark cowlicks and emerald gemstone eyes gave him the energy to look. Birchard aimed his right eye into the telescope's viewer. The battle group lolled at the limit of the horizon, two carriers and numerous escort ships.

"Oh my Goddess. How many attack planes?" he asked.

"A lot."

Before he had been forced to confess, Joseph, like the Captain, had served in the Anarchic States military. A former aircraft mechanic, he would know the exact numbers.

Birchard closed his eyes and straightened. When he dared to look again, Joseph was there, and Birchard wanted to believe everything would be all right. Only it wasn't, and the borrowed time they'd all been living on since Stonewall, when politicians and a dictatorship turned prejudice into policy, would soon expire.

"We don't have long," Birchard said.

Joseph said nothing, only fixed him with a wounded look and nodded.

Birchard wanted reassurance and to reassure. *I love you, Joseph*, he tried to say, but like the ex-military man of few words, Birchard's tongue stilled. A cold winter wind cycloned around the clock tower, and the forces dispatched to cleanse the island of all life moved closer.

* * *

A lilting, melancholy melody drifted out of Lady Judith's cottage, a one-story structure at the edge of the village within clear view of the sheltered lagoon between Sugar Beach and the rocky headlands.

Birchard approached the front door, which was decorated in a mosaic of seashells and bright red holly berries, a sharp contrast to the moody music issuing from inside the cottage. He hesitated from knocking but eventually did. Lady Judith answered the door dressed in a frayed kimono. Eyeliner made from wood ashes had dripped down her face on a cascade of dark tears.

"Birchard," she said, her voice deeper than usual.

Birchard forced a smile. "If this is a bad time..."

Lady Judith answered with a humorless giggle. "Actually, it's a great time. I'm trying to decide on what to keep and what to toss. Come on in."

Birchard entered the house. The once-elegant artwork Judith had been renowned for in her other life, pre-island, which had been smuggled over along with her wardrobe and her music, lay in tatters at the center of the plank floor. So, too, were most of Lady Judith's elegant stage clothes.

"Why?" he asked.

She parroted Birchard's question in response.

"Lady Judith?"

"They're coming back here to slay everyone on their little island ghetto. Perhaps they want your technology, to study what we've accomplished here—the smelting plant, the mechanics of steam. They'll pick through the rubble for anything of value. Original Judith Rathburn paintings still command a high price in the art world, out there." Her blackened eyes took on a distant look before also darkening on the insides. "I'd destroy my art rather than allow it to pass into their bloodied clutches."

"Judith," Birchard started, reaching for her shoulder.

Judith pulled away. Her kimono slipped, and the ugly scar she had been branded with during the days leading up to the relocation became visible. Birchard had seen the burn mark once, very briefly, some seasons back on Sugar Beach. Every day since, the scar had remained out of sight, hidden behind exquisite couture, the last gasp of modesty of a famous creature loved and worshipped by many men, despised by others. That she left the kimono as it was without moving to cover the scar stunned Birchard almost as much as the nightmare brewing off the island's shore.

"I don't care about art, not today," Judith said. "Can you imagine what it was like that day when they stormed into my home, when they set my studio on fire?"

Birchard started to speak but the question, he soon realized, had been posed to the walls, knowing they wouldn't answer.

"They should have killed me then, as they killed Phillipe when he tried to put out the flames. No, instead they dropped me here, an artist with no canvases, no paints nor brushes; a cross-dresser without her Phillipe."

"The Captain has called a meeting in the town square to discuss the carnival."

"The carnival," Lady Judith huffed.

In that moment, her uncommon beauty vanished, and the five years of life on Samer Island heaped onto what she had already suffered caught up, showing clearly in her features, upon her shoulders.

"We have to prepare," Birchard said. "*All* of us, you included."

"I believe that I was." Judith spread her arms, indicating the carnage. "Even if we are to make a run to safety, even then, I know space will be tight, and there are but a few things I wish to bring with me."

Now, Judith seemed willing to invite conversation.

"What things, Lady Judith?" Birchard asked.

Judith plodded into the bedroom. She returned with a swatch of bright purple satin. "Only these. Bold admirers of mine went back, after the Anarchic soldiers left and the fire burned down."

She rolled the cloth between her hands. An oaken, hollow noise rippled through the room and clawed at Birchard's ears.

"Phillipe," said Lady Judith. "I won't leave his bones behind in this cursed place."

* * *

"It is brilliant," said Joseph.

The haunted atmosphere that had followed Birchard since his visit to Lady Judith's cottage on the beach lifted some. He focused on the other man's voice. Joseph, handsome Joseph, stood with his arms folded and was following the test run of the amusement rides the way a cat might a bird or a traveling beam of light, partially hypnotized by raw excitement.

Joseph blinked himself out of the trance and turned away from the amusement park jets making passes around a course on heavy cables and the towering rockets rocketing on circular tracks. Their eyes met and, for the thousandth time, Birchard felt a lesser version of the same spark that had given life to the universe explode within his heart.

"*You're* brilliant," Joseph said.

Birchard stepped closer. The tears he'd barely kept in check at Judith's and after, during this final test of the carnival rides, drove past his barriers. The tears fell suddenly, in torrents. The hard look on Joseph's face softened, as much as a man like Joseph was capable. He growled Birchard's name and extended both hands.

Birchard met him halfway. "I love you," he whispered into the shoulder of Joseph's coat.

"Yeah, me, too," Joseph said.

Birchard gazed up. The barest of smiles cracked Joseph's game face, his war mask.

"Yeah," Joseph repeated, nodding. The warmth and strength of his embrace drove out most of the day's chill. The love in Joseph's twin emerald eyes vanquished the rest. Then Joseph leaned forward, and they kissed.

Somewhere in the distance, a fighter jet screamed across the winter sky.

* * *

The Captain took to the podium. His eyes scanned the crowd. With his heart attempting to throw itself up his throat, Birchard had done the same, taking count of heads, goggles, and hats. The Captain made 311. The entire community was present.

The brass bullhorn fixed into the podium broadcast a sharp whine ahead of the Captain's voice.

"People of Samer Island, my fellow, proud Samers," he began. "Behind us lies the humiliation, the persecution, and the atrocities forced upon us all by the Anarchic States following the events at Stonewall. Knowing this day would eventually come, we have lived our lives the best we could, under far from ideal circumstances. I doubt I alone won't miss the endless meals of salted fish and grilled seaweed."

Enough good-natured laughs and a few amens sounded from the crowd, breaking apart the ominous pall that hung over the carnival grounds.

"We knew our oppressors would return, and also that when they did, it would be to deliver one final stroke of pain and bloodshed. But we will show them that we are not sheep, we are not easy victims. We are the best minds, the most talented artists, and the noblest of lion-hearted warriors this world has ever known. And we will prevail."

"How?" someone asked. To Birchard's ear, the voice sounded like Lady Judith's.

"Because we must," the Captain said.

The fingers of Birchard's left hand wandered and found warmth in another, stronger set. Joseph's intertwined with his.

"We *must.*"

Applause sounded, sparse at first. Others joined in, and the level surged to cacophonous, echoing across Sugar Beach and out across the water, in the direction of the approaching storm. It was the first time since preparations for the winter carnival began that Birchard felt a true measure of hope. His grip on Joseph's hand tightened.

"The hours are short," the Captain continued after the applause powered down. "We'll need everyone's help on final preparations for the carnival, so without further delay, let's make this one for the history books that *will* be written in favor of a handful of Samers who prevailed against the merciless Anarchic States and their war machine."

* * *

Birchard Trent, who had excelled in numerous fields of technology and science at an early age before the relocation, marched with Joseph into the heart of the clock tower. They walked among the gigantic gears and springs to the core, where the energy controls feeding power across the island into homes, businesses and, most importantly, the carnival, were housed.

The Captain stood at the power board, illuminated by the ghostly golden-blue light arcing between the two pylons secretly located in the belfry. The clock tolled five on an overcast December Saturday, the last day that Samers would spend on Lost Hope, a ferrous atoll whose oxidized landscape lay rusty with the color of spilled blood.

A hand-drawn map of Samer Island stood on an easel. Representations of the naval ships they had spotted through the telescope were marked and plotted. The Anarchic States had surrounded them effectively.

Birchard tore his eyes away from the rudimentary sea vessels and instead focused on the concentric circles he, himself, had only recently added to the map in black from one of Lady Judith's eyeliner pencils. The largest circle traveled almost to the edges of the map, well past the Anarchic naval fleet. The others tightened around the island. The bull's eye was within the iron moat surrounding the village, the clock tower at its dead center.

"I thought it fitting that you should throw the switch," the Captain said.

Birchard reached a trembling hand toward the control.

"Time?" asked Joseph.

Birchard glanced at the countdown clock. "T-minus twenty seconds."

The clock ticked down, the last ten almost the longest of his life, overshadowed only by the ugly moment when he'd been dragged across campus blindfolded, his name on the seditions list. Then, Birchard was sure that he was going to be shot like so many others. Those seconds had dragged past slower.

The last of the twenty ran out. Birchard turned the brass switch. The energy crackling between the pylons altered. One side dimmed, while the other glowed twice as brightly. Across the island, lights went out inside bungalows, cottages, and establishments. For an instant, only the clock tower defied the snow-swept darkness.

And then an effulgence of golden light rose up from the carnival grounds and into the overcast sky, a bright beacon proclaiming that the Winter Candlemass Carnival had begun, and a clear target to the enemy jet fighters that were, even then, launching en masse for the slaughter.

* * *

A million golden lights, their bulbs blown from grains of sand meticulously harvested from Sugar Beach, formed constellations around the rocket rides and the jet planes. Calliope horses that Lady Judith had designed and carved from driftwood with the help of numerous other hands galloped around the track to an organ's thrumming beat. Steam billowed. Snow fell. Music and lights defied the approaching storm.

Concession vendors handed out treats to each carnival goer: honey cakes with dried berries wrapped in pale paper painstakingly crafted from bark, crisp water bottled in bottles that had washed ashore over the years or that were smuggled in by the admirers who braved Anarchic blockades of the island, deep-fried fish, golden brown and nourishing.

Each person took their treats and entered the lines, some to the rocket rides, the rest to the jets. The calliope horses raced in an endless circle without riders.

The organ music pumped, striking Birchard's ear like a dirge; a funeral song for the prisoners of Samer Island.

* * *

Four dozen warplanes launched from the decks of the monstrous naval platforms that had hemmed in the island, effectively cutting off the seventy-odd acres of rock that had, in five years time, given rise to a technologically advanced community. The war planes assumed a staggered-wing formation and were ordered to open fire, to level everything and destroy everyone, every last aberrant Samer.

* * *

Lights appeared on the horizon, cold white lights and lights the color of blood. The lights grew brighter as the swarm moved closer.

"Here they come," the Captain bellowed. "Move quickly people. Quickly and orderly."

Whimpers and one shrill scream rose in counterpoint against the calliope's dirge. Birchard stood beside Joseph at the back of the line to the rocket ride, waiting for the last of the designated passengers to board. The lights in the sky grew brighter. Joseph's face, Birchard noted, had hardened once more, but gone was his fear. Now, there was only anger and determination in his expression.

Birchard glanced over to the ten jets on the jet ride. The Captain was helping the last of those designated passengers onboard—Lady Judith, who cradled the swaddle of purple satin in her hands. Despite the magnitude of the moment, he was patient and gentlemanly with her, and, even at the distance, Birchard saw very clearly the spark of something bigger between them that hadn't been able to ignite before, shining now as vibrantly as the million lights of their winter carnival.

The Captain and Lady Judith boarded their jet. Birchard and Joseph hurried up the ramp to their rocket. Inside, the passengers had strapped in and cradled their most beloved possessions. A black and white cat named Ozzie poked her head out of the neck of an older gentleman's heavy trench coat.

"We're going to be okay," Birchard said to Ozzie's protector, who'd once been a poet in that lost life before Samer Island.

He and Birchard raced up the aisle and into the cockpit. Joseph quickly assumed the pilot's controls. Birchard moved before the cranks and the levers, the buttons and bright diodes of the control board linked to the clock tower.

"Do it," Joseph urged. "Punch it, before they get any closer!"

Birchard spun corkscrewing cranks, stepped on pedals, and flipped toggles, a mad sequence of movements, but the proper one. "I'm doing it," he said, keying in the final directive.

The unit puffed steam. Birchard waited for the big green glass button at the center of the console to light. *Green*, though nowhere near the intense color of

Joseph's eyes. It did. He punched it.

Nothing happened. The lights outside swarmed closer.

Eyes wide and unblinking, Birchard muttered an expletive and ran the sequence again, only to suffer the same results.

"*Birch*," Joseph grumbled, the panic in his voice rising, obvious. "The air over our heads is about to fill up with an awful lot of Anarchic warplanes."

Birchard turned. "There's something wrong between here and the clock tower. I'll need to activate the defense manually."

He started back toward the hatch. Joseph caught his arm as he tried to pass. "You can't. I won't leave you behind."

Birchard spun around, seized Joseph's handsome face between his hands, and kissed him. "You have to," he said when their lips parted. "For *them*."

With a tip of his chin, Birchard indicated the thirty other souls strapped into their seats. He pulled free of Joseph. One final glance, and he was gone.

* * *

A sound like thunder crackled through the snowy sky, the unmistakable battle cry of angry birds streaking in formation to attack. The funeral music from the calliope horses had evaporated; Birchard knew by the image of the static merry-go-round that the malfunction originated there, below the circling gears and treads that had been set up to disguise the true nature of their operation to the eyes of satellites and drones. The circling power source had stopped its revolutions. Something in the treads, a gear or rough section of iron pipe, had cut the line to the clock tower. It made ironic sense when Birchard stopped to consider the morbid melody, a funeral song. If he didn't activate their great defense manually and soon, no one would make it off Samer Island. All would die here.

He ran through the lights and the wind-stirred curtains of powdery white, not fully realizing that he would likely not survive the coming barrage or that, if he did, he'd be left behind here, alone on the island. He only thought of the others—the Captain, Lady Judith, and especially Joseph—and crossed the distance to the clock tower, whose face he would always remember had stopped at 5:11. It was the end of an era.

Deafening screams tore across the sky. The atmosphere inside the clock tower was no less turbulent. Energy pulsed through the air, making it ripple under the stress of the massive power being pumped through conduits and conveyers. Steam hissed from vents, enough to cloud the way to the defense controls.

Joseph. Suddenly, tears spilled out of Birchard's eyes, adding to his confusion. He'd taken this same course through the gears, toward the pylons, thousands of times. He could find his way asleep, or blind. But thoughts of never seeing Joseph again threatened to paralyze him.

The clock tower trembled. The lone pylon channeling energy into the carnival crackled with a blinding nimbus of golden light, blue around the edges. Sparks showered down from that smaller but no less spectacular version of the sun.

Steeling himself, Birchard wiped his eyes on his sleeve and soldiered forward. For Joseph. For the Samers. The pylon would shake itself apart if he didn't act soon and discharge the prominence. Were that to happen, they wouldn't need to worry about the attack by warplanes—the explosion would take out all of Samer Island. While approaching the control board, Birchard prayed to Brigid, to the Saints, to the Goddess or God or whatever other deity might be up there listening. He invoked Joseph's name. That seemed to do it.

Birchard came out of the fog and found himself standing directly before the manual defense controls. He quickly ran through the proper sequence of toggles and whirls and reached both hands toward the all-important green glass button.

"For you Joseph, my love."

Birchard punched the button. Nothing happened.

And then, something did.

The destructive energy crackling around the pylon stabilized. A golden effulgence of light formed at the apex of the construct, a sun as bright and beautiful as anything ever seen in the sky. The sun danced at the top of the pylon, radiant and lovely, a vision from mythology, a gift from the gods. There one moment and gone the next, the sun turned black, becoming a toy of the devil.

The black sun went nova, fanning out around the pylon like a vast dark ring tossed around a pike. Racing downward, the energy shot into the conduits and channels underground. The clock tower quaked with its passing, the disturbance powerful enough to knock Birchard off his feet. While on the floor, he imagined what would happen in short order, this insane plan they'd initiated so long ago.

He was right.

Warplanes streaked toward the island, readying to strafe the carnival grounds. The naval fleet surged closer to the shore.

The energy slammed into the ground, traveled through conduits, and into the moat of iron gates surrounding the village. The electromagnetic pulse then surged upward, into the sky, catching the planes upon their approach. Targeting systems shorted out. Avionics followed. Warplanes tumbled out of the sky.

The E-M pulse continued outward and slammed into the naval fleet. Lights went dark. Vessels broke formation and fell off course. Some collided.

Birchard picked himself up. "Go," he shouted out loud. "Get out of here, now— *escape!*"

* * *

The E-M pulse had turned the world dark everywhere, except for the carnival.

"It worked," Joseph whispered. "The pulse knocked out their technology, but not ours, not *the steam!*" He punched in the proper ignition sequence. The rocket trembled. "Hold on, everyone," Joseph called out. "Here we go!"

Jets began moving around the track and gained speed. One at a time, they detached from cables, shooting into a snowy sky no longer filled with enemy fighters. Rockets sped down their tracks, jumping them and assuming formation among the jets. The rocket piloted by Joseph soared up on a golden comet's tail.

Birchard staggered out of the clock tower in time to see the fleet formation rise triumphantly higher, above the fires and wreckage of the downed Anarchic warplanes and the scuttled sea vessels. Golden light far more spectacular than the strings wreathed around the remains of the carnival lit the sky, a tribute to the resourcefulness and determination of the Samers, who had bested their persecutors.

"Go now and live without fear," Birchard said, and though tears streamed from his eyes, a wide and happy smile lit his face.

Only they didn't go, as he implored. A lone light, one of the brightest of the comets, came down from the snow clouds. A rocket landed. The hatch trundled open. Joseph walked out.

"I won't leave you behind, and neither would the others," he said.

Birchard forced his eyes away from Joseph and up into the sky, where the effulgence of lights stood stationary.

"Come on," Joseph said.

Birchard hurried toward the hatch. Joseph pulled him into his arms, and they kissed.

"I love you," Joseph said.

Birchard rested his face in the warm spot between Joseph's neck and check. Then they boarded and the rocket rose back into the sky, where it joined the rest of the fleet high above Lost Hope.

"You didn't follow the plan," Birchard said.

From the pilot's seat, Joseph countered, "Neither did you."

Birchard hid his smile. "So now where do we go? To visit those fun-loving French? Those resolute Russians?"

"I don't think so," Joseph said. "I'm sure the Captain would agree that we stick to our original course and head south, far away from the Anarchic States, where we'll find a safe place to live and rebuild."

The beginning of this new era already seemed uncertain. But the plan had worked, and he was with Joseph, and Birchard somehow knew that all would be okay, wherever they landed.

About the Authors

Hansen Adcock is a writer of short stories and short long stories, in Lincolnshire, UK. His work has appeared in *Chaos of Hard Clay* (Banjaxed Books), and *A Land Without Mirrors* (Fluky Fiction) amongst other places online, in print, and on podcasts. He writes poetry under the name Hansen Tor Adcock, and has a novelette available on Amazon (*Damian's Dream*). He is also the editor and illustrator of *Once Upon A Crocodile* e-zine, and has fibromyalgia and hypermobile Ehlers-Danlos Syndrome. You can find him at www.facebook.com/wyrdstories, on Twitter @Erringrey, or on Pinterest—just search for Hansen Adcock.

Justin Boote is an Englishman living for over twenty years in Barcelona, working as a stressed waiter in a busy restaurant. He's been writing short horror/suspense stories for four years, and to date has published around forty in diverse magazines and anthologies. He has also co-edited and published an anthology featuring a group of writer friends called *A Discovery of Writers*. He can be found at Facebook or at his Amazon author page under the same name.

Gustavo Bondoni is an Argentine writer with over two hundred stories published in fourteen countries, in seven languages. His latest book is *Ice Station: Death* (2019). He has also published three science fiction novels: *Incursion* (2017), *Outside* (2017) and *Siege* (2016) and an ebook novella entitled *Branch*. His short fiction is collected in *Off the Beaten Path* (2019), *Tenth Orbit and Other Faraway Places* (2010), and *Virtuoso and Other Stories* (2011). In 2019, Gustavo was awarded second place in the Jim Baen Memorial Contest, and in 2018 he received a Judges Commendation (and second place) in The James White Award. He was also a 2019 finalist in the Writers of the Future Contest. His website is www.gustavobondoni.com.

Kenneth Bykerk lives and writes in the ghost town of Howells, Arizona, suburb to the slightly larger ghost town of Walker high in the pine forests of central Arizona where he raises his autistic daughter. Lucky enough to live on the land his great-grandfather worked a century before and seriously needing a hobby, a chance comment made while showing a friend the ruins of an old smelter where he would play as a child changed forever how he saw this land. The concrete was not to keep people out... Knowing where the old open shafts and the forgotten graves are found, he began to mine this land himself. The adage to write what you know applies here as Kenneth need only look out his window and wonder what happened in that old stone house across the creek or the stone well just downstream. The Tales of the Bajazid, the history of this mountain valley, spring from the histories of this land and the ruins that haunted his childhood. He at least now has a hobby. These Tales of the Bajazid have appeared in Weirdbook, Sotiera Press, Nightmare Press, Madness Heart Press, Hellbound Books, Darkhouse Books, Stormy Island Publishing, and Thuggish Itch.

Dwain Campbell is originally from Sussex, New Brunswick. After his university years in Nova Scotia, he journeyed farther east to begin a teaching career in Newfoundland. Thirty-six years later, he is semi-retired in St. John's and studies folklore in his spare time. Contemporary fantasy is his genre of choice, and Atlantic Canada is a rich source of inspiration. He is author of *Tales from the Frozen Ocean*, and has contributed stories to *Canadian Tales of the Fantastic*, *Tesseracts 17*, and *Fall into Fantasy 2018*. Neil Gaiman is his hero of the moment, though he will reluctantly admit to a lifelong fascination with Stephen King.

Laura J. Campbell is an internationally published, award-winning author whose works span from science fiction to horror to mystery. In addition to fiction, she has written non-fiction medical and legal articles. Her life goals include using every word in the English language at least once. When she is not writing, she can be found running, lifting weights, or attending rock concerts (usually featuring bands whose lead singers wear more black nail polish than she does). Laura's husband, Patrick, and children, Alexander and Samantha, put up with all of her antics. She has an Amazon page at www.amazon.com/Laura-J.-Campbell/e/B07K6SZJJ9, featuring some of her more recent literary offerings.

Gregg Chamberlain has never been to Arkham, though he understands it is an "interesting" place to visit, and the annual regatta at neighbouring Innsmouth is "unforgettable" according to the local tourism board. He lives a quiet life in rural Ontario, Canada, with his missus, Anne, and their two cats, who may or may not be from Ulthar, but are in complete charge of the household, and know that their humans know it. Gregg has several dozen short fiction credits in various speculative fiction genres, including a few select political sf satire pieces in the B Cubed Publishing *Alternative Facts* anthologies, and in the Scary Dairy Press *Terror Politico* anthology.

Currently, **Stuart Croskell** is teaching English and Drama to kids with special needs. His stories have been published by Storgy Books (print and ebook, 2019), and Owl Canyon Press (Print and ebook, 2020). His writing has been described as "strange and unsettling" (Naomi Booth, author of *Sealed*), and "weird and haunting and totally cool" (Tom Strelich, author of *Dog Logic*).

Lawrence Dagstine is a native New Yorker, video game enthusiast, toy collector, and speculative fiction writer of 20-plus years. He has placed more than 450 stories in online and print periodicals during that two-decade span, especially the small presses. He has been published by publishing outfits such as Damnation Books, Steampunk Tales, and Left-Hand Publishers. He is also author to numerous novellas and three short story collections: *Death of the Common Writer, Fresh Blood*, and *From The Depths* (TBA, with Illustrator Bob Veon). His work is available on Amazon and B&N.com. Visit his website at www.lawrencedagstine.com.

Severely beaten as a child by a WWII hero and combat-induced-PTSD stepfather, **GD Deckard**, as a teen, faced the old man down with a shotgun and earned his blessing to join the military at the time Americans were learning about a country called Vietnam. The "lazy, no good son-of-a-bitch" opted out of combat and hard labor by becoming an Air Force medic, stamping out suffering and misery on Freedom's Frontier at Clark Airbase in Southeast Asia and earning some kind of medal pinned on him personally by then Secretary of the Air Force, Harold Brown, for "Saving lives, et cetera." There followed a summer in Europe ending in the first of happy marriages. Then graduation with University Honors, kids worth dying for and a career in business. Life is good.

Author, *The Phoenix Diary*, Penguin, 2015.
www.barnesandnoble.com/w/the-phoenix-diary-g-d-deckard/1122175645
Founding Member, Writers Co-op. https://WritersCo-op.com
Co-Editor, *The Rabbit Hole* anthologies.
www.amazon.com/Rabbit-Hole-Weird-Stories/dp/1691225355/ref=sr_1_1
Instigator, *SciFi Lampoon Magazine*. http://scifilampoon.com/
Current WIP: Bob vs The Aliens, short stories.
Recipient of the Psi Young award for Creative Biography.

Danielle Davis is a liar, a misrememberer of song lyrics, and a cheater of cards—only two of these are true. She has had dark fantasy published by *Andromeda Spaceways Magazine*, The Astounding Outpost, and over twenty anthologies. You can find out more about her at literaryellymay.com and can find her on most social media platforms under the handle LiteraryEllyMay.

Kevin M. Folliard is a Chicagoland writer whose fiction has been collected by The Horror Tree, Flame Tree Publishing, Hinnom Magazine, Thrilling Words, and more. His recent publications include "Halfway to Forgotten," featured on The No Sleep Podcast, and the Short Sharp Shocks! Halloween tale "Candy Corn." Kevin currently resides in La Grange, IL, where he enjoys his day job as an academic writing advisor and active membership in the La Grange and Brookfield Writers Groups. When not writing or working, he's usually reading Stephen King, playing Super Mario Maker, or traveling the U.S.A.
Author website: www.kevinfolliard.com
Facebook: www.facebook.com/kevinfolliard
Amazon: www.amazon.com/Kevin-Folliard
Instagram: www.instagram.com/Kmfollia
Goodreads: www.goodreads.com/author/show/5266996.Kevin_M_Folliard

John A. Frochio grew up and still lives among the rolling hills of Western Pennsylvania. He has recently retired from developing and supporting computer automation systems for steel mills. He has had stories published in Interstellar Fiction, Beyond Science Fiction, Twilight Times, Aurora Wolf, Liquid Imagination, SciFan Magazine, Helios Quarterly, Kraxon Magazine, and anthologies *Triangulation 2003*, *Triangulation: Parch* (2014), *Time Travel Tales* (2016), *Visions VII: Universe* (2017), *2047: Short Stories From Our Common Future* (2017), *The Chronos Chronicles* (2018), and *Hidden Histories* (2019), as well as general fiction novel *Roots of a Priest* with Ken Bowers (2007), and sf&f collection *Large and Small Wonders* (2012). His wife Connie, a retired nurse, and his daughter Toni, a flight attendant, have bravely put up with his strange ways for many years. His author's webpage is johnafrochio.wordpress.com.

Steve Gladwin is a drama teacher/practitioner, writer and storyteller. He is the author of YA novel *The Seven*, which was short listed for the Welsh books prize in 2014, *The Raven's Call*, and co-writer and story editor of *Fragon Tales*. Recently he has been developing The Year in Mind programme, a new way of approaching change and loss through the seasons, which involved the writing of twenty-four stories on change for junior/primary, YA and adult audiences. In winter 2018, Steve was made an honorary bard by the Order of Bards, Ovates and Druids, for his performance of "The Song of Taliesin" by John Matthews, now a CD. Steve needs to remember that he enjoys writing short stories, but spends far too much time writing long novels with confusing plots!

Kelly Kurtzhals Geiger Kelly Kurtzhals Geiger is a six-time Daytime Emmy-nominated television producer. Formerly a stand-up comedian whose name and headshot still hang on the walls of The Comedy Store in Los Angeles, she is currently pursuing her MA in English Creative Writing from California State University at Northridge. Kelly has published short stories in The Arcanist, Bards and Sages Quarterly, and the anthologies Hell Comes to Hollywood II and Cemetery Riots. Find her on Twitter @kellykgeiger.

Elana Gomel is an academic and a writer. She is the author of six non-fiction books and numerous articles on subjects such as science fiction and narrative theory. As a fiction writer, she has published three novels and more than fifty fantasy and science fiction stories in Apex, Fantasist, Zion's Fiction, People of the Book, Apex Book of World Science Fiction and many other magazines and anthologies. Her latest novel is *The Cryptids* (2019). She can be found at www.citiesoflightand darkness.com and on Facebook, Twitter and Instagram.
www.facebook.com/elana.gomel
twitter.com/ElanaGomel
instagram.com/elanagomel

Max Griffin is the pen name of a mathematician who is retired from academic and executive positions at a major university in the Southwest. He is the proud parent of a daughter who is a librarian, and the grandparent to two beautiful boys. Max is blessed to be in a long-term relationship with his life partner, Mr. Gene, who is an expert knitter. Max's website is at new.maxgriffin.net.

Currently residing in northern Canada, **L.L. Hill**, or Laura, enjoys hiking, photography and planting wildflowers when she's not writing. Her work has appeared in *The Case Files, Volume 2: Creatures* and is to appear in *Blood in the Cogs* by Horrified Press. Visit www.lauraleehill.com for more.

Tim Jeffreys' short fiction has appeared in *Weirdbook, Not One of Us*, and *Nightscript*, among various other publications, and his latest collection of horror stories and strange tales *You Will Never Lose Me* is available now. He lives in

Bristol, England, with his partner and two children. Follow his progress at www.timjeffreys. blogspot.co.uk.

Carl R. Jennings is a man who sometimes arranges words in interesting ways but, more often than not, they're merely confusing and unsettling. Carl R. Jennings has been published in numerous magazines such as Phantasmagoria Magazine and Grievous Angel, and in several anthologies from companies such Third Flatiron, Shadow Work Publishing, and Gehenna and Hinnom Books. His debut humorous fantasy book, *Mister Posted and the Brain Freeze Goddess*, is available on all ebook platforms. For even more useless information, like Carl R. Jennings's Facebook page or follow him on Twitter and Instagram @carlrjennings.

Adrian Ludens is a rock radio afternoon host, hockey public address announcer, bartender and writer. He's published fiction in *Alfred Hitchcock Mystery Magazine, Women's World*, and several dozen anthologies. Favorites include *The Mammoth Book of Jack the Ripper Stories, Gothic Fantasy Science Fiction Stories, Blood Lite III: Aftertaste*, and *DOA III*. He enjoys exploring abandoned buildings and listening to music. Adrian lives in the Black Hills of South Dakota with his family.

Stefan Markos lives in Tulsa, Oklahoma with his wife and two cats. He has resumed writing science fiction after a hiatus of some years, and is a member of Oklahoma Science Fiction Writers. In addition to writing, he also enjoys camping, hiking, fishing, bicycling, and participating in historical presentations and performances.

Jonathon Mast lives in Kentucky with his wife and an insanity of children. (A group of children is called an insanity. Trust me.) He's worked as a pig farmer, a door-to-door insurance salesman, a comic shop worker, a life skills trainer, a video production teacher, a custom window maker, and other various tasks that he probably shouldn't go into, for fear someone may kill him. In fact, sharing that he was a pig farmer may land him in some deep trouble. It's better you don't ask. Just forget you read that. However, if you want to know about Jon, you can find him at https://wantedoneneweearth. wordpress.com.

Andrew McCormick's fiction has appeared in several publications, including Verbsap (online), Tahoe Blues, The Mensa Bulletin, and Edge. Currently, using his background as a former casino pit boss, he has completed a murder mystery novel, set in a casino, in outer space.

Jason J. McCuiston has been a semi-finalist in the Writers of the Future contest and has studied under the tutelage of best-selling author Philip Athans. His stories of fantasy, horror, science-fiction, and crime have appeared in numerous anthologies, periodicals, websites, and podcasts. *Project Notebook* is his first novel. He can be found on the internet at www.facebook.com/ShadowCrusade. He occasionally tweets about his dogs, his stories, his likes, and his gripes @JasonJMcCuiston. You can find most of his publications on his Amazon page at https://www.amazon.com/-/e/B07RN8HT98.

Bruce Meyer is author or editor of sixty-four books of poetry, short fiction, flash fiction, and nonfiction. He was winner of the 2019 Anton Chekhov Prize for Fiction (UK), a finalist in the Tom Gallon Trust Fiction Prize (UK), the Fish Short Story Prize (IRE), the Retreat West Short Story Prize (UK), the Bath Short Story Prize (UK), and the Thomas Morton Prize for Fiction (CAN). He lives in Barrie, Ontario and teaches at Georgian College and Victoria College at the University of Toronto.

Christine Morgan has recently been called "the Martha Stewart of extreme horror" and "the female Edward Lee," but she's also capable of writing calmer stuff when the occasion calls for it. The author of several books and over a hundred short stories, she's a longtime contributor to The Horror Fiction Review and also dabbles in editing. Her interests include history, mythology, folklore, superheroes, crafts, and cheesy disaster movies, and her home life consists mainly of being bossed around by cats.

Peter Emmett Naughton first fell into fiction penning stories to amuse his grammar-school classmates, which helped him overcome his shyness, but resulted in very few completed homework assignments. He is an avid fan of horror movies, especially those with a sense of humor, food served from carts and roadside shacks, and the music of The Ramones, The Replacements, and other bands of like-minded misfits who found a way to connect with the world through their music and their words. He was raised and currently resides in the Chicagoland suburbs with his wife and cats, and his writing has appeared in various publications including the *Apiary, Cemetery Moon, The Literary Hatchet, Graze, Ink Stains, Whatever Our Souls, Dodging The Rain, Sanitarium, No Trace, Dark Lane,* and *The Blood Tomes, Volume 2: Creatures, Novelettes Edition* anthologies. You can visit him online at https://ravenpen.wixsite.com/authorsite.

KB Nelson is a Canadian who started writing poetry as a young child and has continued to do so all of her life. One of her childhood influences was hearing her father read the poetry of Robert Service when her family lived in the Yukon. When not writing poetry, she dabbles in writing short fiction, including slice of life and speculative fiction. She has won awards in both poetry and short fiction. KB has lived in Ontario, Yukon, Alberta, New Brunswick and New Zealand. A mother of two grown sons, she lives with her husband in Greater Vancouver.

Gregory L. Norris grew up on a healthy diet of creature double features and classic SF television. His work appears in numerous national magazines, fiction anthologies, novels, and the occasional script for TV or film. Norris novelized the classic made-for-TV Gerry Anderson movie *The Day After Tomorrow: Into Infinity* (which he watched at the age of eleven), its original sequel *Planetfall,* and is at work on a third release for the franchise. Norris lives and writes in the outer limits of New Hampshire's North Country in a beautiful old house called Xanadu, where he helps run an outstanding writers' group. Follow his literary adventures at www.gregorylnorris.blogspot.com.

Quinn Parker is a screenwriter, editor, and novelist from coastal New Jersey. Having written under many identities, she's been the writer behind *Nova EXE*, *These Walls Don't Talk* and *They Scream*, as well as many short stories. When not writing or working, she's probably at the gym or playing video games. Social media: www.twitter.com/Quinfamy and www.instagram.com/Quinfamy.

Eric Reitan, a philosophy professor at Oklahoma State University, has won numerous writing awards, including the Crème-de-la-Crème Award of the Oklahoma Writers' Federation, Inc., and a fourth place finish in the 2019 Writers' Digest Short Story competition. His short fiction has appeared in such venues as *The Magazine of Fantasy and Science Fiction*, *Gamut*, and *Deciduous Tales*. His most recent nonfiction book is *The Triumph of Love: Same-Sex Marriage and the Christian Love Ethic* (Cascade Books, 2017).

Alistair Rey began his career in Romania writing political propaganda for post-authoritarian governments. He has since advertised himself as an author of "fiction and parafiction," an archivist, a political satirist, and a dealer in rare books and manuscripts. His work has appeared in the *Berkeley Fiction Review*, *Juked* magazine and *WeirdBook*, among other publications. A complete list of works and stories is available at the *Parenthetical Review* website (parentheticalreview.com).

John B. Rosenman has published three hundred stories in *Endless Apocalypse*, *The Dying Planet*, *The Speed of Dark*, *Weird Tales*, *Whitley Strieber's Aliens*, *Galaxy*, *The Age of Wonders*, and elsewhere. In addition, he has published twenty books, including SF novels such as *Speaker of the Shakk* and *Beyond Those Distant Stars*, winner of AllBooks Review Editor's Choice Award (Crossroad Press), *Alien Dreams, A Senseless Act of Beauty*, and (YA) *The Merry-Go-Round Man* (Crossroad Press). MuseItUp Publishing has published eight SF novels and one box set. They are *Dark Wizard, Dax Rigby, War Correspondent*, and six in the Inspector of the Cross series: *Inspector of the Cross, Kingdom of the Jax, Defender of the Flame, The Turtan Trilogy, Conqueror of the Stars*, and *Skyburst*. MuseItUp has also published the paranormal fantasy *The Blue of Her Hair, the Gold of Her Eyes*, winner of Preditor's and Editor's 2011 Annual Readers Poll, *More Stately Mansions*, and the dark erotic thrillers *Steam Heat* and *Wet Dreams*. Musa Publishing gave his sci-fi time travel story "Killers" their 2013 Editor's Top Pick award. Some of John's books are available as audio books from Audible.com. Two of John's major themes are the endless, mind-stretching wonders of the universe and the limitless possibilities of transformation—sexual, cosmic, and otherwise. He is the former Chairman of the Board of the Horror Writers Association and the previous editor of *Horror Magazine*.

Bradley H. Sinor has been published in anthologies by BAEN, DAW, Warner and others, including *The Grantville Gazette* and several Ring Of Fire books. He also has a 1632 novel, written with his wife, Susan P. Sinor, published by BAEN.

Susan P. Sinor (call me Sue) has been writing for around thirty years, since she met her now husband, Bradley H. Sinor. She has had a number of short stories and flash pieces published in various anthologies, published by DAW, BAEN, Flying Pen Press and Yard Dog Press, as well as others. She has collaborated on several stories with Bradley, as well as a novel written with him in the 1632 Universe, which was published by BAEN in 2018. They are now working on a sequel to the novel. They live in Tulsa, Oklahoma with their two feline owners, Mr. Holmes and his sister, Ms. Watson. There, she is involved with some of the many community theaters in the area. One of them, The Spotlight Theatre, has been producing the same melodrama, The Drunkard, for at least sixty-five years. She has played each of the four female characters and currently plays two of them. She has been a member of The Spotlight Theatre for thirty years. You can find Susan on Facebook and Instagram, where you can see pictures of the cats. She is not yet on Twitter, but may succumb eventually.

Nickolas Urpí is the author of the literary war fantasy novel *The Legend of Borach* and has been published in Page and Spine, *The Copperfield Review, HCE Review* literary journal, and *Ripples in Space* magazine, amongst others. A Hispanic author, his writings fuse his studies of ancient history, literature, and philosophy with his crafted prose to immerse the reader in the world of his fiction through vivid settings and characters. An alumnus of the University of Virginia, he resides in Charlottesville, Virginia.

Christopher Wheatley is a writer from Oxford, UK. He has an enduring love for the works of R A Lafferty, Jack Vance and Shirley Jackson, and is forever indebted to the advice and encouragement of his wife and his son.

Martin Zeigler writes genre fiction, primarily science fiction, mystery, and horror. His stories have been published by a number of small-press journals and anthologies, both in print and online. His most recent publications can be found in *Strange Stories Volume I* (edited by Daniel Cureton) and in the November 2019 issue of *The Weird and Whatnot.* Besides writing, Marty enjoys movies, playing the piano, and taking long walks. He makes his home in the Pacific Northwest.

We all know how the stories go:

An unlikely hero will gather a member of every race and every nation
to discover the Fallen Lord's dark secret and cause his defeat.
But Adal is the most unlikely of heroes,
and the stories must be satisfied with the company he leads.

Will the Fallen Lord turn the tales
of the Storied Lands against them?

The Keeper of Tales

STORIES ARE ALIVE.
THEY WILL BE TOLD.

an epic fantasy adventure by

JONATHON MAST

Coming from Dark Owl Publishing, LLC

March 1, 2021

www.darkowlpublishing.com
Where quality fiction comes to nest.

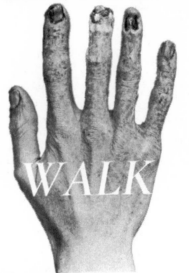

THE DARK

WALK

FORWARD

A HARROWING COLLECTION BY

J O H N   S .   M C F A R L A N D

Available in paperback and on Kindle from

DARK OWL PUBLISHING, LLC

www.darkowlpublishing.com

COMING MARCH 1, 2021!

From Dark Owl Publishing, LLC

THE LAST STAR WARDEN

Tales of ADVENTURE and MYSTERY from Frontier Space, Volume I

BY

JASON J. MCCUISTION

AUTHOR OF
PROJECT NOTEBOOK

www.darkowlpublishing.com

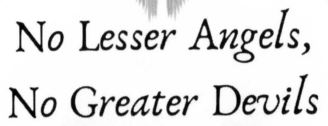

No Lesser Angels,
No Greater Devils

*Beautiful and haunting stories from
the unique and relatable prose of*

Laura J. Campbell

Coming May 1, 2021 in paperback and on Kindle

Dark Owl Publishing, LLC
www.darkowlpublishing.com